Nina Bell has written for most national newspapers and magazines, and has also written a number of radio plays, broadcast on Radio 4. She lives in Kent with her husband David and two teenage children.

The Inheritance

NINA BELL

SPHERE

First published in Great Britain as a paperback original in 2008
by Sphere
Reprinted 2009, 2010, 2011

All characters and events in this publication, other than those clearly in the public domain, are fictitious and any resemblance to real persons, living or dead, is purely coincidental.

A CIP catalogue record for this book
is available from the British Library.

ISBN 978-0-7515-3905-9

Typeset in Bembo by M Rules
Printed and bound in Great Britain by
Clays Ltd, St Ives plc

Sphere
An imprint of
Little, Brown Book Group
100 Victoria Embankment
London EC4Y 0DY

An Hachette UK Company
www.hachette.co.uk

www.littlebrown.co.uk

To Fiona Boucher

Chapter 1

Bramble Kelly slept with her curtains open. She had learned it from her father, who liked to stay close to the weather, and, besides, there was no one outside who could see in. There were only endless rows of low apple trees, dotted with tiny crimson apples, many now fallen in sad, untidy mounds like old ladies' discarded red flannel petticoats. Her father Edward Beaumont had sold the land five years ago but the new owners, a company in Ashford, sometimes didn't bother to harvest the fruit.

That morning Bramble saw a low-lying mist creeping through the orchards, snaking between the trees as if searching for something. Suddenly, she thought she saw evil.

She struggled to shut the window, which was a rickety Georgian sash that stuck and rattled, only responding to careful jiggling. Closing her eyes for a moment she told herself that it was simply an early autumn fog. When she opened them again the mist had gone and she could see the horses jostling by the gate in the paddock, their breath pluming in the air. The young ones danced, their long, elegant legs like springs. Her gaze rested on Sailor, the yard's mischief-maker, a handsome bay gelding with a coat as soft as cashmere. He looked restless and uneasy.

'Horses stop listening at blackberry time,' her father always said. 'They know everything's about to change.'

'They know it's breakfast time, more like,' Bramble muttered to herself as she pulled on her jeans and hurried downstairs.

She paused on the stairs to look through the great arched window over the front door. Lorenden, the house Bramble had lived in since she was born, had been a farmhouse since Elizabeth I's ships had conquered and plundered the Spanish Armada. The house had been built, according to legend, by a crew member of one of the victorious English ships. Only a few brick chimneys remained of that Elizabethan house, but a Jacobean one had been built around them.

The layers of time were tangible. Everyone who had lived there had left a little of themselves behind. At the back of the house there were four steeply pitched clay roofs, while at the front a wealthy Georgian farmer had added a fashionable classical façade, with a pillared portico of a front porch. Bramble, like every inhabitant of the house for hundreds of years before her, looked out of the window at the top of the stairs, checking the sweep of the drive in front of the house and the horses in the field across the narrow lane.

That morning something was not quite right. She stopped and studied the familiar scene. At the end of the gravel drive there were white-painted wooden gates, over which she could see the horses, including her father's retired Olympic champion Ben and Patch, her daughter's old pony. There was nothing wrong, nothing she could put her finger on. She sighed. Tiredness could make you imagine disasters that hadn't happened. Luckily it was nearly the end of the eventing season and the long, dark, cosy evenings of winter beckoned. She clattered down the broad oak staircase, keeping an ear cocked for her father's footsteps. They'd argued last night – bitterly – and she was still angry.

Downstairs in the kitchen Mop and Muddle, the terriers, scuffled eagerly at her toes and Darcy, golden, elegant and lurcher-languid, yawned and smiled his way out of his basket. Darcy was a sofa hound, her father always joked, bred to get to the sofa first. He had been found as a puppy, tied up with a piece of string, his skin raw with mange and his ribs stark through his matted coat. The careless, ignorant cruelty of it had tugged at Bramble's heart and Darcy had come home to the scruffy warmth of Lorenden.

If anything was wrong, Bramble told herself, the dogs would

have known. She struggled with her boots – she must get a new pair, but the farrier's bill came first – and, letting the dogs burst through the door ahead of her, she stepped out into the damp silver light of a September dawn and walked to the stables, the triumph of the Victorian Beaumonts.

Bramble's great-grandfather – who had been a gypsy, Cornish or was the illegitimate son of duke, depending on which family legend you believed – had won a large sum of money on the horses as a young man, and had bought Lorenden to turn it into a stud. With the real gentry out of his reach, he married the only daughter of a wealthy local solicitor. They, too, added their legacy to the house, planting the orchards to ensure an income, creating gardens and building stables that would have befitted a much larger establishment. An Edwardian Beaumont wife had insisted that the house be updated, adding a bay window to the drawing room and a bathroom wing with a spacious cloakroom below. This bathroom had a high claw-footed bath set on a black-and-white floor, and still smelt of talcum powder and linoleum. Bramble's mother had added another bathroom suite, in avocado green, in the sixties. This, like the rest of the house, was a time capsule of its age.

The stables were near the house, through a wooden gate in the garden wall, and were built of red brick in a U shape. A hayloft and dovecote, now a flat for the groom, commanded the centre block, with a weathervane of a racehorse – Mountain Rocket, the one whose winnings had funded the house's purchase – on top. It had been a progressive design in its day: each horse was in a loose box with a view rather than tied up in a narrow stall, and inside the stables there were iron mangers, stone water troughs and cobbled floors sloped for easy drainage. The high roof, in Kent peg tile, was designed for maximum ventilation on hot summer days. Outside, Bramble's father had installed a sand school and a big metal horse walker.

As Bramble went through all the familiar routines, running an eye – or a hand – over each horse to check that nothing had happened in the night and portioning out the feeds, she expected her father to appear, complaining and snuffling as he always did first thing in the morning. 'Have you seen Edward?' she asked as Donna, the groom, came out of her flat, rubbing last night's mascara out of her eyes.

Donna's bleached-blonde ponytail bobbed as she shook her head. 'I've only just got up. Bit of a heavy night. Sorry.'

Most of Donna's nights were heavy. She worked hard and played hard.

Bramble measured out the feeds almost on autopilot: competition mix in the blue bucket for the horse that was still eventing, and a quieter barley blend in the bright green bucket for the mare who'd bucked her owner off three times that week. There were other buckets: purple, lilac, pink, orange and yellow, each allocated to a different horse. Nine horses in all, not counting the pensioners or the youngsters in the field who hadn't been broken in, bringing the count up to fourteen. Bramble tied up a small haynet in each stable to keep the horses occupied, while Donna mucked out, piling up the steaming manure on the muck-heap at the back and sweeping the whole area until it was sparkling clean.

Edward wasn't in the kitchen so she went upstairs to his room. He was always up by seven o'clock at the latest, and usually much, much earlier than that. She tapped on his door then carefully pushed it open, composing the words of her argument in her head as she did so. The bed was rumpled and empty.

'Pa?' she asked.

There was no answer.

'Savannah, have you seen Grampa?' she shouted to her daughter.

'What?' Savannah came slowly out of her room, her mane of curly brown hair tangled with sleep.

There was a direct genetic line – clear grey-blue eyes and thick, irrepressible, corkscrew-curled muddy-blonde hair and the build of a racing greyhound – running from Edward to Bramble and from Bramble to Savannah, although Savannah had inherited the colouring without the build. She had Dominic Kelly's – her father's – stocky, broad-shouldered body. Everyone in Martyr's Forstal remarked that Edward was a remarkably good-looking man for his age, but that Bramble could make more of herself – her curls were cut short in a severe, boyish cap and her style was neat and professional, but hardly feminine. Savannah was curvy, and would have to 'watch it'.

'It's long past time to get up. It's almost eight o'clock,' said Bramble reprovingly to her daughter. 'And do you know where Grampa is?'

'Isn't he in the stables?' replied Savannah.

'No, and he isn't in his room either.'

'Well, he must be somewhere,' said Savannah, closing the door again.

Bramble leant her head against the hall window and sighed, her gaze, out of habit, drifting over the field once again to check the fences, the road and the grazing horses. She'd been looking at horses in fields for so long that she could read their body language from a distance, and could tell from their outlines whether they were frightened or ill.

Something was definitely wrong out there. Bramble remembered the sinuous curves of the mist in the orchard and the sense of dread that had taken hold of her heart. There was the same opaque quality of the air out there. Not quite a mist, but not clear either.

She screwed up her eyes and shielded them with her hand in an attempt to see better against the pale, watery sunlight. 'Savannah,' she shouted. 'What do you think of this?'

Savannah flounced out of her room in too-short, recently outgrown pyjamas, muttering: 'Why do you always have to make such a fuss about everything?'

In the field Ben was alert, his ears forward and tail high, moving restlessly round in a circle and occasionally dropping his head to nudge something on the ground.

'Nothing there,' said Savannah. They looked at each other. 'Well, you know what Ben's like.'

'I might as well check.'

'I'll get dressed.'

They crunched down the gravel drive in silence, Bramble half-believing they were wasting their time.

'That's funny,' said Savannah as they crossed the lane.

'What?'

'There's a parcel on the ground. Or some sort of animal. Perhaps it's a dead badger.'

Bramble saw it too, a dark shape in the long grass. She pulled her mobile out of her pocket as they strode over the tussocky grass and pressed her father's number. He would know what to do.

She could hear a ringing in the grass. 'Pa's dropped his mobile here in the field,' she said.

Savannah ran ahead of her, then crouched down over the dark shape.

For one endless second, Bramble couldn't understand what she was looking at. Time slowed down and hovered in the air.

Edward Beaumont was lying in the damp morning grass at the feet of his old friend Ben, motionless. The horse blew through his nose in a sigh of distress.

Bramble dropped to Edward's side. 'What's happened? Are you all right?' They were, she could see, futile questions.

He mumbled something.

'What?' She leaned down. 'What did you say?'

His voice was thick and indistinct. She couldn't understand.

'I'm calling a doctor. Right now.' Bramble had to concentrate on getting the numbers right. Nine. Nine. Nine. 'Is it the same for mobiles?'

Savannah shrugged, dropping down to hold her grandfather's hand.

Bramble could barely breathe as she gave her name and address. Lorenden, she said, the familiarity of the name calming her. Off the A2 past Canterbury. Follow the signs for Martyr's Forstal, it says a mile but it's more like two and a half, there's an oast house after the railway bridge . . .' Even people who had lived here all their life sometimes got lost in the Bermuda Triangle of fields and lanes, first doubling back on each other then spreading out in an ancient patchwork of meadows, woodland and fields.

The voice pressed her for a postcode. The numbers and letters she had known for so many years jumbled in her head. Eventually she got them straight, her tongue dry and swollen in her mouth.

Is he breathing?

'Yes.'

Is he conscious?

'I think so, he's trying to say something,' she shouted, wanting them to come immediately. 'Please stop asking questions. Just come and help.'

'We need to know the answers,' said the voice. 'They're not slowing down our response. We're on the way. Are there any signs of violence?'

'Violence?' Bramble thought of the evil of the mist, then of her own furious words the night before. 'I don't think . . .' Her voice rose in a sob.

'Please stay calm. We can't help you if you panic.'

'No.' Bramble forced herself to slow her breathing but her voice was still shaking. 'Maybe he fell. Or a heart attack. Or a stroke. I've got a First Aid certificate. What can I do?'

They trailed through endless rounds of questions. There was no bleeding. He was a fit man, he rode every day. He hadn't complained of pain. He hadn't seen a doctor recently – indeed he had hardly ever seen one. He was sixty-nine but you wouldn't think it – he could still do a full fourteen-hour working day. Questions that rolled on and on while Bramble's knees grew damp on the muddy grass, the mobile hooked under her chin as she held her father's dry, papery hand.

'Are you on your own?'

'There's my daughter, Savannah,' she said.

'It would help,' Bramble was told, 'if someone could stand outside the gate so that the ambulance can find the house.'

'We can manage. We'll be waving from the field. But the lane is difficult to find,' said Bramble, trying to see the familiar route through a stranger's eyes – the White Horse pub half a mile before the house, the narrow track winding past the last few hop fields, the caravans for the student workers of a neighbouring farm tucked away behind a beech hedge and the occasional house or farm in the flint and stone mix of the North Downs. The humbler buildings nestled into the landscape as if they had grown out of it. These were the cottages where her father's farmhands had once lived. They had been sold off now: two to second-home owners from London who would not be there on a Wednesday, one to a determined young woman who was prepared to spend two hours commuting to the City on the six o'clock train, and then there was the barn, which was in the process of being converted by an award-winning architect, but was currently a roofless wreck.

'The house has a big, long yew hedge, all curving and bumpy, along the front of the garden,' she said. 'There are some old white gates – they'll be open – and then you can see Lorenden at the end of a short gravel sweep. It's got a Georgian frontage and is painted white. There's a big cedar tree in front . . . the field is exactly opposite the house, on the other side of the road.'

Once again the voice stemmed the flow of pointless detail.

Finally the questions were over and the ambulance, according to the voice, was only about twelve minutes away.

Edward Beaumont moaned softly as he stirred and his daughter looked at her watch. Please come, she silently begged the ambulance, taking off her sweater and folding it carefully under his head. Please come soon.

Edward raised his head and put out a hand. 'Felicity.'

'No, it's Savannah, Pa,' soothed Bramble. 'And Bramble.'

'Felicity,' he mumbled. 'Tell Felicity . . .' The rest of the words were muffled, as if in a rustling paper bag. 'I'm . . .'

Savannah knelt down, and took her grandfather's hand again. 'What is it? Tell me.' She leaned towards him. 'Tell me, Grampa.'

He seized Savannah's arm with surprising strength. 'Felicity,' he murmured again. He said a word that they couldn't hear. They looked at each other and shook their heads. There was another mumble, and then, quite clearly, again, her name. 'Felicity. Tell her . . .'

Bramble saw the light leave his eyes.

'He's still breathing.' Savannah indicated a feather-light rise and fall of his chest and, holding his empty gaze and limp, dry hand, they watched the irregular fluttering of his mouth, the harsh rattle of his breath and then the gradual falling away into stillness.

Suddenly, Bramble remembered her First Aid training and began to work on him, furiously pumping his chest and alternating it with mouth-to-mouth resuscitation while Savannah hovered, frightened. The effort of trying to breathe for two tore at Bramble's lungs, and every time she tried to compress his chest it felt more like trying to knead a lump of meat and gristle.

But she wouldn't give up. She thought that if you kept going long enough you could win. You just had to keep going. You could never give up. Down, down. In, out. Down, down. In, out. Although she knew, in the rational part of her brain, that she couldn't bring him back.

A woman from the ambulance service, dressed in thick, crackly waterproofs, gently took her shoulder and pulled her away. 'He's gone, love.' Bramble heard the words spoken in a Kentish accent above her. 'He's gone. Let us take over now.'

Bramble knew about death. She was an eventer. Seven years ago her husband Dom had ridden into a sunny day and had never come back. He had been killed by every event rider's worst nightmare – a classic slow rotational fall. His horse, taking off a little too fast and a little too soon, had dropped his front legs between the double rails of a log fence and had somersaulted over it, crushing Dom underneath as horse and rider fell. Bramble, who had been waiting to ride the same cross-country course, remembered how time had slowed to a series of heartbeats, remembered the moment when she had known something was wrong, the faces of the people around her, the way no one seemed to know exactly what had happened. The minutes had stretched out then they compressed, suddenly, into a shocking jolt of reality. She had seen the spectators drifting away from the course and back to their cars, silently, with sombre expressions that echoed the numbness in her own heart. From a distance she had heard people offer help and consolation, and she had shaken her head, knowing that she was strong enough to survive.

Looking down at her father's still face, his mouth hanging open and his eyes staring upwards, she wondered if she had been numb ever since.

The ambulance team – a man and a woman – were both crouched over Edward's body, but they straightened up and the man looked at his watch. 'Death pronounced at 8.36 a.m.,' he said formally.

'We'll have to call the police, love,' said the woman, and Bramble nodded. 'Just because it's a sudden death.'

The next half-hour was a jumble of cars arriving and careful, muttered conversations. Looking back on it later, Bramble thought she remembered a marked police car and two young uniformed officers, then an ordinary car and a man in a suit, who asked most of the questions. Bramble and Savannah held hands, but felt embarrassed so Savannah went back to the house to tell Donna what had happened. Bramble offered everyone cups of tea, which they all refused. Eventually the man in the suit, who, she thought, had introduced himself as a detective from the CID, asked Bramble if she was all right. Bramble nodded. Of course she was all right. 'I just feel a bit sick,' she added. 'But it's nothing.'

The detective had a word with the ambulance man, who nodded. 'The ambulance will take . . . your father . . . to the hospital mortuary,' said the detective kindly, and Bramble just nodded again. 'There'll have to be an inquest, but there's no sign of this being anything other than natural causes. The funeral directors will tell you what happens next. And here's my card.'

Bramble put the card in her pocket. It all made very little sense. Inquests, detectives, ambulances . . . this was supposed to be a normal morning.

'Have you got someone who can look after you?' enquired the detective. 'You're shocked, you need to take it easy.'

Bramble looked at him as if he was mad. 'I've got the horses to do,' she said. 'There's my daughter and the groom to help. We can manage . . . but . . . what could have caused it?' She didn't want to admit to their heated dispute the night before. 'Could it have been . . . er . . . stress?'

The ambulance man looked down again, at the now-yellow, waxy face. 'There'll be a post-mortem. Don't worry about it. Edward Beaumont.' He shook his head. 'I'm sorry. I'm so sorry.' It was only then that Bramble realised that she knew him. Mike Tubbs. Of course – Brian Tubbs's son. Brian did some work on the Lorenden roof from time to time. The old countryside where everyone knew everyone else was now enmeshed in the new centralised countryside, where ambulances and fire engines might come from thirty miles away. The woman Mike worked with was a complete stranger, a solid, kindly looking person he addressed as Glenda.

'He was a real local hero, he was,' said Mike to Glenda. 'He did so much for us kids when I was in the Pony Club. We all wanted to be like him.'

Bramble hugged herself tightly. 'Yes, he still does a lot for the

Pony Club.' She swallowed. 'Did, I mean.' It was the first time she had spoken of him in the past tense.

Glenda and Mike rolled his body onto a stretcher, so practised they barely needed to say 'one, two, three'. 'There's a lot of paperwork after a death. Have you got someone to help you?'

'I can call my sister, thank you,' said Bramble. 'My sister, Helena . . .' Her voice choked in her throat, and the rough grass blurred beneath her. 'She lives in London,' she added irrelevantly. 'She'll come down as soon as she can.'

She didn't dare cry, because if she started she might never stop.

As Mike drove the ambulance down the lane he caught a glimpse of a moving shape on his left.

'Bloody hell,' he said to Glenda. 'I haven't seen that before.'

Ben, the old horse, was shadowing the vehicle in a brisk, if uneven, trot along the fence. As it accelerated he broke into a rusty canter. At the corner he stopped, tail swishing, and stood stock still, as if standing to attention while his master was driven away for the last time.

The horse watched the ambulance until it disappeared behind a tangled mess of blackberries and brambles.

'D'you reckon he understood?' asked Glenda.

'He knows. Animals always do.'

Glenda opened the glove compartment and took out a boiled sweet, and offered one to Mike. 'It's always so sad, isn't it?'

Mike managed to remove the sweet paper while driving and popped it in his mouth. 'It's more than sad. Edward Beaumont kept that place together. I don't know what they'll do without him. Mind you, he was a great man but he wasn't easy. That's what I heard.'

'What sort of "not easy"?' enquired Glenda.

'Dunno exactly. I was too young to understand when it all happened, and people didn't used to gossip then the way they do now. They were loyal.'

Glenda thought that people were probably exactly the same as they always had been, but decided not to say so. 'Oh, well, everyone makes mistakes,' she said comfortably. 'Still, there's nothing like a death in the family to stir everything up again.'

'Turns everything right over,' agreed Mike, adding a shout as he was forced to brake suddenly.

The mist had suddenly reappeared, curling over the road in a thick white shroud. Barely able to see six inches in front of his face, Mike slowed to a crawl, guided only by the scratching of brambles against the windows. 'Bloody hell,' he muttered. 'It won't be the last death round here if that mist has anything to do with it.'

Chapter 2

Helena Harris woke at six, startled by a nightmare.

Lying in bed drenched in sweat, mastering her panic, she decided to get up because there was so much to do. She'd often thought it would save a great deal of time and trouble if they could all eat breakfast last thing at night instead of in the morning when there was so much else going on.

A photographer and a journalist were due to arrive at half-past nine. *Fabulous Homes* was featuring the house. Helena had dangled the latest renovations – black floors, black-painted woodwork and an entirely modern use of historic paint shades – in front of a stringer for *House & Garden*. The girl had only come back with a commission from *Fabulous Homes*, which had been disappointing. But still, any coverage kept Helena's name out there, and there was always the possibility that if the acting went . . . well, she didn't like to think about it, but even successful actresses had to have a fallback . . . then she might make her name as an interior designer.

She spent nearly an hour finding the right fashionable-but-casual look, checking her back view, selecting shoes and then clearing every last bit of make-up off the dressing table before tackling the family bathroom. It was such a lot of work having the house featured; sometimes she almost wondered if it was worth it.

Of course it was worth it, she told the mirror, tweaking the straps of her baby-blue silk camisole and rearranging the fall of a matching cashmere cardigan. Blue was the colour of spirituality.

And it suited her blonde English rose looks and lightly tanned, faintly freckly skin. But did she look a bit cold? She checked the weather outside. A thick, heavy mist had settled around the house; she suddenly felt isolated, and frightened again. Did her hair need sharpening up? An arty-looking bob had become her trademark, like Mary Quant's or Anna Wintour's, but you had to keep the swing fresh and glossy. She glanced at her watch. It would have to do.

Blue suited Ollie, too. He had a wonderfully well-washed periwinkle shirt, all baggy and swashbuckling, that she loved him in. It set off his hazel eyes and brown Cavalier hair. 'Your pirate shirt,' she shouted, throwing it into the en suite. 'You must get out of the bath, thingy will be here in a moment. And we need to photograph this room.'

'For God's sake.' Oliver Cooper was not pleased at the interruption. He did his best thinking in the bath, and he simply couldn't make Helena understand that he was unable to write unless he could start the day with an absolutely quiet, private time behind a closed bathroom door, lasting at least half an hour.

Ollie dressed quickly and opened the bedroom door to check where she was, after which he clattered down the stairs and picked up the post. With a quick glance upwards – just in case Helena was peering down the stairwell from above – he rifled through the letters and put two in his pocket. He dropped the others back on the mat, as if they had just arrived.

Helena was too busy to notice. She did a mental check of her children. Eddie said he had a study day and the twins would go into school late. They were only five, they wouldn't miss anything important.

'Ania!' Helena shouted up to the children's floor. 'Can you make sure everyone's in shades of blue, white or cream? It looks so fussy if we're all wearing lots of different colours.'

The au pair appeared at the top of the stairs. 'What?'

'Ruby and Roly. Can you see if they've got something nice in blue? Or blue-and-white. Not too smart, quite casual. Those little cotton sweaters are sweet.' She wasn't sure how much Ania understood. She'd better go up and sort it herself. 'If you want something done, ask a busy woman to do it,' she said under her breath to no one in particular.

'Eddie, are you out of bed?' She climbed another flight of stairs, trying not to feel the tug of a tiny cartilage problem in one knee. Tall London houses kept you fit. She rapped on her elder son's door and pushed it open.

Eddie, gorgeous Eddie, whom she loved more than anyone in the entire world, pushed himself up on his elbows, shaking his tousled curls and blinking at the sudden light. Sometimes people mistook him for Ollie's son, so perhaps, Helena had to admit, she went for a particular type of man. Brown-eyed, tanned pirates and gypsies. Bad boys. Not that Tim Harris had been a bad boy exactly, merely too ambitious to stay around. And Ollie, too, was not exactly bad, just edgy enough to be interesting.

Eddie had soulful dark-brown eyes, thickly fringed with strong, dark eyebrows and long lashes. She'd sometimes thought he should have been a girl with eyes like that, and had always then thought that if he'd been a girl he wouldn't have been her darling Eddie.

'It is a study day, Mum, you know.' He didn't like lying to his mother, but needs must.

'We've got a photographer coming.'

Eddie groaned, flopping back into the mound of stale bedding. 'Why do you do this to us, Mum, why do we have to be photographed all the time?'

'It's not all the time, it's only occasionally, and it's for my job. I need to do these things because I have to stay famous. You wouldn't like to have to go back to Earls Court and being poor, would you?'

'I wouldn't mind,' he mumbled. 'I liked it there.'

So had she, although she hadn't realised it at the time. The nagging worry about money, and whether she was missing out, and if her career would ever take off had been like a current dragging her under but, looking back, she remembered bittersweet happiness. Just her and Eddie, living in a basement. Tim Harris, so good-looking, so successful and so much fun, had not been able to deal with simultaneously being made a father and dropped from a major television serial. He had gone to Hollywood. Helena and Eddie received little news and no money. They had lived on the dole and the odd fifty pounds from Edward Beaumont.

She and Eddie had been everything to each other. When she went to auditions, Polish Katinka in the flat above usually babysat for a few pounds but Helena always took Eddie to parties on the back of her bicycle. In those days nobody had children and Eddie was fussed over for a short time, after which he fell asleep on the coat pile or watched unsuitable videos with stoned producers and actors. Occasionally he went to stay with his grandfather, after whom he had been named.

'He's got the making of a fine little horseman,' had been Edward's verdict, and Helena had clutched Eddie tightly. She had never admitted, not even to her sisters, that she thought horses were frightening and dangerous and she didn't want Eddie caught up in that world. She'd been proved right by what had happened to Dominic Kelly.

For a few years it had looked as though Dom and Bramble might have repeated Edward's success in the eventing world. Dom had won Burghley once, with Bramble coming tenth on the same day, and they'd both featured on the cover of *Horse & Hound*, Dom three times and Bramble once. They were called 'a magic partnership'. They had been beginning to attract real sponsorship and two of their horses were considered to have outstanding potential. Dom had been the outgoing one – a restless, energetic man with a ready laugh and a tactile, intimate manner with almost everyone he met. He rode as if the hounds of hell were on his tail. Occasionally people muttered that he was *too* fast. He had been formally warned, someone said once.

Then he was killed. There had been no reason for the accident. It was a fine, sunny day, with good ground under the horses' hooves. There were no distractions – no stupid spectator flashing a camera or waving a brightly coloured hat. No dog or rabbit had run across their path. The course, although challenging, was well within Dom's capabilities and a safety inquiry came up with no conclusions as to how such an accident could be prevented in the future. To the eventing world it was a tragic accident, something that could happen to anyone. Everyone knew that one fine day, for almost no reason at all, it could be you.

After that Bramble's career went downhill fast. She never rode at that level again, and people began to murmur that the talent and drive to succeed had been Dom's. Without Dom she had slipped in the rankings.

Edward told Bramble that she should give up any idea of making it to the top. 'You're a good, quiet rider,' he said softly, 'and the horses trust you. You're brilliant at bringing them on and turning them round, but you don't ride to win. Your caution gets the better of you. You think too much.'

Helena had seen her sister's stricken face, but thought that her father was right. And she'd been determined, from the very beginning, not to allow Eddie to place himself in that sort of danger. If that meant her changing her life so that Eddie didn't spend so much time down at Lorenden, well, she would change it. Eddie came first.

So she'd married a kind older man, wealthy, amusing and indulgent as a lover, tolerant and kind as a stepfather, and influential in career terms: a banker who sat as a non-executive director on the boards of several theatre companies. He was Helena's sensible choice. He gave her the time to develop her career and provide a secure childhood for Eddie. It was the right thing to do. But she kept Tim Harris's surname – Helena Harris sounded good.

Eight years later Helena was famous, Eddie was at boarding school and her kind, powerful sugar-daddy had turned into a crotchety pensioner who wanted to play golf and bridge and didn't like eating too late.

Then Helena had met Ollie Cooper at the health club where he swam fifty lengths a day. His latest screenplay had just been nominated for an Oscar. He was the son of Norman Cooper, the actor. Ollie understood Helena's life. Helena edged her greying husband out of the house in Primrose Hill and moved Ollie in. 'I'm like Zsa Zsa Gabor,' she trilled at parties. 'I'm a good housekeeper: I always keep the house.' After eighteen months Ollie had proposed to her, in the Gritti Palace in Venice.

'You marry for youthful passion the first time,' said Helena to Bramble on her wedding day. 'And to provide for your children the second time . . .' she surveyed her cream silk suit with satisfaction '. . . and then third time, well, that's Mr Right. The One.'

'Well, anyway,' said Helena, in Primrose Hill with three children and a reluctant husband to get ready for a photoshoot, 'we wouldn't be able to afford Earls Court these days. If we lost all our money we'd have to go to . . .' She strode across the room to rip open Eddie's curtains and picked some washing off his floor while trying to think of somewhere affordable in London. 'We . . . we'd have to go to Catford. That's it. Catford. Now you know we let you come to school in London after your GCSEs only if you promised to work, so get up and get dressed and study and be nice to everyone.'

'Catford would be cool,' said Eddie. 'And I can either study or be nice, but not both. It's just not possible.'

She couldn't help smiling. She did love him so very much.

The doorbell rang. It was Paul the photographer, Tang his assistant, a pile of bags and tripods, and Fi the journalist, who was wearing black and looking dumpy.

'What a lovely sweater,' she said to Fi. 'Is it cashmere? Now who would like coffee and who would like tea? Herbal? Decaff? Green tea?'

'Just builder's, thanks,' said Paul, triggering a faint unease in Helena. It was the second time someone had asked for 'builder's' recently and for a moment she'd thought it was a smart new brand. Was there something retro going on with tea?

Fi followed Helena downstairs into the kitchen.

Helena told her that it had been such a big decision – whether to go with steel, perhaps with lacquered blue door fronts and a huge American fridge, or whether to make it look more understated and furnished. It could never have been country, of course, nothing that reminded her of the cluttered Edwardian dresser and the Aga at Lorenden. It really irritated Helena, the way her father and Bramble lived in a jewel of a country house and did absolutely nothing with it.

'Your kitchen's amazing,' said Fi. 'It's why we wanted to do the house, really. So clever to be so modern and not look like a kitchen at all.'

'We wanted a room the whole family could live in,' said Helena. 'You don't always want to be staring at washing-up, do you? And we wanted a cook's kitchen, of course, because we're both terribly greedy and love food.'

'Love food . . .' wrote Fi. 'And who cooks – you or Ollie?'

'Ollie's a hugely talented cook,' replied Helena.

Fi scribbled a note about Helena Harris being charmingly modest despite her fame. 'So exactly how does it work, this kitchen?'

'Well, of course, we didn't want wall units so we decided to go for something sculptural and boxy in the middle of the room and, as you see . . .' she pressed a button, 'these stainless steel tops conceal the sink and hob. They slide away to make a breakfast bar. When they're closed you don't see anything. And this dark wood is sustainable hardwood, of course. I've got a note about it somewhere.'

'Was it expensive?' asked Fi. 'Our readers will want to know.'

'Oh, I'll give you the designer's brochure, they can tell you. We had ours customised a bit.' They'd also got a discount, what with Helena's name and the promise of publicity – although not quite as much of one as Helena might have liked. The homes companies were never as generous as the fashion ones. Helena always enjoyed borrowing designer dresses for big nights out.

She guided Fi around the house, pointing out that having children didn't mean you couldn't be stylish – 'it's just an attitude of mind and a question of really good storage. Ruby and Roly love picking their toys up and putting them away because the cupboards are such fun.'

The phone rang, and she almost didn't answer it.

It was Bramble.

'Can I ring you back?' asked Helena. 'In about, say, an hour?' She looked at Fi, who nodded. 'I'm in the middle of a photo-shoot.'

In Kent Savannah trailed up the stairs, followed by Darcy. She closed her bedroom door a little more loudly than she'd intended to and plumped down on the bed. The springs creaked. Darcy looked at her, measured the bed carefully and then slithered up beside her, sitting perilously back on his haunches before lurching forward and settling down with a sigh.

She stroked his head and hugged him.

He yawned doggy breath in her face and curled up, falling asleep instantly. She looked at him with love for a moment, then picked up her mobile.

'Grampa dead. Call me. xxx S.' She hesitated before pressing 'send'. It looked very bald, stated in text, but she wasn't sure she wanted to say the words out loud.

'Message sent.'

Savannah lay back on her bed and stared at the ceiling. Normally her choices were between homework and the horses, but neither seemed appropriate. The free hours of the morning stretched ahead of her. She had heard her grandfather and her mother shouting at each other when they came back the night before, and when she'd come down to find out what was happening her mother had stalked out of the room, slamming the door.

Her mother rarely lost her temper. Savannah had looked at her grandfather who had sighed and shaken his head. He'd looked so old and tired. And now he was dead.

Her phone vibrated and she seized it. 'Yeah?'

'Are you OK?' Lottie sounded shocked. 'Katya's taking me to the dentist, but I'd better go outside because there's a "No Mobiles" sign in the waiting room.'

'I think so.' Savannah wasn't sure how she felt, but it was nice to be asked.

'What happened?'

'He fell down in the field. He must have been checking Ben, or something. His eyes went all funny – one was, like, fixed on me and the other kind of floating towards the sky. Then he went all still and yellow. It was horrible. He thought I was my aunt, Felicity. He wanted to tell her something.'

'I didn't know you had an Aunt Felicity.'

'I don't really. I mean, she's my mother's sister and all that but she left home ages ago and she doesn't keep in touch. Well, you know, just Christmas cards and things. She sends me twenty quid usually. So she must be quite nice. We only ever see her on TV, reporting on wars.'

Neither of them were really interested in either war or Felicity, so they fell silent.

'Can I come to yours? After we've put the horses to bed tonight?' Savannah suddenly had a longing for Lottie's light, bright, orderly home.

'Sure. I'll just ask.'

There was a squawking conversation in the background and Lottie's au pair came on the line. 'Savannah! This is terrible. You want I come collect you? Or your mother, she needs you?'

'I don't think she needs me.' Savannah was already walking down the stairs. 'Mum! Can I go to Lottie's? They can collect me after evening stables.'

Bramble, distracted and untidy, stopped rummaging amongst the papers on the kitchen table. 'What?'

'Lottie. Can I go to her house?'

'Oh . . . er . . . well . . . Oh, God, I can't think. Horses. Homework.' Bramble's face was grey with distress and Savannah felt a twinge of conscience. But her mother was almost always too busy to answer questions properly.

'OK. Fine. Whatever.' Bramble clutched her head, then started to open the post. 'Oh, this is such a mess!'

'That would be great,' Savannah informed Lottie, and rang off after another unnecessarily long conversation about whether Lottie would come and help her put the horses to bed provided that her mother didn't find out. Lottie's mother, Cecily, was obsessed with GCSE homework and was making Lottie doing two hours' revision every evening, even though exams were still eight months away.

'Helena's being photographed,' Bramble told Savannah when she eventually came off the line. 'I couldn't tell her about Pa.'

'Who by?' Savannah picked up a pile of books and papers so that she could sit down on one of the kitchen chairs, wishing that sitting didn't make her waistband cut in so much. She shouldn't have eaten those biscuits last night.

Bramble didn't answer her question. 'You're rather pale.'

Savannah was surprised. Bramble was not a fusser, and several of her school friends said they envied her mother's laid-back attitude to parenting. 'At least you're allowed some independence,' was the cry. 'I have to say where I am every minute of the day.'

Savannah sometimes wondered if Bramble cared about her, though, or whether she only really thought about the horses. Sometimes Bramble seemed to look at her daughter through a haze of exhaustion, as if she wondered who Savannah was and where she had come from.

Bramble peered at her. 'Have some breakfast. You must eat.'

Savannah checked the bread bin. There was a stale loaf, with flecks of blue in it. She put the bin lid down, feeling slightly sick. 'Who was photographing Helena? Was it *Vogue*?'

'She didn't say. What about a slice of toast? With Marmite?' Bramble took the bread out of the bin, apparently without noticing anything wrong with it.

'I don't feel hungry.' Savannah pulled at a hangnail and looked out of the window. Life suddenly seemed very insecure and cold.

Helena was giving Fi twinges of repetitive strain injury in her right wrist as she extolled her decorating philosophy.

'I love quite plain rooms with one or two over-the-top pieces. And I can't resist browsing in flea markets and antique shops. I found these art deco lamps in a funny little place on the Left Bank in Paris, for example.'

She also couldn't resist browsing among the mess at Lorenden. There was a delightful bronze horse sculpture that would look beautiful if properly looked after and displayed in simple – but stunning – surroundings. The sculptor had recently enjoyed a revival and Helena had asked her father if she could borrow it. It was in the kitchen, of all places, and completely smothered by rosettes, the occasional scarf and the general detritus around it.

'You can have it when I'm dead, missy,' he'd snapped, giving her a hard look.

Helena slipped her arm through his. 'Oh Pa, don't say such gloomy things. I was only thinking of borrowing—'

'You'd better not think,' he snorted. 'Not if that's where thinking leads.' But he pinched her cheek affectionately.

She'd got back in his good books by asking him about the horses. Some men would have wanted to hear about their grandchildren, she thought. Not Edward Beaumont.

'I understand we need to do the family pic first.' Paul came in, followed by Tang and the cameras. 'Your husband says he needs to go to work.'

Helena could see Ollie signalling. 'Florals are so now,' she said, picking up a cushion. 'If you do them properly. Less is more. Less is more,' she repeated, slightly louder, 'that's what I always say. Have you got that?'

Fi wrote LESS IS MORE in her notebook, and wondered what other jobs might be available for older, slightly lazy journalists. Helena had that special brand of beady-eyed, brittle charm that was quite unnerving, and she kept complimenting her in the most terrifying way. If Fi actually replied she looked astonished, as if Fi wasn't supposed to speak, just ask questions. Was there a real woman underneath it all? Focus on the florals, Fi, she told herself, and turned over the page of her notebook as Helena marshalled everyone.

'It looks great,' said Paul, freezing the viewfinder and beckoning Helena over to check. She had to admit it did: Ollie, lean and muscular with those amazing eyes and his shoulder-length hair, with Roly, his exact image in miniature, divine Eddie and then, of course, Ruby, mirroring her own straight, geometric blonde hair and fair skin. Completing the picture was Oscar, their adorable little Shih-tzu, looking like a very small rag rug. It was what she had always wanted. To be at the centre of a happy, beautiful family in a lovely home.

Chapter 3

Savannah played with Darcy's silky ears as she waited for Lottie to come over. All day it had seemed incredible that there was a world out there, that horses needed to be ridden and lessons given, and that everyone else was going about their business, not realising that everything had changed. Here in the warm kitchen, every surface covered with coffee cups, the house diary, a snaffle, some saddle soap, a tin of tea, several rinsed-out milk bottles, yesterday's papers, half-empty bottles of claret with stoppers in them, her grandfather's boots in front of the old kitchen range and his tweed cap on the kitchen table, everything seemed so normal. But it wasn't.

People streamed through the yard as usual, gasping their amazement and pressing offers of help on Bramble. Donna kept bursting into tears, which made Savannah feel guilty. She felt she ought to cry, but somehow she couldn't. There was a hole in her life and now she felt as if it had always been there, only thinly covered over. The hole that had suddenly gaped open in the most frightening way. Savannah didn't often think of her father – she had been quite young when he died – but surely if he was here he would look after her? And Bramble. Her competent, busy mother, who always knew the answer to everything, was drifting round the yard like a ghost and there was only Savannah left to hold it all together. Or that's what it felt like.

Occasionally the phone rang, and when Savannah walked into Edward's study to answer it, she could sense her grandfather's presence, his faint smell of soap and lemon, of old man and horse, as if he might step into the room and take the call. His desk was piled up with letters and files, a note was stuck to the phone – 'call Nicky' – and old invitations were propped up three deep across the mantelpiece. His diary lay open.

'Who is it?' Bramble came in, hand stretched out for the phone, as if it was so unlikely to be a call for Savannah that it was hardly worth asking. Savannah felt like saying that she did have friends too, you know, but decided that today was not the day.

It was Barratt's, the feed merchant, confirming an order. Would it be all right to deliver around five-thirty?

'Yes, that would be fine,' muttered Bramble. She sighed. 'I suppose I'd better cancel Pa's appointments. I know there's a system, but I've never understood it.' She stood, looking bereft, in the middle of the room. 'And it sounds silly, but I haven't the first clue how to find Felicity. Doesn't she work for CNN? Or is it the BBC? I can hardly start organising the funeral until I've found her, can I?'

Savannah didn't see why not. Well, she did, but if Felicity chose not to bother to stay in contact with the family that was her lookout. She couldn't expect everything to be put on hold for her. 'What do you think Gramps wanted to say to her?' she asked.

Bramble shook her head. 'I don't know. I haven't spoken to her for so long.'

'She hasn't been over since I left St Mary's,' said Savannah. 'Wasn't it Helena's wedding to Ollie? Remember? When she arrived in a helicopter just for the reception, and went off again immediately after they cut the cake?'

Bramble smiled in a abstracted way. 'Oh, I remember that. Hadn't she lured some fighter pilot into diverting his helicopter to make an emergency landing or something outrageous like that? I wonder what happened to him? Still, she got a helicopter ride out of him. Talk about upstaging the bride: Helena was furious.'

Savannah wandered into the hall and looked in the silvered mirror over the fireplace. 'Did Grampa think I was Felicity? I mean, I don't look at all like her, do I? Or perhaps she looked like me when she was my age?' She held her breath for the reply, because it would be very, very good news if this was the case. Felicity was slender, with large dark eyes and chestnut brown hair twisted up with a pencil, showing a long, graceful neck. Her face was framed by a few curls, which looked as if they had slipped out deliberately to flatter. Even the rotor blades of a helicopter had been unable to ruffle her distinctive bohemian style, her swathes of necklaces, bright colours and swirly skirts, which would have looked ridiculous on anyone else. Felicity could carry the look off and make it her own. Felicity the rebel. Aka the selfish one.

Savannah, like the rest of them, had grown up knowing the family roles that had been set in stone a few years after each girl's birth. Felicity was rebellious and self-centred but also brilliant, though she had wasted her talents by not sticking at anything. Helena was beautiful, ambitious and occasionally labelled 'ruthless'. Bramble was the easy baby, the nice one, the one who looked after them all. Bramble always thought the best of everyone, although she could be fierce when it came to looking after her horses.

Savannah thought that Felicity was probably only seen as selfish because she had followed her own dreams rather than the family goal, and she craved to be as careless of public opinion as her bird-of-paradise aunt. But, instead, she felt lumpen, apologetic and chunky. She hated the way her shirts strained at the third button down.

As for her hair, she had inherited the tangled mane of curls that had given Bramble her nickname. 'You look as if you'd been pulled through a hedge backwards,' Bramble's mother had complained, apparently, and her father had added 'and not even an ordinary hedge. A great big thicket of brambles.' After a short period of 'hey, Bramble Hedge' – this mainly from the then fifteen-year-old Felicity – the four-year-old Helena, unable to say her sister's real name of Lavinia, had shortened it to Bramble and the name had stuck. It was, thought Savannah, a lucky escape. Fancy being called Lavinia. People might call you Lav. Mind you, no wonder Bramble had kept her hair so short ever since.

Bramble came out into the hall. 'I can't remember what Felicity looked like when she was fifteen. Pretty much what she looks like now, I think. She used to wear amazing things like hot pants and incredible platform shoes. And false eyelashes like enormous spiders.'

Savannah's shoulders drooped. There was to be no last-minute genetic rescue from the fact that she and Bramble were not delicate, fragile types like Helena and Felicity. 'Proper women' Edward had called them both, and the farrier had once told Savannah that she was a 'nice hefty lass'.

Oh, why couldn't she look like Helena, who was just tall enough to be stunning, but not so tall that she towered over leading actors, with an economical neatness about her – beautifully shaped hands and feet, a heart-shaped face, size six hips and an air of powerful vulnerability. Helena enjoyed – rather too obviously – complaining that everything she bought had to be taken in. And, according to Bramble, Helena's hair, with its studied blonde naturalness, cost as much to maintain as it did to keep a top-class event horse.

'Why don't you try email?' suggested Savannah.

Bramble looked vague. 'Oh, well, I don't . . .'

Savannah sighed. 'I'll do it. There's bound to be something on Grampa's PC.' Making a space in the mess that surrounded the computer she settled down to check her grandfather's email – most of which concerned the yard – and to send, with satisfaction, a message to Felicity.

'I've told her,' she said.

'What?' screeched Bramble. 'You can't tell someone their father's died by email. You should have just told her to phone me.'

'Well, I did what I could. You never said.' Savannah found her mother infuriating at times. So irritating, not to mention unreasonable. 'There's a car.' She ran to the window. 'Lottie's here.'

Bramble, Savannah, Donna and Lottie did the feeds, skipped out any dung in the stables and rugged up the horses. They then carried more rugs out to the remaining horses in the field, haynets slung over their shoulders, their boots slipping in the mud and the first, sharp notes of cold autumn air catching the backs of their throats.

They waited in the afternoon shadows as the horses finished their dinner, scattering the contents of the haynets in a few neat piles on the ground. Sailor was a bit of a bully and was inclined to chase the mares away from their feed and gobble it all down himself. Flocks of starlings swooped in formation overhead, pouring like water into ever-changing shapes before settling into the dark bulk of the trees for the night.

'Do you think Sailor ought to be in at night now?' fretted Lottie over the rhythmic sound of his jaws munching contentedly from the bucket. 'Isn't it getting a bit wintry?'

'Lottie, he's fine,' reproved Savannah. 'Horses are made to live out.'

When Sailor had joined their yard, only two years earlier, Lottie had begged to be allowed to look after him as much as possible, and Cecily Marsh-Robertson had very reluctantly agreed. Since then Lottie had bombarded Edward, Bramble, Savannah and Donna with questions. To Lottie's 'Why do the horses in the field have breakfast? Why can't they just live on grass?' Bramble would stop and reply patiently, 'Lots of ponies would probably be fine in a good field, but horses need anything up to four extra meals a day, plus hay, especially if we are competing them.'

Lottie was also desperately anxious to do everything absolutely correctly, and needed a great deal of reassurance if she did anything even slightly wrong, such as putting a too-heavy rug on Sailor on a summer's evening ('He only needs a very light rug in the summer,' Bramble would explain, 'and none at all if the evening is very warm. And we rug him up in September, when it's chilly, to slow down the growth of his winter coat. It saves clipping him early.') Sometimes, Savannah suspected that her mother hardly knew why she did things, only that they had always been done in that way at the Beaumont yard, and that was that. She could see that Lottie's endless questioning occasionally irritated Bramble, or made her feel that she had to justify herself.

'I suppose so.' Lottie looped her arms around his neck and he raised his head briefly to look at her, as if to say, 'What now?', before dropping his head back down to the important business of what was in his bucket. But it was a kind look. Lottie was his favourite person in the whole world and the only one who could distract him, even momentarily, from his feed. 'He's just so gorgeous. Feel his coat. It's s-o-o soft. I can't believe he's mine.'

Savannah leant against the fence. 'Did you have fog this morning?'

Lottie, still stroking Sailor's neck, thought for a moment. 'No, I don't think so. Why?'

'When we looked out of the window first thing there was a horrible mist thing. As if something had come to get Grampa. Something gross.'

Lottie's brow furrowed. 'It was probably nothing.' She didn't sound certain, but then Lottie seldom sounded certain of anything unless she was on a horse.

'Probably. They've finished. Let's go to yours.' They gathered up the now-empty buckets and once back at the house, Savannah raced upstairs to stuff a toothbrush into her backpack. She was longing to get out of the house, with its burden of grief and disappointment, for as long as possible.

She shot a look at her mother when she came downstairs. Perhaps she should stay with her after all. Perhaps Bramble needed her. She had a sudden longing to throw herself into Bramble's familiar wiry arms, but she couldn't do that with Lottie watching her.

But then she was waving Savannah off. 'See you tomorrow. Don't stay up too late.'

Bramble was fine. She always was. She could cope with anything. Of course she didn't need Savannah.

Cherry Orchards was large, immaculate and Victorian. It had been 'done' by an interior designer and Lottie was based there with a series of au pairs. Her mother divided herself between the house and a flat in London, where she spent two or three days a week, running her company To Die For Bags. Lottie's father, long since married to someone else, lived in Hong Kong and had very little impact on his daughter's life. To Savannah, Lottie often seemed like a wealthy orphan.

'My mother always says she needs a huge drink whenever something like this happens,' said Lottie tentatively once Katya, the au pair, had left them alone in the kitchen with a salad and some quiche. 'There's some vodka in the drawing room.'

Because they were always getting up early to ride in competitions neither Lottie nor Savannah had ever drunk very much. 'We might as well try,' replied Savannah. 'I do feel odd. Very odd. It might help.'

'Shock,' said Lottie. 'You need brandy.' She found a bottle of Cecily's best and they both tried it, screwing up their faces at the fiery taste.

'Maybe vodka would be nicer. With some fresh orange juice.'

It was. Much nicer. They had another, then another.

At Lorenden the house seemed cold and empty without Savannah. An uneasy memory stirred in the silence, of the summer when Dom had died. His face had faded now but Bramble sensed the familiar texture of sorrow, like a faint perfume in the air. It was as if he had returned to take Edward's hand on his final journey.

She must find Felicity. Bramble began to look through her father's desk to find Felicity's number, and checked the diary. Someone phoned and she gave them the news, on autopilot by now, too tired and strung out even to remember their name.

'He was a wonderful man,' squawked the phone. 'I was only really a Sunday rider, but he made me believe I could go out there and ride with the big names. I remember him telling me "eventing is a sport where the amateurs and professionals, men and women, young and old can all compete against each other on the same field". He turned my ideas about myself round. He was an amazing teacher.'

'Yes, he was.'

'And such a charismatic person. He kind of . . . filled the room.'

'Yes.'

'He seemed fine when I spoke to him last week.'

'Yes,' said Bramble, her head still slowly – oh, so slowly – absorbing the full consequences of Edward's sudden death. She must inform the people he coached and cancel his lessons: he only taught once or twice a month, but as a well-known rider he could charge handsomely for an all-day training session. Occasionally he'd stride in muttering, 'Bloody horse box needs major repairs, better get another seminar into the book'. 'Anyway, I've worked side-by-side with him for ten years now,' she assured the caller, 'so it'll be business as usual.'

When she put the phone down she realised she had better contact Edward's solicitor. Did she even know who he used? She knew his accountant, Nicky Dawson, who was still in the office and answered her phone.

Bramble waited patiently through the condolences.

'And he's kept you up to speed with the financial side?' asked Nicky.

'Well, not really. He said it was his money and his business and that he wasn't an old man yet.' Bramble had only tried to broach the issue once or twice and had been brushed off, so angrily she'd never dared try again, although sorting her father out had been very much on her mental 'to do' list.

'I was afraid of that. I know now's not the time to talk about this.' Nicky went ahead anyway. 'I did advise him to make sure there was at least one person in the family who knew what was going on, but he said there'd be plenty of time for all that. I mean, presumably you know the broad picture?'

'Presumably? Yes, of course.' Bramble was conscious that Nicky's words were stirring up a secret worry she'd been suppressing for a while. Money. But surely you didn't have to think about the money on the very day someone died? 'I don't think . . .' she began.

'I'm sorry,' Nicky interrupted. 'I don't want to put you under any pressure. But I do need to talk to you. At least he had a will.'

'Did he?' Bramble had never thought about wills. It had always seemed a long way off, and not something you ever wanted to raise with your own father.

'Oh yes. The only reason why I know is that I asked him once, and he said, "Of course I've got a bloody will, what do you think I am? A complete fool?" I thought it was probably best to leave it there, so I don't know what's in it, or where it is.'

Bramble nodded, suddenly trying to choke back tears. Nicky had painted a perfect picture of her irascible father.

'The awful thing,' said Nicky, 'is that death doesn't leave you any time to grieve. You'd think it was this great big thing – and it is – but in fact, it's the net of constant little things like death certificates and cancelling passports and going through endless papers that ensnares you and catches you out over and over again until you can barely function. At least, that's what it was like for us when my uncle died suddenly.

'I'm sorry,' she added softly, 'but you need to find that will pretty quickly. You need to know what will happen to the yard and what you can plan for the horses. Otherwise you could find yourself unable to pay the bills at the end of the month.'

Bramble still couldn't reply. She understood getting to the end of your energy and having nothing left to give but having to give it anyway. Getting to the end of a long journey and then being faced with another challenge and then, after that, another. She and Edward asked it of their horses – and themselves – over and over again.

'I know,' she said. 'Don't worry, I'll be fine. I can manage.' She swallowed. 'Let's talk later, when I've been through Pa's papers and found out about the will and everything. I'll ring round the local solicitors. He won't have gone far.'

'You don't have to do it right now,' said Nicky gently, but Bramble could hear the urgency in her voice. Not right now, perhaps, but tomorrow. No later. That's what Nicky meant.

'Come and see me when you can face talking about it all. No hurry. Just to warn you, though,' she added, 'the bank accounts will be frozen if they're only in his name. If your name isn't on them, you won't have access to any money until probate is granted. And that can take months. A year, even. Can you sign cheques on the business account?'

Bramble thought of the farrier and the vet's bills, both of which added up to quite staggering amounts at the end of every month. 'No.' She felt a stab of pure white panic, a churning that knotted up her innards.

'I can't sign cheques,' she told Nicky. 'Pa did it all. He told me his pin number so I can get cash out, but that's it.'

'I shouldn't really say this, but draw out as much cash as you can quite quickly. And there's another thing you haven't heard me say: don't rush to let the bank know he's died. Give it a few days until you feel up to it, so that cheques can go through. Oh, and when the liveries pay up this month get them to pay into your bank account and keep a record for the estate. Otherwise your cash flow could get very sticky indeed.'

'I think we'd better talk about that next week.'

'Come and see me any time. I'll move appointments round if I have to,' said Nicky. 'Don't worry too much. And if there's anything I can do—'

'Really, I can manage.'

Scrabbling around the untidy desk, Bramble found a cheque book underneath a copy of the *Racing Post*, and, just for one moment, considered forging her father's signature in order to pay the most urgent bills.

She couldn't make those sort of decisions now, not today, not on her own. Her father had believed that a gentleman didn't talk about money and had snapped at her whenever she had tried.

Darcy stepped delicately into the study and yawned, placing two graceful front paws exactly side-by-side in front of Bramble and stretching his long body backwards in invitation. He cocked his head to one side. A walk would be nice, his bright eyes said, not to interrupt but . . .

He was such a polite dog.

'I don't think so, Darcy.' She stroked him and he wagged his long plumy tail. 'Sorry.'

He circled the study uneasily and whined, before settling down so close to her chair that she risked running over his paws if she pushed it back.

Had she killed her father with that last argument? Had his heart given out with the effort of telling her that she would never be good enough to take Teddy to the very top? And had he been right?

Later that evening she sat in the kitchen cleaning tack, too numb to think, as the day darkened around her. She dipped each stirrup iron into a bowl of soapy water then rinsed it off, the actions so familiar and mechanical they were almost a meditation. She sponged saddle soap onto the bridles, sliding the narrow reins through her hands like ribbons, soothed by the nostalgic aroma of neatsfoot oil, and polished the leather until it was supple and burnished beneath her hands. Only when it was all done, every bridle hanging on its peg, with each gleaming saddle neatly mounted on its rack beneath, could she rest. Lorenden had had a tack room in the stables once, but the insurers had demanded better security for easily stolen possessions like saddles. Now the broad back hall was used instead. The smell of leather mingled with that of cooking in a warm fug of welcome, and the sight of its quiet orderliness never failed to reassure her.

She went over her father's words again and again in her head. Since Dom died she had struggled for success, but it had been very elusive. Every time she came close something went wrong.

To succeed as an eventer you needed courage, hard work, talent and good support but, above all, you needed the right horse and they were very difficult to find. One of their top horses had injured himself in the field and would never jump again. Her father had been offered a huge sum for another when money had been very short. He had measured the potential of the horse against the risk that something might go wrong before he fulfilled that promise, and both against the bills that were coming in. He had sold him. Another, one that she rode for a very pleasant, very ambitious couple who lived nearby, had also been sold when the husband was made redundant. Other horses – a procession of them – just failed to make the grade or were slightly off-colour when it counted.

Or was it her riding? Had her father been right?

'You don't ride to win,' he'd said. 'You think too much. Your nerves get the better of you.'

'Any rider who isn't terrified at the start of cross-country day is either a fool or a liar,' she snapped back. 'Of course I'm nervous. So is everybody.'

'But you don't give your heart,' he said.

'Sometimes I have to get up at four-thirty and don't get to bed till midnight,' she shouted. 'And every moment, and every waking thought and every single thing I do is about the horses. I give *everything*. Everything I have. Nobody could give more.'

He shook his head. 'Since Dom died there's been a part of you shut away.'

'That is so unfair and you know it,' she hissed.

'You are a mother,' he replied. 'And that makes it harder for you.'

'No! That has nothing to do with it.'

She couldn't quite remember what they'd said after that.

And now he was dead.

By this time the light had almost gone. It had all taken her so long, and she was tired. The silence of the house descended on her shoulders like a heavy cloak. 'Pa,' she thought. 'Pa.'

She had never been alone at Lorenden before. There had always been someone – the live-in working pupils, Savannah, Edward, even Helena before she married Ollie, clutching Eddie's hand protectively. This house was made to be filled with bustle and chatter.

The view outside her window, with its faint trace of autumn copper amongst the green leaves, blurred again and she rubbed her eyes. There were so many more phone calls to go; she couldn't start crying now.

Chapter 4

In Primrose Hill that evening it was almost supper-time before the door closed on Fi's endless questions. It had taken all morning to photograph the kitchen, then Paul and Tang spent most of the afternoon fussing over the bathroom, trying to find an angle where the camera wouldn't be reflected in the huge mirrors on every wall.

'They took long enough,' grumbled Ollie.

'It always takes that long,' explained Helena wearily. 'Oh God, and I've got to phone Bramble back. Get me a drink, would you darling?'

Helena heard the news of Edward's death with a detachment that surprised and disturbed her. She didn't feel anything. She would have to pretend. That's what actresses do, she told herself.

Ollie placed a large glass of cold white wine in front of her and she grabbed it greedily. She couldn't let Bramble know how blank and empty she felt and, anyway, it was outrageous that Bramble had let her go on with the photoshoot as if nothing had happened. Bramble was like that, always deciding that she knew best, and it made Helena look so . . . so *heartless*.

'Why didn't you *tell* me?' she demanded. 'How could you let me go on with that shoot?'

'There was nothing you could do.'

'You might at least have let me decide. And why didn't you warn me he wasn't feeling well? We could have come down.'

Forcing her mind to the incomprehensible news that her father was dead, Helena tried to concentrate and say the right things. 'You were with Pa all the time, you must have noticed something wrong,' she added in an effort to redirect some of the guilt she felt for not being there.

'He seemed fine. Just fine. I suppose it can happen any time. Especially as people get older. He was nearly seventy, even if he didn't look it.'

Helena began to sob. 'Sixty-nine is nothing these days. The Beaumonts have always gone on until their nineties. Oh Bramble, I can't bear it. I simply can't bear it. It's all right for you, you don't feel these things like I do . . .'

At the other end of the phone Bramble felt the familiar sense of outrage build in her. She always thought of the right response to Helena about three hours later, and then spent the next three days seething over it. 'Helena,' she said, feeling the conversation slipping away. 'That's really not true.' It sounded weak, even to herself.

Helena worked herself into tears that were only half-acting. 'Nobody in this family ever thinks about how I might feel. It's all horses, horses, horses.'

'Honestly, Helena I do care about how you feel. Truly.'

'Oh, never mind about me,' Helena sniffed. 'I'm sorry. I didn't mean that. It's just all so sudden. It's worse for me because I wasn't actually there. At least you got to say goodbye to him.'

'Well, in fact, it wasn't really like that.'

Helena wasn't listening. 'Did he suffer? Tell me absolutely every detail, I must know.'

But after a few sentences she interrupted again, saying that she couldn't concentrate – the shock was too great – but that she would get into the car first thing in the morning. 'I feel this tremendous homing instinct. Lorenden is calling me,' she said. 'In times like this you need to go home, don't you think?'

Bramble looked out of the window but saw only a deep, black darkness and her own reflection. Night came down so quickly now. She shivered. Perhaps it was time to turn on the central heating. Her father never permitted it before the end of October but, as if experiencing a series of aftershocks following an earthquake, she was jolted again by the thought that he was no longer here to argue with.

'Bramble?' asked Helena sharply. 'Are you still there? Did you hear what I said? I'll come down tomorrow. I want to be there for you. I'll see you then.'

Bramble shook herself. 'No, wait a minute. I mean, yes, I'd love to see you, but I need to know one more thing. Do you have Felicity's number?'

'Oh my God, *Felicity*.' Helena sounded irritated. 'She's absolutely hopeless, never wishes me good luck on any first night, not the faintest clue about any of the children's birthdays – I mean, it's a Christmas card and that's it. Never thinks about anyone else except herself. Didn't she get some amazing new job? In Hong Kong or something?'

'I thought it was Kuala Lumpur.'

'Well, somewhere abroad anyway. Best to try Pa's book, I'd have thought.'

'It's just a question of finding his book,' replied Bramble.

Bramble put down the phone and almost found herself laughing. A conversation with Helena was infuriating – resulting in a mental bruising that often lingered – but you had to see the funny side. Helena would drive you mad if you didn't.

The house rustled. It was now dark outside, the absolute blackness of the fields and orchards falling around her, cutting her off from any human contact.

She got up. She checked the locks on the windows and the shutters all round the house before making her last visit of the day to the stables. She made herself walk across the deserted yard without looking behind her, barely realising that she was holding her breath. The dogs pottered after her, Darcy lifting his leg on the herbs she grew by the kitchen door, the terriers snuffling around after rats.

At the sound of her footsteps, horses lifted their heads over stable doors in curiosity then turned back to their haynets. The security lighting flooded the loose boxes, showing the tubs with their fading flowers set at each corner, the neatly swept concrete and the dark water in the central trough, the post-and-rail fencing securing the fourth side of the quadrangle, even the racehorse weathervane. The lights in Donna's flat were out. She would be in the White Horse, regaling everyone with the dramas of the day. Bramble checked the horses' rugs, topped up water buckets, added some more hay to most of the haynets and skipped some manure out of Teddy's box.

She had to force herself not to run back to the safety of the house and bolt herself in. 'Come on, dogs,' she said, in a high voice. It was so unlike her. She had always felt completely safe at Lorenden. Nothing had changed: Edward's death had been sudden, but clearly natural.

She tried turning the television up loudly, but couldn't help being aware of the occasional shriek of foxes outside, of the swoop of the barn owl and the soft sighing of the wind in the trees.

She jumped up when the window rattled as if someone was tapping on it. After summoning up the courage to peer out she decided it was the whippy stems of the overgrown wisteria being blown against the glass. 'Pull yourself together,' she told herself. 'You don't want to get as neurotic as Helena.' She went round the house and checked the locks again, noting that the wind was rising. They often had fierce storms, which could cause considerable damage, ripping slates off the roof and tearing down trees.

'They come from Russia, these winds,' Edward used to say. 'There's nothing between us and the steppes.'

Bramble had always thought that Germany, and possibly Denmark, might be in the way, not to mention obscure chunks of Eastern Europe, but her geography was foggy and Edward was adamant. Watch out for the wild wind from the east, he always said. It blows hardest when you least expect it.

She was channel surfing in search of distraction when there was a sudden crash and both the television and the lights went out. Bramble jumped, her heart leaping against her chest. Resisting the temptation to burrow into the grubby sofa and pull a cushion over her head, she told herself not to be ridiculous and began to feel her way through the room. There were candles on the mantelpiece, and probably some matches too. The dogs whimpered and pressed their warm, comforting bodies against her leg. They didn't like it any more than she did, and she could hear a low growl rising in Mop's throat.

'Shh, Mop,' she said. 'It's nothing. Just thunder.' Mop gave a thin whine, but Bramble could feel her tail wagging feebly, and Muddle trembled against Bramble's shins.

She thought she heard something else outside – an unspecific man-made sound, not a natural storm noise. Darcy rarely barked, but suddenly let out a throaty 'woof', which was followed by an explosion of yapping from the terriers. She couldn't hear if there was anything out there with all that barking.

Still feeling her way, she checked the table lamps. They were dead. So not a fuse. A complete blackout, probably of the whole area. Her heartbeat rose. She could feel it pattering in her throat, pumping faster than usual, but she suppressed her alarm. This happened, she told herself. Especially during storms. It happened at least twice a year. The Martyr's Forstal electricity supply was famously erratic. They kept a big torch and some candles in the kitchen, just for that purpose.

She edged cautiously down the corridor, finding the torch and lighting the candles with a trembling hand. The light flickered over the kitchen in a grotesque imitation of the happy candlelit evenings they'd spent drinking and laughing with friends around the big oak table. If she blinked she could bring them all back – Dom and Edward, and all the people who'd dropped in, day and night, winter and summer, to drink tea, wine and beer, with homemade cakes or huge chunks of farmhouse cheddar and fresh bread. The kitchen was full of shadows.

There was a sharp rap on the back door. Nobody ever used the front door – it had been jammed shut for at least twenty years. Bramble pushed her hair off her face. It must be the wind again. Or an echo from the thunder that crashed in the distance. Thunder could do funny things. She waited, clutching the torch, hardly daring to breathe.

She had almost convinced herself that there was no one there when the knock came again, distinct and commanding. Bramble picked up the bread knife and wedged it into her pocket, then turned the torch on full blast. Holding it ahead of her she opened the back door very, very slowly.

There, blinking in the glare of the torchlight, stood a man she had never seen before. He was broad-shouldered but graceful, with sloping cheekbones and icy grey eyes that made her think of winter skies.

'I'm sorry I'm late,' he said.

She stared at him.

'I'm Jezzar Morgan, the new nagsman,' he added. 'And by the way, it isn't very safe to have a knife pointing upwards in your pocket.'

'We've never had a nagsman,' replied Bramble. 'I'm sorry, you've come to the wrong place.'

Jezzar fumbled in the pocket of his battered waxed jacket and produced a letter, with her father's distinctive signature scrawled along the bottom of it. He held it out to her. 'This is Edward Beaumont's yard?'

Helena put down the phone and hid her face in her hands.

'What's up?' Ollie came back into the room to find Helena's bag. Discreetly. He needed to nip out to the off-licence before it closed as that had been their last bottle, and he hadn't got any cash on him. Helena never missed the odd twenty-pound note.

Helena tried to look like someone who has been hit by a great tragedy, but she still couldn't feel anything. 'I'm sorry, darling. Pa's died, I'm afraid.' She suddenly felt as if she could hardly breathe.

Ollie straightened up from his surreptitious search. 'No! God, I'm sorry. That's . . . What . . . I mean, how?' For a moment there was something in his eyes. Was it sympathy? Remembered pain? Surprise? Love? Calculation?

He opened his arms and drew her in.

'They think it must have been a heart attack. We won't know till the post-mortem is done. Just like that,' snuffled Helena. 'But it was in the field, next to his old horse Ben. Just the way he would have wanted to go.' She allowed herself to be folded in her husband's arms. It felt lovely and warm and safe, and, for a moment, she just wanted to stay there, pretending that everything was the way it used to be.

Eddie bounded past the drawing room, down the stairs two at a time to the family room in the basement.

'I'm going down to Lorenden tomorrow,' said Helena when the noise of his footsteps had faded away.

Ollie drew back and looked into her eyes; she immediately knew what he was thinking. It was what was so good about them as a couple: they thought the same thing at the same time.

Helena blew her nose. 'It'll all be left to Bramble, you know. Because of the bloody horses.'

Ollie's hands tightened on her shoulders. 'That's not fair on you. Not fair at all.'

Helena laid her head against her husband's chest again. 'No, it isn't,' she said, indistinctly. 'It's not fair, and I'm going to do something about it.'

'Wait,' he said, softly into her ear. She could feel his lips against her hair. 'Wait until you know exactly what the situation is.'

She nodded. Sometimes Ollie was so right. 'I'll get down there as soon as I can, though, don't you think? After all,' she drew away from him and carefully touched under her eyes to tidy away any smudged mascara, 'Bramble needs me.'

'Do you want me to take you?'

She hesitated.

She thought about the extra layer of organisation that would cause – another batch of instructions for Ania. It was all too much to cope with. She just had to get down to Lorenden.

'It's OK. I think I ought to be alone with Bramble. I was a bit snappish with her on the phone, and I didn't mean to be. It was the shock, I suppose, I couldn't believe she hadn't noticed anything wrong with him, but . . .' She kissed him lightly on the cheek. 'I need you to hold the fort here, OK?'

There was that look in his eyes again, just for a second.

He shrugged. 'Sure. I only care about you. You know that.'

Helena looked into his eyes, and felt a deep sense of connection with him. It had been like that the first time they met. Everyone else had melted away. Those moments were rarer now, but they still happened.

The phone rang again. It was Angelina Woody. The supermodel. The wife of vintage rock star Chris Woody. These were the sort of people Helena felt comfortable with. The reason why she had chosen Ruby and Roly's school so carefully. Angelina Woody was an über-Yummy Mummy, with painted toenails and a white-blonde crop, while Chris, with his tangled, greying hair, unshaven face and apparent disregard for the millions that filled his bank account, was so refreshingly different from the usual round of solicitors and doctors that populated Eddie's school on speech day. Helena tried to collect herself.

'Oh, Angelina, that was a simply marvellous party last Sunday.

Roly and Ruby haven't stopped talking about it. It was so clever to think of having a beauty parlour for the little girls, they had such fun. Are you absolutely exhausted?'

'Well, I had to go to Milan on Monday, so yes, I am a bit,' admitted Angelina. 'But I'm glad you enjoyed it. Your little Ruby is such a poppet – do you know she was trying to put nail varnish on everyone's lips?'

Everybody knew that it wasn't the parties you were invited to these days that mattered, but the ones your children went to. Tangerine Woody's party had been unmissable, especially as the children were just still young enough for the mothers and fathers to have to accompany them and be offered champagne with the Woodys.

Ollie had been in his element, lounging in their vast glass and steel kitchen. He was easily the most attractive man in the room – some of the other fathers were beginning to look middle-aged but Ollie was leaner than ever, with shadows under those gorgeous brown eyes. He looked like a ravaged angel, even more dissipated than Chris Woody himself, although his body was gym-fit. When he reached out for another bottle or stretched out to catch a thrown ball he displayed sleek, defined muscles under his tattered T-shirt. Most of the other fathers revealed only occasional glimpses of soft marshmallow flesh. Helena had seen their envious glances and the way they sucked their stomachs in, almost involuntarily.

'Ruby is real sweet,' said Angelina down the phone. She sometimes affected a mid-Atlantic tone. 'I was ringing because I think she might have left a Gucci satchel behind.'

'Um, no, not ours.' Suddenly Helena found it very difficult to concentrate on what Angelina was saying. 'I don't think, anyway.'

'Are you all right?' Angelina sounded genuinely concerned.

Helena hadn't wanted to say anything because she didn't want to trivialise her father's death. You couldn't just come out with it on the phone, as if it meant nothing, but the note of kindness in Angelina's voice slipped under her defences.

'Well,' Helena was horrified to feel real, uncontrollable tears welling up. She couldn't cry over the phone to a woman she hardly knew. 'I'm afraid I've just heard that my father has died.' The words crystallised it into fact. Helena realised that she would never feel her father's bristly cheek brush against hers in a kiss, or hear the sound of his voice shouting for the dogs again.

'I am so sorry.' Angelina sounded sincere. 'That's terrible. My own father left us only six months ago, so I know what you're going through. Is your mother alive?'

'No.' Helena blew her nose, always surprised when anyone mentioned her mother. 'She died a long time ago. When I was very young. I don't remember much about her.' This was not entirely true.

'I'm so sorry,' repeated Angelina. 'I know people always say this, but is there anything I can do for the twins? If you need someone to look after them during the funeral, or anything like that, call me first. Promise?'

Helena was shocked to feel a certain glee at the thought of being able to say that Ruby and Roly were at the Woodys' during the funeral. Chris, after all, was practically Mick Jagger. She thanked Angelina and, once she'd put the phone down, rested her head in her hands. One day, Helena Harris, she told herself, you are going to become a better person. Less snobbish and truly kind. But just for now, you have to stay on top. For Eddie. And Ruby and Roly.

'That was Angelina Woody,' she said, as she put the phone down and picked Oscar up for a hug.

'Really?' Ollie sounded bored, and she remembered that he had been flirting with Angelina at the party. Well, there was nothing wrong with that, Helena reminded herself. She trusted Ollie and they could make the most of it by inviting the Woodys round for Sunday lunch one day. After all, Ruby and Tangerine were such great friends.

But on the other hand perhaps she should have accepted Ollie's invitation to take her down to Lorenden. She'd never turned him away before. Not in anything.

As Helena took another gulp of white wine to calm herself she decided to stop worrying about Ollie. She'd deal with all that later.

Chapter 5

The heavens broke open over Lorenden and a deluge came rumbling down, sluicing the side of the house and pouring in rivulets down Jezzar's boots. Bramble hastily stood back, out of the wet. 'You'd better come in. I'm afraid there isn't any light. We get these power oddities.'

He bent his head slightly to duck through the back door. People were shorter in Jacobean times, when the doorway had been built.

'I don't know what my father said to you,' she said. 'But . . .' she swallowed and turned her head away, pointing the torch towards the kitchen door, past the rows of freshly gleaming tack.

She set off in front of him so that he couldn't hear the catch in her voice. 'But,' she repeated, 'my father died this morning. Quite suddenly, I'm afraid. And he never discussed any nagsman with me.' A small flame of rage lit up inside her, beside the guilt that was already burning.

'I run my father's yard,' she said, lighting two more candles with a trembling hand. 'We have working pupils sometimes, but that's not, presumably, what you're talking about. By "nagsman" I take it you mean someone who knows everything about horses?' Her heart quickened. She ran the yard, her father managed the business. But she wondered exactly how much he had been keeping from her.

Jezzar ignored her last question and stood there, his dark hair plastered to his head by the rain. 'I'm sorry. I really am. Your father was a great man and a very unusual person. I hope I haven't frightened you, turning up so late.' His voice had the upper-class cadence of an Army officer, overlaid with something else that Bramble couldn't quite place. 'And I'm so sorry to intrude. I'll go – I can find somewhere to stay, but—'

'No, wait.' Bramble read the letter in the light of the torch. 'It says here that you're to live in the attic. And compete Teddy and the other horses.' She put the letter down, cold with fear. Her father had engaged another rider. That was what he had wanted to say last night, what she had prevented him from saying when she left the room and slammed the door.

'Teddy's a man's horse,' he'd said.

'I've ridden Teddy since he was a five-year-old. I've made him what he is.'

'He's strong, he spooks at anything and he's difficult to hold. So far, you've got away with it – just – and you've qualified him for four-star competitions by the skin of your teeth. But he'll be taking a step up next season, and he needs the strength of a man on his back.'

Bramble tasted fear in the back of her throat again. It seemed to lie in wait for her everywhere these days, but she refused to give in to it. 'Women are as good as men,' she said. 'There's no difference.'

'They *are* as good as men,' he'd replied. 'But there *is* a difference.'

'There isn't,' she'd shouted, and that's when she'd left.

'You seem to be our new rider.' Bramble forced herself to sound calm. 'And the address he's written to – it's near Newcastle. You must have come a long way.'

Jezzar stood there without replying.

'So if you do go,' said Bramble, on autopilot, 'have you got somewhere to go to?'

'I'll be fine.'

'Nonsense.' Bramble looked at her watch. 'It's nearly midnight and there's nowhere near here that would dream of letting you in at this time. They won't even answer the phone, let alone the door. You'd better stay here tonight.'

He hesitated. 'That's very kind of you,' he said formally. 'I am so sorry to arrive like this. I had no idea.'

'It's no trouble, no trouble at all.' Bramble was back on familiar territory now. She buried the fury deep inside her. 'The bed in the spare room is all made up.'

She thought she saw sympathy in his eyes, but it was hard to tell in the flickering candlelight. 'I'll show you the way,' she suggested.

'A sofa will be fine. Anything.'

Bramble led him upstairs. 'We've got six bedrooms. All with perfectly good beds. So there would be absolutely no point in your sleeping on a sofa.' This isn't fair, Pa, she thought. Not fair at all. Why didn't you discuss this with me properly?

I tried to. Her father's voice floated into her head. You wouldn't listen.

She flung the door of the spare room open, and showed Jezzar the ancient bathroom opposite, the one with the claw-footed bath and powdery, musty smell of childhood and linoleum.

Later, as she whisked up some scrambled eggs for them both, she ran her eyes over the letter again. It was quite clear. It was addressed to Major Jezzar Morgan, who was to train and ride the horses in return for a small salary and somewhere to live.

Eddie Harris was in tune with his mother's moods. Other people – the succession of au pairs, or mothers of his school friends – complained about Helena behind her back but his first few years, as an only child in an adult world, had taught him to listen without being noticed. His mother could be difficult, he accepted that, but she loved her family and she worked very hard to keep them all going. Most people didn't understand what hard work acting was, or why Helena couldn't make costumes for the school play or brownies for the summer fête, but he knew that she did so much for him – well, for them all now – and he wasn't exactly certain what Ollie, so far, had contributed. When Ollie made his mother happy that was good enough for him. When he made his mother unhappy, as he did occasionally these days, Eddie intended to find out why. Helena, he knew, was very vulnerable underneath her stylish veneer. And something had obviously upset her.

'What's up, Mum?' He put his arm round her.

Helena blew her nose and leant against his chest. 'I can't get over how much you've grown.' This was a familiar refrain and had pleased him at first, although he was getting quite sick of it. He waited. Helena could never keep anything from him.

'Grampa's died, I'm afraid.'

Eddie was taken aback by the thud in his chest. It was literally as if someone had punched him hard. 'Grampa? What d'you mean?' He hoped he'd misunderstood somehow.

'Down at Lorenden this morning. Everyone thinks it must have been a heart attack. It probably won't mean much to you, because you didn't know him all that well, but to me, well, he was my father.'

Eddie broke away. 'I did know him! And I wanted to know him better. But you wouldn't let me. And now he's gone.'

'Eddie, Eddie . . .' Helena put out a hand. Eddie was such a sweetheart, he never blew up like the uncouth sons of her friends. 'Don't upset me like this. I can't believe you'd be so cruel as to talk to me in that way. After all, I'm the one whose father's died.'

'Sorry, Mum.' He hugged her mechanically, his mind swirling. He'd always planned to go to Grampa after his A levels and beg to be taken on as a working pupil. Edward Grattan was the only one who could insist that Helena agree to it.

He couldn't believe that his grandfather was no longer striding around Lorenden, eyes narrowed as he assessed a horse or a rider. 'When you're jumping, Eddie,' he'd say, 'remember that the horse is prey. It can see all round itself to see if it's being chased. But there's a blind spot directly in front. So you've got to see ahead on your horse's behalf. You've got to make the demands. You're a partnership, but you're the one in the driving seat.'

Eddie noticed the way Edward's eyes lit up at the sight of him, and he loved sitting with the old man as he showed the boy how to clean a saddle, gossiping about the eventing circuit, complaining about in-fighting in the Pony Club ('no one's more competitive than a Pony Club mother,' he would mutter) and passing on his tips – 'don't use too much oil, it'll rot the stitching'. The smell of saddle soap, horse and damp cloth rose in his nostrils at the memory and he suppressed a whimper of anguish.

He quietly disentangled himself from his mother's embrace and went upstairs to his room, locking the door and turning U2 up as loud as he dared. Then he sank down on his bed, head in his hands, and cried dry, rasping masculine sobs that tore the heart out of him. He had never known such loss or ever realised that pain could be so terrible. Edward Beaumont was as much a part of his life as the sun or the moon – distant, but everlasting and completely, utterly essential if the world was to go on turning.

He stayed there for the rest of the evening, eventually drifting into an exhausted sleep, sprawled across his narrow single bed, still dressed. Helena wondered if she should go upstairs to find out what was wrong, but she didn't quite dare. There was a new maleness to him these days that both impressed her and made her tread more carefully.

It would just be a teenage thing. Even her darling Eddie was bound to have the odd tantrum. It was hormones.

Bramble was sagging with tiredness and grief but this situation was not Major Jezzar Morgan's fault, she told herself. He must be made welcome.

As he walked back into the kitchen the electricity came back on, flooding them both in glaring light. He was unshaven, with dark, heavy stubble that gave him the air of a wolf. A wolf from an icy place, with those blue-grey eyes, she thought, and then she realised who he was.

'I know who you are,' she exclaimed. 'Of course! I must be stupid not to have recognised you.'

He bowed. 'I'm hardly famous.'

'Well, you are, of course you are,' she replied, turning some of the lights off. The kitchen was nicer in candlelight. 'Aren't you half-Russian or something?'

'I'm half Tatar,' he said. 'My mother was Tatar, not Russian. We ruled the Russians. For centuries.'

She could see pride in his slightly almond-shaped eyes – the colour of the sky where it meets the sea on a frosty morning – and in the way he held his powerful, rangy body. 'Right,' she said, nodding. 'I saw an interview. Didn't *Horse & Hound* call you Jumping Jez? On the cover? When you won—'

'When I won Thirlestane.'

'Scrambled eggs?'

'Wonderful.'

'Really, though, why are you here?' she asked. 'I thought you rode for Penny Luckham. She's got a much better string than we have.'

'I did. But she chucked me out. Rather suddenly.'

'Why?'

He hesitated. 'Because I . . . er . . . had an affair with someone else's wife.'

'That's a bit old-fashioned, isn't it? It's hardly going to affect your riding.'

'Penny didn't like it.'

Bramble rifled her memory for gossip. Hadn't Jezzar been living with this Penny woman? 'Oh,' she said. 'Were you and Penny . . .?'

He nodded, shovelling in scrambled eggs as if he was starving.

'I see,' said Bramble. 'And you met my father . . .?' She tried to damp down the slow-burning glow of anger inside her. How dare he? Hadn't she, Bramble, counted for anything?

'He'd always said that if ever I wanted to move down south I should contact him,' said Jez casually.

This was like a punch to Bramble's stomach. So this wasn't an impulse on her father's part. He'd been planning it. The scrambled egg turned dry in her mouth and she took a hasty glug of wine to get it down. 'He never mentioned it. Did he talk about me at all?' he asked.

Jezzar looked surprised. 'You?'

'What did he say?'

'Um, well, just what everyone else says.'

'And what's that?' Bramble steeled herself, knowing he would talk about a talent that had never quite been fulfilled. That after her husband had been killed she'd slipped down the rankings.

Jezzar seemed to be struggling to find words. 'They, er, say that you, er, are . . .' He looked around the kitchen, as if seeking inspiration. 'They say that you're efficient,' he concluded.

'Efficient?' shrieked Bramble. '*Efficient?*'

'You know. Practical. Strong.' He was floundering now. 'You did ask.'

'I can just see it now, on my gravestone: "Here lies Bramble

Kelly. She was very efficient." Great. Is that all?' No one, she thought, would ever call Felicity 'efficient', or Helena. Not because either of them were inefficient, but because there were more exciting ways of describing them. She remembered hearing people talk about Felicity when she was very young. 'A heart-breaker,' someone had said, and someone else had laughed. 'A maneater, you mean.' Then there had been muttering about little pitchers having big ears and *pas devant les enfants*, and the conversation had turned back to the mess farming was in. Efficient. It was hardly going to set the world on fire.

Jezzar looked amused and helped himself to another slice of toast. 'And people wonder why you haven't married again.'

Bramble was taken aback; she couldn't think of what to say for a moment. 'Well, I don't feel it's necessary to jump straight from one relationship to another,' she said eventually. 'And I have a daughter who doesn't need a series of "uncles" in her life. It's only been . . .' Bramble stopped.

Jezzar met her eyes. 'Seven years,' he said. 'It's been seven years since Dominic Kelly died. It was the year I left the Army. I remember reading about it. I'm sorry.' He placed his hand very lightly on her arm in sympathy. She could feel his touch burning through the sweater.

'Not that long, surely,' said Bramble, although the date was engraved on her heart. She slid her arm away and picked up their plates so that she could turn her back on him, making a great deal of noise scraping her egg into the bin, then filling the dishwasher with a clatter. She had the sensation that he was watching her every move.

'Fruit?'

He took an apple, and cocked his head, his eyes appearing lit from behind under the dark brows, his face heavily shadowed by fatigue.

He notices things, she thought suddenly.

She took a deep breath. 'It's none of anyone's business why I haven't married again,' she said, biting a loose edge on her thumb-nail ferociously. She re-filled her glass and reminded herself to be more polite. It was just that she hurt. Every part of her was in pain. Edward was gone. Dom was gone. The holes – and the guilt, and the anger – they left behind were immeasurable.

'No,' he agreed, equably. 'It isn't.' He continued to look at her in the candlelight and she began to feel self-conscious. 'What?' she asked. 'Have I got a smudge on my face or something?'

He laughed and shook his head. 'No, I was just thinking that you were very brave.'

'Not brave enough, obviously,' she said tartly. 'Or we wouldn't be taking on another rider.'

'What time do you start work in the morning?' he asked.

She looked at him sharply.

'I mean,' he added, 'I'd like to help. In return for your kindness in letting me stay the night. Presumably you're short-handed.'

'I start at six-thirty,' she said. It was the closest she wanted to get to admitting he was right.

The following morning Savannah woke up at Lottie's. Her head felt as if it were about to crack open. She'd spent a restless night, tossing and turning as the room spun around her. Several times she'd managed to totter to the loo. She'd been sick twice and so, by the sound of it, had Lottie. Katya had bustled up and down stairs muttering sympathetically. At least it was a Saturday so they didn't have to go to school.

Now her fluting Eastern European tones penetrated Savannah's head like a flight of a thousand arrows.

'I think this is the winter vomiting that everybody talk about. She is sick. A bad stomach.' She was speaking to someone on the phone; Bramble, by the sound of it.

Bramble must have expressed sympathy because she added. 'I am fine. I am not sick. I am from Bulgaria. But Savannah is no eating, and she usually eat much.'

Savannah definitely did not care for the description of herself as 'usually eat much'. 'A moment on the lips, a lifetime on the hips,' she murmured, running her hand across the soft flesh of her belly.

It was definitely flatter. And she could feel the tiny tips of her hip bones. After just one day of not eating. Through the pounding across her forehead it occurred to her that this getting thin might be easier than she had thought.

Savannah put the pillow over her head. If Bramble cared she would come and get her.

On the other hand, she didn't think she could manage a car journey.

Katya tiptoed into the room. 'I'll just leave this bowl by both your beds, shall I? And a little bell so that you can ring it if you need anything?'

Savannah could barely nod before she threw up again.

When they woke up again, the clock said two o'clock.

'Are you feeling OK?' Lottie's voice was hoarse.

Savannah tried moving her head. It ached but no longer threatened to spin off entirely. 'I think so.'

'Do you think we've got the winter vomiting bug?' Lottie managed a giggle.

'I think we might have.' Savannah's stomach still heaved.

'Or do you think it might be a hangover? Katie Browne has them all the time.'

Savannah winced. Katie Browne, who was in their branch of the Pony Club, was super-sophisticated and sexy and known for putting out. She didn't particularly want to be like her, although the sexy bit would be nice.

Savannah closed her eyes and opened them again quickly as she remembered the previous day. Her final sight of her grandfather – his yellow, staring face – had floated through her dreams in a terrifying way, but she couldn't say that she was sad, not exactly. She didn't really think he liked her, let alone loved her, and it was very difficult to love him back.

Which just shows you, Savannah Kelly, she told herself, what a horrible superficial person you are. Fat, superficial and not even clever. She sank back with a sigh, feeling defeated.

At six-thirty in the morning Jez stood in the yard, his hands on his hips, wearing only a short-sleeved shirt and jeans, with chaps on top. Bramble had slept fitfully, woken to the sound of crying and realised it was her own, and had a headache from the wine they'd drunk.

'Aren't you cold?' asked Bramble. He looked so alive somehow, so outrageously – even offensively – vibrant, strong and confident, so, well, so *male*, that she'd had to say something, and it was the first thing that came into her head.

He looked at her quizzically but didn't answer.

Donna, rubbing sleep out of her eyes and with tousled hair, appeared in the yard and stood stock-still in surprise.

'Donna, this is Jezzar. He's come to . . . well, help out for a bit.'

'Everyone calls me Jez.' He extended a hand to Donna, who shook it. She stared at him. 'Hi. Sorry, I've forgotten something.'

She reappeared twenty-five minutes later in full make-up, but by then Jez was vigorously forking dung and straw into a wheelbarrow with fast, economical movements and didn't look up.

Bramble lined up all the buckets for the morning feeds, but found it difficult to concentrate. Was that two or three scoops of sugar beet for Teddy? She lost count several times. She showed Jez the charts on the wall, indicating which horses would go out in the field during the day, who was to be ridden and what work they were to do, and what was left of this year's competition schedule. It was almost over.

'All the horses that live in do a half-hour in the horse-walker first thing,' she said.

'Why not turn them all out?'

'They might injure themselves if they're turned out fresh.'

'Keep them out for longer then.'

'Look,' Bramble's brain was barely functioning with tiredness and shock, and she didn't want to be challenged. 'We have a rota of when the horses go out. They each have their own little patch, roped off with a bit of portable electric fence, so they can all see each other. They're out for about an hour or so. They have a nice time; we don't have any accidents.'

'Horses are herd animals,' he said. 'They need to be out in the field for most of the day. With each other. They'll sort it all out between themselves if you let them.'

'They might fight. Kick each other. Gallop about and catch themselves on something . . .' She thought he must be mad. There was too much invested in Teddy, for example, to let him romp about in the field like a pony.

'Horses need to be horses,' he replied and she bit back a reply.

But they finished their duties in half the time it usually took Bramble and her father, and went inside for breakfast. Bramble put on fresh coffee and made bacon sandwiches, still shaken by her father's assessment of her chances of getting to the top. Could he be right? No. He couldn't. But it ate away at her. It had been such a long time since she'd won anything big. Her confidence had chipped away.

'So,' he said, 'am I hired?'

'What?' She wondered whether Jez could sue them for breach of promise or something if she didn't take him on and felt a twitch of panic. 'Of course, um, I'll stand by what my father promised. If you still want to stay, that is.'

'I'd like to accept,' he said. 'If that's OK by you.'

It was the last thing she wanted, but she didn't have much choice. As he had pointed out, they were a man down and Pa had committed her legally. At least for a bit. Ever since Jez had walked in the door she felt as if she'd lost control of what happened at Lorenden.

'OK,' said Bramble. She had to force herself to get the two syllables out, and immediately jumped up to wash their plates so that she didn't have to see his response.

Later on she watched him work Sailor in the sand school and noted how smoothly the horse responded to him. 'Well, you can ride,' she conceded.

He accepted the compliment without any false modesty. 'Of course I can ride. I'm a Tatar. We're the horsemen of Asia. We ran the horse business in Russia for centuries.'

'I thought you said you were *half*-Tatar,' she replied. She wasn't going to let this ethnic background business get out of hand.

He just grinned and swung onto the next horse in one quick, light movement.

Bramble decided she could leave him to get on with it and took the dogs for a walk, comforted by the familiar sound of birdsong and the scent of damp, fallen leaves. The promise of autumn was on the crisp air, while Darcy and the terriers pricked up their ears, sure of rabbits. She walked through the deserted orchards. Even though her father had sold them, they still used the old paths and tracks around the neat rows of trees. The sun slanted through the trees and she heard occasional soft thuds of falling apples. She picked up a few, stuffing them into her pockets for the horses, and bit into one herself, relishing its firm, sharp sweetness.

Mop and Muddle scuffled around tree roots in endless futile searches, snuffling and determined, and Darcy loped along the rows of trees, occasionally stopping to check the ground. But the rabbits had seen them coming and were long gone.

Bramble loved these fields with all her heart and it occurred to her – for the first time – that she might lose them. Surely Pa, though, would have left her Lorenden and the horses so she could continue his work? Even if everything else went to Helena?

Continue his work. A little voice popped up in her head and asked her about her own work. That is my work, she told the voice, realising, with faint surprise, that she was somehow talking to Jez. There was something about him that made you want to explain yourself.

She tried to shake the introspective mood off but the wind rustled through the trees, whispering questions. Where are you in all this, Bramble? Who are you? She pulled her coat round her and turned up the collar, blocking the gusts from her ears, calling the dogs back to her for reassurance.

She was Bramble Kelly. Dom Kelly's wife. Edward Beaumont's daughter. Savannah Kelly's mother.

But now Dom and Edward were gone. Savannah was almost grown up. She was on her own. The terriers pressed their bodies against hers and turned their faces up to her as if to echo the wind's questions. Don't be silly, Bramble, she told herself. Onward and upward. One step in front of another. Don't look down. And I'm sure you can summon up a few more clichés to suit the situation, she inwardly concluded, with a snap of amusement. She whistled Darcy back from a rabbit hole again, and they turned into the road.

Ben was still at the corner of the field. His whiskery lips brushed the apple she offered him but he refused to take it. Patch snatched it away and tried to rifle her pockets for more. She pushed him away gently – Patch was a greedy pony who, on one of his regular coat-pocket raids, had succeeded in crunching up her mobile phone.

She turned back to look at Ben as she returned to the house. He couldn't really know, of course he couldn't, but the old horse seemed so still and sad.

As she was walking up the drive a London taxi turned in to follow her.

Bramble stopped. She'd almost forgotten Helena was coming down. The big black vehicle looked incongruous against the backdrop of orchards, fields and blackberry hedges. They were at least fifty miles away from Piccadilly Circus.

The door was flung open and a thin woman tumbled out in a flurry of expensive-looking shopping bags. It was as if an alien from Bond Street had landed.

'Helena!' cried Bramble, suddenly glad that her sister had come.

Helena showered the taxi driver with twenty-pound notes and wrapped Bramble up with cries of 'I can't bear it, it's all too, too sad'. Her body seemed so soft and slight against Bramble's strength, as if she might crumple if she was hugged too hard. Her collarbones were now like coat-hangers. Her skin usually had the sheen of wealth and privilege but now seemed tissue-paper fragile.

'Helena!' exclaimed Bramble. 'You're hardly wearing anything.'

'I forgot to grab my coat. I'm freezing.' She shivered and sinews briefly appeared in her neck.

'And you're too thin.'

'Don't be silly, I never stop eating. God it's cold here, I'd forgotten.'

'Come inside.' She felt the familiar weight of Helena's neediness on her shoulders like a lead-lined cloak.

As Helena cuddled Mop and Muddle by the Aga, letting them play games with her fingers, Bramble went upstairs to find something clean and warm for her to wear. Helena only wore cashmere in soft, pampering colours. Bramble wore sensible navy or black fleeces, which were heaved into the washing machine at the end of each day. She hesitated over her favourite sweater before handing it to Helena – it was a black poloneck that fitted her beautifully.

'Here you are.' Helena studied it carefully, but put it on without comment.

'You OK?' Helena asked Bramble.

Bramble nodded. 'And you?' She put the kettle on.

'I just don't believe it. And I'd rather have a drink.' Helena got up and opened the larder door, scattering the terriers. It was a big, old-fashioned walk-in larder, north-facing with a stone floor and marble shelves. Mop and Muddle scurried after her, trying to nip her ankles. 'Pa's best claret? Vodka? Are you allowed champagne when someone dies?'

'I think you should have what you like. Although it is only half-past eleven.'

'What do you want?'

'I'll have whatever you're having.'

'Right.' Helena seized a bottle of champagne, which had been sitting on the floor of the larder since the previous Christmas. Behind her, Darcy slid quietly into the larder. He knew the cheese board was kept in there.

'Watch it, Helena,' warned Bramble.

Helena grabbed Darcy's collar just in time to save the cheddar. 'Honestly, can't you train him better?'

'Lurchers don't train. Not when it comes to food.'

'Did you find Felicity's number?' Helena twisted off the cork with a practised hand.

Bramble shook her head. 'It's the most terrible mess in his office. And I think we need to find the will fairly fast too. I had a tricky conversation with Nic yesterday. It seems Pa might have been in financial difficulty.'

'Was he?' Helena's voice was sharp. 'Not in debt, I hope? We really do need to find his will. But first we've got to get hold of Felicity.' She re-filled her glass and held the bottle out, but Bramble had hardly touched hers.

'Can you remember who she's working for at the moment?'

'I think it's some American news channel. Not Reuters, though.'

'I don't know how she does it.' Helena took another swift sip and began ranging round the kitchen, opening drawers and cupboards, pulling things out and feeling around. 'Do you think there's a lot of money in war reporting?'

Bramble shrugged, wondering what Helena was up to. 'What are you looking for, Helena? Can I help?'

'Oh shit.' Helena held up her sleeve. 'So sorry, Bramble. Your sweater – I caught it on a nail.' She showed Bramble a tear in the sleeve of the black poloneck, and Bramble thought she saw malice glinting in her eyes.

'Helena! You . . .' Bramble reined herself in. It was the story of her childhood: whenever she'd had anything pretty – a new top, or a necklace – Helena had somehow managed to destroy it.

'I'm so clumsy,' wailed Helena as she had done so often when they were children. 'It wasn't my fault. It wasn't a special one, though, was it?'

Bramble got up sharply, to conceal her irritation. Helena wanted an argument. She actually wanted it. And Bramble had no intention of giving her one.

'Come on, Helena, let's clear up his office.' What she really wanted was to hit Helena, and she suspected, from the over-emphasised innocence in Helena's eyes, that she felt the same about Bramble.

'We need to find his will,' she said, keeping her voice unnaturally calm. 'I've phoned round the local solicitors but none of them have it. So it must be here somewhere. If he had one, and Nicky says that he told her he did.'

Helena's eyes suddenly seemed very blue. 'Oh the will, of course,' she said, carelessly. 'I suppose we ought to find it. Not that one likes to think about such things the minute someone dies.'

'We have to think about it,' reproved Bramble. 'We have to know what the situation is. Because of the horses.'

'Ah,' said Helena, and there was no mistaking the sharpness in her voice. 'The horses. Of course.'

'We could start with the filing cabinets,' joked Bramble. 'Under "W" for will. You never know, he might have been that logical.'

Helena's face cleared and she laughed. 'Dream on. You might as well suggest we try "F" to find Felicity. But actually, I think we should grab a pile of bin bags and do it methodically, starting with the top of the desk and the floor and working our way through until it's all tidy. Then we can go through the filing cabinets.'

'Here.' Bramble pulled out a roll of black dustbin bags and handed one to Helena. The sisters smiled at each other, surprising themselves with a sudden flash of comfort. 'Let's do it together. We should each look at everything before deciding what to chuck.'

*

They worked feverishly. Some of it was easy – the outdated newspapers and magazines, the cold cups of coffee, the staplers and pens, the torn, empty envelopes and scraps of desk calendar. None of them had any unfamiliar telephone numbers scribbled on them. Then they made piles on the kitchen table. Bills, personal letters, 'possible chuck later', competition entries, personal, miscellaneous . . .

The phone shrilled and Bramble picked it up. 'Oh, hello Mrs Marsh-Robertson, how are—'

'Is your father there?' Cecily Marsh-Robertson demanded.

'Er, well . . .' Bramble was puzzled. Didn't Cecily ever talk to her own daughter?

'Never mind,' Cecily bowled on. 'You'll do. You can pass the message on. Now I wasn't at all happy with Sunday. Lottie was eliminated, you know.'

'Well—'

'I really think it's time she had a serious horse. She's getting absolutely nowhere on Sailor.'

'But Sailor's a perfect Pony Club ride, he's so honest and . . .'

'Exactly,' squawked Cecily, 'Perfect for *Pony Club*. Lottie's been riding for several years now and she needs a challenge.'

'Really, Mrs Marsh-Robertson,' shrieked Bramble, 'I can't stress enough how important it is that Lottie doesn't get pushed too far too fast. She is only sixteen. Sailor is exactly right for her just now and the next step needs to be thought out very carefully. There's plenty of scope in him yet, and—'

'But . . .' interrupted Cecily.

Bramble overrode her with determination. 'I think Lottie needs at least another year on Sailor – and then we can all make a proper decision about what she should go on to.'

'If you'll let me get a word in edgeways, I think I can be the judge of what's right for my own daughter.' Cecily Marsh-Robertson's voice was steely.

'My father's always believed you should start gently. Not always to go reaching for the next rosette. Sometimes a challenge can be . . .'

'A good thing. Of course you have to keep reaching for the next rosette. And another thing, it's time she focused on something. Had goals.'

'Lottie wants to be an eventer,' said Bramble. 'And what she's doing at the moment is exactly right.'

'Yes, I know. Lottie's told me herself, and I want to know exactly what eventing involves before I decide to invest large sums of money in it.'

Bramble tried to remember how her father brought the sport alive to people who had no idea what he was talking about. 'Back in the nineteenth century, cavalry officers used to brag about who had the best horse, and it would lead to fights. So they started horse trials, which test everything a good army horse needs. There's dressage, which is all about the control and precision of the parade ground, the cross-country phase, which is like riding into battle, and then, because officer and horse both need to show they can still give more, there's a showjumping final to establish the winner. It's considered the greatest test of the partnership between horse and rider.'

'It sounds like some kind of grown-up gymkhana,' said Cecily sharply. 'As I've said before, I don't want Lottie just messing about: it's a waste of her time and my money. Now listen, I want your father to find her a first-class horse. Is he there? I need to speak to him.'

'No, he's dead,' snapped Bramble. 'Yesterday. Quite suddenly.'

'Well!' In the pause that followed Bramble felt as if Cecily regarded this as a cunning ploy to win the argument. 'Well!' repeated Cecily. 'This is terrible. I can't imagine why you didn't tell me before.'

'Savannah's with Lottie at the moment. I thought she might have told you.'

'Of course not. She hasn't had the chance. I'm just on my way back from Berlin. So what's going to happen at the yard? Will you be going on as normal?'

'Absolutely as normal,' stressed Bramble. 'We've got Jezzar Morgan, a top rider, joining the team so there will be no gaps at all. Everything is going from strength to strength.'

'Well, I suppose that's all right then,' conceded Cecily. 'But we will miss your father. He really was an exceptional teacher: I don't know what Lottie will do without him.' With that, Cecily Marsh-Robertson slammed the phone down and Bramble met Helena's eye.

'What do you mean about a top rider joining the team?' asked Helena. 'It's hardly an appropriate time to take someone on.'

'Tell that to Pa's ghost. I'm sorry, I didn't mean to mention it to Cecily, but she makes me so cross.' Bramble rubbed her face in her hands. 'Oh, I can't bear the thought of it. Lottie Marsh-Robertson absolutely adores Sailor. I think he gives her the only unconditional affection she's ever had and her mother's going to sell him behind her back. It'll break her heart, it really will, and then she'll be faced with some brute that's quite beyond her capability and will probably lose her nerve.'

'How grim,' said Helena. 'Anyway, Jezzar Morgan. Jezzar Morgan . . . It's an unusual name. Wasn't there something about him in the papers recently?'

'He's winning quite a few events, he won—'

'Not the horse press. Proper newspapers. Gossip columns. It was some scandal about the woman he was living with, somebody who owns an ancestral pile up north.'

'Penny Luckham. He ratted on her with a married woman. He's told me all about that. What matters is how he rides.'

'It was something worse than that, I think. What was it? Oh, never mind, I'll google him when I get back. Where is he, anyway?'

'Riding out with Donna. He'll be back for lunch, so you can scrutinise him then.'

'Still, I really don't think you should hire staff until we know what's happening. Pa might have left the whole sheboodle to the Injured Jockeys Fund.'

'I'm going to carry on as normal,' said Bramble stubbornly. 'That's what Pa would have wanted. It's what he did want. He hired Jez, not me.'

'Oh well, I suppose we're stuck with him, then. What's he like?'

'Fine,' said Bramble crossly, still shovelling old newspapers into black bin bags. Her pride prevented her from telling Helena about her argument with Edward the night before he died, and besides, she felt guilty. Perhaps Helena would accuse her of effectively killing him.

'He doesn't sound fine from your tone of voice.'

'He's perfectly pleasant. Except that I didn't ask him to come, and now he's here. How would you feel?'

'Just how I always felt,' said Helena, sitting back suddenly, a tear trickling down the side of her nose. 'That Pa didn't care how I felt, or rate what I did or take the slightest notice of me at all. Sorry.' She let out a wail, grabbed a tissue from her bag and hunched up on the floor, rocking with sobs.

Bramble touched her sister's arm tentatively.

'Oh, don't worry about me.' Helena snivelled after several long minutes. 'It's just the shock. Look!' She blew her nose loudly. 'See! Good old Helena back again.' She contemplated Bramble with reddened eyes. 'You know, you ought not to bottle everything up all the time. My homoeopath says that emotions always come back in physical symptoms if you do.'

'Well, I haven't got any physical symptoms,' said Bramble. 'I'm perfectly all right.'

Helena gave her a reproving look. 'Bramble, you are a hard case. A very hard case. Some time, at some point, you have got to let *someone* in.'

Bramble laughed. 'And you, Helena, are a nutcase. Come on, break over, let's get back to work.'

'I mean it,' said Helena darkly, picking up another pile of mess. 'You'll be sorry one day. Oh, why didn't Pa ever throw anything away? What's this?' She showed Bramble a photograph of her father, standing next to a woman and a horse. They were smiling.

Bramble examined it. Photographs looked different when you knew someone was dead, she decided, more unreal. 'Oh, that's Pauline and Teddy. Earlier this year. When Teddy qualified for Badminton. Pa was very pleased.'

Bramble took the photograph. Pauline had high cheekbones, large expressive eyes and good legs. Three things time couldn't erase. Bramble reluctantly put the photograph down, starting a new pile. Goodbye Pa, she whispered silently to herself, pressing a finger against the photograph.

She looked up and saw her sister watching her.

'I'm telling myself I'll think about it properly tomorrow,' Helena said. 'Deal with . . .' she swallowed '. . . it all later. But for now, have another drink.'

This time Bramble accepted the top-up.

'We'll need another bottle.' Helena drained the remainder into her glass, giving it a shake to get the last drops out. She left the room and came back a few minutes later holding the bronze horse from the kitchen. 'Bramble, Pa said I should have this when he died – you don't mind me taking it now, do you? I mean, you've got all this around you to remind you of him, and I'd like just one thing.' Her eyes filled with tears.

Bramble was taken aback. Her father had never suggested that any of them should have anything specific – and, in fact, she wouldn't have dared have such a conversation with him.

'Well . . . I just . . . I don't . . .'

'There's nothing in my house to remind me of him. Please – you have all this.'

Bramble looked at the bronze again. It was a very beautiful sculpture.

'It might be worth getting a couple of the paintings out too,' said Helena, 'and anything else good, in case the probate valuer sees them.'

'*Is* there anything that valuable?' asked Bramble.

'Oh, not really,' said Helena, in a careless tone of voice. 'But we want to keep inheritance tax down to a minimum. Do you want me to have a look around and see what needs protecting from the eagle eye of the Inland Revenue?'

'No, really,' Bramble felt numb. 'It's too early for any of that. We can't start dividing things up until . . . until we've found Felicity. And I don't think we should do anything illegal. If we have to pay tax, then we have to pay it.'

'You're so stuffy sometimes.' Helena stood clutching the horse and glaring at her. 'We might have to give away tens of thousands of pounds.'

Bramble shrugged. 'Then that's what we'll do.' She heard her voice sounding harsh.

'Oh Bramble, I'm so sorry. I didn't mean to upset you.' Helena dropped down onto the floor beside her and began to cry. 'Please forgive me. I'm an insensitive beast. A rotten person, I keep meaning to become nicer but somehow there's never time.'

Bramble hated Helena's scenes. They started small and ratcheted up into major dramas. 'Look,' she said, in order to get this over and done with, 'why don't you take the horse for the time being? Just until we all decide.'

'Really? Oh Bramble,' Helena blew her nose. 'You're such a star, really you are. No wonder we all rely on you.'

Bramble rolled her eyes. 'Let's just keep on looking for Felicity's number and the will, shall we?'

'Well,' said Bramble an hour later, when Edward's study stood unnaturally empty, the papers now in piles. They had found the will, but not Felicity's address. 'In this day and age, with all the different kinds of communication we've got, I don't see how you can actually lose a sister.'

'Oh, we'll find her, don't worry,' replied Helena. 'Let's see that will.'

Chapter 6

Marshes and deserts always reminded Felicity Beaumont of home. Flat acres and gently curving hills under a huge dome of sky hosted a constant kaleidoscope of subtle differences in colour and light, changing every season, every hour of every day – even minute by minute. From rose-edged clouds to brilliant cobalt blues, from a spectrum of greens to a hundred degrees of grey, from straw-gold grasses to hot orange midday stalks, then to dark sepia fringing. She wished she could capture these tiny shifts of emphasis in photographs, but the gradations of light and hue always escaped because the emptiness was too big, and the pictures always turned out flat and harsh. You have to be there – for a long time – to understand it.

Felicity was thousands of miles away from the Kentish fields of her childhood memories, but she felt she was back when she saw how small and random the Louisiana trees seemed against the massive skies, how the storm waters had risen to above her head height and washed the colour out of the land, leaving only grey sludge, brown pasture, broken trees and a tangle of dead vegetation as a high-water mark. There was a single flat road running through the open countryside, almost as if it had been thrown down by accident, and the silence of calamity hung in the heavy heat.

She ran a hand through her hair. It felt unwashed and damp with sweat, and her cotton T-shirt clung to her back in the humidity. She was trying to keep a foothold on a board she'd floated in the sloppy mud, attempting to calm a half-starved horse held in that mud up to its neck, while the fire and rescue team tried to thread slings under his belly. Her back ached with the effort.

Felicity was used to being an observer, seeing suffering but staying detached. She was good at that. But when she'd helped the team get the fire engine and horsebox as close to the muddy ditch as they could, for one second there had been a dart of communication between her and the slate-grey, mud-slathered horse. His eye had caught hers and her heart – that neglected, abused, almost dead core of her being – had responded. Help me, he'd said. Don't leave me.

They couldn't tell how long he'd been trapped: certainly hours, maybe even days. A hurricane had passed over several weeks earlier and livestock everywhere had escaped or been let loose. He had probably wandered into the flooded wetlands in search of green pasture or fresh water, then slipped into the mud-filled ditch. The animal had very little strength left to struggle, but Felicity could see the terror in his eyes.

'We can't do this unless he keeps still,' said the fire officer, exhausted with the effort.

Felicity stripped off her T-shirt and wrapped it tenderly around the horse's head, shielding his eyes. 'I remember my father rescuing horses from time to time,' she said. 'If they can't see they're usually calmer.' The horse was powerful under her hands – he could have knocked her off the board and onto the mud – but he quietened down.

'Find something you can use like a giant needle,' said Felicity. 'Use it to thread the slings through the mud and under him. Some kind of a pole will do. We can't pull him out head-first: if it doesn't break his neck, it'll damage his back for good.' The men worked busily under her instruction, while she talked softly to the dark horse beside her.

When the slings were fixed they pumped water from the fire engine into the mud to loosen it, and slowly, carefully, edged the great machine away. Felicity balanced on her board, then jumped off onto the road, still holding the halter rope.

The mud held fast and the horse barely shifted. Felicity felt his spirit slipping away. 'Come on,' she whispered. 'Nearly there.'

'More water,' said the chief fire officer.

Suddenly, with a gurgle of mud, the horse emerged, staggering on to the road and collapsed on the ground, still in the sling.

'Too late,' said Harry, the head of the veterinary team, dropping down to inspect the prone body. 'No more suffering.' He looked briefly at Felicity crouched over the horse's head and took off his own checked shirt. 'Here,' he said gently. 'Put that on.'

Felicity nearly choked at the kindness and pulled the shirt on over her muddy bra. 'He may still be all right,' she said. 'Give him a little more time.'

His flanks were coated with mud but he had been a prized thoroughbred once. And although lack of food and water had wasted his muscles the shape of his hindquarters rated him a nice jumper, Felicity thought.

Harry shook his head. 'He's almost dead now. I don't think we can do anything.'

'I've seen it before,' said Felicity, trying to buy time. 'At home. When one of my father's horses . . .' She consulted her memory again, rusty and painful. 'Horses sometimes go into a kind of shut-down. Give him a little more time. It's a terrible waste of life.'

Harry put his hand on her shoulder. 'It's all a terrible waste of life. We're dealing with a disaster down here and he's too far gone. You know the rules of war. Don't waste help on those who can't benefit.'

Felicity did know the rules of war. She had seen too much of it. 'Please.' She held Harry's gaze, asserting herself for the first time since she'd joined the team. Felicity had come here to be invisible.

He held it back and Felicity forced herself not to look away. 'Please,' Felicity repeated. 'I'll beg, if that would help.'

'No, lady.' He dropped his eyes. 'I won't make you do that. You're one fizzy lady and fizzy ladies shouldn't beg. How long do you want us to wait?'

'Twenty minutes,' she said. 'Half an hour max. If he's not up by then . . .'

The firemen trundled off and Harry sat in the shade of the horsebox and waited, his hat tipped over his eyes for a restorative burst of sleep. 'I must be mad,' he said to himself. 'We don't have half an hour.'

We must all be mad, Felicity thought, crouching down and sponging the long noble face, revealing a narrow strip of white blaze, then dipping the rinsed-out sponge in fresh water and forcing it between the horse's lips, squeezing it to release a dribble of precious rehydration. We must all be mad to have come to this hellhole in the first place.

Felicity had been curled up on her sofa watching the news, with its panoramic views of floating cars and houses smashed to matchsticks. The reporter, leaning out of her helicopter, had pointed out a horse on a roof. It must have swum when the water was highest and scrambled on, and now, as the waters were dropping, it stood, terrified, without food or water. The roof would never hold if it panicked, Felicity thought.

'Katrina was bad enough,' the newsreader had said. 'These people hoped they would never have to see such devastation again. But Samantha is ten times worse.'

Felicity thought about the other animals, those who had been left behind in the evacuation or swept away from their dying owners or shattered homes. When human life was at risk what happened to the pets and farm animals? Felicity had never thought about it before, and pulled out her laptop to google 'animal rescue + hurricane'.

Please don't email us with questions, the site requested, because we need the time and space to respond to specific reports of animals in need. Go to our FAQs. If you want to raise money for us we'd be grateful. We need animal cages, but don't bring pet food unless you've checked with the shelter first. If you're professionally qualified and want to volunteer to help, please fill in the form and email it back. Don't turn up without a specific request from a shelter team.

Felicity had filled in her form, trying to think of anything that might indicate a professional qualification. In a sudden rush of inspiration she listed her British Horse Society exams. For a moment, old hopes and memories rose like a flock of greylag geese flying across water and Felicity held her breath until the chattering of the past faded into the distance again. Anyway, Americans probably didn't know what the British Horse Society was, although her basic animal first aid training might be useful. Felicity never really believed they would need her.

She didn't believe anyone needed her any more. She had walked out of her life, bought a plane ticket and taken a month's out-of-season rental on a house – well, more of an overgrown log cabin – beside a lake in Virginia. She sat at the end of its jetty every morning drinking coffee and surveying the still water. She watched the great trees begin to turn from green to gold, then red, as she listened to the silence.

And the harder she listened the less real it seemed. As the leaves drifted off the trees the surrounding houses were revealed. Many of them had been built in the confident fifties, then demolished or embellished in the nineties. They were now suburban palaces, complete with several SUVs apiece in the tree-lined drives. Satellite dishes poked out of roofs. Speedboats shattered the quiet of the water. Occasionally a helicopter landed on a little patch of high-maintenance lawn and disgorged smart, wealthy people. High voices called and, at night, the sound of owls was often masked by drunken laughter. But on the end of the jetty you could pretend you were alone.

Inside the house it was like being in a fairy tale in which a wicked witch had waved her wand and turned everything into an imitation of itself. It looked homely, as if the family who owned it were out for the day. There was a fruit bowl on the teak coffee table. Both, on closer inspection, were man-made. Silk pot plants cascaded down the mantelpiece. A row of ornamental copper pans on the wall in the kitchen had 'not for food use' on their bases. A wicker chest of drawers lined in newspaper was made from some form of resin composite. There was a fish displayed in a case on the wall, as if it had been caught in the lake, but which had been made in Taiwan, and vinyl 'terracotta' tiles on the kitchen floor. In the evenings Felicity went out to Grandma Betty's Waffle Parlor or Dick's Diner. In spite of 'Grandma Betty's Biscuit Barrel' and 'Dick's Specials' there had never been a Grandma Betty or a Dick. The food came from vast, anonymous vats and was put together by sullen, underpaid hands. Felicity couldn't believe that any of it had ever grown from the earth. Nothing was real.

When the first news of the devastation had appeared Felicity felt as if the force of nature had risen up in anger to assert itself. There are real winds and trees out there, it screamed. You can turn us into fake stone, plastic and resin, freezing our life force, but we will be released one day and we'll fight back.

The following day Felicity got a call from the shelter. 'So, when might you be able to start?'

She always kept her passport in her handbag, and a knapsack packed with essentials. How often had she got a phone call like this and walked out of her little flat in five minutes? But this was different. She wasn't up against man, protected by her bulletproof vest and the large Press label across her back. She would be up against nature.

'I don't know,' Felicity said. 'When do you need me?'

'As soon as you can get here,' was the reply. 'You need to report for a training day before we can use you – our insurance doesn't cover anyone who hasn't had basic training. Volunteers are doing a week each, but we're short right now.'

'I can come for longer than that,' Felicity said.

'Have you got a tent?' asked the shelter coordinator. 'They've promised some proper volunteer shelters but they haven't materialised yet.'

'Oh yes, of course.' Felicity stopped off at the camping store to buy a little tent, plus a sleeping bag, and, after thinking carefully, some energy bars, several water bottles, a Primus stove, mosquito repellent and a first aid kit. She spent several hundred dollars and the car was tightly packed with things she might need. She didn't contact anyone to tell them where she was going. It was none of their business.

When Felicity arrived she was given a day of training then allocated to a team of four looking after the animals that had been brought into the shelter. Her first job was to wash piles of food bowls to stop them attracting flies and diseases in the sweltering weather, and then on to an interminable round of feeding, watering, cleaning and exercising. The other volunteers complained about the drudgery of it all but, with the first faint lifting of her spirits, Felicity realised that she could do this. It was repetitious and dirty and hot, but it was something that needed doing and

Felicity was good at it. Her back ached, her feet throbbed and her hands were sore, in spite of the rubber gloves, but Felicity felt a sense of purpose that had been missing for some time. And some of the dogs and cats were cute and eager for affection, although others were too traumatised to be handled safely. They had to be held on long poles instead of leads.

In the evening, tiredness permeating into the core of her being, Felicity felt the flimsy sense of being able to cope ebbing away again as she saw the supper of beans and sausages. What would the sausages be made of? Her exhausted stomach heaved at the thought, and she made do with two energy bars before struggling to put up the tent. The ground was hard and stony. She begged an empty cardboard box from the catering area and tore it apart, almost weeping with the effort, so that she could put it under her ground sheet to blunt the feeling of the rocks beneath. In the morning she ached so much she could barely stand upright.

Harry found her as she was queuing for breakfast, trying to identify something healthy on the menu.

'You there,' he said. 'Horses. That right?'

'What?' Felicity had forgotten what she'd put on her form.

'You've got horse qualifications. We need you. We've had several reports of loose horses and horses trapped up towards the north, and I need more people who know how to handle them.'

Horses were part of her old life. Even thinking about them knotted her stomach and made her chest feel tight with tension. To her the smell of hay and saddle soap, laced with the acrid notes of dung, was the scent of long-buried betrayal.

He put his hands on his hips. 'Can you help or not?'

It was the word help that did it. If someone asks for help you have to give it. For the next two weeks, Felicity worked with Harry and Kiefer, a young veterinary student. Every day Harry's Jeep left the centre and picked its way perilously over muddy tracks. They tried to ignore the fly-blown, rotting bodies of cattle, horses and, once, an elderly man slumped on the roadside. ('We can only pray for him,' said Harry, touching her arm. 'There's nothing else we can do.') Felicity pressed her forehead to the Jeep's window. She had seen it all before, but not in America. America,

England – the West – were supposed to be safe. Perhaps nowhere was safe. The thought eased something inside her.

They spent heart-rending hours breaking into houses and dragging open barn doors to find dead, starving or terrified cats, dogs and horses cowering behind them, wedged into impossible places and too afraid to be lured out. They even found a dead stallion, with the bodies of his mares piled up against the corner of a field with nowhere to go. They must have been desperate to be let out, thought Felicity, as they drowned in the rising water. The pastureland was sodden and oily, and she couldn't see any fresh grass or water anywhere.

And then, one day, just as there were more animals leaving the shelter than arriving and gaps were appearing in the rows of stalls and cages, there was a call from the fire and rescue team. A horse had been spotted in a roadside ditch out near the wetlands, trapped in mud. Harry had been asked to go out with the horsebox, and he chose Felicity to accompany him, pocketing his tranquilliser gun and humane killer, in case of trouble.

Waiting in the glaring midday sun beside the horse's prone body, Felicity studied him to see if he had any distinguishing marks. Some people had been writing their telephone numbers in grease on their horses, or shaving something into their coat. If they had time. But she couldn't see anything. There might be a microchip, of course.

Harry shook himself awake and looked at his watch. 'Half hour's up, lady. He can't lie longer than this anyhow.' He began to prepare the gun. Felicity knew he was right. There were no more chances for this horse. She squinted into the sky above and saw a vulture, then another. A third began to circle.

'No!' she shouted, jumping up. 'Go away.' Her words floated away into the emptiness, tinny and small.

But the sudden noise and movement must have alarmed the horse because Felicity turned to see it staggering to its feet, balancing weakly.

'You were right,' said Harry, astonished, replacing his gun in its holster.

'I've seen it before,' replied Felicity, the memories prickling painfully once again, like the return of circulation to a numb limb.

She took hold of the halter and urged him forward towards the ramp of the horsebox, but every inch of him conveyed that he was going nowhere. It's not like you see in the movies. When real flesh gets hurt it goes on hurting. He rolled his eyes and dropped his head.

'Come on, boy. I'm only trying to help you. Come on, darling . . .' The words were unimportant. The endearments Felicity hadn't spoken for so long, the love she had to offer, the openness and honesty that animals can sense . . . Felicity offered it all to him. She hadn't approached a living being like this for so long. 'Please,' she begged, 'don't stop now, not after so much. I'm asking you for one last thing.' The horse elongated himself, between Felicity's hand on the headcollar and its back feet, which were planted firmly outside the truck.

'Pass me a bucket of water,' she said, and Harry handed one to her.

She offered the water but as soon as he began to drink she walked up the ramp, the water bucket in one hand and tugging at the rope behind her with the other. Her back ached again and a mosquito buzzed against her ear, distracting her concentration.

And then he shot up the ramp, clattering the horsebox from side to side. I might as well trust you, he said, as his flanks heaved into place. Felicity heard Harry exclaim softly in relief. She inhaled the familiar scent of horse, running her hands over his slippery, sweaty coat and feeling the hollows of dehydration in his once-powerful haunches. 'Poor old boy,' Felicity murmured. 'You've had a tough time.' She carried on talking to him as she tied him up and slipped out of the jockey door. She didn't quite trust him not to panic yet.

'You've got a great touch,' approved Harry, as he checked that the horse was tied securely. He was rewarded by flattened ears and bared teeth. Harry moved back hastily. 'Guess he's better than he looks. Nothing much wrong with that temper.'

'They recover amazingly quickly sometimes.' Felicity jumped into the cab. The experience made her part of the team. The others talked about where they had all come from. Back at the camp that evening, eating tinned beans and sausages, aching with exhaustion and longing for a shower that was more than a suspended bucket,

Felicity discovered that most people who could drop everything at a moment's notice had something about their lives that didn't fit.

'We don't call ourselves losers,' said Harry, pouring himself a large whisky. 'We call ourselves wild cards. Jokers in the pack.'

Felicity got up. 'I'm just going to check up on the patients. I'd like to see how that gelding's getting on.'

She'd named the horse Merlin. They were naming the animals in alphabetical order and had got to M. Felicity had been asked to pick a name, and a vision of a dark grey speck sweeping high in the wide skies over the Kent marshes had come into her mind. And there had been another Merlin once, to whom she owed a debt. Felicity suppressed the memory.

'Hey, for your English wizard,' one of the volunteers had said.

Felicity shook her head. 'No, a hawk I used to see occasionally at home, actually. Its underside is the same dark grey colour. It's rare. Special.'

'*Ecktually*,' mimicked Harry. 'I love that English accent. So, after this, when are you going home?'

Felicity considered this for a moment. 'I'm not sure,' she said. 'I wasn't planning to go back at all.'

'That's what we all say, darlin',' said one of the other volunteers. 'Don't you worry, we're all running away from something. You're among friends here.'

Chapter 7

Savannah sat shakily at the Marsh-Robertsons' pale ash table, wishing that Cecily hadn't decided to spend what she described as 'quality time' with her daughter. It meant that Lottie wouldn't be allowed out riding that day.

'How are you girls feeling?' demanded Cecily. 'Have a mozzarella ball.' She pushed a plate of what looked like rubbery golf balls at them. 'They're buffalo mozzarella, quite special.'

'Er, no thank you.' Savannah wasn't quite sure if she was up to eating.

'I had a letter about choosing your A levels today,' remarked Cecily, helping herself to a tiny portion of frondy lettuce and a mozzarella ball.

Lottie paled, but didn't say anything, edging her food around the plate and taking an occasional terrified nibble.

'I thought English, History, Mandarin and Spanish,' Cecily declared. 'I think you need modern languages, and China is an expanding economy. 'Pity your maths is so weak. What A levels are you doing, Savannah?'

Savannah murmured that she was leaving school after GCSEs.

'You're *not* doing *A levels*?' Cecily couldn't have sounded more shocked if Savannah had announced she was planning to become a drug dealer. 'But surely you want to go to university? And you must get some proper qualifications, you simply must.'

'I'm not clever like Lottie,' replied Savannah, trying the mozzarella and wishing she hadn't. Her stomach heaved as she swallowed it.

'Lottie's not clever,' said Cecily in a tart voice. 'It's just a question of hard work, isn't it, Lottie?'

Lottie nodded.

'I'm going to be a professional eventer,' explained Savannah. 'There's no point in doing A levels. I've got to get into the junior team and then compete at least forty events a year. I wouldn't have time. Anyway, I'm sick of school.'

'But what does your mother say about it? Surely she's not going to let you leave at sixteen?'

'It's what she did. And Helena. Although Helena went to drama school. Only my Aunt Felicity did A levels and was going to go to university, then . . . I'm not sure what happened. We don't ever see her.'

'But everyone needs A levels,' retorted Cecily. 'They're something to fall back on.'

'I don't want to fall back,' said Savannah. 'I want to win.'

Cecily glared at her. 'What about your grandfather? Surely he couldn't have approved?'

'He does,' said Savannah. 'I mean he did.'

A few months earlier she'd been arguing with Bramble about whether she should be allowed to stay out late for a party and they'd begun to shout at each other. Savannah had stormed out to the stables and her grandfather followed her.

He indicated that she should sit beside him on the narrow wooden bench in the feed store. Savannah dug her nails into the rough surface of the bench, determined that she would stand up to him.

But he hadn't been angry with her. He'd talked to her very quietly and gently. It was all up to her, he explained. Bramble had done well, but she had failed to reach the top and the future of Lorenden now lay with Savannah. They had some good young horses and it was up to her to get herself, and them, to Badminton and Burghley. The Olympics in her twenties. 'You're the next generation,' he'd said. 'But you've got to be utterly dedicated. Only the really committed make it. Now I want to ask you, do you really want to be a professional rider? In your heart of hearts? Because now is the time to say no.'

Savannah was alarmed at the question. 'Of course.'

'Good. I felt I had to ask. Sometimes I see a bit of Felicity in you, and she . . . well, never mind.' For a moment he paused, and the lines of his face settled in deep folds as he seemed to look out across the yard without seeing anything.

'What's wrong with Felicity?' Savannah wondered if she was finally going to be told exactly why a gust of disapproval blew through the room every time her aunt was mentioned.

Edward slapped both knees with the palms of his hands as he came out of his reverie and stood up. 'She's a very talented girl. Well, woman now, of course. She could have been one of the greatest riders of her day. But she runs away from anything difficult and that's not the way to succeed.'

'She's succeeded as a war reporter,' Savannah pointed out. She had watched her aunt on television, on one of the minor news channels, and it seemed to her that someone who would face all that terror and discomfort could neither be called selfish nor lazy. 'That must be difficult.'

'I like to think she's grown up at last,' said Edward. 'Maybe people really do change. Better late than never, I suppose.' His voice sounded doubtful. 'Anyway, Felicity doesn't matter. It's you I want to talk about.

'First,' his attention returned to Savannah. 'Your mother cares about you; that's why she shouts. And she and I both know that you can't mess around like other kids if you truly want to get to the top. Focus, focus, focus. Otherwise, well, you could lose everything.'

She remembered the sunlight streaming in through the fine straw dust, and the smell of linseed oil and hay. 'Everything?' she repeated. 'What do you mean?'

His hand indicated the house and the yard. Lorenden had always been there, at the centre of her life, and so had the horses.

'Everything,' he said. 'We don't have lots of money like some people. We have to work to keep what we've got. If you want to go on living here and competing you've got to be the best. There's no room for second place any more.'

'But what if I'm not? Could we lose the horses if I don't succeed? What would happen to them?'

'That's up to you,' her grandfather told her. 'While I'm still here we'll have Lorenden, but when I've gone it'll be up to you. What I'm trying to tell you is that you can't take anything for granted in life. You have to fight for it.'

And now he was dead.

Savannah looked down at the salad. There was something about the way it swirled that made her feel sick again. 'I'm sorry,' she muttered as she hurried from the table in the direction of the downstairs loo. She just about managed to avoid the floral frills encasing Cecily's Victorian-style washbasin.

'I think we must have the winter vomiting bug after all,' said Lottie later, as they both lay back in bed.

'If this is a hangover I'm never drinking again.' Savannah thought she might die. If only she was in her own high iron bed at home, with its faded patchwork quilt and the illicit warmth of Darcy stretched out beside her. She missed him. And she missed Lorenden, with its red-brick stable yard. She thought of the collared doves that fluttered on the stable roof and the racehorse that swung to point out the direction of the wind. She missed it all, even Edward's authoritarian voice booming out commands over the clop and crunch of hooves on stone and gravel.

Helena and Bramble decided to read the will in the drawing room. Rarely used, it was one of two large rooms on either side of the front door, part of the Georgian farmer's pretensions of grandeur. It had full-length windows, dusty and spanned with cobwebs, with faded hangings draped around them. A marble fireplace and a massive, very ornate over-mantel mirror dominated the room, and ancient Edwardian wallpaper, in navy and gold flock, was peeling off the walls. It all smelt damp and unused.

'Honestly,' said Helena. 'You must feel like Sleeping Beauty living in this place. Waiting for your prince to come and wake you up.' She prowled nervously round the room, picking things up. Now that they were alone there was no reason to delay reading the will. She expected it all to go to Bramble. And she couldn't bear that. Bramble had always been the favourite. The son her father had never had. It wasn't fair. It had never been fair.

'This is rather good, you know.' She put a small porcelain poodle back on the mantelpiece, wondering if she dared open the envelope and what she would do if it said what she thought it would. Thank goodness she'd got the sculpture. That would be worth a bob or two. Helena's eyes flickered over the rest of the room. Nobody wanted heavy dark red oil paintings of ancestors these days, and very little Edwardian and Victorian furniture had any value now, although the Stubbs-type oil of Mountain Rocket, the racehorse that had started everything for the Beaumont family, might fetch a bit. 'The silver's quite nice,' she said absent-mindedly, 'although no one's buying at the moment. The odd piece fetches a bit but mostly people want to buy their stuff from Habitat.' Her voice sounded strained.

She fingered the slim brown envelope nervously. It was marked 'Will' in Edward Beaumont's powerful scrawl. Then the door opened and Jez walked in.

Helena automatically put up her hand to smooth her blonde bob into place. 'Goodness,' she said, sounding nervous, 'there are always so many people coming in and out here. I can't keep track of it.' She tinkled with what Bramble always privately called her 'star laugh', a light, bubbling brook of a sound, almost entirely devoid of humour. 'I'm Helena Harris,' she dropped her voice an octave, 'Bramble's sister. You must be . . .'

He didn't appear to recognise her. 'How do you do?' he said formally, striding across the room with his stalky rider's walk, extending his hand for her to shake. 'I'm Jez Morgan.' He didn't add any further explanation.

Helena treated him to a flick of her head, and the sidelong promise of fun with her eyes.

Helena, thought Bramble involuntarily, don't. Just don't.

'Er, have a cup of tea before you go out, Jez,' said Bramble desperately, dreading being left alone with her sister and the envelope. 'We were just thinking of making one.'

'Or a glass of champagne,' suggested Helena. 'On set we always say that the best way to deal with anything is to have a glass of champagne. I'm an actress,' she added, determined to make Jez notice her.

Jez ignored both suggestions. 'People are beginning to ask about the yard. About what's going to happen. What shall I say?'

'Well, everything will go on as normal,' said Bramble, feeling a flutter of fear and suppressing it.

'Not necessarily,' said Helena. 'We don't know what's going to happen, do we? We haven't read the will, we don't know how to find Felicity—'

'Nevertheless,' said Jez firmly, 'I will tell anyone who asks that everything will go on as normal. That will give you time to decide what you want to do.'

A furrow of disapproval appeared between Helena's brows.

'What shall I do next?' asked Jez, terse.

'Oh, Cecily Marsh-Robertson says that Lottie can't ride Sailor today because she's ill, so that's another one to exercise.'

Helena was restless. She hated the way all conversations in this house revolved around horses. Edward was dead, for God's sake, and it seemed that all Bramble and Jez cared about was this pony and the spoilt kid who rode him. They ought to be reading the will. She caught her breath. She was dreading what it might say.

She stretched up in a fake yawn and noted, with satisfaction, that Jez looked at her breasts. But very briefly, and without apparent interest. Perhaps he batted for the other team, as it were. A lot of male riders did.

'Oh, and Sailor's got a bit of chronic catarrh, which should have cleared up with the last lot of antibiotics, but it still seems to be hanging around. See if you think we need to get the vet out, will you?'

'I'll try some acupuncture,' said Jez. 'I do it by massaging pressure points, not with needles, so it's easy.'

Bramble opened her mouth to tell him not to be so silly, but decided to leave it.

'There's also the old remedy of hanging a string of onions in the stable,' Jez continued. 'I've always found it keeps horses' airways nice and clear.'

'He's not in the stable at the moment,' snapped Bramble. 'Unless you'd like to hang the onions over the gate of the field?'

She then felt guilty about showing her impatience, but Jez had gone, the sound of his boots echoing in the slate-flagged hall.

'I told you,' said Helena. 'This will never work. I'm sure you can find some legal way of getting out of it.'

Bramble wasn't sure if she found Jez or Helena the more infuriating, and decided that, by a very narrow length, she hated Helena the most at that moment. 'I don't want to get out of it,' she said crossly. 'Not yet, anyway. I haven't the time, I need the help and, anyway, I have, by complete coincidence, been trying to convince Pa about trying some alternative remedies for some time.'

Helena gazed at her in amazement. 'You do fancy him,' she crowed. 'I knew you did. You'd never let a man tell you about horses otherwise.'

Bramble was furious. 'That is totally untrue, Helena. You're judging people by your own despicable standards. Everything is about sex for you, but this isn't about men and women; this is about what's right.'

'Everything is *always* about men and women. Pa's dead and now you're deferring to another man.'

'I am not *deferring* to Jez,' hissed Bramble. 'In my world, men and women are equal. In the theatre and TV, maybe men still hold most of the power, and women like you have to suck up to them, but that doesn't happen here. As you well know. And as far as I'm concerned, Jez is *not* a man. He's a colleague.'

'He's an employee,' snapped Helena. 'And if you start to forget that you're in trouble. And don't give me all that superior stuff about being equal. Men and women are never equal. They just aren't and you're naive to think they might be.'

'Helena.' Bramble put a hand out to touch her sister's arm. 'Let's not argue about it. We've got more important things to think about.' She looked at the envelope.

'Anyway,' sniffed Helena, 'Jez may be quite attractive if you like that sort of muscular, outdoorsy Lady Chatterley thing, but I think he's probably gay, of course. Those lovely leather boots are rather too well polished, don't you think?'

'I don't care what he is as long he doesn't frighten the horses,' said Bramble. 'And he's just finished two relationships with different women, so I don't see where he'd be able to fit any men into his rather overcrowded schedule.'

Helena frowned, and looked at herself in the big mirror. Surely she couldn't be losing her touch? A wrinkled monkey-woman in a blonde wig looked back at her, and she turned away in fear.

'The will. I think we should just get on with it, don't you, Helena?' said Bramble, conscious that her mouth was dry with tension.

'Oh yes, quite, of course. I'll read it, shall I?'

Bramble nodded and bit her nails. It was an old habit from childhood.

'"I, Edward . . . blah, blah, being of sound mind" etc, etc . . . let me see . . .' Helena skimmed over the single page, her lips moving silently.

Bramble turned away, a sick feeling in her stomach. She looked over the autumn lawn. Last night's storm had stripped the trees of their yellowing leaves and they lay in soggy heaps on the grass. I don't want to leave here, Bramble thought, suddenly realising what the will might mean. I don't ever want to leave.

It seemed an age until Helena reached the end of the document. She must have read it six times over by now, thought Bramble.

'". . . leave everything equally to my three daughters,"' Helena had her actress voice on again, '"Felicity Jane Beaumont, Helena Mary Harris, also known as Helena Cooper, and Lavinia Rose Kelly, known as Bramble." That's brilliant. Perfect for all of us, isn't it?' Helena sounded relieved. 'How marvellous. There's nothing to argue about and he hasn't left it all to the International League for the Protection of Horses, which was always a possibility.'

'No,' said Bramble, keeping her face turned to the garden so that Helena couldn't see her shock. She'd assumed that her father would leave her the horses. And a way of keeping everything going. Helena was so rich anyway, and Felicity hadn't been home for so long. She'd thought her father would want her to carry on his work.

But obviously not. If he had trusted her to do that he would never have appointed Jez.

There was shame in Helena's eyes, and triumph as she pulled off the black poloneck. 'I'm sorry about tearing this. Really.' She handed it back to Bramble, checking the label. 'I'll buy you another one.'

'It was last year's stock,' said Bramble, taking it back with a sick, cold feeling in the pit of her stomach. 'They won't have any left.'

'I'm so glad he was fair,' burbled Helena. 'It's awful when families deteriorate into squabbling over wills, isn't it, and you couldn't have fairer than this, could you?'

Bramble's natural sense of justice was stimulated by the word 'fair'. 'No,' she said, swallowing her feeling of having been abandoned by her father all over again. 'You couldn't be fairer. We just have to find Felicity now.'

*

They left the room, Helena almost incandescent with relief.

'Don't say anything,' hissed Bramble. 'No one must know. Until we find Felicity.'

Helena opened her mouth to disagree, but decided to avoid any conflict. For the time being. It would be hard enough for Bramble: she would have to sell up and leave. There was no way that she could afford to buy Helena and Felicity out.

But, as she put the kettle on and pulled a chair up to the scrubbed kitchen table, it occurred to her that it might all be for the best. Bramble was so sensible and neatly dressed and, of course, wonderfully tanned and fit, but still so . . . well, so *unfeminine*. It was the only word for it. A great upheaval would do her good. She'd been living in a timewarp since Dom died and, really, she had loads of potential. But she'd better tap it soon, because once she got into her forties and fifties, well . . .

Bramble, her heart throbbing painfully, moved in a dream. 'Lunch, Helena? I've asked Donna and Jez if they want a bite.' She laid the table with cheese and sweet windfall apples from the orchards, then added a punnet of blackberries she'd picked on one of her walks with the dogs, and fresh crusty bread. They ate in almost complete silence. Once Bramble looked up and was surprised to meet Jez's eyes. She couldn't think of anything to say.

'I think an angel must be passing overhead,' twittered Donna. 'That's what they say when nobody says anything.'

Everyone looked at her as if she was quite mad.

Helena wondered what she might do with her slice of Lorenden. She and Ollie had always talked about having a second home, perhaps somewhere in Tuscany or the Dordogne. She hoped this Jez person wasn't going to get in the way. She didn't see how he could really, but she looked at the easy, confident way he sprawled at the table, tipping his chair back on two legs as he talked to Donna. There was something about him she didn't like.

'What about your wife?' asked Donna.

'I'm not married.'

'Got a girlfriend?' Donna arched an eyebrow.

'That,' he said quietly, but very courteously, 'is my business.' He looked at his watch. 'Will you excuse me?'

Donna was unabashed and looked at the clock on the kitchen

wall as well. 'Bugger me,' she said, jumping up and following him. 'Is that the time?'

'I really think someone who's been in the Army ought to have better manners,' said Helena when the door closed behind them. 'And I don't think you should trust him.'

'Oh, for goodness sake, what does it matter?' Bramble wanted to scream. 'Now I know Pa really didn't rate me.'

Helena poured herself another glass of wine and her face grew hard. 'Pa never acknowledged anything I did, never praised me, was never proud of me, nothing I did was ever good enough. He never even noticed me. So don't expect any sympathy from me.'

'That's not true,' shouted Bramble. 'Pa was very proud of you. He always watched *Simon's Way*. I've lost count of the number of times I heard him say, "My actress daughter, very successful, you know she's Mattie in *Simon's Way*."'

'He never said anything to me.' Helena's heart, starved of her father's approval in childhood, snatched greedily at this crumb of comfort. 'Oh Bramble, I'm sorry, I didn't mean to snap. This is all so difficult for me. You don't understand.'

Bramble began to pile plates into the dishwasher. 'Helena, please—'

'At least you had the horses in common,' wailed Helena. 'He never accepted that I had no interest. He even tried to get at me through Eddie. You know, giving him lessons on the quiet, letting him jump long before he was ready, putting him up on Ben and telling him to imagine himself at the Olympics. It was terribly dangerous and irresponsible. I had to put a stop to it.'

'Pa would never have been irresponsible about anything to do with a horse,' said Bramble fiercely. 'If he put Eddie on Ben it's because Eddie—'

Helena put out a hand. 'Bramble, let's not argue. Not now.' Her eyes filled with tears. 'Pa's gone and Felicity's never here. You're all I've got now. Let's be nice to each other.'

'I know,' said Bramble. 'You're right, we shouldn't argue.' She tried to smile and summon up a flip remark to take the heat out of the conversation.

Chapter 8

Rage and fear battled with a powerful sense of justice when Bramble eventually kissed Helena goodbye, pouring her into another taxi with the bronze horse wrapped up in an old blanket.

Possessions are not important, she repeated to herself as she waved her sister off down the drive. Dividing everything equally was fair and right, and what mattered was the family. Sisters matter; possessions don't.

But when she went back into the kitchen the sculpture's absence underlined the emptiness of the house without Edward.

Donna walked in from the pub, her arms crossed. 'So what's the deal with this Jez guy, then? He getting my job, is he?' Donna's skimpy T-shirt revealed a tattoo around her bellybutton, which read 'Benny 4ever'. Benny had been her Pony Club pony, hit by a speeding car on a narrow lane and put out of his agony by the vet forty minutes later. Donna had had three months in traction, then six months of physiotherapy, from which she had emerged with nose and tongue studs, the tattoo and what her mother described as 'attitude'.

'No, Donna,' said Bramble, wearily. 'Jez isn't getting anyone's job. We're short-handed and so we need him.'

'I'm not saying we don't. But what about a pay rise? For my hurt feelings?' Donna's arms were still folded, her stance hostile.

Bramble got up. 'Donna, if you don't deal with it this moment, you're going to know an awful lot more about hurt feelings than you ever thought possible.'

The two faced each other, in a stand-off, until Donna's face broke into a grin. 'Just testing, boss,' she said. 'Just testing.'

Bramble sighed. 'Everyone's testing,' she said. 'And now is not the time.'

As Donna closed the door behind her Bramble wondered whether she should have told her about the will. Donna needed to know what the future held.

So do we all, Bramble said to herself. So do we all. She sank down at the kitchen table, her head slumped in her arms. She wished she could cry, but she was too angry.

Eddie was too shocked by the news about his grandfather to take his usual precautions on his way back from school. Dusk was falling and the returning commuters scurried back and forth across the streets like ants. He noticed, too late, that he had run into the gang.

This was a group of teenage boys, who jeered and whistled as he went past. Occasionally they muttered insults, or called him 'white boy' or 'rich boy'. They were around his age and a mix of races. They were clearly not, and possibly never had been, at school. Eddie usually tried to change his route, but there was a limited number of options between his home and the tube station. Sometimes he didn't even think about the menacing little band, at other times his stomach filled with sick dread as the tube train approached his stop.

As he rounded the corner the gang were waiting for him.

'Hey, rich boy,' said the leader, a massive half-Chinese, half Afro-Caribbean youth. 'Give us your phone.'

'I, er, haven't got one.' Eddie's heart plummeted into the pit of his stomach, and he tried to move away.

The gang surrounded him.

'I think white boy's lying,' said one.

'Yeah, lying's wrong. Don't they teach that at your rich-boy school?'

Eddie was very frightened by now. 'I've, er, got some money.' With shaking hands he pulled out the two twenty-pound notes he'd taken out of the cashpoint that morning.

The gang leader pocketed them with an evil smile. 'What else have you got?'

'Nothing.' He could hear the raw fear in his voice, and they could hear it too.

They laughed.

At that point his mobile rang. A grubby hand delved into his pocket and his mobile phone was waved in front of his face. 'Look, Ty.'

'I forgot about that.'

'Nice phone.' One boy tossed it up in the air and Eddie put a hand out to catch it. The phone was snatched away by Ty, the gang leader. 'I don't think so,' he said. 'Let's see what else white boy's got that he's not telling us about.'

'Nothing, I promise.' Eddie could feel shameful tears starting in his eyes, and he wondered why none of the commuters were doing anything to help him. Presumably all they saw was a bunch of teenagers. They wouldn't want to get involved.

'Kneel,' Ty commanded.

Eddie looked around in desperation.

'They ain't going to save you,' added Ty. 'They as scared as you are, whitey.' He dropped his voice. 'I got a knife.'

Eddie swallowed and sank slowly to his knees.

'Take his shoes.' Ty gave the order, and two boys tugged his trainers off. 'And his keys.'

Eddie thought of his mother and the twins, innocent and safe at home, and the tears slipped down his face. He had, he realised with relief, forgotten his keys that day. Hands rummaged in his pockets and he smelt the tang of unwashed bodies and the stale, sweet smoke on their breath. 'He hasn't got them, Ty.'

'Another day,' said Ty. 'Now run.'

Eddie ran down the road to the sound of their mocking laughter. The chilly, dank puddles soaked his socks and he could feel the occasional sharp stone cutting painfully into his feet.

'And don't forget,' Ty shouted after him. 'We know where you live.'

Eddie leant on the doorbell, and Ania only answered after what seemed like an age.

'Eddie. Why don't you take your keys?'

'Forgot them,' he mumbled, sidling in and upstairs before anyone could notice his feet. He sat down on his bed, his head in his hands, and wept hot tears of humiliation and rage. He wished he had a gun so that he could have shot them, or that he had learned judo.

But he knew that even then he couldn't have fought eight of them single-handed.

So what could he do? He wondered vaguely about calling the police, but the only dealings he'd ever had with the law was on a couple of occasions when they'd stopped either his mother or Ollie for speeding. And what could they do? They wouldn't be there when he came home from school and the gang would certainly take their revenge on him.

He found an old pair of trainers, which were too small, because his feet had recently grown again, and went downstairs to have supper. There was a small cut on one of his feet where he had trodden on broken glass. It was hot and sore against the tight shoe.

A few days later he finally told Helena he'd lost his mobile phone.

Her eyes blazed in fury. 'Eddie, how can you be so careless? We're not made of money, you know.'

Eddie shuffled from foot to foot. 'Um, and I can't find my trainers either.'

'What *is* wrong with you? Well, it'll all have to come out of your pocket money.'

He didn't like to say that that had gone too.

Out in the yard at Lorenden, Bramble, Donna and Jez did evening stables. Bramble was on autopilot. As she walked across the damp grass in the falling light, headcollars draped over her shoulder for the horses that came in at night, she checked the field automatically for anything that the wind or vandals might have tossed into it. Then, after leading the horses in, she went through the feeds with Jez.

On the wall of the feed store, a blackboard with ragged chalk lines listed all the horses and what they ate. 'Basically, there are four categories,' she explained. 'There are the eventers – we've got six, including Teddy – then there are the youngsters out at grass who don't usually get fed. Then Patch and Ben, who are retired and have a small supplement at night, and, finally, there are the liveries – Sailor, and two others we keep for the owners who hunt them in the winter and event in the summer.'

'So fourteen in all, with just nine of them competing? And Teddy's your only top horse?'

Bramble thought she detected criticism in his voice. 'Well, presumably you knew we weren't big when you agreed to come. I know top yards have a lot more horses competing, but we're not at that level.'

'I can change that,' he said coolly. 'That's what I'm here for.'

'Oh good.' She tried not to sound too sardonic. 'Anyway, we've only got one more event this year and that's just a local one that we'll take Sailor to, plus probably the two liveries, if their owners want to come. Possibly one of the younger ones, too, for a bit of experience. The lorry can take five, which is about the most I want to run at any event. We've had a good year, actually.'

'Mmm.' Jez checked over the brands of feed and Bramble tried not to feel defensive.

'We keep a year-to-year diary in the office,' she heard herself beginning to burble under his scrutiny, 'so we can check back on what they've had and what they do best on, but essentially we try to keep to the minimum amount of hard food, plus lots of bulk. And we give them a bran mash on their day off, with some molasses to make it palatable.'

'Bran mash?' queried Jez. 'You're not still using that, are you? Horses have a massive fermentation vat of useful bacteria in their gut and a bran mash completely cleans them out. It takes three or four days to build it up again.'

'My father got to the top on bran mashes.' Bramble tried to sound confident, but she knew her father had been considered old-fashioned. 'And it's not as if I use molasses otherwise,' she added.

'Molasses is fine. Use it every day if you like. Grass is very high in natural sugars and horses are perfectly tuned to digest it. The anti-molasses brigade are confusing horses with humans and thinking their teeth will rot or they'll get too excited, but that's all crap.' Jez folded his arms. 'Bran mashes . . .' he laughed. 'I'd expect that sort of behaviour from the showjumping crowd, but eventers are usually pretty savvy.'

Bramble decided to ignore his rudeness, but she had a nasty feeling he might be right. Her father had always dismissed new feed products and theories as 'a whole lot of marketing junk' and they hadn't revised their horses' diets in decades. It probably was time to take a look at how she could do things differently. But preferably without Jez poking his nose in and being bossy.

Eventually the feeds were done and an air of serenity cloaked the stables as the soothing rhythm of the evening settled in: the sound of horses occasionally blowing through their noses as they contentedly munched, the spiralling lullaby of a song-thrush perched on top of the weathervane and the rasp, rasp of Donna's broom as she swept the yard clean of the last few wisps of hay.

Helena arrived back in Primrose Hill by seven o'clock that evening, unpeeled a roll of notes out of her wallet and paid the taxi driver. The bronze horse seemed surprisingly heavy and she consciously pulled her stomach muscles in tightly, grimacing as she took it from the driver. She daren't do her back in, she simply daren't.

She mounted the steps to the front door, enjoying, as always, the sight of the tall, thin terraced house. It looked, she thought, like a child's picture of a house at night, its windows ablaze with light and warmth. She craned her head round and could just see Ollie's feet in the basement.

The taxi driver hovered. 'Can you manage?' he asked. 'Are you all right?'

'Don't worry.' She swallowed on the sudden, treacherous threat of tears and leaned against the doorbell with her shoulder.

There was a long pause. Where was everyone? She leaned heavily on the doorbell again, pressing it long and loud, and Ollie opened the door, blinking in surprise.

'Oh! I thought you were spending the night in Kent.'

'I didn't say I was, did I?' Helena handed over the sculpture and Ollie sagged under its weight.

'Well, I just assumed . . . what's this?'

'Just bring it into the drawing room.' There was a perfect place for it – at the centre of a low coffee table – and, surrounded by the simplicity of Helena's plain white walls, it sprang into life, hooves pawing the air in a miraculous symphony of balance and strength. There was a breathtaking quality about it, as if the horse might take flight at any moment.

'Is that going to stay there?' Ollie put his hands on his hips.

Helena paused. 'Ollie, what's wrong? You don't seem very pleased to see me.'

'What the fuck do you mean?' he demanded. Ollie was always aggressive when he was wrong-footed, and Helena had occasionally found a surprising number of empty wine bottles in the recycling bin when he was like this.

'Well, where's "Hello darling, how are you feeling?" I have just come from my family home after my father's death, you know.'

'Of course I know. And how *are* you feeling?' Ollie's eyes flickered nervously.

'I'm completely drained, if you must know. Is something wrong?'

'Wrong?' asked Ollie. 'Why would there be?'

Helena was not going to say, ever, that she had never been completely sure of her hold on him. It was very difficult to be married. Her sugar-daddy second husband had adored her, so she'd never had to worry about what he was thinking. Of course, she and Ollie adored each other too, but it was a more equal relationship. As it should be. But Ollie could switch from warm, sexy and loving to cold and angry in a moment, and it made her nervous. She knew it was her fault: she made too many demands on him and, like most actresses, she often put her career before everything else. Since she'd realised that, she'd got better, but she still couldn't get it quite right.

'Come on, I need a drink.' She went downstairs and saw an open bottle. 'After the day I've had.'

'How was it?' replied Ollie, filling her glass and emptying the bottle. He pulled another from the wine rack concealed in one of the kitchen units.

Helena sipped her drink and studied him. Sometimes she couldn't quite read him. Was he angry with her for some reason?

'Should you be opening another?' she asked, looking at the wine bottle. 'I mean, we both have to work tomorrow.'

'Since when were you a model of sobriety?'

Helena hugged herself, suddenly feeling very bleak. 'Pa left everything equally to the three of us.'

Ollie whistled. 'That's a turn-up for the books. I'd have betted anything on him leaving it all to Bramble. What do you think it's worth? One mil? Two? Three, even?'

'Perhaps not that much. The house is in a terrible state.' Years of doing up houses had taught Helena quite a bit about what the maintenance of period homes could involve and she'd always been alarmed by her father's cavalier attitude to planning regulations and conservation officers. 'My family's owned this house for over a hundred years,' he'd snorted. 'I'm not having any Nigel in granny glasses tell me what guttering I can and can't use.'

'Yes, but Pa,' she'd said, 'you *can't* put plastic gutters on listed buildings and, anyway, they often don't work with the roofline. They let water in.' He had merely harrumphed, and the next time she'd gone down she'd spotted the plastic guttering and even, horror of horrors, a couple of double-glazed dormers in the roof at the back. She couldn't imagine the legal to-ing and fro-ing that might be necessary before they could exchange contracts, selling the house. Still, that was all a long way away.

With a moment of anxiety, Helena turned away to the sink so that Ollie couldn't see her taking one of the Valium she kept in her handbag for emergencies, for the nights she lay awake risking shadows under her eyes. She washed it down with the last of the wine in the glass. It would take a bit of time to work and she didn't want to be lying in bed thinking about things. 'And I don't think there's much cash,' she added. 'Maybe even debt. Bramble and I are going to see the accountant next week to find out what the situation really is. I'm bracing myself for the worst.'

'Still,' Ollie said, 'the house is fabulous. Or could be, in the right hands. Not too big. Just right for City bonuses. And City bonuses divided into three . . . Assuming Bramble will sell, of course. It's a bit dangerous, having her living there like that, I'd have thought.'

'Oh, Bramble will always do what is right.'

'Hmm.' Ollie met her eyes. 'It's her definition of right that worries me.'

Helena had an idea. She would quietly make sure everyone

knew Lorenden was for sale. Even before they found Felicity. People would approach them and Helena would have to respond, and Bramble would slowly adapt to the idea that the house was on the market. Helena suspected that she hadn't really taken it on board, and that unless she got things moving quickly Bramble would drag her feet. A quick sale would give Bramble a clean break, which was what she needed. A chance to start again.

Helena was energised by the wine and the thought of marketing Lorenden behind Bramble's back. She began to tidy up, picking up a pile of post. 'Did this come today?'

Ollie shrugged. 'I assume so.'

The top envelope looked like a bank statement but the letter had been folded so that the name didn't line up with the address window. Probably hers, thought Helena, anxious that Ollie shouldn't open it and discover how much she spent.

She couldn't quite understand it. It was a final demand for payment, with threats of legal action. Her brow wrinkled anxiously. Ollie always said she was bourgeois about money: 'You have to think of the wider picture. That money is sitting on deposit earning us interest. Always leave bills until the last minute, it's a sheer waste to write cheques any earlier.'

'Is this yours?' She passed it over. 'I opened it by accident.'

'Fuck that.' He threw the bill back across the table at her. 'I paid that weeks ago.' Then he reached over and took it back. 'Don't worry, there must be some mistake. I'll sort it out.'

Helena forgot about the envelope as a blackness welled up and threatened to engulf her. 'It's not the money,' she said illogically. 'It's that I never got to say goodbye.' With that, she sat down on one of their cold Philippe Starck chairs and began to sob, terrible rib-wrenching sobs that tore the heart out of her and that wouldn't stop. It was as if she would never be happy again.

'I'm sorry,' he said softly. 'I know this is hard for you.' He walked over to her and poured her another glass, kissing her forehead. 'Poor little Helena.'

Later, he undressed her tenderly and pulled a nightie over her head, offering her a last sip of wine then tucking her in. As she slipped into oblivion she felt him slide into bed and wrap himself around her. She fell asleep with the reassurance of his warm breath against the back of her neck and the gentle rocking embrace of his arms around her.

'Poor little baby,' he murmured. 'Shh. Poor little baby. I'm here to look after you. I'm here. I'll never, never leave.'

Felicity worked at the rescue centre for another fortnight, spending any spare time she had with Merlin. When she'd cleaned the mud off his bony frame a criss-cross of tiny cuts – as if he had staggered through brambles – had been revealed and also, less recent but barely healed, whip marks. Some of his wounds were infected and he needed antibiotics.

At first, Merlin was too frozen with pain to acknowledge her, although he seemed easy enough to handle. He remained motionless in his stall, head down and dull eyed, but once the antibiotics started to take effect he grew both livelier and more wary. He was slowly tempted by the buckets of feed she brought, pushing his long nose straight in almost as soon as she set it down. He would pull back as she reached out to stroke him, but he clearly hated having anyone but her around.

'No good getting fond of him,' said Harry the day she managed to kiss Merlin's nose. 'His owners will want him back. He's microchipped so it's just a question of time till we hear from them.'

'Someone's treated him badly,' replied Felicity. 'Even before the storm. He doesn't trust humans. I think we should ask some questions before we allow him to go back anywhere.'

'His cuts are too sore for him to trust anyone much.' Harry strode off, his mind already on other animals that needed him.

Merlin began to look out for Felicity. When she walked down the aisle between the looseboxes his head would appear at the sound of her footsteps, snorting softly with recognition, and his fine ears pricked towards her. He gradually accepted her hands running along the dust and sweat that marked his dark coat. A few days after that, she started brushing him gently, moving slowly and talking softly, running her hands over the wasted muscles and prominent bones, polishing him up to the sheen he must once have had. 'You've had a hard time,' she whispered. 'But you're safe now.' His lower lip drooped in relaxation as he remembered more glorious days, perhaps, then, at the sound of a car accelerating in the distance, his head shot up again.

'Shh, baby,' she murmured. 'Shh.' His head dropped down again, and soon the lower lip followed it, the first indications of trust. She inhaled the smell of horse, the perfume of so many lost dreams.

After three weeks at the centre, Felicity drove into town to find an Internet café. Her laptop was still in the cottage by the lake. There was nobody she wanted to hear from, but the outside world began to tug at her, and one day she woke up with an instinct that told her she needed to be in touch.

The Internet café was run by a young man with a goatee beard, whose badge proclaimed his name to be Sam. He thought Felicity was a young woman when she strode in with her loose, long-limbed gait, scruffy combat trousers and skimpy vest.

But when she paid for a tall cappuccino, bangles clattering along one thin wrist, he saw that her hand was freckled and its skin dull. As he handed over her change he took in the loose skin over bones, a spider network of lines around her bruised bedroom eyes.

Even so, as she walked away from him, her hair the colour of polished leather and twisted up in a chignon held with a pencil, he knew she had class. Whatever age she was – and he couldn't begin to guess what it might be – she was out of his league. He watched her, and so did every other man in the room.

Felicity steadily worked her way through her emails. There were some offers of work, which she quickly replied to with a 'Thanks, but no', carefully leaving the door open for the future, and a handful of catch-ups that she lingered over for a little longer.

Felicity had friends around the world – she might walk into the Café Les Deux Magots in Paris, windowshop the glittering wares of the Kurfürstendamn in Berlin, queue at Hong Kong airport or make her way through the crowds at the Deauville racecourse and suddenly hear a shouted 'Felicity! *Ma chère. Mi amiga.* Ohmigod, what are you doing *here*?' She could rely on finding some kind of contact in the loneliest places: a bear hug in an aid station in Darfur, a warm handshake in a war crimes tribunal in Sierra Leone or a kiss on both cheeks in Sarajevo. She sat with friends around candlelit tables over bottles of rough red wine or tiny shot glasses of lethal local liqueur, switching languages at will. People would register where you came from without judging you for it. Unlike in the English countryside, where the network of old family friendships and relationships were as tightly intertwined as the weave on an antique Turkish rug, its patterns repeating over and over again as century slipped into century. On the noisy boulevards of Paris, in the mosquito-infested swamps of Louisiana or over the intermittent rat-a-tat-tat of helicopters and the occasional sniper in Palestine, they took each other at face value.

But, deep down, Felicity, like Merlin, did not really trust anyone, although she connected well when she chose to. She liked her relationships in boxes – fellow journalists, useful people, old friends, men she might sleep with. Her family was in another box – one she kept locked unless strictly necessary.

Hey, these days, friends have taken the place of family. What was it that drunk journalist had told her, as the bombs crumped down over their heads in Iraq? Oh yes, the family was an outdated societal model. Fine. Who needs outdated?

This year her father had asked her to come back to Lorenden for Christmas and she'd brushed the invitation off, surprised by how much it had upset her. She'd even had nightmares. Why had he chosen to ask her now? She had maintained a strict 'weddings and funerals only' policy, arriving at the last minute, smiling at everyone and making polite conversation, then leaving as soon as possible. It had worked for all these years so why disrupt it now?

She was tempted to delete this latest message from his email address without reading it, except that it was titled 'Please call Bramble'.

Felicity didn't like to think about how small Bramble had been when she left. She had no relationship with the boyish woman her sister had become, who was always busy with the constant stream of people and horses that filtered through Lorenden. Bramble had the life that Felicity had once thought would be hers – the warm, cluttered kitchen, always full of gossip, the stables busy, and the smell of hay, linseed oil and fresh manure in the misty mornings. Felicity didn't want to get drawn into it. Apart from a hesitantly worded card of consolation, and a brief appearance at Dom's funeral, she'd avoided any real communication.

Bramble didn't care about her – she hardly knew her – and that was fine. It was better than Helena's neediness, her boasting of her latest awards or the parties she'd been to, her eyes following Felicity everywhere pleading 'Look how well I've done without you! *Look at me.*' And when Felicity started to appear on television, Helena had tried to appropriate her. She clearly wanted to introduce her 'news reporter sister' at parties. Felicity had quietly rebuffed her.

She opened the email and read it twice, not believing it the first time.

'You bastard,' she shouted, banging her fist down on the table beside her and sending the cappuccino splashing into the air. 'You bastard! You never listened to me. *You never even listened.*'

And she was out of the café, pushing aside tables and chairs, blinded by tears, running away from the pain.

Sam, wiping tables, caught a brief glimpse of her eyes and was reminded of a cornered animal. He hurried over to the computer to mop up the spilt coffee. It had spooled over the floor, but he saw, with relief, that it hadn't touched the keyboard. On the screen the message was still open, unanswered.

'Grampa died suddenly this morning,' he read. 'Please come home. From Savannah.' Well, perhaps it wasn't surprising that the woman was upset.

The café fell silent, everyone staring at the door as if Felicity might come whirling back, but as he closed down the PC the force went out of the air and they turned back to their own business.

Chapter 9

When Felicity got back to the rescue centre, Merlin's box was empty. A girl chewing gum told her that someone had arrived to claim him.

'Who? Where did they go?'

The girl shrugged. 'A horsebox left ten minutes ago. Maybe he was in that.'

Felicity managed to catch up with the horsebox in less than fifteen minutes, but persuading them to stop wasn't easy. The two women driving obviously thought she might be trying to car-jack them, and Felicity wouldn't have been surprised to see them levelling a gun at her. However, being a woman on her own obviously worked in her favour, as eventually they stopped and wound the window down a fraction.

Felicity shouted her story up to them.

'Sorry,' said the woman. 'We've got a chestnut mare here, Lovely Lila, she's called. Here's our paperwork.'

Felicity glanced at the papers. 'Lovely Lila. So that's what she's called. So glad you found her, she's a sweetheart. Thanks for stopping.' She raced back to her car.

'Hope you make it!' shouted the woman driving the horsebox. 'Those insurers want their money back and they'll likely be taking him straight to auction. He could go for meat. There're some better prices coming from Europe now.'

Horrified, Felicity broke the speed limit getting back to the rescue centre and tore in to the makeshift office. 'I need the names of the people who took Merlin, and anything you've got on where they were taking him.'

The man at the office looked up primly. 'That's confidential.'

'Don't you fucking talk about confidential, I saved that horse's life.'

'What's going on?' Harry stood behind her, arms folded across his chest.

'Harry, please help, I'm trying to persuade this arsehole that I need to know where Merlin's gone. Immediately.'

'That's no call to go swearing at people. Now you owe this young man an apology, then I'll see you outside.'

'But . . .'

Harry glared at her.

'I'm sorry,' said Felicity, and the words stuck in her throat. 'But . . . I mean, yes, I'm very sorry.' She left the room and paced up and down the nearly empty barn, almost screaming in frustration.

Several minutes later Harry emerged from the office with a piece of paper. 'You always catch more flies with sugar than vinegar,' he said, handing it over to her. 'Reckon you could do with remembering that sometimes.'

'Oh, thank you, Harry. Thank you. You are a darling. And I'm sorry about the arsehole remark.' She read the photocopy of the paperwork that Harry had got for her. 'I've got to go now, is that OK?'

He grinned. 'Sure. Let me know what happens.'

Felicity telephoned the number on the paper and got a bored insurance clerk just about to go on his lunch break. Forcing herself to remain polite, she managed to extract the information that Merlin was headed for the nearest livestock market. It was about an hour and a half's drive from the rescue centre, and the time Merlin had been released was marked as 9.20 a.m. It was now just past midday, so Merlin might already be there. The insurance clerk refused to give her the cellphone numbers of the company employees transporting him.

She phoned the market. It was closed for lunch. Well, at least that meant they couldn't sell any horses. She revved up the car, reminded herself that getting pulled over for speeding would be a disaster and forced herself to drive at an exact, sedate fifty-five miles an hour towards the small town where the auction was being held.

In Kent, Bramble sat down on a bale of hay in the feed store after evening stables and considered her predicament. Jez was out, and Donna had taken herself to the pub again, so she was alone with the scent of hay and, beyond that, the crisp air of the autumn evening, with its hint of rotting leaves and bonfires. She lay back and began to drift off, into a shadowy world where her father was trying to tell her something.

There was a sudden glow as the security lights came on, and she heard the horses move around, curious to know what was going on.

It was probably a fox. Bramble was almost too tired to get up, but she heard the gate opening and closing softly, and footsteps crossing the yard, stopping, then starting again.

'Hello?' she called. 'Jez, is that you?'

The man standing in the yard wasn't Jez, and between the dark and the security lights she couldn't see his face. He was tall, and quite heavily built.

'Excuse me?' she repeated. 'Can I help you?'

'Bramble!' He moved forward and she could see his face. Toby Fitzroy. A man her father had disliked intensely.

'Toby? What are you doing here?'

They hovered awkwardly. She and Toby were not on cheek-kissing terms, but a handshake was too formal.

'I, er, came to offer my, er, condolences.'

Bramble was puzzled. She hadn't heard his car draw up, and the frost between the Beaumonts and the Fitzroys was such that she would have expected, at the most, a card, or maybe a token appearance at the funeral.

'Thank you, Toby.' She kept her voice even.

'He was a very great man. In the horse world, that is.'

Bramble waited for him to explain further, studying him carefully in the half-light. Toby was a big man – well over six foot – with a powerful body that he barely prevented from turning to fat. The shock of blond hair he'd inherited from his half-Swedish mother Beatrice seemed as thick as ever, although it was fading to white and his eyes, also a Swedish inheritance, burned a brilliant blue in his tanned, lined face. Bramble suspected he intensified their colour with contact lenses. But even Toby's enemies – and he had a few – admitted that he was still a good-looking man, and as a young man had been exceptionally so. And he knew it. Women had always fallen into his greedy hands like ripe plums falling from a tree.

She folded her arms and leant against the frame of the feed store door, puzzled.

'Well, as I said, I wanted to say how sorry I am. And to see if you needed any help. You must be very short-handed.'

'That's very kind of you, but as a matter of fact, we've taken on Jezzar Morgan as a nagsman,' said Bramble, enjoying the look of surprise on Toby's face.

'Oh, really? Jezzar Morgan, eh? Isn't that rather sudden?'

Bramble smiled. 'No, it was decided before my father died.' Nobody would ever know, she resolved, how furious she had been. From now on, as far as the world was concerned, Jezzar was her appointment. She raised her chin in the air.

'Right. OK. Well, that's very . . . er . . . good news. On a very sad day, of course.'

Bramble could almost feel sorry for him.

'Anyway, as I said, please let me know if I can do anything.'

'That's very kind of you, Toby,' she repeated.

'And if you're thinking of selling up . . .'

'I'm not.'

'It's a big place. High running costs. And with your father gone—'

'I'll be taking over.'

Toby leant over so that his lips were close to her ear. 'When you look at the figures, you may find it behoves you to downsize to a smaller yard. Without your father's name, you're not much more than a little riding school that occasionally sells a horse or two.'

'I've got my own name. It's well known enough.'

'Up to a point. You never quite made it to the top, did you? The way things are these days, being an also-ran doesn't do the business.'

'Well, you should know, Toby.'

The shaft went home and she saw a flash of rage in his eyes. 'I know more about success than you ever will.' He gestured to the peaceful yard. 'And it doesn't look like this.'

Bramble swallowed. 'I think you'll find,' she said, 'that things will look very different at the end of next season. We're just beginning.'

'Really?' he said. 'It looks more like the end to me. Anyway, I don't want to argue with you. I just wanted to find out if you'd be interested in offers. For any of the horses.'

'And why would you do that?' Bramble controlled her rising anger.

'Oh,' he said, walking back to the gate. 'For old times' sake, you know. For old times' sake.' He turned round and treated her to a flashbulb smile, the one he switched on for the photographers at smart parties.

Bramble swallowed down nausea. 'Goodbye, Toby,' she shouted. 'And thank you, but it's business as usual here.'

She felt the bile rise in her throat again and, standing over one of the stable drains, she vomited, retching repeatedly out of nerves, exhaustion and shock. As she washed her face and rinsed her mouth out with the icy water from the tap, filling a bucket of water to clear everything up, she remembered when she'd last been sick out of nerves. It had been half an hour before the cross-country at Badminton. Eight years ago.

Except that at Badminton it was all over, one way or the other, in twelve and a half minutes. This could go on for years. For ever, even. She wiped her face with her sleeve and took deep breaths. She would face each fence as it came. Somehow she would keep Lorenden for Savannah.

Teddy's long nose appeared over the top of his loosebox door, and he studied her with a large, alert eye.

Teddy, she thought. Or rather Teddy's owner, Pauline. Lady Rudd. Pauline was more than just an owner, she'd almost been her father's business partner. They'd been working together for more than forty years. Longer than most marriages. And the Rudds were rich. Bramble wondered if there was any way in which she could persuade Pauline to be her backer. Pauline loved buying and selling, and watching her horses win.

She would go and see Pauline. The thought of it comforted Bramble. Since Bramble's mother had died when Bramble was only five, leaving Bramble and Helena in the charge of a series of nannies, Pauline had been like an aunt to Bramble and she was sure she would have some wise advice now. Pauline would tell her what to do.

Felicity got lost looking for the sale room, and was twice forced to double back on a six-lane highway. Eventually she reached a series of barns, parked her car and hurried through, following signs that read 'Office', and launched herself at a sign that said 'Information'. The man behind the desk was handling another query, and Felicity fidgeted until he was free.

'I need to find a horse.' She shoved her photocopy of Merlin's paperwork at him. 'It's urgent.'

With agonising slowness the man consulted his computer. 'He was sold this morning. One of the last lots before lunch.'

'Do you know who to?'

He nodded his head. 'Walt Bird. Just over there, Ma'am.'

Walt Bird was a giant hulk of a man, with a series of overlapping chins and stomachs.

'Excuse me,' said Felicity. 'You've just bought this horse?'

He looked at the paper. 'What of it?'

'I'd like to buy him off you.'

He shook his head. 'No can do.'

'I'll pay more. Much more.'

'Ain't my money.'

'Whose money is it then?'

Walt sighed and his chins wobbled. 'This is the way it works, lady. I'm a kill buyer. I buy a truckful of horses and when it's full I drive them to the slaughterhouse. And if the truck's not full I have to drive somewhere else and buy more horses. That means having to keep the first lot of horses in pens until I get more. And that ain't humane.'

Walt did not look like a man who worried about humanity. Felicity had read about what happened in some of the slaughterhouses. The horses are shot in the head with a bolt to stun them and then their throats are cut and they bleed to death. But the stun gun doesn't always work. The horses know what they are facing. They're not tranquillised because the drug would contaminate their meat. They're terrified.

'Well, if I give you more money than he's worth you can buy another horse. Even if the price rises. And I'll add something extra for your trouble, say a thousand dollars.'

His eyebrows went up sharply, and he looked at his watch. 'Cash,' he said. 'Before the end of the auction so I can buy another horse to fill the truck.'

'Where's the nearest bank?'

The nearest bank was twenty minutes' drive away, and when she said she wanted to take out three thousand dollars, she was asked to wait while her details were checked. The clock ticked away. The auction ended at four-thirty, and it was already twenty past two. Eventually she seized the cash and drove back to the livestock market, where she was forced to circle the car park twice in order to find a parking space. Please, she muttered to the sky, give me a break. Just one break.

A car emerged from a space and she reversed into it.

Walt counted out the money. 'Wait,' he said. 'Till I make sure I can get another horse to replace it.'

Felicity had been waiting all day. She felt sick. Surely Walt wouldn't pass up a thousand dollars? Finally the gavel was lowered on another horse and Walt's consignment was complete.

'Follow me.' He waddled off towards the holding pens, stopping at one packed tightly with untethered horses jostling each other in the gloom, some old, some ill, some angry and some just plain frightened.

'You recognise him?'

Felicity peered at the horses, flank-to-flank, some with the diarrhoea of fear streaking their flanks. They jostled and nipped each other and, in the corner, an old mare cowered with blood dripping from her nose.

'They don't know each other,' said Walt. 'Fightin' for position. Happens all the time.'

Felicity gave a small scream. 'What's that?' A dark horse appeared to have its eye hanging out.

Walt cursed. 'That's what happens when you wait around, lady.

The sooner this lot's at the slaughterhouse the better. The new regulations are making things very difficult for people like me to do their jobs. Now git on and git your horse.'

But Felicity couldn't see him. 'He's dark grey. Almost black. With a thin white blaze.'

Walt picked his teeth indifferently.

'There,' she shouted. 'In the middle. That one.'

'Who's gonna go in and get him?'

Felicity looked at the packed horses. 'I will,' she said.

'Good a way as any to git your leg broken,' said Walt with a grin. 'Or worse.'

Felicity squared her shoulders, making her body as big as she could, and the horses moved away from her as she went into the pen, backing away from the human intruder as far as they could. 'Merlin,' she called softly. 'Merlin.' After moving quietly around, always aware of the big bodies jostling, she thought she saw, in the gloom, a tiny gesture of recognition as a head turned towards her, ears pricked.

'Good boy,' she whispered, as she buckled the headcollar, 'good boy.'

She could feel the other horses closing in again as she led him out, hoping to escape with him, and her heart beat faster, knowing that frightened hooves were only inches away from her feet, and that she could be crushed between heavy, panicking bodies. She thought Walt was enjoying it, and that he'd like it even more if she was hurt. He was, she decided when she saw the glimmer of entertainment in his eyes, a sadist.

'More'n a thousand dollars for a horse only fit for meat,' he said. 'Some folks have more money than sense.' And he laughed at his own unoriginal wit.

With a last look back at the horses she couldn't save, Felicity grabbed the paperwork off him. 'We don't eat horsemeat in this country,' he said, reading her expression. 'In case you were thinking you were better than us.'

'Yeah, well,' she said. And she led Merlin out into the fresh air, away from the fear of death.

As she stood there, in the open air among rows of horseboxes, she realised that until now, in the whole of her adult life, she had never been responsible for another being. Not even a goldfish. And now she had a horse. No home, no job, no partner. Just a horse.

Bramble set off across the fields, calling the dogs. Darcy, who'd been checking a hedge for rabbits, emerged, his tail swishing apologetically from side to side, his head dropped down in a smile. He picked his way carefully over the rough grass, with the terriers scurrying after him.

Bramble sighed. This land was part of her, every inch of it, from the damp thick clay that clung around her feet to the beech and oak trees over her head. She loved the secret network of lanes known only to locals, criss-crossing the fields, the blackberries and rose hips that twined through the hedges in autumn and the poppies that edged the fields in summer.

She followed an almost invisible path along the side of the orchard, the dogs pattering ahead of her, listening to the soft rustle of nature settling itself for the night. A pheasant barrelled out of a hedge in front of her, its wings clattering like a clockwork toy. Bramble called the dogs back and they came reluctantly, deprived of sport.

Alan and Pauline were Edward's oldest friends. Pauline, tall, slim and elegant, had the dignity of a great beauty. Alan had been a captain of industry, knighted for his services to business, and still sat on a number of boards as a non-executive director. Alan and Pauline lived a charmed life, one where there was plenty of money and enough enjoyable work, relative good health and fitness, parties, pleasure and three reliable adult children all making their way in the world. They had a flat in London as well as the Georgian rectory.

Pauline opened the door, immaculately dressed in beige and cream, with a scarf around her neck, pinned to one side with a large jewelled brooch.

'Bramble. My dear,' she said. 'Come in and have a drink. Is Teddy all right?'

Bramble's heart sank at the sight of Pauline's welcoming face. They obviously hadn't heard. She tugged her boots off, avoiding Pauline's eyes, and the door closed on the dogs. They knew the house well, and that they had to stay outside to protect Pauline's sofas from their muddy paws. 'Teddy's fine,' she murmured to the floor.

Pauline looked questioning and called to her husband: 'Alan! Darling! Bramble is here.'

Bramble sat on the end of a sofa, feeling unusually grubby against its impeccable whiteness.

'Bramble. How lovely to see you.' Alan hobbled in. 'Excuse this damned leg of mine, stiff in this weather. You only just caught us. We've been away for a couple of days. Venice, you know. So lovely at this time of year.'

'Vienna, darling,' said Pauline sharply. 'We were in Vienna.'

'Yes, yes, I meant Vienna.' He winked at Bramble. 'All these places sound the same.'

Bramble stared at the floor. 'So you haven't heard?'

Pauline's hand flew to her mouth. 'Heard?'

'I'm afraid Pa's dead. We think it was a heart attack, yesterday morning.' She heard a sharp intake of breath from Pauline. When she looked up, she saw that Alan was grey-faced.

'What happened, exactly?' His voice, in just a few minutes, sounded much older and very frail.

Pauline's face had gone the colour of putty, and Alan tottered out of his chair and slowly lowered himself down beside her on the other sofa, his hands over hers. 'Tell us.'

That is love, thought Bramble. To be with someone for nearly fifty years and still to cherish them. She recounted the story and watched them both shrink into their neatly pressed clothes. Pauline took out a lace handkerchief and dabbed her eyes.

'He was a very good friend,' said Alan. 'To us both.'

'Poor Bramble,' said Pauline. 'This is so terrible for you, dear.'

'I'm fine,' said Bramble. She was worried about the colour of Pauline's face. Nobody really talked about the sadness of losing a friend. Presumably Pauline and Alan had lost several by now, and each time one went their world became a little smaller.

'You must let us know, my dear, if there's anything we can do,' murmured Pauline, her voice trembling.

'Thank you,' replied Bramble, 'but I'm fine.' She could see that there would be no comfort here. Pauline and Alan had aged immeasurably in just a few moments, and were far more vulnerable than she was. All she wanted, at that moment, was to be back at Lorenden and to let the house wrap itself around her. She wanted to be in her own bed, looking out at the orchards she had known all her life. 'There's something else. Pa seems to have hired Jezzar Morgan to ride Teddy.'

Pauline's eyes briefly flashed recognition before she wiped them again with her handkerchief. 'That's lovely, my dear. I'm so glad you've got someone to help you. Isn't that such fortunate timing, in the circumstances?'

'Well,' Bramble steadied herself. 'Pa hadn't actually told me what he was doing. He and I did have a bit of a . . . discussion about whether I should go on riding Teddy.'

'Teddy's a man's horse,' said Pauline, who treated the opposite sex with what appeared to be complete reverence. 'I know he believed that. You're a wonderful rider, my dear, but Teddy needs a bit more strength.'

'I don't . . .' Bramble trailed off. Pauline looked close to collapse. Now was not the time for this conversation. 'Did he tell you about Jez?'

Pauline nodded faintly. 'Your father always made such good decisions. I have complete faith in them. '

So Pauline had been in on it. Clearly neither of them had believed she would ever get to the top. If Pauline wanted Jez to ride Teddy, then there was nothing she, Bramble, could do about it. She swallowed the betrayal and kissed Pauline goodbye.

Alan saw her to the door. 'This will hit Pauline very hard,' he said once they were out of the room. 'She had such fun with your father, following Teddy to events, being an owner.'

'It's business as usual,' said Bramble. 'Really. I'm going to manage.'

'Of course,' replied Alan. She kissed Alan goodbye, and was reminded again, with a spasm of pain, of her father's whiskery cheek and his clean scent of lemon.

But she knew she was on her own now, as she negotiated the familiar, rough path home.

Chapter 10

A week later Helena drove down to Lorenden in the early morning. She and Bramble had an appointment with the accountant, Nicky Dawson. Along the lane, dried-up stalks of the summer's wildflowers were hung with cobwebs. Dewdrops sparkled along the delicate filaments, like thousands of diamond necklaces draped over bare arms.

It really is about time I had some proper jewellery, thought Helena. It's ridiculous that someone in my position only has costume stuff. But it all depended on whether Edward was deeply in debt. A frisson of alarm shuddered through her. It was quite possible that a third of Lorenden might add up to one great big nothing-at-all.

In the yard, Bramble frowned. There was so much administration around death. Visits to solicitors, funeral directors, accountants and registrars. It seemed to go on and on. They were busy enough in the yard anyway, and she didn't like leaving Jez in charge so much when he'd only just joined them. Not that he wasn't completely competent – of course he was – but . . . But. But.

Jez led Teddy out, the horse making it clear with every prancing step that he knew he was a champion. Donna was already up on Tegan. Jez mounted in one fluid movement, adjusting the stirrups with concentration.

'We're down to about an hour's hacking a day with Teddy.' Bramble watched every movement he made. 'No more. Just enough to make sure he doesn't go mad when he goes out.'

'Maybe he should be out more,' suggested Jez, now seated as comfortably on the fidgeting horse as on an old armchair. 'Then you wouldn't have to worry about him getting excited when he's turned out.'

For a moment Bramble saw the paddock as Jez did, through the eyes of a horse, feeling the ripple of the breeze, the crunch of the sweet green grass beneath his feet and, underneath it, the scent of earth and freedom. She shook the image out of her head in irritation. 'He's far too valuable. We have to be very careful.'

'Trust him,' replied Jez quietly. Teddy danced out of the yard with Jez welded to his back. Donna clattered after them.

Bramble stood looking after them, trying not to scream. 'He cannot, simply cannot, take a single order from me,' she said, kissing Helena without saying hello. 'I don't know how Penny whatserface managed. Teddy is the most valuable horse we've got. Everything hangs on him doing well next season. Everything.'

Dawson Daly Accountants was housed in a narrow, wiggly town house in Canterbury. Bramble wished she was somewhere else, and thought of Jez riding down the side of the orchards, past the old damson trees and round into the wide open stubble field with the autumn sun on his face.

Nicky's secretary appeared and told them that Nicky would see them now. Helena and Bramble settled themselves in the two chairs facing the desk.

'Once again,' said Nicky, 'I can't tell you how sorry I am about your father. He is going to be much missed.'

There was a tense silence.

'Thank you,' murmured Helena.

Nicky looked at their faces: 'Right. Let's see. Now how much do you know about how the business was run? You were his partner, Bramble.'

Bramble, reassured by the word 'partner', nodded, but Helena placed a soft hand on Bramble's arm. 'I haven't been involved at all and, also, our father was quite secretive about anything financial, so it might be best if you assumed that we both know nothing and started from the beginning.'

'Right,' said Nicky again, looking uneasy. 'Now. At the

moment there's Lorenden, which encompasses the house, the stables and the little barn, plus the gardens and five paddocks. Your father, as you know, sold off the farm a few years ago, along with the cottages and the bigger old barn.'

Helena and Bramble nodded.

'Unfortunately he didn't sell them at the best time – he certainly didn't realise anything like what they would have been worth today, or even if he'd waited a couple of years . . .' catching sight of their expressions, Nicky added: 'but, of course, we can't talk about what would have been. I just felt I had to explain why there isn't as much money from the sales that have already been made as you might expect.'

She took a deep breath. 'The stables have been losing money for years. I don't know much about this area but, as far as I can see, it's very difficult to make money out of it.'

'Absolutely,' agreed Helena.

'Just looking at the accounts – well . . .' she sighed. 'Am I right in saying, Bramble, that at the heart of it it's simply not a big enough operation to survive in today's market?'

Bramble nodded reluctantly. She had tried to get her father to invest and expand, because making money out of liveries and a handful of active event horses was a perilously hit-and-miss affair.

'There have been other factors in the past, of course,' Nicky continued. 'Obviously the income from farming has been dropping steadily since the late seventies. The economics of a small farm have simply not been viable.'

Helena nodded. 'He should have gone organic. Or something.'

'That would have taken time and money. Which he didn't have,' said Bramble, irritated at Helena's opinion. Helena knew nothing about farming.

'Anyway,' said Helena. 'Go on. Is there anything left?'

'There is a certain amount of money left, mainly in his building society account,' said Nicky, pushing a piece of paper with a list of figures on it towards them, 'but I'm afraid you're going to need every penny of it to pay inheritance tax before you can get probate. There won't be any left, so you'll be facing a cash crisis on the yard.'

'And debts on Lorenden?' asked Helena. 'Mortgages, loans, that sort of thing?'

Nicky shook her head. 'Your father was very old-fashioned about money, and he hated debt. Lorenden isn't mortgaged.'

'Well!' Helena leant back in relief. 'That's all fine, then. Isn't it? I mean, none of us are greedy. We'll just sell Lorenden and split the proceeds. Nothing could be simpler.'

'Well, it isn't necessarily quite that straightforward, because I think you'll have to decide whether you sell it as a business, or whether Bramble relocates the stables while selling Lorenden for its property value alone. Or you may want to try to get developers involved, in which case there may be quite a wait for planning permission – several years, if it's a large or controversial development – or you may even decide to keep the business going and sell at some point in the future, which, in tax terms, could be quite favourable. And none of these options are likely to be immediate – you can't sell anything until probate is granted, and it may take you up to a year after that.'

'A year?' echoed Helena. 'You mean it could be at least a year before any of us get any money? That's going to make life very difficult for Bramble. I mean, I'm all right, and presumably Felicity isn't in any great need, but this is Bramble's life.' She touched Bramble's arm again with a feather-light hand. 'Don't worry, darling, we'll sort *something* out. We won't let you starve!'

'I think cash flow could be a problem for a while,' said Nicky, 'but there are ways of doing things.'

'I want to go on,' said Bramble. 'I'm going to continue with my father's work. For Savannah.'

Nicky looked worried.

'Now, be sensible,' said Helena. 'With your share of Lorenden you can start again. You can buy a little livery stable, give some lessons – you've got a wonderful reputation. And it'll be far less worrying than—'

'I'm an eventer,' said Bramble. 'And so is Savannah. It's what we do.'

'Well, you haven't exactly been winning Badminton, have you?' flashed Helena. 'You've been nowhere near it since Dom died. You *know* this world, there are half a dozen riders at the top who make money out of it and everyone else struggles or is rich anyway. And getting to that level, well, you got close once, but now – well, it's almost impossible. No, I correct myself, it *is* impossible.'

'I won't sell my horses,' said Bramble.

'They're *our* horses,' snapped Helena. 'They're all ours now.' She stopped and put on a conciliatory tone. 'Darling Bramble, I'm so sorry. I didn't mean to be insensitive. But you must admit that you're not making a living out of it.'

Nicky cleared her throat. 'Perhaps this discussion should be held later. Now let's turn to income. You have fourteen horses at the moment – ten you own and four liveries – is that right?' She looked at Bramble, who nodded, almost unable to take anything in.

'Obviously, apart from your father's training commitments and the liveries, buying horses and training them up for resale has been the main source of income over the past few years,' droned Nicky, 'so I've discussed this with him quite often. And I have to say that there have been horses that have barely covered their costs, not to mention several that have become virtually unsaleable because they've failed the vet at the point at which they would otherwise have been sold.'

'That can happen to anyone,' said Bramble. 'It's very common.'

'Yes,' said Nicky. 'Rather the point I tried to make to your father. Several times.'

'On the other hand, we've bought quite a few promising young horses for a couple of grand and sold them on at double or triple what we paid for them.'

'Yes, that's true,' conceded Nicky; rather reluctantly, it seemed to Bramble.

She could feel Helena twitching in her seat, desperate to get involved in the conversation.

'Pa had hardly any owners left, by the look of things. Just Pauline, and whoever they are who own the youngsters. Face it, Bramble, it was all winding down.' She turned to Nicky. 'One thing I've never understood about eventing is the owners. People who buy a horse then pay other people to train it, ride it and look after it, and all they get out of it is watching it compete on some godforsaken windy hillside.'

'It's the same in racing,' said Bramble. 'The owners pay their stabling, trainers, jockeys and so on. It's the way it all works. There's nothing at all odd about it. People find it exciting, Helena, you know that.'

'Exciting?' sneered Helena. 'That's just another word for dangerous. And irresponsible. Besides, in racing there's actually some prize money to make it all worthwhile, and the horses change hands for huge sums, so there's an investment aspect.' Helena couldn't disguise the resentment in her voice. 'Eventing costs a fortune and you don't get anything back. Whereas if you take something like showjumping, at least there's a decent prize structure so people might just feel it's worth loading the horse up in the morning.'

'People lose fortunes on racehorses and showjumpers too . . .' Bramble could feel her cheeks heating up.

'Yes, well,' interrupted Nicky, rustling papers. 'Anyway, we've established that the estate consists of Lorenden, the stables and the horses.'

'The steady money lies in teaching and running courses, a bit from sponsorship, and the big money, if you're going to make it, lies in selling a really top quality horse,' said Bramble.

Helena fixed Nicky with a look. 'What do you think Lorenden – as it is – is worth?'

Nicky steepled her fingers. 'That really is outside my professional competence. You need to talk to an estate agent. And, of course, you can't sell anything until probate comes through, and without Felicity you can't even get that.'

That morning, Savannah was finally considered to have recovered from the winter vomiting bug and was allowed to return from the Marsh-Robertsons' house. She and Lottie were driven back to Lorenden by Cecily.

Savannah hadn't brought clean clothes with her – she'd spent the past six days in Lottie's pyjamas – so Lottie offered to lend her some jeans. But they barely squeezed on over Savannah's hips. 'Never mind, I've got some tracky bums,' said Lottie, pulling out a pair of navy stretch pull-ons. 'And a T-shirt.' The T-shirt was embarrassingly tight, and turned Savannah's top half into a series of bulges. Cecily's eyebrows shot up at the sight of her.

Cecily then had a long conversation, rather impressively in shouted Italian, with the man who ran her factory in Milan. Savannah was aching to be home. Oh why couldn't she hurry up? It was a Saturday. Savannah wanted to feel Darcy's silky head under her hand, and her mother's warm, strong hug, and to see the horses nodding their heads at her over their stable doors. She craved the cooing of the wood pigeons, the eerie cry of the pheasants in the hedges, and the sharp yaps of Mop and Muddle. And she wished her grandfather was still there, because the thought of life without him was frightening.

Darcy was curled up outside Teddy's stable when Cecily drove in. She braked in the middle of the yard, jumped out and fluttered about calling for Bramble, while Savannah sank to her knees to greet her dog. He was very pleased to see her. Tail-waggingly, wrigglingly pleased. She was the only one who let him sleep on her bed.

She suddenly saw a pair of beautifully polished boots and followed the line of them up to a tanned face with high cheekbones and slightly slanted blue-grey eyes gazing down at her.

'Hello,' he said. 'You must be Savannah.' He put out a hand to help her to her feet. She clutched it, then felt embarrassed to still be holding it when they were both standing up. It was warm and strong, and, for a brief second, made her feel protected.

But she could feel, as usual, the blood rushing into her face. She hated blushing and tugged her hand away. Darcy pressed himself against the stranger's leg and wagged his plumy tail again.

'Well, I've brought the invalid back!' Cecily often spoke in exclamation marks. 'But she's still a bit peaky. Hello? I'm Cecily Marsh-Robertson. Sailor's owner.'

Jez shook Cecily's hand. 'I'm Jez. I'm managing the yard here now.'

Savannah couldn't think of anything to say. Bramble had explained Jez briefly and, along with Lottie and a great many other teenage girls, she'd pored over an interview with him in *Horse & Hound*, but it was all still very surprising.

'Oh, I'm so glad!' exclaimed Cecily. 'I don't know how Bramble does it, looking after all this and running the . . .' She trailed off because she was never quite sure exactly what Bramble did do. 'Anyway, here's Savannah, looking a bit thinner I'm afraid, although actually that's rather nice, don't you think?! Savannah is such a pretty girl underneath all that . . . er . . . hair.' Sometimes Savannah could see why Lottie said that Cecily was the most embarrassing mother in the universe.

Jez looked carefully at Savannah, as if he really saw who she was. 'She's a very pretty girl anyway,' he said kindly.

Savannah felt herself going an even deeper shade of scarlet, and wished the earth would swallow up Cecily and her four-by-four. 'Where's Mum?'

'In Canterbury with Helena. Donna's making some tea. Have you got a bag?' He reached into the car to help her with it, and Lottie wriggled her way towards him. 'Hi, I'm Lottie. And no, Savannah doesn't have a bag.'

'Oh, hello.' He stopped courteously. 'I didn't see you there. Have you been ill too?'

But, as Lottie later pointed out, the winter vomiting bug was a bit of a conversation stopper – certainly not very sexy – and they could hardly mention that they'd first thought it was a hangover with Cecily hovering.

'I'll be back,' said Cecily. It sounded like a threat. 'Around five.'

With a huge sense of relief, Savannah and Lottie watched Cecily roar off down the drive before racing into the kitchen to find Donna. She would know what was going on.

The familiar clutter enveloped Savannah like a warm embrace. Home. Sometimes it irritated her to death, but every time she went away, even just for a few days, she longed to be back. She loved it so much.

'Hiya, ' said Donna, plucking a teabag out of her mug with her fingers and tossing it into the sink. 'As you can see, things have just got a whole lot more interesting round here.'

'Well that went all right, didn't it?' said Helena as they got into the car. 'I was terrified that Pa might have mortgaged Lorenden to the hilt and gone in with the kind of dodgy moneylenders who shoot your kneecaps off if you don't pay.'

'Were you?' Bramble was upset. 'Listen, Helena, I want to buy you and Felicity out. I don't know how much it'll take or how I'll raise it, but if you give me time I'm sure I can do it.'

Helena's mobile burbled a Scottish reel. She delved into her capacious basket, rummaged briefly and pulled the phone out. 'Hello?' she shouted.

'Oh, I'm good. And you? Good. Just dealing with my father's

accountant, you know.' She laughed. Bramble thought she sounded shrill and forced. 'As if there wasn't already enough to do . . .' Helena snuggled down in her seat, turning away from Bramble very slightly.

Bramble concentrated on the roundabouts on the way out of Canterbury.

'Right. What did they say?' shouted Helena.

There was quite a long silence.

'Oh. Fine. Fine. But really it was only . . .'

There was another silence.

'Yes, but do you know who . . .'

'Right. Right. So that's the direction they're going in . . . For fuck's sake, that was the day after my father died. And I'm not sure when I've got time to . . .'

'Right,' said Helena again. 'OK. I'll see you then, in that case, but . . .'

The last pause was the longest of all. 'You too,' said Helena eventually. 'You too. Lots of love.' She switched the phone off and threw it into her basket. 'Just my agent, Caroline.'

'Bad news?' The hill ahead of them fell away, opening up to Bramble's favourite landscape. Home.

'There was a part I didn't get. Not that I really wanted it, of course. But she wants to talk to me about the future. You know I'm thinking of giving up Mattie? They're absolutely furious about it, of course, and they're demanding she talks to me about it. We've all been given scripts for the end of this series and they're going to shoot a death and funeral scene for each of the four main characters. So none of us, in theory, know who's going to die. But you can get a pretty good idea, from who's talking about being optioned for another series.'

'And you?' asked Bramble.

'Oh, do you know, I think I've had enough. Really had enough. No time off for Pa's death. Well, they say they'll rejig the schedule so I can go to the funeral but that's all. After everything I've done for the series. I've opened supermarkets and leisure centres and gone on talk shows, been interviewed ad nauseam for women's magazines. I mean, my life's hardly my own any more. If I want to remember where I had dinner last night I only have to look in the gossip columns.'

'Mmm,' said Bramble, who had noticed that these days there was rather less of Helena in the press than there had been. 'Anyway, don't you get paid for supermarkets and leisure centres?'

Helena snorted. 'A few grand. A very few grand, I might stress. It's hardly worth putting your make-up on. No, I do it for *Simon's Way*, to keep it in the public eye. Melissa's far too inexperienced, and at the moment she's at that stage of her career when it's all for her own profile. When she does do interviews she barely mentions the series.'

'She's good, though,' said Bramble, without thinking.

'Oh, well, if you like that sort of thing. I think the public's going to get very sick of her very quickly.'

Bramble could see Helena's colour mounting and decided to distract her. 'You'll never guess who came round the other night.'

'No, who?'

Bramble told Helena about Toby Fitzroy's visit.

Back in the kitchen at Lorenden, Donna unwrapped a stick of chewing gum. Savannah was surprised. It seemed a curious combination with tea. 'I've given up. Smoking.'

'Again?'

'Well, you know. But Jez said that *he* gave up when he ran out of puff half way round a cross-country course. It wasn't the horse that was unfit, he realised, it was him. And since then he hasn't smoked. He says we should all remember we're athletes too.'

Savannah was impressed. Edward had threatened Donna with the sack countless times when he'd caught her smoking, and she had merely responded by finding new and ingenious places to smoke.

'So what's been happening?' she asked, feeling nervous.

Donna leant forwards, chewing vigorously. 'Well! Your mum thinks she runs the yard. And Jez thinks he does. And they don't agree on anything.'

'Who do *you* think runs the yard?' asked Savannah. This seemed to her to be definitive.

'Your mum's got a lot of the old man's ideas, and she's kind of stuck on them, like it's never occurred to her to do anything different, and she's really, really careful about everything, which is good. But Jez, well, I think he's a bit of a horse whisperer. But it's your mum's yard, she owns it, so I suppose . . .' She didn't sound certain.

Savannah could see Lottie chewing her nails, looking anxious. Lorenden was a second home to her, particularly as her first one was so unsatisfactory, and she looked worried by the changes.

'Pauline rang. Sorry,' Donna corrected herself viciously. 'I mean Lady Rudd, of course.' Donna hated being made to use Pauline's title. 'She was all gushy – you know how she is. *Said* she's very excited about Teddy being ridden by such a talented hotshot.'

'Hasn't she been round to meet him?' asked Savannah. 'She usually comes over most days.'

Donna shook her head. 'Hasn't been here once.'

'That's odd. Don't you think? What about the other owners?'

'Very excited. Can't keep away.'

'I should think they are,' said Savannah. 'But why on earth has someone like Jez come here? Couldn't he have had his pick of yards, particularly when he's just had such a successful season?'

'I thought of that.' Donna's eyes sparkled. 'So I've been talking to the girls.' Donna was plugged into a network of grooms across the length and breadth of Britain, and there was very little that escaped her. 'Teddy has qualified for Badminton, so maybe he came because of that.'

'Wouldn't loads of people be offering him Badminton horses?' asked Lottie.

Donna shook her head vigorously. 'No way. Badminton's a four-star event and even the Olympics are only three-star. There just aren't many horses that are up to it, and once you've got a horse-and-rider team that's qualified you probably wouldn't want to change. So if you're a rider and you lose your owner and their horses suddenly, like Jez has, you could take years to find something else you could qualify on, however good you are. But that's definitely not all. When things ended at Penny Luckham's, the police came to take him away.'

'No!' gasped Savannah and Lottie together.

'What could it have been?' asked Lottie.

Donna shook her head. 'No one knows.'

'Drugs?' suggested Lottie.

Savannah raised an eyebrow. 'Someone who doesn't even smoke?'

Donna shrugged. 'Doesn't mean he doesn't. But I don't figure him for a space cadet, he doesn't seem the type. It could be something that doesn't mean anything. Like unpaid parking tickets.'

'Shouldn't my mother be told?' asked Savannah.

Donna unwrapped another piece of chewing gum and added it to the first. 'Nope. Think about it. She finds out. She tackles him. They have a blazing row. He leaves. And where are we all then?'

Savannah and Lottie silently agreed.

Donna looked at her watch. 'Fuck, is that the time? Anyway, telling your mum? I say don't go there. Just don't go there.'

As Helena turned into the drive she looked at Lorenden with new eyes, taking in the cracked, grubby white stucco on the front, the wisteria that needed cutting back to let light into the long windows over the lawn, the sealed-shut stagnation of the front door and then, as they walked round and in through the back door, the four steep, sharp, mottled dips of the old roof at the back. Who would buy it?

'Why did Toby come round, do you think? He's not after Lorenden, is he?'

'I wouldn't have thought so,' replied Bramble. 'It's not much bigger than his farm manager's house. And he hates us – he wouldn't want anything to do with it.'

'Why?' Helena's eyes noted more details she'd forgotten: the fine old door handles and stone flags on the floor. People dreamed of finding houses like this.

'I don't know,' admitted Bramble. 'I thought you might, as you're older than me.'

Helena suppressed a stab of panic. Older. That was what everyone kept saying at the moment. Old. She was only thirty-nine. And a bit. Technically. At least that's what she told everyone. 'Why should I know?' she asked Bramble sharply, feeling the fear eating away at her as it so often did these days.

'Just that you might remember more of what happened when we were little.'

'No,' said Helena, noticing how battered the big kitchen was and wondering whether it would frighten buyers off or be part of the attraction. 'No, nothing comes to mind. The first time I can recall Pa saying anything at all about Toby was not long after Felicity left, but I wouldn't necessarily have remembered much before then anyway.'

'Helena,' said Bramble, suddenly. 'Helena, please let me make this work. All I ask for is time. Either I'll raise enough money to buy you out, or I'll do what you want and sell Lorenden, but I need at least two years to do it. I want to prove I can turn out horses and riders the way Pa could. Otherwise, if I have to sell now and break everything up, I think Savannah and I will just disappear. We need the Lorenden name. For a bit longer, anyway. And Savannah needs to do her GCSEs and find her feet. Please. You don't need the money now, do you?'

'No, of course not. But what if you don't make a go of it? What if you lose money? Then it's my money you're losing, and I have to think of Eddie and the twins.'

'We'll work something out,' begged Bramble. 'There'll be a way of adjusting it. If I lose money I get less when we divvy up in the end.'

'Unless you lose it all, of course,' replied Helena. 'Anyway, we can't agree on anything until Felicity arrives. That's what Nicky said. We have to wait for Felicity. Meanwhile, though, we need to get the estate agents in. Just for valuations.'

'I'm too busy,' snapped Bramble.

'Don't worry,' replied Helena, allowing her tone to ooze just the right amount of sympathy. 'I can do it.'

Game to me, she thought. Bramble walked right into that one.

Savannah knew that Bramble and Helena had gone to talk to Nicky about money. She'd found out from Donna. Almost all her information was now obtained like this, or by eavesdropping, as Bramble was both abstracted and secretive.

'Mum.'

Bramble, chopping onions, didn't look up.

'Excuse me? Mum? I am here, you know. I do exist.'

Bramble looked startled. 'Sorry. I was thinking.'

'What about?'

'Sorry?'

'I said, what were you thinking about?'

'Oh, nothing. Nothing much. Well, if you must know, I was wondering what to do about finding a new farrier now that Martin has retired.'

Correction: Bramble was not only abstracted and secretive, she was lying through her teeth at every opportunity.

Savannah sat down. 'I'd like to know the truth, Mum.'

Bramble looked wild-eyed. 'What? What do you mean?'

'Are we selling Lorenden and the horses?'

'No!' said Bramble a fraction too loudly. 'We are not. You mustn't worry yourself about things like that. Everything is going to be all right. There are a few . . . temporary . . . difficulties because of Grampa dying but it's nothing for you to worry about.'

Savannah's stomach contracted in fear. She was sure that Bramble wasn't being truthful – or not wholly truthful – but equally she didn't quite feel brave enough to press her mother any further. It might be worse than she imagined.

'Is Felicity going to be back for Grampa's funeral on Friday?'

'We've left messages everywhere we can think of. I'm sure she'll come when she can.' Bramble didn't sound sure of any such thing. 'Anyway,' she added, 'what about your homework?'

As Bramble had asked this already – twice – and both times Savannah had reassured her that she didn't have any, Savannah merely sighed and stomped off. What was the point of telling people things that they didn't listen to?

It was almost dark when she got back from school these days. Jez was in the yard, distributing the evening feeds, Sailor was looking over his stable door in search of mischief, and Teddy's gentle, intelligent face appeared at the sound of her footsteps. He whickered softly and blew on her face in welcome.

The night before the funeral, Helena staggered into Lorenden with a basket bulging with goodies. 'One must do one's bit,' she'd said to Ollie, on the way down in the car. 'Eddie,' she turned round to the back seat. 'Don't forget to do your bit too, will you? Offer to help with the washing up or something. It will all be absolute chaos because Bramble just won't fork out for proper help.'

She sighed. 'She is hopeless, sometimes. Do you know, she didn't even want us to have a marquee? Half of Kent will be coming back to Lorenden after the funeral and there simply isn't room for everyone inside. But Bramble is absolutely obsessed with money. I do love her, of course I do, but sometimes she just doesn't realise that there are more important things in life than how much things cost. I said we'd pay, that's all right isn't it? After all, we need to help her in any way we can.'

Ollie grunted. 'Any progress on selling?'

'I've booked Smallwood's, they're probably the best local firm, and then a big national one, Trott & Tanqueray. They're coming to give valuations the morning after the funeral. I thought we needed someone who knew the local market and someone else with vision and a good grip on the London scene. All those City bonuses. Not that I can really do anything until we find Felicity. We've left messages everywhere, she must know. If she's such a hotshot reporter there should be teams of people in touch with her all the time. Anyway, she can't blame us; we've done what we can. It's up to her. Bramble's probably heard by now, I expect. People don't go missing these days, not with mobile phones everywhere.'

But Bramble hadn't heard from Felicity, and was worrying about holding the funeral without her.

'Well, we can't cancel it now,' said Helena. She unpacked some cheeses from a deli in Marylebone High Street, organic cheese biscuits, elderflower water, olives, a pineapple and a big box of Godiva chocolates.

'Pa would have wanted us to go ahead. Give him the send-off he deserves. I've brought some soaps by the way, for the bathrooms, and some scented candles.' She plonked them on the table. 'People always forget about the basics when they're planning parties.'

'It's not a party,' said Ollie. 'It's a funeral.'

Helena glared at him. 'You know what I mean. We still need extra lavatory paper. People don't stop—'

'Yes, fine, we get your drift.' He dumped several crates of champagne in the larder and brought out a bottle of claret. 'This looks about right for this evening. Shall I open it, Bramble?'

Bramble, cutting up sausages for the following day, nodded.

'Now you have made sure there are plenty of nibbles for vegetarians and people on dairy-free or wheat-free diets, Bramble, haven't you?'

'Bugger the vegetarians,' said Bramble. 'Anyway, there's plenty of cheese. I got a value pack from the supermarket.'

Helena tutted. 'Oh, people only eat organic cheese these days – the supermarket stuff is full of growth hormones and bound to give one cancer. Really, Bramble, don't you *ever* read the newspapers? Where are you going, Eddie?' She swung round sharply to see Eddie edging out the door.

'Off to the stables with Savannah, Mum.'

Two furrowed lines tried to appear between Helena's botoxed brows, but she decided to get on with arranging the flowers. Lucky she'd thought to bring some down; it wasn't the kind of thing that Bramble ever managed to get together. 'Then we can go through my eulogy together, can't we, Ollie? We'll take the main spare room, shall we? As Felicity hasn't turned up?'

The house without her father seemed grey. Helena noticed again how shabby it had become, and how much mess there was everywhere. 'It's going to be a nightmare to clear out,' she said later that evening to Ollie. He was curled up in the big four-poster bed, with a jug of Edward's best claret on the bedside table.

He looked up over his book and raised his glass in reply.

'I wish Felicity would bloody well get in touch,' Helena muttered, vigorously rubbing cream into her face in front of a silvered mirror on the dressing table. She wiped the cream off with a tissue. 'She's a clever woman, she'll see the point of getting Bramble to move on. Bram's been stuck in the same old rut since Dom's death and this is our chance to help her out of it, don't you think?'

Without waiting for Ollie to reply, she walked over to the bed and slipped off her silk dressing gown. She noticed his eyes slide across her breasts and down over her hips (nice and slim still, she noted, turning quickly to check herself in the pier glass on her side of the bed). Ollie's eyes followed hers and she realised too late that her bottom was perfectly reflected in the glass. Bother, she thought, I should have brought a nightie.

She got in with her back to him, continuing to chatter on as if she hadn't noticed his gaze. 'We must help her, Ollie. She'll cling on here as long as she can. Otherwise she's trapped. Just look at the way she dresses, all dark fleeces and sensible jackets. You can hardly tell there's a woman underneath it all.'

Helena pulled the duvet up to her chin and picked up a book from the bedside table. An old paperback with a worn spine. Something about hunting. She sighed and put it back again. 'She's weighed down by all this clutter,' she prattled on, trying to put off having to deal with the warm hand snaking across the bedclothes. 'It's far too large a house for one woman to look after. The sooner she and Savannah are somewhere a bit smaller and brighter, and easier to look after, the better, if you ask me.' She finally ran out of breath, aware that her voice had risen and was sounding rather squeaky.

'Well, that was a long rant. Is it over now? All off your chest? And, speaking of chest . . .' Ollie's hand slowly drew the patchwork quilt down to reveal her breasts, reached for her nipple and tweaked it suggestively. 'Have we ever done it in a four-poster?'

'Yes, when we went to that hotel, remember?'

'Mmm.' Ollie's hand continued to travel down. 'Perhaps you'd better remind me.'

She removed his hand. 'Not tonight, Ollie. Of all nights. It's my father's funeral tomorrow.'

She thought he might be angry, but he merely kissed the hunched shoulder she turned to him.

'Sorry, babe. Sleep well. Do you mind if I read for a bit?'

Head thick with sleeping pills, she murmured a suggestion that they should go somewhere nice soon and try out a four-poster bed that didn't have years of dust in the hangings. Then, before she dropped into the darkness that the pills so obligingly provided, she thought that Ollie was really being very, very nice about all this. His own father had died just a few years ago, so he presumably understood, but even so . . .

The following lunchtime, Martyr's Forstal rustled and hummed with anticipation. Edward's friends donned black suits and dresses. They straightened unfamiliar, throat-constricting ties and brushed their hair with extra care. It was a bright, clear day. Purple elderberries and wild rose hips danced in the hedgerows, punctuated by scarlet sprays of hawthorn. In a few secret corners, sloes tumbled in a tangle of green, copper and brown.

Pauline made a light lunch for Alan, indulging in an interesting daydream about it being Alan who had died, rather than Edward.

'They haven't managed to find Felicity yet, have they?' she asked, merely to have something to say. Alan was hardly likely to have heard any gossip that she hadn't.

'Mmm?' Alan looked hunted.

'Felicity?' shouted Pauline. 'You know. The oldest.' She raised her eyebrows meaningfully at him.

'Hmm. Hmm. Of course. Couldn't forget Felicity.'

Pauline gave him a piercing look, because Alan forgot everything at the moment. It was very boring.

'Well, of course after . . . frankly, I'd be surprised she'd want to show her face round here. I know you thought he was a little bit hard on her about . . .'

Alan was gazing out of the window.

'Alan! Are you listening to me?'

'Harrumph. Of course. Edward very hard on her. Very hard on all those girls, if you ask me.'

Sometimes Alan could be quite surprising. 'What do you mean?'

Alan turned a bland expression to her. 'Never took any notice of the pretty one. No wonder she's a . . .'

'Actress?' asked Pauline sharply.

Alan flapped his hand in irritation. 'Actress, actress, that's what I meant.'

Pauline was intrigued. She didn't often have anything that she regarded as a conversation with Alan these days. 'Well, it didn't do Helena any harm. She's very successful.'

'Hmmph. And he turned Bramble into a boy. Made her the son he never had.'

'She doesn't make the best of herself,' admitted Pauline quietly.

'What?' Alan was also going deaf. 'Mind you, she's a fine looking woman.'

Pauline sighed. Really, Alan made no sense at all these days.

Not like Edward: his brain had been as sharp as a pin. Her eyes filled with tears and she carefully soaked them up with the tip of a piece of kitchen roll. Mustn't let her mascara run.

Alan rustled through the post and the papers. 'Things aren't getting any cheaper.' He sighed. 'Just not getting any cheaper.' He ripped an envelope open. 'What's this? What's this? A hat? It seems an awful lot for one hat.' He waved the piece of paper at her.

Pauline didn't really believe they were having money problems, but she decided not to challenge him. 'I had to have something special to say goodbye to Edward in,' she wheedled. 'Don't you think?'

'Whenever you buy a new hat, I always know you're up to something,' said Alan, looking at her thoughtfully from under his bushy white eyebrows. 'And the bigger the hat, the more the mischief. You can't fool me, you know.'

'Don't be so ridiculous, Alan.' She shouted so that he could hear, because she was too irritated to repeat herself. With her head bent over the bread board, she failed to notice his expression.

Even though it was Edward's funeral, the routine had to go on. Bramble, Donna, Savannah and Jez – with the addition of Eddie, who was thrilled to be part of the team – were all up by half-past six, mucking out, measuring out feed and riding the horses out. There was a heaviness in the air. They had all, even Savannah, been to too many funerals, all round Britain, in France, even in Germany, Holland – across the seven seas, in fact, anywhere where an eventer had been killed riding across country. They all lived in the knowledge that the next bad fall could be theirs, no matter how good they were.

At least Edward had died at home, and at sixty-nine. It was better than Dom's thirty-one. Bramble sat down on a hay bale, dropped her head in her hands and sighed.

A shadow crossed the floor. 'If there's anything left to do I can do it,' suggested Jez, standing in the doorway.

'I can manage,' she said wearily, struggling to her feet, and picking up several buckets. 'Anyway, it's nearly done.'

He cleared his throat. 'I . . . er . . . that is, I mean . . .'

Bramble wished he'd get out of the way. She couldn't push past him, but she was late. There were sandwiches to make and she had to explain the workings of the tea urn to a local girl who'd come in to help.

'I . . . well . . .'

It was unlike Jez, not that she knew him very well, to be awkward. For a moment her heart stopped. Suppose he was going to say he was leaving? 'What is it?' Anxiety sharpened her tone.

'I could help more,' he said, studying her with his observant eyes. 'If you let me.'

Bramble's instinct was to push him away. Help was a nuisance. It involved gratitude, awkwardness, the possibility that he might want something in return. Help meant intimacy.

'I'm fine,' she said for the twentieth time that day. She was Bramble, who looked after everyone else. She didn't want people looking after her.

Cecily Marsh-Robertson had a business to run – To Die For Bags was gaining cult status in all the right places – but Edward Beaumont's funeral was important. Most of the people who mattered in Kent would be there, and she wanted to make some discreet enquiries about some warehousing just off the A2 that she had her eye on. And of course what would it look like if Lottie didn't attend? She yanked her daughter out of school, furious with her appearance. Why couldn't the child make an effort? It reflected so badly on *her*.

'It's an expensive uniform and a top school. You haven't even tucked your shirt in. And you've got an ink mark on your hands and a ladder in your tights. How could you? You knew you were coming to Edward's funeral.'

Blushing and stammering, Lottie tried to explain that she had only just nicked her leg on a nail running towards her impatient mother's car.

'Could I put my jeans in the back of the car? Then I can help with Sailor—'

'No,' hissed Cecily, irritated by the slowness of the tractor in front of them. 'Don't you dare mention that bloody horse to me again today.'

Lottie cringed in the passenger seat. She was worried by

Edward's death, because she knew that her mother respected him and she'd always felt that Sailor was safe in his care. Cecily was already muttering that she didn't think Bramble was quite up to it, and they might have a look round for something better.

'I'm going to have a word with Toby Fitzroy today, if he's there,' said Cecily. 'Now there's a man who knows about horses.'

Bramble hoped that once the funeral was over she might be able to sleep. She'd never been an insomniac before. All her worries magnified themselves several times over every night, as she watched the moon come up over the trees and listened to the low whoop of the barn owl swooping over field mice. For the first time in her life, the faint ghostly shrieking of dark country nights made her shiver.

First, there was the problem of money, which had been a nagging worry for some time, but which, after their meeting with Nicky, had expanded into something so huge that Bramble barely dared contemplate it. There was Savannah and her brittle vulnerability, and Jez, who she was secretly rather nervous of. And then there was Helena and the way she ranged round the house, picking things up and turning them over as if she was valuing everything. No single incident was worth making a fuss about, although Bramble did try to head her off from time to time. Even so, the tiny queries and minor appropriations dribbled on.

It was time to get ready for the funeral. Bramble tried to cover up the dark circles under her eyes with an old foundation that she hadn't used for months. The pump firmly refused to dispense anything. Bramble shook it, and pumped it vigorously. With a raspberry noise, a large gob of foundation shot out and landed on her jacket.

'Oh hell.' She used a towel to wipe it off furiously. Helena appeared behind her, knocking on the bedroom door in passing. 'Oh by the way, do you mind if I take this? It's absolutely valueless, of course, but I think it's rather sweet.' She showed Bramble a little silver jug.

Bramble never used it. 'Yes, yes, whatever. Do you have any foundation I can borrow? Mine's just spat its last drop all over my jacket.'

Helena's eyes lit up. 'Come with me: I'll get you sorted.'

She pushed Bramble down on her bed, took out a huge tool box of make-up and set to work.

'No, really, Helena, I just need a small amount of foundation. I'm busy, I've got to . . .'

'I won't take a second. Now close your eyes.'

Bramble could feel a sponge tapping all over her face. 'You'll make me look like a clown.'

'I'm going to make you look like you. Only better.'

It seemed like an eternity before Helena stepped back. 'There! You really do look great, you know. If only you'd let your hair grow a bit; just enough to soften your face.'

'It's so thick,' grumbled Bramble. 'It gets in the way.'

'Well, I'm not going to sympathise, because most women would kill for thick hair.' Helena packed up her tools with satisfaction, and Bramble allowed herself a fleeting look in the mirror.

All trace of tiredness had vanished and there was a sparkle in her eyes. She looked like the old Bramble. The Bramble who married Dom and was heading for the top. The Bramble who laughed.

Helena placed a hand on Bramble's shoulder and met her eyes in the mirror. 'I wish I could make you see how gorgeous you could be. It's just a question of making a bit of effort.'

Bramble was surprised to see tears glimmering in the corner of her sister's eyes, and felt them rise in her own. She brushed them away. 'Thanks. Look, the cars are here.'

Two long black cars parked outside the door, one for Ollie, Helena and Eddie, the other for Bramble, Savannah, Donna and Jez.

Savannah had never seen Jez in anything except jeans or breeches before, and thought he looked great. She carefully analysed each item he was wearing so she could remember it: a black polo neck (*much* nicer than a shirt and tie), a grey herringbone jacket (*lovely*, why hadn't she ever realised how nice men looked in tweed?), and charcoal trousers. Dark and respectful, but not too formal, thought Savannah. Free and cool rather than corporate. All the other men looked trussed up in comparison.

She liked Jez. He bothered to be nice to her. She had found

herself talking to him constantly – in her mind. In his actual presence she often felt tongue-tied. The only thing that worried her was not telling her mother about the incident with the police, but Jez couldn't have been involved in anything serious. She was sure of it.

Outside the church, she couldn't help an involuntary gasp as she saw the coffin. It didn't seem possible that Grampa could be inside it. He didn't belong in there. He belonged outside in the sunlight with the rest of them.

Jez squeezed her shoulder and she was immediately thrilled by his touch.

Bramble hadn't realised how many people would come – riders from all around the country, even from overseas, children from the Pony Club, the Lord-Lieutenant, the High Sheriff and the Mayor, the local MP and most of the town dignitaries, the owners of all the horses at Lorenden, even Cecily Marsh-Roberston, smart in black trousers and a nippy jacket, mobile clamped to her ear. Friends, pupils, rivals – so many people whose lives Edward had touched. The Estonian eventing team, who he'd once had a contract to train, were all there. Bramble even saw Glenda, the ambulance woman who'd attended the 999 call, and her eyes filled with tears, touched that someone whose connection with her father was so tangential had thought enough of him to give up an afternoon to be here.

She realised Jez was just behind, and surreptitiously sniffed back her tears. She didn't want him to see her crying. Beyond him was Toby Fitzroy, glad-handing everyone in sight.

'Quick,' whispered Bramble. 'Pretend to be saying something very important to me. I want to avoid Toby.'

Jez looked surprised for a moment, then grasped her arm and steered her down the aisle, head bent into hers. 'Quite right,' he said. 'He's a dreadful man.'

'I didn't know you knew him.'

Jez looked back over his shoulder at Toby, who seemed to be heading in their direction. 'I sold him a horse once,' he said. 'Never again.'

Bramble couldn't help smiling. It was obscurely comforting to know that Jez hated Toby as much as she did.

'Do that again,' he said.

'Do what?'

'Smile. You have a very pretty smile. I expect lots of people have told you that.' Bramble hated compliments and wanted to pull away, but Toby was still heading in their direction so she decided to pretend she hadn't heard.

'Look,' Jez said, pointing to a carved plaque with three Beaumont names on it. 'Are those your ancestors?'

She nodded. 'Pa always said he wanted his ashes thrown across the Vicarage Vee at Badminton. He didn't want headstones or inscriptions.'

'You were obviously very close to your father.'

'Well, not so close that he felt he had to discuss anything with me before he took you on.' She hadn't intended to allude to this now, but the hurt was still too fresh. As soon as she spoke she realised that her words sounded grudging and petty. 'I'm sorry, I didn't mean that.'

Jez's looked at her carefully.

'Sorry, it's not your fault.' She felt gauche. 'Really, I didn't intend to be rude, I was just joking.'

That intense gaze again.

'Toby's sitting down now, I'd better get on,' she said. 'Thank you for helping me hide.'

There were people standing in the side aisles and packing the back of the church, and the heavy doors were propped open so that those who couldn't get inside could hear.

Bramble couldn't help looking round for Felicity. Surely she would come. She would do one of her dramatic appearances – dropping out of the sky by parachute, perhaps, or arriving in a chauffeur-driven Rolls-Royce. It was impossible that she could have missed every single one of the flurry of messages that had been sent.

'There are so many people,' whispered Savannah, sounding frightened, and Bramble clasped her hand for comfort as they walked down the aisle after the coffin.

All Bramble was aware of, as the service rolled on like a newsreel of someone else's life, was the warmth of Savannah's hand in hers, clutching her tightly.

*

Helena stepped lightly up to the pulpit. 'My father,' she began, 'Edward Beaumont, was born in 1934, and his childhood spanned the Great Depression and the Second World War. He taught us that even if you lose a battle you can win the war, that you should never give up and that each and every one of us can turn our dreams into reality.

'He knew how to encourage the young – young children as well as young horses – and my sisters and I always knew that we could reach for the top. He did not believe in giving a child what he or she wants, rather in helping them understand that if you want something, you yourself can get it.

'Like most young boys of his class and generation, he was expected to follow the traditional sequence of Eton, Cambridge and the Guards, after which he would take over the family farm. What he actually did was run away from school to work in an Irish racing stable at the age of fifteen, where he stayed, becoming a jockey and then a trainer, until his own father fell ill.'

Did he? thought Bramble in astonishment. I never knew that. Or did I? A sharp sense of loss pierced her heart and she gazed ahead of her, willing herself to note the way the autumn sun shone through the stained glass of the church window.

'He came home, and continued to build his riding career while running the farm, winning a gold medal at the Olympics at what now seems the relatively late age of forty-six, long after most athletes – even riders – have given up their hopes and dreams. From then on, he focused on producing the best and most brilliant event horses, as well as training up the next generation of top-class athletes, many of whom I see here today.'

Helena suddenly stopped talking as the church door creaked. There was a brief murmur from outside, the sound of a slammed car door and an exclamation. A woman walked into the back of the church, her heels click-clacking against the stone.

The whole family turned round, but the sunlight streaming through the church door made the stranger a silhouette. They couldn't see her face as she was wearing a broad-brimmed hat.

Ollie nudged Bramble. 'Is that who I think it is?'

They all turned. The outline was right – a fashion plate cut-out of a stylish and confident woman. Two-dimensional. The

Felicity they had known had always made an entrance, had never hurried, had always been a little bit late. And her hats were legendary.

Bramble turned with the rest of them, feeling rather than hearing the ripple of interest from the back of the church. She screwed up her eyes to see better, her heart quickening. The woman, her face still obscured, seemed to be searching the pews for them. Bramble raised a hand to her and saw her hesitate, then walk down the aisle towards them, the tap of her heels echoing Bramble's heartbeat. 'Savannah,' she whispered, 'it must be Felicity.'

The sun disappeared behind a cloud and the stream of bright gold light dazzling them all was stemmed. The rays of dancing dust vanished, leaving only the failing light of an old church on an October afternoon. The woman's face briefly emerged from the shadows.

Bramble craned her neck. If it was Felicity, why didn't she walk straight to the front? She saw a glimpse of tanned skin and the point of nose. Felicity? It could be. It could still be.

Finally, seeming to find the person she sought, she edged into a pew several rows behind Bramble. She was kissed by someone, then shushed down in her seat by a man. As she picked up her hymn Bramble saw her full face and didn't recognise her. She was nobody special. Everyone rustled and settled themselves again, and Bramble's, Savannah's and Eddie's shoulders dropped in disappointment.

Helena took an audible breath and carried on, with only the slightest tremor in her voice betraying her distraction at the interruption.

'Above all,' she continued. 'My father taught us to reach for success. And he taught us that no one can succeed on their own – that we all need a team behind us.' Helena paused, thinking of all the pastries and drinks she always bought for the production staff, and how hard she tried to remember everyone's birthdays. And yet there was a whisper against her on the set of *Simon's Way*. She was sure there was.

With a jolt she realised that everyone was looking expectantly at her. She collected herself. 'We learned that you can't simply buy success with the most expensive horses – you have to work for it. And, finally, even if your greatest dream seemed smashed beyond repair, you can pick it up and slowly, painstakingly, put it back together again.' She paused for effect.

She then carefully named all Edward's grandchildren and their role in his life. With a graceful flourish and a funny story about his time as Master of the local hunt, recounting an occasion when the hounds had streamed into the butcher's shop and come away with strings of sausages, leaving the butcher's customers shrieking and the counter in chaos, Helena wound up with: 'We will miss him very much.'

People were openly sobbing as Edward's coffin was carried out of the church. It was to be taken discreetly to the crematorium accompanied only by Bramble and Helena, while the rest of the family and the other mourners made their way back to Lorenden. The family trickled out into the bright, thin air. Bramble, feeling the cold on the tips of her fingers and her nose, heard Savannah sobbing softly and led her aside to give her a hug.

'It's so awful, Mummy,' mumbled Savannah, suddenly sounding very young. 'It's horrible now he's gone, everything's different and I hate it. What's going to happen to us?'

'Nothing, darling, I promise.' Bramble would have promised Savannah the earth and moon to comfort her. The warm, soft body in her arms, smelling faintly of shampoo and Helena's jasmine soap, her shoulder blades shuddering against Bramble's arms with the effort of crying – this small, vulnerable being was all that mattered to her. 'It's very sad about Grampa dying, but we can keep his memory alive. Every time we ride a horse, or walk through the fields, it'll be as if he's still here. Really.'

Savannah nodded. 'Promise everything's all right? Promise?'

'I promise.' And I will make that promise good, thought Bramble. 'Wipe your eyes.' She patted away a little smudged mascara from Savannah's eyes.

Savannah moved off to talk to Eddie, and Bramble felt her own eyes fill again. She wondered if she could possibly wipe her nose on her sleeve before it began to run.

'Here,' said a voice. 'Have my handkerchief.'

She looked up at an open, smiling face with a smattering of

freckles and into a pair of hazel eyes squinting against the sun. 'Nat,' he said. 'Nat Croft.'

The new farrier. 'Oh, yes.' Bramble blew her nose as discreetly as she could. 'Of course.'

'Every novel I've ever read has made it clear that men should always carry a clean handkerchief because at some point in their lives there will be a pretty woman needing to borrow it,' he said. He had the crazy, flyaway hair of a mad professor, but it was curiously attractive on the stocky, solid body of a blacksmith. 'And handkerchief ownership is what makes a hero.'

Bramble couldn't help laughing. 'What about abseiling down the face of a building with a huge box of chocolates? Or slaying dragons? Or saving the world in forty minutes?'

'I fear you've been reading some very trashy literature. You must let me lend you some proper books.' As Nat chatted easily to her, she felt an unfamiliar prickle as her skin came alive and her body woke up. He was an attractive man, and he seemed to be interested in her.

How can you think like that at your father's funeral, she admonished herself, blowing her nose again and thinking that she must move off and greet more people.

But somehow she couldn't quite make herself.

Eddie felt only darkness and numbness. He wanted to jump up and scream at his grandfather. To ask him why he had left him now. The ceremony seemed pointless, just an excuse for his mother to buy something new that flattered her slim figure, and for Ollie to dig out the hip flask he took to cricket or rugby matches and fill it up with brandy.

During his mother's eulogy he was soothed by the sound of her voice, although fresh waves of sorrow swept over him at the thought of all the things he hadn't known about Edward.

'Let us pray,' intoned the minister.

Eddie prayed for deliverance from the gang on the street corner. If only his grandfather was here, he could talk to him about it. Helena would get hysterical: she was quite capable of trying to take them on herself and getting knifed for her pains; Ollie would laugh and do nothing.

And he prayed to be allowed to ride. To open the door every morning, knowing that the stables were there, and that there were horses to be ridden out, trained and competed. But now there was this Jezzar Morgan person. Eddie had hoped to suggest that he changed schools and came down to Martyr's Forstal to help out now that Grampa had died, but there was obviously no point now. The need to be here, at Lorenden, doing what he was sure he was born to do burned in him. He was hungry, so very hungry for the horses that Savannah seemed to take for granted.

As if his mother would let him anyway. But she'd be sorry if the gang killed him. With a sick shiver, Eddie realised that they could. They really could. You read about it in the papers every day.

As Helena left the relative warmth of the church and stepped outside into the cold air, Ollie was beside her, a light hand protectively on her bottom, steering her past the over-bright flowers and towards a tasteful series of evergreen hedges. They stood there, Helena accepting everyone's condolences and congratulations on her eulogy, until Pauline and Alan appeared.

'Helena. My dear,' said Pauline. 'What a wonderful send-off for your father. He would have loved to have been here. You're looking very smart; we don't often see such high fashion down here. And don't you think Bramble is looking so pretty today too?'

Helena was pleased. 'She let me make her up at last. I've been trying to persuade her to take care of herself.'

'She's always been so overshadowed by you. I don't think she realises how much she's got to offer.'

Helena was taken aback. She opened her mouth to protest.

'And she does so much,' added Pauline.

'We all do,' said Helena. 'Us mothers. When we can.'

'Well, I don't suppose she lets you very often.' Pauline smiled. 'She's got used to being the one who has to make it all right for everyone.'

The remark was delivered with such sweetness that Helena only felt its jellyfish sting a few minutes later, after she and Pauline had exchanged a few more polite remarks and moved apart.

The journey to the crematorium was the bleakest part of the day. When the curtain slid over their father's coffin Helena, her face the colour of plaster, turned to Bramble and hugged her. Bramble hugged her back tightly, feeling her sister's body choking with sobs and the damp of her own tears sliding down her cheeks.

'I'm glad it was just us,' said Helena, drawing back and fumbling for a tissue. 'Do you think he's at peace now?'

Bramble shook her head. 'The mist got him,' she blurted out, hardly knowing what she was saying. Helena would understand, she thought, she always said that everything happens for a reason.

'What?' asked Helena.

Bramble never cried in front of her family – or in front of anyone if she could help it – and she struggled to control the chunk of grief rising in her throat. 'There was a mist,' she managed to say in a whisper, the muscles around her mouth barely under her control. 'It was . . . an . . . evil mist in the orchard the morning he died,' she gasped. 'It was looking for him and it got him. I don't know how to get him back.'

Helena folded her sister in her arms. 'Shh. Shh. You're imagining things. It was just the weather. We can't help feeling that it reflects what happens to us, it's completely natural. But it doesn't mean anything.'

Bramble relaxed into her embrace for a moment, feeling the tears come, then she pulled away and brushed them aside with her hands. 'You're right. I'm being silly.' She swallowed. 'But Felicity ought to be here.'

Back at the reception, the respectful hum quickly rose to a roar. People packed into the marquee and were even forced out to shiver on the lawn. Darcy nosed around the tent, ever-hopeful, followed by the terriers. They liked parties. Parties meant opportunities. Dropped sausages, unattended plates, guests who liked dogs enough to pass on titbits.

Savannah took a bottle of champagne round in each hand, although her progress was hindered by a number of people stopping her to tell her – often through a spray of quiche crumbs – that she had grown, that she was the spitting image of Bramble when she was young. Occasionally someone dropped their voice and asked if Felicity was expected.

She saw Alan standing on his own and poured him another

huge glass of champagne. Pauline was always trying to restrict his intake.

'Very kind, very kind,' he said. 'You're a chip off the old block.' He patted her arm. Savannah tried to wriggle off but he wrapped a claw-like hand around her wrist. 'I've known you since you were born,' he said. 'I've always thought you were the best of the three.'

Savannah realised, with a sinking heart, that Alan had mistaken her for a youthful Bramble. She smiled patiently, deciding not to muddle the old man further by trying to explain. He leant in closer. 'Just wanted a word,' he breathed. 'Pauline,' he said. 'I'm sorry she's caused so much trouble. She likes trouble, you know. Thrives on it. Shouldn't say so, of course, but I wanted to warn you . . .' He looked at his glass, and Savannah refilled it again. 'Thank you, my dear, thank you. Now, what was I saying? Oh, yes. When Pauline's upset she can cause an awful lot of . . . trouble,' he repeated, clearly on an endless loop. Savannah surreptitiously glanced at her watch.

Alan took another large slug of champagne and moved even closer to her ear. 'Bit of advice for you: marry for love, whatever anyone says. Don't go up the aisle thinking "this chap's all right". Go up thinking that you'd do anything for them. Because you'll have to. I loved Pauline the day I married her, and I love her now. But she's dangerous when she gets an idea in her head. Forewarned is forearmed, that's what I say.' He tapped his nose meaningfully, but his eyes were far away. 'Good girl,' he said, releasing her. 'Glad I managed to have a word.'

Helena held court with a glass of champagne in her hand, kissing cheeks and signing napkins for children. Ollie stood beside her in the pose of a royal escort, proud, slightly distanced, occasionally extending his glass when someone came near with a bottle. Bramble caught sight of herself in the hall mirror out of the corner of her eye. She was now red-faced and her hair was sticking up like that of a disreputable lurcher. The merry-go-round of plates, sandwiches and sympathetic faces speeded up as the afternoon drew to a close. Always with an eye on the door – telling herself that she wasn't waiting for Felicity, just checking – Bramble edged through the crowds with bottles under her arm, throwing replies to condolences over her shoulder with brisk efficiency.

'So kind of you to come,' Bramble said. 'Have a cheese sandwich. So kind of you . . . have you got a drink?' Every time someone tried to take a plate or a bottle round, Bramble seized it back and pushed whoever it was away. 'Don't worry, I'll do that. Now, you remember . . .' At one point she spotted Darcy slinking out of the marquee with an entire quiche, the foil dish sticking out of his mouth like a piece of African lip jewellery. Large chunks of quiche dropped in his wake, to the great excitement of Mop and Muddle. She couldn't be bothered to worry about it now.

A hand took the bottle from her. 'I'll take that round, shall I?'

Bramble turned to see someone smiling down at her. Nat Croft.

'Oh, hello again.' There was a reassuring strength and stability in the ordinariness of his face.

'By the way, I meant to say that I've moved into a cottage just down the road,' he said. 'So you must come round some time.'

'Oh,' she said. 'Well, thank you.'

'I just wanted you to know that I'm here. If you need me,' he added. 'I know it's not easy trying to be a single parent and hold everything together.' He smiled ruefully. 'I've been there. Got the T-shirt. In fact, I'm still there with the T-shirt on. Now, which end of the marquee is thirstiest, do you think?'

'They're all behaving as if they were in the Sahara.'

He smiled – a relaxed, crinkly smile – and raised the bottle to her in a salute. 'Off I go across the desert. Tell them I died with my boots on if I don't make it back.'

Bramble watched his back disappear into the crowd, feeling warmed by the smile. She knew that she was going to be seeing more of Nat Croft. And she liked the idea.

Savannah was just heading back to the kitchen to get more bottles when a large arm appeared in front of her face, blocking her way and pinning her to the wall. 'Well, well,' said a deep voice. 'So it's the latest little Beaumont on the scene.'

Savannah jumped. It was Toby Fitzroy, quite drunk. She turned her face away from the wine fumes and the smell of cigarettes.

'Excuse me.' She tried to duck under his arm but he grabbed her wrist.

'Where are you going?'

'Er, to get some more champagne.'

'Really.' His voice was mocking. 'I thought perhaps you were running away from me. You Beaumonts are good at that.'

Savannah faced him, flattening herself against the wall and noticing how hard and rough his skin seemed close up. 'I don't know what you mean.'

'I bet you don't.' He laughed. 'And do you know why your Aunt Felicity isn't here to pay her respects to your dear departed grandfather?'

'She's abroad.' Savannah wished she didn't sound so much like a little girl.

Toby pressed his face very close to hers. 'She didn't want to show her face. Didn't dare. Well, she's bound to come back. For the inheritance. Tell her she owes me, OK?'

'Why don't you tell her yourself?' Savannah tried to move his arm, determined not to feel frightened. Toby laughed and walked away.

As Nat crossed the marquee, re-filling glasses and charming old ladies, he caught sight of a face he thought he recognised. Well, well, well. Major Jezzar Morgan.

How had he got down here? And, more importantly, what was he up to?

Nat Croft resolved to keep a close eye on him. It might be worth warning Bramble about Jez.

On the other hand, Nat knew that he was new down here too. Best not to rock the boat straight away.

By five o'clock the last guests had trailed off, with murmured offers of help and slurred goodbyes.

Bramble's feet hurt. She wasn't used to wearing high-heeled shoes for so long. She and Helena, both clutching dishes, staggered from the marquee back to the kitchen.

'Eddie!' said Helena sharply. 'And Ollie. Savannah. Help us clear up. You can't leave everything to us.'

'Felicity didn't come,' Bramble said sadly to Helena.

'No. She couldn't be bothered.'

'I had a very odd conversation with Alan,' said Savannah. 'He was going on about something about Felicity.'

'Alan's a bit like a mobile going in and out of range,' said Bramble. 'You think you're having a perfectly good conversation with him and then you're suddenly lost in white noise. I think Pauline's having a hell of a time with him.'

There was a rumble from the road and the sound of gravel under large wheels. Helena let out a sigh of exasperation. 'For heaven's sake, what now? There's a bloody horsebox coming down the drive. You'd think people would be more considerate, wouldn't you?'

Bramble squinted. The sun was dropping fast, enveloping them all in a misty dusk, turning everything into shifting grey, brown and purple shadows. A wood pigeon cooed and the brakes on the horsebox grated as it ground to a halt.

'Ridiculous time to arrive,' said Helena. 'I don't suppose it's anyone for the funeral. Get rid of them, Ollie, would you? Now isn't the time for business. Bramble's exhausted.'

'No,' said Bramble, putting a hand on Ollie's arm. 'I'll deal with it.'

She heard Helena splutter behind her. 'We need to be just family tonight,' she grumbled. 'I don't think we should have any outsiders. You know, once you lot start talking about fetlocks or martingales or whatever you don't stop. The rest of us just have to hang around for hours.'

The horsebox had parked by the stables.

'Who is it?' asked Savannah.

Bramble swallowed. 'I can't quite see in this light.' She suppressed a stab of anxiety as she hurried forward.

'It's a rented horsebox,' observed Eddie.

'Rented or not,' retorted Helena, 'I don't care.' She stood on tiptoe and peered into the gloom. 'You must ask them to go.' Her voice quavered.

Jez came out of the feed store. He looked at the horsebox for a few seconds then he strode towards Bramble. His feet crunched the gravel in the silence, and in the distance a dog howled. Jez put his hand on Bramble's arm, leaning in to speak softly in her ear. 'There's only one driver,' he said discreetly, 'and whoever it is might be ill.' Bramble felt the warmth of his breath against her cheek.

'What did he say?' snapped Helena, hurrying to join them, almost overbalancing on her heels. 'Who is it?'

Bramble could now see a figure hunched over the wheel, as if praying or gathering strength for one last effort. Then the driver straightened up and jumped out of the cab.

Bramble found herself looking at a tired-looking woman of around fifty, in a thin black T-shirt, a swirly black skirt and a black cowboy hat and boots. A collection of silver and turquoise bangles circled one wrist. Bramble had the brief impression of looking into her eyes and seeing a vision of hell.

Bramble blinked, unable to speak, and the expression in the woman's eyes vanished, to be replaced by wariness and exhaustion.

'Oh bugger,' said Felicity. 'I've missed it, haven't I?'

'Yes.' Bramble folded her arms. 'You have.'

'And I dressed in black specially. Oh well, who was it who said "Never apologise, never explain"?'

'You, apparently.' Helena's voice was acid.

'Well, in fact it was first said by Disraeli,' said Ollie. 'What he actually said was "never complain and never explain". Then John Wayne said "never apologise, never explain, it's a sign of weakness". In *She Wore A Yellow Ribbon*. A film.'

'Thank you, Ollie, for the encyclopaedic references,' hissed Helena. 'So useful to know.'

'What have you come as?' asked Ollie with what appeared to be genuine curiosity. Bramble suppressed a smile. Felicity had dressed as different people throughout her life. They'd had the elegant woman who'd arrived in her lover's Aston Martin, and the war reporter who'd descended from the helicopter six years ago. Earlier Felicitys had encompassed the good-time girl in Capri pants and sunglasses and even, briefly, in the eighties, a short period of brightly coloured power suits and high-necked blouses with bows, when she'd been trying to set up a publishing company in New York. This Felicity looked bleached out in her black clothes, almost as if those other Felicitys had been a photograph and this was the negative of herself. Her face was colourless, her lips blending into her features. Her body language was still defiant and graceful, but her eyes were darkly shadowed.

'I was rescuing a horse from a hurricane,' she said. 'It took longer than I thought to get him over here, but I couldn't leave him behind.'

'I thought you didn't ride any more.'

'I don't,' said Felicity. 'But I've bought a horse, because if I didn't buy him I don't know what would have happened to him. He might have finished up in a tin of dog food. He's an ex-racehorse,' she added, with a slight return of colour to her face. Bramble opened her mouth to ask about quarantine and regulations, but closed it again. If anyone could get round all that, it would be Felicity.

'There are such things as mobile phones,' grumbled Helena, also trying to adjust to the new Felicity she saw in front of her. 'Or even email. Not to mention old-fashioned post.'

'We're all being very English, aren't we?' said Ollie. 'What about "Hello Felicity, how *are* you?" Or welcome. Or something. Well, I'm going to say it.' He stepped forward and wrapped her in a drunken embrace. 'Felicity. We're delighted to see you. Better late than never, as the actress said to the bishop. Come in and have a huge drink.'

Felicity carefully peeled his hands off various parts of her anatomy. 'Hello, Ollie.'

'Yes, of course.' Helena surged forward with a cry of delight. 'Felicity, darling, has it been a terribly long journey? You do look a bit tired.' She air-kissed Felicity's cheeks. 'Now where's your luggage? Eddie can take it up to your room.'

'Let's have a look at this horse.' Bramble helped Felicity drop the ramp, and they all gathered round.

There was a thumping noise as an elegant steel-grey horse, with long, intelligent ears and flaring nostrils, looked out at them, outraged. 'What now?' he seemed to be saying. 'How dare you?'

'Wow,' said Savannah. Helena and Ollie edged backwards, as a crash came from the horsebox.

'This is Merlin,' said Felicity. 'Don't worry, he's an absolute sweetheart underneath it all.'

The animal that came barrelling down the ramp, snorting and jerking his head, did not look like anyone's sweetheart. Felicity maintained a steady soothing monotone, but he reared up suddenly, backing away on his hind legs and wrenching the rope out of her hands. He dropped down again, between Helena's cream Mercedes and Jez's ancient sports car.

'My car!' screeched Helena. 'Do something, Bramble.'

'He'll be OK,' said Bramble. 'He can't go anywhere. Just keep calm and your car will be fine. It's important not to panic him.'

Felicity approached him cautiously, but he edged away from her.

'Be careful,' said Bramble. 'He might barge out past you. He could knock you over.'

She had hardly finished before Merlin did just that, and there was a cry of pain from Felicity. Helena screamed.

Jez stepped forward and quietly took hold of the lead rope, and began to talk to Merlin in a soft undertone. He led him to the nearest stable and shut him in.

They all stood in silence as Jez walked back. 'See,' said Felicity through gritted teeth. 'He's no trouble at all. He's just a pussycat.' She hauled herself up, hanging on to Helena's car.

'So where are you going to keep him?' asked Bramble, realising, for the first time, that Felicity's brown eyes were exactly the same shade as their father's. The colour of earth and dark bay horses.

'Well, I thought perhaps he could stay here,' said Felicity, her face suddenly lighting up with Edward's wry, but charming, smile.

Bramble had the brief impression of the real Felicity behind the series of different faces she'd worn throughout her life.

'Of course you can both stay. It's your home.'

Felicity closed her eyes and leant back against the car. Then, almost silently, she slid to the ground.

They stood in a circle, horrified. It was Jez who came up with a blanket, wrapped it around the limp Felicity, then picked her up and carried her into the house.

'It's been a long journey,' he said, as if to a child. 'But you're safe now.'

Chapter 11

Felicity opened her eyes to find herself in a dream. She was lying on the old leather sofa in the study at home. Her father, a young man again, was moving round the room. She could smell his polished boots and hear the firm tread of his walk. Outside the window, in the falling light, an old chestnut tree spread its generous branches, its prickly green fruits just beginning to drop to the ground.

Perhaps I've died, she thought, and tried to sit up. Through a haze of nausea she could see a familiar mess of papers piled up around the room, the overcrowded noticeboard, with rosettes pinned up around it, and the oil painting of her mother in a pale blue backless ballgown over the fireplace.

A throbbing in her foot informed her that she was still alive and, moreover, that she had been hurt. She suppressed a gasp, and clenched her fists.

'Are you all right?' Everyone – Helena, Bramble, Savannah, Eddie and Ollie – clustered into the room.

'Fine.' She winced. 'I think Merlin trod on my foot, though.'

'She'll need to go to hospital.' This from Helena. It was funny, Felicity thought, how the minute you were ill or hurt everyone talked about you in the third person. 'I've drunk far too much to drive,' Helena added. 'And so have the rest of you. We'd better call an ambulance.'

'I do *not* need to go to hospital. An ambulance would be quite absurd,' said Felicity. 'It's only a bruise.' The row of faces seemed rather far away, as if she was at the bottom of a well and they were all peering down at her.

'I think you probably need to see a doctor,' said Bramble anxiously.

Felicity tried to smile. 'You know us eventers. We run a mile at the word "doctor".'

'Well, I don't think you're going to run anywhere at the moment.'

'I need a good night's sleep.' Felicity closed her eyes again. 'It's been a long journey, that's all.'

The man who'd carried her in, the one she'd thought was her father, leant over her, his face almost as close to hers as a lover's might be. 'Where does it hurt?' His voice was low, almost rusty, as if he didn't talk very much. Now she could see him properly he looked nothing like Edward Beaumont. His dark hair was short, but growing and starting to curl out from around his head in spikes. He needed a shave. It made him look like the devil. She felt sick again.

'Only my foot. There's nothing else wrong with me. Who are you?'

'I'm Jezzar Morgan,' he said. 'The new nagsman.'

For a moment she thought she recognised him as a fellow adventurer, someone like herself who didn't belong anywhere. Then she thought she might be half-delirious.

That's not right, she thought. Pa would never have had a nagsman. Pa. Where was Pa?

Oh, I remember. He's dead. That's why I'm here. She struggled to organise her thoughts.

'I'm afraid your room's turned into a bit of a junk heap,' said Bramble. 'But I'll get the bed made.'

A frisson of shock ran through Felicity at the words 'your room'. She'd forgotten she had one. She'd assumed, insofar as she'd given it any thought, that the little room tucked between two of the main bedrooms – where she'd slept from the day she was born until she'd left home at nineteen – would long ago have been turned into an en-suite bathroom or a walk-in wardrobe, or maybe a room for one of Edward's working pupils.

But when she finally half-hobbled – and was half-carried –

upstairs, wincing with pain, she saw that it had barely changed. The same old white-painted iron bedstead – a comforting, old-fashioned size half way between a single and a double – still had its faded silvery velvet quilt. The cabbage-rose wallpaper that she had loved at eight and despised at eighteen was only slightly peeling in places. The shelf on one side of her bed held her much-thumbed old paperbacks – *My Friend Flicka*, *Thunderhead* and *National Velvet* – along with her childhood collection of china horses and her moth-eaten teddy bear. He was facing the door, as if he'd been waiting for her.

'Ted,' she said, trying to laugh rather than cry. 'Someone should have thrown you away years ago.'

Someone had shoved the old dappled rocking-horse from the playroom in here, its tail long since gone, and there was a sewing machine and a few suitcases that had obviously been dumped out of the way, but, apart from the closed-up smell of dusty fabric, she could have left it yesterday.

'I'm sorry it's so untidy. We didn't know you were coming.' Bramble tugged at a curtain, once a glazed cotton chintz to match the wallpaper, its folds now bleached into stripes by the sun. After some fiddling, the curtains closed, setting off a puff of dust. Helena, behind Bramble, coughed theatrically. 'My goodness, Felicity can't possibly sleep in here. Felicity, don't worry, you can swap rooms with Eddie, that would be far better.'

Felicity sank down on the bed, shedding her bangles onto the little rosewood chest next to the bed and tugging the boot off her now-swollen foot. 'I'm not going to sleep in there,' she said firmly. 'I'm fine here. Really.' She wanted them all to go, to stop fussing. She wanted to open the cupboards and drawers, but she was dreading the thought of what she might find there.

Her old self. The person she'd been running away from all her adult life.

She sank back. 'Please go,' she whispered. 'Sorry. I'll be more sociable in the morning.'

They all shuffled out, with promises of glasses of water and suggestions of paracetamol and things to eat, but she simply shook her head and crawled under the covers, still dressed, in search of oblivion.

Before she slept she thought she smelled a waft of lily-of-the-valley but it slipped away from her. She had worn Diorissimo when she was younger – her mother had thought it suitably innocent and flowery – but even if there was an old bottle left here it would have lost its scent years ago.

Helena pulled Ollie into their bedroom.

'Did you hear that?' she hissed. '"Us eventers"! She's reverting to type.'

Ollie was carrying a bottle of wine. He opened it and poured some into a glass. Three coffee mugs and piles of scribbled-on or screwed-up papers left over from writing Helena's speech were strewn around the room.

'She was concussed,' he said. 'Anyone could see that. I heard a crack where her head must have landed when that bloody horse knocked her over. She wasn't making sense.'

'Well, it's pretty worrying that when she doesn't make sense she thinks she's back eventing again,' said Helena. 'It's that horse at the bottom of all this. She's brought that . . . that . . . Merlin here, which means she's back for good.'

'Jesus.' He rolled his eyes. 'Only maybe, though. Not necessarily.'

Ollie and Helena's eyes met. Each knew what the other was thinking.

'She's not getting back into any helicopters or chauffeur-driven cars, is she? And she's on her own. Exhausted. To me, she looks like someone who's run out of places to go.'

'You're being overimaginative. As usual,' snapped Helena. She paused. 'But you're right, there's no sign of any man, is there?'

'Mind you, she's getting on. Not so easy to get men.'

'Felicity could always get men.' Helena didn't like any reminders of age. 'And she always comes with one, as if to show that she doesn't need us. But if Bramble and Felicity are here together, single, it will be much harder to persuade them to sell this place.'

'Maybe the horse is just one of her phases. Like the time she sailed round the Caribbean on an old fishing smack, selling things from island to island.' Ollie drowned his glass of wine and refilled it almost immediately. 'You know Felicity, she'll be off as soon as she feels better. I'm betting she'll want to grab the cash and go.'

Helena's nerves were so frayed she forgot to reprove him for the second glass of wine. 'I hope so. But, potentially, it could be a lot more complicated now.'

'If you're right we may never get our money. Fuck.' With the expletive, Ollie threw his glass at the fireplace. It shattered against the marble and a thin trickle of red wine stained the dusty hearth.

'We bloody well will,' said Helena, bending down on her hands and knees. She picked up pieces of glass up carefully and folded them away in some newspaper. 'I'm not going to let anyone take my inheritance away from me. I promise.'

The morning after the funeral Savannah had to force herself to get out of bed. With every movement a deep exhaustion sucked her back into bed.

Wearily, she pulled on some jodphurs – noticing that they weren't as difficult to zip up as they had been – and went down to the stables to help with the wake-up routine. The last, crumpled pelargoniums fluttered in tubs around the yard and the swallows darted and swooped like tiny indigo and white jets, ready to leave for the winter.

Savannah felt out of sorts. Nothing seemed quite right. She was cold one minute, then taking her jumper off in a sweat the next. She sighed, inhaling the sharp ammonia smell of the stables. Bramble was making a list of who was to ride when. 'You, Donna, Eddie and Jez,' she said. 'Hack out this morning on Tegan, Errol, Chancer and Teddy. Is Lottie coming today? I want Sailor to do some flat work this afternoon. So if she's not coming, you need to get that in hand, Donna.'

Savannah let it all pass over her, and did her chores with her feet weighed down by concrete boots. Tegan was being mareish, putting her ears back and giving her the evil eye. Savannah was too tired, and too abstracted, to take much notice. She was thinking that it would be good if she could get a little bit thinner, just so that things were a bit more comfortable. It would be nice to feel more confident, too, and not to have Helena eyeing her with disapproval. Yesterday it had been easy to eat less, but today she knew she would be tempted. But if she planned it all first, it should be do-able. She lugged the saddle over to where Tegan was tied up, and Tegan turned her back on her.

'Oi. I don't like rude horses.'

The mare pushed her nose into the air and swished her tail angrily. 'I don't like being ignored,' she seemed to reply.

They skittered out of the yard in a string: Jez, Donna, Eddie and then Savannah. Tegan hated being last and kept snatching the reins out of her hands, bounding forwards and having to be told who was in charge. 'You're not listening to me,' muttered Savannah. Tegan's reply was that Savannah was not worth listening to.

They turned off the lane and down a narrow path, where autumn fruit – dark purple sloes and damsons, rosy crabapples and bullaces like clusters of green marbles – brushed against the riders' legs and the horses' coats. Once they'd been part of the orchards but, too fiddly to harvest commercially, were now wild, straggly bushes and sprawling hedgerows, surviving in any little corner they could find.

And then they were out in the open field, with its poplar trees and high beech hedge, and, after a few circuits, cantering at Jez's command round the edge of the stubble, away from the rising sun. Tegan was determined to race and she pulled and tugged at her reins. Before Savannah could take control properly a rabbit bounced, dipping and scurrying, across her path and dived into the hedgerow.

Tegan spun sideways. Deliberately naughty, not really frightened, Savannah thought as she pitched over the horse's shoulder and into a blackberry bush.

She was dimly aware of Jez vaulting off Teddy, catching Tegan and handing the horses to Donna and Eddie before coming over to kneel down beside her. 'Savannah?' He touched her shoulder gently. 'Savannah, Savannah?'

She sat up, feeling shaky as he helped her out of the thorny mound of vegetation. 'I'm fine. Really.'

'Where are you hurt?' His face seemed very close.

'I'm not hurt a bit.' Savannah tried not to cry. 'Here, help me up. That mare aimed me for the blackberry bush, she really did. She was trying it on.'

He moved her right wrist up and down carefully, and then the left.

'Nothing's broken.' She showed him her hands, covered in scratches.

'Ouch,' he said. 'That must hurt. But why weren't you wearing gloves?'

'Forgot,' mumbled Savannah. In fact, she'd left them behind in the kitchen and hadn't had the energy to go back and get them.

He touched her face gently. 'And your face. A nasty scratch.'

'It's fine.'

'How many fingers?' asked Jez, holding his hand up.

'Four,' said Savannah. 'And I know today's Saturday. And don't ask me who the Chancellor of the Exchequer is or what seven times eight comes to because I couldn't have told you before I fell off.'

Jez smiled faintly. 'All right, what did you have for breakfast?'

For a moment, Savannah went completely blank. Perhaps I have got concussion after all, she thought. She rubbed her face with her hands and remembered that she hadn't eaten anything. 'Er . . . I haven't had breakfast yet.'

'Hm,' he said. 'Not a good idea to ride on an empty stomach. You didn't have the strength to handle Tegan. Or the concentration.'

'It was the rabbit. Look, I'll get back on and show you.'

'I think we'll head for home,' said Jez. 'I saw you. I don't think you've recovered from that winter bug, and I don't think you should ride until you have.'

'Really, I'm fine. I just felt a bit faint. Give me a leg up.'

He studied her carefully. 'You and Felicity. You're obviously cut from the same cloth. There's no telling you, is there?'

'No.' She mounted again, but as her heartbeat slowed down she could feel the blood pumping through her hands, spreading the stinging sensation across them. She'd been silly about the gloves. But she was warmed by Jez's concern, and the feel of his hands on hers had been a sensation like nothing she'd ever experienced. Savannah had always listened to the other girls giggling about the boys at school with complete indifference. A boyfriend had always been something she expected to get around to one day, not something she wanted immediately. She was conscious of being out of step with her friends – with the exception of Lottie – and worried that there might be something wrong with her.

Jez's face next to hers changed all that. She wanted him to notice her, to want her, and when she settled into the saddle, wincing, and met his concerned eyes a flash of communication sprang between them. He looked straight into my soul, she thought. I know he did.

By the time they got back, and she'd taken Tegan out to the field, the adrenalin of the fall had started to ebb away, leaving sensations behind: a bruise on her shin, an ache in her bottom, the soreness of the scratches, a blow on her elbow, a crick in her neck . . . she put Tegan's saddle back on its rack, feeling tireder than ever, but still lit up inside with the memory of the way Jez had looked at her.

The saddle was next to a row of hooks, which were always piled up with coats in a jumble of textures and muddy, bracken colours. She brushed against her grandfather's old tweed jacket, scratchy and smelling of him, and it hit her, properly, for the first time. He wasn't coming back. Not ever.

She fingered the jacket and buried her head in it as tears rose up. I should have been nicer to you, she thought. You were a bit fierce, but I wasn't really frightened of you. Not deep down. I could have been nicer. I could have loved you and I didn't.

She felt a hand gently touch her shoulder. 'When you're sixteen,' said a low voice, 'the dark seems very dark. But it won't always be like that, I promise.'

She turned and Jez held her tightly, as if she was a child.

'You don't understand,' she sniffed. 'I didn't really love Grampa, and now he's gone and I'll never get the chance.'

He drew back and wiped her tears away with his thumb. 'Look at these,' he said softly. 'You don't cry like that unless you loved someone. And he knew it.'

'You think so?'

'I know so.' He stroked her hair gently.

It was so different being in Jez's arms, so different from her mother's soft embrace or Lottie's bony welcome. He felt strong and warm. And safe. She wanted to stay there for ever, because then nothing and no one could hurt her. She sobbed for herself and for Bramble, for her Grampa, for her fear of losing Lorenden and the horses and Jez, and for the frighteningly unclear future that lay ahead for all of them.

'We decided to let you sleep.' Helena made an entrance into Felicity's room and wrenched the bleached-rose curtains apart. Sunlight streamed in through the dust.

Felicity hauled herself up, feeling drugged. 'What time is it?'

'Nearly ten.' Helena sounded victorious. 'You've been asleep since early yesterday evening.'

Felicity tried to shake the fustiness out of her head, as Helena advanced on her with a tray. 'I don't know what you like,' she said, 'but fresh orange juice, toast and home-made strawberry jam usually go down OK. Unless you're wheat intolerant, of course. Or diabetic?' She peered at Felicity. 'Or on the Hay diet? Or Atkins?'

'No, toast and strawberry jam is cool.' She thought of the tins of combat rations she'd eaten in the last few years, the snatched sandwiches and fast food, the occasional proper meal, enjoyed all the more for its rarity.

'And coffee,' said Helena, manoeuvring the tray across Felicity's knees and straightening her pillows. She plumped herself down on the end of the bed. 'I brought a cup for myself, I hope you don't mind.'

'No, no. Of course not.' The sunlight hurt Felicity's eyes. Helena noticed and jumped up, adjusting the curtain and coughing, waving her hand in front of her face.

'Right,' said Helena, when they'd settled down again. 'It's lovely to see you.'

Felicity's mouth was too full of toast to reply. 'Mmm,' she murmured, wondering where this was going. Because going somewhere it was. She recognised Helena as a woman on a mission.

'We're really glad you managed to make it. You see, you're an executor of Pa's will and we can't do anything without you. You don't have to stay an executor, of course, but there are legalities to complete first even if you want to back out.'

Felicity was too astonished to reply. She put her toast back on her plate and watched Helena.

'And, of course,' said Helena, 'one-third of what the solicitors call "the estate" is yours. What's left of it. We're down to Lorenden and the horses, I'm afraid. Pa died just before everything finally fell apart.'

'Mine?' asked Felicity, almost unable to comprehend what her sister had said. 'What do you mean, mine?'

'Pa left it equally to the three of us. Absolutely the right thing to do, of course.' Helena bared her teeth in an unconvincing smile. 'I mean, we're sisters, after all. Equality is very important in families. So, you see, we need you to sign papers and things before we can sell up.'

'Sell?' asked Felicity.

'Sell,' echoed Helena firmly. 'There's no other way of dividing it all up. Bramble will want to go on with the riding thing somewhere else, of course, but she'll be relieved not to have to manage something this size. It'll be the making of her, really it will. And it's not as if you would ever want to live here, is it?'

'No,' replied Felicity, bemused.

'So the sooner we sell the better. Bramble, in particular, really needs to get settled somewhere that she can call her own, although, of course, she's far more emotionally attached to this place than either you or I are. Naturally.' Helena's smile this time was conspiratorial. 'You see, she thinks she's not really worth anything and that people only came here for Pa's name and expertise. The sooner she gets out on her own, making her own way, the sooner she'll understand that, really, as a person, she too has value.'

Felicity was still too surprised by the whole conversation to reply.

'So what I wanted to ask you,' continued Helena, 'is whether you'd help me make this as easy and smooth for Bramble as possible. Help me to help her, if you know what I mean. She's had such a tough time with Dom dying, and she never fulfilled her early promise as far as the riding went, and she's had to bring up Savannah on her own . . . I'd like her to feel that we are really behind her.'

'OK,' said Felicity equably. 'I don't have a problem with that.' Inside, a fuse began to burn. Bramble was the one who'd had it all, who had had their father's love and attention, who hadn't had to leave home at nineteen and make her own way in the world. And now she was being asked to make things easier for her. Felicity didn't know what easy was. She'd never had it.

'Good,' said Helena. 'I just wanted to have a word with you first. Make sure you understood. She's very stubborn, you know, like Pa.'

'I would have thought . . .' said Felicity, sipping her coffee in the hope that it would clear her head '. . . I would have thought . . . that he'd have left it all to Bramble. So she could carry on here. I'd have thought that's what he would have wanted.'

'Well, he clearly didn't.' Helena paused. 'He more or less told me that he knew Bramble would never be . . . well, you know, truly first-rate, and that he knew he had to make some tough decisions. I mean, if he'd thought Bramble *could* carry on, was even capable of it, he wouldn't have appointed that . . . that—'

'Yes, who *is* he?'

'He's called Jezzar Morgan. Major Jezzar Morgan. An ex-Cavalry officer who's been trying to make his way as an eventer. Half-Russian apparently. Or Tatar, as he calls himself. But he's broke – or seems to be – so he's here. Basically to ride Teddy for Pauline, I suppose. There aren't any other owners worth mentioning left.'

'Who was riding him before?'

Helena shrugged. 'Bramble.'

The sisters looked at each other.

'You see,' said Helena softly, 'Pa finally realised she would never get to the top. But Teddy could, so he had to get someone else in.'

Felicity didn't reply. She was feeling too drained.

'So,' Helena got up, but she was watching Felicity carefully. 'What have you been up to recently? Still doing wars?'

'Up to a point. You know.' Felicity lay back on the pillows again, and closed her eyes against Helena's inane questions. If Helena was going to treat 'doing wars' like 'doing lunch' she didn't deserve a proper reply.

'I think we should get you to a doctor.'

'No,' said Felicity. 'No doctors.'

'Does your head still hurt?'

'No, it's just a bruise on my foot, I keep telling you.' Felicity decided not to mention that when she had woken up to go to the loo in the middle of the night, she hadn't been able to put any weight on the foot at all, and she had had to crawl, hauling herself up by hanging on to the washbasin.

'Oh, well,' said Helena. 'Just call if you need anything. I'll be around.'

Felicity nodded, and after Helena left she manoeuvred the tray, with its half-eaten toast, on to the floor.

She couldn't understand it. There had been Beaumonts at Lorenden for over a hundred years, and now her father had thrown it all away by leaving a third of it to her, someone who had promised never to come back. Felicity levered herself up and looked in the dusty mirror. She still hated the face that stared back at her. Even hearing that her father had acknowledged her in his will hadn't changed that.

She fell back on the bed and lay there for another half-hour, watching the leaves outside blow in the wind, drifting across the window, and realised that, for the first time in her life, she had real options. This could be her chance to start again.

Nat Croft appeared in the yard just as Bramble had time to draw breath. For once, she wished she'd put on some make-up.

'Oh, hi,' she said, wondering if he'd notice if she slipped upstairs. 'I was just going to have a coffee. Fancy some?'

'I'd love some.' His eyes crinkled at the edges when he smiled, she noticed, and his chunk of mad-professor hair blew in the breeze. 'I left a jacket behind yesterday.'

Bramble nodded to where the marquee company was taking the tent down. 'Not in there, I hope.'

'No, somewhere in your hall, I think.'

She nipped upstairs and purloined one of Helena's cashmere cardigans from a pile of clean laundry, brushed her hair and put on a discreet slick of lipstick.

Downstairs again, she filled the kettle and cleared some clutter off a chair so that Nat could sit down.

'So,' he said in a companionable way, 'how have things been? So far?'

She told him about Felicity's arrival with Merlin. And the fact that Sailor had just lost a shoe. And the bank accounts had been frozen until they got probate. He listened attentively, and she found herself saying more than she'd intended.

'And Helena is fussing about saying we've got to ring the estate agents and get Lorenden valued. The thing is,' she twisted her coffee mug round in her hands. 'We – that is, Pa and I – never really thought about what would happen if he died. We didn't expect it to happen yet. He's left everything equally divided between the three of us, which means I've got to sell up and re-establish myself somewhere else. Just when Savannah's doing her GCSEs and we're about to break back into the big time with Teddy, and . . .'

He placed a large, strong hand on hers. 'It will all work out. Things have a habit of turning out for the best. I used to have a high-powered banking job. You know, lords of the universe and all that. Bonus cheques that looked like telephone numbers. But one day I realised how meaningless it all was and walked out.'

'How long ago was that?'

'About six or seven years ago.'

'You don't look like a banker.'

'I don't suppose I look like a farrier either.'

Bramble laughed. 'No, you look like a . . . I don't know, a philosopher. Or one of those playwrights who live in Hampstead and write in sheds at the bottoms of their gardens.'

'A philosopher!' He laughed. 'Well, perhaps a bit. Now then, my philosophy is that if you start with the things you can sort out, then everything starts to look a little less impossible. I've got my kit outside in the car and an hour to kill before I'm due anywhere. So let me pop a shoe on Sailor and solve at least one of your problems. Call it a demonstration of my skills.'

Bramble felt her usual resistance when someone offered help. She was used to exchange – the cash-poor horse world survived on it – but she didn't want anything for free. You might feel obliged. She looked at his open, honest face and changed her mind.

'That colour suits you,' he said, gently laying a large, capable hand on the cardigan sleeve to make his point.

'Thank you,' she said, allowing the hand to rest for a moment before she pulled away and led Nat to the yard.

'Sailor's the ideal horse in every way, except he doesn't like being shod, for some reason, so he could be tricky. He might try to sit on you.'

Nat nodded, and took his tools out of the back of his van. Once he'd wrapped his thick leather apron around himself he assumed the sturdy, bulky appearance of a farrier. Bramble felt more confident.

He nodded again, and waited. He had a curious quality of stillness.

Sailor, thought Bramble, would sort out whether he was a good farrier or not.

'Mmm.' He stroked the horse. 'Lovely boy. Now why don't you like being shod?' He ran his hand gently over Sailor's face and ears, and blew softly into his nose, talking to him in an undertone, murmuring soft endearments. Sailor blew back at him and responded by nibbling his jacket.

Nat worked quickly and competently. She found herself watching his hands, noting strength, gentleness, confidence . . . she shook her head. She needed sleep. God, how she needed sleep. Sailor stood absolutely still and, after a few minutes, closed his eyes and leant against Nat.

'You seem to have the magic touch,' said Bramble with relief. She realised that she'd been hoping he would be good.

'Ah, well,' he said. 'That's what blacksmiths are. Magicians. Or so the ancients thought. St Dunstan had a prayer against the "spells of women, witches and blacksmiths". Even though he ended up as the patron saint of blacksmiths.'

'What, all women?'

'All women,' said Nat to Sailor's hoof. 'They were considered dangerous creatures in pagan times.'

'What made you decide to become a farrier?' He seemed so unlikely.

'I wanted a proper job. Something that needed doing. Something honourable. I became a blacksmith first. There. Shoe done. Did you know . . .' he looked directly at her '. . . how many phrases in the English language are based on the blacksmith's work? Irons in the fire, forge ahead, a drawn-out argument that comes to a point . . . they all come from the smithy.'

'You've hit the nail on the head?' offered Bramble.

He grinned, packing up quickly and deftly. 'Aren't you the bright spark?'

'You didn't, presumably, change careers because of a few clichés?'

'No. After I'd done a bit of time as a blacksmith, making wrought iron furniture and sculpture, I realised I wanted to work with horses. It seemed more necessary. Who really needs an iron sculpture in their life?'

'I don't know about need,' said Bramble. 'But we were thinking of something to remember my father by. That sort of thing.'

He nodded. 'That sort of thing can be important, I agree. But I wanted day-to-day work. So here I am. For now. And I do the sculpture in my spare time.'

He stood up and gave Sailor a mint. 'All over now, my beautiful. He's not difficult at all.'

She put out her hand to pat Sailor's neck, but Nat intercepted it. 'You're still wearing your wedding ring. I heard about your husband. I'm sorry.'

Bramble was embarrassed. 'Well, it was a long time ago. I just never took it off. It seemed like . . . I suppose . . .'

'Really saying goodbye?' Nat's eyes sought hers.

'I suppose so. I don't think about it any more.'

'Do you still miss him?'

Bramble took her hand away. 'He's gone now. He's completely and utterly gone. For a long time it seemed as if he might still be here, just around the corner or in another room, but now . . .' she shook her head.

Jez drew up in his old sports car and parked beside Nat's van.

Bramble felt the air change as Nat bent over to zip up his bag without glancing in Jez's direction.

Jez jumped out and looked at him. Nat straightened up and, for a moment, they locked eyes.

'Hello, Jez,' said Nat evenly, turning away to lob the bag into the back of the van. He slammed the door.

Jez looked as if he might reply, but then turned on his heel and went inside.

'I'm sorry,' said Bramble. 'I'm afraid Jez is a bit abrupt sometimes.'

'I know,' replied Nat. 'I've met him before. Before here, I mean.'

'Oh, where?'

Nat took a deep breath. 'Look, it's none of my business. And I don't gossip.' Surprisingly, he touched her cheek briefly. 'Now remember, concentrate on sorting out the things you can sort, and have faith that the big stuff will deal with itself.'

Bramble allowed herself to feel comforted.

'Call me,' he said. 'If you need a friend.' He jumped into his van and drove away.

Helena had been watching at the window, and was infuriated to see that Bramble was outside the front of the house when yet another car pulled up in the drive. The chief negotiator for Trott & Tanqueray got out of his car. She rushed out.

'Bramble, don't worry about this – I can sort Mr . . .?'

'Edwards.' He extended his hand.

Bramble hovered, but fortunately Donna came out of the stables wanting a second opinion about possible heat in Chancer's leg, and she quickly disappeared.

Helena and Mr Edwards exchanged condolences, comments about the weather and the general state of the property market. 'I'll show you round, shall I?' suggested Helena. 'Would you like a coffee?'

Over the kitchen table, Helena explained that there were three executors. 'But we all get on very well, so you won't have any of those family arguments I'm sure you have to deal with all the time.' She then took him everywhere, hurrying him past the stables so that Bramble couldn't come out to say that they weren't sure about putting the house on the market. She saw Eddie schooling Errol and her heart hardened. She had to get rid of this place, before her son got any more ideas about being the next Beaumont rider.

'So what do you think about the development potential?' she asked.

*

Pauline dressed very carefully. Out of habit. There didn't seem much point now, but she had never gone out without her make-up on, and she wasn't going to let herself down. Not like Alan. He was in the drawing room in his favourite armchair. Snoring in the middle of the day, his jaw slack and his clothes awry.

'Mrs Dawkins, could you keep an eye on Sir Alan?' she called. 'I'm just popping over to the stables for a minute.'

'Right you are, Lady R,' replied Mrs Dawkins cheerfully. 'Don't you worry.' She was the only person who knew how vague Alan was getting and, in some ways, was the only person Pauline really trusted to keep it to herself. She didn't want people to talk, and to start crossing their names off invitation lists.

She drove over to Lorenden in her little runabout. She wanted to touch something of Edward's again. She would brush against his coat in the hall, or surreptitiously wrap her hand around his old tweed cap. She wondered if she could slip it into her handbag and keep it, to weep over in secret.

They had had such fun together. It seemed only yesterday that she'd travelled to Aachen in Holland with him, and to Germany. And France. They'd crossed on the ferry like lorry drivers and eaten in the freight canteen with a dozen other riders and grooms, all heading in the same direction.

'He's envying me,' said Edward, of a fat, belligerent lorry driver who glared at them over his bacon and eggs and his copy of the *Sun*. ' He can't understand why I'm surrounded by so many beautiful women.' But he'd looked at Pauline when he said that, and she knew his words were meant only for her to hear. The other grooms and riders had been fitter, younger and more tanned than she was, but they were a cloud of butterflies. She and Edward, as owner and rider, then owner and trainer, had been together longer than most marriages.

It felt like last month, and now it was all over. Going through the hall at Lorenden she managed to wangle his favourite scarf – a slubby, checked wool strip – into her bag. It was the first thing she had ever stolen in her life.

'Bramble, darling, it all went brilliantly yesterday,' she cried, gushing to hide her embarrassment. 'Your father would have loved it. You're such a clever girl.'

'Oh, Helena did most of the organising,' said Bramble, getting up to kiss her on the cheek. 'Listen, Pauline, we want you to have something to remember Pa by. Would you like to choose something?'

Pauline flushed. She couldn't admit to the scarf; it was too intimate. 'Oh,' she said, looking round for inspiration. 'The little clock on the shelf above the door,' she said. 'I remember him winding it up every Sunday evening. It was the sign that we all had to stop celebrating and go home to bed.' As Bramble took the clock off the shelf and handed it to her – it was a very pretty little clock, she thought, very sweet – she added that they had done a lot of celebrating. 'It's all I can remember of your father,' she said. 'The celebrations. Maybe not so much recently . . .'

Pauline's heart crashed against her ribs in a sudden roll of drums as she saw someone else come into the kitchen. She tried to take a deep breath, clutching at her throat to steady herself, but it almost choked her.

'Hello, Pauline,' said Felicity, manouevring herself on one leg and sitting down at the table.

Pauline pulled herself together. Her mother had taught her never to show feelings in public. 'Good morning, Felicity,' she said. 'I didn't see you at the funeral yesterday.'

'No, I missed it, I'm sorry to say.'

'Oh well.' Pauline got her breath back. '*Plus ça change*, as they say. Bramble, darling, I can't stay, I just nipped in to talk to Jez about next season.'

'Jez?' asked Bramble sharply. 'You can talk to me about next season.'

'Of course, of course. You're just so busy that I . . .' Pauline backed away. 'Don't worry, let's deal with next season nearer the time.'

And she almost ran out of the kitchen, just making it to her car before her legs collapsed under her. Perhaps she was having a heart attack. She wouldn't mind if she was. Perhaps this was what Edward had felt, his heart thumping and his lungs striving for huge gulps of air.

But by the time she got home she was fine. She walked into the drawing room in crisp, determined strides.

'Felicity's back,' she shouted at Alan. 'And Bramble gave me this clock to remember Edward by.'

He flinched at the sudden noise, and his head wobbled as he opened his eyes. 'What?'

'Felicity's back,' she repeated in a more normal tone.

'Edward will be pleased,' croaked Alan.

'Edward's dead,' Pauline hissed. 'We went to his funeral yesterday.'

'Is he?' asked Alan. 'That's a shame. That's a terrible shame. Well, I'm very sorry to hear that.'

Pauline could hardly bear to remain in the room with Alan. She hated him sometimes, she thought, as she placed the clock on the mantelpiece and remembered all the happy times it had marked. She actually hated him. It wouldn't surprise her at all if he did it on purpose. She took the scarf out of her bag and smelt it, hardly able to bear the pain.

At Lorenden, the telephone rang for what seemed like the hundredth time that day. 'Hello,' said Bramble.

'Oh, hello. It's Nat here.'

On the phone, his voice sounded gravelly and tobacco-stained, and tinged with something Celtic.

'Oh, Nat,' she said, wondering if he'd left something else behind. 'Hello.'

'I . . .' he cleared his throat '. . . wondered if you'd like to come to a private view of my sculpture. It's being shown in Emma's Gallery in Faversham, in West Street.'

'When?' asked Bramble in surprise.

'On Thursday. At seven o'clock.'

'That would be very nice.'

'I'll see you there then.' He put the phone down.

'What was that about?' asked Savannah.

'I don't know,' mused Bramble, still gazing at the phone as if it could tell her whether there was the faintest possibility that she'd just been asked out on a date, or not. Surely not. It was a party. He would have invited lots of people.

'Well why are you smiling?'

'I'm not.'

A frown appeared between Savannah's brows. 'I wish you'd stop treating me as if I was about three.'

Bramble decided not to have another argument. 'Sorry,' she said. 'I don't mean to.'

'Yes, you do,' replied Savannah fiercely. 'If you didn't mean it, you'd stop it.'

Chapter 12

Savannah flounced out of the kitchen. Helena went to the study to start phoning, leaving Bramble and Felicity facing each other over the table.

'Hi,' said Felicity, lighting a cigarette.

All the exotic, flamboyant versions of her sister that Bramble had glimpsed over the years metamorphosed into a tired-looking woman sitting in a kitchen, looking quite ordinary. 'Oh yes, well, hello.' Bramble felt awkward. 'How's your foot?'

'My big toe's broken.' Felicity lifted it up and placed it on a chair, twisting herself sideways so that she could rest it there. 'At least, I'm pretty sure it is.'

'So, hospital after all?' Bramble waved Felicity's tobacco smoke out of her face.

'Maybe hospital later. I don't think there's a lot they can do with broken toes.'

She and Bramble faced each other.

This is the sister who got the life I was going to have, thought Felicity.

This is the person who left us when we needed her, thought Bramble. The big sister I heard so much about. So talented. So bad. 'Actually, we try not to smoke in the kitchen now,' she said, waving her hand in front of her face again. 'Savannah was asthmatic when she was little and—'

'I started smoking just after you were born,' stated Felicity. She stubbed the cigarette out in her coffee mug. Its noxious fumes curled up through the room, poisoning the air.

'Really? Why was that, do you think?' Bramble got up and started to empty the dishwasher.

'Dunno. House full of baby stuff, small new being around the place. Everybody fussing. I suppose I thought I'd better grow up pretty quick. Anyway, Helena got really clingy and it was a way of getting away from her.'

Don't try to make it my fault, thought Bramble, clattering about and putting things away. She finished and banged the dish-washer door back. 'Do you want to see Merlin? He's banging on the door of his box and shouting a bit. But otherwise he seems fine. If you want to see him, I've got some crutches upstairs I can lend you. From when I broke my leg.'

Bramble fetched the crutches and Felicity manoeuvred herself outside. 'I didn't know you broke your leg. When was that?'

'I came off at a one-day event at Tweseldown. Over a log.'

Felicity concentrated on swinging herself along to the yard. 'Nothing's changed, has it?' she said, stopping to catch her breath. 'It all even smells the same.' It hurt, she realised; it hurt that it was all still there, and had always been there, and that she had been banished from the patchwork fields and rambling hedgerows, heavy with fruit.

At the sound of her voice, Merlin raised his graceful dark head over the top of the stable door. He whickered at Felicity and looked curiously at Bramble.

'Merlin,' she murmured, rubbing his forehead. 'How's my baby?'

'Your baby,' said Donna, pausing as she swept up a pile of dung and a few last stray wisps of hay, 'has got Attitude.'

'Yeah, well,' replied Felicity. 'All the best people do.'

'What are you planning to do with him?' asked Bramble, watching her sister out of the corner of her eye. Even in faded jeans and on crutches, Felicity had a kind of magic centre to her, with those bruised bedroom eyes and commanding way of holding herself. Bramble could see that Felicity had this impact on everyone, even Mop and Muddle, who wriggled at her feet, ignored, begging for tickles.

'Planning,' repeated Felicity. 'Planning? I couldn't say I'd got that far. I've just been trying to save his life. And then I got the email saying Pa had died, and there was nowhere to leave a horse. I tried to call a couple of times, by the way, but by the time I'd found the number . . . then no one was in and I didn't want to leave a message . . . you know how it goes.'

'He is beautiful,' mused Bramble, because it was easier to talk about Merlin than to ask Felicity where the hell she had been for most of her life. 'And young, too.'

'He's four. That's old in racing. It's the same in the States as it is here: it doesn't matter what they've achieved – if you can't breed from them they can be pretty much thrown away once they've finished at the racetrack.' Felicity continued to stroke him affectionately. 'He looked like nothing on earth when we rescued him, just a broken-down nag. We don't know how long he'd been loose, but even so, he must have been looked after by someone who had no idea how to feed a thoroughbred, and I expect they just turned him loose in a field and thought that would be enough.' She sighed, and looked up at a muddy old horse tied up a few stables away, waiting patiently for Donna to groom him. 'That's never Ben, surely? Pa's best-ever horse? Is he still alive?'

'He's thirty-four,' said Bramble with pride. 'Very few make it that far.'

Felicity hobbled across the cobbles, the crutches slipping on the smooth, worn surfaces. 'Do you think he remembers me?' She fondled his mane. 'I went with Pa and Pauline to buy him.'

'Pauline?' asked Bramble. 'Was he hers originally?'

'No, Pa always took Pauline when he chose his horses. He said she had an eye.' Felicity kissed Ben on the muzzle. 'Poor old boy. He looks so sad.'

'Was that after Mum died?' Bramble didn't know why she suddenly felt so threatened by this information. It was hardly new. 'Felicity, I've wondered this before: when Pa and Pauline were younger, do you think they . . .'

Felicity stopped. 'Bramble, leave it. It all happened a long time ago and they're all dead now. Except for Pauline, of course. Let them sleep in peace.'

'But they're not,' said Bramble. 'Pa isn't.' She took a deep breath. 'The morning he died I saw this mist creeping through the orchards, as if it was looking for something. And I've never felt so terrified in all my life. That was before I knew he was dead. I don't think I've ever really seen evil in my life, but if I did that's what it would look like.'

'Believe me, evil isn't a mist,' said Felicity. 'I have seen it and I can tell you it isn't. When I left here I discovered that anything bad that happens here is tiny. It's nothing compared to the horrors of war. I've seen children with their hands chopped off, done out of sheer malice, and . . .'

Bramble was irritated. Felicity always had to upstage everyone. 'Yes, I know a mist creeping through your orchard isn't on a par with men chopping people's hands off, or slavery or bombing . . .'

'It really isn't.'

'But the mist got him and we need to get him back. He's not at peace.'

Felicity gave a short, bitter laugh. 'Too right he's not. But that's his problem, not ours.'

'You know he was trying to tell you something when he died?'

'I don't care.' Felicity's voice was flat and careless. 'He had thirty years to tell me anything he wanted me to know.' Felicity thought of her father, intractable, controlling, lacking in compassion. 'Come on, Bramble. You're just in shock and imagining things.'

'He was a good man.'

'I simply remember him as someone who didn't let anything get in the way of what he wanted.'

'Felicity,' said Bramble, who couldn't bear the worry any longer. 'Has Helena told you? Pa left everything equally to the three of us, and we're all also executors.'

'Lord, I don't care about the money.' Felicity yawned. She began hobbling back to the house again. 'Just divide it up however you want to and give me whatever's mine.'

'It's not quite that simple. Helena wants to sell as soon as possible. And I don't,' said Bramble, deciding not to beat about the bush. 'I need time to get Savannah through school, and to establish my own name without always being seen as Pa's sidekick. If we break up the business now it'll be much harder for me and Savannah to make it on our own. This is my home. I don't want to have to leave immediately.'

'So I've got the casting vote?' Felicity stopped at Merlin's box and caressed him again, but Bramble thought she saw the shutters go down in her face. For a few minutes she had been a real person, but as soon as you asked anything of her she retreated.

'Wow,' said Felicity. 'Quite a heavy trip. Pa really knew how to tie us up in knots, didn't he?'

'I think he was trying to be fair,' said Bramble.

Felicity laughed harshly. 'Oh, really? I don't buy that, I'm afraid. I think he was trying to get me back here and into the family again. Manipulating us from the grave, that's what I call it, just like he always did when he was alive.'

'Why are you so angry with him? What did he do?'

Felicity ran a hand through her hair, and Bramble noticed that it was no longer the sleek chignon even of yesterday. It was as if she had fallen apart on getting back to Lorenden. 'He didn't do anything. That was part of the trouble.'

'It's hard for me to understand if you speak in riddles.' Bramble tried to keep the frustration out of her voice. 'Tell me, please. What went wrong?'

Felicity sighed. 'It's all too long ago. The past is a bucket of ashes, as they say. Carl Sandburg, an American writer,' she added, at the sight of Bramble's furrowed brow. 'My foot's hurting. Let's go back to the kitchen.'

Bramble wondered if Felicity always retreated behind quotations when you got too close. 'I'll take you into the hospital, shall I?' she suggested, as Felicity hopped in the back door.

'Don't worry,' said Helena, popping her head out of the study so quickly that Bramble thought she must have been watching them. 'I can do that. You're so busy.'

Helena and Felicity were away almost all day. Helena phoned to say that Felicity had been right – her big toe was broken, and the hospital had also diagnosed dehydration and exhaustion. 'They want to keep her in overnight, but she doesn't want that. So I'm bringing her home,' she told Bramble on the phone. 'We'll be back by supper time.'

They all did evening stables together – Bramble, Jez, Donna, Eddie and Savannah, helped by Lottie.

'Fancy a drink?' asked Donna, as they put away brooms and

stacked the wheelbarrows up on their sides against the wall. The soft sound of horses contentedly munching settled over the evening.

'I've got to do supper,' said Bramble. 'But thanks.'

Cecily Marsh-Robertson sent her driver to pick up Lottie. Savannah went back to the house, still feeling desperately tired. She was aching all over and had the shivery feeling that came from adrenalin rushing into her system after a fall then draining slowly out again. She found another sweater hanging on the crowded pegs in the hall. She was supposed to be getting on with her homework, but it was mainly reading. If she curled up in one of the big armchairs she could give it a quick glance, and could probably count on remembering most of it.

Her favourite chair was a faded green velvet wingback, one of a pair which faced the bay window. It was Savannah's spot. Ever since she was tiny she'd curled up there to read, watching the swallows dart and twist across the lawn in the summer, the rain in the winter or, in the distance, the horses. She pulled one of the heavy velvet curtains around the chair and turned it into her own secret spot. It had always been a good place to hide. Settling herself down with a copy of *The Old Man and the Sea*, her least favourite English set text, she drifted off into a doze and woke up to hear Bramble asking Helena and Felicity where Savannah was. Before she could answer, Helena said that she thought Savannah was upstairs.

'Oh good,' said Bramble. 'Because I don't want to discuss any of this in front of her. I think it's so important for her to feel secure, particularly in GCSE year.'

'Children are tough,' said Helena. 'They cope much better than we give them credit for.'

'All the same,' replied Bramble. 'This is her home and I don't want her to worry.'

'We have to make some hard decisions here, Bramble,' said Helena. 'This is not just about Savannah. Anyway, we should begin. I think we're all agreed that we need to make balanced, sensible decisions for the long term. For all of us.' Savannah heard a rustle of papers and the sound of the three women making themselves comfortable on the two big sofas by the fireplace.

'Shall we light the fire, Bramble?' asked Helena.

Savannah heard her mother agree, and the sound of rustling as it was lit.

'Right,' said Helena. 'The position is this: I've been going through the books and talking to people, and we have a number of options. First, we will probably get the most money by selling Lorenden to developers.'

'Developers?' asked Bramble in agitation.

'Developers, of course,' said Helena with satisfaction. 'The uplift would be quite substantial.'

'Bramble, don't jump to conclusions. Just listen,' admonished Felicity.

'We can almost definitely get planning permission to turn the stables into, say, four three-bedroom homes, and the garage, well, it's an old coach house and could probably be turned into a dwelling too. Although there are a couple of trees that would need to go to provide a proper access road.'

'Some of the trees have protection orders,' said Bramble.

Helena shrugged. 'Quite frankly, who's going to notice if we cut them down? And even if they do, what's a little fine compared to the money we could get? Especially as there's a possibility – though only a small one – that the main paddock over the road could be bought for housing. There are some old plans, apparently, that show there used to be buildings there, farm cottages. If that's the case, then we could get up to two million pounds for it all.'

Bramble's heart dropped. 'But what if we – or whoever buys it – doesn't get planning permission for *dwellings*?' There was scorn in her voice. 'How much would it be worth then?'

'Well, they *say* just under a million. But Lorenden is so special,' Helena purred. 'It's very important we don't undervalue ourselves. People will pay anything for something as unique as this.'

'People will pay what it's worth,' said Felicity harshly. 'That's how it goes. You needn't fool yourself about that. There's a cost per square foot, and per square acre, for this part of the world and, one way or another, that's what Lorenden will fetch.'

'Now, admittedly, as an estate for a wealthy city escapee,

Lorenden has just a few shortcomings,' continued Helena. 'The cottages, oast house and the big barn have already been sold off and people who pay top money don't want other people living that close. Whole estates, with privacy and staff accommodation and so on, get the best prices in the current market.' She sighed theatrically. 'Pa was so short-sighted sometimes.

'Also Lorenden needs pretty much complete renovation. Although it's perfectly liveable in, it's the sort of house where, once you start doing things, it will all unravel and, although a lot of people dream, it's only a certain kind of buyer who can genuinely cope with all that.

'And, of course, it's also possible to sell it as an equestrian business but the house is probably too valuable. People wanting to start a horse business will want to put their money into their horses, not into the house. Although it's certainly worth marketing it as such.'

'But . . .' said Bramble. 'Getting planning permission that would enable a sale to developers could take up to two years anyway. That's how long Pa had to wait to do up those barns.'

'Not that long, surely,' said Helena sharply.

Savannah heard the indrawn breath that signalled that Felicity had lit a cigarette and was inhaling. 'Personally, if you ask me,' Felicity's words were exhaled with the smoke, 'I think this is too important to decide in a hurry.'

'But I feel that it's important for both Bramble and Savannah to move on,' squeaked Helena desperately. 'I think they'll blossom when they're out from under Pa's shadow.'

'But if we move out now and start somewhere else we'll lose all the reputation of Lorenden and some of our owners will go elsewhere.' Bramble took a deep breath. 'We made our income, Pa and I, mainly from his teaching and selling on horses. The liveries keep everything going, but there's not much left over for us. But Pa's was the name behind it all. I was only ever seen as his assistant. And now he's gone, no one will rate me on my own if we break up the business immediately and start up somewhere else. Savannah and I will just disappear. We'll never keep going. I need a chance and so does Savannah. This is our home and our work. We can't simply be turned out of it. You don't need the money immediately, do you, Helena? I'll turn this into a viable business and it'll be worth more at the end. You can all be partners.'

'It's a nice idea,' drawled Felicity, as if she was enjoying keeping them both on their toes, 'and I do agree that you can't be thrown out at a moment's notice. But there's absolutely no point, either for you, Savannah or any of us, in wasting the next few years and getting the estate into debt. I've never had any money, I've lived from one freelance assignment or salary cheque to another, all my life. This is big for me too, you know.'

'That's why it's so important we don't make a hurried decision,' begged Bramble. 'We can't just instruct estate agents and wrap everything up immediately.'

'On the contrary,' said Helena. 'If we instruct estate agents, then get an offer in – or perhaps even two or three – *then* we're in a position to make a decision. Based on hard facts. We can't just sit around and do nothing.' Her voice sharpened. 'And I think that if you want to start your own thing, the sooner you do it the better, and you also need to live somewhere a bit easier to look after. A little cottage or a modern house would give you and Savannah a chance to devote all your time to the horses without worrying about guttering.'

'I don't worry about guttering.'

'I can see that,' said Helena. 'But meanwhile water is getting in and doing a massive amount of damage.'

'The gutters are fine for the time being,' said Bramble.

'Oh, don't be so literal. You know what I mean. Roof tiles, windows, rising damp, whatever. Lorenden potentially has it all, and you don't have the time or money to sort it out.'

'The house is OK,' said Bramble. 'It's not in any immediate danger. Obviously it needs a bit of repainting and . . .'

'It's *more* than a bit of repainting, it's—'

'Helena!' Felicity spoke sharply. 'Bramble. Both of you. Please. We're getting away from the point.'

'This is the point,' replied Helena.

'Let me say something,' interjected Bramble. 'Felicity has brought Merlin here and she doesn't know what she's going to do with him. Give me two years to turn him round, Felicity.'

'Two years!' screeched Helena. 'Anything could happen in that time, Bramble. You might lose even more money than Pa did. After all, if he couldn't make it work – and he was the top rider of his day – what chance have you got?'

'I have got a chance,' said Bramble. 'I can be more businesslike than he was. And if Felicity does want Merlin to have a future – well, that can take a while,' she added. 'Racehorses need to learn to think differently, and we don't know what's happened to him since he left the racecourse.'

Savannah strained her ears to hear a response from Felicity. Surely she must have some opinion on what Merlin should do next?

'I'm sorry,' said Felicity, after a pause, 'but this is all too heavy for me. I think we should cool it for a bit.' She didn't sound sorry at all, and Savannah wondered if her aunt was as big a bitch as everyone had always made her out to be.

'Well, I seem to be outvoted.' Helena was almost choking with rage. 'As far as getting anything actually done, that is.' Savannah didn't think she had ever heard her sound so angry. 'If we just let things drift on we will lose money. A lot of money. Especially if there's a property downturn.'

'There's a very large gap between making a decision too quickly and letting things drift,' said Felicity, sounding irritable. 'I've said what I think, I can't say any more.'

But you haven't, have you? thought Savannah. You've said precisely nothing. Just a few outdated hippy clichés.

'More coffee, anyone?' asked Bramble, and Savannah thought her mother sounded strained, close to tears even.

'Lovely,' murmured Felicity and Helena together, both voices equally tight. There was a chink of cups and the sound of pouring.

'Speaking of Savannah,' said Helena. 'She's looking so much prettier now she's lost a bit of weight. You want to watch that, Bramble,' she spat out the words viciously, 'and make sure she keeps it off. Being fat is just the worst thing for a teenage girl. They miss out on everything. Boyfriends, parties, fun . . .'

Savannah turned so cold with horror that she could barely hear her mother bleating something defensive about Savannah's weight being fine. Bramble would always stick up for her, anyway, and would tell any sort of fib to smooth things over, Savannah knew that. All she could think about as they wittered on behind her was that word: fat. Helena had called her fat. An image of herself with a white, fleshy tummy roll, dimpled thighs, plump calves, shirts that would barely button up and a double chin imprinted itself on her mind. Fat. Of course Jez – or anyone else – would never fancy anyone like her.

'Oh Lord, this paper needs a witness to our signatures,' said Felicity. 'Is Jez about?'

The three of them left and Savannah, barely able to hold her head up, slid out of the room and went upstairs to lie on her bed and stare at the ceiling. Fat.

As her grandfather had said, it was up to her now. She needed to ride to win so that they could keep the horses and her mother could stay in business, and she needed to learn about dieting. She'd missed a few meals and lost a bit of weight, but she'd also been catching up occasionally, wolfing down great slabs of bread slathered in butter and jam, or shovelling in a whole packet of biscuits two at a time. Once she'd been so hungry she'd eaten frozen peas – the only thing she could find – still frozen, as if they were ice cream. She needed to find out exactly how you lost weight properly. She would read everything she could find on the subject and be the best dieter there was.

There was a soft 'wuff' from outside the door. Darcy wanted to be let in, but was too polite to bark loudly. He slid in when she opened the door, grinning and lashing his tail from side to side. She stroked the top of his silky head. He didn't care if she was fat or not.

'We can do it,' she whispered. 'We can do it.'

Helena came down to the kitchen the following morning. 'Where's the little clock that used to be on the shelf above the door?' she demanded.

'I gave it to Pauline,' said Bramble.

'What?' shrieked Helena. 'It's one of the few things round here that's actually worth anything.' She clutched her head. 'You fool! You complete and utter fool! It's worth about thirty thousand pounds! You'll just have to get it back. Say you made a mistake, or it belongs to Great Aunt Edna. Anything!'

Bramble paled. 'I suggested Pauline take something as a reminder of Pa and she chose the clock. I'm sorry it was so valuable, but there's nothing I can do about it.'

'You can. You can go and ask for it back. Pauline won't mind, she's incredibly rich.'

'I can't do that.'

'Oh, I get it. Pauline's your most important owner and you can't offend her. So Felicity and I have to lose the equivalent of ten thousand pounds each? And we've got to pay inheritance tax on it!'

'Pauline is an old friend.'

'Well, if you won't go and get it back I will,' declared Helena.

'No! You can't do that. Felicity, you agree with me, don't you?'

Felicity had been sitting drinking coffee. 'Don't get me involved in this. I haven't come back to sort out your arguments.'

The other two stared at her.

'I don't *do* that older sister thing, coming in and looking after everyone, remember? I didn't do it when Mum died, and I'm not doing it now. I am officially no good, completely irresponsible and rotten to the core.'

'Don't be ridiculous. You *are* involved in this,' said Helena. 'It's your clock as well.'

Felicity looked surprised. 'It's Pa's clock.'

'Ye-e-s.' Helena spelt it out, as if for a child. 'And Pa is now dead, so it's *our* clock. Which Bramble has given away without our permission.'

Bramble could see Felicity panicking, like a horse that believes itself to be trapped, about to kick itself into greater danger. 'Felicity,' said Bramble. 'It's all quite all right. We don't need you to be an older sister or to look after us, but it's partly your clock and you have a right to a view on whether I should have given it to Pauline or not. And if not, what should be done about it.'

The shutters had come down in Felicity's face again. 'Look, what none of you seem to grasp is that I don't care about anything that goes on here!' She shouted so loudly that Bramble thought that she perhaps cared a great deal.

'Felicity,' she soothed, in the tone she might use with Sailor when he had taken fright at a flapping paper bag. 'Felicity, it'll be all right. Whichever you choose.' The words didn't matter, just the tone. She looked at her steadily, until Felicity got up with her coffee.

'Oh, for fuck's sake. Helena: the clock stays with Pauline.' And she walked out, slamming the door.

'Why can't I get anyone in this family to behave responsibly about money?' Helena was almost too angry to speak, but she concealed her feelings carefully. She was not going to accept this. She was not. She intended to think about it all carefully, and do something before she found herself conned out of everything, with just a worthless holding in some horse business that could never pay up.

And Felicity was no help at all. She never had been. Helena remembered Felicity as a goddess, sometimes taking her into her confidence and showing her the new clothes she'd bought, at other times shutting the door in her face. When Bramble had been born Helena had felt shut out, had seen the intimate bond between mother and baby and how her mother looked at her with irritation when she tried to paw her for affection. She'd run to Felicity but she had gone off into another distant world, to do with boyfriends and parties and smoking. Helena had been utterly banished – from the nursery and from the party. She had that same feeling now, and she was also getting it when she went on to the set of *Simon's Way*. Panic began to choke her.

Really, it was all too much! When most people's parents died they just sold up and divvied up. It was perfectly simple. And that's what needed to happen here.

But she had filming to do and Ollie had to get on with his work. And Eddie – who seemed to be striking up a very unsuitable friendship with that minx Donna – couldn't miss any more school. They must leave. Now. This moment.

'So much better to travel before the traffic gets going,' she said crossly, trying to round up her men. 'Eddie!' She hurried him past the stables, but he stopped.

'Mum,' he touched her arm. 'I want to talk to you.'

'Not now, Eddie, not now.'

'It's about school.'

This stopped Helena in her tracks.

'I've made some calls. I could start at the school Savannah goes to next week. And I could stay here, I'm sure Bramble would have me. I would only have missed a few weeks of term and I could help out here. It would be so much better, I could concentrate and really work without all the London distractions, and—'

'Are you mad? Are you quite mad?'

'No, Mum, I really want to stay and . . .'

'Do you have any idea,' spat Helena, 'how many sacrifices I have made for your education, and now you want to throw it all away because of *horses*?' She raised a hand. 'No! Don't interrupt me. I *know* we're talking about horses and some mad dream you've got about riding. Is this Bramble's idea? Just because she doesn't value education, there's no reason why she should drag you down with her.'

'No, it was mine, I rang Savannah's school—'

'Savannah's school is a state school. You go to one of London's top private schools. There is no comparison.'

'Universities want students from state schools,' countered Eddie, recovering from the initial impact of Helena's tirade.

'Don't you get clever with me, young man. Get into that car now, this minute, and I don't want another word out of you.'

Ollie punched him on the arm maliciously. 'Timing is all, my boy. That's an important lesson to learn in life.'

'But Mum . . .'

Helena glared at him with such fury that he subsided. She turned to her husband. 'Ollie, can you drive or shall I? Have you been in the pub?'

Ollie shrugged. 'I did some research. Found a wonderful old boy, an absolute mine of information. I could have spent days in the Imperial War Museum and never got such fantastic material. And all for a couple of brandies.'

Helena's eyes went as hard as boiled sweets. 'Brandies. Oh dear, I think I'd better drive.' She sighed. 'Sometimes I think I have to do *everything* around here.'

'You don't understand,' said Ollie, 'what a writer needs to do. We have to tap into people's feelings, their emotions, their memories . . . you can't do that in five minutes over a cup of tea. You have to invest time in people.'

'I'm surprised they've got any memories left after a couple of your drinks,' retorted Helena. 'Bramble, darling, thank you so much for everything. And we'll talk. Soon.' She mimed speaking into a telephone.

Ollie rolled his eyes at Bramble as Helena revved up in irritation. 'Madam hasn't a clue, has she?' He waved a regal hand. 'Bye, darling, it was lovely.'

Bramble could see, by the angle of their heads and the odd, sharp hand gesture, that they were still arguing as the car jerked away. She waved as it disappeared round the corner. She had never known a couple who so perfectly illustrated the saying 'can't live with each other, can't live without each other'. Any one of their arguments would have led to divorce in almost any other couple but, just when it looked like one of them would walk off for good, Helena and Ollie would look at each other and they'd be like honeymooners again. Bramble almost – but, then again, not quite – expected them to go on like that for ever, shouting at each other into their nineties.

At least Felicity had been tugged back into the family. Now Bramble needed to keep her there. Felicity's words, 'I don't do that older sister thing', triggered faint memories of people saying 'I suppose Felicity will come home now that Rose is dead, Edward, to help you look after Helena and Bramble?' And her father's face going very stiff and pale as he said that it really wasn't Felicity's sort of thing and that he wouldn't expect it of her. 'You have to let young people hoe their own row in life, you know.' And he would manage a faint laugh and change the subject.

But if Felicity stayed they could buy Helena out.

Along the telegraph wires, strung between the stables and the house, the swallows were lining up to leave for the winter, jostling each other and fluttering off, then landing again in another spot. The journey ahead would be long and dangerous and some of them would die.

Bramble shivered and quickly walked inside. Perhaps, one day, she could accept that she, too, might have to leave her home. But not yet.

Chapter 13

Already late at seven o'clock on Saturday morning, Bramble yanked open one of the doors on the side of the horsebox and began to pull out boxes in search of studs. It was the last event of the season, a small local one at an estate called Fordham Castle, and she was taking Savannah, Lottie and Donna, with four horses.

The horsebox had been her home from home since March – as it was every summer – and, although she tried hard to keep everything in order, there was a whiff of end-of-season chaos emanating like a faint smell from the neatly stacked crates. The studs she screwed into the horses' shoes to prevent them slipping should have been found in a small plastic box in a large crate marked 'S', but it was not. On the inside of the door, Bramble had taped up a typed list – which was beginning to peel off – clearly stating what should be kept in each box. Box S contained spurs, studs and the spanner to tighten them with, a sewing kit, sweat rugs, surcingles, sponges, sweat scrapers . . . if it began with 'S' it went into box S.

Only it hadn't. She clambered up into the cab and pulled the glove compartment open, only to discover a half-eaten Crunchie bar and some scrawled notes. She rifled through these in the hope – disappointed – that her father might have scribbled something important on them. She found several silks in the Beaumont colours – lilac and green – scrunched up under mattresses or tucked behind cushions, and gathered them together so she could wash and iron them in time to use them next time one of them did cross-country. A rummage inside the living area in the horsebox, opening up the drawers on the tiny kitchenette and pulling open the big drawer under the banquette that folded out into Edward's bed yielded more stuff, some of which needed throwing away, but none of it a box of studs. There was a huge double mattress over the driver's cab – big enough for both her and Savannah to sleep on – which things gravitated to and she winkled a few other bits and pieces out of there. She sighed. A headcollar, for heaven's sake, and Savannah's stock. This, a white cravat worn for competitions, had a tendency to disappear under cushions and in the bottom of bags, and Savannah was often heard screeching in despair as it emerged, crumpled and grubby, just seconds before she was due in the collecting ring. Bramble sighed.

Then she checked the cramped caravan-style shower and loo unit, discarding a nearly empty bottle of shampoo and a cracked, black-veined sliver of soap. No stud box anywhere. Everything needed a good clear-out before the winter, but she didn't have time.

Time. Time. She was haunted by it. Sometimes Bramble had nightmares that she had travelled miles to an event, only to discover she'd left something vital behind. In these dreams she packed and repacked, never getting it right, occasionally almost surfacing to realise that it was a dream before sinking back down into an endless scurrying against the clock. She was not fussy by nature, but she'd been forced to become meticulous, checking and rechecking all the equipment before and after each event, repairing and replacing everything as soon as it was damaged. It ground her down, this endless exactness, this knowledge that if you didn't get it right – if you brought the wrong gloves and the reins slipped through your rider's hands in torrential rain, for example – the consequences might be horrific. Or even if they weren't, it could be the difference between being placed and not winning anything, and if you failed to win too often . . .

Donna hadn't yet learnt this lesson. 'Donna!' she called. 'Donna, have you got the studs?'

Donna was bent over one of the horses' legs, putting on bandages. 'I think I put the box in my bag.'

'Well, don't,' snapped Bramble. 'Put things back where they

belong.' She slammed the side doors shut and walked up the ramp to check that the saddles, bridles, haynets and rugs were all safely in the compartment behind the living area. She couldn't leave it to Donna; they'd finish up without something really important, like a saddle.

'I've checked everything,' said Jez. 'Shall I load?'

Bramble stopped. Was he criticising her? Or did he think she was criticising him? Or was she going mad with tiredness and too much to do? She just stared at him, unable to think of anything to say. 'Yes,' she said eventually. 'Now. We're running late.' She went back to the kitchen where Felicity was frowning into a cup of coffee.

'Sure you don't want to come?'

'With these?' Felicity pointed to her crutches. 'No way.'

Bramble sighed. Felicity seemed so angry with the world. She could at least try to be nice.

In the yard, the horses, their elegant necks plaited up, knew what was happening. They blew through their noses in anticipation, and Tegan stood on her hind legs when Savannah tried to lead her towards the lorry. Lottie was leading a restless Sailor round in circles, and Donna was hurriedly redoing the plaits of an over-excited Chancer.

There was a clatter and the lorry rocked from side to side as Tegan, led by Savannah, shot up the ramp in a rush, followed by Lottie and Sailor. Haynets were adjusted, Donna and Jez got the last two horses on and the girls jumped up on to the worn leather seats of the cab, both pale with excitement. Mop and Muddle hated to miss anything and, just before the cab door was closed, they wriggled up in a fizz of terrier enthusiasm and settled on the girls' laps, paws on the dashboard and whiskery noses pointed eagerly towards their destination. Everybody – dogs, horses, girls – knew they were going to a party. A frisson of nervousness shuddered through them all.

As Bramble slowly drove away she saw Ben in the field, looking sadly at the departing horsebox. Once all the fuss and preparation had been centred on him; now he was left behind. He hung his head, dejected and bony.

★

'Muffin?' asked Savannah, passing a bag along. Bramble took one, but Lottie's smile was small and tight. 'No, thank you.'

'Nervous?' asked Bramble.

The girl nodded. 'Just a bit. I don't want to let Sailor down.'

'Don't worry about him. He's a star. You're both stars.'

'Mummy's coming,' said Lottie. 'With my godfather and his girlfriend. And Mummy's new man. They're bringing a picnic.'

No wonder Lottie was so uptight. Cecily had never come to see her daughter compete before.

'She says she wants to see me win.'

Bramble didn't say that, if Lottie's mother had wanted to see her win, she should have come to almost any of the events she'd done so far. Lottie and Sailor were going well together, but you couldn't bet on a win, not ever. Anything could happen.

'Well, that's nice, isn't it?' she suggested.

Lottie's white face implied otherwise.

Just over half an hour later they rolled in to the open field and parked the lorry at the end of a jagged row of horseboxes and trailers. These ranged from sleek, gleaming six-horse lorries to ancient, crudely converted cattle trucks and muddy trailers. No two were exactly alike, so it was easy to pick out friends. And enemies.

'What's Toby Fitzroy doing here?' frowned Bramble at the sight of a massive pale blue pantechnicon with 'Toby Fitzroy Eventing' painted in huge capital letters across both sides. 'He doesn't usually bring on young horses, so I wouldn't have thought he'd bother with something like this.'

'Perhaps he's got a working pupil or a groom riding,' suggested Savannah.

The hills rolled and dipped around Fordham Castle in a patchwork of greens and browns, and a skylark twirled higher and higher over the busy ground. Mothers bustled in and out of horse boxes, adjusting studs in hooves, straightening plaits, issuing last-minute instructions. One lunged a difficult pony round and round in a circle while another crouched down with a stopwatch, directing a last-minute rehearsal of the dressage test. A horse whinnied to a friend over the revving of a lorry. Mop and Muddle, tied to the side of the lorry, twitched with anticipation. So many dogs, so little time, that was their motto. There were terriers to be yapped at, retrievers to be thoroughly sniffed, lurchers to torment . . . even a pair of red setters peering lugubriously out of the back of an estate car.

Jez's car rolled up and parked across the nose of the lorry, and Donna tumbled out, full of chatter. Lottie led Sailor out in silence and checked him over, tacking him up with quiet efficiency while Donna lost the studs again and Savannah suddenly got panicky about tying her stock. Bramble, used to dividing herself between getting the horses ready and calming the girls down, became aware that Jez was always a step ahead of her. She finished screwing the studs into Tegan's shoes and found that Jez had done both of the other horses, and had tied Savannah's stock in just a few seconds, bringing colour to her face.

Just as Lottie was about to warm Sailor up for their dressage test, Cecily Marsh-Robertson appeared in a silver Porsche with tinted windows. She parked directly behind the lorry.

'We have to get the horses in and out,' said Bramble. 'And no, not alongside, that's where we tie them up.'

'I could move Jez's car and they could park in front,' suggested Donna. 'If he doesn't mind, that is?'

Cecily treated him to a dazzling smile. 'That is simply so sweet of you.'

Bramble wasn't sure she could cope with Cecily right under her nose, especially when a balding man in fiercely fashionable glasses hefted a large wicker picnic basket out of the boot and unfolded five director's chairs, blocking off access to and from the lorry.

'We'll need to lead the horses through there,' said Bramble.

A deep furrow appeared in Cecily's brow. 'Well, where *do* you suggest we sit?'

After Bramble had arranged their chairs, Cecily mumbled an introduction, waving a hand in Bramble's direction. Bramble knew that Cecily regarded her as one of the servant class, paid to do as she was told and not to speak up. The man – Matthew – gave her a vague nod, his eyes sliding over her towards the castle.

'Beautiful setting,' he murmured.

'Mmm,' said Cecily. 'And look, Bramble actually lives on the lorry when she travels to events, don't you? Have a look, Matt, can you imagine it? Her father was still sleeping in there in his late sixties.'

To Bramble's fury they both clambered into the living area. 'Christ!' she heard the man say. 'It's a bit cramped, isn't it? Why don't they stay in hotels?'

Bramble thought she heard Cecily whisper something about 'hard up' and as they edged back down the tiny pull-out steps again she couldn't help sticking up for herself. 'In fact, we prefer staying on our lorries. You're in your own space, all your friends are around you in their lorries, so there's a great supportive atmosphere, and we're close to our horses and where we're going to compete.'

They both stared at her – briefly – as if she was mad, and took no notice. 'Have a melon ball,' said Cecily, picking up a Tupperware container. Matt took one. 'The one thing you need at these sorts of places is something light and fresh,' she trilled. 'There's so much fast food everywhere. Try one, Jez.' She thrust the container at Jez, who was tightening Tegan's girth while the horse flicked her tail angrily.

'Don't be ridiculous,' he said, not even bothering to turn round.

Cecily tightened her lips and snapped the Tupperware container shut.

That was all they needed. Jez upsetting the clients.

Cecily's mobile burbled. 'Darling? You're here? Good. It's all terribly sweet, isn't it? I think Lottie's going to be doing some . . .' she raised her eyes at Bramble '. . . dressage in a minute. *Dressage*. It's a series of exercises. You know, walk, trot and canter in circles. Yes, dreadfully dull, but they have to do it. Where are you parked? Where? Oh, yah, I know where you mean. I'll send Lottie over and she'll show you where we are.'

Bramble choked back the retort that dressage was at the core of all good riding, and anyone who could work successfully with their horse in these 'dull' circles was properly placed to succeed at both showjumping and cross-country. But it would do her no good to antagonise Cecily further, and, anyway, she wouldn't listen. Cecily hated being corrected.

Sailor threw his head up, obviously alarmed by the way Cecily was flapping her hands.

'I think I ought to go and warm up, Mummy,' said Lottie. 'I'm on in twenty minutes.'

'Yes, really, she ought to . . .' added Bramble.

'Nonsense. There's always time for good manners. Get off that horse now and go and get Colin and Harriet. They're in a black Mercedes over by the gate,' shouted Cecily. 'Really, children today have no idea.'

Sailor was clearly in no mood to prance about in a piddling dressage test, instead pointing his ears forward to the cross-country jumps. Let me at 'em, his body language declared, as he tried to back away from Cecily and the melon balls. Lottie came running back, breathless. 'They're coming now,' she said to Cecily.

Cecily tutted. 'You should have waited for them.'

Bramble legged Lottie up again and they escaped, Bramble and Jez following, half at a run, down the hill to where the dressage arenas were marked out with white poles and letters set into the grass.

'We've hardly got time to warm up,' said Lottie, thoroughly nervous and close to tears.

'Just do what you can,' said Bramble. 'And have faith in Sailor. You're a great team.'

'Take a deep breath,' advised Jez. 'People sometimes forget to breathe when they're doing a dressage test.'

Lottie gave him a tiny smile and obeyed.

Bramble and Jez watched Lottie closely as the dressage judge tooted her car horn to indicate she should start her test. Sailor trotted slowly and carefully down the centre line, but there was no doubt about it, Lottie's mother had knocked her confidence. Sailor, indignant at his rider's distraction, was swishing his tail from side to side and shaking his head furiously. 'They're usually much better than this,' said Bramble.

Jez, arms folded, continued to watch Lottie intently.

There was a kerfuffle behind them as Cecily and Matt caught up. 'I still can't quite understand the way the scoring works,' demanded Cecily.

'Marks out of ten are given for each movement, and then collective marks – also out of ten – at the end for the horse's paces, rider's position and so on,' advised Bramble. 'If this was a pure dressage competition, the person with the highest number of marks would win, but because here Lottie has to go on and do showjumping, followed by cross-country, where mistakes are penalised, it's reversed – the marks she *doesn't* get are penalties, so the lower the dressage score the better.'

'And how's it going?'

Bramble shook her head. 'Difficult to say. It all depends on what the judge thinks.'

Lottie and Sailor left the ring looking dejected. Bramble went up to comfort Lottie. 'Not too bad.'

'It was the worst test I've ever done. Does Mummy know?'

Bramble patted Sailor's neck. 'Mummy hasn't a clue what's going on, so don't you worry about that. And there's still the jumping and cross-country to come.'

They all watched Savannah conduct an extremely good dressage test, and only a few minutes later Donna, too, did a nice one.

'Well,' said Cecily to Matt, Colin and Harriet. 'They all look the same to me, but I'm sure Lottie's was the best. Shall we have a little explore, Matt?'

Harriet shivered. 'I'm cold.'

A few minutes later Cecily clocked the biggest lorry of all: Toby Fitzroy's.

'Look,' she said to Matt and the others. 'Toby was MD of the company that originally bankrolled To Die For Bags. Seven years ago now. Toby! Darling! How simply amazing to find you here.' She advanced on him, cheek extended for a kiss.

Toby's eyes flickered over her with the experience of many years of womanising. 'Cecily.' He kissed her. 'What brings you here?'

She introduced everyone and explained that her daughter, Lottie, was an extremely talented eventer. 'Everyone says she could go to the top and she's had such a successful season that I thought it would be fun to come and watch her. But what are *you* doing here?'

'Just a favour for a couple of friends, really – I've let them borrow my lorry, because theirs has broken down. I event myself, of course, but at rather a higher level. Can I tempt you all to a glass of champagne?'

Getting four of them on board and into the accommodation at the front of Toby's horsebox was quite a performance, but once inside Cecily realised she'd been missing a trick stabling Sailor with someone like Bramble. This was where Lottie belonged. While the inside of Bramble's horsebox was like a caravan, with cheery red-and-white checked curtains, a microwave and two gas rings, this was more like a nightclub with low-voltage lighting and beige suede banquettes. Toby pressed a button and the seating area slowly extended out to the side. 'Nice to have a bit more space,' he chortled. 'Veuve Clicquot, do you?' He took a bottle of champagne out of a small fridge.

'I gather you're one of the best eventers in Britain,' she said, willingly talking about horses for the first time in her life. Best to lay it on thick: men liked that.

'Oh well,' he filled her glass. 'One tries.' His eyes glittered with interest as they darted again over Cecily's small, but delectably pushed-up, cleavage.

Toby asked her what level her daughter had reached: 'Is she doing JRN yet?'

Cecily hadn't the faintest idea, and mentally reminded herself to text her assistant with 'JRN – find out what it is'. 'Actually,' she parried, 'I'd be hugely grateful of your advice. I'm just not sure what direction Lottie should take. I mean, do you think she's wasting her time at little events like this? I'd like to make sure she's mixing with the right people, if you know what I mean.'

Toby's eyes gleamed in understanding. 'Well, eventing is *the* smart end of horses. When I'm talking to the bank about renewing their sponsorship, I always say that it has more AB people than in any other sport.'

'Not that I'm a snob, of course,' insisted Cecily, 'I just want her to feel at home. What about showjumping?'

'Oh, lots of money there,' said Toby, 'but it can be, you know, a bit, er . . .'

'Nouveau?' suggested Cecily, with a tinge of anxiety.

'Well, you can get a few dodgy types. There's a joke that in eventing you can leave your car door unlocked with your bag on the seat,' he leaned back and examined his glass, 'but that if you go showjumping you have to nail everything down.'

Cecily giggled.

'Although, of course,' he drawled, 'the showjumpers are equally rude about us. They say we're spoilt little rich kids.'

'Do you know Bramble Kelly?'

Toby's expression changed. 'I knew her father better. He was a bastard. And Bramble is coasting on her father's reputation. I don't think you'll see anything much come out of that yard now he's gone.'

'Really?' Cecily was astonished. Everyone always spoke so reverently of Edward Beaumont. She hesitated. She hadn't necessarily wanted to be found out bad-mouthing Bramble, but her finely honed instinct for survival told her that Toby Fitzroy would like nothing better.

'We keep Lottie's horse with her, and she trains Lottie. She's been brilliant so far, but Lottie needs to move on. She's way beyond Pony Club level, but Bramble doesn't agree. She always wants to keep her back.'

'Lost her nerve,' said Toby. 'Women do.'

'Well, yes, that's all very well.' Cecily had never experienced the Fitzroy charm up close and it was difficult to breathe easily. 'But it's no reason for her to keep Lottie back.'

'How old is she?'

'Just turned sixteen. But she's very tall and experienced.'

'Mmm. Well, of course, part of the problem is that her own daughter comes first. If a horse is any good she'll want it for Savannah.'

'Oh my God, I never thought of that.' Cecily sipped the cold, delicious champagne. Bramble only ever offered her mugs of tea or instant coffee. 'You see, I'm too trusting. It's my main fault. I always see the best in people.'

Soothed by two-and-a-half glasses of champagne, Cecily and her party emerged from Toby's box an hour later and looked at the proceedings with new eyes. Judging by what he'd told her, there seemed to be some very rich and influential people in the world of eventing. Toby's friends, Sally and Gemma, looked romantically athletic in their skin-fitting cream breeches, immaculately tailored black coats and hair tied back in elegant chignons. They had virtually ignored Cecily as they bustled about, conferring with Toby and helping the groom get their horses ready.

Cecily wasn't used to being overlooked. She had perhaps, she mused, not quite realised the potential of this horse world because everything had always seemed so understated, even scruffy. Think royalty, old money and big business. That's where she should be selling her handbags. And she'd been letting her daughter run about in a tatty old lorry with a couple of has-beens.

Toby escorted them all to an open tent where the dressage scores were written up on a whiteboard. Cecily ran her finger down to Lottie's name. 'Forty-five,' she said. 'Is that good?'

'Depends what the others have got,' explained Toby. 'Look, here's Savannah's. Twenty-nine. The lower the better, remember. Well, there you are then. Savannah's got a superior horse, therefore Savannah gets higher marks in her dressage test.' He made a quick calculation. 'Lottie's ninth at the moment.'

Cecily was mortified. 'Oh well,' she said. 'We only do it for fun, of course.' Inwardly, she fumed.

'I buy and sell a few horses,' said Toby. 'Give me a ring.' He passed his card over and winked. 'Call me soon. I might have just the horse for you.'

My life is over, thought Pauline, as her little runabout jolted down the hill and over the grass towards fence four, the Garden Rails. She and Alan were fence judging, volunteering their services to monitor one of the cross-country jumps, spending the day counting the riders through safely and making sure that any refusals, run-outs or falls were noted. She hadn't wanted to get up that morning, but then she hadn't wanted to get up ever again. Only the mantra 'what would people think?' had forced her up, into the bath and in front of the mirror.

She'd always loved fence judging – it was a chance to be involved behind the scenes and, when she and Alan were younger, they'd done some really special three- and four-star events, getting invited to the parties and camping out in the lorry park with the competitors. Now it was just an opportunity to put something back into the sport she enjoyed, an occasional day out, a favour for a friend on the committee . . . but her friend had been Edward, and she'd always, unconsciously, been looking to him, observing each rider closely so that she could discuss it with him later, commenting that this rider was over-horsed or that one needed to ride steadier. There didn't seem a lot of point in doing it without him, but if she pulled out what would people think?

Their day started, as always, with the cross-country jump judges' briefing, which took place in a tent big enough to hold anything up to ninety people. Pauline waved to fellow judges, all of whom they'd seen over and over again that season. 'Who are all these people?' Alan whispered in her ear.

'You know,' hissed Pauline. 'They're our friends. Most of them, anyway.'

Then Alan covered up his mistake, as he did so often nowadays, by going on the attack. 'Nonsense, there are lots of new people here. They don't look as if they know what they are doing. Fence judging's an expert job, you know. You can't have just anybody doing it.'

Pauline sighed. 'Alan, I'm sure they're all quite capable.' She smiled at someone, then at someone else, but didn't want anyone to get too close and risk them hearing Alan talking nonsense. She steered him to a seat. Life was going to be so lonely if he was really going senile. It suddenly seemed lonely enough as it was.

The jump judge organiser banged the table and began his briefing, and Pauline let her mind drift. Her life was over, she thought again. And Alan – well, Edward's death seemed to have wrenched him out of his intermittent fog of vagueness and plunged him into full-blown senility.

Note down the time the rider passes your timing marker, droned the organiser. Remember to confirm the rider number. Blow the whistle to get the public off the course. A step backward is a refusal. Call first refusal clearly and loudly. Then second refusal. After the third refusal ask the rider to leave the course by the most convenient route. Don't let a concussed rider get back on. Don't let any rider get back on if there's the slightest chance they might be concussed. Above all, keep your radio with you at all times. Pauline listened with half an ear, wondering if the packed lunch would be nice, whether there'd been too little rain and the ground would be too hard, and, lastly, sadly, did she really have to get Alan to a doctor? She would see how things went today, see if he made too many mistakes, and decide then.

They parked next to the jump and took out two folding chairs and a picnic table, setting out their Thermos of tea and a bottle of water. She handed the whistle and the clipboard to Alan. He looked blank.

'Don't forget to blow the whistle when the rider's approaching,' she said. 'To clear everyone out the way.'

She pulled out an extra scarf and tied it round her throat as protection against the wind. 'What?' she demanded, seeing his blue eyes watering with rage, wind or tears – she had no idea which. 'Why are you looking at me like that?'

'Do you think I'm daft?' he asked, and his fists clenched. 'We've done this for years.'

She thought of saying, yes, daft is exactly what I think you might be, but backed off at the last moment. 'You just seem a bit vague today, that's all,' she hedged.

He harrumphed and limped off to plunge the timing marker into the ground, and Pauline watched him. He placed it exactly a hundred yards before the jump. So he'd lost none of his fussiness. She heaved a tiny sigh of relief. So far, so good.

As she watched him standing beside the marker, ready with his watch and clipboard to mark the riders' numbers and times as they came through, he seemed the old Alan again. Perhaps he wasn't as bad as he sometimes seemed. And if he missed a rider number – just stood there gazing into space as one galloped past – she could still cover for him. She knew almost every rider and horse in the South of England – even beyond – and barely needed to see their numbers to know who they were.

After the dressage, Bramble and Jez went with their riders and horses to the practice area. 'Can you look after Savannah and Donna?' she asked Jez. 'I want to concentrate on Lottie because she's really upset. She doesn't show it, but I've never seen her so rattled.'

Donna had a pole down on one of her horses and then, later, three refusals with the other. Bramble frowned.

'What do think, Jez? We're hoping to sell these on next spring and we won't get what we hope for with performances like that.'

Cecily's group came up behind them. 'Is this where we stand?' they twittered to each other. 'Everyone seems to be wandering everywhere. Are you sure we're in the right place? Aren't there any seats? You'd have thought they'd have a grandstand or *something*.'

'I've no idea how these little country events work,' said Cecily, balancing with difficulty on her high heels. 'I usually only go to the polo at Smith's Lawn. Ask Bramble, she knows.'

Bramble thought of pointing out that they wouldn't need binoculars, but decided to go for the short and simple. 'There are ten jumps,' she said, trying not to sound clipped. 'And they have to jump over each one without knocking any poles down. Within the time.'

Cecily glared at her. 'Yes, thank you Bramble, I'd never have guessed.'

A cluster of competitive mothers had their programmes open and were writing everyone's scores in it with pencils. 'Really, half the dressage scores haven't even gone up yet,' muttered one. 'I can't tell *how* we're doing.'

A girl cantered into the ring and dropped three fences. Her mother tutted, hurrying to take her horse from her at the end of the round. 'I need better boots,' the child complained. I can't ride in these. It's all right for Lottie Marsh-Robertson, she's got Ariats.' She slid off and walked away, her buttocks, in tight jodphurs, swaying sulkily from side to side.

'Oh look, it's Lottie,' said Cecily, raising her binoculars, then lowering them again as she realised she could see rather better without them. 'You heard that,' she whispered. 'They're all so envious of her. But it's pure ability, of course.'

Bramble could tell that Lottie still hadn't recovered her concentration and got round the first few jumps with luck more than judgement. She was bottling up Sailor's energy – he was fighting for his head – then firing him directly at the jumps. Bramble shook her head as Sailor nearly refused on the fourth, making a huge cat jump at the last minute. Lottie seemed to collect herself and they bounded gracefully over the next four in an easy, apparently effortless, rhythm.

'Come on, Lottie!' shouted Cecily, waving. 'Come on!'

Lottie looked quickly at her mother and Sailor, so sensitive to his rider's every move, checked briefly. Bramble inhaled sharply. They were taking off too late and Lottie wasn't really in control.

But Sailor, wonderful horse that he was, tucked his feet up out of the way and took Lottie over. 'He really looks after her,' Bramble said to Jez, and his face cracked open in a rare, but sunny smile.

'He's a great horse for a young rider,' he said. 'And she's got talent, too, if she could get over the shyness.'

'A clear round for Lottie Marsh-Robertson and Sailor Sailor,' crackled the commentator, 'so there's nothing to add to their dressage score of forty-five.'

'*Forty-five* really isn't good enough,' said Cecily, now primed by Toby. She tottered over to her daughter, trying to balance on the uneven ground. 'That was all right but the dressage should have been better,' she hissed. 'Remember we've all come to watch you.'

Savannah jumped clear too, and then it was time to hurry over to the cross-country course, to find a place that offered the best view of as many fences as possible.

Bramble and Jez walked to the point of the hill where the fields and woods dropped away from them in undulating folds. Neat, manicured farmland and woodland, cultivated for centuries and still studded by only a few black-and-white timbered cottages, spread as far as the horizon, where a distant haze signalled the nearest town, almost out of sight.

Cecily Marsh-Robertson and her party wandered into view.

'Hey, Bramble,' Cecily called. 'Where do we watch this thing from?'

'About here is good. You can see the first three jumps from here, then if you rush across over there . . .'

Cecily treated her to a frosty smile. 'Where's the finish?'

'By the start. Look, there's the last jump.'

'We've another competitor on the course,' said the commentator, 'number eighty-three, Lottie Marsh-Robertson on Sailor Sailor, safely over the first three jumps and heading down now towards the Arbour.' Lottie and Sailor disappeared out of sight, down the hill towards a knot of green trees, and Bramble held her breath. She overheard Cecily complain that it wasn't like racing or polo at all, and that she was surprised more spectators didn't get injured. 'I'm sure the course is roped off at proper events.'

There was a tense silence, while in the distance a horse and rider emerged from the trees, went through the water and then galloped back up behind the hill, out of sight again.

Cecily tapped her foot impatiently. 'Of course, Sailor is only a Pony Club pony,' she said to Matt and their friends. 'The ones that win are on decent horses.'

'Sailor's not a pony,' said Bramble indignantly, not caring that Cecily wasn't talking to her. 'He's a small but excellent horse. He and Lottie have been very successful so far, and there's plenty of mileage in him, at least for the next few years.'

Cecily looked irritated and faintly surprised, as if the chair she was sitting on had suddenly addressed her. They caught a quick flash of Lottie and Sailor down in the valley, galloping uphill.

'Lottie Marsh-Robertson has come through the water fast but safely,' broadcast the commentator.

A few minutes later Lottie came in sight over the hill and was heading towards the last few jumps. She was well within the time. 'A nice fast round,' said Bramble.

'Well, thank goodness for that,' said Cecily walking back towards the finish, looking bored. 'Let's go and have some lunch. Matt?'

As Cecily's party walked back towards their car, Sailor's hindquarters thundered ahead of them. Bramble prayed for the last jump.

Sailor ran out.

Lottie brought him back round to try it again and he popped over without difficulty. Lack of concentration, thought Bramble. She saw her mother and lost it. There was no other reason for them to make a mistake at the very last jump.

'Was that a fault?' queried Cecily.

Bramble nodded. 'In fact, in this section there are twenty penalties for a run-out.'

'Twenty!' Cecily scowled, and her party disappeared to open the massive picnic basket.

Bramble returned to the lorry where Lottie was patting Sailor. 'He did so well,' Lottie said, 'I'm so proud of him. That last jump was my fault.' She unsaddled him, and began to sponge him down.

Bramble went back to the course to watch Savannah and Donna. Savannah had another clear round. 'She's in line to win,' said Jez.

'I hope so,' replied Bramble. 'It might cheer her up. She seems to have taken Pa's death quite badly.'

Jez didn't answer for a while. 'When you're sixteen,' he said eventually, 'you feel things very deeply.'

Bramble looked at him. For a moment she wanted to ask what had happened when he was sixteen, but he had a closed look on his face, as if he had said too much already.

'Do you think she'll be all right?'

Jez considered her question for some time. 'I think,' he said slowly, 'that you need to watch her at the moment. But yes, in the end, she'll be all right.'

He said it with such finality that she believed him, and some of the worry seeped away.

They reached the lorry and could hear Cecily's voice.

'Have you any idea how embarrassing this is for me?' she queried. 'I mean, I've brought three people down all the way from London to see you win, and all you get is faults. And you've made such silly mistakes. Just letting Sailor stop whenever he feels like it. Mind you, that horse isn't good enough, it really is time we got you something decent.'

'It was my fault, Mummy, I promise. I wasn't concentrating properly, I should have used my stick but . . .'

'There's no point in us spending all this money if you're not going to concentrate. This riding business costs a fortune, you know, and you're a very spoilt girl. Just think of all the girls who would love to have all the privileges you have. They'd concentrate all right. I think we should sell Sailor and—'

'I will concentrate, I will. Please, Mummy, please. Don't sell Sailor. I will be good, I really will.'

'I should think so too. This is a preparation for life, you know. You don't get prizes for coming second in the real world, and unless you pull yourself together you're going to be a complete and utter failure at everything.'

Bramble nearly stepped forward to rebut Cecily Marsh-Robertson, but stopped herself just in time. Antagonising Cecily any further wouldn't help Lottie and, shamefully, she couldn't afford to lose a customer. When Cecily stormed out of the lorry Bramble tiptoed in. Lottie was sitting in the dim light.

'Are you OK?'

Lottie nodded. Bramble could just see a tear trickling down her cheek. She crouched down beside her. 'You rode brilliantly. You were just a bit put off in the dressage and towards the end of the cross-country because your mother was there with all her friends. I will tell her that, you know. So she understands.'

'She won't. And please don't make her any crosser. I let Sailor down and now she wants to sell him.' Lottie's voice was almost inaudible through suppressed tears.

'I'll do everything I can to stop her.'

'No one can stop Mummy,' whispered Lottie.

Bramble intended to do her very best to do so. She scrabbled through the mess to find some tissues and passed them over. 'You're a very good rider, Lottie. With your focus, determination and ability to work hard you can achieve anything you want to. Anything. I'm going to tell your mother that.'

But Lottie couldn't hear praise. Bramble left the lorry quietly.

'Hello,' said a voice. 'You look like you need a stiff drink.'

When Bramble saw the smiling, tanned face, with its tangled grey hair, she felt a rush of warmth.

'Oh Nat, hi. I need about six drinks. But I've got to get this lot home first.'

'What if I buy you a drink in the White Horse tonight, once you've got everything sorted?'

She laughed. 'It sounds very tempting.' She thought of Dom suddenly, and how lovely it had been to go through the day together at the end of an event, by the fire with glasses in their hands. But Dom, who had seemed just out of sight, round the corner or in another room for so many years, was suddenly as two-dimensional as a black-and-white photograph, dog-eared with time – someone she had known many years ago, in a different life.

'Come on,' he urged. 'I can run to a plate of chips and one of their homemade meat pies, too.'

He seemed very solid, very comforting, and Bramble crumbled. She could let herself go with him. 'OK,' she said with a smile.

'Around eight-ish? See you there.' He raised a hand in farewell and strode off across the grounds. Bramble watched him go. After Helena's rapaciousness, Felicity's anger, Savannah's sullen pickiness, Jez's refusal to accept her decisions and Cecily's continual fault-finding, it would be heaven to spend the evening talking to someone who seemed to be on her side.

Donna ran up to say that the prize-giving was about to start and that Savannah had won.

Savannah was presented with a cup – an award established by a long-dead Master of Foxhounds in memory of his daughter – and she hurled herself into Bramble's arms in delight. She was whirled round by Jez, and then waved the cup in the air before putting it down on the ground so that she could help the committee take down the marquee.

A silver Porsche swayed across the field, purring through the crowd, and Cecily Marsh-Robertson gave a regal, but slightly irritable, wave from the driving seat, bumping over the rough ground as if it was a Knightsbridge street.

As she passed by the committee stopped dismantling the marquee.

'She's driven over the cup,' cried Savannah, pointing to an object on the ground that looked very much like a crumpled silver pancake. The tail-lights of the Porsche disappeared past the castle and vanished from sight.

'That car,' said Alan, who had hobbled up the hill on foot after a very satisfying day's fence judging, 'is brand new and costs a hundred thousand pounds.'

'That cup,' said Pauline, immensely relieved to hear Alan so coherent, 'is a hundred years old and has the names of all the past winners on it.'

Unaware of the appalled faces in the rear-view mirror, Cecily

Marsh-Robertson was thinking furiously. Toby had been right – Savannah had won because she had a better horse and her teacher, Bramble, was only interested in her own daughter. Cecily resolved that she was going to take a lot more interest in Lottie's little hobby from now on.

Chapter 14

Even in the safe, centrally heated world of studios and Primrose Hill, Helena's late autumn days seemed darker than usual. She sensed that her career was slipping downhill, but she couldn't work out why. At first, she tried to ignore the signs.

She called her agent for reassurance. There was nothing she could put her finger on exactly, just a feeling that when she walked on set a draught of unease blew around the room.

Caroline was evasive.

'Just be careful about things like punctuality and learning your lines,' she said. 'Lots of early nights, darling, and don't worry.'

Helena was outraged. 'I'm the most punctual person on the set. I always have been. There was just that one time, and my father'd died, for heavens sake.'

'All I'm saying,' said Caroline, 'is that you can never be too careful in this job. Be whiter than white, darling, whiter than white.'

'I'm about as white as you get. Not like that Calum, and half the production team who are . . . are . . . are . . .' Helena tried to think of what the cool phrase for taking cocaine was at the moment '. . . well, sticking things up their noses.'

'That's a different sort of white altogether and you'd better stay away from it.'

'Of course I'll stay away from it. I wouldn't dream of taking anything except a drug that's prescribed for me.' Which was almost true, because she did take the odd sleeping pill from time to time, and, occasionally, borrowed some from a friend when she ran out, but didn't everyone?

Caroline started to be slower about returning her calls and generally the phone rang less and less. Or so Helena thought.

She stared at her mobile, willing it to ring. She'd placed it next to her landline. That, too, was silent. She'd left two messages for Caroline that morning, asking her to get to the bottom of the atmosphere on set over the next series. Her dignity prevented her from leaving another. She checked her email as often as she dared – although *that* would definitely be bad news, as it would mean that Caroline couldn't face talking to her.

Even the thud of the post on the mat made her heart beat faster, until she shuffled through the pile with gradually increasing disappointment – flyers for National Trust membership and home insurance, a school fees reminder, two or three credit card bills and a thank-you card. This last she opened feverishly, thinking it might be an invitation. She cast it aside in irritation. It was very nice of people to write thank-you letters, of course it was, but she thought they were getting fewer invitations these days. She sensed an invisible withdrawal, as if people had been told, 'Helena Harris and Oliver Cooper are no longer hot'. Possibly not even lukewarm. As if the word had got out that Helena and Ollie now belonged in a different sphere from other successful couples. Everybody else knew that Mattie was being killed off.

Then she told herself that she was being paranoid. At the end of the last series, Pete Young, the director, had congratulated her on her performance. He'd said he couldn't do it without her. He'd told her that Mattie was one of the greats. 'They call it *Simon's Way*, but it's *Mattie's Way* really, isn't it?' She clung to the memory of that conversation. They couldn't drop Mattie, surely they couldn't? All the production team had told her how professional she was. What a pleasure to work with. She made sure she was never too grand, not even when she was talking to the lowliest runner. She always thanked people for everything they did and complimented them on what they were wearing. She'd brought in a great tray of patisseries for the whole team on the last day of shooting. She never spoke about anyone behind their back, never gossiped, never complained. She smiled and was patient and did what she was told. A trouper, that's what the sound engineer had called her.

But Pete Young had moved on and the new director looked at her with a cool, calculating eye. He didn't seem to listen to anything she said. There was a new producer, too. Both had been brought in to 'revitalise' *Simon's Way.* Two of the camera-men and one of the production assistants had departed, each for a different, excellent reason, but the rumour mill was churning. Their replacements didn't seem aware of how important Helena was. Instead of a five-minute round of kissing and greeting, she often slipped into the studio unnoticed these days, almost with the sensation that she'd become invisible. Now there was always a crowd gushing respectfully round Melissa, the actress who played her on-screen daughter Zoe. Yesterday, Helena had found herself contemplating a row of backs. Eventually she had said 'hello', and it had come out as a squeak. Everyone stopped talking and, after a short pause, Melissa had complimented Helena on her shoes and her sweater, both of which she had worn the day before.

Perhaps she should have been more starry? Perhaps nice didn't get you anywhere any more? Her panic-stricken thoughts went round and round on a never-ending treadmill. She knew that viewer research was being done – had already been done – and she wasn't sure that the viewers would love Mattie as much as Pete and the production company did. Viewers might see her as old-fashioned, outdated, past her best . . . her mind was slipping inevitably towards the word she feared most: old.

She dragged her thoughts back. Nearly forty is not old. Her publicity pictures said she was thirty-eight. She had managed to stay thirty-seven for two years. She would be thirty-eight for another two. And she had Lorenden to sell at the best possible price. It was obviously going to be all down to her, as both her sisters would either keep it or let it go to any old person they liked the look of, and there was a difference of thousands – even a million – if you got it right.

No, she wasn't past her best. Take Mick Jagger. And Paul McCartney. And Leonard Cohen. Old no longer mattered. She focused her mind on positive thoughts over and over again. Positive Mental Attitude. That was what you needed.

Mick Jagger, Leonard Cohen and Paul McCartney were men. No! She paced up and down, her heels click-clacking on the lacquered oak floor. Think about Joan Baez, then. And Dolly Parton. Sharon Stone. She picked up the newspaper and flicked through it.

The main feature hit her between the eyes like a bullet. It was an interview with Melissa. Melissa, the interview said, had turned a background role in the series *Simon's Way* into a star performance. She'd been nominated for a Bafta for her role in a very successful small film. She was becoming something of a cult figure, turning down more parts than she accepted. She'd declined several top Hollywood roles because she wanted to stay in England with her banker husband and ten-month-old daughter. (Huh, thought Helena, no one *really* turns down Hollywood roles – she just didn't get the part.) The next paragraph informed Helena that one American director had decided to shoot Melissa's scenes in England in order to secure her services. She was being talked about as the new Keira, the new Nicole, the new Julia. But she was, the reporter said, unmistakeably herself. Her role in *Simon's Way* was being expanded. She was extraordinarily convincing as Helena Harris's on-screen daughter – 'a slimmer, more elfin version of the older woman'. Each word was like a hammer blow, putting the nails into the coffin of her career. 'Slimmer,' she said out loud. '*More elfin,*' she hissed. 'OLDER WOMAN!' she shouted at the wall.

She threw the paper down, then snatched it up again, unable to resist torturing herself. Other roles were being written especially for Melissa. But the young actress intended to do the school run herself. She believed in cooking an organic meal for her husband every evening. Family would always come first: 'I don't believe in having children and leaving their care to other people,' she said. 'Motherhood will always be my most important job.'

Helena crumpled up the newspaper and threw it away, fuming. I too have turned down important roles for my family, she told herself. I too have done the school run and cooked organic food for my husband. And she'd been so kind to Melissa, giving her advice and guiding her gently when she was an ingénue straight out of drama school. But when the interviewer had asked Melissa which actresses she admired, she hadn't mentioned Helena. You'd think she could have had the good grace to acknowledge the woman who'd made *Simon's Way* the success it was. But Melissa was a survivor, an arch-manipulator. Helena suspected that the pressure to maximise Zoe's role at the expense of Mattie's had come from Melissa herself, despite her innocent, doe-eyed prettiness and apparent lack of pushiness. Perhaps Melissa's refusal to mention Helena was a compliment of a kind, that the younger woman didn't dare acknowledge that Helena was a threat. Yes, that was it. It was a compliment, it meant Melissa rated her. Not that she'd forgotten that she existed. Helena swallowed and clenched her fists. Positive Mental Attitude.

Eddie, too, was trying to convince himself that a positive mental attitude would help. When he left the tube station he walked along the central white line of the main road, ignoring car horns blasting and the risk of motorcycles threading their way through the traffic. He strode purposefully, his eyes on the road, checking everything out with his peripheral vision, then he would turn in to his road very suddenly. Once out of sight, he ran, clutching his house keys in his pocket. Every time he slammed the front door behind him his heart felt as if it was beating out of his chest, and he often found his forehead streaming with sweat. That was Strategy One. It couldn't be used too often, or they would lie in wait for him nearer his front door.

Strategy Two was not to go home at all, but to stay with friends. Strategy Three was to stay at home, pretending to have study leave and Strategy Four, which he had dismissed after careful consideration, was to tell the police and, by extension, his mother. However he didn't see what the police could do and he was terrified of retribution. If the gang thought he'd set the police on them, they would definitely beat him up. As for Helena – she would make the most terrible fuss, and the next thing he knew they'd all be in the papers, or in a minor celebrity magazine, with Helena photographed looking tearful and talking about how she had coped with her 'torment over her son's bullying', and leading a campaign to get policemen back on the beat. And that would bring down an avalanche of teasing at school, although he didn't care so much about that.

One evening they caught up with him just as he turned off into his road.

'Hi, rich boy.' It was Ty, the half-Chinese one who was blocking his way.

'Hi,' said Eddie, trying not to sound too middle-class, and stepping aside.

Ty blocked him again. 'Hi,' he mimicked in a high-pitched tone. 'Rich boy's getting friendly. We'll be invited to his place soon.'

Eddie forced himself not to look at his house in case they followed his gaze and worked out which one it was.

'We want money,' hissed a voice at his ear. 'And you got it.'

He felt something round and hard in his side. 'That's right. It's a gun,' hissed the voice, 'now get your money out now.'

Eddie's throat went dry. 'I don't have any.'

'Rich boys always have money.' They seized his backpack and tipped it out over the pavement while Eddie felt his knees begin to shake. He'd done self-defence classes, but throwing someone to the floor on a padded gym mat seemed completely unrelated to tackling a group of street-hardened youths with a gun. Even if it was probably fake, maybe even just a bit of piping.

His books sprawled across the pavement and into the gutter, and a photograph fluttered out. Ty giggled. 'Who's this geezer with you? Your lover, gay boy?'

'My grandfather,' said Eddie hoarsely. It was the only picture he had of them together.

'Your grandfather. How sweet is that?' The boy tore the photograph into tiny squares and flung them into the wind. A few blew into the road and cars passed over them, obliterating them in the grimy tarmac. Eddie forced himself to feel nothing. A photograph didn't matter.

'You tell your grandfather you has to have money in future, right? You don't come down dis road without it again.'

Chapter 15

Bramble and Nat went to the pub together several times. He shod a couple of horses. He suggested the cinema on Friday night and Bramble, who usually fell into her bed exhausted, and was often asleep by ten, felt oddly revitalised by having less sleep rather than more.

Nat occasionally touched her arm or her shoulder, and she was always aware of the warmth of his great body beside hers. They slotted together, she thought. They were friends, but there was something more there, waiting in the wings, a kind of tingle, sometimes a warmth . . . above all, it felt easy. She didn't have to prove herself to him.

The fourth time they went to the pub together, Bramble, washing her hands in the cracked peach-coloured basin in the ladies at the White Horse, looked at herself in the mirror. Her hair had grown out a little. It bubbled around her face, softening her features.

Perhaps she would let it grow a bit more. Cutting her hair had been like shoeing the horses: something to get done because it was thick and springy and could be a nuisance when it was longer. But she felt like a change.

Or was it that she felt changed already? She was more alive, as if her skin was thinner and there was electricity in the air. Something clattered into the basin and she saw that the third finger of her left hand was bare. There was a strip of white flesh where her wedding ring had been. She fished around the plughole, extracted the ring and held it for a moment, then took a deep breath and slipped it into her pocket. She looked at the cracked glass inset into the peach-tiled wall, and saw a woman with large brown eyes and smiled. She saw a woman who could be beautiful.

Is that how a marriage ends, she thought? With a ring falling off a finger and being tucked away in a pocket?

She opened the door of the ladies. Her marriage had ended seven years ago when Dom was killed. It was time to move on. Perhaps there was something about being out with a man, even one as friendly and undemanding as Nat, that made her feel different about herself.

When she returned to her seat, Nat had ordered another drink.

'I gather you knew Jez before?' she said, deliberately lifting the glass in her left hand, wondering if he would notice the ring of untanned skin on her finger.

'Mmm.' Nat chinked his glass to hers. 'Cheers. Yes, I did. Why? Has he said anything about me?'

'Nothing much. Just that you and . . . er . . . Jenny lived nearby for a couple of years.'

'How much do you know about him?' he asked.

'Not all that much. Just his background and that he was in the Army, and . . . why?'

'It's not for me to pass on gossip. There are always two sides to any story.'

'I'd like to know. He's living in my house, after all.'

'Don't let it go any further,' said Nat. 'I'd hate to be unfair to him. And I don't have any proof that all or any of it's true.'

'Go on.' Bramble was beginning to feel nervous.

'He lived with a woman called Penny who was quite a bit older than he was – she must be, what, late forties, even mid-fifties, by now – something like that. And she had the big house, and the stables and the smart horse box, and he had . . . well, charm and good looks. People thought, probably unfairly, that he was only with her so he could compete on the horses from her yard – in it for the money, basically.' Nat checked out her expression. 'Personally, I don't think it was that calculated. But I think there may have been at least some element of convenience in the relationship. He was officially her nagsman: he rode and trained her horses, and ran the yard, but everyone knew what the set-up was.'

Bramble thought it was typical of Nat's careful, balanced approach to life that he was so keen on putting Jez's behaviour in the best possible light. 'What happened?'

'He started having an affair with a married woman in the village we lived in,' said Nat. 'And when Penny found out about it, she threw him out. She packed his bags and left them outside. And, er, after that . . . look, are you sure you want to know all this?'

'Yes, yes. Of course I do.'

'He claimed she hadn't paid him for three months, so he broke into the house and took three hundred pounds and her grandfather's cufflinks. The police were called and they arrested him, but charges were dropped.'

'That's terrible. Just terrible.' Bramble was appalled.

'As I said, I don't think you should discuss this with anyone. Things are very complicated between couples and, well, if we were all judged on what we did wrong in an affair . . .' he laughed in a self-deprecating way '. . . well, none of us would look very pretty.'

Bramble was silent.

'And if it's any justification, I understand that she really hadn't paid him for three months. He was owed the money. And more.'

'That doesn't make it right.' Bramble was conscious of a huge sense of disappointment, as if Jez had let her down personally.

'Money is difficult in relationships. I got shafted, so I know what it's like. Jenny, my wife, was awarded our home and custody of our daughter, and I got nothing. The judge didn't think I deserved to play a part in my daughter's life and now I live in a rented cottage and see her whenever Jenny lets me. Which isn't often.'

'That's awful,' said Bramble, liking him more because he hadn't told her this before. And because he hadn't immediately gossiped about Jez – she'd had to force it out of him.

He took her left hand and held it. 'You're not wearing your ring?'

'It fell off.'

He turned her palm over and kissed it. She felt his lips against her skin and trembled.

'Welcome back to the world,' he whispered, gently holding her face in his big hands, very gently kissing her lips and lingering briefly – so briefly that she almost thought she might have imagined it.

'I wondered if I could ask you a huge favour?' Nat, drawing back, cleared his throat.

'Of course.' She sipped her wine, its warmth hitting the back of her throat and making her feel just slightly dizzy.

'There's a party being given by a vet's surgery I often link up with. Ten years of practice or something, and I've been invited with a partner . . .' His face, leaning towards hers in the flickering light of the pub's log fire, looked almost handsome, a tanned hero's face with lines that showed that he had lived.

'You wouldn't, by any chance, be able to come with me?'

'Oh.' Bramble took a deep breath.

He wrapped his hand round hers as it lay on the table, and it felt strong and protective. She thought of moving her own hand away, but she didn't really want to. 'Well,' she said, 'I . . . I'd love to come. Thank you.'

He squeezed her hand and let it go. 'Thank *you*.'

'Is it formal?' she asked, 'because I haven't got . . .'

'Don't worry,' he smiled, 'just party-ish. You look good in everything'. Sometimes, when she was with him, little chinks of happiness broke through the clouds of day-to-day life. And, deep down, there was something rather lovely about the idea of going somewhere with someone and belonging to them for the evening. She was getting sick of always having to go everywhere alone.

When he dropped her back at Lorenden he leaned over and kissed her again, and left her smiling, wanting more.

Felicity spent most of her time asleep. Her broken toe made her feel tired, as if the blood had drained out of her. And she was still angry. She was angry when it took her half an hour to get dressed in the morning. She was angry when she saw her father's writing on a piece of paper. All the anger she thought she'd forgotten came bubbling up. The post-mortem from her father had come back, and it had been his heart, after all. Sometimes Felicity thought her own might give out under the sheer weight of the fury she carried around inside her; that she might collapse with a heart attack herself.

So, he had given her a third share of Lorenden? Bully for him. Too little too late, as far as she was concerned. She was determined not to take sides, because that would draw her back into the family, so she didn't say anything when Helena used Bramble's absences from the house to sneak estate agents in. And she didn't tell Helena when she overheard Bramble tell people that Lorenden was not for sale. As she lay on her bed, smoking and staring at the rose-print wallpaper, she wondered why she was bothering. It was so clear that the only option was to sell up and split it between the three of them. Why didn't she just say 'OK, I agree with Helena, let's whack it on the market as soon as probate comes through?'

She didn't know. And that made her angry too. What am I doing here? She should have dumped Merlin and left him. Bramble would look after him, and she could have stowed the brief days with him back in the part of her heart where intimacy was kept locked away.

Felicity absent-mindedly went to slip her silver bracelets up her arms, but found they weren't there. You didn't wear jewellery in a stable, and now she was home she'd automatically gone back to the old ways without thinking.

That was the problem: without thinking. Her brief flight with Merlin had reminded her that with horses you had to be yourself. You couldn't fool them with glitter or wit, or a change in hair colour. 'Horses are prey,' her father had said. 'They survive by reading your body language. They are acutely aware of you, of what you're feeling and doing, more aware sometimes than you may be of yourself. That's what they respond to.'

Not like people, who could be deceived by what you wore and how you talked. She had rescued Merlin from the slaughterhouse on impulse, and had then arranged for him to come to England. Once on her own, in the rented horsebox, she had driven as quickly as she could to Lorenden but, without realising it, she'd got involved with him, and now she was here, and there didn't seem much chance of her getting away for a couple of months.

She used the excuse of her plaster cast not to go near the stables again, because the stables made her angry too. It hurt too much to smell the warm scent of horse and Merlin didn't need her now that he was here. She'd got close to him and nearly lost him. She didn't want that to happen again. They could look after him: Jez and Bramble. He'd be better off with them.

She lit another cigarette with the stub of the last and coughed. She supposed she ought to make a will herself. The terriers scratched at her door and whimpered to be let in. Why couldn't they leave her alone? Eventually she opened the door and two warm little bodies jumped on the bed and licked her face.

'Yuck,' she muttered. But she drew them to her and tickled their tummies absent-mindedly.

It was a shock to think that she now had enough money to have to make a will, and also that there was no one she particularly wanted to leave it to. It would be very convenient for everyone if she died quite soon and left everything to Bramble and Helena, or even to Savannah. They'd be hugely relieved, secretly.

She ought to write the most irritating will possible – maybe leaving it all to Retraining of Racehorses, or to Merlin himself. That would annoy Helena more than it would Bramble, though.

For the next hour Felicity amused herself, between cigarettes, by thinking up the most inconvenient will possible. She would divide it into complicated fractions – seventeenths, perhaps – and leave parts to her family and some to people who would be very difficult to find. What about that freedom fighter she had slept with among the bombed-out ruins of Sarajevo? What was his name again? Perhaps she should just leave her estate to be divided between all the married men she'd had affairs with, so that private detectives would have to be engaged to find them and they would be forced to explain their sudden little windfalls to their wives. She laughed briefly, and coughed again, and was surprised to feel tears start in her eyes.

'I am not a victim,' she told herself furiously, wiping them away. 'I don't do self-pity.'

She concluded by deciding that there was one person she could leave it all to, with the absolute guarantee that everyone in her family would be equally enraged – Major Jezzar Morgan. She chuckled again. And they would think she'd slept with him.

It was almost worth writing out the will leaving it all to Jez then throwing herself in front of a train. She could imagine the arguments, shock, outrage and surprise it would cause.

The phone rang in the kitchen at Lorenden, and Bramble answered it. 'Eddie! How are you?'

'Uh, fine.' This was followed by silence and Bramble strained to understand it.

'Uh, I, um . . . wondered if I could come down this weekend. And ride.'

'Of course. You know we always love to have you. Is Helena going to bring you or do you want to be picked up from the station?'

'Uh, er . . . Mum doesn't know . . . do you mind not mentioning it?'

Bramble took a deep breath. 'Eddie, I can't lie to your mother about where you are. Not even by "not mentioning it". But surely she wouldn't mind you coming down here? Do you want me to ask her?'

'No, no . . . please don't.'

'I could easily. I could speak to her now.'

'No, don't. Uh, sorry. Goodbye.' The phone went dead.

Now what was all that about? Helena was obviously really angry with them all if she wasn't even allowing Eddie to come down.

Meanwhile, the phone in Primrose Hill had gone so quiet that Helena occasionally lifted it to see if it still had a dialling tone. Perhaps it was the time of year. Although October was usually a busy social month.

It finally rang one afternoon, echoing over the hard floors and bare walls. Helena took two deep breaths before answering it.

It was Angelina inviting her to a 'girl's lunch'. 'I thought you might still be feeling low about your father.'

'Oh I do, I do. Terribly low. I never expected to feel so . . .' Helena's mind was still whirring over Mattie's television future and her role in *Simon's Way* '. . . well, just low. It's just so kind of you. It's at times like this that you really appreciate your friends, isn't it?

'Will we be seeing you at the Bonds'?'

'The Bonds'?' Helena thought furiously. The Bonds had an annual party. Everybody who was anybody was invited. If you were successful you would be at the Bonds'. If you were on the way out, they were the first to know and they would be quite ruthless about striking a pencil through your name. But surely it was usually held near Christmas?

'You do know them?' queried Angelina. 'Jonno and Lulu?' Jonno and Lulu Bond, often referred to jokingly as the Bondages because of their sexy theme parties, were a husband-and-wife team. They produced and directed everything. Everything you'd ever want to be in.

'Of course I know Jonno and Lulu.' Helena tried not to snap. 'But there are so many invitations at the moment that I keep forgetting . . . can you just remind me?'

'Their Christmas party. On November fifth this year. They're so original, aren't they? A Christmas party on bonfire night.'

Helena thought that the entire world might be going completely mad. 'Oh God, *that*,' she improvised. 'Well, of course we'll go if we can but it is *so* busy . . .'

'Well of course we're busy too.' Angelina sounded irritated to be out-busied. 'But we don't like to let Jonno and Lulu down.'

Helena raced up to Ollie's office. 'Have we had an invitation from the Bondages? For some idiotic Christmas party on Guy Fawkes night?'

Ollie swung round. He was leaning back in his chair, hands linked behind his neck, looking out the window, as far as she could see. 'For God's sake,' he said. 'I am working, you know. You've just broken my train of thought.'

'Sorry. But is there any post I haven't seen?'

Ollie indicated his desk. There was a pile of papers on it. 'Only yesterday's. I was going to bring it downstairs later on.'

Helena rummaged frantically through the mess and picked out several unopened envelopes. 'Is that it? Is there any more?'

Ollie shrugged. 'I've been thinking about more important things.'

'Well, I've been thinking about whether we're being invited to fewer parties because I might be dropped as Mattie,' hissed Helena, who could see from the franking on the envelopes that there were no invitations there. 'You don't get much more important than that.'

Ollie raised an eyebrow: 'World peace? Making poverty history? Stopping half-arsed groups of terrorists getting their hands on atomic bombs?'

She put her hands over her ears. 'Stop it! Stop it now! I'm talking about important to *us*. I don't care about world peace and terrorism, I care about my family, about keeping my home, and my children in their schools, and . . .'

'. . . and whether you'll go on being invited to parties and can afford designer gear. Yeah, yeah.' Ollie managed to find a space for his feet on his desk and picked at his teeth with a matchstick. 'And it's *our* children by the way. *Our* home. Unless I'm just the hired help round here.'

'No, sorry, you're right. I didn't mean it. I meant us. We. Ours. That's all that matters to me.' Helena tore one of the envelopes open. 'Shit, Ollie, what's this? Twenty thousand pounds on a credit card bill?' She held it towards him.

He took it from her and looked at it. 'Don't be silly. It's two thousand.' He stuffed it into his pocket. 'Give me a break, Helena.'

'Sorry. Sorry.' She started to bite her nails and stopped herself. 'I'm just so worried about this Mattie thing.'

He took his feet off the desk and picked up his pen. 'Well, if you lose Mattie you can find another part. You're a star.' In the one tiny corner of her mind that wasn't numb with panic, Helena thought she detected a note of bitterness in his voice.

'You don't understand,' she screamed. 'I've *never* been successful at anything except Mattie. I was earning eight thousand a year when *Simon's Way* came along. Bit parts and the odd radio play. I've never, ever done anything else well. Ever. If I lose Mattie I lose *everything*. I failed to get the last few parts I went for. I fail to get pretty much anything I go for at the moment.' She stopped. She had never let her guard down like this. Not to Ollie, or anyone else. You could never let anyone see how frightened you were, how weak or how vulnerable. Not even your husband. You must pretend, pretend, pretend and, if you carried on, the pretence eventually became a reality. She could not even *say* the word 'failure', or she would be letting it in the door. And now she had admitted it. Out loud. She had said 'fail' twice and that door had opened, revealing a black, yawning chasm on the other side. She might never be able to close it again.

She gazed at Ollie, terrified, willing him to say something, anything, that might make it better for her.

His eyes hooded as he withdrew his attention from her. 'I'm sure everything will be fine,' he said wearily. 'But you *must* let me work. I simply can't achieve anything when you go on at me like this. Now it'll take me hours to get my concentration back. You've virtually written off the whole of my day.'

'Yes, of course,' she whispered. 'Sorry.' As she closed the door, her mobile rang. The number on the display was Caroline's. Her hands were shaking so much she could barely press the answer button or register where she'd thrust the unopened letters. Nothing else existed except the phone and the message it would convey. 'Hello?' she asked, trying to sound normal.

'Well,' said Caroline in her gravelly voice, 'Helena darling, what can I say?'

Savannah studied the subject of food as hard as she worked for her GCSEs. Harder. She found every single calorie booklet, fat counter, diet article and recipe book that she could and began to take over the kitchen at home. That way, she could remain in control and make sure that no one presented her with an unexpected, irresistible blackberry-and-apple crumble or extra crisp, fragrant roast potato. Bramble was too busy to question her new interest and Felicity praised her for her efforts. 'This is delicious, Savannah,' she'd say. 'How clever you are.' Being praised by Felicity was like being awarded a medal. Savannah saw how sharply she spoke to everyone else. And Jez smiled his appreciation, or placed a hand on her shoulder.

All round, it was a win-win situation.

She thought about food all the time. Every hour that passed without eating was a victory. Every night that she went to bed feeling hungry was an indication of success. Every time she felt sick or weak from lack of food, she reminded herself that you had to suffer if you wanted to win. 'I'll get to the end of mucking out this stable, or writing this essay,' she told herself, 'then I'll let myself have a black coffee or a Diet Coke.'

Sometimes she was aware of Felicity watching her. 'You're doing a lot of cooking,' she observed.

'Well, it's to help my mother. She's so busy.' Savannah treated Felicity to the kind of smile she reserved for teachers, dressage judges and Masters of Foxhounds.

'Can I help at all?'

'No, thank you,' replied Savannah. She didn't want Felicity finding out what she was really up to, as she had an idea that Felicity might be an awful lot more difficult to fool than Bramble and she didn't trust either of them not to try to make her eat fattening things. It was quite strange, suddenly having a relationship with someone who had never been anything more to her than a signature on a Christmas or birthday card. But the signature had always been accompanied by a fiver, then a tenner, so Savannah had always liked Felicity, in a vague, impersonal way.

'Felicity,' said Savannah suddenly, one day.

Felicity stopped at the door. 'Yes?'

'How did you become a war reporter? Was it something you always wanted to do?'

Felicity smiled. 'I had an affair with the managing director of the TV news company and he thought I'd be good at it. And I was.'

Savannah swallowed. 'Wasn't it . . . scary?'

Felicity nodded. 'It was exciting.' She smiled slightly. 'People don't like to admit it but wars are always exciting. Like going across country on a horse that's too much for you, in atrocious weather, and going clear all the same.'

Savannah wasn't sure what else to say. Felicity left the room and Savannah turned back to the biggest thing in her life at the moment: food.

It's not as if she wasn't being careful. She was. She was supplementing her diet with vitamins and minerals. She weighed out meat, fish and chicken with pinpoint accuracy, stripping each portion of any trace of fat, filling her plate with piles of vegetables. Her stomach became distended and painfully windy. She was left feeling unsatisfied, and desperate for a taste of sweetness.

But sweet was evil. And if she ate butter Jez would never love her. Jez had crept into her dreams. Donna, one day after evening stables, invited her up to the loft and they cleaned tack together, watching a DVD of a romantic movie.

'He reminds me of Jez,' said Donna, as the hero had a predictably argumentative first exchange with the heroine. 'It's that combination of blue eyes and very dark hair. And the unshaven look. It gets me every time.'

'Jez's eyes aren't blue,' replied Savannah. 'They're a sort of grey-blue. Like a pebbly beach in winter.'

Donna looked at her thoughtfully. 'Fancy him then?'

'Of course not.' Savannah blushed.

'You do,' shrieked Donna. 'Don't blame you, though, so do I. Tell you what, let's have a race. First to get a proper kiss gets him. Until then, all's fair in love and war.'

Savannah was horrified at the thought of competing with sexy, confident Donna. 'Um, I . . .'

'There you are, then.' Donna held out her hand and slapped Savannah's to seal the deal.

Food began to get between Savannah and Lottie. Lottie had always hung around the yard as often as her mother would allow, between violin lessons, French club, yoga and whatever lesson or activity was currently deemed the best way of stimulating young minds and bodies. She'd been sent to an expensive private school with a long day, but at weekends she not only groomed and fussed over Sailor with all the lovingness of a lonely child, but helped out wherever else she could in the yard, completing each task with intense, careful seriousness.

But she'd always been skinny, like a string bean, and rarely finished her plateful. Her most irritating habit, in Savannah's mind, was the way she was always leaving half-eaten Mars Bars or Twixes around. They tormented Savannah. 'Aren't you going to finish this?' she'd demand. 'It's such a waste.'

Lottie looked surprised. 'You have it.' Savannah instead broke it into tiny pieces and threw them into the rubbish bin one by one, stirring the contents of the bin as she did so. She couldn't quite trust herself not to fish it all out and eat it unless it was so thoroughly mixed in that she could barely detect the shards of chocolate in among the detritus of tea leaves, old curry and plastic wrapping.

Lottie gazed at her, worried. 'Are you OK?'

'Of course, I'm absolutely fine,' said Savannah, pretending that what she was doing was normal.

She began to slip food through her fingers at the table, into the willing mouths of Darcy, Mop and Muddle, although they occasionally gave her away by wagging their tails enthusiastically and licking their lips. 'I dropped something by accident,' she would say.

She no longer cared about telling the truth.

Chapter 16

Helena frequently drove down from London, apparently with the express purpose of trapping Felicity in a corner.

'You see, Felicity, I can see everyone's point about maintaining the status quo until Savannah leaves school and Bramble gets more established,' Helena waved her hands in the air to demonstrate, 'I *can see*. I *am* sympathetic. But the problem is that there'll never be a convenient time to sell. There'll always be a Burghley or Badminton, or the Olympics or the World Games or whatever . . .'

'You obviously have great faith in Bramble if you think she's going to make all those,' observed Felicity.

'Well!' Helena, flustered, started back-tracking. 'It was a manner of speaking. *Of course* I have faith in Bramble, although she's obviously not quite going to get to that level. But everyone says Jez could and he's here . . . come on, Felicity, you know what I mean. How am I going to suddenly say, OK everyone, out now, two or three years down the line?'

'Well, it's what you're saying now.'

'And no one is taking a blind bit of notice, so that rather proves my point. It isn't fair.'

Felicity thought she heard the cry of a neglected child in Helena's voice. It's not fair. She refrained from saying, as their father would have said, 'Yes, well, life isn't fair.'

Helena got up and prowled round the room. 'Oh, I hadn't noticed that.' She stopped at a little oil painting tucked behind a lamp. 'I don't think the valuer saw that. Shall I take it up to London and have it looked at?'

Felicity shrugged. She was too tired to deal with Helena. She couldn't decide about Lorenden. She could barely decide what to wear, or what to eat. As her toe healed she expected to feel better, and ready to leave again, but she couldn't find the energy. The days and nights of sleeping were ebbing away and being replaced by an inability to sleep at all.

At night terrible images from wars she had covered flickered constantly through her brain and she struggled into consciousness, sweating and sobbing, over and over again. She would feel for the lamp, always wondering where it was, and where she was, and then, switching it on, would be overwhelmed by sadness – yet obscurely comforted – at the sight of the wallpaper. Sometimes she slept with the light on.

During the day she was so tired she could barely open her eyes. Somewhere the brave woman who had flown into places most people were trying to get out of had turned into someone who jumped at shadows. The toe was healing quickly, but she clung to using one crutch. I'm still hurting, she told herself. Still hurting. I can't make a decision yet.

'Wait until probate comes through, none of us can decide until then,' she told Helena, wearily.

They were suddenly plunged into a bitterly cold November. The wind off the marshes cut across Bramble's face like a knife, and the coppers and golds of autumn turned quickly to the greys, purples and browns of winter. On the edge of the fields, drifts of teasel heads were outlined in frost, and the horses' breath plumed in the morning air.

The horses relaxed in the fields on their annual holiday. They were turned out more than usual – all day – in groups of three or four to a field, growing thicker, furry coats and enjoying a certain amount of muddy self-indulgence. Jez was proved right – there were no more injuries than normal, and even Bramble conceded that the horses seemed more relaxed.

Merlin was another matter. He had so much to learn. A race-horse is never mounted from the ground – jockeys are always given a leg-up or use a mounting block. Bramble and Jez taught him to allow people on board from a foot in the stirrup. They rode him at a walk every day to build his muscles up, then started him trotting. But he couldn't rid himself of the habit of going from zero to flat-out in five seconds. Taught to start galloping immediately from the stalls at the start of a race, he was quite capable of surging forward at the least encouragement – which, for him, meant a twitch of the reins, the brush of a heel – and he was off, soaring across the fields then, equally suddenly, stopping hard. He unseated everyone, even Jez, and his speciality was the 'whip round'. This was a lightning movement, guaranteed to get eject his rider out of the side door without having to go to the trouble of bucking.

He was suspicious of most things, and hated leaving the group. Bramble was patient, urging him to trot away from the others for a short time then rejoining them before he had a chance to get too worried about it. He danced sideways and pulled to rejoin his stablemates.

'Racehorses,' she sighed to Jez one day. 'I know all horses hate leaving the herd, but racehorses . . .' She shook her head. 'They've spent their lives being exercised in strings and raced in groups – I really wonder if he'll ever be really happy out on his own.'

'He needs time,' said Jez, 'that's all.' The winter shadows drew in round them and the hard yellow stable lights flooded the cold yard. 'One day Felicity will be able to ride him.'

Felicity was standing beside them – yet not quite there, in her own dream world as usual – leaning on one crutch. They both looked at her.

'I'm only just out of plaster,' said Felicity, 'and I don't ride any more.'

'Hmm,' said Jez. 'That toe should be strong enough now.'

Felicity flinched, as if he'd hit her. 'I haven't ridden for thirty years, and I couldn't ride Merlin even if I did start again.'

'Wait,' said Jez, looking at the stables. Lottie had just returned with Sailor. He strode across the yard and Bramble could see patches of sweat where his T-shirt clung to him, outlining the sinews of his powerful shoulders. She wondered why he never felt the cold. It was almost arrogant to wear cotton in the winter like that.

He returned with Sailor, still saddled up, and a riding hat in one hand, which he thrust at Felicity. 'Up you get.'

'What?' Felicity stared at him.

'You need to ride. Because with a talent like yours – I've seen the photos – you need to get back to competing. It's the only way you'll start living again.'

He handed Sailor's reins to Felicity, bent down and, before she could protest, lifted her lightly into the saddle.

Bramble suppressed a stab of jealousy. She wanted Felicity to ride again, but she'd grown up with the tales of the magical girl who could ride anything, the champion that never was, and she'd always assumed that she, Bramble, was second best. She followed Jez and Felicity to the sand school, trying not to feel left out.

Helena tapped on Ollie's door.

'Yes!' he shouted. 'What the hell is it now?'

She stood there, mobile in hand, trembling. 'I'm sorry,' she whispered, her voice quivering. 'I'm so sorry. I've let you down. I've let everyone down.' She dreaded what Ollie was going to say. She dreaded being blamed for piling the pressure on him, for forcing him to write when he wasn't ready because she wasn't earning.

'What?' He pushed himself away from his desk.

The tears spilled down her cheeks. 'Mattie.' She tried to compose herself and to speak clearly. 'I've lost Mattie. It's top secret and we can't tell anyone, but they're not renewing my contract, so it must be me they're killing.'

Ollie stood up and pulled her to him. 'Don't cry, darling.' They stood clasped together, rocking back and forth, as he whispered comforting, gentle, reassuring phrases. 'Don't cry. It'll be all right. I'll look after you. There'll be another part. You deserve a break. We can manage. Dearest. Honeybunch. My darling.' All the things she had longed for him to say. She began to cry, jerkily and noisily, the kind of crying that she never did on television – wild, desperate, choking sobs that racked her whole body and almost suffocated her. Her face was wet and even her hands were running with tears. It was only the thought of her nose and the terrible inelegance of not having a handkerchief that eventually slowed the torrent. Ollie passed her a tissue.

I didn't cry like this for my father. She suppressed that treacherous thought. These tears are probably for him, too. The shock. Grief emerges at curious times. Of course I am not the kind of person who grieves more for a lost job than for a dead parent. She suddenly had a sharp pang for the warm, cluttered kitchen at Lorenden, even the sub-zero temperatures of the echoing hall and the big, squashy sofas and beds. It was still home, and her father was still there. In the next room, somehow, never quite in her line of vision, just out of earshot. She must go down again soon and begin to sort through the stuff she'd left there since childhood. It was a comforting, bittersweet thought. Lorenden was still there.

Ollie steered her to his chair and sat her down, waiting for her to finish blowing her nose and wiping her eyes. 'Tell me exactly what Caroline said.'

Helena gulped. 'She said she'd done the best she could for me in the circumstances. I didn't dare ask what circumstances. I suppose there must have been some terrible viewer research. They must have said I was boring or stuck-up or irrelevant in today's multicultural society or something. Too middle-class. Or middle-aged. Too married. Not edgy enough. I don't know. Mattie's going to get breast cancer and it's going to turn out to be much more serious than anyone thinks. They want me to die sooner rather than later because they don't want to end the series on a downer. They want Simon to start dating again and, get this . . .' Helena laughed wildly '. . . they want me to come back as a ghost and tell him I want him to make a new life for himself. He's supposed to be holding back out of grief, but I tell him to move on. I'm supposed to say, "Go ahead, just date that nineteen-year-old girl," or "Do spend the night with my oldest friend," or whatever!' Helena began to cry again. 'As if I would. As if *any* woman would. But Caroline was pleased she'd negotiated the ghost scenes because it means a bit more exposure, a bit more money. A stay of execution, she called it.' She blew her nose again.

'Well, at least we'll get a decent amount of dosh from this series,' said Ollie. 'And it'll give you time to get Lorenden sorted. So we do have a bit of breathing space.'

Helena, who had never wanted breathing space – she wanted to work, and she wanted it passionately – nodded and blinked.

'Has Caroline got any other roles you might go for?'

'I'm going in to see her later this week.'

Ollie pulled up a stool and took each of her hands in one of his, kissing the tightly clenched knuckles in turn. 'Good. Positive mental attitude. Remember?'

Helena nodded, trying to ignore the tight, sick feeling in her stomach.

'Good girl,' he repeated. 'You'll be back in before you know it.'

Helena nodded again, determined to suppress the thought that she might not. 'It's a *good* thing, my leaving the series,' she said, resolving that from that moment onwards, she would be 'leaving' not 'losing'. 'There are so many things I want to do and, really, I'd gone beyond Mattie.'

'Of course you had.'

'And I need to spend more time with my family, too. Eddie's A levels are more important than any television part, and Ruby and Roly need more of my attention. This'll give me a chance to focus on the more important things in life. The things that matter. You, for example.'

'Me? asked Ollie. 'What about me?' She thought he sounded slightly hunted.

'Well, I need to give you more time and space to work. And if I'm less busy then I won't have to keep relying on you for trivial things like picking up the twins from school when Ania has her classes.'

'Oh, that.' He sounded relieved. 'Of course all that would be a great help. A very great help.'

'I can't tell you how much this means to me, Ollie,' Helena's eyes were stinging with tears that threatened to flow again. 'Knowing that you're there for me. Knowing that I can rely on you.'

'Oh, you can rely on me all right,' said Ollie in a hearty voice. 'I'm the one person you can always rely on. Listen: let's neither of us do any work today. Let's celebrate. The start of your new life. Your liberation.'

'It is, isn't it? A liberation. A chance to escape. Of course, I've been wanting to do something different for years, but they were always so keen to do another series. There are so many other things I need to do.' She felt across Ollie's desk for another tissue.

'Way to go, baby, way to go. Now, I'll take you out. To . . . where would you like to go?'

'I'd rather not go out just yet.' Helena was aware that, at her age, a crying session like this could not easily be eradicated, even with copious applications of Touche Eclat. That only a good night's sleep could restore the dewy freshness to the delicate skin around her eyes and get rid of the last traces of bloodshot whites. It would be a disaster if she was seen looking upset. She needed the rumours about Mattie quashed, not stoked.

'OK.' Ollie stood up. 'I'll go to the deli and get us a special lunch.'

Helena hoped he wouldn't want sex afterwards. Still, he was being so sweet that perhaps he deserved it. Not a good idea to forget that a man needs regular servicing. She giggled at the thought.

Ollie smiled. 'It's good to see you cheering up already. Come on. Sit on the sofa. Put on your favourite music and chill.'

As the front door closed behind him she wondered if losing Mattie had, after all, been the best possible outcome, however painful it was now. She felt so much closer to Ollie. This could be exactly what they needed to revitalise their relationship. Sometimes it really wasn't a good idea for one partner to be much more successful than the other, particularly when the more successful one was a woman. Her having a bit of downtime (but not too much, she hoped) could be the balance that they needed as a couple. Dear Ollie. She would have a few months out and really look after him, and make sure that he had the conditions he needed to finish his screenplay. By that time she'd be back in business again and they could both go back to where they were.

Yes. Losing – no, *leaving* – *Simon's Way* really was a cause for celebration. She decided to go down to the cellar and get a very special bottle. When they'd married their wedding list had been placed with a prominent wine merchant. 'We've got all the things like toasters and pillowcases,' she'd told people. 'We've both had houses for ages. So we thought it would be a bit different to start a proper cellar. Wine that you lay down for drinking in five or ten years' time.' She and Ollie had planned power dinner parties with outstanding wines as well as intimate evenings with a few friends –

or even just each other – tasting the best of the best. Being able to say, 'Oh, I often think Puligny Montrachet is a bit over-rated', and to gain a reputation for fine entertaining. 'We'll drink better wines and drink less,' they'd told each other, laughing and toasting their future in their favourite champagne. They both liked Veuve Clicquot. They were so well matched. Yes, the wine cellar had been part of the dream of their brilliant, perfect lives together.

The wine itself, of course, had needed a few years to reach its best, but what with doing up a new house, having the twins and *Simon's Way*, there hadn't been time for much more than an annual party with cheap champagne. They had even left the wine in cases, stacked one on top of the other, always meaning to get proper racks some day. But now, she thought, part of her come-back could be a series of very carefully orchestrated dinners to maximise networking opportunities. She knew she could get a few key people pinned down – Angelina and Chris Woody, for example – get everyone else in by dropping their names. People would know that Helena Harris was still a Player.

Buoyed up by the prospect of a plan, she negotiated the steep, narrow steps down into the cellar, and surveyed the choice. Would a white be cold enough? It was chilly down here, and she could always bung it into the freezer for half an hour while Ollie was shopping. Aha. A very nice . . .

She opened the box. It came open easily, as if it had already been opened. And the box was empty. They must have used it up without noticing. Careless of them. They'd always promised themselves they wouldn't glug these wines down.

She opened the next box. It, too, was empty. She was irritated. By the third, she was getting worried. She opened thirty-six boxes, her anger mounting with each box. Every single one was empty.

'Ollie,' she said, as he came back through the door just before one o'clock. She thrust an empty cardboard box at him. In the other hand she held an empty wine bottle, garnered from a pile that she had discovered in the cupboard in his room.

'What exactly is the meaning of all this?'

Chapter 17

Felicity landed in the saddle with a brief sensation that her limbs had become oddly disconnected, before they immediately settled into the ways and shapes that had been hard-wired into her brain from her earliest days. For thirty years she had been half-Felicity, and now, high enough off the ground to see things differently, she was whole Felicity again. Sailor's saddle creaked as he walked forward, and it took barely a few seconds to adjust to his stride.

'I can't do this,' she said to Jez in sudden panic, as the old feelings overwhelmed her.

He led Sailor into the school without answering and, once inside, he closed the gate and turned to her. 'Walk on,' he commanded.

And Felicity set out, her pelvis swaying in time with Sailor's gait. She circled the arena, gradually easing into it, noticing that the trees had grown taller since she last rode here and were now obscuring the view of the fields, that she could see across to the house and that the roof was missing a few tiles. But above all, coming through with every step, there was a sense of unity with Sailor, the warm smell of horse rising up from the wonderful, powerful muscles beneath her, capable of surging forward at her command.

A group of people gathered to watch her, the way they always do when someone rides, thought Felicity with sudden recognition. Donna, always glad of the chance for a break, eating a KitKat, Bramble resting her chin in her hands, elbows on the wooden rails, watching intently for any sign of danger, the dogs, always alert to any new developments, Lottie and Savannah, heads together, probably criticising her style – well, that's what I would have done at their age if a middle-aged woman had suddenly got on my horse – and Jez, poised to instruct, his body language telling her, and Sailor, that he was in charge so nobody needed to worry about anything . . . all these thoughts drifted through her head as she gathered up the reins and felt the contact of Sailor's mouth on the bit.

'Trot on at H, then twenty-metre circle at A,' called Jez.

She was surprised to feel herself slotting into the old rhythm as easily as if she had ridden yesterday, but there was no doubt that her body was older, stiffer and less strong. Her fitness let her down and she had to catch her breath. She picked up within seconds, her breathing deeper and sharper in time with the rising trot. She was out of condition. She shouldn't be puffing like this but, otherwise, it felt so . . . so right.

After twenty minutes of trotting, in circles, serpentines and figures of eight, changing direction under Jez's command, he asked if she'd like to try a canter. She urged Sailor forward, feeling the smooth, rocking-horse motion beneath her, hearing the rhythmic creak of the saddle again and looking between his ears at the ground ahead. On a horse you are a god, she thought, a being with superhuman strength and speed. The ancients knew that. How did I manage to forget it?

Jez signalled to her to slow down to walk and came towards her. 'I think that's enough for today.'

She leant forward along Sailor's neck to speak to him as she took her feet out of the stirrups and slid down to the ground. Her legs trembled with the unfamiliar effort.

'Well?' Bramble was waiting.

Felicity knew exactly what they were doing. Get Felicity back on a horse, and then she'll stay. Bramble didn't care about her, only about keeping Lorenden.

But you can't stay angry on a clear November day. The last sunshine is too precious. Felicity, warmed by the blood coursing through her veins, smiled. 'Good. It was good. But don't go thinking I can go back to what I was. I'm a hell of a lot older for a start.'

Jez ran up Sailor's stirrups and took the reins to hand him back to Lottie, who was hovering with a polo.

'None of us can ever go back,' he said in a low voice, that only she could hear. 'But you can choose how you go forward.'

Helena and Ollie screamed at each other about the wine. Ollie said that Helena was a controlling, selfish, manipulative bitch and Helena shouted that Ollie had betrayed her and that she could never forgive him. Eddie came in to find a CD and hastily backed out again.

Ollie pointed out that living with Helena was so stressful that it was no wonder that he drank. 'You make me drink,' he shouted. 'It's all your fault. I was almost teetotal when I met you. But you have to have the best of everything, and everything has to be done your way. I've tried to fit in, and keep up my writing, but it's tearing me apart. Tearing me apart, do you understand? I've given you everything, what more do you want? My lifeblood?'

Helena sank down on the huge white sofa with her hands covering her ears. 'Don't say any more. Don't say a word!'

Ollie collapsed beside her. 'We need some changes,' he said, after fifteen minutes punctuated only by Helena's breathless, squeaky sobbing. 'Both of us. A new beginning. We have choices.'

Helena, facing the end of her marriage with terror, gazed at him almost without hearing. 'We do?'

'You've got this great break now you're free of the series. This fab chance to start again,' he said, placing a cautious hand on her shoulder. 'We can be different. We can cut the stress. If you can change, so can I.'

'The thing that's stressing me is this business with Lorenden,' said Helena, closing her eyes and leaning back against the sofa. 'I just feel as if my sisters are trying to do me out of what is rightfully mine, or even if they do intend to sell they'll wait so long we'll hit a downturn in the property market.'

Ollie got up, walked round the back of the sofa and began to massage her shoulders. 'You're so right, darling. So right. They're taking you for a ride and I, for one, won't allow it.' He dropped a kiss on the top of her head. 'We're in this together, aren't we?'

Helena's hand crept up towards his. She felt bruised, like someone who'd fallen into a turbulent, icy river and been rescued. 'Oh, Ollie.' She squeezed his hand. 'Ollie. Please. As long as you can cut down on your drinking.'

He rested his lips in her hair. 'Of course, darling. I would do anything for you, you know that. Anything.'

Bramble lay in bed at night with figures whirling round her head. There were such huge differences between the various valuations of Lorenden. One minute she had worked out how she could get a mortgage to buy Helena out – but that always relied on Felicity wanting to stay – and then she'd be dividing up what they might get into three, taking off inheritance tax and wondering where on earth she could find a house – a bungalow, or perhaps even a caravan – with stables and paddocks for that price. If she had to leave Lorenden, she wanted to carry on somewhere else, but that wasn't going to come cheap.

Nat reassured her constantly: 'You will find something else you like. You do need to leave Lorenden. Buy your own place. Be your own person.' He also encouraged her to think that developers wouldn't be such a bad thing. 'Someone will do it. Lorenden has changed every hundred years or so for centuries. You can't freeze it the way it was when you were a child.'

'You don't understand,' she said, and he laughed.

'Nobody understands anyone else.'

The more she relied on Nat, the less she trusted Jez. Every time he said something she wondered whether to believe him.

He walked through the kitchen one evening, having spent an hour in the pub.

'I've heard a rumour that Pauline might be selling Teddy.' His face was deadpan. 'At least, that's what they're saying.'

'What? Who's saying? How do you know? She'd never do that without telling us.' Bramble turned cold inside. Pauline hardly came over any longer. She had been one of the most frequent faces around the kitchen table. Bramble had thought she was too busy with Alan. There were rumours circulating about how vague he was getting.

'I heard,' he said. 'On the grapevine.'

'Well, perhaps you didn't hear right,' replied Bramble, picking up the phone and dialling. 'Pauline? How are you?'

Pauline trilled about how cold it was, and how winter always made everyone feel sad, and whether Bramble had had a flu jab.

'Pauline, I've heard this ridiculous rumour that I thought I ought to mention . . . people are saying that Teddy's for sale.'

There was a silence at the other end of the line.

'Bramble, darling, you really mustn't listen to gossip.'

'So he's not?'

'Well, people are always asking me if I will sell, of course. Perhaps that's what you've been hearing. Let's have no more talk like this. Now, we haven't seen you for ages. When can you come round for a drink?'

Bramble put the phone down after a short conversation about how Alan was. 'She's not selling him. You know how rumours get about.'

Jez shrugged and left the room.

It was difficult, working with a man. No, she rephrased that: this was a world where men and women were equal. But it was *different* working with a man who was her own age and with roughly her level of experience. Her father had been older and it was his yard, the occasional male working pupil much younger and deferential. Now she might theoretically be in charge, but Jez walked in his own skin and every time they clashed, Bramble could feel a hot, pink blush creeping up her neck. She only ever thought of a good retort about three hours later.

She examined every possible infringement of respect over and over in her mind. She grumbled to Felicity, who wandered in looking for a glass of wine.

'Does he leave the yard untidy?' Felicity asked.

'No, but . . .'

'And he cleans the tack properly? Doesn't leave jobs for you? Empties and cleans out the horsebox? Is a good rider?'

'Horses go well for him,' admitted Bramble.

'So what *is* it, Bramble? What is wrong?'

'It's his *attitude*,' she'd blurted out. 'I can't describe it.'

'But what about *your* attitude? Has it occurred to you that this is mostly in your head, and that's where you need to sort it out?'

Bramble opened her mouth to say something but words failed to emerge.

Felicity was looking amused. 'I thought you were so sensible and easy-going. Isn't that what everyone says about you? Don't tell me you've grown up and found out that the world isn't such a lovely place after all?'

'Perhaps,' hissed Bramble, 'if this is so unlike me, and I'm normally an easy-going person, then people might consider, for one moment, that I might have a case and that I'm not actually going mad.'

'We're all mad,' said Felicity. 'But that doesn't mean it's Jez's fault.'

'I don't know why you're taking his side.'

'It's not a question of sides. It's all about the efficient running of the yard. I think you resent Jez because he's not Pa. It's Pa you're angry at.'

'You're one to talk,' retorted Bramble. 'We're living in suspended animation here because you're so angry at Pa you can't make up your mind. You should come back here – you know you should – and run the yard with me. This is where you belong.'

The words were out. Bramble hadn't meant to say them, not yet. And she hadn't meant to say them so angrily.

Felicity turned pale. 'I'm not coming back,' she said. 'Just because I'm not sure what I'm doing, it doesn't mean I'm back to stay. And if you think it does I'll leave tonight. I don't want any illusions. I don't want anyone thinking I'm letting them down when I do go.'

'No,' said Bramble. 'Don't go. I didn't mean it. Let's just muddle along as we are.'

'I can't be your saviour, Bramble,' whispered Felicity. 'I can't even save myself. Please don't rely on me. I'm no good.'

'Save me? I don't need anyone to save me. I suppose you feel sorry for me, poor Bramble with the husband that died and who's never left home, while you're the big-shot war reporter who's travelled all over the world . . .'

'What? What on earth are you talking about? The only person who's feeling sorry for *you* is you yourself.'

'Are you accusing me of self-pity?'

'No, I'm accusing you of not facing the facts. Pa has died and things will change. Deal with it.'

'Do you think I don't know that?' Bramble suppressed tears. 'But don't go now.' She struggled to keep her voice even. 'Merlin needs you.' She couldn't quite force herself to say, 'I need you.'

'Merlin?'

Bramble nodded. 'Now you're fit again, Jez and I thought you could start exercising him.'

'Now I know you're trying to murder me.'

'You need to make decisions about him, about what he's going to be,' added Bramble. 'Ever since he's been here you've completely ignored him.'

Felicity shrugged. 'You can do all that.'

'No, we can't. He's yours, and we could do with the help in the yard.'

'I could pay livery.'

'No, it's partly your yard. There's no way I could charge and, I suspect, no way you could pay. Anyway, you're not scared of hard work, are you?'

Felicity's smile was a sunburst, dazzling the room the way she always had over the years, when she used to return in exotic outfits, laughing and drinking before flitting off again like a butterfly. 'No, I suppose the one thing you can say for me is that I'm not scared of hard work. Anyway, back to the beginning of this conversation, why not give poor Jez a break,' she added. 'He's not the cause of your problems.'

'Poor Jez, yeah,' Bramble tried to make her own voice jokey.

'He's good, you know. I've been away all this time, but you can always tell, can't you?'

'Fucking horseman of the East,' muttered Bramble crossly. 'Next you'll be saying it's in his genes. All those thousands of years of Tatar horsemanship.'

Felicity smiled. 'Maybe we're all the result of what our families did a thousand years ago. Did you know the Tatars could make their horses sit?' she asked, as if looking for a change of subject.

'I don't want my horse to sit,' said Bramble through gritted teeth. 'Particularly not when I'm riding it.'

They both laughed.

But it went on.

'What's this "Dreyfuss" at ten? In the diary?' asked Bramble, steadying herself one morning as she walked across the yard. An almost invisible film of black ice coated the puddles.

Jez forked manure neatly into the wheelbarrow and straightened up. Much as Bramble hated to admit it, his strength and vigour was well beyond hers and Donna's. Or even her father's. Jez was spare and lean, all muscle and sinew and bone. He worked quickly, at twice the speed of anyone else and achieved three times as much, and Bramble couldn't help resenting it. It made her feel uneasy, as if her role was being chipped away. She was used to being the strong one, the person everyone looked to when there was a problem.

'Dreyfuss,' she repeated. 'Who is he?'

'He's the new farrier. You remember, old Roberts retired?'

'Where did he come from?'

Jez went back into Teddy's stable and continued mucking out. 'I found him.'

Bramble followed him. 'Well, how do we know he's good? What do we know about him?'

Their eyes met as Jez, having filleted the manure from the straw with a practised shake, flicked it onto the wheelbarrow again.

'Jez. *Please* don't make these decisions on your own. This is *my* yard, and I've lived here all my life. If anyone knows where to find a good farrier *I* do.' She could hear herself sounding like a toddler having a tantrum. 'Jez, it's not fair to me if you run this yard as if I wasn't here. Anyway, I've decided to use Nat as our farrier.'

Jez spat to one side of the pile of manure. 'Dreyfuss is better.'

Bramble frowned and tried to make a joke of it. 'That's a bit rustic of you, Jez. Look, it's my yard and I decide who shoes my horses.'

Jez glowered back. 'Nat's no good.' The words hung in the air.

No good as a farrier, or just no good? Bramble didn't want to ask. 'I've seen him shoe Sailor. He knows what he's doing.'

It was a stand-off. Bramble was determined not to back down and glared at him.

He stared back, steadily looking into her eyes.

'Tell me why you don't like him.' Bramble hoped it didn't sound like a plea. She wanted to hear Jez's side. She wanted more than that – she wanted a logical, honest explanation of what Nat had told her. She wanted to know that Jez wasn't a thief or an opportunist . . . or a liar.

Jez continued his steady gaze and she felt herself being tugged into it, as if dragged under by a deep, powerful current beneath the sea. It was like the playground game where the first person to look away is the loser.

Except that the longer they regarded each other the easier it was. She felt her irritation and distrust drain away. All that she needed to know was there, in front of her, in the connection being forged between them. He was like a shaman, drawing her into his heart of fire.

She didn't know how long they stood there. Jez's mobile phone sounded, but he took no notice.

'It's your phone,' she said gently, hearing her own voice a long way away. 'Don't you want to answer it?'

His eyes still held her. 'Look,' she said, conscious that it was she who was yielding to compromise. 'Why don't you use Dreyfuss if you want to, if you're making the booking, and I will call Nat when I do? It makes sense to have two farriers, after all, in case one person is ill, or away or something.'

The tones of his mobile died away and the yard was silent again.

'Fine,' he said eventually. 'If that's how you want it.'

Which one of them had given way?

It was acutely infuriating, having someone like Jez working for her, because he had such pride. He seemed unable to say 'I'm sorry' or 'I was wrong' or 'I won't do it again'.

Chapter 18

Helena decided to use her new free time to plan her life properly.

First, she would get everyone lots of presents. She set out to comb the West End. A v-neck sleeveless cashmere top for Ollie – no two, because they were so useful. Another cashmere top, this time for Savannah, in large and black. Black was so slimming and a black poloneck was classic. And it wasn't as if Helena was buying cheap cashmere either; all these were quality and would last a lifetime. Cheap never works, Helena told herself. She got a selection of clothes from Marks & Spencer for Ania, so that she could change them if she didn't like them. For Eddie, a top-of-the-range electric guitar – Eddie needed an interest in life that had nothing to do with horses – and Ruby and Roly were ready for their first proper bicycles, as well as a television for their nursery.

Every now and then she wondered if she might be spending too much, but Ollie would get a good chunk of money when his script was finished and he spent all day working in his office. He kept regular hours – he closed his door at nine in the morning, emerged for a one-hour lunch, then back again until six. In the evening they shared a bottle of wine, and if they opened another one it was usually at Helena's request rather than Ollie's. When Helena asked, tentatively, if the script was 'on target' he glared and told her that everything was 'fine'. He usually added 'back off', but was otherwise generally in a good mood.

Helena glowed with her own generosity and also treated herself to a selection of new dresses for the party season. To stay on top she had to look on top. It was investment dressing. She checked out the latest must-be-seen lunch venues and caught up with all her girlfriends. *Simon's Way* was shot three times a year, so she'd lost touch with so many people. It was heaven to linger over a glass of champagne and catch up with what everyone was up to.

She was surprised to get a call from Eddie's teacher, wanting a meeting. Perhaps they wanted to discuss whether he should go for Oxford or Cambridge once he had his A level results.

Jez found a buyer for one of the young horses, and at a good price too. Bramble spent hours in the evening over the accounts and she had just about managed to work out what the finances were. Things were tight, but they could hopefully be turned round. It would be good if they get could get one more owner – someone who would keep their horses with her and pay for their training and entries. Bramble could have filled her own diary seven times over in taking riding lessons at thirty pounds an hour, but it left her no time for training the horses and running the yard, and, even if she worked all the hours in the day, it didn't make quite enough money to live on. Her father, with his reputation, had charged much more. Even so, they had Teddy, and with Teddy they had a chance at the big time. Plus the other young horses, any of which might – or more likely might not, but Bramble didn't want to think about that now – turn into a Teddy one day.

They sold Chancer and watched him go. He was a nice young gelding with a certain amount of promise, and Bramble thought he was going to the right rider. She and Jez hoisted up the tailgate of his new owner's lorry and bolted it without regrets.

'Let's have a drink in celebration,' she offered. She got out her cheque-book and wrote out a sum for Jez. It was his percentage for helping turn Chancer into a profit. He followed her into the kitchen – empty of people, for once – and she dug out one of Pa's better bottles. 'Salut!' She lifted her glass.

He raised his, meeting her eyes.

Helena sat in front of Eddie's tutor, Mr Swift, hardly able to understand what he was saying.

'What do you mean, Eddie has been truanting? He goes to school every morning, he always has.'

'I have his attendance records here.' Mr Swift pointed to the papers on his desk. 'And his grades have collapsed. He is in danger of failing his A Levels.'

Helena was completely nonplussed. 'But he spends hours in his room working.'

'He may spend hours in his room, Mrs Cooper, but Eddie is clearly not working. Has anything happened in the family recently? I don't want to pry, but sometimes this kind of thing is a reflection of a problem at home.'

Helena was outraged. 'We don't have problems at home. At least, well, his grandfather died a few months ago, but I didn't think he was all that close to him . . .' she trailed off, remembering Eddie's reaction.

Mr Swift looked at her steadily. 'It might be worth discussing it with Eddie.'

'He won't talk to me,' admitted Helena. It hurt to say it; each word stabbed her. She and Eddie had always been so close. So close. 'Surely it's just the usual teenage rebellion?' she suggested.

'Being a teenager is difficult, and teenagers themselves can be very obstructive, but there's usually a reason of some kind behind really challenging behaviour. It can't simply be ascribed to hormones. Also, Eddie is a little old to fit into the usual teenage pattern of rebellion – he is already eighteen, after all.'

'Yes, of course. I'll talk to him,' promised Helena, swallowing tears and gathering up her bags hastily. She couldn't bear it. Not her darling Eddie. Perhaps he was being bullied. Maybe he had been closer to Edward than she'd realised. Or could it be that minx Donna? Or another girl? Was it puppy love? Helena left Mr Swift's office like an avenging angel, determined to get to the bottom of it once and for all.

The following afternoon, Jez and Bramble hacked out Merlin and Teddy. Merlin's steel grey coat was now glossy, defining the shape of the muscles beneath. He walked like a star in the making, with a long stride and an imposing sense of himself. Jez, a dark jacket zipped up against the weather for once, had the same athletic grace.

They talked above the bluster of the wind. 'We need to buy a few more horses, don't we? If we could do a Chancer a few times a year it would make quite a difference.'

'I could do a trip to Ireland,' offered Jez. 'I've got some good contacts there.'

Bramble stiffened. Edward had always gone in the past; it was her turn now. 'I was thinking of going,' she said. 'We can't both be away at once.'

They were in stand-off again.

They reached the long field and its apparently endless stretch of bare earth, where they galloped the horses to maximise their fitness. It finished at the foot of a small but steep hill, which worked out lungs and hindquarters. 'A pipe-opener?' suggested Bramble, distracted by the exchange. 'They need a good gallop.'

Jez nodded. They shortened their stirrups and the horses, picking up on the tension immediately, broke into a jog, eager to be away, until, at their riders' command, they sprang forward.

Merlin, with his racehorse training, took the lead. Bramble dug her heels into Teddy but was almost taken by surprise at the sudden surge of power beneath her. They moved up alongside Merlin's pumping haunches, his shoulders and forelegs like relentless pistons. Bramble, allowing herself just one glance sideways, saw Jez laughing with the joy of speed.

And then it happened. Teddy, who preferred to be lead horse, was determined not to be beaten. He seized the bit and Bramble felt all control snatched away, as her thighs began to ache from half-standing in the saddle. Suddenly she knew terror. Complete fear. She was riding a high-speed train and, for no more than ten seconds, was powerless to stop. In spite of all her skill and all her strength, they were going over an edge.

At the foot of the hill both horses slowed and she took the reins back again, regaining mastery. They reached the top almost alongside Merlin; she could hear both horse and man breathing as they dropped to a trot, then a walk. Bramble, tears carved into her cheeks by the cold wind, caught her breath, shocked by what she had discovered about herself. You could get away with a few seconds out of control on a bare field in the middle of nowhere. Competing at the highest level, it could mean the difference between winning and losing. Serious injury or a fall. Life or death. Her father had been right: she couldn't ride Teddy to the top.

Jez wheeled Merlin round and, coming alongside, high-fived her.

Bramble high-fived him back, still trembling and also furious with herself.

'Are you OK?' he asked, suddenly concerned. Beyond him she could see Lorenden in the lee of the hill, like a white wedding cake in the winter light, protected by its land.

'Of course,' she gasped, her throat sore from trying to get her breath back in the biting winter air. She could see rivulets of sweat running down Jez's face and could feel it on her own skin too, drying immediately in the wind. He reined Merlin in and they both halted, facing each other.

'What's wrong?' He could see through her.

'You go to Ireland,' she said, not quite sure why that was her answer. 'The yard needs new contacts.'

A kestrel hovered and the brown, empty hop fields and leafless fruit trees dropped away on all sides of the hill. Jez grinned and, digging his heels into Merlin, set off towards home, a dark horse and rider silhouetted against a vanilla sky.

Her heart was still beating in double-time.

Chapter 19

Nat took Bramble to the party. There were over seventy people crammed into an Italian restaurant with a disco in the basement.

Bramble had a system for getting dressed smartly in the minimum time: a classic little black dress or a pair of black trousers and a jacket. Usually it worked, but now her little black dress looked drab, the trousers and jacket too professional.

With her share of the money from Chancer's sale, she decided it was time for a revamp. Nothing dramatic, just an update. Felicity came with her, looking around the racks with a practised eye.

'I suppose I need some new stuff too,' she said. 'Although I'm pretty much broke.'

Bramble froze. If Felicity was running out of money she might want to sell Lorenden. 'What do you think?' she asked, fingering a sequin top distractedly.

'You could wear it,' said Felicity. 'You could wear anything, but there's something about a woman in a red dress . . .' She took a deep crimson velvet dress off the rails. 'Try this. You've got great legs, you can take short.'

It fitted Bramble perfectly, clinging to her greyhound body, softening it in all the right places. 'And these,' Felicity picked up a pair of faux ruby earrings. 'They're the colour of the roses in the garden at Lorenden. Now that your hair's a bit longer and not quite so severe, you can do the gypsy look. With high heels, of course.'

For half an hour it was like having a real older sister. Someone who cared, who knew more than she did.

And then, on the journey home, the question of money came up again.

'Has the solicitor said when probate is likely to come through?' Felicity asked.

Bramble shook her head. 'It could still be months, even a year. I don't know why.' She concentrated on driving. Probate meant having to make decisions about Lorenden.

'You could buy quite a nice little cottage with your share.'

Bramble detected a touch of malice. 'If we sold Lorenden I'd have to buy another business as well, don't forget.'

'Oh, there'd be enough left over to invest in some good horses. I'm sure you could rent a yard quite easily.'

'This is my home,' said Bramble, through gritted teeth. 'I am going to try to work out a way of staying. Take out a mortgage, do bed-and-breakfast or something . . .'

Felicity laughed. 'Bed-and-breakfast isn't going to service the loan you'd need to take out, and anyway, why give yourself the hassle? When you could do it another way?'

'My business is based here. Everybody knows me.'

'Everybody knows you as Bramble Kelly of Lorenden,' said Felicity. 'That's what you don't want to give up. Being the person who lives in the marvellous, big house? You wouldn't feel so important in a little cottage, would you?'

Bramble tried not to crash the car. 'I don't care about what people think. And I don't feel important: I just love my home.'

'Everyone's idea of themselves is so bound up in their houses,' said Felicity, languidly. 'That's why I got out ages ago. I saw the way Lorenden made us think we were better than other people.'

'So,' said Bramble, struggling to keep her voice even. 'You've decided, have you? As soon as probate comes through you'll be siding with Helena and we'll be selling?'

'I didn't say that,' replied Felicity. She lit a cigarette.

'And please don't smoke in the car.' Bramble realised her father had been right: Felicity was a troublemaker.

That evening, Bramble found a bottle of bath oil, given to her a few years earlier, and made herself lie in the bath, ignoring the monkey chattering about chores on her shoulder. She took the time to add blusher to her cheeks, to draw the lipstick more carefully, to slip the dress on so smoothly that it was like a caress. She stopped in front of the mirror and saw someone different.

'That's about as good as it gets,' she said to herself. 'Bramble Kelly, you have passed the trot-up.'

'Mum,' said Savannah, passing on her way upstairs as Bramble was coming down.

Bramble forced herself not to throw her coat over her dress.

'You look OK. Quite nice, in fact.' Savannah then ran up the stairs and closed her bedroom door.

Bramble managed a smile.

Jez walked into the hall from the kitchen. 'Has anyone seen Bramble?' He stopped and looked up at her, and Bramble forced herself to carry on walking down the stairs. It felt as if she was on a catwalk.

His eyes followed her down every step until she stood beside him, the high heels raising her eyes almost – but not quite – to the level of his.

'Nice dress.' He cleared his throat.

'Thank you. I'm going to a party with Nat.'

An expression – she couldn't work out what – crossed his face and he started to say something.

She tried never to mention Nat's name. She looked down at the bows on the toes of her shoes. They looked pretty. But not very Bramble.

Neither of them moved. She heard his voice, very close. 'Are you sure you know what you're doing?'

'I'm not doing anything.' She didn't have to explain herself. Not to Jez. 'Just going to a party. That can't hurt me.' She looked up defiantly. 'Nat's a nice man,' she added.

Jez turned away. 'No, he's not.'

'Look, either tell me what you've got against him or stop all these dark hints and thunderous looks. If there's something I need to know . . .' She thought, once again, that he was going to say something, but she was disappointed.

'Ask him yourself. You have to make your own judgements.'

Bramble hovered. 'Why were you looking for me anyway?'

'Oh, um, nothing much. Just to say that Pauline phoned and wants you to call her back.'

They went through to the kitchen and Jez opened the little door beside the chimney breast that led up to the attic flat. This was the very oldest part of the house – an Elizabethan firebreast that had survived from the very earliest building here, with a tiny, curving, neck-breakingly steep staircase, its steps worn and almost too narrow for modern feet. It wrapped itself around the chimney with only two doors out – one to the spare room and the other, on the floor above, to the attic. Jez stopped, as if wondering whether to go upstairs. Bramble could see the lights of Nat's car in the drive. 'Bye, Jez.' She made her voice sound casual.

Before she could leave, he caught her arm. She could feel his fingers through her coat. 'What has Nat Croft said about me?' he muttered in a low voice.

'Nothing,' she said, pulling her arm away. Bramble was a hopeless liar.

'Bramble,' he called as she went outside.

She turned. 'Yes?'

'Be careful.' His face, by the staircase door, looked down at her with condescension. Or was it disdain?

'I can look after myself.' Tucking her legs into Nat's car and pecking him on the cheek, she thought that she had spent far too much of her life being careful.

The restaurant was packed. Nat hung their worn-out jackets on a crowded peg behind the restaurant door and Bramble saw him, for the first time, in a suit. It was dark grey and well cut, with just one button and he was wearing it with a navy open-necked shirt. He looked – Bramble had to admit – more imposing. He looked like someone in authority, not just the friendly guy she had drinks with from time to time. Formal clothing suited his classic face, made the hair seem less scruffy and more arresting.

'Hi Nat!' Someone slapped him affectionately on the back. He seemed popular, she thought.

'You look great,' he said, looking down at her with a twinkle in his eye and crooking his elbow towards her. 'Hold on tight or you might go down in the scrum. Let's find a drink.'

She tucked her hand into his arm. It felt natural and right. He efficiently elbowed their way to the bar and got her a glass of white wine. The room was so crowded that hardly anyone seemed to notice that they were arm in arm, but she could feel the warmth of his body against hers all evening. And the noise was so loud that he had to bring his lips close to her ear. 'Remember, you don't have to drive tonight. Have another drink,' he murmured, beginning to introduce her to people. Many were old friends she hadn't seen since the summer. 'Bramble, you look amazing,' they said. 'Fab dress.' 'I like your hair longer.'

It was fun, belonging to someone again after all this time. Even if only for one evening.

Helena struggled through the rush-hour traffic, Mr Swift's words swirling through her mind.

Ania was ironing in front of the television. The twins were eating fruit on the sofa.

'Where's Eddie?' Helena demanded.

'Upstairs in his room.'

She stormed upstairs and flung open Eddie's bedroom door. The room was empty. 'Ania!' she shouted. 'Ania, come here this minute! Where is Eddie? Where *is* he?'

Ollie came out of his office. 'What's all this noise about, Helena? How am I expected to work like this?'

As Ania came up the stairs the doorbell rang.

'Open that, will you, Ania,' called Helena. 'Ollie, we must talk about—'

Two men walked into the hall. One was burly, the other shorter but equally thickset. Both had shaven faces, blunt-cropped hair, blue shirts with cheap ties and big, strong-toed boots.

'Oliver James Cooper?' asked the burly man, holding a note-book and pencil.

'What's this?' asked Ollie. 'Who are you?'

'Bailiffs.'

'Bailiffs?' gasped Helena. 'There must be some mistake.'

'No mistake.' He began writing. 'Wide-screen TV – get the make on that, will you, Rob? DVD. What are these?' He indicated the mound of expensive-looking carrier bags propped against the wall in the drawing room. Helena's newly purchased presents.

'They're mine. You can't take those.' Helena, trembling with shock, grabbed them. What was happening? Why wasn't Ollie doing something?

Large, powerful hands removed the shopping bags. 'Sorry, madam. He's your husband: you're liable for his debts.'

'No, that can't be true.' She tried to tug the bags back without success. 'Go away! Or I'll call the police.'

'Call who you like, madam,' said Rob, rummaging through the layers of delicate tissue paper with enormous tattooed hands. 'New sweaters. Cashmere, it says on the label. Write it down, Andy. And a nice pair of cufflinks here: Bond Street.'

'Stop! Stop! We'll sue. We'll sue. You can't do this . . . this . . . in front of our children!'

'I suggest you send the children downstairs, madam,' said Andy.

Helena made frantic signals at Ania, who retreated to the basement with Ruby and Roly. Faint wails trailed up the stairs. Ollie did nothing.

'Do you know who I am?' demanded Helena.

Andy and Rob, supremely indifferent, hardly gave her a second glance. 'We know what your husband's debts are, madam, and we're here to collect them.'

'I shall complain to your superior!' Helena struggled with tears. The two men went on writing, looking round the room. 'This doesn't happen to people like us. Surely you can see that?'

'That 'orse sculpture,' said Andy. 'Worth a bit, wouldn't you say?'

'That was my father's.' Helena darted forward. 'You can't take that. You wouldn't dare.'

Rob picked up the sculpture as if it weighed nothing and tucked it under his arm. 'Perhaps, for the time being, we'll just have this. On account, as it were. Means we can leave the presents. Do you a favour, like.'

'What do you want?' screamed Helena, tugging uselessly at his elbow. 'Give that back to me now! It's . . . it's . . . it's not even mine. It belongs to my sister.'

'In that case, she can claim it back from us. Once we've been paid. Until then, we can take anything in this 'ouse.'

Helena's hair fell over her eyes, obscuring her vision, as she hung onto Rob's arm, trying to dig her high heels in to the polished wooden floor to stop him leaving. She found herself inexorably slithering along behind him, his shiny blue jacket tightly gripped under her fingers. 'How dare you? Stop!' she screamed, still trying to pull him back. 'Stop! I'll pay. I'll pay.'

Rob handed the bronze horse over to Andy. 'Three thousand, two hundred pounds.'

'Ollie? Is this true?'

Ollie coughed. 'I, er, may have forgotten to pay a credit card. But it was an oversight. An oversight, do you hear?' His voice squeaked. 'We'll complain to the highest authority.'

'Three thousand, two hundred pounds,' reiterated Rob. 'Or we take the horse.'

Breathless with panic, Helena found her handbag and got out her cheque-book, writing out the cheque with a shaking hand.

'If it bounces, we'll be back,' promised Andy, dropping the horse on the floor. It landed with a bang on its side, and Helena rushed to pick it up. It wasn't broken, but the floor had been dented.

'You've marked the floor,' she cried.

'We'll be back,' Andy repeated. 'If the cheque bounces.'

'You haven't heard the last of this,' she screamed after them, slamming the door then turning to see the frightened faces of Ania, Ruby and Roly peering up the basement stairs, and Ollie retreating towards his office.

'Ollie!' she screeched. 'Ollie, what the hell's happening here?' She bounded up the stairs after him. '*What* is all this about?'

Ollie got to his office just ahead of her, nipping in and closing the door. Helena heard the key turn in the lock. She rattled the handle. 'Let me in, Ollie, this minute. THIS MINUTE. Do you hear? I want an explanation.' She rattled the handle again furiously and began to kick the door. 'LET . . . ME . . . IN!'

Eddie opened the front door and saw his mother hammering on Ollie's door on the half-landing. He stood, lanky and adolescent, arms hanging down at his sides.

'You!' she whirled round. 'And exactly where do you think you've been?'

'Uh, I had a late class.' He began to sidle down the stairs to the kitchen, but Helena caught his shoulder. 'No you didn't,' she hissed. 'Because I've been talking to the school. They called me in, do you understand? Me. I had the humiliation of being told that you're truanting. Like a common street kid.'

Eddie wrenched his blazer out of her grasp. 'He . . .' he jerked his head up towards Ollie's door, 'seems to be doing a better job of humiliating you than I ever could.'

'Don't you dare talk back to me. After everything I've done for you. You're letting me down. And yourself. You're going to blow everything if you don't pull yourself together.'

'I don't care. I don't want to do A levels and I don't want to stay at that school. Not for another moment because—'

'You don't want to do A levels? Are you mad? Are you *quite* mad? How are you ever going to get on in life?'

Eddie carried on down the stairs, not answering her, and Helena grabbed his blazer again. Ollie took the opportunity to leave his office quietly, locking the door and tiptoeing towards the front door. Helena caught the edge of his socks in her eyeline and rushed upstairs again. 'Where are you going, Ollie? Answer me! I need to talk to you.'

Ollie slipped out the door. 'It's all a mistake,' he said hastily, his voice trailing out across the street. 'I'll pay you back when the script is finished. I've got to interview someone. Back soon.' He gave a little wave and set off briskly, crossing the road and disappearing down a nearby alley. Short of standing on the doorstep screaming, there was nothing Helena could do, and she didn't want the neighbours to alert the press.

Eddie was downstairs, nonchalantly drinking a large glass of milk. Ruby and Roly were huddled on Ania's knee, reading a story. If you looked in through our basement window from the outside, reflected Helena, from the winter darkness into the false sunshine of the halogen-lit kitchen, you'd think we were a normal family.

But we're falling apart. She took a deep breath.

'Please talk to me, Eddie.'

'OK, OK,' he said, rolling his eyes, 'don't worry, I'll stop skipping classes.'

She wasn't sure whether to believe him, but there wasn't a lot more she could say.

'But Mum,' he said. 'Ollie: he's no good.'

'Don't,' she whispered, pulling him out of Ruby and Roly's hearing. 'It was about money, all that shouting. Ollie is very vague about things like that and he forgot to pay a bill. Then it was handed on to professional debt collectors for some reason. It's a bit of an extreme measure, but it's the sort of thing that happens to him because his mind is on other things. Geniuses often are difficult to live with, and you know that *Vogue* called him one of the finest writers of his generation.'

'*Vogue*,' sneered Eddie.

'*Vogue*,' repeated Helena firmly. 'And lots of other people. When he comes back, I'm going to talk to him and get him to give me all the bills in the first place. It was for a very small sum of money – only three thousand pounds. Nothing really, when you look at all this.' She waved a hand at the immaculate room. 'I got a cheque for thirty thousand this morning, for my last round of Mattie.'

'Look Mum,' he said suddenly, his voice hoarse. 'I don't want to stay at school any longer. I hate it there. I hate my A levels. I don't want to go to university, I want to be a rider.'

Helena gazed at him in horror. This was her worst nightmare. Beyond her worst nightmare. 'No!' she shouted. 'Go upstairs to your room! Now. You don't know how much I've done for you, and this is how you repay me. Don't come down until you're ready to talk sense.'

Eddie strode upstairs and slammed his bedroom door.

Helena had been there when Dom was killed. It was a gloriously sunny day, and both Bramble and Dom were competing. Helena, along with a few dozen other spectators, had found a knoll with a view of three or four cross-country jumps, and she'd settled down on the grass, sunning her legs, watching riders gallop out of the trees and down to the ditch, over the water, then up and round over a couple of brush fences before disappearing off towards a sunken road. She lay back and dozed, not bothering to listen to the commentary until everything stopped.

She sat up. 'Is there a delay of some sort?' she asked her neighbour.

The woman frowned. 'I think there might have been a fall.'

'Did you hear whether my sister or her husband have started?' asked Helena slightly anxiously. 'Dom Kelly or Bramble Kelly? On Jack of All Trades and Sugarplum?'

'I think I did hear a Kelly, but I wasn't concentrating.'

The commentator crackled about it being a beautiful sunny day, and said that he wanted to thank Wellies & Co. for sponsoring the event for the third year running.

'It's always a bad sign when the commentator talks about the weather,' said Helena's neighbour. 'Or the sponsors. It means there's a hold-up they can't talk about.'

'I think I'll go and find out.' It took Helena about twenty minutes to trudge back over the hillocky grass to the beginning of the course. She wasn't really worried, just uneasy.

'Did you hear? A horse has been killed,' someone said in passing. Another person suggested that a rider had been knocked unconscious. Nobody seemed to know who.

Helena struggled against a sea of people going in all directions. They were quiet and subdued.

'What's happened?' She stopped someone who looked official.

'A rider's been . . . um . . . hurt,' he said.

'Is it my sister?' screamed Helena. 'Bramble Kelly?'

A moment of hesitation flitted across his face. 'I don't know,' he said. 'Try the secretary's tent.'

Helena began to run, breathlessly pausing to ask people on the way. 'Do you know what's happened? Have you heard who it is?' Everybody thought it was something different, no one knew anything for sure.

She sagged in relief when she saw Bramble trying to control her horse in the start box. 'What's the delay?' Bramble leaned over to call to Helena, her face tense. 'I've been held here for forty minutes. Nobody's telling me anything. Who's hurt?'

'I think there's a fence being repaired,' lied Helena. 'Where's Dom?'

'He went two before me. I hope he's all right.'

Edward Beaumont walked briskly up the slope, his face ashen, and grabbed Helena, pulling her behind the portaloo near the start box. 'Dom's been killed,' he whispered. 'I'll take Sugarplum, and you look after Bramble. Make sure she doesn't see him, all right? She mustn't see him.'

Helena was shocked and tried to think straight. 'What if she wants to? Surely she ought to be allowed to?'

'He doesn't look as if he's sleeping peacefully,' hissed Edward. 'When half a ton of horse lands on you at thirty miles an hour everything goes everywhere. Do you understand? Blood, guts, eyeballs, the lot!'

Helena recoiled in terror. 'It can't be Dom,' she said. 'We were going to have a drink together . . .' She couldn't comprehend that Dom, who had been laughing and joking with her a few hours earlier, was no longer going to claim his drink.

'Just get on with it, Helena. Look after her.' And Edward strode towards Bramble and took her horse's bridle.

Helena watched her sister crumple, and visions of Dom, crushed and bloody, danced through her mind for months afterwards. 'Blood, guts, eyeballs . . .' She couldn't shut the images out.

Seven years later, staring in horror at her son's angry, retreating back, hearing him say he wanted to become a rider, she swallowed back the sickness that rose in her throat. It couldn't happen twice in one family. It would be totally irresponsible of her to allow him to endanger himself in this way.

Then she went back downstairs to take over from Ania, shepherding Ruby and Roly up to their beautifully decorated nursery, smiling and checking that they had brushed their teeth properly, reading their favourite book to them without skipping pages. Helena, as so often, felt that she was acting the role of perfect mother while her mind was elsewhere. She hoped the twins couldn't see that.

After three books they still showed no signs of going to sleep.

'Mummy,' said Ruby suddenly. 'Who were those men?'

Helena smoothed her daughter's hair back. 'Just horrid people who came to get some money off Daddy. It was very naughty of them. Daddy's going to complain. But they won't be back, so you mustn't worry about them.' She had a thought. 'And you mustn't tell anyone about it.'

'Can't I do it for show and tell?' asked Roly.

'No!' shrieked Helena, caught unawares. She dropped back into her dulcet good-mother voice. 'Sorry, darling, I meant no. Anyway, there's nothing to show.'

'We could take the horse.'

'Horse?' Obsessed by her fear of Eddie riding, Helena had a brief, hysterical image of Bramble loading up one of the horses and driving it into London, and the whole school gathering round to hear that Helena Harris had had bailiffs in the house.

'Grampa's statue,' added Ruby.

'Oh that. No, darling, absolutely not. It's too valuable, and anyway, the nasty men must stay a secret.'

'Why?'

'They just must.' She rose briskly. 'Now go to sleep and forget all about it.'

Helena paced up and down for the rest of the evening, ears straining for the sound of Ollie's return. She tried his mobile. It was off. She even walked down to the pub, braving the cold, the dark and the insolence of two drunk teenagers. He wasn't there. Over and over again, her finger hovered over her address book, then she closed it, not wishing to admit to anyone that she didn't know where Ollie was. Three times she opened the front door, thinking she heard his step outside, only to see a stranger hurrying past in the lamplight. She searched every drawer for another key to his office door. She didn't find it, but she found envelopes. Opened ones, and ones that had been shoved carelessly away unopened. There were about twenty in all.

She sank down in a chair and began to go through them one by one. Each one filled her with increasing fear and anger.

And still Ollie didn't come back.

Savannah caught sight of herself reflected in the window. The darkness outside turned the windows at Lorenden into mirrors, but even broken up by the panes of glass it was obvious that she was still much bigger, in every way, than everyone else. She was also feeling uncomfortably full because she had just wolfed down three chocolate bars. She hadn't been able to help it.

She raised her chin. She was tempted to make herself vomit

them up, but she wasn't going to make the mistake of becoming bulimic. She now knew too much about nutrition to go down that route. She would add some extra exercise into her routine and would cut down a bit tomorrow. Not much, just for a few days until she worked off the chocolate bars.

She sighed. It was so up and down this dieting thing, and it was taking over her head. That day she'd woken up early to go running and had an apple and a black coffee for breakfast, checking the calories. Make the numbers balance, she told herself. It's all about getting the numbers right. There are only a few more pounds to lose and everybody has noticed how much healthier and prettier you look. Even Helena's sharp eyes had skimmed over her body with approval, and she had rewarded Savannah with one of her cast-off sweaters. 'It'll fit you perfectly once you've lost a few more pounds,' she'd said.

She noticed that Jez watched her, with eyes that saw everything. Jez could see that she was lumpy and fat, not like the petite blonde she'd spotted him with in the White Horse. You have to get thinner, whispered Savannah to the windows and the faded, silvered mirrors that caught her at awkward, ugly angles, and you have to stay strong to win. You have to be the best. Sometimes she thought she floated, invisible, through the house, burning up with an inner fire but numb to everything else, revelling only in the thought that at last she was getting her life together.

Felicity woke at three o'clock, her heart pounding in double time and the usual cold terror gripping her bones. She switched on the bedside light and tried to focus on the room. There would be no more sleep tonight. She put on a pair of jeans and pulled a sweater over her head, and crept downstairs. She noticed that Bramble's door was still open and that the bed hadn't been slept in. She pulled the door closed. Bramble might not want Savannah to know.

The dogs blinked sleepily, thumping their tails but declining to get out of their baskets. She put the kettle on and began to make herself a herbal tea, opening the cupboards and, not for the first time, being assailed by memories as she did so. Nothing had changed. The cupboards still smelt of spices and coffee, as they had in her childhood, and the same glass storage jars and pale green tins, marked 'tea', 'coffee' and 'sugar' sat on the same shelves.

She heard a car outside and expected it to be Bramble, but it was Jez. 'Hello,' he looked surprised. 'Couldn't you sleep?'

She shook her head. 'Peppermint tea?' she offered.

He laughed, his eyes glittering and his hair dishevelled. She thought he might be slightly drunk and wondered where he'd been. There was nowhere local that stayed open this late. He disappeared upstairs and came down with a bottle of single malt whisky.

'I'll never sleep if I drink that.'

He poured two glasses. 'You're not sleeping anyway.' He swilled it round in the glass, and the light shone against the gold liquid. 'Want to tell me why?'

Felicity shook her head. 'Shit happens. To everyone. Talking doesn't make it un-happen.'

He nodded in agreement, sprawling back on the kitchen chair with his long rider's legs. 'So,' he said after a companionable silence. 'Are you sticking around this time?'

'Are you?' she flashed back, and their eyes met.

He acknowledged the question with a raised eyebrow, but didn't reply.

'Well, we're a right pair of gypsies, aren't we?' said Felicity, feeling the whisky burn its way down her throat. 'And Bramble isn't. Bramble has roots. I envy her.'

'She was born with them. You don't acquire something like that – you come into this world able to make a home.'

'Or not,' said Felicity quietly.

'Not everybody needs to be the same,' he replied. 'What's going on with her and Nat?'

'Not a great deal so far,' said Felicity, thinking of Bramble's empty bed. 'But if you know something against him you should say. Sooner rather than later.'

'I knew his wife, Jenny, before she met him. Not like that,' he added hastily, at Felicity's expression. 'She was just a friend. A lovely, pretty, happy girl. He wrecked her life.'

'Was he violent?'

'You don't need to be physically violent to leave scars. I don't think that fists were his weapon of choice.'

'So how do you know what really happened?' asked Felicity. 'We've all been in destructive relationships. You need to know both sides, and even then you can't judge.'

He nodded. 'That's why I don't say anything.' He poured her another slug of whisky. 'Have you ever been married?'

Felicity nodded. 'It lasted six weeks. We got ourselves married by the British consul on one of the Caribbean islands. I can't even remember which one. I don't know where he is now. It was a sort of joke.' She swirled the peaty liquid round her mouth and swallowed. 'Still, it was fun while it lasted.'

'Does anyone here know?'

Felicity threw her head back and laughed. 'No, it was a long time ago, when I was still too angry with my father to want him anywhere near my life.'

'Was?' asked Jez.

'I'm still angry,' admitted Felicity. 'But he's dead now, in case you hadn't noticed.'

Felicity liked to challenge men. It excited her, making them care about what she said. The words hung in the air between them and Felicity met Jez's eyes. They were calm and appraising.

'Don't you ever take anything seriously?' he asked.

'I'm beyond redemption, haven't they told you that?' She looked up at him from under her eyelashes.

'No.' Jez refused to flirt. 'All they've said is that you were a brilliant rider.'

'Ah well, that was a long time ago. In another country and besides, the wench is dead,' she quoted. Or misquoted. Whatever; he'd get her drift.

Jez merely continued to look at her.

'So, what about you? Have you been married, I mean?'

'No,' he said. 'I don't make promises I can't keep.'

Nat's party soon became nicely fuzzy around the edges, as two hastily gulped glasses of white wine hit Bramble's empty stomach. Nat looked after her without crowding her, making introductions then backing off to let her talk on her own account. There were one or two people she knew – the equine vet, of course – and plenty of gentle, unsurprising gossip. Nat's hand, in the small of her back, supported her.

The disco pumped out nostalgic eighties music and Nat caught her hand. 'C'mon.'

'I can't dance in these shoes,' she laughed. But she could. At first her body felt clunky and disconnected, then she let the music take over. Nat was a good mover and she mirrored him to the pounding beat, as if the thinnest of silk ribbons wound back and forth between them with each step, drawing them together.

'That's me done for.' After half an hour it seemed quite natural to lean on Nat, gasping with laughter. The music softened and the sinuous tones of 'Lady in Red' rolled across the floor.

'You have to stay for this one,' he whispered, drawing her into his arms. 'Lady in Red.'

As they rotated slowly, she could feel the heat of his body melting against hers, the slightly scratchy quality of his suit and the feather-soft whisper of his lips on her ear. 'OK?' he asked at the end, and they drew back from each other slightly, their mouths only millimetres apart.

'I'm flagging a bit.' Someone proferred a plate of dried-up pizza slices but Bramble wrinkled her nose. 'I ought to eat something, I suppose, before I drink any more.'

'What about scrambled eggs back at my place?'

It was just what she felt like. Nothing elaborate. And she was curious to see where he lived.

The cottage had Kent peg tiles and a cat-slide roof, with two little dormer windows. The front door had an old knocker and, inside, a huge inglenook fireplace and a large sofa dominated the sitting room. It was shabby, cosy – even pretty.

'Did you do this all yourself?' she asked in the kitchen, which was a narrow corridor of very ordinary kitchen units, but painted a soft shade of blue.

He nodded. 'When I moved in I took a paintbrush to the place. Then I bought a whole load of furniture in house clearance sales. Jenny got everything. She got the house, so she had to have the furniture to go in it.'

'That's not fair,' said Bramble, taking her glass back to the sofa.

'You need furniture too. Don't judges do a fifty-fifty split on property and possessions?'

'I wouldn't want to turf my own daughter out of her home. No, it's right that Jenny and Gemma got everything. I wouldn't have dreamt of fighting it.'

'That was generous of you.' Bramble studied him, and he looked embarrassed.

'Well, it would only be giving money to the lawyers, wouldn't it?' he said, turning away to put another log on the fire. 'I'd rather they had it.'

Bramble smiled and he handed her a glass of red wine before sitting down comfortably beside her. 'Why did you split?'

Nat paled. 'She had an affair,' he said. 'She made a complete fool of me. Everyone knew. I was commuting to work every day, so I was out all the time, and she was sleeping with another man. In our bed, I think.'

'That's awful. Did you . . . er . . . discover them?'

Nat shook his head. 'They were too clever for that. Eventually she told me she was in love with someone else and moved out. I had no idea. I thought I had a happy marriage and a loving wife. Everything changed in an instant.'

'Is she still with him?'

He laughed bitterly. 'No, he wouldn't leave his wife. I felt sorry for Jenny, in a way. He let her down, but it was all too late by then for us to try and go back.'

'I'm sorry.' Bramble put her hand on his arm.

'It's not as bad as someone dying,' he said. 'At least we all get to try again.' This time, when he kissed her he didn't stop. And she didn't want him to, as he tipped his face up towards hers, touching her lips tenderly with his own, and then the taste of man and red wine in her mouth, and a sudden longing flooding through her, a warm, liquid rush of desire that she'd thought she might never feel again.

He gently guided her upstairs to his bedroom. There were two doors, both open, and she stopped to look into the smaller room. It had a single bed, with a pink bedspread and two dolls on the pillow.

'I decorated that room for Gemma. She's never been allowed to come here.'

'Oh no. That's so sad!' Bramble's heart went out to him. 'So, if you want to see her, you have to go all the way up to Newcastle?'

'When I get a free weekend, yes, that's what I do.' He kissed the side of her neck, drawing the hair away from it with his hand. 'But it's a long way. Once I went all the way up there only to find that Gemma had gone out to a party. I had to come back down without seeing her.'

'But that's so awful, Nat. Can't you go to court or something?'

'When parents go to court it's the kids that suffer. No, I have to be patient and hope that Gemma knows I love her. You have lovely hair, did you know that?'

Then he undressed her, kissing every part of her body as he revealed it, murmuring that she was beautiful. She covered her breasts, ashamed of the silvery lines that snaked across them, but he kissed her hands away and she soon forgot to be shy. He even managed to be discreet as he rustled a condom from his bedside drawer, making it feel like something considerate and intimate rather than a barrier between them, and she cried out with pleasure when he entered her.

'I'm not hurting you, am I?' he asked, his voice full of concern, and she smiled with joy.

'Far from it,' she replied, pulling him to her. She had never expected it to feel so . . . so right. Nat, with all his quiet devotion, was a man she could trust. And trust opened up pleasure and happiness and a wonderful feeling of abandonment. Bramble let herself enjoy the rising urgency of his thrusts until that elusive explosion of ecstasy.

'Good?' he asked, stroking damp tendrils of hair away from her face.

'Good.' She snuggled down into his arms, already feeling warm and sleepy.

'What's the attic like to sleep in?' asked Felicity, back in the kitchen at Lorenden. 'When we were children it was full of junk. We used to play hide-and-seek there. I remember an old birdcage, lots of bits of broken furniture, some uniforms from the First World War . . . it had a very low ceiling, as far as I can remember.'

'It's still got a very low ceiling,' said Jez.

'Perhaps I should come up and see how it's changed?'

A mile away, in her elegant bedroom, Pauline couldn't sleep either. Every time she went to Lorenden to visit Teddy, and saw the anticipation in his pricked-forward ears or heard his soft whicker of recognition, she also saw Felicity's scornful face. When she leant against her horse's neck she ached for Edward. It was so lonely without him, and so, so lonely to go to the house where she had once been an integral part of everything that went on and to feel herself a visitor. It was all new. The girl Donna had been appointed by Edward only a few months ago, replacing a head groom who had been with them for ten years. Then Jez. Then Felicity back. All of them laughing and talking while Edward's ashes lay waiting to be scattered over the open fields.

I want him back, thought Pauline, hurting too much to cry. I want him back so much.

Alan moved in his sleep, then opened his eyes.

'Can't you sleep?' His hand reached out and turned on the light.

Pauline wondered if this was the old Alan, who'd always looked after her, or the new, irritable, absent-minded man who treated her as a cross between a warder and a servant.

'Oh, you know I never sleep these days.'

He felt for her hand and wrapped it in his, and she felt comforted.

Alan and Pauline had had a deal, forged at their wedding ceremony at St Margaret's, Westminster, in 1954. She offered him beauty, a well-organised life and discretion, and he repaid her with wealth, success and adoration. As a young man he hadn't been considered attractive – he was only five foot seven and quite slight, with a pale, gingery complexion – but he came from a wealthy background. There had also been a certain amount of talk about him being an up-and-coming fellow on the political scene, but he could never have married a stunner like Pauline, one of the most beautiful debs of her generation, without the money. Marriage was the only career that Pauline had been bred for, and she was ambitious, although slightly hampered by the fact that her father owned a chain of shoe stores and was therefore considered 'trade' (she had just managed to squeeze into the debutante circus through her godmother). She had had several proposals, but had judged Alan the best bet in the long run. Everyone had been rather surprised, particularly as Pauline was a few inches taller than her groom and would therefore never be able to wear high heels again.

Pauline had really wanted to be an event rider, but in the 1950s women couldn't compete on the British team, and, anyway, there was no money in it. Her father had made it clear that she had to marry well, because the shoe shops would all go to her brother. The year they married a woman won Badminton for the first time, but it was too late for Pauline. 'Your husband will expect you to be at home for him,' said her mother, 'looking after his children. When a man comes back from a hard day's work, he needs a wife, not a stable girl covered in mud.'

It had been one of Alan's grand gestures – for her thirtieth birthday – to buy her a horse and introduce her to Edward Beaumont, who was going to ride it for her, so she could go to the events and be part of it all as an owner.

Yes, the deal had worked very well for nearly fifty years but, looking at his watery blue eyes and age-spotted hand, she wondered what would be asked of her next.

'You're up to something,' said Alan. 'That's why you can't sleep.'

'No, I'm not.' She slid her hand away, switched off the light and turned away from him. 'Don't be ridiculous.'

'Pauline,' he said.

She pretended to be asleep.

'Pauline,' he repeated. 'You can be very destructive at times.'

She ignored him, but it occurred to her that, as well as missing Edward, she also missed the old Alan, who'd loved her completely and accepted everything she did without a breath of criticism.

At five o'clock in the morning Bramble slipped out of Nat's bed and began to dress. He pulled her back towards him.

'Don't go.'

'I must,' she said softly. 'I don't want the others to know that I was out.'

'They'll have to know some time,' he said, holding his eyes steady with hers.

'Yes,' she agreed, feeling happy. This wasn't a one-night stand. 'They'll have to know. But not yet.'

'You're a tough woman, Bramble Kelly.' He drew her on to the bed and kissed her thoroughly.

She disentangled herself, laughing.

'Saturday night?' he asked. 'A film and a curry?'

'Saturday night.'

She went home feeling happy. The early morning mist curled out towards her as the taxi turned into the lane and, for a second, she caught her breath in fear.

Then she told herself not to be so foolish. As Helena said, you can't read meanings into the weather.

Chapter 20

Winter crept by, pounding Lorenden with snow, rain, hail, drizzle, the sharp east wind and the odd chilly ray of sunshine. Savannah took over the kitchen, poring over recipes and calorie booklets. She particularly liked to bake biscuits and cakes, which she offered to everyone but never ate herself. Sometimes she took them upstairs to Jez's attic rooms, tapping nervously on the door. He was always pleased to see her, although sometimes there was someone else there, usually a beautiful woman who would treat Savannah dismissively, as if she was a little girl.

Bramble took tentative steps into a relationship with Nat. He always phoned when he said he would, he often texted her during the day to say that he was thinking of her and he frequently alluded to something in the future together – a cinema visit, a walk with the dogs on the coast – without making her feel trapped. It was nice to be happy, Bramble told herself, as she walked the dogs through the orchards. Nat gave her nothing to worry about and he was completely reliable. His solid, unquestioning devotion made her feel safe.

Even though they had passed the winter solstice, the days seemed longer and darker, and were bitter, damp and often windy. Sometimes it was too icy to take the horses out on the road, and twice snow fell, carpeting the fields in white. The hot water finally packed up for good and the boiler had to be replaced. The new one didn't work with Lorenden's antiquated piping and the plumber had to return, while Bramble, Felicity and Savannah slept in gloves, socks and sweaters.

Ben lost weight and condition. Since Edward's death he'd almost stopped eating, and now his haunches were bony and his head drooped.

'There doesn't seem to be anything actually wrong with him,' said Jez. 'He's just old and sad.'

'What do you think?'

Jez folded his arms and circled the horse, studying him carefully. 'He looks terrible.'

'We can't let him go on, can we?'

Jez shook his head. 'He doesn't seem to want to.'

Bramble found some mints in her pocket and Ben nibbled feebly at her hand, but failed to take them. She put an arm round his neck. 'Oh Ben, not even up to a mint?'

The old horse stood there, motionless, and his head sagged a little lower.

She patted him and swallowed tears. 'OK. Let's call the kennels.'

'I can take care of it if you want.'

Bramble turned away to hide the tears welling up, and she shook her head, not trusting herself to speak. She swallowed. 'You call Johnnie,' she said hoarsely. 'But I'm going to be there.'

Jez went inside to call the huntsman, who would come to put Ben down. His carcass would be fed to the hounds. It would be his 'one last ride across country', considered to be an end for the finest of horses, freeing their spirits over the land they'd jumped in life.

She tied Ben up and began to groom him. She knew the old boy found it soothing, and it seemed important that he go out looking his best. She brushed the mud away from his belly, sponged his face and combed his mane. Then she worked methodically over his gaunt frame, brushing as carefully and thoroughly as if he were about to do a dressage test. It took her nearly three-quarters of an hour, and his lower lip drooped in pure relaxation, his eyes closing peacefully. He rested one back hoof and dozed off, as if dreaming of better times. When she finished, he put his ears forward with pride, towards the horsebox in the yard. I'm back in business, he seemed to say. Going places. This time

I'm not going to be left behind in the field while lesser horses compete. I am still a champion. He held his head a little higher.

Johnnie arrived in his truck, and she led Ben to the field with the best grass. He took a few mouthfuls before stopping, as if to say, 'That was very nice, but no more for now'.

'I'm sorry,' said Johnnie. 'He's a wonderful old boy.'

Bramble nodded.

'Do you want to hold his head?' asked Johnnie. 'Jez can do it for you.'

'I'll do it,' whispered Bramble. She gave the whiskery muzzle a last kiss and thought she heard herself say 'goodbye'. Then she nodded to Johnnie.

There was a soft 'whump' as the bullet hit him between the eyes. Ben dropped to the ground instantly.

Bramble left Jez and Johnnie to winch Ben's body onto the truck, the memories coming thick and fast as she walked across the muddy field. Ben had been with Edward since he was four and Bramble remembered the day he'd arrived at Lorenden.

Ben was gentle enough for the old stable cat, Tiggy – now long gone – to sleep on his back, but had gone on to win Badminton and her father's Olympic gold. He'd become a star in his own right, and a collage of his press cuttings hung in the downstairs loo, ringed by rosettes and photographs. Edward had always said that riding him after riding any other horse was like driving a Ferrari after a journey in an old banger. There were so many happy memories, triumphs and laughter and a sense of purpose and achievement.

But he could be temperamental. Boy, did he have star temperament, mused Bramble. Only Edward could make him do something he didn't want to do.

Like live. He didn't want to go on without Edward.

The sense of her father swept across her, engulfing her in a tide of sadness. She could almost feel his bony arm, his scratchy coat, and see his weatherbeaten smile. His voice whispered in her ear, but she couldn't hear what he was saying.

'What do you want?' she shouted to the wind. 'Tell me what I should do.' The words disappeared across the fields, drifting like children's balloons then fading into the distance. There was no answer, just the lingering feeling that there was something important she had missed.

She spent the afternoon sorting papers and deciding which events they should enter next season. Darcy came into the room and whined at her several times, then curled up at her feet; even Mop and Muddle seemed to have lost their sparkle. She wondered if dogs could scent death.

Jez came into the kitchen at three o'clock, his face pale under the olive skin. 'Are you OK?' he asked.

Bramble didn't meet his eyes. 'Fine,' she managed to say.

'I'm really sorry,' said Jez. 'He was special.'

Bramble nodded and blinked back her tears. She clenched her fists tightly under the table. She would not have pity from Jez, she would not. She would not be pitied by anyone.

'Well, anyway,' she cleared her throat. 'Do you, er, want a cup of tea?'

'I'm fine.' Jez spoke quietly. 'What about you?'

'I'm fine, too,' she said hastily. 'Well, I suppose we'd better get on.'

'You were brave. To be there for him.'

The large rock of pain that had settled round her heart so long ago moved up to her throat, blocking any words. Without looking at him, she shot out the back door. Everything seems to be falling apart, she thought, choking back tears. I don't think I can do this alone. Perhaps Helena is right – I can't manage without Pa. Or without Dom. She realised, with a jolt, that she had barely thought of Dom for days. Weeks, perhaps.

Sorry, Dom, she muttered. I can't even remember the colour of your eyes. Even his infectious, shouting laugh, the biggest thing about him, seemed like something she had read in a book about someone she had never met. Forgetting its timbre seemed the ultimate betrayal. Bramble wished she could cry, but there were no more tears left for him. He had gone completely.

Unlike her father, whose presence permeated every brick and stone at Lorenden, infiltrating her thoughts like a guilty conscience. What did he want of her? Why did it all feel so jagged and unfinished? She felt very alone until she remembered Nat's big, comforting bulk, protecting her against the winter night.

Savannah was furious when she got home. 'I wanted to say goodbye to Ben. You should have waited.'

'He was suffering,' explained Bramble.

'Then you could have come and got me. School would have understood.'

Bramble couldn't explain that she had given up. That it was as if her entire body and mind had shut down, that she had needed to get it over with. She didn't want Savannah to think she was cracking up.

'I'm sorry,' she said wearily.

'Sorry isn't good enough.' Savannah stormed out of the house in tears and, out of the window, Bramble saw Jez catch her by the arm.

The phone rang. It was Nat.

'I've just heard,' he said. 'You should have called me. I would have come immediately.'

'Well.' Bramble couldn't bear feeling so very lonely for another minute. 'Why not come now?'

'I'll be with you in ten.'

Eddie had developed a strategy. Two days a week, he left school at lunchtime, calculating that his tormentors would still be in bed. The other three days, he went home with friends, sleeping on a variety of mattresses, sofa beds and bunks. Helena, slumped in a fog of bad temper and worry, seemed barely to have noticed, and Ollie, Eddie suspected, preferred him out the house as much as possible. Only little Ruby and Roly crawled into his bed on the nights he was home and asked him where he'd been. Then one of them usually wet Eddie's bed, after which they returned to their own.

Eddie had become adept at changing sheets, or sleeping across his bed to avoid the damp patch and generally sleeping anywhere that didn't involve the journey home in the evening.

He liked his friends' houses. Nobody seemed to take too much notice of him. His favourite was Rufus's. Rufus's mother, a stout, red-faced woman in elasticated waistbands – she was so unfashionable that Helena barely considered her human – was orderly and kind. Eddie's backpack and coat were hung neatly in the cloakroom and the front door was closed. Eddie, tucking into home-made stew, could forget everything.

Rufus was also pleasantly undemanding and they mostly talked about how the school team were going, or what Chelsea had done. Rufus, though, was in love with a girl from a nearby school.

'So where are you going to try for?' he asked Eddie one day. 'You know, which university . . .'

'I'm not going to university,' said Eddie. 'I'm going to be a rider.' It was the first time he'd said the words out loud as if they were a fact and not a dream or a question. Or a plea. He would be a rider. Saying them made it seem as if it might all really happen.

Rufus nodded as if he understood. In fact, it made no sense to him, but hey, most things didn't make much sense when you thought about them. 'Cool,' he said, accepting.

'Now boys,' said Rufus's mother, putting her head round the door. 'One hour's prep after supper, then bed. You know the rules. No TV. No Game Boy. No PlayStation. Not during the week.'

Eddie didn't mind. Rufus's house was safe, and that was all that mattered. Rufus and Eddie laughed and joshed each other as they went upstairs.

But, even to Rufus, Eddie didn't confess that he was afraid to walk down his own street.

The night before Jez left for Ireland, Pauline rang Bramble.

'I've got a buyer for Teddy,' she said brightly.

'But you said you weren't selling.' Bramble was aghast. Pauline's words made no sense to her at all. Surely she couldn't be taking Teddy away, just ten weeks before Badminton.

'I didn't *say* I wasn't selling. You rang up and asked me if you could sell him. I wasn't the one to raise the subject. After our conversation, I mentioned it to someone I met at a party and he was interested.'

'But . . . but . . . that's not what I said. I said . . .' Bramble wondered if she was going mad.

'Well, I hope you're not suggesting I'm senile. I'm quite clear about how the conversation went. *You* rang *me* to talk about selling Teddy. You needn't worry about getting your commission: Edward was the one who made him what he is so I'm very happy to pay that.' Pauline's voice, usually so creamy-sweet, was hard and businesslike.

'Pauline, I don't care about the commission,' begged Bramble. 'Just don't sell Teddy.'

'I've made my decision now. I can't go back on it.'

'Who have you sold him to?'

'Toby Fitzroy.'

'Toby Fitzroy! But he's a terrible rider. And he ruins his horses.'

'Toby Fitzroy is very experienced and well known on the eventing circuit,' reproved Pauline.

'Yes, that's why we all know what an appalling rider he is.' She made one last effort. 'He buys wonderful horses and destroys them. He's gets to the top events because he's got so much sodding money that all he really has to do is buy a good horse and sit on it. And he can't even do that without breaking their hearts – or their legs. Pauline, you love Teddy.'

Pauline's voice began to sound wavery and old. 'Oh Bramble, don't make this harder for me than it already is. Of course I love Teddy. Don't you realise how upset I am? But it's all too painful, it reminds me of your father, who was our oldest, oldest friend. And we can't afford Teddy; the price of everything has gone up so shockingly, and we're on pensions, you know . . .'

There was nothing that Bramble could say. She put the phone down, numb, after Pauline told her that Toby's horsebox would collect Teddy the following day. She had obviously been unable to pluck up courage to make the call until the last minute.

Bramble stared at the phone. Everything they were working towards had gone. Teddy was their only big horse. Their only chance to prove themselves. She felt sick, too sick even to be angry. It was all gone. Down the pan.

Pauline put the phone down with a sense of satisfaction. That would show them. Nobody cared about her. They thought she was a silly old woman who'd be happy to pay all the bills while they galloped her horse up hill and down dale without a care in the world. Felicity was probably gossiping about her even now, telling them all that Pauline had been in love with Edward.

Pauline had always, always been loyal to Alan and utterly discreet. Those girls knew nothing about loyalty and discretion.

Pauline raised her head with dignity and went into the flower room to arrange flowers for a dinner party that evening. She hadn't been totally honest when she said she'd sold Teddy. She'd sold half of Teddy. She was going to go to the parties at all the great houses and castles, only this time with Toby Fitzroy, who was a charming young man and knew how to make an owner feel appreciated.

She cut the ends off a bunch of roses with a vengeance. Of course, Toby was hardly a *young* man – fifty if he was a day – but he seemed like one to her. Like those girls who didn't know how lucky they were. Well, they were *women* really, with responsibilities to their husbands and children. She shook her head. Women should know better. Eventing was dangerous and they had their families to think of.

Alan bumbled in. 'Who was that on the phone?'

'Bramble.' Pauline straightened the roses and carried them off to the drawing room.

Alan followed her. 'What did she want?'

'Oh, I was just telling her that I've sold Teddy to Toby Fitzroy.' Telling Alan was the worst of it, the bit she dreaded most. She went back to the kitchen and started pulling ingredients out of the fridge to make a Hollandaise sauce.

'Selling Teddy?'

'Well, it was Bramble's idea really.' Pauline had almost convinced herself that this was true. 'She rang me a few weeks ago and started rambling on about selling Teddy and getting some commission, so when Toby approached me . . .' She fitted up the hand-held electric whisk and turned it on, blending an egg unnecessarily loudly so that she couldn't hear what he had to say about it.

He switched the whisk off at the plug. 'Why did you do that?'

Pauline pretended to rummage in one of the drawers for a piece of equipment. 'Well, you're always telling me how short of money we are. Toby gave me fifty thousand pounds for half of Teddy and is doing a very special deal with livery and training fees. I'm saving us so much money, I'd have thought you'd be pleased.'

'You're destroying everything that Bramble has worked for. Just because she isn't Edward.'

Pauline straightened up and looked him in the eye, angrier than she had ever been before. 'Tough,' she said.

Choking back tears, Bramble stormed up to Jez's attic flat and flung the door open. The rooms were almost empty. Tidy. Shabby. Clean. And with very few signs of occupation. There was a suitcase on the floor, and a pile of CDs beside the television set. And a single coffee mug, unwashed in the sink. Jez was a man who travelled light.

'Jez! Jez!'

'Bramble?' He came out of the shower room with wet hair and a towel wrapped round his waist. A herringbone of dark hair traced a line down his flat abdomen.

She didn't apologise. 'Have you been talking to Toby Fitzroy?' she demanded.

'No, of course not. Why?'

'Because he's bought Teddy, that's why, and you knew all about it.'

'Toby Fitzroy, oh shit. Let me get dressed.' Jez disappeared behind a door and came out a few minutes later, pulling a sweater over his head. 'Let me get one thing straight. I did *not* know about it. I heard some rumours in the pub, and thought Pauline seemed disengaged enough from us for them to be true.'

'It's a disaster,' said Bramble, almost shaking. 'Teddy's our only chance. What can we do?'

Jez shook his head. He looked shocked.

'I don't think we can afford to buy any more horses now,' she said.

'We've got to take risks. If we don't keep going forward we drop back.'

Bramble suddenly realised that Jez's dream of winning Badminton, and representing Britain, had been knocked back. Again.

'Jez, I'm so sorry.' She put a hand on his arm. 'I didn't think. This is just as bad for you as it is for me. Worse. I'm so sorry.'

He looked down at her from a long way away. 'It happens,' he said, his face expressionless. 'You know.'

Bramble did know. Over the past seven years she had twice had an owner sell a promising horse from under her. There was too much money involved – people couldn't always turn it down, even if they wanted to. 'Is there any way we can get a four-star horse, or even that you can ride for someone else? Isn't there anyone else needing a rider?' She racked her brains.

'There are more good riders than there are horses.' Jez's voice was flat. 'It's only ten weeks to Badminton and I don't see another ride coming up in time.'

'No.' There was nothing more to say. 'Oh, why did she do it? She said they were short of money, but . . .'

Jez laid a hand on her shoulder. 'It doesn't matter why she did it. She's done it, that's all.'

Bramble touched his hand with hers, in sympathy. 'I'm so sorry, Jez. So sorry. You came all this way for Teddy.'

He didn't speak, and she wondered if he was angry with her, if he blamed her for not keeping Pauline happy. She was suddenly aware of his body so close to hers. She could see the texture of his skin and the dusting of dark hair along his arms.

'You know something?' She suddenly felt it was important to tell him the truth.

'What?' He looked down at her, and she thought she detected something that almost seemed like tenderness.

'I couldn't have ridden Teddy. Not at the major events. I lost control of him, just for a few seconds, when he didn't like Merlin racing ahead of him. And then I knew it could happen again. Easily. Maybe when it really mattered. I was . . .' she swallowed '. . . terrified. I've never been that frightened on a horse before.'

Jez lifted a strand of hair that had fallen over her eye and smoothed it back. 'I thought something like that had happened.'

'I think I've probably been fooling myself all this time. I should probably face up to it, shouldn't I? Somewhere along the line I've lost my nerve and that's why I've never got to the top. Pa was right.'

Jez shook his head. 'That's not what he said. He said you couldn't ride Teddy. He was just too big. You know that.' He smiled down at her. 'We'd better concentrate on getting something fantastic in Ireland now, hadn't we?'

Bramble could barely breathe. She had intended to insist that they couldn't afford to go to Ireland and buy horses now, but she didn't want to sound . . . silly.

'We're not going to let this stop us,' added Jez, and she believed him.

'No, you're right.' Bramble forced herself to smile back at him and go downstairs again, still shaking with shock.

Once in her father's study, Jez's words faded away and her sense of failure cloaked her. She sat quietly in the dark for a while, and tried to tell herself that her dream wasn't over. That somehow she could still go on.

The phone rang. It was Nat. Her eyes filled with tears. She wanted to go over to his cottage, curl up in his arms and die.

Nat laid a fire, poured her a glass of wine and was philosophical, as she'd known he'd be. 'Well, you know,' he said in his rich voice, as he dropped down on to the sofa beside her, 'sometimes this sort of thing can be a turning point. Maybe you'll look back on today and realise that as one door shuts another door opens.'

'I just feel that I'm never going to get there. It all comes so close and then it slips away again. It's happened again and again over the past seven years.'

'Hold on to that thought,' he advised her. 'And when it stops making you feel frightened, then you'll be ready to decide what to do next. You have options, you have so many options. You don't have to be Bramble Kelly, the rider.'

'This is me, Nat, this is what I do. If I don't have this, what do I have?'

'You have me.' He drew her close to him.

'Pauline sold Teddy because I came back,' said Felicity.

'Felicity.' Bramble tried to tread carefully because she hadn't quite relinquished the dream that Felicity might ultimately stay at Lorenden and that they could buy Helena out, but she couldn't quite conceal her irritation. 'I honestly don't see how you can be that important. Sorry, but you know . . .'

They were getting Teddy ready, packing up his boxes of kit, sorting out what was theirs and what belonged to Pauline. Pauline had declined to come and see him off: 'It'll upset me too much' was her excuse.

'I'm not saying it's the only reason,' said Felicity, picking an old sweet wrapper out of one of his boxes and re-rolling the bandages. 'But you must have noticed the way her face changes when she sees me. She looks as if she'd swallowed a lemon.'

'Don't worry about it.' Bramble was sharp. For a second she allowed herself to think that if Felicity hadn't come back, Teddy would still be at Lorenden, and then she suppressed it. She'd always somehow thought that if Felicity came back into their lives everything would be all right again, and it occurred to her that she had no idea why this belief was so firmly rooted in her head. It certainly hadn't come from her father.

'He knows something's up.' Bramble indicated Teddy's head over the top of the stable door. He knocked at the door with his hoof and snorted. The horse moved restlessly round his box and reappeared, as if to ask what was going on. Everyone was ringed around, looking at him – Savannah, Lottie, Donna and Jez, plus a few other people, a livery owner and a woman who lived in the cottages – who were specially fond of him. Several friends had popped in. Horses coming and going was always an event. Felicity and Donna put his travel boots on and rolled a bandage round his tail. 'There. All ready.'

Bramble was still scribbling notes for Toby and his grooms: 'Watch out when you're loading and unloading, he can barge out over you. He loves company – don't ever leave him alone or he goes demented . . .' 'What else?' she asked Donna.

Donna was crying as she patted his neck. 'He's a perfect gentleman in the stable,' she sniffed, 'but he's bloody minded out of it.'

'You'll have a life of luxury,' said Donna to Teddy. 'Don't forget us.'

'He won't forget us.' Lottie opened a packet of mints. 'Horses never forget anything.' Teddy accepted a mint like the gentleman he was, rolling it off her hand with velvet lips.

Toby's vast pantechnicon backed up the drive. It was too big to come in forwards, as it wouldn't be able to turn round.

'He's got a smaller, two-horse box, you know,' said Bramble. 'In matching colours,' she added crossly. 'I reckon he's showing us what a big willy he's got by using that one.'

'He's come in person,' Felicity said, as Toby jumped down from the cab and walked towards them with a cowboy gait, his grooms following behind him. 'And he's come in force. He doesn't need two grooms to load a horse.'

'He's here to crow, obviously. Do you think he dyes his hair? It can't still be blond at his age, can it?'

Felicity and Bramble walked to meet him.

'Hello Toby,' said Felicity.

'I'm so sorry to be taking your horse away,' he said. 'But you know how it is in this business.'

'You've been waiting thirty years to say that,' said Felicity.

'Well,' he said, with the grin that charmed hostesses from Morocco to Mustique. 'Perhaps I have. And, do you know? It was worth it.'

Chapter 21

Helena lay awake at four o'clock in the morning, listening to the distant sirens of the city and the swishing of cars driving past. Her over-strained ears picked up a scratching sound from the front door.

She was downstairs in a flash, to see Ollie, with matted hair and filthy clothes, closing the door quietly behind him.

'Where have you been?'

He jumped. 'You gave me a fright.'

'*You* gave *me* a fright. I had no idea where you were,' she whispered furiously. 'I've been checking the hospitals. Lying to the children. Not getting a wink of sleep. This is the second night you've been away. Do you know how worried I've been? How terrified?'

Ollie ran his hands through his filthy hair. 'Oh, God, I'm so sorry. I've been, um, actually I don't know where I've been.' He sank down on the bottom stair and began to cry great, choking male tears. 'I walked. I walked and walked. I was afraid to come home. To look you in the eye. I'm so sorry,' he sobbed. 'So sorry for everything.'

Helena was wrong-footed. She'd expected blame and anger, not complete collapse. She squatted down beside him and put her arm around him tentatively. 'Why didn't you trust me? We can talk.' She thought of the terrifying pile of letters, and swallowed. 'Whatever happens, we can face it together.'

He raised a tear-stained face to hers. 'Helena, I don't mind what happens as long as we're together. Please, please, just tell me you've forgiven me.'

'Of course,' she said. 'You know I'd forgive you anything. But we must . . . sit down and talk about it all.'

He nodded. 'Not now, though. I have to sleep. I don't think I've slept . . .' he swayed as he got up, and Helena caught his elbow.

'Come on, my darling. Bed. This minute. We'll talk later.'

He fell face down on the bed fully clothed. 'Talk. Yes.' In a minute he was snoring noisily.

Helena inhaled. He smelt like a tramp. She'd driven him away. It was all her fault. Guilt swamped her anger as she tiptoed away to sleep in the spare room. Forgiveness was one thing, sleeping next to someone who smelt that bad was quite another. Those envelopes, piled high with their frightening secrets, could wait. She didn't want anything to come in the way of getting Eddie through his A levels. And, of course, getting Lorenden sold. Because it was beginning to look as if she couldn't wait a year to get her hands on the money.

The phone had started to ring again, but instead of party invitations and requests from her agents there were stern-voiced people on the other end, demanding payment. Some of them phoned every day and Helena had gone out to buy a phone that would screen calls. Two of her cards had been rejected when she tried to pay for it, but the third, luckily, had gone through.

'It's quite ridiculous,' said Helena. 'I will complain.'

Bramble, out hacking on Merlin one morning, saw a shrunken, shambling old man in one of the fields. She blinked. It was Alan, usually so dapper.

'Alan!'

He peered at her. 'Hello, darling.' Alan called everyone 'darling'. 'We haven't seen you for ages.'

'Er, no. How are the family?'

'The family?' Alan looked mystified.

'Have any of them been down recently?' Bramble bowled on.

'Well, someone came. Can't remember who.'

It hardly seemed worth pursuing the conversation, but Bramble had one more go. 'We were so sorry to lose Teddy to Toby Fitzroy.'

A little comprehension glimmered behind Alan's eyes. 'Bad business that. Toby Fitzroy. He won't forgive you, you know. Never has. Stupid boy.'

It was hopeless. Alan was making no sense at all. 'Are you all right?' asked Bramble.

'Fine, darling,' said Alan. 'Never better.'

'Are you going home?'

'Home?' he repeated. 'That's right. Home. Lovely to see you, darling. Give my best to your father.'

Bramble hoped he could still find his way across the fields he'd known all his life, and kept a discreet eye on him until she saw him outside his own gates.

Everyone – Bramble, Felicity, Jez, Savannah and Donna – worked with a sense of defeat. Teddy's box seemed very empty. His presence, like Ben's, had been immense.

And so was Merlin's, Bramble realised suddenly. Here was another horse who walked like a champion, she thought, watching Jez lead him in from the field. Now that there was no Teddy, he seemed to come into his own. She went into the kitchen and found Felicity reading the newspaper. 'Felicity, you've got all Merlin's paperwork, haven't you?'

Felicity looked wary, as if this was another trick. Every day she made a different excuse as to why she could ride Sailor but not Merlin, and Bramble, reluctant to put anyone up on a horse if they didn't feel right about it, hadn't pressed the point any further. And, as for helping out in the stables, Felicity threw herself with great vigour into occasional jobs – often very dirty or unrewarding ones – and she cleaned Sailor's tack after she'd ridden him, but otherwise she kept her distance. She was infuriatingly perverse: if Bramble asked her to do something there was always a reason why she couldn't carry out the task, but then occasionally a major job had to be done – unloading the hay bales, for example – and Felicity would set to without a word. Everything she did, she did well. But the message was clear: I'm here on my own terms. Don't count on me, I'm not part of the team.

'Merlin's paperwork,' repeated Bramble. 'You do have it?'

'Sure. It got passed on by the insurance company. Do you want to take a look?'

Bramble went through it all. He was four years old and officially called Overnight Flight. 'I wonder what his stable name was,' she said.

Felicity shrugged. 'It's bad luck to change it, so I'd rather not know. He'll always be Merlin to me.'

Bramble frowned with concentration. 'He's a fast learner and, although he's got plenty of spirit, he also wants to please. I think we should aim him at the Young Horse Championships.

'I don't think he's ready,' said Jez, putting the kettle on to boil. 'I think he needs a lot more time. I'm betting he's got some bad memories. Probably around racing and competing in general.'

Bramble tried not to feel irritated, and looked at Felicity. 'It's your call. Do you want me to see what he can do?'

Felicity yawned. 'Do what you like.'

Helena had intended to talk to Ollie about the envelopes, but Angelina threw a party, so there was no time. Then she decided that it would be better to tackle the subject once she had a new part, so that they might have a better idea of where they stood. By the time she'd got an appointment to talk to Caroline, and attended a few auditions, they'd slipped back into their old life. The pile of envelopes receded in her mind and she managed to find ways of ignoring any fresh ones that arrived.

She visited the doctor, who prescribed some anti-depressants and a few sleeping pills. Life drifted by in a pleasant, slightly headachey haze, and she felt one step removed from the outside world. It was all temporary, she told herself. Just until she was established again. She was talking to a hot new production company about a comedy series, and they'd promised that the part was almost hers.

One morning Ruby had a sniffle and a slight temperature, so Helena bundled the child into their huge double bed, got in with her and cuddled down, settling Oscar on the other side. Protected by the small, warm bodies, she drifted off, one ear cocked as usual, waiting for the call that would tell her she was back in business.

The late-morning sound of the doorbell, insistent and repetitive, penetrated her consciousness. Helena sat up, her heart beating loudly in dread. Oscar cocked his ears, and let out two short yaps.

'Shh, Oscar.' She fondled his silky head. 'We don't necessarily want people to know we're here, do we?' She tiptoed down the stairs in her stockinged feet and peered through the spyhole, unable to restrain a gasp when she saw the two bulky shapes on the other side. She crept away from the door.

'Mrs Cooper.' The voice booming through the letterbox made her jump. 'Mrs Cooper, we have a court order. We're the bailiffs. And we know you're there.' Then a minute's silence. 'Mrs Cooper?'

'I know my rights,' shouted Helena, in a shaky voice. 'I don't have to let you in.' She tiptoed down to the kitchen, opening the fridge door and pouring herself a glass of white wine to steady her nerves. There was a tap on the basement window and she nearly dropped her wine. The two men loomed through the glass. Helena hastily shut the slats of the blind, trying not whimper in terror.

The phone rang. 'Hello?' she whispered.

It was Caroline. 'That part you went for,' Caroline dived straight in. 'It's no go, I'm afraid.'

Helena had been counting on it. 'Shit! But they were so keen.'

'They aren't now.'

'But why?' pleaded Helena, her heart beating a tattoo. 'Couldn't you persuade them?'

'They've been asking around.' Caroline knew that her job, as an agent, was to be truthful when it mattered. 'The word is that you're unreliable. The rumour is that you might be drinking a bit too much.'

'Me? Drinking! That's . . . that's absurd! Who is spreading these lies? Can we sue them? It's that Melissa, isn't it? She's jealous of me, she always has been.'

'When did you last have a drink?' asked Caroline.

Helena looked at the empty glass in her hand. It didn't count: she was in shock. She deserved it. 'Ages ago. I can't remember when. Really, this is outrageous. Someone is determined to wreck my career. It's so unfair. I have such a healthy lifestyle – ask anyone. I only eat organic food, go to the gym four times a week, always have my two litres of water a day . . .' she trailed off.

'It doesn't matter how much water you drink. There are stories going round about you falling apart while shooting the last series.'

'My father'd just died. And that was all Melissa putting spin on nothing . . .'

'Look,' Caroline sounded weary. 'I'm here if you want to talk. Any time.'

'I just don't know what to say. This is so stressful.' Helena put the phone down. Maybe people were muddling her up with Ollie. She shivered, poured herself another glass and went upstairs to get a sweater, Oscar pattering after her.

As she reached the top of the stairs she heard Ruby shriek. The little girl came barrelling out of the bedroom and clung to Helena's legs, sobbing in fright.

The bailiffs were in Ollie and Helena's bedroom.

Helena, too, screamed and dropped the wine glass in her hand. Oscar began to yap.

'As you know your rights,' said one, 'you'll be aware that we're allowed to enter through an open window.'

Stunned, Helena, still with Ruby clinging to her leg, staggered to the window and looked out. They'd propped a ladder up against the house.

'How dare you terrify my child in this way?' she demanded. 'I could have you put on the paeodophile register for this.'

They ignored her, and began unplugging the flat-screen TV that she'd bought Ollie as an extra Christmas present.

'Very nice. Top of the range. And new, if I'm not mistaken.'

Helena picked Ruby up and tried to comfort her. She clung, whimpering, to Helena's neck. Helena cleared her throat. 'I shall call the police.'

The two men barely glanced at her. 'People often do,' said one. 'The police don't care. You're a debtor.'

Helena realised that she had crossed to the other side. She was no longer a law-abiding, tax-paying citizen to be respected and protected, but an almost-criminal, to be pushed around and scorned by authority. She felt utterly powerless.

'I don't even know what bills my husband hasn't paid.'

'He hasn't paid any of them, by the look of it. But we're here for council tax arrears.'

'I'd like to see your identification,' she asked primly. 'Otherwise I'll have to assume that you've broken in.'

As the bailiff thrust his identification towards Helena, Oscar, believing his mistress to be under attack, rushed forwards and sank his teeth into the sturdy calf above the steel toe-capped boot. The man hopped and swore.

'Cute dog.' The other bailiff's huge hands picked up Oscar as the little dog yapped and snarled uselessly. 'Second hand goods, stuff like televisions and the like, well, you wouldn't believe how little they fetch. But a dog like this . . . what do you think, Andy?'

'Five hundred at least,' Andy said, rubbing his leg.

'Don't you dare. Don't you dare. I'll call the RSPCA,' Helena screamed, over and over again. 'You've no right, no right at all. Oscar's a living creature. He'll be frightened without us. He's part of our family.'

'This is your last warning.' Andy threw the still-snapping Oscar back onto the bed. They strode out of the bedroom, down the stairs and out the front door, still holding the television and DVD player, tossing her a receipt. 'Be clear about this, Mrs. We can get in. Any time we like. And we can take what we want. Legally. It's time to pay up.'

'Don't let them take Oscar,' screamed Ruby. 'And don't let them take me.' It took Helena half an hour to disentangle a sobbing, frightened Ruby from her arms, and then she had to clear away the broken wine glass.

At Lorenden, Felicity, leaving her room, saw a ray of light pointing a finger across the landing carpet. Her father's bedroom door was open. Since he'd died, only Helena had been in there, coming out with a pair of cufflinks and a tiepin that she'd suggested should go to Eddie. But now the dust danced in the sunlight and the old rosewood chest of drawers stood between the windows, where it had always been.

She took a deep breath and went into the room. It still smelt of him, of his soap and his well-polished boots, of beeswax, musty carpet and closed, empty room. A few bluebottles lay dead on the windowsill.

Bramble was behind a wardrobe door, and jumped out of her skin when she saw Felicity. 'Oh, it's you.'

'I saw the door open and . . . thought you might want some help.'

'Oh, right. Yes.' Bramble indicated a pile of dustbin bags on the bed. 'We sort. Anything valuable or sentimental, we save to discuss with Helena. Everything else, out. I'll finish the wardrobe and you take the chest of drawers.'

Felicity began to open the drawers, pulling out their meagre contents. Most of Edward's clothes were so well worn that, although they were well-cut and made of fine material, there was nowhere for them to go except out. 'Not even a charity shop, what d'you think?' She tipped out the bottom drawer and threw most of its contents away. The drawer was lined with paper, which also flipped out. There was a letter hidden underneath, in her mother's writing. Felicity knew the cursive script so very well and her heart turned over.

Bramble's head was back in the wardrobe, and Felicity slid the letter into her sleeve. She would show it to Bramble later – of course – but just now she wanted her mother to herself.

She was the only one of the three of them who really remembered her, after all. Bramble had only been five when she died, and Helena nine, but Felicity had had her whole childhood, and her teenage years, with her, and losing her had been like losing everything. She had never thought, when she left Lorenden, that her mother would be gone before she came back. But she'd died. And they hadn't told her in time. Felicity gave a whimper of pain.

Bramble's head shot out of the wardrobe. 'Are you OK?'

'Yes, fine.' Felicity shook her hand. 'Just pricked my finger on an . . . er . . . old tiepin. Silly.'

The shape of the writing brought the memories flooding back. Of her mother saying that she was relying on her to help with the little ones, especially after Bramble was born. Helena had always been chasing after Felicity wanting to be like her, pathetically demanding her privileges in spite of the ten-year age gap, but Bramble had been so small she had captured Felicity's heart. She remembered how she'd loved seeing the toddler come running towards her on short, fat legs, arms outstretched, giggling. There was very little left of that laughing affectionate child now, just a self-contained, rather serious woman. Although that, too, had been there at an early age: Bramble had played on her own for hours, with intense concentration, building a brick tower up as high as she could then, when it fell down, building it up again, always determined to get it one brick higher.

'What?' asked Bramble, catching Felicity's eye.

'Sorry,' said Felicity. 'I was just remembering . . . things.'

'Well, while you're about it, perhaps you'd like to remember why Toby Fitzroy has it in for us.' There was a plea in Bramble's voice, muffled by the inside of the wardrobe.

Felicity hesitated. This was verging on dangerous territory. She decided to take the risk. 'When Pa was just beginning to be really successful, Toby was about nineteen and *his* father thought riding was a waste of time, but if a Fitzroy was going to do something he was going to do it well. He used to buy Toby good horses, top equipment, training, everything . . . but he really put him under pressure. We'd hear old man Fitzroy shouting at him sometimes – you know how sound travels when people have arguments in horseboxes. Toby had to prove himself or join the bank.

'Toby was particularly excited about one horse, but he had a bad day on him at Wylye and the old man pulled the plug. In those days, patriotism was considered an important part of sportsmanship, and the British selectors put pressure on the Fitzroys to sell the horse to Pa. In those days, Toby's parents and ours were great friends, along with Pauline and Alan and a few other couples – they all used to go on holiday together. Pa told Toby's father that Toby was never going to make it as a rider – and Pauline backed him up, so Hugh Fitzroy sold Pa the horse and ordered Toby to join the bank or be disinherited. So that was the end of Toby as a professional rider, although he obviously started competing as an amateur once he made enough money to finance it. He blamed Pa for stopping his career at a critical point, and for destroying his father's faith in him because of wanting the horse.'

'Which horse was it?'

'The first Merlin. Merlin's Magic, the one he nearly took to the

Olympics. I went with Pa to fetch him, and Toby took me to one side and promised to destroy us. He told us that the Fitzroys never let anyone take anything from them. He said I'd see.'

'And then Merlin died of colic, isn't that right?'

Felicity nodded and, joining Bramble in the wardrobe, wrenched the remaining suits off the rails, flinging them on the bed. 'Now then, these suits can only go to the tip.'

'Why did you call the horse you rescued Merlin?'

'No reason, really,' said Felicity. 'They needed an M and it popped into my mind.'

'We've all had horses sold from under us,' said Bramble. 'We don't bear grudges for decades. But I'm surprised Pa never told me. It doesn't show him in a great light, I suppose . . .'

'Toby can't bear not to win, I know that,' said Felicity. 'He had to win everything at Pony Club level, he was top of his class at school and in all the sports teams. I think he was head boy. You know the kind of kid who's never met failure and doesn't know how to cope when it does eventually hit him. Then he went on to be a brilliant banker, and made another fortune to add to the one he started with. But he presumably reached a ceiling in terms of competitive riding, and perhaps really believed that if he'd kept going when he was young he would have got to the top there too.'

'Spoilt brat,' muttered Bramble, straightening up and taking out a photograph tucked into the corner of her father's mirror. It had been there so long she had ceased to notice it.

'Look.' She handed it to Felicity. It was a picture of the three of them, Felicity on a horse, with Bramble, as a baby, on the saddle in front of her, and Helena on a pony, her legs too short and her hat too big, grinning broadly. 'I never knew Helena rode.'

Felicity studied the picture, a feeling of warmth flooding over her in spite of herself. They'd been a happy family once. She'd almost forgotten that. 'Helena was so desperate to do everything I did, and everyone expected me look after her, especially out riding. She used to pester me and wanted to ride the horses I rode, which was ridiculous considering how young she was. One day, probably not long after that picture was taken, I let her ride a pony I knew she couldn't possibly handle. He took off with her, dumped her in a hedge and she broke her collarbone. She was screaming in pain and I told her that if she didn't get straight back on she'd never ride again, because horses would always know that she was frightened of them. She didn't get back on, and she didn't ride again. It was my fault.'

Bramble, tying up dustbin bags, didn't seem to think this was such a crime. 'Don't you think that, if she'd really wanted to, she'd have tried again whatever you said?'

'Maybe,' said Felicity, feeling one small edge of her iceberg of guilt melting at Bramble's brisk, matter-of-fact approach. 'Maybe you're right.' Something shifted inside her and she felt easier.

'What I don't understand, though,' said Bramble, 'is why Toby blames you in particular. Rather than Pa.'

Felicity rummaged through her mind for a suitable excuse, but the phone rang, making them both jump. She picked it up. 'It's for you,' she said, holding it out to Bramble. 'It's Nat.'

For a moment they looked at each other and Felicity thought that Bramble was going to refuse the call so that they could go on talking. She handed Bramble the phone, picked up the full dustbin bags and left the room. She thought she'd better get out before this turned into some terrible clichéd family memory-fest, complete with weeping and promises.

And she wanted to read the letter she'd found. Not for what it might contain – it was unlikely to be very interesting – but to hear Rose Beaumont's voice again as it leapt off the page.

Chapter 22

Cecily Marsh-Robertson pressed an entryphone button on a brick pillar in the middle of swathes of unspoilt countryside. Toby Fitzroy's vast wrought iron gates, inscribed with the name Beckett's Park, swung open slowly and impersonally. The gates and the entryphone seemed incongruous in the middle of nowhere, but Cecily supposed Toby needed good security. She bounced over a cattle grid and followed the winding drive for another five minutes. On one side she could see the fences of a cross-country course and, on the other, paddocks with a couple of mares and foals browsing the grass. As she approached the thicket of trees that concealed the house, she spotted two arenas. There was someone riding in each of them – in one, a girl without a hat, and with a long, flowing ponytail, was obviously practising a dressage test, and in the other, another girl jumped under instruction.

There were signposts: estate office, stables office, main house and stable cottages. She took the drive to the main house, following it round a generous, immaculate gravel curve and parking outside a massive porch.

The front door was almost three times her height. She was used to immense wealth in London, but the houses themselves were never built on this scale. Cecily suppressed the thought that it reminded her of a very grand prison, and concentrated on the tasteful landscaping around a fountain in the centre of the drive.

The door swung open to reveal a beautiful blonde woman. The

housekeeper? The live-in girlfriend? The cleaner? Toby's daughter? It was getting increasingly difficult to tell by people's clothes and mannerisms, thought Cecily crossly. She hated not being briefed properly. Before coming that day, she'd ordered her PA to draw up a one-page paper on junior eventing, and she now knew that Lottie should be doing the Junior Regional Novice series with a view to being on the South East team for the national championships. And she also knew that the Pony Club was a good route through, and that she should be heading for the nationals there too. Neither of which she seemed to be achieving under Bramble's tutelage.

Toby strode to greet her across a vast marble floor. 'Cecily! My dear!' He kissed her on both cheeks. 'How terribly kind of you to come. Can I get you anything?'

After a hurried negotiation he turned to the blonde. 'Laura, we'll both have peppermint tea. In the morning room.'

After sipping tea in a huge pale blue room with chintzy sofas and portraits, they toured the stables.

'When I inherited, the stables had been in use for over two hundred years . . .' he pointed to a row of speckled red-brick buildings with roses clambering up the side. 'But it seemed madness not to start from scratch so now they're staff quarters, except for the bigger one at the end, where Klaus lives.'

Cecily nodded. Klaus Jürgen, her PA had briefed her, was the captain of the German team and was based with Toby because Britain was at the heart of international eventing.

Toby led her away from the old stables to a massive modern barn, walking past a yard where five gleaming horseboxes of various sizes were parked, three with Toby Fitzroy Eventing and two with Klaus's name and a great deal of German sponsorship inscribed on the side. Since seeing Toby at the Fordham Castle event, Cecily had studied brochures carefully enough to know she was looking at over half a million pounds worth of transport.

'These are the stables,' said Toby, indicating a vast metal-roofed barn. 'We can house twenty-four horses in here, along with the tack room, the feed room, the hydrotherapy unit – basically, everything is together under one roof. We can drive the lorry in under cover when we get back and unload horses in the dry.' He laughed. 'It saves a lot of time, I can tell you, just to be able to unload and get them straight into their stables without having to dry them off because they've got wet between the lorry and the stables.'

It was like a factory, thought Cecily, impressed, designed by a businessman who had really researched his stuff. 'How many horses do you have?' she asked, her voice sounding small under the height of the barn roof.

'I have sixteen at the moment and Klaus has six, so we do have a couple of vacancies. I always have at least one top foreign rider based here, it's a marvellous learning curve for me and anyone who stables their horses with me.' He winked at her.

Cecily's briefing had included the fact that it cost approximately twenty thousand pounds a year to run one event horse, if you included feed, entries, veterinary and physiotherapy treatments, equipment, training . . . sixteen by twenty thousand . . . her sharp financial brain boggled at the figure she came up with. Toby was paying over three hundred thousand pounds a year to keep this show on the road. And the prize money at all but the most important events rarely topped a couple of hundred pounds. It was madness, thought Cecily. At least in racing and showjumping there was proper prize money. But Lottie needed to be part of this world. Here she would make the right contacts . . . even ultimately marry the right man. What Cecily could earn through her company paled beside the enormousness of this kind of wealth.

He showed her round. The horses were in blocks of six, stabled together for age, competition level and temperament. Some stables had windows outside, some were more private than others, some nearer the action. 'Each horse is different,' said Toby. 'Some horses love a view, others will jump out the window if you give them one.' There were charts neatly tacked to the walls: feed charts, exercise charts, charts of who was competing where. A hydrotherapy machine – 'all my horses have hydrotherapy as a matter of course after competing or hunting' – a horse walker and another barn, used as an indoor school, completed the set-up.

'It's stunning,' said Cecily, thinking of the ageing buildings at Lorenden. Of course, Bramble always kept the stables as neat as a pin, but the rest of it looked . . . well, old-fashioned.

'This is our latest horse,' said Toby, 'Lady Rudd's Be Good Be Clever.'

'Oh, I know Pauline quite well,' said Cecily, vaguely recognising the handsome head that turned to look at her. She fancied she saw reproach in Teddy's eyes. 'What are you doing here?' the horse asked, adding 'traitor' before turning back to his hay.

Cecily blinked. She was imagining things.

'She was a very old friend of Edward Beaumont's and she agonised over moving him here,' said Toby, 'but in the end she owed it to the horse. Everyone loves Bramble, of course, but Edward had "winner" written right through him like in a stick of rock, and Bramble simply doesn't.'

'What about the new man, Jezzar Morgan?'

'The Russian? You know, I wouldn't trust him. Penny, his previous owner, is an old friend of mine and she told me a few things about him.' Toby shook his head. 'Bramble must know all about it, of course, you don't get many secrets in this world, but also that boyfriend of hers trained as a farrier only a few miles away from where Penny was based and he will have told her what Morgan is really like.'

'What sort of things?' Cecily was alarmed. 'I mean . . . Lottie . . .'

'He does have rather a reputation with women,' admitted Toby. 'Penny's daughter was a bit older than Lottie but, at one point,' Toby lowered his voice, 'I gather he was sleeping with mother *and* daughter. So he's not, shall we say, *discriminating*.'

Cecily was appalled.

'But, of course, it's not the sex thing that matters,' Toby continued. 'What people do in the privacy of their own horseboxes is their business. But he . . . well, I gather he also stole some money and, really, if you can't trust someone with money, you can't trust them with your horse, don't you think?'

Cecily nodded. 'Or your child,' she added.

'Or your child,' he agreed. 'And what worried me was that Bramble hadn't even *told* Pauline, which I think is most unprofessional of her. When I mentioned it, Pauline was shocked. Very shocked. As you can imagine.'

'Quite.' Cecily was quite shocked herself.

'So,' said Toby, signalling to one of the grooms, 'shall we get Hannah here to put Vincent through his paces and you can see what you think?'

As they watched Hannah, who was around the same build as Lottie, take Vincent over a series of jumps, Toby talked about where Lottie should be in a few years' time and how, if she kept her horse at Beckett's Park, she could tap in to the expertise he had on hand. Cecily hardly bothered to watch Vincent; Toby obviously knew what he was talking about.

'Don't get me wrong,' he said. 'I think Bramble's done a wonderful job, for both Lottie and Sailor. She has a real strength in bringing on young horses and riders, but she can only take them so far. And when I saw Lottie riding Sailor at Fordham Castle that day, well, I thought, here's a *jolly* good little horse and rider, but it's not a combination that will ever get to national level.'

At that point, Cecily finalised her decision to sell Sailor.

When Jez arrived back from Ireland with the horsebox, Bramble and Savannah rushed out in excitement, followed by Felicity, Donna and Lottie. He'd rung to say that he had bought Frenchie, a seven-year-old who he thought was ripe for some early-season events, and who could then be taken further or sold on as a 'ready-made' eventer. 'Lots of potential,' he said. 'He won't necessarily go all the way to Badminton, but if not, we can certainly make a profit on him.'

He led out a delicately beautiful chestnut gelding. 'Hmm, chestnut,' said Bramble. 'Red-headed and temperamental.' She ran her eyes quickly over him. 'But he's certainly nicely put together – the dressage judges will like him.'

'You should see the jump in him,' said Jez. 'And he's honest – look at those big ears.'

'What's the link between honesty and big ears?' asked Lottie.

Once again, Bramble was caught out by Lottie's eager questioning. 'I don't know really, it's just something people say. They think big ears on a horse are a sign of being genuine. And a kind eye.'

Lottie looked puzzled.

'There's another one in there!' called Bramble. 'You've brought back two.'

'Ah.' Jez smiled. 'This one is special. She's for you.'

'Me?' Bramble wondered exactly what he meant.

Jez led a skewbald mare down the ramp, and Bramble's first panic-stricken impression was that she was hardly more than a pony – not much over fifteen hands. Her winter coat was so abundant that it almost concealed a delicate part-thoroughbred outline.

'Very pretty,' said Donna, approvingly. 'Lovely little mare. Under all that hair.'

'But that's what she is,' added Bramble. 'A little mare.' Humiliation flooded over her. She had told Jez that she'd been frightened of Teddy, and this . . . this . . . *pony* was his response. Something small and safe. 'I'm five foot eight, Jez. She's too small for me.' She tried to keep the tears of frustration out of her voice.

'I've ridden her,' said Jez. 'I'm over six foot. And she's good.' He patted her neck. 'She's very, very good.'

'So how come we got her with *our* budget?' demanded Bramble. She was vaguely aware of everyone else melting away from the sparks in the air, and of Frenchie being led off by Donna.

'The senior riders think she's too small and the juniors can't handle her. But if you turn her into a star, any foal she has will be worth a lot. She's got great potential.'

'Make her famous? Jez, are you mad? It doesn't work like that, you know that.' Bramble concealed her face by checking the horse over. She felt the strong legs and powerful hindquarters ripple under her hand. 'Well, obviously I can't tell in one glance, but if she's as good as you say she is, she's the sort of horse that ambitious Pony Club parents would pay a fortune for, even if she is a bit of a handful.'

Jez shook his head. 'That type want ready-made winners. This mare is only halfway there. And you're the best at getting a horse from halfway there to where Teddy is now.'

'I'm hardly going to win Badminton on a shaggy little pony, am I? Oh Jez, this means more money going out, no money coming in again. Why did you do it?'

'Because she reminded me of you.'

The air was silent between them.

'And why's that?' Bramble folded her arms, trying not to cry.

'She's brave and careful,' said Jez. 'It's an unusual combination.'

So Jez was being kind. Her anger drained away. She ought to be grateful. She had told him that she'd lost her nerve, and buying her a little mare with a few problems was his way of encouraging her. She didn't think she could handle such kindness from him. It underlined how far she'd fallen from the elite group of riders that everyone looked up to. She was embarrassed, now, to think she had ever believed she belonged there.

'She's also stubborn and determined to do things her own way,' added Jez, with a smile. 'You know what they say: you tell a gelding but you ask a mare. Well, this mare insists you say "please", and even then she'll make up her own mind.'

'Come on, Shaggy,' she said, taking the lead rope from him.

'She's called Chequerboard Charlotte,' Jez called after them. 'But everyone calls her Chessie.'

'I don't care,' said Bramble. 'While she's here, she's Shaggy.' She knew that it was considered unlucky to change a horse's stable name, but she was too miserable to care.

The following day, Bramble sat in the big chair in her father's office. It now had neat rows of files and, although there were still envelopes, magazines and newspapers on every surface, they were ordered in organised piles. Bramble knew where everything was, and what it all meant. Outside the window, the ground under the trees was patterned with purple, white and yellow as anemones and crocuses pushed through the remains of last year's fallen leaves. The first tips of green were beginning to spatter the winter browns, and the horses at Lorenden were ready to compete again.

The phone rang. It was Cecily Marsh-Robertson. 'I've sold Sailor,' she said, without preamble. 'I decided that it was time to take a stand. Lottie is wasting hours every day at your yard—'

'That's because she wants to,' interrupted Bramble. 'I think she enjoys it.'

'Enjoying herself?' Cecily sounded outraged. 'What good does that do her? She's not learning anything.'

'She's learning the value of hard work,' said Bramble.

'I don't want her to be a groom,' replied Cecily. 'And that's all she'll be fit for if she goes on like this. Anyway, it's pointless arguing. The Turnbulls are having Sailor because Georgie is just about right for him, and I've bought a very suitable next-stage-on horse from Toby Fitzroy. He'll be stabled there, of course, it'll cause much less upheaval.'

'Which one?' Bramble's stomach flipped. Cecily really was taking Sailor away, and a lost livery meant another set of bills that couldn't be paid.

'A chestnut. Vincent van Gogh, I think he's called.'

'Vincent's called Vincent because he's talented but a bit mad,' exclaimed Bramble, worried for Lottie as much as for the finances of Lorenden.

'He'll get her to the nationals, that's all that matters. And probably even on to the international circuit.'

'She's far too young for that,' said Bramble. 'She's actually one of the most brilliant and talented young riders I've had, but she really needs another couple of years . . .'

'Well, not this year obviously,' said Cecily, as if Bramble was being very stupid. 'Or even next, but we want her to get there as soon as possible after that, and it just wasn't going to happen with you holding her back.'

'Listen, I've got a teenage daughter myself, and I really do urge you to—'

'Well, that's another thing. I can't help feeling that Savannah comes first and that Lottie is always a long way down the line. I want Lottie to be at a yard where the focus will be on her, and Toby's agreed to take her as a pupil as a special favour to me. He doesn't normally do teaching. And, as you know, he is one of the most experienced . . .'

'. . . twats in the business.' Bramble finished the sentence for her, fuming. 'Lottie has always had the best of my attention, she's never come second.'

'I really don't think there's any point in discussing this any further. The Turnbulls will send a horsebox for Sailor tomorrow, your fees will be paid until the end of the month and, in the meantime, I expect you to keep completely quiet about all this. Lottie is not to know, she'll get absurdly upset.'

'But she needs to say goodbye, she adores Sailor . . .'

'Precisely. She's far too fond of that horse, and a long, hysterical goodbye will only make it all worse. I do know what's best for my own daughter, you know.' And with that she slammed down the phone, leaving Bramble shaking with rage.

Perhaps she shouldn't have changed Shaggy's stable name, after all.

Chapter 23

The Turnbulls, who had bought Sailor, arrived with a horsebox during the school day and he was loaded in. This time, the group that gathered around him to say goodbye was smaller, and the atmosphere was even heavier. Just Jez, Bramble and Donna, and none of them could bear to speak unless they had to. Bramble felt she was betraying Sailor as well as Lottie, and every time she walked past the empty stable it was as if she'd been punched in the gut. Jez, carrying a saddle back to the house, stopped beside her.

'Poor Lottie,' said Bramble.

'Poor's the word,' said Jez. 'We can't afford to lose that livery. Have you done the entries for Stileman's yet? I'd like to take Frenchie.'

Three days later, during evening stables, a taxi rumbled up the drive, and a pale-faced, red-eyed Lottie got out.

'You let him go. You promised you wouldn't,' she said, facing Bramble squarely. 'You didn't even let me say goodbye.'

'I tried,' said Bramble. 'I . . .' She opened her mouth to blame Cecily, but shut it again. 'I'm sorry, Lottie.' She tried to put an arm around Lottie's shoulders, but the girl moved away and went into Sailor's stable. She sat there alone for half an hour, before coming into the kitchen and politely thanking Bramble for everything she had done. Bramble knew she had failed, failed in her duty of care towards a pupil, someone young and vulnerable she had been responsible for.

'Come and see us whenever,' she urged. 'Are you doing Ardingly? There'll always be a Jelly Baby for you in our box.'

Lottie didn't smile. 'Thank you. I don't quite know what Toby has in mind for me.' She slipped quietly back into the taxi.

'Toby's not going to stop until he's completely destroyed the Beaumont yard, is he?' said Felicity after the taxi had disappeared.

Felicity watched Sailor go. She should go, too, before her presence destroyed Bramble's yard. She was sure her presence had triggered Toby's spate of vengefulness. He might well stop if she went.

And there were the bad dreams, which had come back. All her life Felicity had found that the best way to get rid of nightmares was to move on. The excitement of a new plan, a new challenge, new people . . . it pushed anything bad into the background. Felicity was a traveller by nature, she knew that, and her solution to life's problems was to leave the difficulties behind.

Only she was beginning to notice that they followed you. At a distance. Whether it took two weeks, two months or two years, at some point she would wake up in the middle of the night, hating herself again, and once that happened the only way was to leave. Going home, like going anywhere, had been exciting, and she'd surprised herself by uncovering good memories – the taste of an autumn apple straight from the tree, the smell of log fires on the winter air, the sight of white daffodils nodding their heads in the lawn and, most recently, the return of the swallows with their promise of summer. They were nesting now, partnered for life as she'd always assumed she and her sisters would be. In fact, none of them were. Not her father and mother, nor Bramble or herself. Well, maybe Helena was happy with that drunk of a husband. Happy endings are for the swallows, she thought, watching them swoop and twist around the stable roof. Not for us.

Still, as she'd said to Jez, bad things happen. Particularly around her. Perhaps she sought them out. Perhaps that's why she'd become a war reporter. But she didn't want to do that again either. She had begun to feel like a leech, feeding on other people's suffering.

That evening, after Bramble left for Nat's cottage, Felicity went upstairs to her bedroom. She re-read the letter that she'd found in her father's bedside chest of drawers.

'My dear Edward,' Felicity read. She smoothed out the paper as the words blurred before her eyes.

'And you *are* still dear to me,' continued the sloping, elegant hand, 'in spite of what I've just discovered. I'm writing this to leave in the drawer beside my bed. You will find it when you clear out my possessions, after my death. Perhaps I'm being cowardly in not having it out with you now, but I couldn't bear to see the betrayal in your eyes. You still treat me very tenderly, and I'm grateful for the pretence between us. It is better than nothing, and I know that, although you no longer desire me, you do still love me. In your own way.

'You are still dear to me, because we share three daughters and more than twenty years of our life together. Nothing can take that away from me, although I am about to lose everything else. The doctor has told me that I probably only have a few weeks left to live. I'm trying not to be bitter. I'm trying not to blame you.

'I have found out, you see, about Her, as the women's magazines would put it. You can imagine how I found out, of course. It doesn't surprise me. The best friend – how very clichéd. Couldn't you have been a little more original?

'But, as the magazines would also say, any man married to a sick wife, a wife who has been unable to fulfil her marriage contract in bed for over three years, well, such a wife must expect such things. It still hurts, though. If I was a well woman, perhaps we would divorce but, then again, if I was well perhaps it would never have happened.

'But I am writing to you about the girls. You will want to marry Her if she can get divorced, but don't let her cut you off from them. They will need you so much, even Felicity. I was wild like her at her age, and then I met you and you showed me how life could be different. You saved me, with your ambition and your desire to succeed and your determination. Without you I would have settled for second best. I would have settled for a man who bored me, a life of bridge and dry martinis. So thank you for that.

'You see I'm counting my blessings, which is what Father Anderson has suggested I do. Making my peace with God and the world. I would like to wish you happiness with Her, but I can't quite do it. I just want you to put the girls first, to keep talking to Felicity, to pay attention to Helena and not to take Bramble for granted. Felicity has been holding things together in this family for far too long, and she needs to be free to be young while she can be. Helena needs a different audience and a larger stage – she has chosen to reject your world because she's proud and ambitious, and she knows she'll never be as good a rider as Felicity – and as for Bramble, of all of them, she's the one who's inherited your determination. But it's harder for a woman. A woman doesn't always know what she needs to be determined about. It's not such a straight road. Don't turn her into the son you never had. Let her be herself, and she'll find her own way through.

'Above all, don't forget that your ambitions are yours alone. They can't be handed on as part of an inheritance, like a gold watch. Let them have your love and their own goals. That's all they need.

'There's so much more to say, but the light is fading and I don't want to say anything I might regret. Only that I love you. Still. *Rose.*'

Felicity had read it and re-read it with relief, with rage and with sorrow. Relief that being 'wild' was something that could be handed on, like green eyes or dark hair, and therefore wasn't necessarily her fault. That her mother hadn't seen her as spoilt and selfish, the way everyone else had, but as 'holding things together'. And her mother's illness? Felicity tried to remember those days, filtering the memories through new knowledge. She remembered that once she'd learned to drive she always drove Helena, then also Bramble, to school and picked them up again at the end of the day. She had helped them with their homework and given them supper. Her mother had often 'not been feeling too good today'. But, now she thought about it, what had actually been wrong with her? Not a sudden heart attack, as everyone had been told, but a slow slipping away? She needed to check the dates on the letter against the dates of everything else – and perhaps talk to people who'd been around in those days – in order to work it all out.

And Bramble had been right about Helena: she'd chosen to

give up riding, not been frightened into it by Felicity. Her father's infidelity was hardly news – she'd known about that for a long time. And she'd despised him for it. It was part of the reason she had left. She didn't want to see him with Her, as her mother would have put it. She wasn't going to have the charade of a happy family played out in front of her.

But there were also things she didn't quite understand, and she wasn't going to show Helena or Bramble the letter. Or at least, she was going think about it carefully before passing on any more pain from the past. They had loved their father, both of them. She thought they probably both suspected him of having an affair with Pauline, but, from the way they phrased their occasional questions, she thought they automatically assumed that anything physical had happened after their mother died.

So I was a proper older sister once, she thought, folding the letter away. 'Holding things together here' were precious words, and she could remember how it felt. She had the same set of choices in front of her now: she could either stay, and try to hold everything together again, or leave and let them sort themselves out. And if she stayed, might she be trapped here for ever? She remembered thinking before that she might never get away, that she was needed too much. They would never let her go, there would always be something to pull her back.

She took a deep breath, put the letter into her backpack, along with some tightly rolled clothes, and went upstairs to tell Jez that she was going. He could pass the message on.

'What about Merlin?' He stood up and looked down at her, disapproving. But she was used to disapproval.

'I'll write. I'll give him to Bramble.'

His expression made her feel guilty, but she was used to that too.

'Look, I'm going to say goodbye to Merlin,' she insisted, 'and then I'm off. You can't stop me. At least Toby might stop trying to destroy Bramble if I wasn't here.'

Jez's face, for a moment, seemed very close to hers, and she thought he was going to say something else.

But he let her go, and she descended the narrow staircase that curled down from the attic, and walked unsteadily across the yard, stopping for a moment to sense a change in the weather. The electrical tension of a storm hovered and the air – too hot for spring – was oppressively still. She would be gone by the time the first drops fell and there would be a new Felicity, she would change herself all over again. Or she could find somewhere to end it all. Maybe that would be best.

As she walked, engrossed in getting away, her instinct tried to register the fact that Merlin's head had not appeared over the stable door at the sound of her footsteps. Her ears, missing the low whicker with which he greeted her approach, sent an alert to her brain. She suppressed both messages.

And when she looked over the door and saw him lying down, she tried to reassure herself that he was just resting, although she knew, deep down, that something was terribly wrong.

Merlin raised his head and peered round at his belly and, before she could take it in and fully accept what she was seeing, he began rolling and kicking vigorously.

'No, Merlin!' She rushed for a headcollar and buckled it on amidst flailing hooves. 'Up, Merlin, up,' she whispered to the horse, overwhelmed by the sheer size of him on the floor. He staggered to his feet, obeying her with an effort. '*Good boy*,' she crooned, trying to create a fragile thread of trust that could pull him through the pain, '*good boy*.' A sheen of sweat soaked his coat where her hand touched it, and his eyes were glazed with fear. Felicity hadn't had to deal with a case of colic for over thirty years, but there was no mistaking the symptoms. A horse could all too easily die of a twisted gut. 'Come on,' she urged, 'please.'

The darkened house seemed a long way away.

Jez,' she called. 'Jez. Jez, help.' She led Merlin towards the back door, aware of his breathing behind her, and his urge to roll.

The kitchen door opened.

'It's Merlin,' she shouted. 'Colic.'

Jez called the vet and he arrived within the half-hour to examine the trembling horse.

'It's hard to tell how bad it is,' said the vet, 'but I don't need to tell you that if he needs surgery there's only a fifty-fifty chance he'll make it through.'

Felicity nodded.

'I think the only thing we can do is to set our alarms at intervals,' said Jez, 'and take turns to check him and walk him round for five or ten minutes every half an hour or so. I'll turn and turn about with you.'

Felicity nearly cried. 'No,' she said, wearily. 'I can do it. I don't sleep anyway.' She thought he was going to protest, so added sharply, 'Go away, please. I'll do it. There's no point in both of us being exhausted tomorrow.'

She dragged a pillow and duvet down into Merlin's stable and pulled in some straw bales just as the horse began to sag and sway, about to go down again. 'Oh, no you don't,' she said, seizing the rope quickly and pulling him out of the stable to walk round again.

Merlin placed a soft, trusting velvety muzzle on her shoulder, but she saw his nostrils lengthen in pain, with deep grooves of tension down the side of his nose. Her heart turned over.

Round and round the yard they went, then they circled the garden lawn, lit only by the light of the moon. Felicity heard the soft snore of the barn owl, the final screech of its prey, and all the rustling noises made by the creatures of the night. She could feel her T-shirt clammy against her back and the occasional trickle of sweat down her face. It cooled instantly against her skin. In the moonlight there were menacing shapes and movements in the shadows, but every time she approached them, her heart beating at twice its normal speed, they turned into bushes or disappeared completely. The ghosts were out there, but she walked to face them and they melted away as she approached.

'You're only spirits,' she said. 'You don't have any power over me any more.'

She thought she felt them brush past her as they fled, but it was only the leaves of the trees on her bare arms.

'I wish I could sing,' she said out loud to Merlin, who was treading behind her like a guardian angel. 'I could sing to you then.' The sound of her voice seemed to calm him, but she couldn't think what else to say.

Poetry. If she could remember any, she could declaim poetry. 'Do you like Browning?' she asked. She thought Merlin nodded, his head swaying from side to side as they plodded on.

'Boot, saddle, to horse, and away!' she declaimed. 'Rescue my castle before the hot day' – they clopped slowly round in a circle again – 'Brightens the blue from its silvery grey, Boot, saddle, to horse, and away!'

It had a comforting rhythm to it and, unable to remember the next verse, she repeated the first. Seeing Lorenden's tall Georgian chimneys against the moon, and the sharp zigzag of the back roof, she wondered if she should fight to rescue her own castle. 'I wasn't going to come back, Merlin, and here I am, leading a horse round all night as if thirty years had never happened.'

'Boot, saddle, to horse, and away!' she recited one more time, sensing him try to go down again. 'Rescue my castle before the hot day, Brightens the blue from its silvery grey,' she whispered desperately. 'Boot, saddle, to horse, and away!' The dew on the grass soaked the hem of her trousers, chilling her ankles, and the owl repeated his heavy, sighing call.

At intervals, when Merlin seemed easier, she lay down on the straw bales, pulling the duvet over her ears against the sharper cold of the first hours of the day. As soon as she drifted into sleep, and saw the shadowy hands and faces that had pursued her all her adult life, Merlin's restlessness woke her.

'No, Merlin, up you get,' she said wearily, urging the sweating horse on, forcing him through the night. 'Come on,' she said out loud. 'How many times do I have to save your life? Boot, saddle, to horse, and away! Off we go.'

As they circled, she remembered the second verse: 'Ride past the suburbs, asleep as you'd say;/Many's the friend there, will listen and pray/ "God's luck to the gallants that strike up the lay." Strike up the lay, Merlin, means a song about fighting the Roundheads, if I remember rightly. Boot, saddle, to horse, and away! Well that was a lost cause. There's a verse about "my wife, Gertrude", who laughed at the thought of surrender.

'That's what I thought, Merlin, I said I would never surrender, but I had to, like Gertrude must have done in the end.' She felt Merlin's silky coat, still damp with sweat, and they trudged on.

'Shall I tell you, Merlin, shall I tell you why I left? You won't feel sorry for me, or judge me, or tell me what to do.'

Merlin's head nodded at the sound of her voice and his hooves trod softly behind her through the velvet darkness.

By the time she finished talking there was a thin sliver of grey light across the horizon as the rain gathered overhead. She heard the tentative, twirling song of the first bird and the staccato chirrup of the second in answer. Merlin's movements were more fluid and his breathing easier as the pain ebbed. She led him back to his box and lay down on the straw, only dimly aware of someone wrapping the duvet round her and Jez's hand taking the lead rope from her hands.

As she dropped into the deepest darkness of real sleep, she thought she could hear work beginning in the yard and smell the freshness of rain. It fell, drumming on the stable roof.

Chapter 24

That evening, Felicity surprised Bramble by joining her for evening stables. Jez, straightening up from examining Frenchie's hock, looked at Felicity and something passed between them, but before Bramble could wonder what it might signify, Helena's cream sports car zipped up the drive and skidded to a halt.

Helena jumped out. 'Great news!'

'You've got a new part,' suggested Felicity.

Helena paled. 'Oh that, no, I'm not really looking for anything at the moment. I'm putting my family first. And you're not supposed to mention Mattie. Not to anyone. Who's going to die is deadly secret and the tabloids are offering thousands for it.'

'Of course we won't,' replied Bramble, irritated.

'No, what I've got here is really important. Let's go inside.'

They followed her, leaving Jez and Savannah in the stables.

Helena slapped a piece of paper down on the kitchen table. 'Probate! Ta da! Now we can really get on with it.'

Bramble's heart thudded in her chest and for a second she felt dizzy. The kitchen swung round. Felicity's easy outline froze and she folded her arms over her chest, suddenly as defensive as she had been on the day she'd arrived.

'Right,' said Helena. 'Decision time. We need to make a decision about who are the best estate agents and find out what the market will offer for something like this.'

Bramble clutched the back of the kitchen chair and looked round at the beloved room, with its old stone floor, clutter and view of the garden. The Aga and its rail, where she hung damp socks and numnahs, the old pine door and the shelf above – where the clock had been – with its toppling cookery books. It wasn't possible that she might have to leave and never come home again.

'Bramble,' said Helena. 'It makes sense, you know it does, and it's only fair. To get some offers in and find out what it's all really worth.'

Bramble looked at Felicity desperately, but Felicity was staring at the floor.

'I need the money,' added Helena in a whisper.

'And I need time. For my home,' said Bramble. 'And my business.'

'It's about my home, too,' said Helena, almost unable to get the words out. 'It . . . well . . . if I don't get some money soon, I think the bank . . .' She took a deep breath. 'We might lose the house. We'd have nowhere to go.'

Bramble was shocked. 'Helena, I had no idea. That's terrible.' She tried to think of a solution. 'Look, why don't you rent it out for a bit and come here, we'd love to have you and . . .'

'That way, you could keep Lorenden?' Helena sounded cynical.

'Helena, I'm only trying to help. I was going to say "it would give you a breathing space". Until you get a new part and Ollie finishes his script.'

'It would never work. I don't want to be here, I want us to sell. We need the money.' Helena brushed Bramble's offer away. 'Felicity, please, you're the only one who . . .' She broke off as 'The Dashing White Sergeant' burbled out of her bag, and prodded her mobile. 'Hello? Hello?'

There was a silence.

'That's completely untrue,' shouted Helena. 'I simply can't comment, I'm afraid, except to say that if you print that I will sue.' Helena shook the mobile. 'Did you hear that?' she raised her voice to a shriek, '*My father died recently. Please* allow us some space to grieve. Oh no, she's gone.'

'The range round here is very dodgy,' said Bramble, hearing her own voice wobble. 'It comes and goes.'

Helena snapped the phone off again and flung it back into her bag. 'Some shit has sold my story to the press. My leaving the series. Making it sound as if I'm completely over.' She swung round to Bramble and Felicity. 'It must have been one of you, I haven't told anyone else. Have you said anything to anyone? What about Donna? She'd sell her own grandmother, I bet. Or Jez. I bet it was Jez.'

'Of course, I haven't said anything to anyone,' said Bramble. 'And Jez couldn't be bothered.'

Felicity shook her head.

'Anyone could be bothered if they were short of money,' screeched Helena.

'Well, it wasn't Jez,' said Felicity. 'Or anyone else here. So forget storming out there and accusing them.'

Helena blew her nose. 'This is so awful. I could be accused of being unprofessional. I might never work again because people think I'm leaky. It's my career on the line here. It's supposed to be a secret, it's supposed to be the great ratings-puller. I need a drink. Have you got anything?'

'I really do think you're exaggerating,' said Bramble, unable to concentrate with the threat of losing Lorenden hanging in the air. 'It's only a tiny gossip-column story. Haven't you always said that it's best to ignore everything that's written about you and carry on as usual?'

There was a half-empty bottle of Merlot with a stopper in it beside the sink, and Bramble gave it a quick sniff. A bit vinegary, but it would do. She sloshed it into a tumbler and handed it to Helena, who drank it down as if it were lemonade. 'Haven't you got some decent stuff?'

'Have a cup of coffee,' suggested Bramble. 'It's better for you. Come on, Helena, I think you've got this out of proportion . . .'

'Nobody respects my feelings in this family. I *feel* upset. I *feel* I've been made to look unprofessional. And that might not be important to you, but it matters to me.'

'Well, you can't blame any of us,' said Felicity firmly.

Helena slammed her tumbler down on the table. 'Why does no one in this family ever support me? If someone here has . . .' She burst into tears. 'Everything's going wrong. Absolutely everything,' she sobbed, sinking down into a kitchen chair, her head in her hands. 'The bailiffs have climbed in the bedroom window and tried to kidnap the dog, Eddie's grades are going down and he's out all the time, Ollie won't talk about it, and all I get are bills, bills, bills. I'm so frightened about money that I can't even walk past a bank without feeling sick. And you two are down here with the horses, always putting them first, never listening or thinking what it might be like for me, having to keep it all together for my family.' Her voice dissolved into hiccups. 'Where's that fucking drink? Here,' she grabbed a bottle, opened it and poured out three glasses.

Bramble had been looking forward to a glass of wine but, looking at her sister's flushed, coarsened cheeks, decided that it didn't seem like such a good idea after all. She shook her head. 'I've got to get up at six tomorrow as usual. Can't do it if I drink.'

'You should lighten up,' said Helena. 'You're still a young woman. You should be having fun, not behaving like some middle-aged matron.' She often got vicious after a couple of glasses of wine, then claimed not to remember it later.

'Helena, this is important. I don't think you should have any more.' Bramble tried to take the bottle off the table.

'Cheapskate,' hissed Helena. 'I suppose you feel superior to me.' She emptied her handbag of bills and spread them over the table. 'Look at these, Mother shitface Superior. I bet you've never seen bills like this.' Her hand, shaking, shoved a bank statement under Bramble's nose and she was forced to take it.

'Is this a typical supermarket bill? For one week?'

'That's food,' Helena said indignantly. 'It's my basic right to feed my family good quality food, not mass-produced rubbish. You can't blame me for that. I admit I spend a bit more because everything's organic, but only pennies. And worth it. You shouldn't ask why my food is so expensive, you should be asking why your food is so cheap.'

Bramble decided not to. 'But you owe fifteen thousand pounds on this one card alone,' she said, looking at another bill.

Helena let out a wail. 'Don't be so vile to me. You really are being beastly, I can't bear it. Let's stop this now before one of us says something we'll regret. Come on, Bramble, do have a drink and we'll talk about it all tomorrow.'

'What are these payments of four thousand pounds a month?'

'Our mortgage,' said Helena. 'Everyone has a large mortgage. It's madness to think small in the property market. You don't understand. Anyway, once Ollie stops drinking and finishes his script – and once we've got Lorenden out of the way – everything will be fine. You see,' she leant forward, her eyes not quite focusing, 'this whole business, it's putting me under such stress. We've got to make a decision. It's driving me mad. We have to sell, you know that.'

Felicity sat down next to Helena and put an arm round her. 'Come on, Hell's-bells.'

Helena sobbed on her shoulder. 'You always used to call me that. When I was little.'

'Because you made such a hell of a lot of noise,' admitted Felicity, letting Helena cry on her shoulder for a few minutes.

When she looked up, her face decisive, Bramble caught an edge of a memory, as if she knew this Felicity from a long time ago.

Felicity remembered walking into the dark with Merlin the night before, and the way the menacing shapes had dissolved into air as she walked towards them. This was no different, she told herself. She could face up to her responsibilities and be an older sister without it sucking her in for ever. She had been running away from people needing her for too long.

'Bramble,' she looked at her directly. 'I'm sorry, Helena's right. It makes sense for us to put Lorenden on the market now. It's really the only option. You're not in a position to buy us out, and we haven't got a proper idea of what it's worth anyway. But . . .' she raised her hand as Bramble tried to speak, '. . . I think that it's reasonable to say that Bramble at least has this season here, isn't it Helena?'

'Suppose someone wants a quick sale? Because they need to move urgently?'

'There's never anything quick about this sort of a sale,' insisted Felicity. 'Realistically, if we had an offer tomorrow it would still be months before they moved in, and they'd want to do work anyway. No, if we're going to be sensible we have to accept that nothing's going to happen immediately, and that at least gives Bramble some of the time she needs.'

'How can I run the place with closure hanging over my head?' demanded Bramble. 'What about Donna? And Jez? They'll probably leave.'

'In which case,' Felicity took a deep breath. She stretched out a hand to Bramble, and thought about Merlin's footsteps treading behind hers through the night and the trust he had placed in her. 'You've got me,' she said, accepting that she'd come home at last. 'I'll stay for as long as you need.'

Bramble took the hand reluctantly, squeezed it and released it, reassured in spite of herself. 'OK.'

Felicity was back. At last. Deep inside Bramble, a little girl who had spent for ever waiting anxiously for someone she loved to return, agreed, finally, to go to sleep now.

'What means most to me,' sniffed Helena, always one to milk a scene, 'is that this is the first time that anyone in this family has ever admitted that something I said makes sense.'

'That's probably because it's the first time anything you've said *has* made sense,' said Felicity with her old asperity.

Savannah came in. Bramble thought she looked very pale. 'What's this?' Her mouth trembled. 'I heard you say you were putting Lorenden on the market.'

Bramble leapt up. 'Sweetheart, we don't have a choice . . . it won't sell for ages . . . you mustn't worry . . .' She put a hand out to her daughter, who brushed it off.

'Savannah, darling, it will all be all right,' added Felicity. 'If Lorenden sells – and it won't be soon – your mother will have the money to buy somewhere else.'

Savannah briefly looked surprised at the new authority in Felicity's drawling, husky tones. 'I don't want somewhere else. And what about the horses? Will we have to sell those too?'

'Savannah. For goodness' sake, don't get bogged down in detail,' said Helena. 'It's none of your business, it really isn't.'

'It *is* her business,' said Bramble, flashing a look of anger at Helena. 'And we won't sell the horses. Of course we won't. Except the ones that were going to be sold anyway.'

'And what about Jez?'

'He'll move on,' said Helena. 'But he would have done anyway. People like that always do. You're just a step on his way to the top.'

Savannah hesitated, looking very young and frightened. Bramble wanted to fold her in her arms and rock her gently, as if she was a small child, and reassure her that everything would turn out for the best. 'Savannah.' She put a hand out to touch her arm.

After a moment's hesitation, Savannah turned away. 'Oh, leave me alone,' she said.

'No, Savannah, come back. I'm just about to do sausages for supper,' said Bramble, conscious of a note of pleading in her voice. 'They'll be ready in about twenty minutes.'

'I don't want any sausages,' replied Savannah. 'Sausages make me feel sick.' She left the room and slammed the door.

'She's very attention-seeking at the moment,' said Helena. 'You want to watch that.'

Savannah went upstairs, trembling. Lorenden would be sold. Jez would leave. And her life would be over. She was amazed to realise, as she closed the door of her own, precious bedroom, that the thought of Lorenden being sold was hard enough to imagine, but that Jez going seemed like an even bigger abyss. She could talk to him. He never told her to do homework or stopped talking when she came into the room.

She must find him now: he would know what to do. Jez would do something. Jez would save them.

Perhaps he'd gone to the pub. He often did. Savannah put on make-up, layering it on, then wiping most of it off, and chose a pair of tight jeans. For a moment, when she looked in the mirror, she felt good about herself, but as she turned her bottom looked huge and she nearly decided not to go. But, instead, she pulled on a baggy black sweater that made her look thinner, scraped a little more make-up off and went downstairs looking almost the same as usual, before tiptoeing out the door.

It was a long, dark walk to the White Horse, and Savannah, wobbling in her best shoes, wondered if she was being silly. Occasionally a car whizzed by, far too fast, lights on full beam, not expecting to find a girl walking alone at night. Each time she shrank into the hedge and had to disentangle herself from the hawthorn and brambles that caught at her hair and her sweater. Every so often one of her ankles turned on the uneven verge, and the tangle of weeds at the side of the lane clawed at her clothes, as if to drag her down into a pit of terrible tiredness.

But Jez was there at the bar, laughing at something the barman had said. He looked at her, penetrating the bright, brave disguise she'd taken so much trouble over.

She blushed. 'I . . . I . . .' she said. 'They're going to sell Lorenden. I overheard them. I don't think they were going to tell me.' Humiliated, she could feel a tear trickling down her cheek. She quickly brushed it aside.

He put a hand on her shoulder. 'Sit down.' He propelled her to a seat in the corner. 'What do you want to drink? I haven't eaten yet, have you?'

'Sparkling mineral water,' said Savannah, grateful for the distraction of scouring the menu board for something that wasn't too fattening. In the end, she settled for a Caesar salad without dressing, but found it difficult to eat. She was too self-conscious to relax. Bits of lettuce kept getting stuck in her teeth.

'So. The decision has been made?' Jez tore open a packet of peanuts and swallowed the whole lot in three big handfuls.

Savannah nodded, transfixed by the number of calories he'd just consumed without thinking. 'Please don't leave,' she blurted out. 'We need you.' She could feel her face burning crimson, and more tears welling up. She was so clumsy. She wished she was sexy and clever.

Jez studied her for a few moments. 'First, of course they were going to tell you. Selling a house is a very public thing, and I know your mother would never do it behind your back. Even if she could.'

Savannah nodded, wiping away another tear and hoping he hadn't noticed.

'And, Savannah, I'll always be your friend. Whether I'm working at Lorenden or at another yard, I'll always be there. You know how it works – we all meet each other over and over again at events, we all travel together and spend whole days together, and park our horseboxes alongside each other. We won't lose touch. I won't let us. That's definite.'

'But, without you, how are we going to win? I know this season has only just begun, but we've still won more than we have before.' It only occurred to Savannah, as she was speaking, that this was the case. It had been so stop-start that it had been difficult to see the victories for the disappointments.

Jez thought before replying. 'That hasn't just been down to me. You mother is an incredibly talented rider, you know, if only she'd believe in herself, and I see a touch of that in you too. I think you've both got to stop over-analysing everything and just go for it. If that's what you want, of course.'

'Of course it's what I want.' Savannah looked ahead to a lifetime of seeing Jez, competing alongside him in teams or against him as an individual, being in his world forever as a friend, and then, as he realised how good she'd be for him, as something more. Her parents had been a husband-and-wife team competing with and against each other, lots of people were. It was her destiny. Provided she could get thin – and stay thin – and as long as she worked really hard on her riding, she could achieve it all.

'So, what do you think about Merlin and how he's coming along?' Jez changed the subject.

She leant forwards, instantly interested. 'Well, I think Mum's managing to teach him to canter at last. Although he still has her off sometimes.'

Jez nodded. 'He is coming along nicely, and she's good with him. But I think he needs a lot of time to chill out. These days, everyone wants instant winners and some horses need to grow up. They're like some people: they just need to ride and work without too many challenges while they sort themselves out.'

Savannah's eyes filled with tears again, unexpectedly, and she stared at her salad.

'Remember, it's not easy for you to adjust to your grandfather's death. You're having to take on some pretty big changes in your life. Don't give yourself too hard a time.'

She thought carefully. 'I admired Grampa a lot, but he was quite scary. I think I disappointed him.'

'Savannah?'

She looked up and found his eyes very close to hers. As if he could see everything she was thinking. 'You weren't a disappointment to him,' he said gently. 'He talked about you to me. He had great faith in your ability. He said you would be the next great Beaumont rider.'

The weight of her grandfather's expectations settled heavily on her shoulders, and she nodded. 'He told me that once. But I don't know if I can do it.'

'You can,' said Jez. 'You can. In ten years time you and I will be on the British team together. You've got the talent and you've got the drive, and that's half the battle.'

'What's the other half of the battle?' she asked, laughing shakily.

He laughed with her. 'I don't know. Luck. Good horses. Back-up at home. And you've got great back-up in your mother.'

Her mother was another thing that made Savannah feel guilty and irritated. 'Oh, Mum's pretty distracted with Nat at the moment.' Too late she remembered Bramble warning her not to mention Nat and Jez to each other.

Jez's face darkened. 'Do you get on with him?'

'He's OK. He doesn't really notice me.'

'Well, he should,' said Jez fiercely. 'You deserve to be noticed.'

This cheered Savannah up. 'Why don't you like him?'

He laughed, as if her question was a joke, and rumpled her hair teasingly. 'Tell me about you, though. Have you got a boyfriend?'

She turned scarlet. 'Erm, no.' She wondered why he was asking. Because he fancied her?

He continued to study her, his eyes searching hers. He was graceful, she thought, watching the way he moved. People didn't often talk about grace in men, but the way he was so comfortable in his body, and that sureness and liquid strength that dancers and athletes have – to Savannah, this defined sheer beauty. Lucky him. Savannah's body felt cumbersome in comparison. Perhaps she should work out more.

She summoned up some courage. 'Have *you* got a girlfriend?'

He laughed again. 'No, not really.'

Savannah plucked up her courage. 'What does that mean?'

'It means, I never seem to find anyone who I want to spend the rest of my life with.'

'What sort of a woman are you looking for?'

'It's hard to say. I know that I want to succeed as an eventer and that's such a full-time job that I could only marry someone who cared about it all as much as I do. But maybe if I really loved someone I'd give up everything for her. What do you think?'

'If she really loved you, she wouldn't want you to change. She'd want to be totally involved in what you do,' said Savannah. 'I know I would.'

He smiled and touched her cheek. 'Then I'd better wait for you to grow up, so that I can marry you,' he said lightly, getting up. 'C'mon, let's get back.'

Chapter 25

Bramble drove to Nat's cottage. With its big inglenook hearth, log fire and saggy, squashy sofas, it had become a sanctuary. No one could get at her there. She banged on the door and breathlessly poured out her indignation.

'They want me to sell up in the middle of the season,' she gasped. 'Moving is a major thing and I'm likely to be away competing half the time. Summer is frantic enough as it is, without packing up over a hundred years' worth of family life as well.'

He poured her a drink and sat her down. 'One thing at a time. Felicity and Helena can pack the house up; neither of them are working.'

'But it isn't *their* house,' shouted Bramble.

He studied her carefully in the silence that followed. 'It is, you know.'

Bramble looked away. 'Anyway, even if we do sell I don't have time to go looking for somewhere else to live.'

He took her hand gently. 'You and Savannah can always come here.'

'Here?' She snatched her hand away.

'I'm sorry. It's a bit soon to be talking like this, but when you feel something's right . . .'

Bramble felt a sense of rising panic. What did Nat expect of her?

But he seemed to read her mind. 'All I'm saying is that you don't have to be homeless. You can come here for a few weeks, or even months, while you sort yourself out. Savannah can have Gemma's bedroom. Jenny still hasn't allowed her to come down and spend the weekend here.'

For a moment, Bramble felt indignant on his behalf. How dare this Jenny keep a father and daughter apart? How could she be so selfish? Then she remembered her own predicament. 'What about the horses?'

'Livery somewhere? Or perhaps Helena's right. Perhaps it is time to start again. You don't have to be your father, you know. You have a very good reputation of your own: it's just a different one. Perhaps it's time to think about the real Bramble, and what *she* wants, rather than trying to live up to your father's expectations all the time.'

'But . . .' Bramble saw her future spread out ahead of her, being a riding instructor, living in Nat's little cottage . . . not being Bramble Kelly any longer. Being somebody else.

'You will have options,' he said. 'You get a third of Lorenden.'

She sat there, cradling her glass of wine.

'Listen, I don't want to pry, but if it would help to talk to me about what exactly is involved in terms of money, then I wouldn't tell anyone, and I was in the financial world.'

Bramble had done the sums already. She knew roughly what she might get, once inheritance tax had been paid and the estate had been divided into three.

'Hmm,' he said when she told him. 'Yes, that's about what I thought. Many people would be happy with half that amount. You can buy a very nice house.'

'I don't *want* a very nice house,' said Bramble, slightly surprised that Nat had already been doing his own calculations. 'I want to run an event yard and produce top-class horses. I want to win.'

'There comes a time,' said Nat slowly, 'in everyone's life . . . where they have to face up to the fact that their childhood dreams are never going to become a reality. I was going to be a millionaire by the time I was thirty, but if I had been I wouldn't be here sitting beside you. And when I look at my life in this rented cottage, earning my living honestly by my hands . . . well, I would have been horrified if you'd told me ten years ago that this is what I'd become. But you know? I've never been happier. It is *much* better than constantly striving for something that, in the end, may not even be worth having. I am so, so much richer in every way.'

Perhaps he was right.

'You have to think about what really matters in life,' he said. 'And for me, that's the people I'm with.'

The estate agents, two eager young men in shiny, dark suits, came to measure up for the brochure, both as friendly and enthusiastic as puppies, yapping about open days, development potential and 'uplift'. They seemed to see nothing incongruous in telling Bramble how exciting it was to find something so unspoilt and historic, and making it clear that any buyer would probably change it completely and totally. They chattered away: 'What do you think? Two hundred grand of work?'

'Could be up to a mil. Depends what they want. But I reckon it's a total refurb. Nice sunny day for the photographs, though.'

Bramble had put off telling Jez until the last minute. He was working Merlin in the sand school, and she watched the way the beautiful dark grey horse had come on. When first faced with jumps in a school, he'd had no idea what they were and had simply demolished everything. Now he was pinging gracefully round. One, two, three, over. One, two, three, over. It was like watching music.

Jez trotted over to her. 'What do you think?'

'Coming along.' She took a deep breath. 'But not fast enough to save Lorenden.'

Jez got off and unlatched the gate, leading Merlin through. 'The house is on the market?' It was barely a question.

She nodded.

He seemed unconcerned.

'Will you go?' she asked.

'Do you want me to?'

Bramble was surprised to feel a jolt of fear at the thought of him leaving. 'I . . .' she began.

A silence opened up between them.

'Well, I . . .' She'd intended to say that she thought he should start looking for other yards as soon as possible. Do what was best for him. Put his career first.

'I think . . .' She swallowed. 'In fact, I . . .'

He watched her the way he always did.

'I would . . . um . . . like you to stay,' she blurted out. 'For as long as possible, I mean. Until you find something else, of course.' She could feel her cheeks heating up. 'I mean, don't rush. Take your . . . er . . . time. That is, if you like. If it suits you.'

'Then I'll stay. As long as you need me.'

She managed a shaky smile.

He wasn't going to make it easy for her, but she thought she saw the ghost of a smile as they returned to the stables.

Merlin's saddle rested on the stable door while Jez scraped the sweat off the horse's grey hide. Bramble waited for a moment, feeling that there was something more to say, watching him deftly flick off the moisture with a sweat scraper. Droplets of water glinted in the sunlight.

'I think Shaggy would be a brilliant next step for Savannah,' she said.

Was that disappointment in his eyes? Jez barely stopped working on Merlin. 'OK. Just be aware that she's not a novice ride.'

'Savannah's hardly a novice.'

'No, but . . .' he turned to face her. 'Is she OK?'

'What do you mean?' Bramble spoke sharply, out of fear.

'She's lost a lot of weight.'

She had noticed, but she hadn't thought it important. 'She's no thinner than Lottie.'

'True, but Lottie's built like that and Savannah isn't.'

Bramble thought about it. Savannah was two inches shorter than she was, and she had inherited Dom Kelly's stocky build, with its broad shoulders and sturdy hips, rather than the Beaumont greyhound shape. Lottie's long, slender limbs were born to her, too – she was already nearly six foot tall. She sighed. If Savannah was measuring herself against Lottie then she would never feel thin enough.

'Do you think I should be worried?'

Jez shook his head. 'I don't know.'

'I do ask her if she's eating enough,' said Bramble. 'She tells me not to fuss. If you get the chance, can you talk to her?'

He nodded and turned back to Merlin.

Perhaps Nat was right. The people in her life – and that had to be Savannah above everything – mattered more than her ambition or her home. Bramble walked back to the house, telling herself that, this time next year, she wouldn't see the rosebuds on the walls emerge from their winter hibernation. If the estate agents were right, and the new owners – whoever they might be – wanted to gut everything, there might not even be any rosebuds.

'Bramble,' Jez called.

She turned. 'Yes?'

'It's madness to try to live a dream.' His eyes locked on hers.

Her shoulders dropped. Even Jez thought she would never make it.

'But,' he added, 'to try to live *without* one is insanity.'

She smiled.

'It's a Tatar proverb,' he added.

'It's a question of which dream,' she said.

Helena held the telephone in a sweaty palm. She had just opened a letter from the mortgage company, and unless they received a cheque soon they intended to repossess the house. Ollie refused to come out of his study so she decided to phone his agent, Theo, to find out when his next payment was due.

She was put through immediately. 'Helena. My dear. What can I do for you?'

She tumbled out a muddled explanation about cash flow and crossed wires. It would never do to allow anyone to know how bad things were.

'I'm sorry,' said Theo. 'I don't understand.'

Helena swallowed. 'I just wondered when Ollie might expect his next payment. He's, er, not around at the moment so I can't ask him.'

'Payment for what?'

'Well, the screenplay he's been working on for the last year, of course. The one he's just finished.'

The silence on the other end of the phone told her everything she needed to know.

At five o'clock in the morning Felicity woke up gasping for air. She had dreamt that her father had come back, in a thick, choking mist like the one Bramble said she had seen curling round the orchard the day he died. The sensation was so real that when Felicity switched on the light and surveyed her tiny rose-print bedroom she could almost smell him. The clammy air flooded her lungs, depriving her of oxygen.

'What do you want?' she whispered when she got her breath back, although she barely believed in ghosts. 'What do you want from me?'

'It isn't over,' said a voice in her head, and she realised that she was still asleep and tried to switch the light on again with limbs that could barely move. Her own voice – or perhaps it was her father's – said that someone else would die and she struggled, again, to wake up properly.

'What isn't over?' she tried to ask over the weight pressing on her chest. 'Who are you?'

'I'm sorry. I'm so sorry.' The reply was a breath of wind through the curtain and the rustle of leaves outside the window, and she woke, properly this time, her heart thudding.

It was almost light and, now fully alert, she could see that there was a mist outside, lying low and heavy in the road, waiting for an unwary car to come round the corner too fast. It had been one of those half-dreams, part real and part not. She'd had them before. She pulled the curtains open – she might as well get up – and when she was dressed she looked again: the mist had gone.

As soon as the clocks went forward the sun began a steady assault on the landscape, first encouraging abundant growth and then baking the ground into hard terracotta. Jez, Savannah, Donna and Bramble competed two or three days a week, watching the sunny days with increasing concern. Good going turned into hard going, which rapidly turned into no going at all. Going cross-country would be like galloping down a road, risking injury to their horse's legs.

They had a few triumphs. Savannah was doing well enough to be considered for the South East team for the Junior Regional Novice championships, and Jez, who was taking any rides he could get, seemed omnipresent at the top of the leaderboard, but for every win there seemed to be a failure: a horse lame, a sudden stop in front of a straightforward jump, an inexplicably poor dressage score, or just a day when no one could quite believe in themselves.

When Bramble told Donna that Lorenden was being sold, she burst into tears, but revealed that she had had job offers from other people.

'You should take them, Donna,' advised Bramble. 'We're two horses down, we'll manage.'

'I feel awful. I don't have to go yet.'

'Don't worry. Do what's right for you – we'll make it work somehow.'

Felicity, dressed in jodphurs, stood in the doorway. 'Right,' she said. 'It's time for me to ride Merlin.'

'Are you sure?' Bramble felt the old insecurity bob up. Felicity could do anything. That's what they'd always been told. If Felicity came back, then she'd be the next great rider in the family.

'Sailor got me back into shape. Now I'm ready for anything.'

Donna gave her a leg-up.

'Keep your hands quiet,' warned Jez. 'He's very sensitive and you'd be halfway to Canterbury before you know it.'

They clattered out of the yard: Bramble on Shaggy, Jez on Frenchie and Donna on Paddy, one of the young horses. Merlin, ears forward, felt young and keen. And powerful.

'It's like riding a motorbike after travelling by train,' gasped Felicity as they streamed out along the old stubble field, now replanted with rapeseed. 'Sailor was a dear, but he wasn't like this.'

'Are you OK?' Bramble trotted alongside. 'Merlin's got a much bigger stride.'

'I'm more than OK,' Felicity called back as they accelerated up the hill, her ears echoing with the pounding of hooves as Merlin stretched himself out, thundering up the track with the joy of a superbly fit athlete. 'I'm bloody fantastic.'

Then, suddenly, the 'driest spring for thirty years' turned into the wettest one since Victorian times, with day after day of sheeting, wind-blown rain. Once or twice a week Jez, usually accompanied by Bramble, Donna or Felicity, set off in the lorry, but when they got to the event they sometimes even decided not to run the horses in spite of the long journey and the expense of getting there. Jez rode for other people as well, picking up twenty-five pounds per horse, but this source of extra income dried up as owners decided not to risk their horses on the slippery ground.

The team came back in the evenings or early the following day, admittedly often with a smattering of rosettes, but also with frustration for what might have been. Simply because of the weather they were competing half as often as they needed to. Events were cancelled. Cheques were returned. Never had success seemed more elusive.

They had one clear week. Bramble and Felicity took Merlin to a small local event, just to see how he coped. The horse's excitement mounted with every stage of preparation: the plaiting up, the travelling boots, the rug, the back of the lorry being lowered in the yard . . . by the time they loaded him he was in a frenzy of anticipation. Or fear.

When Bramble heard a series of thumping and crumping noises coming from the back of the lorry as she turned onto the motorway, she asked Felicity to investigate.

Drive slowly, she told herself. Don't be distracted.

'He's trying to kick his way out,' said Felicity, edging carefully back to investigate. 'I don't understand it, he was quite quiet when I brought him over.'

'He knows he's off to a party,' said Bramble, remembering Jez's assessment that Merlin had some bad memories associated with competing. They both crossed their fingers in hope that he, and the lorry, would survive the journey.

When they arrived, Merlin was trembling and covered in blood. In spite of the protective travelling boots, he'd managed to kick himself, tearing long scratches in his skin.

'We can't enter him like that,' said Felicity.

Bramble cleaned him up, risking a kick in the hand, the chest or the head. 'They're just superficial scrapes. They've almost dried up already.'

After a word with the judges and the on-field vet, they were told Felicity could go ahead. If she could ever get as far as the arena. Desperate for the comfort of being in the middle of a racing pack, Merlin refused to pass anywhere where two or more horses were tied up together, shying towards them and bucking when Felicity tried to move him away. People dived out of her path, grabbing buckets and moving their own horses round. 'Just sitting on him when he's standing still is like trying to ride a washing machine on its spin cycle,' said Felicity. Her shoulders and arms were already beginning to ache with the strain of holding him back. 'I'm really quite nervous.'

By the time they reached the collecting ring both she and Merlin were drenched in sweat. When the horn was sounded she managed to persuade him to enter the dressage arena, but he was still dancing on his toes, tossing his head as he faced the judges. Where's the race? Where's everyone else? What this all about? Felicity tried to communicate calmness and security throughout her entire body, holding herself still and strong For a few minutes the memory of their daily lessons came back, as he worked in supple circles at walk and trot, but as soon as he was asked to canter he lost it, breaking into a gallop, almost flying away. Out of the corner of her eye, as she struggled to control him, Felicity could see the dressage judge looking visibly startled.

'None of my horses have ever come *bottom* of the dressage before,' commented Bramble as they checked the scores on the board an hour later. 'There's nothing like a change, I suppose.'

Felicity was surprised at how much she cared. From the moment she had stepped out of the horsebox into the half-remembered atmosphere of diesel engines, burger stalls, hay and hoof oil, all whipped around in a cold wind, she had wanted to win.

'Never mind,' she said tightly, 'it's early days yet.'

The showjumping was slightly better, as he had something to focus on, but he was still fighting. After struggling round the arena while waiting for the starting bell, Felicity pointed him towards the first jump but when she asked him to take off he hesitated. A fraction too late, he gave a massive spring and his powerful hindquarters propelled them over. She heard a pole rattle down behind them. 'You can do it, Merlin, you can,' she whispered. Even though he was trying to go too fast and getting confused about when he was being asked to take off, the power of his jump was awesome. They finished with twelve penalties – something of a triumph, as it meant he'd cleared seven of the ten jumps.

'Not bad,' said Bramble. 'For a firecracker like that.'

On the cross-country Felicity could barely get him into the starting box. He hated being asked to leave the horses in the lorry lines behind the course, and when she finally heard the starter shout 'three, two, one, GO and good luck' they shot through the start and cantered sideways for a few moments until she got him listening to her. But, once out of everyone's sight, he steadied, ears pricked forwards. He tried to skitter sideways when they went into the shade of the trees, and she had to encourage him through the water – he teetered on the brink for so long she was expecting the fence judge to call 'first refusal' at any moment but suddenly she could feel that he was with her, wanting to do well as much as she did, his hooves eating up the ground beneath them at a steady pace. She felt the wind on her face and heard his breathing finally settle into a rhythm, almost too late. But it was there. The talent and the love of going across country was there.

'That horse will be big one day,' she gasped to Bramble once she had managed, with some effort, to slow down after galloping through the finish.

'But one day is a long way away,' sighed Bramble. 'Jez was right. He's got a lot to learn. There'll be no quick victories here.'

'No,' admitted Felicity, as the red haze of competitive adrenalin slowly left her body. 'But I'll tell you what, Savannah will be riding him to four-star victory before you know it.'

'If only you knew how often we've said *that* of a horse,' muttered Bramble, irritated that Felicity was prepared to pronounce Merlin a top grade horse on the basis of one disastrous competition. 'Never mind, Merlin, you did your best.' She patted him affectionately and took the reins. 'You're just terminally confused about coming out to party and, instead of a nice orderly race track with lots of horses doing the same thing and going in the same direction, everyone's milling about all over the place and you're expected to do your stuff on your own. We'll have to get you used to it.'

'If a horse starts off wrong,' said Felicity, 'it's so difficult to get them right again. They hang on to their memories and it holds them back.'

And so do we, Bramble thought suddenly. Perhaps I, too, am hanging on to memories of achieving medals and trophies as a junior rider and it's time to let them go.

As the season progressed the rain continued. 'It's two steps forward and one step back, isn't it?' asked Bramble, unloading the lorry with Jez one evening and trying hard to breathe some life into their efforts.

'Frenchie still gets so tense in the dressage,' said Jez. 'I tried working him for an hour beforehand to take the edge off him.'

'Did it work?'

Jez shook his head. 'Next time I think I'll take him straight from the lorry into the dressage arena so he doesn't get time to think about it.'

Bramble sighed. Horses were full of frustrations. 'There's a sort of horse Rescue Remedy we could try.'

Out hacking, the horses slithered in the mud and they dared not jump them, except in the sand school. She watched their condition, so carefully achieved, melt away as they bored of going round the school. The yard smelt of damp and her socks seemed permanently wet.

Badminton – where Jez should have ridden Teddy – came at the beginning of May. Jez, Bramble, Donna and Savannah took three horses to a minor event on the same day. As they watched Savannah's marks creep up the leaderboard they held their breath, finally forgetting everything else, and when Savannah won her section it was as if the sun had come out again.

Bramble hugged her daughter. 'Amazing, amazing, amazing!'

Jez whirled her up into the air, and she shrieked, and Donna jumped up and down singing 'We are the Champions'.

'I *never* thought we'd win with that dressage score,' said Savannah. 'I can't *believe* we went clear in the jumping – you heard that pole rattle – and, did you hear, Lottie was eliminated . . .' she chattered on, reliving every element of the day with all its ups and downs and maybes.

They saw Cecily driving off, furious, leaving Lottie to come back with Vincent and the groom. 'Oh, poor Lottie,' cried Savannah. 'Shall I go and see if she's OK?' She raced over, buoyed up with confidence for a change.

'What do you think about Lottie's new horse?' Bramble asked Jez.

'Too strong for her,' he replied. 'She's a tall girl but she's very slight. And she's not riding him as he should be ridden.'

Lottie appeared at the door of the lorry with Savannah. 'Savannah rode so well, didn't she?' Her cheeks were flushed with pleasure for her friend.

'And so did you, Lottie,' exclaimed Bramble warmly. 'Vincent is not the easiest horse and you did very well to get a clear round in the showjumping.'

But she knew Lottie was deaf to all compliments: 'Mummy's awfully cross.'

'Cecily was watching her by the water,' explained Savannah, 'and she shouted "Use your whip, he needs to know who's boss", and the judge counted it as unauthorised assistance and eliminated her.'

'I wouldn't have taken any notice of anything Mummy'd said,' said Lottie.

'Of course you wouldn't,' soothed Bramble. 'It's so unfair.'

Savannah and Lottie went off, heads close together, to the secretary's tent to give back their competitor numbers.

'Thank God for that,' murmured Bramble. Since Lottie had left their yard Savannah's social life seemed to have disappeared completely. 'Perhaps she'll stop this dieting thing if she's got her friend back.'

She thought Felicity looked concerned. 'Perhaps.'

Helena finally cornered Ollie – literally – by picking up a knife and holding it to his chin, trapping him in the kitchen. It was a Global, one of the best, and very, very sharp. Helena suppressed the thought that if she became a murderer she'd make sure she did it with the right logo on the blade.

Ollie looked alarmed. 'There's no need for that, Helena.' He held both hands up.

'You are not writing a film script,' she screamed at him. 'You never were. You've spent the last year in your office drinking.'

'Well, I can't write with you in this state, that's true,' replied Ollie, 'you've no idea how difficult you make it for me to work.'

'You've been pretending that you've got a deal.'

'Yes, my dear little competitive wife, because you wouldn't have let me have a moment's peace if I hadn't. You'd have been on at me day and night—'

'Only because I don't want us to go bankrupt!'

'Yes, well, that's not how genius works. We can't just sit down and turn it on like actors can. You made me live a lie because you have such ridiculous ideas about what we need. I can't go out to work like you can, taking on any tinpot, mindless role that's offered to you. I mean, "Mattie". It's hardly Chekhov, is it?'

'I work because I have to,' said Helena. 'I work because there are five people depending on me.'

'*You* work because you like the fame and spending lots of money,' replied Ollie. 'Don't deny it. We wouldn't be in half this trouble if you hadn't insisted on a new kitchen when the house we bought already had a recently fitted one.'

'You can't have a country kitchen in the middle of Primrose Hill,' shouted Helena. 'Not these days. It would have made me look like a mad bag lady.'

'And what about the three shower rooms?'

'Today's houses need to have almost a one-to-one ratio of bathrooms and bedrooms,' said Helena. 'We were bringing the house up to present-day standards. It's an investment.'

'Well, it cost a lot. And what about the new granite flooring on top of very nice stripped floorboards? And the twins going to the most expensive nursery school rather than the playgroup round the corner?'

'Round the corner? Round the corner? They'd have been knifed on their way in in the morning.'

Ollie looked pointedly at the Global. 'Only by their mother, it seems.'

Helena placed the tip of the knife against the bottom of his chin. 'DO NOT LAUGH AT ME. This is serious.'

'Er, shall we sit down and talk calmly?' He edged towards the door.

'I have been trying to sit down and talk to you for months,' she hissed. 'All you ever do is go to the pub, and now look what's happened.'

'I've been sorting things out. I've made some very valuable contacts. You don't meet the right people by sitting at home and waiting for them to knock on the door.'

'No, the only people who knock on *our* door are the bailiffs.' She jabbed the knife up in the air again. 'And don't think you're getting out the basement door, because I've locked it.'

'I was only trying to reach my sweater,' said Ollie plaintively.

'So tell me,' she fumed. 'These marvellous contacts. How are they going to help us? Are they going to stop us going bankrupt?'

'Well, they are, actually. D'you mind if I sit down?'

Helena sat down opposite, laying the knife on the kitchen table but keeping her hand on it. 'Well?'

'OK,' admitted Ollie. He slid an envelope across the table. She didn't want to open it. 'Is it bad?'

Ollie shrugged.

Helena opened the letter with trembling hands. The mortgage company was giving them a week to leave the house.

'They don't give us much time,' she said in a whisper.

'That's the way it goes. It's not our house any more.'

'What about the other debts?'

'Once we've moved it'll be less easy to find us. They're big corporations, they're inefficient. We need to lie low for a bit and most of them will write the debts off. In fact, the sooner we get out the better. Those bailiffs will come back any moment.'

'So we've lost the house completely?'

'They'll give us any money left over once they've sold it,' said Ollie. 'We can add that to what you get from Lorenden, and we can start again.'

'I've got a huge tax bill,' whispered Helena.

'You'll have to pay that, I'm afraid. There's no getting away from the tax man. But don't talk to any of our other creditors. Just send all the recent letters back with "not known at this address" scribbled on them. My man in the pub says that some of them will go bankrupt before we do, and after a bit they stop chasing minor sums. Personnel change, companies go under, debts get bought and sold . . . It's all one great big muddle.'

'But that's fraud,' gasped Helena.

'Not if we leave without telling anyone. We truthfully won't be known at this address. Hand the keys back to the mortgage company and walk away. We'll have to talk to the bank and ask them to freeze the loan, but the rest of the stuff, let's just see who eventually manages to find us. And we need to take anything we really want with us before the bailiffs can get their hands on it too.' Ollie's eyes were alight with excitement. 'I know a man with a van who'll come at night—'

'Probably because he's a burglar,' flashed Helena. 'Those are the only sort of vans that move furniture at night.' Surely this was all a dream, a terrible nightmare and she would wake up soon? She couldn't be going to lose her beautiful, precious house, the pinnacle of everything she had achieved.

'The letter says a week.' She read it again, shaking with shock.

'I got it yesterday. And the bailiffs could be back first thing tomorrow morning.' Ollie quietly took the knife from her. 'Let's start packing. Give me any bills that have come in recently: I'll write "Return to Sender" on them now.'

'But where do we go?' asked Helena. She had come so far and had lost it all.

'Lorenden, of course.'

Bramble had recorded cross-country day at Badminton and, along with Jez, Donna, Savannah and Felicity, they watched it when they got back, with plates of curry on their laps. After a relatively dry beginning, the heavens opened and rider after rider struggled through torrential rain. It drummed down like a refrain in Bramble's ears. You should be here. You should be here. Never had the top looked so far away. The Bramble who had ridden that course, and had made it to the top twenty, was someone she could hardly remember. Someone she could walk past without recognising.

Toby and Teddy lumbered out onto the course. The commentator called him a 'veteran of the circuit – this is Toby Fitzroy's eighth Badminton'.

'That's all they can say about him,' said Donna. 'It's not as if they can call him popular, or successful or a promising rider.' She giggled and everyone else tried to smile.

'I was talking to Hannah, his head groom, the other day and she says he's always buying new kit for vast sums of money – if it's not expensive it can't be the best. He's on saddles at the moment, apparently, and has found some international saddle-maker who charges a fortune to tell him his current saddles are putting all his horse's backs out.'

'It's probably having to jump huge fences with a great lump like Toby clinging on that's hurting their backs,' said Bramble. 'He keeps himself in shape, but he's a big man.'

Teddy galloped bravely over the first few fences, but it became obvious that Toby's habit of hanging on to the reins had damaged the good-hearted horse's confidence. Approaching the fifth fence, the Beaufort Staircase, Teddy responded to contradictory commands – Toby's urging him forward with his legs and hauling him back in the mouth – by almost slithering to a halt in front of the first element, then clambering overs it.

'Poor Teddy,' shrieked Savannah, as horse and rider picked their way down the steps. 'It looks so uncomfortable.' Teddy landed at the bottom unbalanced, with his feet in the wrong place to tackle the narrow pile of logs at the bottom. He ran out and Toby circled him again, using his whip hard.

Bramble sighed. Teddy did not deserve such treatment. He was a horse who would jump anything if you presented it to him properly. Toby skidded round the rest of the course, coasting on luck rather than judgement, and twice Teddy got him out of trouble by twisting to get over a jump or adding in a stride when Toby hadn't calculated it properly. They eventually blundered into the main arena, clearly exhausted but Toby punched the air. He was fifty-seventh out of a field of sixty-one.

They all looked at the screen in silence.

'He's just not a good enough rider,' said Bramble. 'If he didn't have this obsession with riding at the highest level, and didn't face himself and his horses with such huge fences, he'd be fine. But he can't accept his own limitations.'

The others were glued to the screen as the current leader, Betsy Parker, an American rider, came on to the course, but Bramble's mind was still on Toby's ambition and whether, in some ways, it matched her own. Suppose she, like Toby, had been wealthy enough not to have to sell the best horses that had passed through her hands; perhaps it would have been her up there, with other people commenting on her riding and seeing what she could not. She had dismissed him as a spoilt brat, but why shouldn't Toby be allowed ambitions? Why didn't she find his determination and commitment admirable?

She puzzled over it for a while, as the American rider managed one of only two clear rounds within the time so far. Then she realised that growing up meant self-knowledge and, at fifty-two, Toby hadn't grown up enough to realise that he was out of his class. Perhaps she should learn from that.

'If Jez had been riding Teddy he'd have got into the top twenty,' said Savannah.

Jez grinned at her. 'Yep.'

It must be nice to be so confident. Nobody said anything about what would have happened if Bramble had ridden Teddy, and Bramble held back the thought that she was also actually half-relieved not to have been clambering nervously over the enormous fences and dithering for terrifying half-seconds in front of huge drops on such a large horse.

'Well *you* won today, Savannah.' She tried to bring the earlier sense of victory back into the room. 'You're on your way to the nationals. And then it'll be you up there, instead of Toby.' But she was so distracted that she didn't notice that Savannah had used a napkin to cover up the curry remaining on her plate.

With her lean frame and up to ten horses to ride every day – not to mention the hard, physical work in the yard – Bramble had no idea what to do with a daughter who hated her body and was prepared to starve it into something it should never be.

Later that evening, her tiredness gone, Savannah looked at herself in the mirror as she zipped up a pair of jeans that Felicity had discarded, a pair of slinky size tens, much smaller than any Savannah had ever owned.

High on the adrenalin of success, she saw shining eyes, flushed cheeks and a pretty, heart-shaped face. 'I'm a winner,' she told herself. 'I can do whatever I like. I can get thin. I can win Lorenden back for Mum. And I can win Jez.' Every touch of his hand – the way he lightly legged her up into the saddle or embraced her as the commentator announced her as the winner – set her on fire. She could scarcely sleep for happiness and excitement.

Outside, the water sluiced down the guttering and rushed over the flagstones.

Chapter 26

The gang were waiting for Eddie as he loped back from watching television at Rufus's house. He'd persuaded Rufus to watch eventing instead of football and, while his friend had been only half-watching, playing a game on his laptop and texting his girlfriend at the same time, Eddie, sitting forward on the sofa had absorbed every movement of leg and arm, the approaches to each fence, drinking in the interviews and the commentators' remarks and committing them carefully to memory. These were his heroes. One day he would be one of them. On the way home, he was still thinking about Toby and Teddy, and how he might have ridden the horse better, when he heard footsteps behind him.

'Oi,' shouted a voice, and a bolt of high-voltage fear shot through him. He lengthened his stride – imperceptibly, he hoped – but footsteps thudded up behind him and he broke into a run, swerving in front of a car, which hooted at him. He just managed to spring out of its way and back into the middle of the road, running down the central reservation in the face of two lanes of headlights, running his lungs out but still aware that the gang was somewhere behind. Looking over his shoulder, he thought he saw a dark shape setting out to thread its way through the traffic after him.

He dodged through a small gap that opened up in the flow of cars – resulting in a cacophony of horns – and reached the other side. He stopped for a few seconds and looked across the road, his sides heaving. Ty was directly opposite him, only partially masked by the moving traffic, then completely obscured by a bus. When the bus passed, Eddie could half hear, half lip-read the boy's shouted message. 'We know where you live. You are dead.'

An articulated lorry flashed past and Eddie took advantage of its cover to dive behind some garages, clamber over a wall and begin running again, into the warren of buildings behind. This estate, a sixties development with an interlinking mesh of driveways, footpaths and culs-de-sac, was not just on the other side of the road, as far as Eddie was concerned, but almost the other side of the world. Helena had always pronounced it dangerous and evil, full of drug dealers and muggers. She had managed to blank it out of her vision, and the vision of her children. They barely saw it when they went past it every day. This, in all probability, was the gang's home turf, but he'd have to take that risk, just to get away from them.

A few people – an old woman toting a carrier bag, a pair of girls, younger than he himself was, each with a pram, and a shrivelled, wrinkled tinker of a man sitting on a step drinking – looked at him curiously but, schooled by Helena's determination that everyone on the estate was dangerous and would harm him, he ran on. But he got the feeling that an increasing number of invisible eyes were watching him, and that a whisper of communication had already swirled round the buildings. He heard a shout. They were closing in. He must find his way out, to an ordinary road with shops in it, or a bus route, or a tube station. Somebody, somewhere who could help him. He raced round a corner to be faced by the dead end of a high brick wall.

Helena sat, motionless, in the twilit kitchen until she heard the doorbell ring. Only a few months ago the bell had been a harbinger of excitement – friends dropping in, delicious mail order parcels being delivered, children returning from school . . . Now the sound filled her with terror and she clamped her hands over her ears.

Ollie came down a few minutes later. 'Mick and the gang are here.'

'Mick?'

'Man with a van. Several men with a truck, actually.'

'We can't go now. Not this minute.' Helena was shocked into standing up. 'Eddie's not here.'

'We may not have another opportunity. We go now, or we go under.'

'I don't believe it. We're fleeing our home like common criminals. All because you lied to me about having work.'

Ollie seized her shoulders. 'This, Helena, is all *your* fault. You had a very nice house without a mortgage we could have lived in. Instead, we bought an even nicer one. You spent hundreds of thousands of pounds changing it completely so that it could be featured in *Fabulous Homes*,' he sneered at the title '. . . *you* insisted on us having parties, holidays and expensive clothes, and chartering that yacht that time. You got into my head, with your rampant consumerism and obsession with the right labels and made me believe that no one is worth anything unless they're wearing the latest shoes. Think about the spending that goes on in this house: how much of it is down to you?'

Helena was stunned into silence.

'Right. You see? Practically all of it. When did I last buy anything? Or ask for anything, for that matter? No wonder I couldn't write. Look at yourself, Helena, and take responsibility for once.'

Helena was still in shock. 'But your drinking . . .'

'Is irrelevant. It's the only way I could cope. It's not as if I'm an alcoholic, for God's sake, just someone pushed too far. I say it again, take responsibility, Helena, take responsibility. For once in your life.'

Ollie was enjoying this, thought Helena as she watched her husband stride round the house as if he was planning a military exercise. Mick and the gang had brought piles of removal boxes and Helena took all her clothes off their rails and threw everything in, then upturned the drawers and threw their contents in too. She flung any shoes she could find on top.

'Half an hour a room,' said Ollie, 'no more. But I'll keep one set of keys and sneak back later if we really miss something.'

It was like a nightmare: Ollie was planning to burgle their own home.

She went up to Eddie's room and made sure that everything of his was packed, even checking under the bed. Teenage boys didn't have much, but he had some old toys and books, and two teddies. They had been with him since Earls Court.

'Leave those,' said Ollie, 'they're just rubbish. You're spending too long up here.'

'No, no, he'll want these.' Helena brushed aside a tear.

'Mick and the gang are packing the drawing room and the kitchen.'

'Do you trust them? Are you sure they won't steal things?'

They left the sleeping twins till last, then woke them.

'We're going on a fun adventure,' said Helena. 'A treat.' Roly and Ruby, only half-aware of what was going on, were tucked up in the back of the car with their duvets, pillows and favourite toys. She continued to dial Eddie's number frantically. 'I still can't find Eddie, I can't go without Eddie.'

'We may have to,' said Ollie, lugging a box of books down the stairs. 'Here guys, these can go.'

'Where's the horse sculpture?' Helena asked, rushing distractedly from one room to the other. 'Pa's sculpture?'

'In the van somewhere. Now hurry up!' Ollie took her by the shoulders.

A few people walked down the lamplit street and looked curiously in, but fortunately none of the neighbours came out to ask them what was going on.

Ania came back from an evening at the cinema. 'What is happening?'

'We're going abroad,' said Ollie. 'Here, look, have you got a friend you can stay with till you find another job?'

'Well, yes, but . . .'

'Here's compensation.' Ollie peeled some notes off a roll.

'Ollie, where did you get that from?' screeched Helena.

'Never mind. I've got us enough cash to last for a bit.'

'But where from? Is it legal?'

'It's perfectly legal. Now shut up and get on with it.'

'Mrs Cooper, what is happening? Please tell me.'

'There's nothing to tell, Ania. I'm sorry this is so sudden. We've decided to move.'

'In the middle of the night?'

Helena gripped Ania's arms. 'I'm so sorry, Ania,' she repeated.

'I hope you'll be all right. But please don't talk about this to anyone.'

Ania was too astonished to respond.

'Can you find somewhere this evening?'

'Yes, yes, my friend Maria. Her employers are away, but . . .'

'Then go. We're leaving in a minute.'

Ania went upstairs, counting her money. Helena tried to see how much it was. Quite a lot. Hundreds of pounds, maybe more.

'Can we leave a note for Eddie?'

'No, you stupid woman, we *cannot* leave a note. We might as well send a forwarding address to the bailiffs. Ring round his friends' parents. If you know their numbers, that is. If you were a proper mother, you'd know exactly where he was.'

Helena curled up on the stairs in pure pain, then pulled herself together and began to rifle through the boxes for various class lists. Her back ached, her feet hurt and she was more tired and confused than she'd ever been. Nobody ever talked about bankruptcy. She'd once had a friend who'd alluded to 'having to get out of the house terribly quickly' and another who had disappeared from the scene for several years, but she'd never heard much more. People might discuss their irritable bowel syndrome, sexual intimacies or experience of childbirth in gory detail, but they always skimmed over anything like bankruptcy with a self-deprecating laugh.

'You go,' she told Ollie. 'You take the twins and keep an eye on Mick and the van. I don't trust him not to drive it straight to Dover and across to the markets of Europe.'

'He's a mate,' said Ollie scornfully.

Helena sat in the almost empty house, trying to imagine where Eddie might be. He would be at a party. It would be too noisy for him to hear his phone. Or staying overnight at someone's house, with his phone left downstairs in his school bag.

I have never been so frightened in my life, she thought. I don't know where Eddie is. My child is missing.

The house already seemed to belong to someone else – to another time, another family, another woman called Helena. Stepping outside, desperately peering up and down the street for Eddie, she no longer knew who that woman was.

Chapter 27

Savannah woke up and traced her hands over her hip bones. Were they a little softer than yesterday? Her mind, caged by thoughts of food, calculated how little breakfast she could get away with, until she realised that she'd been woken not by the alarm but by the sound of children shouting. She went to the window and saw Ollie and the twins. She got dressed, forcing her reluctant, tired limbs into clothes and went to find out what was going on.

'Mum.' She tapped on Bramble's door. 'There's a van downstairs with a whole load of men,' she said. 'And Ollie's there, with the twins, who are racing round the yard.'

'What?' Bramble shook herself awake. It was already light. 'What's the time?'

'Half past five.'

She and Savannah looked at each other. 'At least it's sunny,' said Bramble, checking the weather. 'We desperately need the ground to dry out a bit.'

'Ollie says they've come to stay. All of them.'

'Where's Helena?' asked Bramble.

'In London, waiting for Eddie. He's out at a party or something, apparently. Ollie says that their house is being repossessed.'

'Oh no! That house is everything to Helena.' Bramble threw herself out of bed and pulled on her clothes. 'This is a disaster. On top of losing Mattie – she'll go completely mad.'

'Perhaps they could live here permanently,' suggested Savannah, biting her nails. 'And then we wouldn't have to sell.'

Bramble stopped and stared at her for a moment, gave a short, humourless laugh and then began to pull on her clothes.

'So I'll take that as a no, then, shall I?' Savannah sighed.

While Bramble was making tea in the kitchen, men shuffled in and out with pieces of furniture. 'Look, excuse me . . . I know I suggested, but Ollie . . . I don't think . . .' She tried to stop a short, thickset man, but he simply said 'Mind out, love, this is heavy,' and staggered past her.

'But you can't just . . .' Bramble's mobile rang and Savannah answered it as Bramble tried to tackle Ollie about why he'd turned up with a van full of furniture and how long they were planning to stay. 'We need to discuss—'

'Can you ask Bramble how long I should wait before I ring the police about Eddie? Or Felicity? She probably knows about these things,' gasped Helena, sounding panicky. 'He's not home yet and I've tried all the friends I know.'

Savannah passed the message on, a chill catching at her heart. This wasn't like Eddie.

Bramble seized the phone. 'He's stayed out all night before, hasn't he?' Savannah could see her mother frown as she saw, through the open kitchen door, three men strong-arming a huge double bed up the stairs. 'Well, I'm sure that's OK then. Don't worry, he'll turn up. Listen, Helena, about all this furniture . . .'

It was almost as if Helena had planned Eddie's disappearance, thought Savannah in a cynical moment. Normally Bramble would have been heading the men off, querying whether the bed should come in before they'd agreed how long everyone could stay. But with Helena so frantic, she knew her mother wouldn't want to add to her problems. Still, the furrow between Bramble's brows deepened as Ollie's computer was whisked upstairs.

Savannah could still hear Helena's voice squawking on the mobile as Ollie came in, with a pile of books in his arms. He took the phone from Bramble: 'Helena, don't be so daft. If you call the police then everyone will know where we've gone. For goodness' sake, he's a kid, he'll have dossed with a friend. You know teenagers,' he shouted. 'Out on the razzle as usual. Stop fussing.'

'Helena thinks he might have run away because she won't let him be a professional eventer like Pa,' said Bramble quietly to

Savannah, as Ollie clumped upstairs. 'In which case, I'm sure he'll be fine. He'll turn up soon.' But Savannah could see that her mother was worried. Still, it stopped her noticing that she, Savannah, had only had a black coffee for breakfast. It was a victory.

'Ollie doesn't like Eddie, does he?' observed Savannah, clattering a clean plate into the dishwasher to give the impression of someone who had had some toast.

Bramble paused, as if she hadn't thought about this before. 'I think it's always difficult with stepfathers.'

Out in the yard Felicity was bent over, running her hand up and down Merlin's back leg.

'I can't *feel* anything wrong.'

Bramble came round the corner to hear Jez saying, 'Trot him up again and let's see.'

'Let's see what?' Bramble was sharp.

'Merlin and Frenchie seem to have kicked each other in the field,' said Jez, focusing on the horse as Felicity trotted him away from them. 'Frenchie's got a bruise, and we think Merlin might be lame.'

'I told you so!' Bramble was infuriated. 'If you turn valuable horses out together, they're bound to hurt themselves.'

'If you don't turn valuable horses out,' said Jez softly, 'they're so fresh when you ride them you can't do any proper work with them. This is the first injury we've had in the field since I've been here.'

'Well, that's just luck. This was always an accident waiting to happen.'

'How's Frenchie?'

'I'm icing him now,' said Donna from the other side of the yard, wrapping a cool pack round Frenchie's leg and twisting a bandage over it. It doesn't look too bad. He should be OK for the weekend.'

'He'd better be. It's his first Novice outing.' She shook her head in despair, although she had a sneaking feeling that Jez had a point. Every yard always had to deal with a stream of injuries, but under his laid-back approach, they did seem to have had fewer than usual.

But she could barely concentrate. For a moment, under the harsh electric light in the kitchen, she'd seen Savannah differently. She had looked like an old woman, with a mouth that seemed to be all teeth, and dull skin stretched tightly over bones. But that was just the worry about Eddie, surely? Then she'd blinked, Savannah had moved and the schoolgirl face had returned, not so pretty as it had been, admittedly, but children changed so fast at her age.

Merlin trotted up sound, apparently none the worse for wear after all.

'You see,' said Felicity. 'Jez was right. Jez, what do you think about . . .'

Bramble interrupted to tell Felicity about Eddie going missing, suppressing the nagging worry about her daughter, along with the feeling that she had lost control of her own yard.

'Ollie's right, up to a point,' replied Felicity. 'The police won't take any notice of an eighteen-year-old boy staying out all night. Even so, I don't like it. He's usually pretty reliable, isn't he?'

'Very,' said Bramble.

'If he hasn't been found by lunchtime I'll go up to London and help Helena look for him,' promised Felicity.

'Felicity,' Bramble suddenly felt the need for reassurance. 'Savannah . . . Do you think . . .?'

'Do I think she's eating far too little? Yes, I do,' said Felicity, decisive as usual. 'But it's less clear what you can do for her. I think it could be linked to Pa's death, you know – for the second time in her life she's lost a father figure, and I think she might be very frightened.'

Upstairs, Savannah gazed in horror at her hairbrush. She was sure that she'd cleaned it yesterday, tugging out the hair wound round the brush, but there seemed to be more now. Too much for a few minutes brushing, surely. Or maybe it was normal? Of course it must be normal. She stared at her face in the mirror, terrified. Was that her scalp she could see through her hair? Fear tore at the hunger inside her. At least she'd only had black coffee for breakfast.

It would be all right. She could control it. If you lacked confidence because you were fat, or if you were frightened, you should go on a diet and get thin, and then you would be able to do everything you'd ever dreamt of and people would respect you more. Men would fall in love with you; women would envy you. You would look good in everything. Yesterday, in the paper, she'd seen a photograph of a woman who'd jumped from a bridge. Her first thought had been, Why did she need to commit suicide? She was slim. Didn't she know how lucky she was?

The main problem in the country today was obesity and everybody eating far too much. That was what the television told her every night. And, of course, there was no such thing as being too rich or too thin. She must remember that, remember it all, and it would all be all right.

She took a deep breath, pinched her thighs – hard – with hatred and started her work. She had discovered, to her surprise, that exam revision was one place she could lose herself, where no one would bother her and where thoughts of food faded to manageable levels, although sometimes it, too, revolved around her head in endless loops as she tried to sleep.

Bramble was just about to drive Felicity to the station when Helena's sports car turned very, very slowly into the drive, making slightly too wide an arc. It crept towards them, eventually dribbling to a stop.

Bramble and Felicity looked at each other. Helena's style was usually so nippy and determined. The car door opened and Eddie unfolded himself from the driver's seat.

'I didn't know you could drive,' said Bramble, horrified at his appearance. His lip was swollen and cut, his face was dirty and there was a huge bruise over his eye. 'And what happened to you?'

'I've only had three lessons,' he replied. 'But I'm insured to drive if there's a full licence holder in the car.'

'A conscious full licence holder,' said Felicity, opening the passenger door. 'Helena doesn't qualify. And you ought to have L-plates.'

Helena's head was thrown back and she was snoring, breathing very slowly. The smell of vomit filled the car.

'Mum had to have a drink,' he said, wincing as he leant against the car. His clothes were damp and filthy. 'It was my fault, she was so worried about me.'

'She *was* worried about you.' Felicity spoke firmly. 'But the decision to drink was hers. It was nothing to do with you, whatever she says. How much do you think she's had?'

'I think she might have had several bottles of wine,' admitted Eddie.

'Eddie, what's happened to your hand?' Bramble indicated his left hand, which had swollen to twice its normal size and was loosely wrapped in a bloodstained scarf.

'Someone stamped on it,' he said. 'Several times. I had to come here: Mum said we couldn't tell anyone where we were.'

'I'll take you to hospital while Felicity takes Helena up to bed.'

'No.' Felicity took the car keys out of Bramble's hand. 'I'll take them both to hospital. You may not recognise alcohol poisoning when you see it, Bramble, but I do, and Helena needs a doctor just as much as Eddie does.'

'Are you saying that you drove down here, with that hand and heaven knows what else . . .' asked Bramble ' . . . with only three driving lessons behind you, all because Helena was drunk?'

Eddie managed a painful smile. 'I made her promise that I could become a professional rider first. I got her to put it in writing on the back of an envelope. So that's all settled.' Bramble saw his eyes light up with anticipation. 'I'll need to be able function properly when I'm injured, after all, so it was good practice.'

Chapter 28

'Eddie's been stalked by a local gang for months, but he didn't want to tell anyone,' Bramble told Nat, when he came round the following evening. Helena had spent twenty-four hours in hospital, on a drip, while Eddie's hand had had six stitches. 'I was able to watch the showjumping at Badminton on TV in the waiting room,' he'd said cheerfully, 'so it wasn't too bad at all.'

'They chased him on his way back from Rufus's,' Bramble continued, still horrified by what he'd been through, 'and he fled into the local estate, where he got lost. He thought he'd got away but, by coincidence, probably, they found him again just as he was nearly back home again at about three, and they beat him up. Apparently, they were kicking and stamping on him while he was on the ground, when two men and an old woman came out of the flats in the estate and started screaming about calling the police. The woman took him in and cleaned him up, and one of the men drove him home. He's in terrible pain: apart from the broken hand it's what the doctor calls "only bruising" but he can hardly move. I can't believe how brave he's being, he just keeps asking after Helena, and telling us he's getting into practice for what it feels like falling off four-star horses.'

Nat shook his head in sympathy. 'He could have been killed. Or permanently injured. And Ollie and Helena have moved in with you? Just like that? How do you feel?'

'It's my fault as much as anyone's,' sighed Bramble. 'I did suggest it in passing a few weeks ago, because I knew Helena was worried. But she rejected it out of hand and I didn't think any more about it. And it *is* partly Helena's house, after all. But it's my *home*, and they just swept in, and I knew she was so upset about losing Primrose Hill and worried about where Eddie was, I didn't feel I could challenge her. While she was lying in her hospital bed, claiming to be suffering from "exhaustion" she apologised so profusely for landing them all on me that I found myself reassuring her that it really doesn't matter. But it does. Do you think I'm being selfish? After all, legally, she has just as much right to live at Lorenden as I do. And I did invite her, in a way.'

'I think you've got to sell this house,' said Nat. 'It's dragging you down, entangling you in all your family's problems. You can't move forward until you do.'

'And Felicity and Jez have taken over the yard,' Bramble laughed, trying to make a joke of it. 'They're a gang of two. Every time I say something, they stop talking, look at me, wait for me to finish and then go on talking as if I wasn't there. I feel as if I'm about five and they're the grown-ups.' She'd meant it as a funny story, but realised there was real resentment in her voice as she spoke. She wasn't sure she liked the person she was turning into.

'He's always been overbearing,' said Nat. 'He may well be manipulating her sexually as well.'

'What?' Bramble spluttered into her drink. 'What do you mean?'

'It's his modus operandi.' Nat stroked her cheek. 'Move into a yard, hit on the senior unattached female and take over. As he can't have you . . .' He squeezed her thigh affectionately.

Bramble thought about that first night, when Jez had arrived in the storm, and the tension that had crackled between them. The way he'd watched her move around the room, challenging her in almost everything they'd talked about. But since Nat had become a permanent fixture in her life that electricity had gone. She and Jez were just friends now. If such a thing were possible. Colleagues might be a better word. She sighed. 'I honestly don't think he would do something quite so—'

'I do,' said Nat sharply. 'You're being naive. Men are just as calculating as women when it comes to money in relationships. He's probably after her for her share of Lorenden.'

There was something wrong about that statement, but Bramble couldn't quite put her finger on it. She closed her eyes. It had been another long day. She leaned back on the sofa, looping her legs over Nat's, luxuriating in the comforting warmth of his solid body.

'Bramble,' said Nat gently, placing his hand on her cheek again. 'You are not your sisters' keeper. And you've let yourself get into the habit of thinking you are.'

'I suppose not.' She finished her drink and put it down. 'Who else do we have, though, if we don't have each other? Helena's marriage seems to be deteriorating beyond the point of no return, and Felicity's on her own. And I . . .'

'And you have me.'

Bramble hesitated, and thought how sweet he was. She picked up his hand and kissed it. 'What would I do without you?'

Nat left his hand touching her face. 'I want to talk to you.'

'You are talking to me,' replied Bramble, laughing.

'No, I mean seriously. In the last few months I've been happier than I've ever been. I think we're good together. I think what you've done is amazing, both with the horses and Savannah. It's not easy bringing up a teenage girl on your own, and that's why I want to be at your side. You look after everybody, and I want to look after you.'

'Well, yes, but Savannah is . . .'

'Bramble, we can look after Savannah together. She needs a father desperately.'

'But Helena and Felicity are . . .'

'Please stop thinking about everyone else and think about yourself for a moment. I want to marry you. Please say yes.'

A wave of both terror and elation washed over her, as if she was being unexpectedly swept away in a torrent of icy water, but she held it back with another sip of wine. Anyone would feel like that, facing such a decision so suddenly.

She thought about not being lonely, and having someone to talk to, to bounce ideas off . . . someone whose arms would be warm and welcoming at the end of a long, hard day.

'I want us to be together,' he said softly. 'To be together properly without everyone else interrupting us all the time. And, call me old-fashioned if you like, but that means marriage to me. I want a real commitment and I hope you feel the same.'

'Yes,' she whispered, a choke of emotion rising in her throat, 'yes, I'd like that very much.'

A huge burden – one she'd hardly known she carried – dropped off her shoulders. It all seemed so clear and so right. Something in the maelstrom ahead was sorted and clarified. And, together, they could provide a secure home for Savannah.

Chapter 29

Savannah was on her bed, revising for her French GCSE with Darcy curled up beside her, when there was a knock at the door. She sat up, hoping that she looked less exhausted than she felt. 'Come in.'

It was Bramble, who crept in looking apologetic.

Now what? Savannah made space for her mother on the bed.

'I've got something to tell you,' said Bramble, sitting down.

Savannah hoped it wasn't anything dreadful, like having cancer.

'Nat and I are getting married. I wanted you to know first.'

It was as if someone had punched Savannah in the stomach. She stared at Bramble.

'He's a good man,' said Bramble. 'And he wants to make us both happy.'

'I was happy,' replied Savannah, studying her patchwork quilt. One square was a washed-out blue with little stars, another a faded pink with white polka dots. She clung on to the familiar detail because it would never change. In a frightening flash of perception it occurred to her that perhaps her mother hadn't been happy herself, that the magical childhood that Savannah remembered, where everyone had loved her and she'd been included in everything that her mother did – perhaps that hadn't been happiness. She didn't dare lift her eyes to Bramble for fear of what she might see there.

Bramble put a hand on Savannah's arm and Savannah slid it away, in case Bramble was trying to see if she'd lost weight. She curled up in a tight ball.

'I'm not sure that you are happy,' said Bramble gently. 'I'm worried about how little you eat. You're getting very thin.'

'I eat lots.' Savannah tried to think of a way of convincing her mother. 'I had a peanut butter sandwich, a banana and a KitKat for supper,' she lied. 'I just don't like beef stew, that's why I wasn't there with everyone else.' This intrusion into her eating habits made her feel panicky, far more panicky than her mother marrying Nat did. Nat was OK, but she hadn't envisaged him hanging around for ever. 'So when are you getting married?' she asked, to divert the conversation.

'We don't know yet. Maybe next year. Do you mind?'

'It's fine,' said Savannah to her own knees. 'I really don't care.'

'Savannah?' Bramble spoke gently. 'Look at me. I'm not going to get married without your . . . your blessing.'

Like hell she wouldn't. Grown-ups always did exactly what they liked. And what was this stupid blessing thing anyway? They weren't religious, neither of them.

'Savannah?' Bramble touched her shoulder and Savannah twitched away.

'OK. OK, you have my *blessing*. Is that all?'

Bramble kissed the top of Savannah's head. 'This is about you just as much as it's about me. I love you very much and you'll always be the most important thing in my life.' She left the room and closed the door softly behind her.

Savannah very much doubted that. Nat would be the most important thing in her mother's life from now on. As her mother had said earlier, there were always problems with stepfathers.

'How did she take it?' Nat was waiting anxiously, sitting at the bottom of the stairs. He laughed. 'I feel like a nineteenth-century suitor waiting to ask a father for his daughter's hand in marriage. Only in reverse. In fact, do you think I ought to talk to her myself?'

'No, I don't think that's necessary.' Bramble didn't want him to see Savannah's reaction. 'She's basically OK, but I think it's been a bit of a shock.'

Nat kissed her on the lips and she felt a brief, warm jolt of connection between them. ' It'll be better when we have our own place,' he said. 'Somewhere for you and me and Savannah. Then she and I can really build a relationship.'

'What about Gemma?' Bramble was surprised that he mentioned his own daughter so rarely. 'Surely it's time I met her?'

'Sadly not. Jenny is so vindictive, she'll set up a screaming match and go back to court and try to get more money off me because I'm getting married, or reduce my access even more. Really, I promise you, leave this to me. I'll work something out. Well, shall we tell the rest of them? They're all in the kitchen.'

The kitchen was full of people, and the supper plates were still scattered across the table. Ollie had opened a bottle of wine and was sitting on the edge of the sink blowing smoke out of the window, Helena was flicking through a glossy magazine, Felicity and Donna were deep in discussion over saddles and Eddie, deathly pale, was almost asleep at the table. Ruby and Roly – who should have been in bed hours ago – were running in and out of the garden playing tag with the terriers. Bramble clutched Nat's hand. It was warm and firm. 'We're in this together,' he whispered in her ear, and she immediately felt better.

'Er, everybody.'

Ollie threw the cigarette out of the window and jumped down from the sink. He tapped the wine bottle. 'Bramble's trying to say something, everyone.'

Bramble looked at their upturned faces and the words nearly died in her mouth, but she felt Nat squeeze her hand. She cleared her throat. 'Um, we – that is Nat and I – well, we're . . . we're getting married.'

There was a shocked silence, then Helena leapt up, squealing in delight. 'How heavenly! When? Do let's have a wedding before we leave Lorenden. I can organise it all, it'll be such fun.'

And they were all up, kissing her cheek and pumping Nat's hand, asking 'when, when, when?'

'We don't exactly know,' said Bramble, blushing.

'But soon,' added Nat, squeezing her hand again.

As soon as her mother's footsteps died away, Savannah slipped off her bed, opened her bedroom door cautiously, checked that no one was about and quietly went through to the spare room –

where Eddie was staying – and unlatched the little door to the attic staircase. She tiptoed to the top and found the door open. Jez was standing at the dormer window looking at the stars, listening to music. The piece he was playing was wild and haunting, and she would remember its notes for the rest of her life.

He turned round when he heard her. 'Savannah! What's up?'

She was shivering. 'Mummy's getting married. To Nat.'

'What?' he sounded vague, then looked at her properly. 'What did you say?'

She summoned up all her courage and flung herself into his arms. 'Mummy. And Nat. Please stop them, I know you can. You hate him too, don't you?'

He drew back and examined her face. 'Savannah. Why don't you like him? Has he . . . has he hurt you in any way?' She could tell from his voice that he really cared and was tempted to invent something, just to hear that concern again.

'No, nothing like that,' she cried hysterically. 'He's too nice and he says things at the wrong time and he tries too hard to be liked. He wants me to like him . . . but I don't. I *don't* like him.' She hadn't known, until this moment, that she felt like this.

Jez held her in his arms, and she was struck by the hardness of his muscular body. 'Savannah, those are not crimes.' He sighed and kissed the top of her head. 'You're very young and you don't really know him.'

'I don't want to know him,' she murmured into his chest.

They stood there, Savannah revelling in the safety and security of his arms. No one had ever made her feel like this, so protected and so . . . so . . . loved. Surely Jez must be in love with her or he wouldn't be holding her like this, as if she was precious. This is a magical moment, she thought, Jez and I. Alone under the stars, holding each other, with the music and our skin on fire where it touches each other.

He sighed again, resting his chin on the top of her head. 'Dear little Savannah.'

She dared not move. She listened to the slow thud, thud of his heart against her own swift one, like the beat of a waltz played by a magical band. He smelt of hay and hard work.

'I will try to find out,' he said eventually, 'if there's any reason why Nat shouldn't marry your mother. But . . .' he turned her face up to his and held it, so she was forced to look into his eyes '. . . I want you to promise that if he hasn't actually done anything wrong you'll do your best to get on with him.' He gently wiped a tear off her cheek with his finger. 'Do I have your promise?'

Savannah would have promised him anything. 'Of course,' she said, confident that Jez would do something and that everything would be all right. 'Of course.' On an impulse she laced her arms around his neck and kissed him on the lips.

'You're sweet,' he said, and she felt his mouth on hers, answering her desire, then suddenly responding to her with the intensity she had dreamed of as their bodies melted together. She yearned for more, was hungry for him and reached for him in a way that she had never known she could.

'I'm sorry,' he said, drawing back after what seemed both an eternity and a fraction of a second, his slate-grey eyes burning into hers. 'That was wrong of me.' His voice was hoarse. 'You should be in bed. You should go.'

'No! I'm not a child, you know.'

'No, Savannah, you are not a child. You're a very lovely young woman, but you must go to bed and stay away from people like me.'

But I love you, she wanted to cry out. I can't stay away. Trembling, she traced the shape of his face with her finger and saw her own desire reflected in his eyes. She was never quite sure if she'd imagined it, or whether she reached up and kissed him, or whether it was he whose mouth dropped on to hers, but their lips met again, tenderly and briefly.

'We're opening a bottle of champagne downstairs,' said Helena's voice from behind them. 'I wondered if you'd like to join us, Jez, to toast Bramble and Nat.'

Savannah jumped out of her skin and away from Jez, but he faced Helena squarely. 'That would be very nice, Helena. I'll be down in a minute.'

Helena looked from Jez to Savannah, her eyes glittering, and Savannah shrank against the window. 'I'll be down in a minute too, Helena, I was just asking Jez his advice about how I should . . . er, manage Shaggy at Mulberry Hill if she . . . um, won't go in the ring.'

Helena stood there for another full minute but then, under Jez's steady gaze, was forced to turn round and go downstairs. 'Very well,' she said in clipped tones. 'I'll see you both in the drawing room.'

It sounded like a threat.

Chapter 30

At first, Helena was too shocked by her departure from London to think about Savannah and Jez, and what it might mean. She woke up on her first morning back at Lorenden and unpacked her bags, folding up her clothes in an old cherry wood chest of drawers that needed careful jiggling as they opened and closed. At home in Primrose Hill she had a walk-in wardrobe, and everything was kept in wire baskets or on shelves. She leaned against the window and felt sick. Thirty years ago her childish nose had been pressed to the same slightly rippled panes. She had looked at the same orchards, at the orderly rows of pink and white blossom on the trees and heard the coo of the wood pigeons in their branches. She had promised herself that she would get away and be someone in the real world, no matter what it took. She was going to be rich. Rich enough to have the treats she wanted, not to be told 'no' over and over again because the horses came first.

And here she was, back again, with nowhere else to go.

Bramble tapped on the door. 'Helena?'

They sat in the kitchen over mugs of tea, and Helena tried to explain their flight.

'But in this day and age, with all the surveillance there is, and all the computers, how can you just disappear?' asked Bramble.

'Well, we're not exactly disappearing, just getting some breathing space. And we won't be here long. Just until . . .' The depth of the gulf between this week and last yawned ahead of her.

'There are now a lot of us living here. Perhaps we should do a rota,' said Bramble.

Helena gazed at her without comprehension. 'That's a good idea,' she said. 'Otherwise I expect it'll all be left to me as usual. Perhaps we should get someone in—'

'Helena,' Bramble tried to suppress rage. What did she mean, all left to her? 'There isn't the money.'

'Just a student, or something. An au pair. Nothing that costs too much.'

'Helena, anything is too much. We can't borrow, there's no way of paying it back. Helena, I need you – and Ollie – to help out.'

'Well of course I'll help out.' Helena sounded offended. 'I mean, you know me. I'm the sort of person who can never sit down unless everything's sorted.'

Bramble gave up. She hoped she had made her point.

'Anyway,' said Helena, 'what about your wedding? You must have a marquee, of course.'

Savannah came in and made herself a black coffee.

'Savannah, have you eaten?'

'Yeah, yeah.' She was about to leave but Bramble, too jangled by her exchange with Helena to be careful, stopped her. 'You're not going out again until you eat this toast.'

Savannah picked at it, cutting off the crusts with generous margins. The phone rang and while Bramble answered it Savannah slipped away, jettisoning the toast in the yard where Darcy snarfed it down gratefully. He sniffed around the yard for more unexpected surprises.

As the days went on, Helena never mentioned Jez and Savannah's embrace to Bramble, although her eyes darted from Savannah to Jez every time they were together. Helena decided that her new role was that of home-maker, the woman who bravely gives up everything to look after her family. So she kept herself busy making strawberry jam, in pretty little pots with 'Helena's Strawberry Jam' on the labels, and planting salad mixes, dressed for the part in a floral pinny.

Savannah and Eddie took their exams. Not that Savannah's mattered, of course: Helena couldn't believe that Bramble was letting her leave school at this point in her life. Her sister was so irresponsible. As a mother. Helena enjoyed expounding her theories on Bramble's shortcomings to Felicity, although Felicity was irritatingly unwilling to be drawn into taking sides.

The new *Simon's Way* series was due to be aired and Helena would be very much back in the public eye, although she hoped bailiffs didn't watch it.

And life wasn't too bad at Lorenden. There was something surprisingly comforting about its shabby embrace. She explained to Ruby and Roly that they were like the Railway Children and that they were now poor, but that it would all turn out fine in the end. She had the sense that Eddie had escaped her, which was faintly disturbing, but he seemed happy and she shuddered daily at the thought of what might have happened if they'd stayed in London. He returned to his old school by day to take his exams, cheerfully enduring a commute of almost four hours a day. Then he spent all his time riding or working in the stables. Helena had given up trying to stop him. For the time being. Ollie said that Bramble had asked for no alcohol in the house during the day, and so he spent most of his time in the pub. 'I promised Bramble,' he said cheerfully. 'Bramble and I have an understanding.'

Helena limited the number of people she called – down to about twenty or thirty *closest* friends – and portrayed their flight as finally deciding to get out of dirty, crime-ridden London for the sake of the children. 'It's so wonderful,' she said, trying to block out the sound of Roly's Game Boy. 'Seeing them race around outside and have the wonderful freedom I had as a child. And, of course, I need to tune into my roots,' she said. 'Discover the real me.'

In fact, the real Helena was indeed tucked away in the attics and orchards of Lorenden and the last thing she wanted was to face her. Since moving up to London to be an actress at the age of eighteen, she had got so used to greeting every setback with a smile that she no longer recognised despair when she saw it in the mirror. She had to be cheerful for the children, in order not to frighten them, and put a positive spin on everything with friends because otherwise she would drop off the 'must have' list, both professionally and personally. Nobody liked self-pity and nobody wanted a loser. And as for Ollie, well, after all those lies she would obviously have to divorce him, but not now because she needed to keep her head below the financial parapet. Divorce, she told herself, would be a huge opportunity for personal growth. Again. Helena wondered how much more she could personally grow.

But sometimes she looked across the fields and sky and thought that there was too much space and silence. She, Helena, might come unravelled in such a place, her time no longer occupied by searches for the perfect tile or the most desirable shoe.

She showed prospective purchasers around Lorenden, and quickly learned to tell the difference between developers and what she came to think of as real people. The developers marched briskly round the house, occasionally tapping a wall, and never asked questions. They could see most of what they needed to see on a Land Registry map. Real people spent hours going round and asked hundreds of questions, most of them completely daft. 'Do you get a lot of noise from the motorway?' was one of the most frequent and, as the motorway was twenty minutes' drive away, Helena got quite snappish. The number of people who decided they loved the house but couldn't manage the commute was another frustrating one – why were they looking at a house so far away from where they worked in the first place? Then there were people who wanted a project, but were deterred by the amount of work Lorenden potentially needed, and others who wanted to open up the whole of the ground floor into one huge glass-and-steel kitchen–living space but were put off by the restrictions of it being a grade two listed building. The initial frenzy of interest slowed to a trickle and one developer told Helena that the main problem with it as a development site was access. 'You won't be able to use the drive, not for twenty-four houses,' he warned. 'You'd have to cut that tree down over there and widen the old bridlepath.'

'I think that cedar's got a protection order on it,' ventured Helena.

The developer laughed. 'Just cut it down. You risk a fine, but it's nothing compared to the potential profit.' Helena's fingers hovered over Tree Surgeons in the Yellow Pages. And she could also see, quite clearly, where Bramble was going wrong with Savannah and was invigorated by the prospect of a good family row. She thought – and felt it was her duty to say so – that Savannah had a very unhealthy crush on Jez and that Jez was undoubtedly abusing the trust of a sensitive young girl. She wasn't quite sure why she hadn't actually mentioned that she'd seen Jez kissing Savannah in the attic, but she suspected that Bramble – who only ever thought the best of everyone, as family legend went – would be fobbed off with some story, which she would believe and Helena would be positioned in the role of trouble-maker. As usual. No one in this family respected her opinions. She began to sow suspicion before making any specific accusations. Savannah was being unduly influenced, she maintained, and Bramble must put a stop to it.

'Well, I don't think that I actually have the right,' said Bramble. 'Technically Savannah is old enough to make up her own mind and, as far as I can see, Jez hasn't done anything I could stop.'

'I don't know how you can stand back and see your own daughter suffer.'

'Jez isn't making her suffer. It's this dieting thing.' Bramble wondered whether she should speed up their wedding plans, to give Savannah some security. Should she wear a long dress for her wedding, or a nice tailored suit? She glanced in the mirror. A very different Bramble looked back at her, a pretty woman with dancing eyes and springy curls. She must cut her hair, though: it was beginning to look unprofessional.

'But the age gap!' shrieked Helena, buzzing like a mosquito in the background. 'Thirty-six and sixteen, surely you can see that it's just not on.'

'Well, your friend Angelina is only thirty-two and Chris Woody is fifty-seven. That's an even bigger age gap.'

'Bramble! Stop being so reasonable this minute. You know that's not the same. Think about what's best for Savannah.'

Bramble had to admit that Helena was succeeding in making her feel uneasy about it all. 'But he's done nothing wrong, and neither has she . . .' She didn't believe any of it, and thought Helena was just troublemaking.

Apart from her campaign against Jez, Helena also enjoyed

reinventing herself as an English Martha Stewart, and 'because they were so poor' revelled in gathering flowers from hedgerows to arrange in vases. 'It's the new chic,' she said, wondering if bailiffs read women's magazines and, if not, whether one of the glossies would like to feature her new idyllic rural lifestyle. On one of her flower-gathering expeditions she came back shrieking, 'Bramble! It's the paparazzi! They've found out where I'm hiding.'

'What?'

'I should have known! *Simon's Way* goes back on tonight! There's about twenty of them out there, just at the corner of the drive, with all their tripods and long lenses and . . .'

Bramble strode down the drive to find out what was going on. She came back five minutes later. 'Helena, they're bird-watchers. A very rare double-breasted tweed jacket or something like that has been spotted in the Long Field.'

'Well!' said Helena, still flustered. 'They looked like paparazzi to me.'

With the long summer evenings, Bramble and Jez were able to fit in more teaching and improve their cash flow. After putting their own horses to bed at five o'clock, a horsebox or trailer would draw up in the yard and one or both of them would teach until seven. Eddie was in hard training, as he'd been promised his first proper event, an Intro class at Mulberry Hill, a new fixture at the end of September. Jez was schooling him on Dollar, a young but steady horse that Bramble knew would never make the big time but would, she hoped, be sold profitably as a next-horse-on for an ambitious Pony Club rider.

'He was born to ride,' said Jez after one of his lessons with Eddie. 'Not many people are.'

Savannah would be riding too, on Shaggy, who was emerging as the yard's charmer, although she could be spoilt, sulky and bad-tempered when she wasn't in the mood.

In the middle of August, the A level results arrived.

'Two Cs and an F,' said Eddie cheerfully. 'Told you I wasn't university material.'

Helena let out an eldritch screech. 'It's those horses, you weren't concentrating.'

Eddie just laughed. 'C'mon, Mum. My first exam was two days after our moonlight flit.'

Helena burst into tears. 'All the sacrifices I've made for your education, I can't believe you would do this to me. We must get them re-marked, or complain. Or what about a crammer?'

'What about letting me get on with my life?' He put his arm round her and passed her a piece of kitchen towel. 'Here, blow your nose. Crying gives you wrinkles.'

Helena blew her nose. She knew that she had lost all authority over Eddie when he'd been driven home, covered in bruises and very frightened, only to find her too drunk to stand. She was still very ashamed, and found that she now hesitated before pouring herself a drink. Often she closed the fridge door and made herself a cup of tea instead.

At the end of August, the GCSE results arrived.

'Well?' Bramble was permanently on edge when it came to Savannah. Almost everything seemed to end in her stomping upstairs and closing her bedroom door, especially just before a meal.

'They're OK,' said Savannah, going pink.

Helena sighed. 'I don't know, you and Eddie have had every opportunity, and you don't realise how important these exams are. To your whole futures. I can't believe . . .'

Bramble took the piece of paper from Savannah. 'Savannah, eight As and a B. That's fantastic! Brilliant!'

'What?' Helena asked sharply. 'Of course, she's a girl. The system is skewed in their favour these days. Still, Savannah, well done.'

Over the next few days, Helena told a number of stories about pushy mothers she'd known who pretended not to care about exams, but were secretly having their children coached privately.

Bramble was pleased because Savannah so badly needed some confidence, but as Mulberry Hill came up she grew increasingly uneasy, without being sure why. She wondered if Jez rated Eddie as, potentially, a better rider than Savannah. She loved Eddie, of course she did, but he wasn't as good as Savannah. Was he? Could he be? Was she pushy, as Helena implied, letting both Savannah and Eddie ride above their level of competence?

Perhaps anyone who knew what eventing entailed always worried.

Helena began having appointments with her accountant to work out the best route to divorce.

'He says it's much better for me not to work much because I don't want to have an enormous income,' she said. 'Particularly if most of the money for the property was mine in the first place. Really, it would be madness for me to take another part now.'

But a debate began to build around *Simon's Way*. Once the story about Mattie's death had leaked, a number of viewers had complained that it offered a negative image of breast cancer and denied sufferers hope. Even breast cancer surgeons weighed in: 'In the early episodes, Mattie was diagnosed with a stage one, easy-to-treat cancer,' wrote Professor R.L.D. Brown, 'and I would advise most women presenting with these symptoms that they have an excellent chance of survival. To have a major television series depicting this particular kind of breast cancer as ending in death will panic thousands of patients unnecessarily. I deplore the irresponsible . . .'

'The scriptwriters wanted to add more drama by giving an all-clear that eventually proved to be wrong,' crowed Helena. 'They should have used better medical advisers.'

'I wouldn't have made that mistake,' said Ollie.

The producer put out a press statement saying that they had shot four death scenes, and that it was still undecided as to who was to die.

Then, when an older female Cabinet minister was pushed out and replaced with a woman twenty years younger, Helena told Angelina in strictest confidence – knowing that Angelina was having lunch with a friend on a tabloid newspaper – that the whole Mattie thing had been about age discrimination and that the production company had decided to make Melissa the female lead for future episodes because any woman over thirty-five was considered 'not sexy enough'. When the tabloid rang her to confirm the story she said she couldn't possibly comment, and that Melissa knew much more about it than she did. 'Don't quote me, I really don't want to cause trouble and I do admire her – she's so determined.'

Some very satisfactory items appeared in the paper, which, combined with the business of the Cabinet ministers, triggered off a debate about older women in the workplace being pushed out by younger women, and whether ageism was the new racism.

Eventually the producers took the step of saying that they would have a public vote, setting up phone lines that viewers could call in. 'Text or ring 1 to save Simon, 2 to save Mattie, and so on.' Interactive drama, the papers said, was very now, and in ten years time critics expected all series to be finalised in this way.

'It's all so stressful,' wailed Helena, her eyes shining. Caroline, her agent, pointed out that although the producers were pleased with the publicity as the viewing figures rose, they were concerned about being associated with ageism or frightening breast cancer patients.

'Well, they should have thought of that in the first place,' rejoiced Helena. 'It's nothing to do with me.'

Chapter 31

The Mulberry Hill team consisted of Bramble, Jez, Eddie and Savannah, and they were taking Dollar, Frenchie and Shaggy. Felicity would stay behind to oversee the rest of the yard.

Shaggy, once she had put on weight and muscle and got familiar with her surroundings, had been crowned Queen of the Yard. Bramble had often noticed that horses were quiet when they first arrived, only revealing their full personalities once they'd settled in, and Shaggy's quirkiness was more defined every day. The other horses deferred to her, and her temper was legendary – it was a general joke that her motto was 'Bugger off, it's my stable'. However, her honesty and bravery when faced with a cross-country course made up for her moods. Savannah was to ride her at Mulberry Hill to see if she might be a better option for the junior teams than Tegan.

If they ever got there. Bramble had checked and triple-checked the equipment in the lorry – grooming kit, dressage saddles, jumping saddles, stirrups, martingales, studs, spares in case of broken girths or reins, hoof oil, grease for the horses' legs so they'd slip over any fence they accidentally scraped, rugs, feed, water buckets and carriers . . . the list went on, finishing with several large bags of Jelly Babies for sugar boosts. Eventers are split into those who live on Haribo sweets and those who prefer Jelly Babies. Bramble belonged to the latter camp. Their overnight kit and the kitchen supplies – masses of pasta and jars of sauces, packets of biscuits and bags of fruit – had all been stowed away too.

The other two horses had also clattered on board, even Frenchie who could be tricky.

But Shaggy put her foot down. All four of her feet, in fact, firmly square at the bottom of the ramp. Bramble gently tugged at her headcollar and Shaggy stretched her neck out, lengthening herself considerably, but remaining immoveable.

They tried treats. Shaggy viewed them with disdain. Bramble backed her away from the ramp and forwards again, in Monty Roberts reverse-psychology style. Shaggy backed and went forward. Up to a particular point, where she stood fast again.

'My dressage is at four, and Jez's is at five,' said Savannah anxiously.

'I know. I know.' When applying for the event, Bramble had ticked the box to say that Savannah and Jez could do their dressage the afternoon before, because she'd thought it would give them more time on the day itself. She was now wishing she hadn't.

Shaggy lifted one front hoof and Bramble whispered encouragement. 'Good girl. Come on, easy now.' The hoof hovered over the ramp and descended slowly. They all held their breath. Shaggy replaced her hoof, exactly at the spot she'd lifted it from. Bramble was strongly tempted to whack the infuriatingly immoveable behind, but she'd tried that once and the mare had stood on her hind legs, squealing. Half a ton of enraged horse in a smallish space was never a good idea.

Eddie and Jez got a rope and slung it behind her hindquarters, attempting to move her forwards by sheer force. 'One, two, three, heave!'

Shaggy looked mildly offended but stood four square.

'We've been here for forty minutes,' said Savannah.

Bramble had a sudden stab of panic. It was as if Shaggy knew that they shouldn't be going. But that was ridiculous – she'd been difficult to load before, although never quite this bad.

Jez took Shaggy's lead rope from Bramble, whereupon she went straight up the ramp.

'You see,' he said triumphantly, before being almost knocked off his feet as she turned round and rattled straight back down again.

'Excuse *me*,' he muttered, dusting himself down, and Shaggy flicked one ear towards him as if to say 'I hear what you say . . . but

I'm not taking any notice.' She stood at the bottom of the ramp, every fibre of her being registering intransigence.

'Should we try taking the others out, to see if she goes in better as first horse?' suggested Savannah.

Helena came running out into the yard, waving her phone. 'I've had a call from Caroline. The producers of *Simon's Way* have had millions of calls from viewers – the final tomorrow is going to be one of the biggest hits of the year. At least that's what they think. You will be back, won't you?' Her eyes were shining.

Shaggy took advantage of the distraction to step backwards.

The other horses, now fidgety, came out and were walked round the yard. Shaggy peered into the interior of the lorry, stretching her neck out again as if to suggest that she might, possibly, think about going on board.

But not yet.

Bramble waved at Helena, hoping that this would be sufficient acknowledgement, but Helena hovered, obviously wanting to discuss the programme further.

Jez wrapped the rope round Shaggy's nose to give himself more control and began backing her up, then bringing her forward, backing her up and bringing her forward.

Eventually, with a massive sigh, she tired of the game and tiptoed carefully – and agonisingly slowly – up the ramp, was boxed in and given a haynet. Her velvety nose, fringed with rapidly disappearing wisps of hay, appeared over the partition, with an expression that said, 'Well, what are you all hanging around for?'

'Of course,' exclaimed Helena anxiously. 'I might not have got enough votes. Even though the publicity was all so favourable. They might still think I'm . . .' She trailed off, reluctant to expose her underbelly of insecurity in front of her family.

'I'm sure they've voted for you,' said Bramble.

'I did,' added Savannah, relieved that Shaggy was now on board.

It had taken an hour and twenty minutes. Bramble was heading towards the driver's side of the lorry when Jez jumped up into the cab and began adjusting mirrors. She hesitated.

It was the kind of thing that still caught her out. Jez always assumed he would drive. And he was, in truth, a slightly better driver. Watching the strong, lazy way he turned the steering wheel, and his relaxed control of the great lorry, she knew that he'd find three hours' driving easy. She was confident enough in her ability to get them all safely to their destination, but was always slightly on the edge of her seat, peering ahead for problems, aching in her shoulders and neck by the end of the journey . . . no, it wasn't that she *wanted* to drive.

But she resented Jez's masculine assumption that he could do everything better than she could.

'You will be back in time to see the programme tomorrow night, won't you?' Helena waved them off.

Chapter 32

By the time they arrived at Mulberry Hill Savannah's nerves were at screaming point. She would have given everything she had in the world to be going home again.

'A rider's no good unless they're slightly nervous,' said Jez, looking at her pale face as he checked Shaggy's girth.

'I get *too* nervous.'

'Of falling off?'

'Not that exactly.' Savannah tried to put her feelings into words. 'It's the dressage that gets me: I feel as if it's out of my control. If I get a judge that doesn't like me, I'll never get a good mark.'

Jez's face lit up with a surprising smile. 'If you stay in control you won't get a judge that doesn't like you. Go on out there – you know it's the basis of everything else you do on that horse.'

Savannah set off towards the practice area, followed by Bramble and Jez. She worked Shaggy in circles, practising the more difficult moves, until Jez came up. 'Don't over-practise,' he advised. 'You risk reinforcing bad habits before your test.' Feeling the horse tense up under her, Savannah let her go in one last circle in a big, bold, elastic trot and then straight into the dressage ring at the sound of the judge's horn.

'There's my girl,' said Jez.

Bramble watched intently as Shaggy and Savannah seemed to float across the ground. 'There's no doubt,' she said, 'that they've come on a lot. Under your coaching,' she added, with an effort, because it was true.

'She's still got a bit of a way to go,' muttered Jez, as Shaggy swished her tail and shook her head in irritation at their first halt in front of the judges.

They watched intently – Bramble could barely breathe – as Savannah and Shaggy executed several beautiful fluid circles and serpentines at a trot and a canter, then made a silly mistake.

'Bit late into the walk,' said Jez, 'they won't like that.'

The pair slowed down to their walk, Savannah loosening the reins and Shaggy stretching her neck out and walking freely. 'Good,' murmured Bramble, feeling the release of tension. 'That looked nice.'

Savannah collected Shaggy up again, and they were off into the last few movements, drawing to a final halt and salute in front of the judges.

'That wasn't too bad,' conceded Jez. 'It was a good test. Not perfect, but . . .'

'It never is perfect,' sighed Bramble. 'That's the problem with dressage.'

That evening, after Jez's dressage on Frenchie – from whom they were hoping for a good performance, leading, fingers crossed, to a quick sale – they all walked the cross-country course. The countryside was hilly green Home Counties, farmed for millennia, divided up into neat fields by hedges and fences and punctuated with occasional dark patches of ancient woodland. The September air was damp and soft, and the reds, golds and burnt oranges of autumn were just beginning to turn.

The house, Mulberry Hill, dominated the landscape, and had obviously been built by some Victorian magnate as a display of his wealth. With its turrets and gables, it was an imposing, if not exactly beautiful, backdrop.

There were seventeen obstacles for Eddie's section while the others, riding later, would jump a full twenty-two. Bramble stood by each one and measured the height of them against her own body, thinking, as always, how she would approach each fence, inhaling the exhilaratingly fresh smell of birch and pine and then remembering, with a thud, that she was now the teacher, not the rider. Perhaps she should have ridden Shaggy. But no, Savannah came first. Savannah was the one with a future.

'This one looks worse than it is,' she told Eddie of a pair of rails with a ditch below it. 'The course designer's put a ditch below this – you see – to make riders perceive it as bigger.' She touched him on the arm. 'We call it a rider-frightener, but the horse knows exactly how high it is. Horses don't imagine the worst the way people do.'

Eddie nodded, but she thought he looked nervous. 'They now insist that you have to go over a jump not under it,' she added, to make him laugh. 'Since a horse and rider managed to clamber down into the ditch and *under* one of these things in 1984.'

Jez jumped up onto the bank and called the others up. 'Look,' he said. 'You're going to leap up on this bank, down again, and you won't know exactly where your horse'll land until he does, and then you've got to point him at that narrow jump immediately. You'll have to make an instant judgement as to whether you take one stride or two, and if you get it wrong, the horse'll run out.' Eddie and Savannah paced it, with serious expressions on their faces.

It wasn't too challenging for experienced riders like Savannah and Jez, thought Bramble, and where the fences were more difficult, Eddie had easier alternatives he could take. There was nothing to worry about. Nothing at all, she told herself.

By the time they had finished, the dressage scores were up on a whiteboard outside the secretary's tent. 'Jez, you're in the lead so far,' said Bramble, with the tension of knowing how easily the magic could slip, down one place at a time, as other riders did their tests and got better marks.

He shrugged. 'For now. But Savannah's score is very useful, and her class is complete. You're placed third so far, Savannah, so there's everything to play for tomorrow.'

Lottie had invited Savannah and Eddie to spend the night in Toby's pantechnicon. 'It's got a Sky TV and media centre,' said Lottie, 'and his collection of DVDs is amazing.' Bramble cooked them all supper in the Lorenden lorry.

'You need complex carbohydrate to give you stamina,' advised Jez, looking at Savannah's plate. 'The days are gone when eventers could live on black coffee, chocolate and nerves. We're professional athletes now.'

Savannah divided her plate of pasta into four sections as usual, managing to throw away or feed the dogs with three-quarters of it. She finished up with half an apple then, while the others were talking, laughing and nibbling cheese, she cleaned the kitchenette thoroughly, wiping down the tiny worksurface and taking the rubbish bag out so that no one would notice that she'd thrown most of her food away. If she could have refused Lottie's invitation, she would have, because Lottie would have peanuts or crisps, or force her to have a slice of the groom's birthday cake, or a high-calorie glass of fruit juice or a mug of cocoa. But Bramble insisted that she go: 'Enjoy a luxury mattress for a change.'

The Fitzroy horsebox was certainly more luxurious than anything Savannah had ever seen before. She and Eddie clambered up behind Lottie into its beige interior.

'Wow.'

'Look.' Lottie played with the light switches. 'Bright lights, sexy lights. Bright lights, sexy lights.' She unfolded a banquette and hauled out some bedding stowed beneath it. 'This is your bed. This is Eddie's. Hannah sleeps in there . . .' She opened a door onto a small cubicle with two bunk beds. And this . . .' she pressed a button and a pull-out extended the lorry's side outwards creating a double bed area '. . . Ta da! Is my bed!' She jumped on it and curled her legs under her. 'I think this is where Toby and my mother . . .' she let the words hang.

'Are they . . .?'

Lottie screwed up her nose. 'I think it's going badly. Mummy's in a terrible mood, especially with me because I never win any more.'

'You do!' said Savannah out of loyalty, although she knew Lottie had had a very bad season.

Lottie shook her head. 'I haven't even been placed in any of the Junior Regional Novice events, and Mummy was so furious she made Hannah take me out of the area, up to somewhere in Lincolnshire or something, and when I came third there she rang up the South East regional selector and said . . .' Lottie imitated her mother's voice '. . . Lottie's had a *very* successful time in Lincolnshire, I just wondered if you might be wanting her for the nationals.'

'No!' exclaimed Savannah. 'How *embarrassing*. What was the answer?'

Lottie shrugged. 'Mummy was told that the team was already full so of course she was furious with Hannah for not telling us before we went to Lincolnshire.'

'Was it?' asked Savannah.

'Don't think so.' Lottie was matter-of-fact. 'Like, I mean, you have to be at least first, second or third at least twice in a regional class, and even then everyone's got to believe in you before they invite you to the nationals, so they're really going to want me, aren't they? The muppet who comes last all the time.'

'Well, not last, surely? I've seen you get some really good dressage scores.'

'Well, I might as well be last,' said Lottie. 'I am now officially crap at riding. According to my mother.'

'That is so not true. She doesn't know anything about it.'

'And guess what? Mummy's been sending a car for me twice a week to collect me from school, so that I can have extra riding lessons. And we've been for training days with practically every accredited trainer in the country.'

'What, a whole private day's training all to yourself? How amazing.' Savannah looked at her friend's face. 'So why isn't it working out?'

'I'm a bit frightened of Vincent,' admitted Lottie. 'He's OK in the school, when we're being taught and everything, and I have learned a lot. It's getting better, but he scares the shit out of me across country. He just takes hold of the bit and goes, and I have no control. It's like trying to ride a rocket. Half the time I come off, or he ploughs into the jumps or runs out.'

'Have you explained that to your mother?' Savannah was worried. It was so unlike Lottie.

Lottie nodded, her eyes filling with tears. 'She says I'm just being silly, and that he's a really expensive horse and much better than Sailor. And that Toby is a really well known event rider, better known than your mother or Jez, and he has the most amazing stables, so he knows what's best. So it must be my fault, because I'm not trying.'

'Vincent's a man's horse,' said Eddie suddenly. He'd been flicking through DVDs, apparently not listening. 'He's too strong for you, and he's used to having Toby's steel thighs wrapped around him and a solid hunk of weight on top. You're a good rider, but a horse like that only respects weight and force.'

'Yes, well,' laughed Lottie. 'Mummy only respects weight and force. And Toby's steel thighs.'

They tried to concentrate on a film, but Lottie fell asleep. Savannah huddled up under a duvet with her teddy, going through the cross-country course in her head, over and over again, mentally marking out strides before slipping in and out of a headachey doze. Tomorrow was too important to screw up. She had to come in the top three if she was to qualify for the finals at Weston Park. The selectors wanted consistency, not occasional flashes of brilliance.

That morning, while packing up, she had come across a tiny bear that her father had won for her at a funfair many years ago. It was the only thing she could remember him giving her and, on an impulse, she stowed it in her bag. Perhaps everything would be different if he hadn't died. Perhaps she wouldn't have got fat in the first place.

Bramble woke up in the middle of the night and couldn't get back to sleep. She clambered down from her mattress over the cab as quietly as she could, to fetch a bottle of water. Jez was asleep on the pull-out banquette, and she could hear the steady rise and fall of his breathing. His face in the moonlight was only inches away from hers, a few impish tendrils of dark hair giving his formal haircut an edge of rebellion.

Watching him was comforting. She no longer felt quite so alone.

His eyes snapped open. 'Can't you sleep?'

They looked at each other with a kind of recognition that made her feel she could answer honestly. 'Do you ever get a bad feeling?' she asked slowly. 'Do you ever wake up thinking something terrible's going to happen?'

Jez stretched out his hand and took hers. 'Come here.'

'The day my father died, I thought I saw something evil.' The words drifted into the darkness and it seemed quite natural to edge onto the banquette, lie down and curl up against him. 'I've got that same feeling now.'

They lay talking as the moonlight crept under the gingham curtains, and Jez told her about his family. Stalin had purged the Crimea of Tatars, and his mother had nearly been sent to a death camp but his father, an officer in the British cavalry, had somehow saved her. 'My parents were both so young – my mother was only eighteen – and they were so terribly in love that they never wanted anyone else around them, not even children of their own. I came along at the last minute, many years later, and gave them a bit of a shock, I think. Although my mother was wonderful; the best mother anyone could ever have.'

'How romantic,' said Bramble. 'What about your father?'

'He was a hero, during the War,' said Jez, 'but—'

'How romantic,' said Bramble. 'A real hero.'

'Yes,' said Jez, 'but in peacetime he gambled away everything he had and died leaving her destitute.'

'A risk-taker. There's nowhere for people like that to go when a war's over.'

'Except here.'

'Well, there's always a war somewhere,' said Bramble. 'Perhaps that's why Felicity . . .' She sat up. 'Jez, I'm not a natural risk-taker, am I?'

She could see his pale wolf-like eyes in the moonlight. 'I don't think it's natural, for mares or for mothers, to leave the herd and go into danger. And that's what riding across country is.'

'But a mare – or a mother – *can* do it. They can.'

'Yes,' he said. 'But it's harder.'

'The night you arrived,' she said, the thought emerging out of nowhere, 'I thought you looked like a wolf. Knocking on my door like a character in a fairy story.'

'The wolf is our symbol.' His voice was a storyteller's caress. 'Several millennia ago, the Chinese were fighting the Tatars and they utterly defeated us. They set out to kill every single Tatar but, to show their contempt, they left one baby alive on the battlefield.

'That baby was found by wolves, who brought it up as their own and, in time, it found a wolf as a mate and the babies of that union are the ancestors of today's Tatar race.'

Bramble began to drift into sleep, lulled by the age-old power of story to soothe and console.

'Tell me,' said Jez. 'I've often wondered . . . why does nobody ever mention your mother?'

Bramble's eyes fluttered open. 'She died when Helena and I were quite little. We don't remember much about her, that's why we don't talk about her. Only Felicity really knew, and she hasn't been here until now.'

'And now a question for you,' she added, just before slipping into darkness. 'What happened at Penny Luckham's?'

'Things went wrong,' said Jez. 'Go to sleep now.'

And she did.

Eddie's dressage, plus the showjumping and the cross-country for them all were scheduled for the following day. Bramble woke up to the pitter-patter of rain on the lorry roof, and saw the shape of Jez's shoulder beside hers. She could feel the heat of his body against hers and lay very still.

He turned to look at her. 'What's the weather forecast?'

'Not too good,' she whispered.

Jez swung himself out of bed and stood up.

Bramble was used to the forced intimacy of a horsebox living quarters, but even so, there suddenly seemed to be not enough space or air for them both. Jez slept in his boxers, and his lean, powerful, well-muscled body seemed so . . . well, so close.

This was going to be difficult, thought Bramble. She had spent the night with him. There had been nothing sexual between them – nothing at all – but she still couldn't tell Nat. He would never believe her. And she didn't want to keep secrets from the man she was going to marry.

As if Jez could hear her thoughts, he looked down at her and their eyes locked. Bramble wondered what he could see. She knew she should have cut her hair months ago, and it was probably standing on end in corkscrew curls.

'I like your hair long,' he said into the silence. 'You look like a gypsy, or a flamenco dancer – all wild and full of life.' He took a lock and wound it round his finger. 'When I first came your hair was so short you looked like a choirboy.'

The air seemed very still and Bramble could hear the rain again, softly playing out a rhythm over their heads, as the lock of hair slipped slowly out of Jez's grasp.

Blushing, she rolled out of the banquette and clambered back into the darkness of her cubbyhole, feeling around for a hairband to tie back the rebellious mass. She wriggled into some jeans under the duvet and slipped down to the main living quarters again, stowing the bedding out of the way and trying to seem businesslike. 'Yes, well, I need to cut it. Tea? Coffee?'

He pulled on a pair of jeans, then a polo shirt over his head. 'Don't,' he said softly.

She pretended not to have heard.

Helena woke late. She raced downstairs, catching sight of the orchards outside Lorenden through the big hall window. The trees were shrouded in a mist that curled towards her as she watched, wrapping itself around her heart, choking it with cobwebs of cold, damp silk. For a second she knew real heart-stopping, gut-wrenching fear, but she shook it off. Tonight was the night of the *Simon's Way* final. The votes were in. Her fate was decided.

Ollie, looking gaunt and with matted hair, was in the kitchen gazing into a black coffee.

'You look terrible,' she said.

'Such sympathy from my loving wife,' he sneered at her. 'As a matter of fact, I slept very badly. Worrying.'

'I expect you didn't sleep because you'd had too much to drink.' Telling herself not to respond further, she filled the kettle quickly, peering outside and trying to make herself feel better.

He glared at her and lit a cigarette. His hand trembled slightly and his wrists were painfully thin. He was a mess, thought Helena. A complete mess.

'Are you really going to drive in this?' He inhaled heavily. 'Sometimes, you do my head in. Risking your life just to see your beloved son jump a fence. Get real, Helena, get real.'

'It's just a late summer mist, I'm sure it'll burn off. I've got to see Eddie,' said Helena, feeling that clutch of fear again. 'I've got to be there for the jumping and the cross-country. To show I support him.'

'You really don't. He'll understand. He can see what it's like.'

Helena glugged back her coffee. She would drive very carefully, she told herself. Not rush.

'Well, don't blame me if you kill yourself,' said Ollie. 'Bloody fool woman. But it's all Eddie with you, isn't it? What about Ruby and Roly? Not to mention your darling husband. Has it occurred to you that I might worry about you? Might care if you kill yourself?'

'My darling husband,' hissed Helena, 'is a soak. That leaves me looking after everything. I don't neglect Ruby and Roly, you know I don't. But *just occasionally* I need some support from you, and *today* I'm leaving *you* with them. Don't get drunk, don't drive them anywhere and don't lose them. Is that too much to ask?'

'I think I can just about manage that,' he replied, breathing a trail of smoke out through his nostrils. Helena waved it away irritably. 'And *don't* smoke in the house,' she added.

As she hunched over the wheel of her little car, peering through the mist for signposts, she wondered if the twins were indeed safe with Ollie. Was she neglecting them? And him? Did he really care about her, after all? She was so furious about the debt that she had barely spoken a civil word to him for months. Was she doing the right thing? Should she try to be more understanding? She nearly missed the turning on to the A2 in the fog and, on the main road, a huge black car came up behind her far too quickly. Her heart began to beat faster, and her mouth dried out. She would get to the Mulberry Hill one day event or die in the attempt.

She didn't mean that. It was just an expression. She was only nervous because of the *Simon's Way* final.

At Mulberry Hill, the horses were stabled in rows of temporary canvas looseboxes. The ground around them was awash with mud, churned up by a constant procession of hooves and feet and exacerbated by a leak from the main tap. Bramble slithered along to Dollar and Shaggy's stables, mud spattering up as far as her face as people led their horses out. To save her competitors' cream breeches, she led the horses back to the lorry, to saddle up where conditions were relatively dry.

'What do you think of the course?' she asked Jez, who had walked it again with Savannah and Eddie, talking them through how they should approach each jump.

'It's OK,' he said. 'It's been properly looked after, especially around take-off and landing.' His eyes met hers, and she remembered the way they'd talked through the long dark night. Talk, she told herself, is fine. Talk is nothing to worry about.

'It should be fine,' he added. 'If the weather doesn't get much worse. One could wish for slightly better conditions for Eddie, as he's done so little compared to Savannah, but...'

They both looked at the sky, the drizzle slicking their hair down.

'Where are my cross-country gloves?' shouted Savannah. 'And my medical armband? Shit, this rain . . .' She clambered on to the driver's seat to use the rear-view mirror to tie her stock, her fingers fumbling with nerves. The sweet, tangy scent of mane and tail conditioner, with its clinging citrus aroma, mingled with the smell of grass, damp horse and anticipation.

Bramble inhaled, breathing in the excitement of competition. 'You're doing your showjumping first,' she said. 'You can find your gloves afterwards.'

The rain paused briefly – but ominously – as if giving itself an opportunity to take a deep breath and draw in even darker clouds. Bramble worked with Eddie and Savannah, putting jumps up for them and watching every move they made. Her heart was in her mouth as Savannah was called into the showjumping ring.

Shaggy cantered in without hesitation. Bramble found herself clutching Jez's arm in the tension.

'You beauty,' said Jez under his breath, 'you beauty.'

They watched intently, Bramble still trying to suppress a sense of impending disaster. She thought Savannah seemed a little off-balance at first, going a little too fast at the first jump. Everything was fine, she told herself.

She cleared it. 'God, that was lucky,' breathed Bramble

Savannah focused, got Shaggy under control and carefully took the rest of the jumps in a steady rhythm, wobbling one and taking off a bit too early at another but getting away with both.

Bramble's shoulders dropped in relief. 'Well done,' she said, taking Shaggy from her. They stayed to watch Lottie, who also had a clear round.

'I think it's all coming right for her at last,' said Bramble.

'Lottie's come on a lot,' said Hannah, Toby's groom, appearing beside her. 'At first she was off more often than she was on.' There was a note of disapproval in her voice. 'That mother – she's got the goal posts in the wrong place, if you ask me. But . . .' she zipped her jacket up tightly against the wind '. . . the extra training does seem to be paying off. She's worked hard, that kid has. Very hard.'

Eddie's round, a little later on, was more of a concern. Dollar fought him from the moment they entered the ring, rolling his eyes dramatically at the judge's tent. Bramble watched intently, concerned that the combination of a relatively green horse with an inexperienced rider might be too much for both of them. On the other hand, Eddie was certainly capable of handling Dollar under normal conditions and they both had to learn. She winced as Eddie fired the horse at the first three jumps – 'far too fast' she muttered under her breath – and heard the rattle of the poles going down. As if he'd heard her, Eddie collected himself and settled into a reasonably creditable round, although he also dropped a pole at the triple. 'Not *too* bad,' said Savannah charitably. 'Twelve penalties. It is his first time, after all.'

'Hmm,' said Bramble. 'I'd like to see him take it all a bit more slowly.'

The rain started again, and Bramble's unease spilled over into panic. She looked round for Jez and then, on an impulse, walked briskly to the secretary's tent. 'It's Bramble Kelly,' she said, 'and I want to withdraw Silver Dollar X and Chequerboard Charlotte.' She knew Jez would make his own mind up.

'Not Shaggy,' said Savannah's voice behind her. 'I'm riding. Third in the dressage and clear showjumping is too good to let go, and I think I can ride this course well. Please don't try to stop me.'

'Savannah, it's not safe.'

'If it wasn't safe they'd cancel the event, wouldn't you?' she turned to the official.

'Well, I don't think . . .'

'Would you cancel this event if it was clearly too dangerous for horses and riders to take part? Yes or no?'

'Yes, of course,' said the woman. 'But that doesn't mean—'

'You see.' Savannah turned back to Bramble. 'Stop treating me like a child. I can handle it. Do you understand? I *can* handle it. How are we ever going to get anywhere if you don't trust me?'

'I do trust you,' said Bramble. 'Of course I trust you.'

'Then let me ride.'

'And me,' said Eddie. 'I can do it. I will take it slowly, I promise.'

Bramble hesitated, sick with terror, then, feeling that there was no real reason to worry, she nodded. 'OK. But please, *please* be careful.'

Savannah rolled her eyes. '*Of course* I'll be careful,' she screeched, striding out of the secretary's tent.

'I'm sorry about that,' Bramble said to the secretary

'I know what teenagers are like. She's probably scared stiff underneath all that bravado.'

'I'm sure she is,' replied Bramble, her heart turning icy cold.

Back at the lorry, she checked the cross-country times taped up on the lorry door over and over again. Eddie was going at the end of his introductory class, while Savannah, one of the first in her section, was to go soon afterwards, and Jez and Frenchie were towards the end of the afternoon.

'You've already told us all that twice,' said Savannah, ratty with nerves, checking Shaggy's tack and tightening her girth for the third time. 'I still can't find my cross-country gloves.'

Eddie was green. 'You OK?' Bramble asked him. 'You really don't have to ride if you don't want to.'

'Of course I want to,' said Eddie. 'I want to more than anything. I just think I might have eaten something.'

'It gets everyone like that,' said Bramble, hoping Helena would arrive in time to insist he pull out, then realising that Eddie was probably the most determined rider she had ever met. Short of handcuffing him to the lorry, there was nothing either of them could do.

Eddie tried to smile at her, but had to stagger off into the bushes. He came back wiping his mouth. 'Sorry.'

Lottie, looking pale and tense, appeared and handed him a tissue. 'Here. It always happens to me, too.'

'Oh, hello Lottie,' said Bramble. 'When are you on?'

'Just before Savannah,' said Lottie. 'The three of us can all ride down to the start together.'

'That'll be lovely,' said Bramble, to three pale faces.

'Bramble,' said Lottie. 'Eddie says that Vincent is a man's horse, and that Mummy should sell him. If she doesn't let me have another horse – and I don't think she will – can I come and help out at Lorenden?'

'Of course,' said Bramble, impressed at Eddie's grasp of the situation. 'As long as we're there, of course. But there'll always be a place for you in my stables.'

'If I do well today,' added Lottie, 'she might buy me something else, of course. It's failure she hates.' She looked up the hill at a horsebox a few rows up. 'Oh look, that's the Turnbulls' box. I wonder if Sailor's here? Do you think they'd mind if I said hullo?'

'I don't think they'd mind at all.'

'Perhaps I'd better wait until afterwards, though,' said Lottie, looking wistful. 'Everyone's so busy before.'

Bramble nodded, lifting Dollar's hoof to check his studs. 'Good luck, Lottie,' she called after the tall, waif-like girl, heading miserably back to the solitary splendour of Toby Fitzroy's lorry.

Her mobile rang as soon as she'd hoisted Eddie up. 'Darling,' said Nat, 'how's it going?'

'A bit frantic.' Bramble cradled the phone under her ear. 'I can't really . . .'

'What's Savannah's score so far?'

'She's doing really well, but . . .' As Eddie and Savannah rode off to join Lottie and go down to the start she found Savannah's cross-country gloves. 'Oh shit, I don't know what gloves Savannah's got with her. In this weather, she'll never get a good grip on the reins with her ordinary gloves.'

'She'll be fine. And Eddie? No disasters there to worry Helena?' He laughed jovially.

'He's doing OK, but . . .' She signalled to Jez that he should follow the riders and that she would catch him up

'I do love you very much,' said Nat.

Jez was still in earshot, locking up the lorry.

'Mmm, yes, same,' she muttered.

'Are you all right?' demanded Nat suspiciously. 'What's happened? Is everything OK?'

'Yes, absolutely fine,' she snapped. 'But I *have* to go.'

When Felicity saw the mist it reminded her of the end of summer and that twitch of excitement and terror that heralded a new term. Coming home had been like a long, hot holiday, but, like the swallows she felt the urge to move on, away from the gentle death of autumn. It had taught her one thing. She'd always thought she was running away, away from the memories and the arguments and the disapproval. But it wasn't just that. She was someone who would have gone anyway.

She didn't know where this knowledge came from – perhaps from having the time to see the difference between the birds that leave and the ones that stay. Or perhaps from the slow, repetitious work she'd done on Merlin, the endless hours of walking and trotting to bring him back to fitness, while her mind eased into a kind of meditation. She had one more conversation to have – with Pauline – and then she would pack her bags and leave.

She put Merlin's bridle over her shoulder and the weight of his saddle on to her arm and left the house. He lifted his handsome head and whickered at the sight of her. He was now a very contented horse.

'Time for a nice, gentle hack,' she said.

Or was it too foggy? She looked at the thick white air again. It should lift soon.

At the fence judges' briefing at Mulberry Hill, Pauline and Alan settled themselves in a row of chairs. The organisers were old friends and had invited them to spend the night at the house. But Pauline's heart wasn't in it. She tuned in to conversations around her.

'Oh, the summer's been hectic,' trilled a woman with a long, battered rainproof coat. 'We've been *everywhere*. You know we fence judged at the European Championships?'

'Of course, we're never at home,' countered someone else.

'We've said we'll take it to the London Olympics and then we simply must stop.'

Pauline closed her eyes and wished the metal folding chair was less hard and cold, as the Cross Country Steward rapped on the table, cleared his throat and began to explain the day. She knew it all by heart.

'We haven't got radios for everyone,' he said at one point. 'So if you've got a radio, you will need to cover for several fences.' He read out who had radios, and which fences they were to cover.

Pauline and Alan were not allocated a radio. The woman with the battered coat – who appeared to be called Maggie Something – had the radio that would cover Alan and Pauline's fence, the oxer at fence 17.

After the briefing Maggie Something smiled at Pauline with long, yellow teeth. 'They always allocate the radio to me. I suppose you can't beat Olympic experience.'

Pauline just smiled politely and checked out the lunch they'd been given. 'Cheese rolls,' she said. 'Rather nice bread, though.'

'The lunches at Gatcombe are much better than this,' said Maggie. 'And, of course the French lunches at Le Lion d'Angers . . .'

'We'd better take up our positions, don't you think?' Pauline put her hand in the small of Alan's back and steered him out before he could embarrass her. The car bumped uncomfortably over the ground to their fence. It was a pair of rails – quite straightforward, but needing a certain amount of judgement – and it was one of the most distant fences, hidden from most of the rest of the course by a clump of trees.

'I could have done with a radio,' thought Pauline. She could only just see Maggie, at the top of the hill, but Maggie could presumably see her quite well. Alan bumbled into position, stabbed his timing stake in and the drizzle began again.

'The ground's not too bad, really,' said Pauline, almost to herself, studying the fence again. 'As long as everyone knows what they're doing, there shouldn't be any trouble.'

Having left Shaggy with Eddie, Savannah vomited in the Portaloo beside the starting box. Hardly anything came out – it was a dry-retch of pure terror. She looked at her grey face in the dusty mirror. The trouble was that she felt so weak. She often found that cutting down on food conjured up a magical light-headness and injected her with both confidence and feverish energy, but suddenly the course ahead might as well have been forty miles. Every step was a fight against exhaustion. She felt shivery inside. You can do it, she told herself. It wasn't like this when your father died. It was good going. Just a freak accident on a sunny day. Accidents can happen any time. You just have to hope it's not your turn today.

She could barely remember Dom – when he hadn't been travelling round the world, competing or looking for horses to buy, he'd been working from six o'clock in the morning until late at night.

'If you're up there somewhere, Dominic Kelly,' she said to her reflection, 'look out for me.' As she stepped out of the tiny cubicle and back into the wind and rain, a little voice inside her added: 'Just for once.'

Once in the open air, Savannah's head started to hurt. Every step across the uneven ground was an effort.

Helena drove very slowly and, looking at the clock on the dashboard, realised that she was going to be late. The radio reminded her, over and over again, that tonight was going to be the finale of this series of *Simon's Way*, that viewers had been voting for the characters they wanted to stay in. She didn't know what frightened her more, the thought of the figures ticking over – thousands and thousands of them, voting for Melissa, or one of the men, then just a few hundred for boring old Mattie – or Eddie doing his first proper event, starting out on a path that might lead him to a future like Edward Beaumont's. Or Dom Kelly's.

The fog was continuous, all along the M25, and then down the A23 and, once onto the minor roads, she could barely see the signs or turnings she was looking for. She was beginning to get very frightened. Larger cars, with their fog-lights full on, tailgated her in frustration and her confidence was slipping. Between the blinding glare in the driving mirror and the thick soup ahead of her, she could barely function. She would miss the dressage and the showjumping, she thought, but that didn't matter. She'd make it for the cross-country, and that was the important part. Every so often she pulled up to allow a larger car or a van past, then re-joined the road, her shoulders screaming in tension. She phoned Bramble again.

'Don't drive too fast,' advised Bramble. 'Eddie's doing his cross-country last, right at the end of his section, and Lottie and Savannah start immediately after him, so they're all going out at about midday.'

Helena flipped the phone off and edged nervously out into the narrow road once more. How was one expected to find the right road in this weather? The trouble with the countryside, she thought, was that nobody there *wanted* you to find them. They liked to keep their lanes a nice secret. Was this the right fork? Another van filled her rear-view mirror with harsh light and the driver hooted at her. Fuck you, she muttered, almost sobbing. Fuck you.

Horses and riders, increasingly mired in mud, continued to struggle past Pauline and Alan as the drizzle intensified to a downpour. Pauline's glasses were beginning to fog up. She heard Alan's whistle, followed by the sound of thundering hooves. A competitor emerged from the now-driving rain, slithered to a stop in front of the fence, turned and rode at it again.

'First refusal,' called Pauline, trying not to get her marking sheet wet and finding it almost impossible to see the rider's number. She didn't recognise either horse or rider.

After a fractional hesitation, the horse heaved itself over and the rider lost a stirrup. They disappeared into the scrub, the rider barely in control. Shortly afterwards the horse emerged, reins trailing, and set off with its rider hopping after it.

Pauline tried to blink away the water in her eyes. 'Did you get that rider number?' she shouted at Alan.

'Of course I did.'

'What is it?'

Alan didn't reply.

'Oh, for goodness' sake,' she muttered, slightly worried. She could hear another rider coming and monitored it as it jumped safely and thundered up the hill, then went to retrieve the list from him.

It was completely blank. 'You haven't filled anything in.'

'The weather,' he blustered. 'It's impossible. No one could . . . um . . . what did you say?'

Pauline, staring at him in horror, realised that Alan's fine intelligence had been hiding a surprisingly rapid deterioration in his mind. She'd had no idea he was this bad. 'You've forgotten, haven't you?'

'Forgotten what?' he demanded.

'Forgotten why you're here.'

'Well, why am I here?' he asked, as if it was a perfectly normal question and she was being the unreasonable one.

'Alan,' she said. 'Sit in the car. Another horse will be through soon and I'll have to manage on my own.' She took the whistle from him and, as he staggered towards the car, she realised that she probably couldn't even trust him to do that. If she'd had a radio she'd have called for help, but there wasn't time to get up to Maggie's fence before the next competitor. She checked her mobile phone. No signal. And here, at the farthest reach of the course, in this weather, there certainly weren't any spectators she could call on.

Pauline straightened her shoulders as a clap of thunder broke overhead. She would just have to cope. She peered into the sheeting rain, choking with loneliness and hurting beyond belief for the loss of the Alan she had known – and, she realised too late, had loved. Another clap of thunder made her jump. Surely someone would come and tell her the event was cancelled.

But the next rider was upon her, a shape in the storm galloping suddenly out of the murky wall of water. She seized her soaking list and tried to focus. It was impossible. She took her fogged glasses off. Her brain wouldn't let her fully understand what she was seeing.

Later she struggled to untangle the mess of flesh and hooves by telling her story over and over again, hearing a cry that she would hear in her sleep for the rest of her days. She saw the horse take off a stride too soon and slip, registered the way its legs dropped down between the double rails and then she heard her own voice in a terrible scream inside her head as the whole huge body seemed to catch on the front of the fence and somersault over, landing, as if in slow motion, on its rider beneath.

Helena drove in through the Mulberry Hill gates as the thunder broke overhead. She dropped down the hill to where all the horseboxes were parked, and took a deep breath, still trembling from the journey. There were dozens of boxes and it took her a while to find Bramble's. There was nobody there.

She phoned Bramble again, but heard an answering ring from under the driver's seat of the box.

Funny, she thought, Bramble never loses her phone. Not when her horses and riders are competing. She tried Eddie, whose phone was switched off, but that was less surprising as, by her reckoning, he should be out on the course at any minute. She might even have missed him. She grabbed Bramble's phone, changed into her wellington boots, locked the car and hurried towards the gap in the hedge where other riders and spectators seemed to be heading.

She could hear the commentator talking about the weather. 'It's been an exceptionally rainy September,' he crackled, 'but with the help of our sponsors, crackle . . . crackle Agrivators, something, something, something. Hiss, crackle. We'd like to thank . . . for their . . .' The words went in and out of Helena's head.

She remembered the day Dom had died: 'It's always bad news when the commentator talks about the weather. Or the sponsors. It means there's a hold-up they can't talk about.' They were words she would never forget.

Helena began to run, slipping and sliding in the unwieldy boots. She stopped a rider coming the other way. 'Has anything happened in the cross-country?'

The rider nodded. 'I think there's a delay of some kind. It's been going on for about ten minutes.' She seemed unconcerned.

Helena told herself that it was nothing, that cross-country delays were as common as . . . well, quite usual anyway, and steadied herself as she rushed to find Eddie. Please, please, she told her thumping heart, don't let anything happen to Eddie. Or anyone else, of course.

She was gasping for breath by the time she got to the secretary's tent, where three women were huddling over a list. There was an air of tension.

'Excuse me,' Helena sobbed. 'I want to know what's happening.'

'We haven't got any details,' said one. 'There has been an accident, but we don't know any more than that. We'll let everyone know as soon as we can.' She spoke urgently into a phone, but shook her head at the other two when she had finished.

'But my son,' screamed Helena. 'My son. Eddie Harris, and my niece, Savannah Kelly, are they on the course?'

The women looked at her with some sympathy, and bent over the lists again. 'It's hard to tell exactly where we've got to. Quite a few people have withdrawn, and some have gone out of number order,' said one gently, avoiding Helena's eye. 'Listen to the announcements, or you could check the start box. The official there should know who's on the course.'

'Thanks.' Helena got directions to the start and hurried towards it. She stopped a bedraggled group of spectators. 'Does anyone know what's happened?'

'Someone's fallen off.'

'A horse is down.'

'There's a delay because a fence has broken.'

The commentator thanked the local estate agency for sponsoring the jumps, and went on to describe their work in sub-Saharan Africa. What? Helena, struggling through the mud, couldn't care less about their charity efforts.

'This is a special announcement,' cried the commentator. 'Special announcement, please, for everyone with horses. We're bringing the air ambulance in, so please ensure your horses are safely tied up or in their lorries. Please be aware, we are bringing the air ambulance in. Secure your horses properly.'

Helena caught her breath. Please, she sobbed under her breath. Please. The air was almost pure water now, pummelling down onto the slippery ground, driving into her face so that she could barely see or breathe. The announcer crackled again: 'Owing to the worsening weather, the event is now cancelled. We apologise to . . .'

It was impossible to recognise any of the scurrying people with their coat collars pulled up and their umbrellas tugging in the wind. All the horses and riders looked the same to her, black boots, cream jodphurs, heads down, moving carefully in the mud.

But there ahead of her, unmistakeable, was Bramble, her hair plastered to her head by the rain, leading Eddie's horse. Riderless.

Helena sank to her knees, and curled up in anguish on the sodden ground. Please, she sobbed, clawing the mud. Please. Eddie was gone, she knew it. There was no point in going on any more.

'Maggie,' Pauline had screamed into the hill, an endless second after the horse and rider fell. 'Radio! Radio!'

But the wind was going in the wrong direction and the water muffled her voice. It was like shouting from the bottom of a lake.

'There's another horse coming.' Alan, shocked into reality by the sight in front of him, burst out of the car. 'Stop,' he called, waving his arms. 'Stop. Stop. There's been an accident. You must stop.'

To the oncoming horse, his blurred outline must have seemed like a ghost in the rain. The animal slowed for a few strides, then jerked violently away from the shouting shape, disappearing into the weather, its rider trying to cling on.

'Radio! Radio!' shouted Pauline again, as the horse that had fallen struggled to its feet and stood, its head hanging down and sides heaving.

Pauline was torn between grabbing the reins, stopping any further riders from taking the fence, trying to do something – anything – for the crushed body on the ground. 'Take this,' she ordered Alan, handing him the reins. 'And stay here. *Don't move.*'

Alan stared in horror at the broken body. 'I don't understand,' he quavered, with the voice of a much older man. 'What's happened? What has happened?'

'Just don't move.' And Pauline set off, as fast as her shaking legs would take her up the slippery, muddy hill, trying desperately to breathe properly, to inhale enough oxygen into her screaming lungs to get her up there and able to summon help.

★

Bramble saw her sister coiled in the mud as if physically injured. 'Helena!' she cried. 'Helena, get up now!'

Helena stood up and howled like a wolf. 'I knew it. Eddie. Eddie's gone.'

Bramble, trembling with terror herself, slapped Helena's face. 'Shut up. Listen. And help me. You have to help, or we'll never find them.'

'Find them?' asked Helena, blank with terror. She had mud on her face, and all down her clothes.

'Eddie and Savannah are missing. They both seem to have been out on the course when there was an accident, along with a couple of other riders, but I can't find out what or who, and . . .' Bramble took a huge lungful of air '. . . I've only just been handed Dollar, who was found wandering around the horsebox lines.' She saw Helena struggle against panic, and then focus.

'We're going to find them,' whispered Helena. 'Don't worry. They'll be all right.' She hugged Bramble. 'I promise.'

'Yes,' repeated Bramble. 'We'll find them.'

'Bramble, what's happened?' A horse appeared out of the rain. It was Jez on Frenchie.

Bramble told him what they knew.

'You go,' said Helena. 'You go on Dollar. With Jez. You can find them faster if you're mounted.' She held out a map of the course in a shaking hand. 'I'm going to station myself in the secretary's tent, and I'll make them tell me everything they hear.' She took a deep breath. 'And here's your phone, so call me.'

Bramble hesitated.

'Go on,' said Helena, surprised at her own calmness. She could face whatever came next. 'All that matters is finding them.'

Bramble and Dollar followed Jez and Frenchie as they negotiated the mud and the crowds, stopping every so often to scan the horizon.

'Right,' he said, once they were out on the course. 'We split. You check the fences and I'll check the woods.' He dug his heels into Frenchie's sides and they vanished into the murk.

By now Bramble knew that the accident had happened down at the most distant clump of trees, and she was riding towards it when her phone rang. It was Helena. Her heart was thumping as she answered it.

'Eddie's safe,' Helena gasped. 'He came off and got a bit lost in the rain, but he's fine. He's absolutely fine. But Bramble . . .'

'Yes?' said Bramble, her teeth chattering. She was so frightened she was barely able to function. Savannah. Her little Savannah.

'We still don't know anything about Savannah. It's chaos out there, and no one seems to know who the rider was who . . .' Helena trailed off. 'But I can't find out any more.'

When Dom was killed Bramble had been held in the start box, waiting for almost thirty minutes, not knowing what was happening, tense, but not terrified. It had never occurred to her that Dom could be hurt. It would be someone else. Now she knew differently. Now she knew that accidents happen to people you love.

'It's fence seventeen, right?' she asked.

Helena murmured something to one of the organisers and confirmed that it was.

The announcer came on again. The air ambulance was cancelled.

'Not as serious as they thought,' said Helena, still on the phone, desperate to comfort. 'That's good news, isn't it?'

Or there's nothing an ambulance can do, thought Bramble. You only cancel an air ambulance if it's too late.

She rode down the hill to the group of trees, where a crowd of officials, an ambulance and St John Ambulance personnel clustered around the oxer.

'I'm sorry,' said Maggie officiously, emerging from the ring of backs. 'No one can come any nearer than this.'

'I think I might be the rider's mother,' said Bramble, sliding off Dollar but afraid to go any further. Afraid to know the truth.

She vaguely registered, with distant surprise, that Pauline had come up behind her and was trying to give her a reassuring hug. She could hear words but couldn't understand their meaning. 'The horse,' she asked, her words sounding thick and far away to her own ears. 'Was it a coloured horse? A skewbald?' But she didn't dare hear the answer. If no one told her it wasn't real.

I could have been a better mother. I haven't been watching and while I was looking the other way, at Nat, at Lorenden, at Pa's death, my child slipped away from me. She wasn't experienced enough to ride Shaggy in this weather. She didn't have the right gloves. I should have stopped her.

She was aware of someone speaking gently to her, tugging her arm, trying to tell her something, but she was deaf with fear.

Out of the trees, through the rain, she could see a horseman, like a vision, gaining shape and definition as he approached, an apparition turning slowly into flesh, carrying some kind of a load. As he came nearer she saw the outline – the triangle of his shoulders and the way he moved with his horse. And she could see what he was carrying on the front of his saddle.

It was Savannah. Jez's eyes were on Bramble's as he rode up to the ambulance, and gently lifted Savannah off the front of the saddle as the paramedics came forward with a stretcher. 'She's barely conscious,' he said, as they arranged her limbs on the stretcher and covered her with a blanket. 'But she'll be OK.'

'Savannah.' Bramble dropped down beside her, sobbing. 'You're all right, you're all right.'

Savannah opened her eyes. 'I'm fine,' she said weakly, trying to smile. 'Just felt a bit dizzy. Got carted by Shaggy and fell off.'

Bramble rolled off Savannah's sodden gloves, noting that she must have picked up a pair of old ones, and that, instead of the knobbly, extra-grip surface of a pair of cross-country gloves, the palms of these were just wet, slippery leather. A cloak of guilt settled around her shoulders. She should have chased after her daughter with the gloves. And Savannah's hands were so cold.

The paramedics lifted the stretcher into the ambulance and closed the doors.

'I'll come with you,' said Bramble, trying to get in after her.

'No.' Savannah's voice was weak. 'Look after Shaggy. I think she might have hurt herself.'

'We'll take her to St Catherines's Hospital,' the paramedic told Bramble. 'You can catch up with her there. She'll be quite safe.'

Bramble drew back as the ambulance drove away, then turned to look at the quiet circle around the shape on the stretcher, the body covered with a blanket.

'So who?' she asked, although, of course, she knew.

'Lottie,' said Pauline gently. 'It was Lottie Marsh-Robertson. Vincent came at the jump too fast, she couldn't hold him and he didn't take off properly. He put down between the rails and they somersaulted over.' Her eyes were red and her face was gaunt with grief. 'I'm so sorry, my dear, there was nothing I could do.'

Nobody spoke as they walked back to the horseboxes, where riders, grooms, owners and friends were packing up with sombre faces, their faces wet with tears and rain.

Helena held Eddie's hand.

'Hannah, poor Hannah,' said Bramble as she saw the groom, head bowed, leading Vincent back to the lorry lines. 'Shall we help her get Vincent home? She'll be in shock.'

'I'll do it,' said Eddie, suddenly no longer a teenager but a grown man. 'I'll go with her in her lorry and make sure she's OK. Mum can take you to the hospital to be with Savannah.'

'Poor Lottie,' whispered Bramble. 'She never did get to see Sailor.'

Chapter 33

Bramble and Helena found Savannah lying in a cubicle in casualty, waiting to be seen. The electronic noticeboard told them that the average time patients had to wait was three hours.

They bought metallic-tasting cups of coffee and made conversation. The hours ticked by very slowly. Visions of Lottie – mucking out the stables, asking endless, intense questions, kissing Sailor's nose, winning her first Pony Club trophy – drifted through Bramble's exhausted mind. She had failed her. And poor Cecily. Poor, poor Cecily.

Eventually a tired-looking doctor appeared and the curtains were drawn. Savannah needed to go for an X-ray. There was a further wait until the results came through.

'You don't need to stay, Helena, we'll get a taxi back.'

'Nonsense. It'd cost a fortune.' She pulled Bramble aside and spoke in a whisper. 'I take it you're not going to tell Savannah about Lottie just yet?'

After a muttered discussion over Savannah's bed, the tired-looking doctor said he'd like to admit her.

'What's wrong?' Bramble's heart stopped.

'The X-rays are fine,' said the doctor. 'She's got some quite severe bruises, which will be painful for a few weeks, that's all. But she's seriously underweight and dehydrated, and I think she needs to be put on a drip.'

He talked to her about anorexia. I'm as bad as Cecily Marsh-Robertson, thought Bramble. So focused on the future that I didn't see how my daughter was in danger. She sat, stunned. Suddenly everything was different. It wasn't just dieting gone too far: Savannah could die.

Helena gripped her arm. 'Bramble, listen to me. Lots of kids go a bit wrong with eating. I did myself.'

'When?' Puzzled, Bramble rifled her brain for any memory of an eating disorder.

'A couple of years after Felicity left, when I started to develop. I got so frightened by the whole idea of growing up, and having to be responsible for everyone, I just concentrated on getting thin.'

'Responsible for everyone?'

'Mummy had died, Felicity had left and you were only small. It was just me and Pa in the house and I felt I had to make it up to him that the others weren't there. I remember ironing his shirts when I was about ten, just because I thought, poor Pa, he's got no one to look after him.'

Bramble couldn't believe that she had forgotten this about Helena. She could dimly remember her ironing, but she'd never given it a second thought. 'What happened then? And what cured you?'

'I'm not sure. I think maybe I'm still a bit . . . well, you know how fussy I am. I saw an article the other day. Apparently people like me, who are stringent about cutting certain things out of their diets, are called orthorexic now. It's such a help to have a label, don't you think?'

Bramble couldn't take it in. She couldn't take anything in. Not Lottie's death or Savannah's diagnosis. Helena's words floated across her brain. 'But you were cured?' she asked desperately. 'You do function?' Or perhaps she didn't. She thought of Helena's drinking, her thinness. Helena had always seemed so on top of everything. 'Helena . . .'

Helena gave her a flashbulb smile, the one that sparkled for photographers however she felt. 'I'm fine. Of course. I'm totally over it. One day I went up to London for a party, met Tim Harris there and he seemed so exciting . . . and you were quite happy with Pa – neither of you seemed to need me any more. I felt really guilty about it, though, I still do. I kept telling myself that if Felicity could leave, then so could I.'

'Well you don't need to feel guilty. We were OK.' Bramble remembered the chaotic kitchen and the untidy house. 'Helena . . .' She hesitated. 'Speaking of guilt, Felicity feels really terrible about putting you off riding, but I don't ever remember you wanting to ride.'

Helena shuddered. 'No, I barely remember myself. But when I was about five everybody kept telling me I ought to be more like Felicity, and I thought she was wonderful so I kept trying to be good enough to get her attention. I wanted her to be proud of me. Then one day I demanded – absolutely *demanded* – to get on a really naughty pony of hers. She was always saying "No, Helena, you're not old enough" and things like that, which made me so mad that I insisted. Of course, it carted me and dumped me, and I broke my collarbone. That gave me an excuse to say I never wanted to ride again. Looking back on it, I never really cared about riding at all, just about getting Felicity's approval.'

'Felicity thinks it's her fault.'

'Well, she tried as hard as she could to stop me, so I don't see how it could be.' Helena yawned. 'Anyway, it doesn't matter. Once I stopped riding I started dancing and singing classes, which I was much better at, and nobody ever compared me to Felicity there.' She flicked through magazines for a bit, then looked up. 'She does care, doesn't she? Felicity, I mean. In spite of pretending to be so cool and remote?'

Bramble nodded. 'I think she was trying to escape the big sister role, and now she realises it's what she is. Have you noticed how bossy she's got?'

Helena shuddered. 'Don't. She stopped me from opening a bottle of wine the other day. Said it was too early.'

A nurse appeared and said that a bed would be ready in about three-quarters of an hour.

Helena looked at her watch, and Bramble remembered. Tonight was the final episode of *Simon's Way*. 'Helena, go home. Watch the final. We'll be OK.'

'No, I'm staying to see Savannah in, then I'm taking you home. I can catch up later.' Helena was white-faced. 'I told myself that if Eddie and Savannah were all right I'd be grateful for everything else. I promised myself I wouldn't care.'

The nurse looked excited. '*Simon's Way*? Oh my goodness, you're Mattie, aren't you? There's a TV in the patients' lounge – there's never anyone in there.'

A faint colour came to Helena's cheeks. She couldn't help being pleased.

They heard the clack-clack of confident heels on hospital linoleum and looked up to see a slim figure with a flowing coat striding towards them, owning the corridor.

'Hi girls,' said Felicity. 'I've come to join you. I thought there must be a TV somewhere here.'

Helena sat on the edge of a plastic chair and blew her nose as the opening credits of *Simon's Way* came up on the screen. She no longer felt alone. Her sisters were there, one on either side of her. Felicity produced a bottle of champagne and three plastic cups: 'To Mattie.'

They lifted their glasses. 'To Mattie,' they echoed.

'Right.' Helena faced the television set, trying not to clench her fists. 'I'm ready.' If the votes were with her, they could go back to Primrose Hill. Not that one series would pay off all of the debts, but they could restructure, maybe downsize.

I've faced the worst, thought Helena suddenly, I've faced Eddie being killed, so I can face anything else. Nothing can frighten me any more. There'll be no more running. We'll pay off the debts. I don't care if we live in a little house and nobody invites us to any parties. I'll still be me, Helena, and I'll still have my family. She straightened her shoulders almost involuntarily.

Bramble looked at her sister's reddened eyes. 'Are you OK?'

Helena nodded bravely. 'Never better. Really.'

'Will you know when the final scene starts? After all, you must have been there for all the different endings.'

'It's difficult to say,' said Helena, frowning as the story rolled on. 'I think they're cutting it differently.'

The nurses kept putting their heads round the door and making encouraging remarks. Helena accepted them all graciously, although inside she was screaming.

After a tense twenty minutes, Helena pointed. 'There,' she said.

'That's my deathbed scene, with everyone surrounding me. You see, I'm telling Simon I want him to be happy with someone else, and he's saying he doesn't need anyone else.'

She got up and walked to the window. 'Well,' she shrugged. 'At least I got a bit of notoriety out of it. I must be a bit more marketable than I was.' But maybe she was less marketable. After all, the great British viewer had just voted her off the screen. She swallowed. 'It's all rather an anticlimax, isn't it?' she added. 'Eight years of Mattie, and then it's just over. Like that.' She summoned up the flashbulb smile again. 'Never mind, Helena's Country Jams and Chutneys beckons. Or Helena's Best Bed-and-Breakfast in the World. I'd be good at that, wouldn't I? I'm so fussy, I'd have the most comfortable rooms in town.'

'No, stop,' said Bramble. 'What's that?'

'My funeral.' Helena barely bothered to turn back to the screen. 'First they show my deathbed scene, and then my funeral.'

'Well, if it's your funeral, why are you in the front row in an absurd hat?'

Helena let out a shriek and crouched down by the television set. 'I don't understand. Why would they show my death scene and then someone's else's funeral?'

'Who is it?' asked Bramble, along with eight million other viewers. 'If Mattie's there in the church, passing lace handkerchiefs down the pew to everyone, who is it who's died?'

'It's Simon,' said Helena. 'Look!' As the credits rolled, there was a flashback of Simon taking Mattie home after a miraculous recovery and helping her unpack, then going out into the garden and dropping dead of a heart attack.

'They've cut all the alternative death and funeral scenes around so they're completely different from how they looked when we shot them,' said Helena, numb. 'Poor Simon. Poor, poor Simon.'

Her mobile began to ring. 'Hello?'

It was Caroline, her agent. 'Congratulations,' she said. 'I heard from the TV bosses just before the programme went out. Apparently you got more votes than anyone else. By quite a margin.'

Helena laughed. 'Well, with Simon gone, I don't see that *any* of us are going to get our contracts renewed.'

'No,' said Caroline. 'They decided the publicity had gone a bit too far this time. But they want to talk to you about something else. I'll call you tomorrow.'

'What was it Pa used to say after he won?' Helena lifted her plastic cup with a real smile this time.

'One for all and all for one,' said Felicity and Bramble in unison, lifting theirs. 'The three musketeers.'

Nat was waiting for Bramble when she arrived back late with Helena and Felicity. He'd been celebrating Helena's victory with Ollie, but the shadows in his eyes spoke of Lottie.

He drew her into his arms, then made her drink something hot.

'This is terrible. Terrible news. Tell me what happened.'

Bramble shook her head. 'I'm too tired. It's . . .'

'Don't talk then,' he said. 'Come up to bed and sleep.' He tucked her in, and when she woke up in the morning he was there and she wasn't alone.

'I've been a bad mother,' she said as soon as she opened her eyes. 'Savannah is really dangerously underweight and I never noticed. And I should have stopped Cecily Marsh-Robertson from buying Vincent. Somehow.'

'Stay here. I'll get you a cup of tea first,' he said, his big form swinging out of bed and reaching for a towel, 'then you can tell me all about it.'

She looked at the clock. 'The horses. I must get up.'

'Felicity said that on no account were you to go near the stables today.' He grinned down at her, his face crinkling up and his mop of grey hair standing on end.

'You do look disreputable,' she said, 'like a mad wizard.' She was surprised to find herself laughing, and then she stopped.

'It's OK to laugh.' He spoke tenderly. 'Life goes on. And, just for the record, you're a very good mother.'

She swallowed back tears and he kissed her. 'Wait here, and I'll be back with tea and breakfast. I don't suppose you've had anything to eat since . . .'

'A sandwich?' She tried to remember. 'About eleven o'clock yesterday?'

She drifted back into a doze, thinking that she really did love Nat, for his calmness and the way he never judged her, but was woken by his mobile phone ringing from his trouser pocket. She hesitated before answering it, even going to the bedroom door to call him, but there was no answer.

Oh well. They would be husband and wife soon. With no secrets.

Well, almost no secrets. She didn't count the night spent talking to Jez, curled up against his warm body.

She picked it up.

'Sorry?' A woman's voice, tentative, almost frightened. 'Nat?'

'No, it's Bramble. His, er, fiancée.' Such a silly word. 'Can I give him a message?'

'Oh! I didn't . . . um, that is, better not, perhaps, um, I should call back some other time.' The woman sounded flustered.

'Shall I tell him who called?'

'Jenny,' she said. The voice was a crushed whisper.

'Oh, Jenny!' said Bramble, unthinking. 'It's so nice to . . .' she tailed off. Nice? Was that the word you used to a bitter ex-wife? 'So, er, nice to speak to you at last,' she added in a rush.

There was an astonished silence and Bramble's heart sank.

'Well, congratulations,' said Jenny, eventually. 'Er . . . I didn't know . . . I hope you'll both be very happy . . .'

'Hadn't Nat told you?' Bramble was sure that Nat had said he had, and that Jenny had reacted very badly. She struggled to remember what Nat had actually said, but it was all a blur of work and never having enough time to talk. Could she be imagining things?

'Oh no. No, no. I mean, well, no. He doesn't tell me anything. I mean, why should he?'

'Well, I wondered if Gemma might like to be a bridesmaid but . . .' Bramble trailed off. She didn't want to start an argument.

'Oh, that would be lovely! She would adore that.' Jenny still sounded astonished.

Bramble thought that Nat had said he'd already asked her. 'It won't be for a bit because there's been an accident to a friend of mine, but . . . can I have your telephone number so that I can call you when we do go ahead?

Jenny dictated it. 'And I've got a number for Serena, if you want it, although she's probably moved on from there.'

'Who's Serena?' asked Bramble.

There was another silence. 'Serena's Nat's stepdaughter,' said Jenny slowly. 'From his first marriage.'

Bramble's heart contracted. 'But I thought you were his first wife.'

'Oh no, I was his second wife. Susan was the first. She died in an accident when Serena was about fourteen. She's twenty-eight now and hasn't been in touch for a while. Look, I'm sorry, I probably shouldn't be saying all this.'

'Of course.' Bramble's mouth felt very dry all of a sudden. She needed that cup of tea. 'Well, I hope I can meet Gemma soon, that she can come down.'

'Gemma would love to,' said Jenny warmly. 'It's always been a problem because she's too young to travel down on her own, and it's very difficult for me to take the whole weekend driving her down and back again.'

Bramble took Serena's number down – next to Jenny's – in a daze and put it in her pocket.

Nat came back with the tea and took a look at her face. 'What's happened?'

'Jenny phoned.'

His face darkened in fury. 'I told you she was a troublemaker. Why in hell did you answer the phone?'

'I thought it might be someone needing a farrier. She told me about Susan. And Serena.'

'Oh I'm sure she couldn't wait to tell you. I bet it came up in the first half-dozen sentences. She's a manipulative bitch. I should have been the one to tell you about Susan and Serena.'

'Well, yes, you should. Why didn't you?'

'Because it hurt so sodding much. Serena walked out on us when she went to university and only gets in touch when she wants money. I tried to be a father to her and I can't bear to talk about either of them, not to people who don't know, and then as time went on it became more and more difficult to say, "actually, there's a stepdaughter I haven't mentioned". Can't you see that?'

'Well, I can, sort of, but shouldn't we have had the conversation by now?'

'We were going to,' he said. 'So many times. But something else always cropped up. You have a very busy life, Bramble, and it's sometimes hard to get your attention long enough to talk about something really important.'

Bramble sagged, thinking of Savannah. 'I know. I'm sorry.'

He sank down beside her and took her hand. 'No, I'm the one who should say sorry.' He shook his head. 'I don't believe it. One short conversation with Jenny and she manages to destroy your trust in me utterly.' He sounded despairing.

Bramble shook her head. 'She hasn't destroyed my trust in you. But I do wonder what else you haven't told me.'

He closed his eyes and spoke very softly. 'I wanted to forget about Susan, OK? You've lost your husband, I've lost my wife. I don't see the slightest point in raking up the past and upsetting ourselves. And because Serena never gets in touch, I kept telling myself that I'd wait until we had time to talk about it properly, without interruptions. The most important thing to me is the future. Our future. Does that make sense to you?'

'Well, yes, it does, but I . . .'

'But three minutes on the phone with my ex-wife has changed that, has it?'

'Of course it hasn't,' Bramble burst out. 'I don't care what she says. I still love you, of course I do, but—'

'You do?' He grabbed her arm fiercely and she winced. 'Sorry. I didn't mean to hurt you.' He let her arm go and spoke more gently. 'You can't imagine what that means to me. I've got so used to people believing her lies, her side of things, looking at me as if I was a monster, it's never really occurred to me that someone might believe in me. Not her. *Me*.'

'I do believe in you.' Bramble was close to tears. 'But please, please, in future tell me things. However painful they are. I can't trust you if you don't.'

He held her tight. 'I will. Of course I will. I've never been able to trust anyone else before . . . except Susan, of course, and when she died . . . well, I married Jenny on the rebound. I should never have done it, I know that now, but hindsight's all very well, isn't it?'

A chilling thought struck Bramble. 'Do you still love Susan?'

Nat tipped her face up towards him. 'Dearest, darling Bramble, you are the one I love. I loved Susan and now she's dead. That's all. She's gone. She's really gone. To be truthful, I barely think of her, although I feel a bit guilty saying that. You're what matters now.'

'You're sure?' Bramble was too tired to function.

'I'm sure.' Nat kissed her, warm and tender.

'Now we have to talk about Savannah.'

'Yes,' he said. 'Savannah comes first now.'

Over the next few weeks, Savannah sat through a number of sessions with the hospital doctors, her GP and a kindly therapist called Vikki, feeling nothing but a sense of distance from them. She pleasantly agreed that her father dying when she was eight had been traumatic, and that this 'illness' – as they insisted on referring to it – had most likely been triggered by her grandfather's death, especially as she had been with him at the time. Finding answers seemed to make them happy, and somebody might as well be happy. She would never be happy again. Lottie would never come back.

And she thought the therapists were all fools. She could barely remember Dominic Kelly and most people her age had had at least one grandfather who'd died, admittedly not necessarily in front of them, but they must think she was very fragile if she couldn't cope with what had to be a normal life experience. It hadn't seemed to occur to them that she had to be thin to succeed, and they were trying to make her eat so she'd turn back into the fat lump she'd been before Jez came. Jez would never have kissed the doughy girl she'd been then.

Bramble and Helena had driven her back from hospital the morning after Mulberry Hill. Through her exhaustion she was dimly aware of a tension in the car, probably, she thought, because the doctors had said something to Bramble about her weight, but she'd been too shattered to take much notice. All the way home she drifted in and out of a doze and dreamed, because Jez had come to rescue her as she'd known he would.

She could dimly remember riding up to fence 17, the oxer, a man waving at her in the rain, and Shaggy spooking away from him, bolting towards the fields. She'd been thrown off balance, losing a stirrup, and couldn't regain control, especially as, without the knobbly texture of her cross-country gloves, she didn't have enough grip on the wet reins. She'd had to cling on rather than ride. There had been one terrifying moment when Shaggy made one of her gigantic leaps over a gate, jolting Savannah sideways. When Shaggy jumped she always felt enormous, like a much bigger horse, and landing knocked Savannah again and she slipped out of the saddle. Her brain retained a fuzzy memory of hanging down by Shaggy's pumping shoulder for a few seconds, then her limbs were banging painfully on the ground in a tangle of hooves and earth. She thought she'd tasted some mud, but everything had been spinning round very far away, and her body throbbed with white-hot pain. Lying in the mud, wet, icy cold to her core, defeated and weeping, unable to gather the strength to move, she waited for Jez to come.

And he did. Sweetheart, he'd called her, and she could hear love and concern in his low tones. She'd reached out, sobbing like a baby and he'd picked her up, and she'd known she was safe.

Until they'd told her about Lottie. Savannah still didn't believe it. She could feel Lottie at her side and knew that she could turn round and talk to her whenever she wanted to. Except that she turned, and Lottie wasn't there. Savannah couldn't understand how Lottie could have gone for ever.

'She can't be dead,' was all she'd said when Bramble had told her. 'We rode down to the start together. The three of us. Eddie, Lottie and me. We were all together.'

Felicity watched the starlings gather, forming and re-forming in strange and wonderful shapes in the air as it sang with their chatter. The swallows had gone, discreetly. One day they simply weren't there. She wondered what urge drove them to fly thousands of miles, over the Pyrenees, across Spain and Morocco, then further still over the vastness of the Sahara desert, often dying of starvation or exhaustion, until they reached the southernmost tip of Africa. Only to make the dangerous journey back again six months later.

If she could, would she tell them not to go? Would she reach out and urge them to stay where the trees and hedgerows were bursting with ripe fruit, and the last of the wild sorrel still green enough to be gathered? Mushrooms with exotic names nestled under the falling leaves – trompettes de la mort, chanterelles, girolles and hobgoblin ceps – while the woods echoed to the whispers of cobnuts, hazelnuts and walnuts dropping to the ground. There was so much to stay for.

Riding out three or four horses every day, Felicity felt her body grow hard and strong, and the shadows begin to leave her mind.

Lottie's funeral was held in the tiny village church where she'd been christened, and mourners spread out of its door, down the path and across the gravestones. Cecily, her face like a death's head, head-to-toe in black as if she'd been dipped in ink, walked down the aisle alone, her head held high. Lottie's father was back from Hong Kong, holding on to his current wife and Lottie's two step-brothers tightly, as if he was afraid of losing them too. Everyone was there – the mothers and children from the Pony Club, a coachload of weeping girls and sombre teachers from Lottie's school, Toby's grooms, all the different trainers and riders that Lottie had been working with over the summer – the light gone from their faces, each wondering if they could have taught her something more, just one thing that might have saved her life. Most of Martyr's Forstal was there, to say goodbye to the skinny girl who'd always smiled when she passed them on the lanes, Pauline, grief carved into deep lines on her face, arrived with Toby, whose tan looked old and yellow.

'I don't know how he dared come,' hissed Savannah. 'He more or less killed her by selling her Vincent.'

'Whatever else you can say about Toby,' said Felicity. 'He's never lacked courage. And it wasn't just Vincent being too strong that killed her.' Savannah watched him covertly. There was something about Toby that always made her feel very uneasy. She didn't think Felicity had told her everything.

And still they came: the staff of the feed merchant's, the tack shop, the old farrier, Roberts, the back person who came once every eight weeks to check their horses' backs, even the livery stable where Lottie had first kept Sailor arrived in a pale, silent group. The organisers of Mulberry Hill emerged from a car together, their faces set. There would be an inquiry, of course, but it was hard to see what could be improved upon. The weather, although poor, had hardly been unique and had worsened so quickly that even if Pauline had had a radio, it was unlikely the event would have been cancelled in time to stop Lottie's last jump. As people continued to walk up the lane, and cars negotiated the narrow passing spaces, Felicity reckoned that there must be over four hundred people there. Everyone who could was touching someone else – hands clasped, shoulders encircled, elbows linked – as if only by holding on very tightly could they stop them slipping away too. It was as if they had suddenly been shown how narrow the line was between life and death.

'Lottie was so quiet and shy,' whispered Savannah. 'She'd never have imagined that so many people loved her. I wish she could see this.'

Felicity turned her head sideways to look at her niece and saw her head bowed, exposing the knobbly bones of her neck. A large tear dropped down onto Savannah's hand. 'She was such a good friend to me and I didn't see her enough. She asked me to do things and I didn't go.' Her bony shoulders shook as she clutched Bramble's hand tightly and the protective bulk of Nat shored them up on the other side. Felicity studied his broad shoulders, and hoped he was going to be good for Bramble. She turned and her eyes met Pauline's in the pew behind. It was a challenge and they both knew it.

After the funeral, Helena was determined to make Eddie see sense. She sat herself down in the kitchen in Lorenden. He leant back against the worksurface, drinking lager out of a can.

'Now do you see what I mean?' demanded Helena. 'Now you know why I didn't want you to get involved down here.'

'I still want to be an eventer,' said Eddie. 'Lottie's horse was too strong for her, everybody knew that.'

'There's always an excuse. All my life I've heard these excuses. It was always somebody's fault, some reason why any sensible person wouldn't have ridden, or wouldn't have ridden in that way. The truth of the matter is,' she thumped her hand on the table, 'that it's a dangerous sport and even the best rider on the best horse on perfect ground can be killed or horribly injured.'

'They can be,' said Eddie. 'And I won't forget that. But most aren't.'

She fixed Eddie with her brilliant blue eyes, which were shining with tears. 'Do you want to finish up like Dom or Lottie?'

'I won't finish up like them. But please let me be sad about Lottie without turning it into a lecture on how I should live my life.'

'Eddie, it is dangerous,' she shouted.

Eddie leant down and rested his elbows on the kitchen table, taking one of her hands in each of his, curling his fingers round hers, squeezing them gently. 'Mum, I want this more than anything. My life would mean nothing without it. It's what I think about when I go to sleep at night, and then again first thing in the morning. Every book I read, every programme I watch, every single second of my day – all I ever think about or work towards is how I can be a better rider. Haven't you ever felt like that about anything?'

A tear trickled slowly down Helena's cheek and she studied his hands carefully, as if memorising every line and whorl. 'Yes,' she whispered after a few moments. 'Yes, I do know. It's how I feel about acting. The others,' she said, smiling at him through her tears, 'people who don't feel like that about something, they don't understand, do they?'

Eddie smiled back and kissed her cheek. 'Thanks Mum, you're the best. Always the best.'

At the other end of the kitchen table Savannah, trying to pick at a slice of toast, watched him with huge, hungry eyes. Eddie, over the top of Helena's head, thought his cousin was beginning to look like a sad little goblin.

'Eddie is so emotionally mature for an eighteen-year-old boy,' Helena told everyone over the next few weeks. 'He and I are one of a kind. I suppose I've just got to be brave about it.'

Chapter 34

Savannah was being weighed weekly, but she was continuing to lose ounces rather than gain them. Bramble was terrified.

'It's very important to have family meals,' said Vikki, the therapist. 'And not too late either. You all need to sit down around six or six-thirty and eat together. By seven o'clock she'll have made herself something on her own and it won't necessarily be the right sort of something.'

'But,' said Bramble, recognising the truth of this, 'I'm usually teaching then and it would mean cooking at about five instead of doing the horses' feed.'

'Mrs Kelly,' Vikki's pen was poised over her notes, 'what is more important? Your daughter's supper or the horses'?'

Bramble knew what her father would have said to that.

Nat suggested that he attend a session, but Savannah blocked it.

'I'm hoping that when we marry, and have a home of our own,' Bramble told Vikki, 'then Savannah might feel more secure. At the moment everything's so up in the air, it can't be helping.'

'Mmm,' said Vikki, frowning over her notes. 'You may be right.'

'I don't know what to do,' Bramble said to Helena. 'Nobody seems to be getting through to her.'

Helena finally told her that she had seen Jez and Savannah in the attic on the night of her engagement. 'I know you don't tend to believe anyone when they say anything against Jez, Bramble, but I think that he is part of Savannah's problem. And you know from Nat that he's quite capable of having an affair with a very young girl.' Bramble remembered the night she had spent with Jez in the horsebox and felt totally, utterly betrayed.

Not because of anything sexual, but because they had talked through the darkness and she thought they trusted each other. She thought they'd been honest.

As she walked, trembling with rage, she remembered lying there, skin against skin as if it had always belonged there. She felt raw and exposed at the thought that, secretly, his hands had been touching her daughter's face and his lips had kissed hers. It felt dirty, like those three-in-a-bed romps you read about in cheap newspapers or the sad, salacious stories like the one Nat had told about Jez having had an affair with the mother and the daughter.

She found him in the stables, rugging up Shaggy, and her last hope sputtered and died when she saw, from his eyes, that he knew exactly why she was there.

'I'm sorry,' he said.

'Sorry?'

'About Savannah.'

Bramble felt tears rise behind her eyes as she heard the finality in his voice. These weren't the words of a man who was in love with her daughter. They were the words of a man who was ashamed.

'You kissed her.'

Jez started to say something, but stopped. He nodded.

'So whatever that kiss meant, and whatever lay behind it, you're not planning to be around in Savannah's life?'

He shook his head. 'I never meant to hurt her. Please believe that.'

'What were you thinking of?' she flashed. 'She's so young and so vulnerable. She looked on you as a father.'

His face was stony. 'I will tender my resignation, of course.'

'You mean leave us?' Although it was a warm evening, Bramble was chilled. 'Go? What, immediately?'

His face was very close to hers and very bleak.

'But what about your career? And who will ride the horses?'

'You will,' he said. 'You need to get out there and live again.'

As she turned away, unable to reply, he spoke again. 'Can I say goodbye to Savannah?'

'Try not to hurt her any more than you have already,' said Bramble, walking away to hide her fury. She would like to kill him.

'Bramble . . .'

She stopped. 'Yes?'

'You,' he said. 'You can get to the top yourself. Shaggy will take you. If that's where you want to go. Don't bury your ambition in Savannah: it's not good for either of you.'

Bramble walked away without replying, tears stinging her eyes. So it was all her fault, was it? Jez was just attempting to shift the blame.

Savannah was having supper with Donna. Finding it impossible to have the daily family meal as recommended by Vikki, her mother had introduced an informal rota of people who prepared food for Savannah and ate with her. Donna, with her microwaved meals in her little dovecote flat, was the easiest to deal with. Donna didn't watch every mouthful she ate and didn't treat her like a sick child.

'So,' said Donna. 'Got a boyfriend?'

'Sort of.' Savannah blushed. Keeping her feelings for Jez a secret was so difficult. She longed to talk about him, about the way he'd taken her in his arms, about the kiss, about everything she felt and the way he always spoke so directly to her, as if she was someone special. She had to talk to someone but Lottie was gone. The gap she left was huge. 'Well, not really. I wouldn't call him a *boyfriend*.'

Donna eyed her up. 'Still keen on Jez?'

'No! Well, I mean, yes, but . . .' Savannah was enjoying this, in a way, hugging her memories to her. It made her feel quite hungry and she forked another mouthful of shepherd's pie into her mouth.

'Has he kissed you?' asked Donna shrewdly, and was rewarded by Savannah's eyes shining back at her.

'Have you slept with him?'

Her fork hovered on its way to her mouth. 'No, we're . . . we're taking things slowly.'

Donna sighed. 'The thing is, Savannah, you don't know anything about men. You're never their girlfriend until you've slept with them. You shouldn't trust Jez, anyway. He's the sort of man who sleeps with everyone.'

'No he isn't. And how would you know?'

'Because,' Donna's eyes gleamed. 'He's shagged Felicity. I saw her come down from his flat one morning.'

Savannah put down her fork. How many calories had she ingested? How could Jez love a fat girl?

'Well,' she said, trying to appear calm. 'That was before us.'

But Donna's words shattered Savannah's dream, and she left shortly afterwards. Nobody could fancy her, Savannah, not if they'd had Felicity. Or anyone else. The difference between a short kiss and someone who had spent the night – perhaps many nights – was so huge that she suddenly questioned everything about their single, precious embrace. Had she forced herself on him? It must have embarrassed Jez so much. She was now flooded with mortification. The whole perspective of the relationship tipped in her mind, distorted into something clinging, meagre and pitiful. She saw a schoolgirl crush, not true love.

Perhaps that's what everybody saw. Helena might not have said anything to her face, but would have told someone – probably everyone – behind her back, and in the end everyone would want to know what had happened and would be laughing. She would have to say . . . well, what could she say? She clambered blindly out of the dovecote, and stumbled away from the stables. She didn't deserve to live.

'Savannah.' She heard Jez's gentle tones as he found her sitting at the bottom of the garden, and her heart leapt.

'Savannah, I'm leaving—'

'No,' she screamed. 'Not because of me? Don't say it's because of me!'

'Shh,' he said. 'It wasn't your fault. It wasn't your fault at all.'

'So it *is* about me, Helena must have been saying stupid, stupid things . . .'

'Savannah, have you talked to your mother about this? Or anyone else?'

'No. *Please* don't say anything, I couldn't bear it. I feel so stupid.'

'Of course I won't talk about it. You're not stupid,' he said. 'You're fantastic and if I was twenty years younger I would have fallen in love with you. But I'm too old.'

'You're not. You're not.' Savannah seized his hand and great tears splashed down on to it. Don't leave us,' she sobbed. 'We can't manage without you. Grampa's gone, and now Mummy's marrying Nat and Helena and Felicity are living here, and it's all horribly different and it's not home any more. You've brought us so much luck, please, please don't go.'

Jez put an arm round her. 'I need you to promise me something.'

'Anything.' Savannah turned her face up to his.

'You need to eat. What you're doing to yourself now risks everything. You won't be able to compete without strength and fitness. You're risking the collapse of your organs, you may not be able grow up properly and have babies, and starvation turns your brain off and stops you having fun with your friends.'

'I don't care about fun, I haven't got any friends. And I'm frightened.'

'Savannah, look at me. You're one of the bravest and most determined people I've ever met. Use that courage now.'

Helena, peering out of her bedroom window, saw Jez holding Savannah tight. 'My God,' she said to herself, hurrying downstairs to break them up. 'Nothing will stop that man, will it?'

Chapter 35

Helena tore a screaming Savannah out of Jez's arms and half-dragged, half-carried her back to the house. Savannah sobbed in her room for two hours, refusing to talk to either Bramble or Helena. Eddie came back from a hack and went upstairs.

'She won't talk to me either,' he said.

Bramble left a tray of food outside the room but it sat there, untouched, until the evening. And so did the next tray, and the next.

'She's not eating anything,' she said to Helena the following day, terrified.

'If this goes on,' replied Helena, 'you'll have to section her.' At Bramble's horrified face she added, 'Send her to a mental hospital under section something or other of the Mental Health Act because she's a danger to herself.'

'I know what sectioning is. And Savannah would never forgive me.'

'Oh well, children don't starve themselves,' replied Helena.

'Yes, they do,' said Bramble, desperate and frightened. 'Felicity, please, please do *something*.'

Felicity went upstairs and pressed her mouth to the keyhole, knowing that it would act as a tiny microphone. 'Savannah?'

There was a silence and Felicity was about to try again when she heard a muffled voice. 'Toby Fitzroy says you owe him one. And that we Beaumonts always run away.'

Felicity was about to say she didn't know what Savannah was

talking about, but she was too tired to go on pretending. 'Toby Fitzroy's right,' she whispered through the keyhole.

A moment later the door flew open. 'Toby Fitzroy's right? No one's ever said that before in this house.'

'Well, maybe they should have done.' Felicity sat back on her heels wearily. 'I do owe him one and I did run away. And that's what you're doing now, not eating and locking yourself in your room.'

The door slammed shut again.

Ten out of ten for tact, Felicity, she told herself. That didn't work. 'I don't want you to make the mistakes I did,' she said, through the keyhole. There was no reply.

Just as Felicity was about to go downstairs again, Savannah flung her door open. 'Why did you leave?'

She thought, for a moment, that Felicity was going to tell her, but then her eyes shut down. 'When I look at you,' she continued. 'I see myself. Just rebelling in a different way.'

Savannah had no idea what she was talking about. It was the sort of thing adults said when they were drunk. If you didn't escape quickly they'd repeat it over and over again.

She was about to shut the door again, but took a deep breath. 'If you tell me – honestly and truly, and not trying to hold anything back, and not lying to stop me worrying, and all of that crap my mother does – why you went I'll come out.'

'Only if you eat something first.'

Savannah's grip on the edge of the door tightened. 'I can't,' she said eventually. A tear trickled down her face. 'I just can't.'

Felicity opened her arms and drew her in. 'Come downstairs and try. I'll tell you everything, I promise.' She held Savannah's face between her hands. 'And then, Savannah, dear one, please, I know somewhere they may be able to help you. But you'll have to stay there for several weeks, more even. And you'll have to trust me.'

Savannah nodded. 'OK.'

The next few hours were a jumble of telephone calls and hastily packed bags, and then Savannah found herself in the back of Helena's car, with her mother holding her hand, and Felicity in the front passenger seat. There was no time to talk, but Felicity had promised and Savannah felt too tired and scared to want to hear any story now. Felicity would tell her, she said, as soon as she was feeling strong enough.

She was checked into a small white room, with two neatly made beds in it, each with a pine bedside table, chest and wardrobe. It made Savannah think of a prison cell, except that out of the window she could see fields and trees, their leaves turning to bronze, gilt and copper. Vikki came to tell her that there would be a meeting that evening, at five, and that Savannah need only introduce herself and listen. Everyone was here to help her. There was no reason to be nervous.

As she kissed her mother, and Felicity and Helena, goodbye a huge sense of relief washed over her. Someone else would take this horrible, scary burden away and give her back her life.

Back at Lorenden, after the twins had been put to bed and Ollie had gone to the pub, Felicity opened a bottle of wine and pulled out three glasses.

'No thanks.' Helena put the third wine glass away and pulled out a tumbler.

Bramble and Felicity stared at her.

'Don't tell me you'll be checking in yourself,' said Felicity lightly. 'I gather that rehab offers the most fabulous networking opportunities these days.'

'Actually no.' Helena poured herself a glass of orange juice. 'The old Helena would have been straight in there, finding out where all the A list go to dry out, lining up the magazine features for when I came out, being photographed with new best friends who'd "been so there for me".'

One thing you could say for Helena, thought Bramble – she knew how to laugh at herself.

'But this is for me,' continued Helena. 'The real me, not some-one who sees their life through the pages of a magazine. I want to stop drinking. I don't want life to be a blur. I know I'm brave enough to take what comes. And when I look at poor little Savannah – well, it makes me ashamed of myself.'

'Why you?' flashed Bramble. 'Surely if anyone should feel ashamed it's me.'

Helena and Felicity stood poised, frozen, as she saw them both try to think of a reassuring reply.

'Bram, darling, you've done your best,' said Helena. 'You've had to run a business and bring up a daughter on your own. No one could have done more.'

'You were just busy,' added Felicity. 'That's all. You couldn't help it.'

'We need to talk.' Bramble went straight round to Nat's after she'd checked the horses for the last time that night.

Jez had gone. Completely. First she saw that his car was missing. She'd tiptoed upstairs to his flat, knocking hesitantly on the door. It swung open. All trace of him had disappeared in a few hours.

She walked round the flat, ducking under its low eaves, remembering the evenings they'd sat over the kitchen table discussing the horses, his easy strength in the yard, his sudden smiles when she said something funny, and his habit of quiet watchfulness. It had made her feel safe, as if someone was guarding over her.

How could he have done it? Even if Savannah had thrown herself at him, there was no excuse she could bear to hear. She now realised, too late, that she had come to trust him at a very deep level as a friend – no matter what everyone had said about him – and that ultimately he had failed that trust. It hurt. She couldn't pretend otherwise.

She closed the door behind her. Nat was her life now. She had to talk to him.

'I don't want us to get married for about eighteen months,' she said.

'Hey! What's this all about? Whoa, just calm down, Bram.'

'It's Savannah's anorexia. I have to put her first.'

'But I want to be in this with you, for us to handle it together.'

Bramble was silent for a moment. 'She could die, Nat. It's serious. She weighs six stone. We thought we'd got on top of it, and I think for a bit we had, but it's been so busy recently. That's why I need to minimise any distractions. I need to get myself straight, get Savannah straight and then marry you, knowing I've done everything I can do.'

'OK, OK, I can see that you won't want a big party and everything. But that doesn't have to mean us not going through with it. Let's cancel everything except the ceremony itself, and just you and me . . .'

'No,' said Bramble. 'I can't do it without Savannah, and I can't do it with her the way she is now.'

'I just want us to get on with the rest of our lives.'

'So do I,' replied Bramble. 'And we can.'

'But . . .' He looked angry. She had never seen him like that, and her heart beat faster, almost in fear. 'I feel you're not properly committed to me, so I can't . . .'

'Can't what?' She was horribly aware that Nat had supported her, comforted her and been behind her every step of the way, and that she had not repaid this support.

He slammed his fist down on the table between them. 'Never mind.'

'Tell me.'

'If we'd bought somewhere together, somewhere that was ours – well . . . oh, it's no good. This isn't an appropriate thing for us to be talking about.'

'It is appropriate,' Bramble assured him. 'I am committed.'

'There's a live-work unit for sale down the road, with a workshop. If I could buy it I'd be able to expand and have a proper forge. Do railings and other ironwork as well as farriery. Take on an apprentice, build something for our future together. Not waste more money on rent. I want us both to fulfil our dreams – surely you can understand that.'

'Live there?' asked Bramble alarmed.

'Rent it out. Or live there. Whatever suits us both.' He emphasised the word 'both'. 'It's the reason I want us to be a team. So we can make these decisions together.'

'Why can't we take these decisions together anyway?'

'Well, because as a freelance who's only been working for a few years it's not that easy for me to get a mortgage without some kind of security. And if we had a house together it would be security. But I can hardly ask you now, can I? To act as security on my business?'

'You can,' said Bramble, before realising what she was saying.

'Of course you can. I've got my share of Lorenden. It's not cash, but it could be security.'

'I couldn't do that. Not unless we were married.'

'Of course you could. Of course.' At last there was something she could do for him.

'Could you?' His face cleared. 'Bramble, it would make all the difference in the world to me. It would show you had faith in me. And faith in us. It's not as if I'd ever have any call on the money. It would just be a bit of paper.'

'Don't worry,' said Bramble, wishing she didn't feel a twinge of uneasiness about the whole thing. She must be generous. And he was right, they both needed their dreams.

He kissed her. 'You're fantastic. I'll support you and you support me. It's what partnership is all about.'

Savannah came home from Hightrees House, as the clinic was called, in the middle of her second week as a reward for gaining a small amount of weight and sticking to the rules. Darcy and the terriers were overcome with delight. She sank down on the familiar old sofa and breathed in the scent of horse, polish, cooking and just the faintest trace of dog as if it were the most expensive perfume in the world.

'You promised,' she said to Felicity. 'To tell me everything.'

Felicity took a deep breath. She had never told the story to anyone, except Merlin, and she was afraid of resurrecting that terrible burning anger, or the humiliation, or the sense that nothing would ever be right again. She looked at Helena drinking her tea, and thought about how Helena was facing her demons.

It was her turn now. You're a war reporter, she told herself. You've spent your working life telling other people's terrible stories, your own is not so bad as some of the things you've seen.

'Right,' she said, when they'd all sat down on the big sofas in the drawing room, warmed by the fire. 'When I was eighteen, in the early seventies, London was where it was at. Down here was twenty years behind and I had the sense that there was a great big party somewhere, happening without me. Parents seemed fusty and hopelessly outdated, and nothing they said seemed relevant. I wanted to be a top rider but I also wanted fun, and that's what Pa didn't seem to want me to have.

'Fun round here meant a bad lad called Ricky Mitchell. He was twenty-nine and from the wrong side of the tracks – his grandfather had been a gypsy, his father had been inside – he had eleven brothers and sisters and he was everything Ma and Pa didn't want for me.

'But he had long dark hair and a moustache, like Che Guevara, and he lived in a squat – a beautiful old Georgian house in Canterbury. He dealt in dope and a few other things, and his life was one long party. And he was gorgeous, with his complete disdain for everything about the world I'd come from. Here, at Lorenden, we had formal dining chairs round a huge mahogany table, in his house there were bean bags on the floor and a hookah pipe. We had oil paintings of our ancestors but he had posters on his walls. When he started being interested in me it was the most exciting thing that had ever happened. Of course, when he came back to Lorenden the parents kept saying things like "he's not quite our class, darling" and "have you noticed the way he uses his knife?" which made me so furious and so determined to prove that they were wrong about everything.

'Pa mainly cared about Ricky's effect on my career. He kept telling me that I couldn't afford to play all night then work all day. I said, why not, that's what you do – in those days they drank and partied in a way that would seem quite astonishing today. And I kept saying that they were being hypocritical in criticising weed when alcohol was just as toxic and much more aggressive. I really did believe, like lots of my friends did, that the world of drugs was more honest and more meaningful than the one of alcohol, that people who drank had fights whereas those who took drugs connected with each other at a purer, more fundamental level. And, of course, anything they said about sex seemed downright daft – we didn't have Aids then. Love was free, or so we thought.

'So I used to slip out of the house and spend the night at Ricky's, sneaking back at about four or five, before Pa and the rest started in the stables. Ricky introduced me to amphetamines and coke just so that I could keep going, and because I'd find it almost impossible to sleep after that I got sleeping pills from my doctor for when I needed them. I lived on a chemical rollercoaster.

'Pa had just been selected for the Great Britain squad, and everyone was absolutely sure they'd be in the final line-up for the Olympics, but then his horse, Breezy, slipped a tendon – which, as you know, is catastrophic –and he was left without a horse. He'd had his eye on a horse called Merlin's Magic, which belonged to Toby Fitzroy. As you know, pressure was put on Toby's father and he lost Merlin to Pa. He bought it with Pauline as a joint purchase. Toby was furious. But Pa had a stunning couple of seasons on him. They were selected for the British team, and we were going to the World Championships – even being talked of as almost definitely heading for the Olympics.

'Then our parents went away for a weekend – which was very rare – and left me in charge. Bramble and Helena went to stay with Pauline and Alan because their children were about the same age, and I was left with the grooms. So I decided to give a party and gave the grooms the night off.

'The word went out – through Ricky, I suppose – and suddenly hundreds of people turned up, loads of them I didn't know, and they trashed the place. They stubbed cigarettes out on the carpet, spilt wine and beer over the furniture, broke things – at one point I even found a naked couple in one of the bedrooms. I told Ricky it was beginning to get out of control, but he told me to cool it and passed me another joint. I'd already had quite a cocktail – he'd given me some coke and I'd been drinking since the afternoon.

'At this point a huge black car drew up, and out poured these scary looking guys, and what I thought of as a really old man. By which I mean he was around fifty, with a paunch, and wearing a suit. They walked into the house in a group, with the old guy at the centre, and after a few words with Ricky he pointed them upstairs.

'"That's Mr Big," Ricky pulled me to one side. "He is the Man."

'"What man?"

'"God, you're so stupid sometimes. That's Ron."

'"Ron who?"

'"Ron None-of-your-business. Come and be nice to him." He grabbed my wrist. "Very nice."

'"I asked him what he meant and he said, "Don't play the virgin with me. You know what nice is."

Felicity swallowed. This was the bit she was most ashamed of.

'He told me,' she could barely force the words out, 'that I had to have sex with Ron to pay for the drugs I'd taken.

'"But you took the drugs too," I said to him. "You sold them all over the place. What about the money from that?" Then he told me that if I loved him, I'd do it.

'I said that if he loved me he wouldn't *ask* me to do it.

'He said that we'd agreed that sex was the least important thing in our relationship.

'I said that didn't mean I had to sleep with someone to pay for drugs.

'"Why not?" he said. "That's the way you're going, you might as well start now."

'That was when I realised what I was getting myself into. I had never heard of pimping and was only vaguely aware of various ex-girlfriends who "owed him money" from time to time, but I now suspect that getting young girls into drugs then easing them into prostitution was one of his sidelines, even then. I'd never thought about how the waifish girls that drifted through his parties actually paid for their habit, or to what extent he controlled them.

'He thrust me into the spare room where Ron was already unbuckling his belt. Ricky slammed the door and left me there.

'I screamed and managed to grapple the door open again, but there was another man stationed outside the door and he threw me back in. And another of them shouted that . . .' Felicity's voice dropped so that it was barely audible '. . . that after Ron had finished, they'd all like a go. There was a man there with a tattoo of a rearing horse on his arm, I think, but I can't remember much about his face. Or any of their faces. It's all a terrible blur.'

'But that's . . . a terrible crime,' said Savannah. 'Weren't they afraid of you calling the police?'

'With all the drugs we had in the house? No, the police were the enemy, as far as I was concerned.'

★

Felicity remembered the disconnected way her brain had struggled to sober up, half drunk, stoned, hearing her own voice come out disjointed and slurred, unable to think or walk straight but still aware of the danger she was in, the sweet smell of the marijuana, the music and laughter drifting up from downstairs, and a muscular arm with a tattoo of a horse – she remembered thinking how odd that had been – somewhere. She couldn't remember who he was or what part he'd played in it all.

She could remember cowering on the bed and beating the big man with her fists, kicking uselessly. He dodged her the first few times then cuffed her to the floor, breathing heavily. 'D'you want me to call the others in to make you behave? Cos I will. I don't mind an audience.' His voice was gravelly, as if he smoked too many cigarettes.

She could remember his weight, and the pain and her shame and the way he went on and on, grunting as she shut her eyes and held herself still and stiff. At one point he stopped and propped himself up on his elbows. 'C'mon, loosen up, you won't get a lot of business like this, you know.' She kept her eyes tightly shut. 'You go down this route, girl,' he said, thrusting again. 'You want to put a bit of effort into it. Punters . . .' thrust '. . . don't pay top whack . . .' thrust '. . . for something as stiff as a board.'

When it was over he put his lips very close to her ear. 'You're mine now,' he said in his rasping voice, breathing heavily. 'And don't ever think about getting away. You do what I say. Understand?'

Then he rolled over and sat up, sitting on her as if she was a cushion. Tears squeezed from her eyes and she could barely breathe. The careless use of her body like this cheapened her almost more than the original rape had done. 'I've got something,' he said. 'To say thank you.'

He pulled his trousers towards him, and she saw him take a syringe out. Some of the drunkenness and the dope had ebbed away and things seemed clearer. If you go this route . . . he'd said and he was right. What he had in that syringe would blunt the impact of what came next. She need hardly notice the next few hours. She would hardly need to notice anything again, except the desire to blot everything else out, always. Somehow, muggily, she managed to work it out and shook her head.

'Suit yourself,' he said. 'But it'll make it easier.' He nodded towards the closed door. 'Some of the boys can be a bit rough and you won't feel no pain with this.'

She almost agreed. She was almost grateful to him. She hated herself for that: for the gratitude, for the twitch of feeling that made him her protector. But she lay still as he got up, wiping himself down with the edge of the bedspread. He began to pull his trousers on, facing away from her, and she waited until he was putting his second leg in then rolled over and bolted for the other door, the one in the corner that looked like a cupboard but led up to the attic staircase and down to the kitchen.

His shout of rage and the heavy footsteps of other men followed her as she skidded down the tiny, curving staircase with the speed born of a lifetime's experience.

At the bottom she ran into the tattooed arm again, and her memory blurred. She remembered a struggle. How had she escaped?

But she did. She was out of the kitchen and into the yard before they could follow, although she couldn't go far in bare feet and she knew they'd have no trouble catching her up once they were outside. Looking around for somewhere to hide, her heart thumping out of her chest, she saw her favourite childhood hidey hole, the cedar tree. Ducking down and swinging up into its spreading skirts, she clambered as far up as she could. She was heavier and less agile than she'd been at ten, and there were spiny fronds to negotiate as well as the thick older branches.

She heard them burst out into the yard when she was about ten feet off the ground and flattened herself against the tree's scaly trunk, winding her legs round and holding herself so still that even though torches flashed in and around the tree no one thought to check the higher branches.

But it was hard holding on. Her limbs began to ache and she couldn't keep her breathing quiet enough. It seemed to echo in the branches of the tree, the needles moving as she gasped.

'Fuck this,' said Ron. 'I know how to get her out of wherever she's hiding. She needn't think she can get away from me. Get one of those horses out. That one. Come on.'

She could see the yard lights go on and hoped they wouldn't

illuminate her hiding place. But she was lucky – by blackening out everything on its margins, the glare made it safer. There was shouting as, with fumbling fingers, one of them was ordered to put a headcollar on a horse.

'He's big, Guv,' she heard a man say.

'I'm fucking big,' came the hoarse reply. 'Who are you most frightened of?'

She heard the measured sound of hooves on stone and, illuminated in the yellow light, proud and graceful, stood Merlin's Magic.

Felicity didn't tell her sisters and Savannah every detail. She kept the weight of Ron's flesh, the smell of his spicy, rancid breath and the taste of his sour, unwashed skin to herself, but she told them how Merlin's Magic, her father's top horse, came out of his stable trusting the men who led him. 'He'd always been treated properly by people,' she said. 'He had no reason to be suspicious, and he had a wonderful easy-going temperament. He was curious. A lot of horses would have been nervous or difficult but Merlin just stood there like a champion.

'Ron got out a knife and waved it in the air, walking round the yard. "Right," he shouted. "I'm giving you a count of ten to come out of your hiding place. We know you're here somewhere."

'The yard was completely quiet and I was sure they must hear my breathing, but I was determined to cling on. I was frightened for Merlin, but I didn't think there was much Ron could do to him – a horse's skin is very thick, after all. If Merlin felt threatened or received any kind of a blow it was much more likely that he'd kill Ron rather than the other way around.

'"If you don't come out . . ." he shouted, "the horse dies."

'I knew that a man couldn't really harm a horse single-handedly,' said Felicity. 'I couldn't go out there. I just couldn't. I . . .'

'Of course you couldn't,' said Bramble. 'No one could. And a horse can defend itself against one man. It's much bigger and stronger.'

'That's what I thought. I was just waiting for Merlin to lash out but Ron suddenly plunged the knife right down the centre of his neck – which must have taken incredible strength – and Merlin reared up. It all happened so fast I couldn't quite understand it at the time, but Ron must have hung onto the knife just for long enough so that Merlin's weight going up and Ron's going down drove it in deeply. Far further than Ron could ever have managed unaided.

'And Merlin was terrified. He lashed out and began careering round the yard, flinging Ron to the ground and possibly trampling on him. He – Ron – was screaming and there was a crack when he hit the stone, so I think he must have been injured, and his men were shouting and running to their cars. There was a lot of shouting from the house too and everyone started to pour out, screaming as Merlin managed to get out of the yard and into the garden. The other men helped Ron into a car, but there was a moment when he stopped, hanging on to its roof, and he shouted so loudly that everyone stopped.

'"Just remember," he bellowed. "You're mine now. You may think you've got away with it this time, but I'll find you."

'The rest of the party vanished – someone had obviously spread the word – and I came down the tree to find Merlin. I nearly slipped on dark puddles of his congealing blood – I didn't know what it was at first, this sticky stuff on my feet – and as I went round the corner into the garden I saw him still going round in circles, still fleeing, except that he was weakening. He began to stagger and then he buckled at the knees and slowly went down on the grass. It took just minutes for him to lose so much blood that he couldn't keep going.

'By the time the police arrived – someone must have called them, but I don't know who – his breathing was intermittent: giant, rattling breaths, with huge gaps between them, and his eyes had gone dull. His chest would rise, as if to take another huge breath, and then there'd be silence while I held his head and sobbed that I was sorry. He died as the vet arrived – he'd bled out. Ron had hit the carotid artery.

'The vet told me later that the chances of actually getting a knife deep enough, and in the right place, had probably been less than one in a million, and of one man doing it unaided – well, it was technically possible, but he wouldn't have believed it if he hadn't seen the single, deep slash himself. "It was unlucky," he said.

"Whoever wielded the knife obviously knew nothing about horses or he would never have tried anything like this. Much more likely to have got himself killed." Most horses would have probably survived, though, but Merlin's thin, fine thoroughbred skin, and the fact that he was clipped, meant it was quite possible to slice through like that and hit the carotid artery.

'Telling Pa was terrible. Not only was it a horrific way for a beautiful, innocent animal to die, but that was his chances of representing Britain at the Olympics gone completely. And all his other chances gone too, until he could find another horse of that quality, and you know how rarely they come along and, if they do, how long they take to get to their peak.

'He was icy and furious. When he saw the house, with its roaches and Rizlas and condoms littered about, he ordered the police to arrest me. "You'd better arrest my daughter for possessing drugs," he said. "I think she may have been dealing."'

'So I was taken away to a police cell and interrogated. They told me I could go to prison for years unless I told them everything. I told them a bit about Ricky, but I didn't dare say much about Ron and I certainly didn't tell them about the rape. You didn't, then – I knew that rape victims were treated as little better than tarts in those days and I could hear that man's harsh voice in my head telling me that I'd never get away from him. I believed him. Looking back, I know I was in shock and I was terrified. I wonder if I should have told them everything, but I was desperate to get as far away from that voice in my head as possible.

'Even when I tried to think about it logically and clearly I knew I had to keep quiet. It was so muddled. How could I identify any of those faceless voices, that tattooed arm, the bits and pieces I could remember – how would any of it identify anyone safely? And even if it did, how could I stand up in court and have my behaviour read out and questioned and criticised? I would never be believed, would I? The whole lot of them would say I'd consented. I'd asked for it, don't you think?'

'In the end they let me go without charging me over the drugs. "With any luck, you've learned your lesson," they said.

'When I got home, Pa and I had a screaming match because I

didn't think Pa should have tried to send me to prison, however bad I'd been, and I sobbed that I was so desperately sorry. And so traumatised.' Felicity remembered the sense of unreality and the piercing loss of the happy, partying Felicity she had once been. She'd known that Felicity could never come back.

'I tried to tell him, but he didn't listen. He was so furiously angry he kept stopping me and saying, "Well, what *did* you expect, the way you've been leading your life?" He made it clear that I'd had it coming, whatever it was.'

'Couldn't you even tell our . . . mother?' asked Bramble, stumbling at the unfamiliar word and wondering what sort of a mother she could have been. To Bramble she was a shadowy figure in photographs, but surely, if she knew anything of what Felicity had gone through, she would have ripped Ron apart with her bare hands?

'She wasn't very well. She had to know something of what happened, of course she had to, but everyone kept trying to keep details from her. I think they even managed to convince her that Merlin had died of colic. I did tell . . .' Felicity paused. 'I told Pauline. She was the closest female friend the family had.'

'What did she say?'

'That I only had myself to blame, running around with scum like Ricky. She agreed to speak to Pa, but advised me that he was unlikely to think any better of me.

'And everyone went on screaming at me, until I eventually shouted that they were hypocrites, pretending to be so straight when all the time Pa was having an affair with Toby Fitzroy's mother. "That's how we got Merlin," I yelled, when he was in the kitchen with our mother and Pauline. "It was all sex. Nothing to do with patriotism at all."'

'Toby Fitzroy's mother?' asked Helena. 'Not Pauline?'

Felicity nodded. 'Beatrice Fitzroy.'

Helena and Bramble looked at each other, astonished.

'And, with that, I packed and left,' continued Felicity. 'I knew that Pauline had told Pa about the rape and I needed him either to be on my side or out of my life. Yet he still told me that he could never forgive my endangering an innocent horse, no matter what I'd been threatened with. Those were his exact words.

'So I told him that I would never, ever spend another night under his roof. And I needed to get away from here, to make sure that that rasping, threatening voice could never find me again. I had no idea how powerful he might be.'

'And then Mummy died,' said Helena. Her voice sounded bleak.

'Yes,' replied Felicity. 'I was told she'd had a heart attack, and Pauline pretty much told me that I was to blame. It was the shock of hearing about Pa's unfaithfulness. I was living in Paris by then and I came back for the funeral. Pa could hardly look at me. Although since then I've found a letter that says she'd been ill for a long time and, in fact, she knew about Pa and Beatrice. So it wasn't me who blew that one wide open either.'

'He can't have loved her very much if he was having an affair with Toby's mother.'

'Oh, he did love her. In his way. I don't think he thought affairs counted. But Toby's father thought they did, and he divorced Beatrice, so that's another thing that Toby holds against us. Toby believes Pa – aided by me and my big mouth – stole his success and split up his family.'

'Beatrice Fitzroy,' said Helena again. 'I was so sure it was Pauline. And I always thought maybe it was just a flirtation. At least until Mummy died.'

'How terrible for you,' said Bramble to Felicity. 'You must have been so lonely, with no one on your side.'

'Grampa did forgive you,' said Savannah. 'He tried to say that. His last words.'

'He has been trying to make contact recently,' agreed Felicity. 'But he failed me, first by calling the police before hearing my side of the story and then by not defending me against Ron and his revenge. He said he would never forgive me and I said I would never forgive him.'

There was still a missing piece of the jigsaw, thought Bramble. Something she should have picked up on, something important, but she couldn't quite put her finger on it.

'But Savannah,' said Felicity, remembering why she had agreed to tell her story, 'what you need to know is that you can't always see what everything's about when you're going through it. The letter I found, one that our mother wrote to Pa – it made me see that I only saw one view of it all, and he only saw another. Her heart attack wasn't sudden. She had been ill for some time and was increasingly dependent on me to run the house. And Pa expected me to ride to the top. Coming back here, after all these years of running, of changing my address and my job over and over again – and having a lot of good times as well as bad – I've realised that I wasn't just running away from Pa and the threat of Ron. I was getting away from what everyone expected of me. And I think maybe it was in my nature too. They all wanted me to stay, but I'm like the swallows, I had to go. I just wish that, like them, I'd come back.'

'What about Ron?' asked Bramble. 'Is he still around?'

'I don't think so. Over the years I managed to find out bits and pieces – it was what got me into journalism – and there was a small-time gang run by a man called Ron in the East End. I saw a fuzzy photograph, which I'm pretty sure was of him. He was jailed fifteen years ago and died there, aged about seventy-three. And Ricky's dead too – he had a motorbike accident.'

'Well, shall we talk about something cheerful?' trilled Helena. 'I've just had a call from my agent and the producers of *Simon's Way* are offering me big money for the new production. It could be that the only problem I'll have is that this time next year I'll be earning so much I won't be able to divorce Ollie.'

There was a movement from the armchair in the bay window and, red-eyed and unshaven, Ollie rose up like an avenging angel. He must have been there all along, concealed in the big wingback armchair facing out of the bay window. 'Helena, my darling, you are magnificent. You've been listening to the most important story of your childhood and you haven't heard a word.'

Helena went white and clutched her heart with a dramatic gesture. 'Of course I have. I heard everything.'

Ollie walked over and grasped her shoulders. 'So what, my little ostrich, do you feel? Bramble was only five, but you were nine. You must have noticed something of what was happening all around you. Tell us what you *felt*. If you're capable of being that honest with yourself or anyone else.'

Helena's face crumpled. 'You want to know how I felt?' she

shrieked. 'Well, Bramble might think it was lonely for Felicity, but I was totally alone too. *Totally*. There were people screaming, shouting and crying behind locked doors, and no one ever told me what was happening. I thought the world was falling apart and then, when Mummy died, it did.

'Pa spent all his time with the horses and Bramble, every minute, she had all his attention, all his love and everybody thought I was old enough to cope. I had to do everything and nobody seemed to care. I ironed and made beds and burnt myself when I tried to cook . . .' She blew her nose. 'At least we had a family before . . .' she shook her finger at Felicity '. . . before you decided to find yourself in the drug dens of Canterbury. But then it was Pa and Bramble, and you weren't there so I had to do everything on my own.'

'I'm so sorry, Helena,' said Felicity. 'I had to go. I *had* to. I know everyone thought I was selfish, not staying to be the big sister you all needed, but I could see my life disappearing before I'd lived it.'

'You left me alone with *them*,' screamed Helena. 'It was always horses, horses, horses.'

'Just like it's always acting, acting, acting with you,' said Ollie, his voice silky. 'Tell me, is there a single moment in the day when you're not Helena Harris, the actress, and you become Helena Cooper, the wife and mother?'

'Don't be ridiculous,' replied Helena. 'I'm totally a wife and mother now.' She suppressed the thought of how she acted, how even making strawberry jam in the kitchen was played to an invisible audience and re-shaped for a possible bit of publicity. 'I've always set aside time for my family. My acting takes up nothing like as much time and attention as Pa's riding did.'

'It was his job,' said Bramble. 'It was how he earned his money.'

'Oh, it was more than that.' Helena looked up, her face blotched with anger. 'It was his vanity. His pride. His dynasty. That's why you were so important once Felicity went. You were going to be the next Beaumont rider. Nobody thought about how I felt.' She continued to sob. 'Nobody cared about me.'

Ollie, slightly mocking, looked down at her. 'This may come as a shock to you, my sweetheart, but I do.'

'Oh fuck off,' she snarled. 'You only care about your next drink.'

'I'll be in the pub,' said Ollie, 'if anyone needs me.'

'Wait!' screamed Helena, as he slammed the door. 'I didn't mean it! I love you! I do! Wait for me.'

Chapter 36

'The letter,' said Bramble. 'Can I read it?' She held out her hand, and Felicity took the well-fingered document out of her bag.

'I still have to talk to Pauline,' said Felicity, 'but she won't see me.'

'I'll ask her.' Bramble was struggling to come to terms with the fact that the father she had loved and respected seemed to have failed both her elder sisters. 'And I'll come with you.' She held Savannah's icy hands in hers and rubbed them. 'When I've taken Savannah back.' She mustn't let her daughter slip away from her; she must learn from her father and Felicity.

'It was a terrible story,' said Savannah in the car going back to Hightrees House. 'How could Grampa be so awful to her? After what happened?'

'He thought she was ruining her life as well as his,' mused Bramble. 'I think he probably thought that if he was firm enough about it, he could save her.'

'To be the next Beaumont champion?' asked Savannah. 'That's all that mattered to him, wasn't it?'

'I'm sure it wasn't just that. He would have cared about what she really wanted, too, every parent does. If she hadn't been so proud and stayed away so long I'm sure they would have made up.' Bramble hugged Savannah as she handed her back to Vikki. 'See you tomorrow?'

Savannah nodded. She looked very fragile.

Bramble turned back to her. 'You know that you could never

disappoint me, don't you? All that matters is your happiness. Nothing else. Nothing else at all.'

'I don't know how to be happy,' whispered Savannah. 'That's what frightens me.'

When Bramble got back to Lorenden she and Felicity set across the familiar fields together, the dogs pattering behind them and the damp of sunset on the leaves brushing against their sleeves. Bramble was lost in thought.

'Do you think,' she asked Felicity, 'that you *can* get to the top without it being too destructive for the people you love? Do you think ambition just eats everything in its path, and that's why Pa was like that?'

'I don't know. I've never wanted to risk it.'

They arrived at Pauline's gate. The lights were on, and both cars were at home.

'We need to talk,' said Bramble, as Pauline opened the door.

'Alan went into residential accommodation today,' replied Pauline, her eyes dull. 'I've put him in a home. That's what they'll say, isn't it? People will think I've let him down.'

'Oh Pauline, I'm sorry!' Bramble touched her arm. 'We'll go away and come back another time.'

'No, sit down.' Pauline sounded as if she no longer cared about anything. 'We might as well.'

'We've got a letter here from our mother,' said Felicity, and Bramble handed it over. 'We found it in Pa's things.'

Pauline took it reluctantly, then handed it back unread. 'It's none of my business.'

'You can read it if you like. If you don't believe me. In it she makes it clear that she knew all about Pa and Beatrice before I told her. She even thought they'd marry.'

Pauline tightened her lips. 'He would never have married that woman. She was . . . a piece of madness. She was just a flirt. She had to have every man dancing to attention. But once your mother was dead and Bea divorced, well, the time was never quite right. Your father had to build up his career again, thanks to you, and he had to work all the hours God gave him. We bought horses together, he and I – it took a lot of time and hard work to get a horse that good again.'

'And a lot of Alan's money,' said Felicity.

'Yes,' said Pauline. 'Alan was very generous. I wanted to build up a world class stable of horses, and so did your father.'

'And Beatrice Fitzroy didn't quite fit into those plans.'

'No,' said Pauline. 'She didn't. If your father had really loved her . . .'

'You made sure that he didn't,' commented Felicity.

Pauline smiled in acknowledgement of her power. 'Maybe.'

'So our mother didn't die because of Felicity's behaviour. She was dying anyway?' asked Bramble.

'Felicity's behaviour would have hastened her death, I'm sure. Felicity told her that Edward had been unfaithful.'

'But she already knew,' said Felicity. 'Before the party and the death of Merlin. It's all here in the letter. I checked the dates, both the date of the party and that of my mother's death. This letter was written six months before the party and eight months before she died, and it speaks of her only having weeks left to live. But she survived all that time, even after what happened.'

'It's not an exact science, you know. Even doctors can't tell precisely when someone is going to die.'

'No,' replied Felicity, 'and I don't doubt that my mother was very upset by everything I did, which I deeply regret, but if someone who is expected to live a few weeks survives eight months, I hardly think her death can be considered hastened, as you put it.'

Pauline sat in silence, her nostrils slightly flared and a look of distaste on her face.

'Were you in love with my father?' asked Felicity.

'Love! What we had was far deeper and finer than that. We were partners. I expect you think that means we had sex, but I was always loyal to Alan.'

'And Pa wouldn't have you. That was what hurt, wasn't it? You, one of the most beautiful women of your time, and a man wouldn't have you? You couldn't forgive me for knowing that.'

Pauline threw up her hand, as if to ward the accusation off.

'You had no idea about Bea Fitzroy, did you,' continued Felicity, 'until I blew that little secret? That's why you hated me so much.'

Pauline's eyes flashed in fury. 'Felicity, it wasn't just Edward's chance of going to the Olympics you wrecked, it was mine too, remember. I was going to go as an owner, it was my dream, and you, you . . . you didn't care about that, did you? You didn't care how many hopes you shattered as long as you could fuck your moustachioed criminal, thinking you were being so cool.'

Bramble and Felicity froze. They had never heard Pauline swear before.

'Fuck is a good Anglo-Saxon word,' said Pauline. 'And at least it's honest. And yes, I was upset about Bea and your father – I thought he was letting the side down, having an affair when Rose was so ill.'

'What exactly was wrong with her?' asked Bramble. 'I was always told that she'd had a heart attack.' Everyone – perhaps encouraged by Pauline – had always said, in hushed tones, that the stress generated by Felicity's wild behaviour had effectively killed her.

'She did,' said Felicity. 'Her heart was weakened by the chemotherapy of the time. It was very toxic in those days. On her death certificate, which I tracked down recently, two causes of death were given: the heart attack, which finished her off, and the bowel cancer that wore her down. I also managed to talk to her doctor, who still lives near here, and he confirmed it. The cancer – which kept coming back – and all the different treatments they tried proved too much for her in the end.'

'Cancer?' Bramble was surprised. 'Why didn't anyone ever say that she had cancer?'

'People didn't in those days,' said Pauline. 'Cancer was something that no one liked to talk about. It was so often a killer, and people who had it kept it to themselves. And, of course, no one would have wanted you girls to know. It would have upset you.'

'*Those days*,' said Bramble, 'were only the early seventies. Not long ago.'

'Oh, some people had started to be more open even then, especially when some of the treatments started to be successful.' Pauline sounded disdainful of them. 'But Rose was a very private person and there was no way she was going to go round telling all and sundry she had bowel cancer.'

'If I'd known she was really ill, not just a chronic invalid, I would never have left,' said Felicity. 'Someone should have told me. I would have had the chance to talk, to take care of her, just to be there in her last weeks . . .'

'If you'd been the sort of daughter who supported her family rather than rebelling against them, I'm sure someone *would* have told you. But it was up to your parents, and perhaps they didn't feel they could trust you.'

Bramble was stunned.

'There's one thing I want to ask,' Felicity faced Pauline. 'That's what I've come about. Did you tell my father about the rape and what I was threatened with when I asked you to?'

Pauline took a deep breath. 'Not exactly. I told him something . . . but I didn't think he needed to hear the finer detail. Oh, don't look at me like that; you didn't really want him to know or you would have told him yourself!'

Felicity went very white. 'Perhaps you're right. So he never properly knew what I went through?'

'Well, not until someone else told him. About a year ago. He came to me and asked me if it was true, and I said it was. That was when he changed his will. Originally he was going to leave everything to Bramble, so that she could continue with his work, but he said that repairing the family was more important. He felt he owed you, Felicity. I think that's when he decided to bring someone else in, to help Bramble. He thought she needed a partner, someone who wasn't part of everything that had happened to Dom, who could get her to look at things differently.'

'Someone told him a *year* ago?' asked Bramble, barely noticing the reference to herself. 'Who?' Once again, she had the niggling sensation that they were all missing something.

Pauline shrugged. 'It must have been someone who was there. I never told anyone, I promise you that. It was a big party, you know: I'm surprised the story didn't go right round the county.'

'But it didn't,' said Felicity. 'If anyone else had known, it would all have got out at the time and we'd have heard about it. No, the only people who knew about the rape were the men involved, the other people at the party knew nothing. I don't think people even realised much about the death of Merlin. Everyone seemed to accept that he died of colic.'

'Well.' Pauline shrugged. 'In that case, it must have been one of the men involved.'

'They were East End thugs – apart from Ron, they'd hardly have known either who I or Pa was. And both Ron and Ricky died years ago. Anyway, why tell him now?'

'Well, you must have told somebody who told somebody who told him. Or perhaps he'd been thinking about it all and was slowly putting two and two together. I've absolutely no idea how it happened and, if you'll forgive me, I'm feeling very tired.'

'Oh, I'm sorry.' Bramble jumped up.

'At least I now know why he was trying to get in touch with me,' said Felicity.

'You must understand,' said Pauline urgently. 'Your father needed someone to put his interests first. Your mother had been ill, on and off, for years. You, Felicity, were . . .' she shook her head '. . . going off the rails in a very frightening way, and then he had two small girls dependent on him, added to which he was representing his country at the highest level. That alone takes 110 per cent of someone's attention. He needed back-up, and he wasn't getting it. People in your father's position need to be single-minded. That may seem tough, but life is tough, especially competitive life.'

'But if he'd really loved me—' started Felicity.

'Oh, of course he loved you. Don't be so self-pitying.' Pauline's eyes were rimmed in red and she took out a delicate lace handkerchief and dabbed them, careful not to disturb her make-up. 'He and I talked about you for hour after hour, about what was best for you. We thought you'd perhaps had a bit too much responsibility for the little ones in the early days of Rose's illness, that maybe he'd come to rely on you too much too soon, so we thought that if we let you flounce off you'd get it all out of your system and come to your senses.' She faced Felicity squarely. 'We thought it might do you good to get away from home for a bit, but he couldn't just forgive you, not like that. It would be giving out quite the wrong message. We both thought you had to find out that you couldn't make something right just by saying sorry. You had to learn that life wasn't one big party.' Her voice quavered.

'I'm sorry,' said Felicity. 'I was very young. I didn't realise.'

Pauline studied her. 'Yes, you were.' She spoke more gently. 'I tried to tell myself that. But I couldn't forgive you, and I couldn't encourage Edward to forgive you. Not then. But I never thought you'd stay away so long. I thought you would be back. You're both so alike, you and Edward, you never give in. If I'd known . . .' her voice trailed off. Then she made a massive effort: 'I'm sorry too.'

'But why blame Bramble, why desert *her* after he died,' Felicity stood up, 'taking Teddy away just when she really needed him?'

Pauline had never cried in front of anyone before. It was completely counter to her code of behaviour, but she couldn't help her eyes filling again and her voice was so low they could barely hear it.

'Really, Felicity, I do think you are the most self-absorbed person sometimes. It was *nothing* to do with all that, or at least hardly at all. I just couldn't bear going to Lorenden and your father not being there. It hurt so much. All right, you *were* there, Felicity, with your knowing eyes, making me feel guilty and reminding me . . . But mainly Toby offered me a deal I couldn't refuse, when I was at my lowest. In every sense of the word.'

Felicity walked out without saying goodbye, but Bramble held back.

'Pauline,' she said. 'I'm sorry too. I know that when Pa died I was too bound up in everything to see how you were feeling, and I didn't take the time to make you part of the yard I was running. I should look after my owners, and I didn't look after you. I do know that.'

Pauline nodded. 'Possibly, my dear, possibly, but I still shouldn't have done it. Please wait for just a moment.'

Bramble hovered in Pauline's immaculate cream sitting room until she came back with an envelope. 'It's your commission. I know we mentioned it before, but I was too ashamed to get around to paying you what you deserved for working with your father to make Teddy what he is today. It's been on my conscience for a while. When I saw that dear sweet Lottie die like that it made me realise that petty feuds are . . . well, so petty. So unimportant in comparison. Even Edward and Bea – it really didn't matter in the end. His friendship was what I valued.'

Bramble kissed her. 'Pauline, our families have been friends for ever. And I've missed you.'

Pauline patted her hand. 'And I've missed you too. Now go and marry your charming farrier and make all your dreams come true.'

It wasn't until later that evening, when Bramble sat down at her father's desk to write the cheque into the account book, that she looked at how much it was for.

It was a cheque for fifty thousand pounds. There was a note attached: 'This was what Toby paid me for a half share of Teddy. The money belongs to you, so that you can do whatever you want to do. Your father had great faith in you, and so do I.'

It was all very well for Pauline – and Jez – to talk about dreams, thought Bramble, but they didn't have an anorexic daughter and a future husband relying on them.

Bramble knew she had a choice. Try to win again, no matter what it cost her and the people she loved. Or choose the safe route: sell Lorenden and the horses then walk away with her inheritance, to put the people she loved first.

Chapter 37

Eighteen months later, Bramble slipped on a pair of cream trousers and a soft raspberry wool jacket, tailored to create curves on her angular body. She had thought carefully about what to wear – of course, everyone always did – and had decided that she would stick to her own style, tailoring and trousers, but that she wanted colour too, not just cream or white. Helena had given her huge smoky eyes, like a cat's, and teased Bramble's hair out into a pre-Raphaelite cloud. She had let it grow at last, but had had it trimmed and shaped. Looking in the mirror, she knew Jez had been right. It suited her neat outline to look a little wild. She looked like a different Bramble – more confident and powerful. Someone you might turn to look at when she entered a room.

Not that she ever thought of Jez these days. She read about him in the horse magazines and, occasionally, even the newspapers. Helena had shown her an interview with him in some women's glossy and she'd seen him on television, after the cross-country at Burghley, saying that his horse had given him a fantastic ride and thanking his owners. Once or twice she'd seen his name up on the lists when she'd been competing, but something had always conspired to prevent them from meeting, like a horse going lame, the ground being so hard that one or the other had withdrawn or even, on one occasion, they had missed each other by moments, as Jez pulled out, in his smart new lorry with 'Jezzar Morgan Eventing' and several sponsorship slogans inscribed on the side, just as she'd been driving in. He hadn't noticed her or recognised the battered old horsebox.

Bramble slid her engagement ring back onto her newly manicured fingers. Her nails were still short and businesslike, but they had a pale flesh polish on them and the ring sparkled on the third finger of her left hand. Soon there would be another ring there. She zipped up her new, soft beige suede ankle boots and she was ready.

'You look fabulous,' said Helena, discreetly adjusting her own make-up in the mirror. This might be Bramble's day but, of course, Helena herself would be recognised.

Bramble had often thought that it was a day that would never come.

Shortly after Felicity had told them all her story, they'd received an offer for Lorenden from a developer who'd inspected the old county maps showing that there had once been cottages in the field across the road – indeed the field shelter with its corrugated iron roof was, when you looked closely, the remnant of one of them. Planning permission to build eleven houses on the field had been applied for, but had been turned down, thus losing them the sale, but another developer had come forward, one with a passion for history. He was now applying to reconstruct the original grouping of half a dozen cottages in vernacular style, using local materials and creating something that was both historically appropriate and ecologically outstanding. There was, apparently, even some excitement about the prospect of such housing being built and the neighbours, who had mounted a vigorous campaign of objection to the first developer's proposals, were cautiously enthusiastic about the plans of the second, especially as they were beginning to see that such a development might well add value and prestige to their own homes.

But it had all taken eighteen months, during which Bramble, Felicity and Helena – who had finally given Ollie an ultimatum to stop drinking and had separated from him – had lived together and run the Lorenden yard.

Bramble and Felicity had concentrated on Shaggy, as well as two ex-racehorses they were turning round for specific clients, bringing on the three young horses that Edward had bred and, finally, a gentle but steady programme aimed at ironing out Merlin's quirks and channelling his obvious talent. Shaggy was a rule unto herself – she'd be the sweetest horse in the stable all week, then, if you were ten minutes late for her feed on Saturday she'd stamp on her bucket and flatten it. She loaded smoothly and happily nine times out of ten, and on the tenth it could take half an hour to get her in the lorry. Bramble, remembering Mulberry Hill and the day Lottie had died, always wanted to withdraw on these occasions, but Felicity stopped her: 'Don't go down the route of lucky signs and omens,' she insisted. 'It'll damage your performance. Good preparation and concentration, that's all you need.'

Bramble, when she saw the mists in the orchard, never allowed herself to feel that sense of suffocating fear again. Or was it that the mist was different? She closed the shutters firmly on such thoughts.

In the first few months, after evening stables, Bramble got into the car and drove to Savannah at Hightrees House, where she now shared a room with another girl, who was in for self-harming.

'Everybody's really weird here,' Savannah said. 'But they're nice. We sit in circles and talk about ourselves. They've all had terrible lives.' She bit her nails nervously. 'And I haven't; I've been so lucky. I don't belong here.'

Bramble told her that she was not planning to marry Nat for at least a year. She was rewarded by a smile.

She and Savannah had sessions together with Vikki.

'I rang the junior regional selector,' said Bramble, 'and she was very nice. She said she quite understood you wouldn't be well enough this year, but she'd look forward to following your progress next year.'

'Next year!' Savannah sat up. 'No! That's too late. I'll be fine by next week, I know I will.'

'We don't want to place any time pressures on you,' said Vikki.

'But next year's too late!' cried Savannah.

'You'll barely be eighteen,' said Bramble, puzzled. 'It's not too late at all.'

'It'll be too late to save Lorenden,' said Savannah, as if Bramble was very stupid. 'Grampa said it was all up to me.'

Vikki and Bramble looked at each other.

'It's not up to you, Savannah. Lorenden will be sold some time, definitely,' said Bramble. 'And you and I can set up a yard together if that's what you want. But you don't have to.'

'But will we be able to afford it? If I don't get sponsorship? Suppose the old horses, like Patch, have to go?'

'Savannah,' said Bramble. 'What did Grampa say to you?'

'He said he didn't want me to turn out like Felicity.'

'It seems as if Pa put the fear of God into her,' said Bramble over a late supper in the kitchen. 'Made her feel as if everything hung on her shoulders. And, of course, she's so inexperienced that she thinks sponsorship would save Lorenden, when it's actually peanuts most of the time. There's no way a girl in her teens or early twenties could ever have earned enough, and Pa should never have let her think she could. I'm so angry with him.'

'Now you know how I feel,' said Helena.

'And me,' added Felicity.

'If only he was here . . .' said Bramble, fuming.

'But he's not,' said Felicity in a wry tone. 'We've got to make our own mistakes now, we can't go on blaming him any more.'

'I miss him so much,' said Helena in a small voice, 'that I can hardly bear it.'

Savannah was warily unravelling her life.

'So when was it decided that you would leave school at sixteen to pursue a riding career?' asked Vikki. 'Did you feel pressured into it, coming from a famous riding family?'

Savannah explained that all she'd ever wanted was to be a professional eventer and that she had, in fact, had to fight Bramble hard to get her to agree. 'I was so happy when Mum finally gave in last year, I just knew that was what I wanted to do with my life . . . and I still do,' she added hastily, as Vikki made notes.

Vikki let a silence hang in the air.

'Really,' added Savannah. 'And anyway . . .'

Vikki studied her carefully.

'. . . I'm seventeen now. It's too late for me to change my mind.'

'Savannah, nothing is too late when you're seventeen.'

⋆

'We need to talk about Jez,' Vikki said at the next therapy session.

Savannah twisted in her chair. 'I feel so-o-o stupid.'

'You weren't stupid,' said Bramble, flushing with her own guilt. 'It was his fault, he should have known.'

'What should he have known?' asked Vikki. They talked over how Savannah's feelings had become an obsession.

'We didn't do anything, I promise,' said Savannah, forced to remember, now that she could stand back and see things more clearly, that she had been the one to press kisses on him. With a flood of mortification, she now remembered the strength of his arms. Pushing her away. Gently disentangling himself after that first brief touch of their lips. She had not been loved. She had been rejected.

'He was just friendly and nice, and I thought . . . It was so scary at home when Grampa died, and Jez made it safe for us. For me, anyway. But I can see that now. I'm not . . . not . . . thinking about him like that any more.'

'Why not?' asked Vikki gently.

Savannah flushed. 'When Donna – that's our groom – told me that he'd shagged Felicity. She's my aunt,' she added. 'Donna saw Felicity coming down from his flat one morning. And then I realised that we'd only had a silly kiss, and not even that, really. He obviously only wanted Felicity. He probably thought I was an immature schoolgirl.'

Bramble could barely believe it. Jez, in the space of only a few months, had been making love to Felicity, flirting with Savannah and then the night – now embarrassing to think of – with herself. Savannah must never find out. Even though, of course, nothing had happened between her and Jez. When he'd first left she'd hoped they could stay friends, but she didn't want friends who betrayed her.

Nat, once again, had been right all along.

On the way home she resolved to make it up to Nat. She would sign the piece of paper that secured Nat's business against her share of Lorenden.

'We've been talking about Lottie,' said Vikki, at the next session.

Savannah's heart twisted in pain and she wanted to change the subject, the way she did when people tried to talk to her about Lottie. 'I can't really believe she's not there any more,' she whispered. 'And I feel really guilty, not eating, when she died like that. She would love to be alive, and eating muffins – she loved muffins – and riding Sailor.'

'And you?' asked Vikki.

'I want to be alive, of course . . .' said Savannah hesitantly. 'Of course.'

Vikki listened quietly, and Bramble held her breath.

'And I've been thinking about Felicity and what she told us. How Pa said once that I reminded him of her. I thought that meant I was bad, but maybe he meant someone who wanted something else.'

Vikki exchanged looks with Bramble as Savannah curled into a tight ball and began to cry. 'Lottie should be here, she shouldn't have been the one to die.'

'It's all right.' Vikki spoke gently. 'You can let yourself enjoy life again. It isn't wrong to want to be happy.'

'It's too late,' sobbed Savannah. 'I've screwed everything up so much. Here, Mum,' she got a small badge out of her pocket, 'it's Lottie's Pony Club badge. I found it in my box. I was going to ride in the nationals for her. Will you keep it for me? And wear it when you compete somewhere special?'

'Why can't you wear it when you compete somewhere special?' asked Bramble.

Vikki and Savannah looked at each other. 'It's OK,' said Vikki softly. 'It's OK to want something different.'

'You see, Mum, would you mind terribly . . . I think I'd like to go back to school next year and do A levels. I want to go to university, I think – oh, I don't know what I want to do, but I don't think I can be the next Beaumont rider after all. Or at least not yet. When Grampa asked me if I really wanted to be a rider, I suddenly thought, Oh! Maybe I don't want to after all. I think he saw that, but I was too scared to change my mind. Not after trying so hard for so long.'

It wasn't easy after that – nothing you really wanted was ever easy, thought Bramble, and this would probably all stay in

Savannah's head for life – but Savannah tried. Most weeks she gained a few ounces, and occasionally she lost them again, and, at the end of six months, she was still underweight but she had gained half a stone. 'You have to get to a certain weight,' said Vikki, 'to turn your brain on properly again. Then you can really get better.'

'I will,' declared Savannah. 'I'm going to get better for Lottie. So as not to waste life.' She went to a new school – a sixth form college – and turned her powerful work ethic, learned from the horses and the routine of the stableyard, to catching up with her studies.

Bramble looked at herself in the mirror again, at the cloud of hair and the raspberry jacket and felt the butterflies in her tummy. Savannah would be out there with all the others, waiting for her, looking pretty and definitely more confident, with a friend from her new school, a boy called Tom who always seemed to be near her. You could never say you'd won – there was always another hill to climb – but she thought that Savannah was fine for now.

Helena's mobile trilled.

'Hi.'

'It's me,' said the laid-back voice that still made Helena's heart leap.

'Hi Ollie.' Helena kept her voice calm. She never wanted him to see how much she still loved him. The house in Primrose Hill had sold, for far less than Helena thought it was really worth, its air of desolation having done it no favours. Helena had insisted that the money left over go to pay their debts. 'I've faced the worst when I thought Eddie was dead,' she'd told Ollie. 'And then again when I thought I'd been voted out of *Simon's Way*. Now I know I don't mind being poor.'

'Hardly poor,' Ollie had said. 'You've got a third of Lorenden if you'd only get on and sell it. I think you're all clinging on, making excuses because you can't let go. You've got to say goodbye to that father of yours and move on.'

Helena had told herself that while she was working again it made no financial sense to divorce Ollie legally, but she'd asked him to move out and stop drinking. He now rented a room from Nat, and the two of them got along surprisingly well.

'How's Bramble doing?' asked Ollie.

'I've just got her ready. She looks fantastic. Everything's going swimmingly. We're just about to—'

'I'm ringing up to propose.'

'Propose what?'

'I'm ringing up to propose that we get back together. Nat and I are sitting here talking about the meaning of love, and I still love you.'

'Are you two drinking?' asked Helena suspiciously, who thought that two men talking about the meaning of love at half-past three on a Wednesday afternoon was a very unlikely scenario unless they were on to the second bottle. 'You promised you wouldn't. And Bramble wouldn't want Nat to get here looking like an old tramp and stinking of booze.'

'We could renew our vows,' he said, ignoring her question. 'In the old church at Lorenden. Have a bit of a party.'

'We could . . .' Helena was excited. 'But we'd have to earn – both of us – and not go into debt again.'

'Well, if you can stop shopping,' he said. 'I think we could do it.'

'And if you could stop drinking.'

'Oh Helena.' The exasperation in Ollie's voice came clearly down the line. 'You won't face up to the mess you've made of your own life. You've always got to find someone to blame, and that someone is always going to be me.'

'No, stop,' cried Helena. 'I'll change, I promise I will . . .'

But the line was dead.

Helena knew she had no time to think about calling him back. This was Bramble's day. With her heart breaking, she straightened the little brooch on Bramble's jacket, pasted on her actress smile and the two of them got into Helena's car.

After parking the car, Helena and Bramble showed their security passes and walked under the huge limestone arches of Badminton House and through to the stable quadrangle. A procession of proud, beautiful horses were being led round the yard, every one plaited and groomed to perfection, at the peak of fitness, their gleaming bodies packed with finely-honed muscle and their pricked ears showing their excitement. Every few minutes a horse peeled off to take its turn to trot up in front of Badminton House, the judges and the first eager spectators. Once passed as fit to compete, it was led back again, while others – eighty-six of them in total – emerged from the stables and joined the flow. There among them, stepping out as elegantly as a ballet dancer, was Shaggy, led by Felicity. They looked up at the stable clock.

'It's time,' said Felicity.

'Yes,' said Bramble, her stomach churning. 'It's time.'

Helena slipped out to the front, behind the ropes that separated the spectators from the horses, and found Eddie, Savannah and Tom, who had bagged her a place on one of the huge haycarts parked in front of the house for those who wanted to watch the trot-up. Eddie and Tom stretched out their hands to help her clamber up, and Helena clocked a few heads turning to recognise her with a feeling of satisfaction. And that Tom was a nice young man, she thought, giving Savannah's friend a second look. She wondered if Savannah realised how often he looked at her. It would be good for Savannah to have a boyfriend, very good.

Inside the stable yard, Felicity handed over Shaggy's lead rope and slipped her rug off. Bramble led the horse out to the outer courtyard and turned left under the great arch, to come out in front of Badminton House. Shaggy's hooves, dancing with anticipation, crunched on the gravel and a sea of faces watched every movement. The only people that mattered, however, were the ground jury, a trio of formally dressed and serious-looking officials.

The first inspection at Badminton on the Wednesday afternoon. They had made it. So often in the past eighteen months she had despaired of ever getting here.

'Number twenty-seven, Chequerboard Charlotte, owned by Mrs Bramble Kelly and Miss Savannah Kelly, and ridden by Mrs Bramble Kelly,' declared the commentator and she jogged forwards, extending into a run to trot Shaggy along the graceful Palladian frontage, past the ground jury, turning her round at the end and running back, trying to keep her steps even and smooth in the new suede boots. Shaggy swung alongside, occasionally whinnying or throwing her head up, fired up with the tension of the occasion.

The three members of the ground jury debated between themselves and she was asked to trot up again. Bramble's heart plummeted. They weren't quite satisfied.

The second run was harder, because her breath seemed to be stuck in her throat. She thought of all the times she and Felicity had got up at five to jog before morning stables. 'Think of the trot-up at Badminton,' Felicity had said over and over again in the cold and the dark. 'You've got to be fit for that.'

Felicity had never for one moment – not even when Shaggy went lame or had a sore back, or refused to go into the showjumping arena or got over-excited in the dressage – ever allowed Bramble to think that they wouldn't get here. Bramble ran up and down again, thinking of Felicity's fierce determination and how it had propelled her through, and telling herself that Shaggy was 100 per cent fit and that the ground jury would see that. They couldn't have come so far just to be turned away at the door. Barely one horse in a hundred failed at this point.

The president of the ground jury raised his bowler hat to the commentary box.

'Number twenty-seven, Chequerboard Charlotte, has been accepted.' The commentator noted the raised bowler hat and its significance, then she was back through the arch again, Felicity laughing in relief.

'Did you see?' whispered Savannah to Tom on the haycart. 'Mum's wearing my friend Lottie's Pony Club badge.'

Tom discreetly entwined his fingers with hers. She was aware of the warmth of his body and the electricity where they touched.

In the stables, all anyone could talk about was the weather. The past five weeks had been unusually hot and dry, but rain was forecast and although the organisers had prepared the ground beautifully, adding topsoil and working it in, they were reluctant to water too often in case they were swamped by a deluge. The clear blue skies and the heat – almost a baking heat for early May –

contradicted the weathermen. With the World Championships that year, albeit another four months away, several riders in national teams had withdrawn their horses, citing the hard ground and concern for their horses' legs. The majority, though, looked at the preparations and held their nerve. It'll ride OK, they said to each other, but there was a question mark in everyone's voices.

There was the usual rash of articles trying to predict the eventual winner. About a dozen riders were repeatedly named – the head of the German team, Klaus Jürgen; Betsy Parker, the top American rider; Britain's four World Championship hopefuls; two or three riders who had already won Badminton and were still at the top of their game; plus a handful who were just beginning to make their mark, and who might give the established names a run for their money. Jezzar Morgan was named as one of these. Properly funded at last, with wealthy owners based near Cirencester, Jez had had several good two- and three-star wins so far in the season, and had been lucky enough to be offered a last-minute Badminton ride on a top horse, Fireflight, whose rider had broken his leg. 'One to watch' was the pundits' view.

Bramble had barely been mentioned, although there had been two lines in one pre-Badminton round-up: 'Bramble Kelly, who was married to top rider Dom Kelly (killed at Thurlwood eight years ago) has been making her own name in the sport over the past few years. This is her first four-star since her husband's death, and her so-far successful partnership with quirky little "pony" Chequerboard Charlotte could yet provide some surprises.'

What sort of surprises? Bramble decided not to think about what they might have meant. Her goal was to get to the top twenty, the televised showjumping finale on the Sunday afternoon. That would tell everyone that Bramble Kelly was no longer just Dom Kelly's widow or Edward Beaumont's daughter, but a rider in her own right. And it would make any foals Shaggy might have very much more valuable.

Looking at the entries, she could see more than twenty riders who belonged up there ahead of her.

Bramble's dressage test was on Thursday, at midday, and throughout the night she'd woken at almost hourly intervals, hoping to hear rain on the roof of the horsebox, hearing low murmurs and the occasional shout of laughter from the other boxes. The eighty-six competitors and their entourages were all packed into three lorry parks, and there was hardly space to put up a picnic table and a few folding chairs between each horsebox. She and Felicity were staying in the lorry; Savannah, Eddie and their friends were sharing a caravan on the campsite, and Helena was in a hotel, although they all often came back to the lorry for meals. Nat would be coming up for Thursday. The lorry, therefore, was like a shrunken-down version of the kitchen at Lorenden, always full of people, gossip and the smell of food or brewing coffee. Only at night was it quiet, creaking as Bramble or Felicity turned in their sleep.

Bramble got to the stables at eight-thirty to plait up Shaggy. A heat haze already shimmered over the grounds and the mare was fired up and ready to go – perhaps too fired up – so, aching with lack of sleep, Bramble saddled her up half an hour early to work off the excess energy in the practice arena.

'Doing Pony Club, are you?' Toby Fitzroy, looking like a Jane Austen hero in his cream breeches, black tailcoat and white stock, cantered into the practice ring on Teddy. His test was just before hers.

'Small is beautiful, didn't you know?' she flashed back, squinting up at him in the sun. Yellow rape fields spread out in the distance, and the blue-and-white striped marquees of Badminton fluttered like tents at a medieval tournament. She could feel sweat trickling down the back of her neck. Teddy turned his ears towards her in recognition. She imagined that he was saying he wished he was still with the Lorenden yard, but if any horse could offer Toby the victory he craved it would be her dear Teddy.

Shaggy looked like a patchwork donkey compared to him and the other magnificent dressage machines that seemed to be trotting on air. These would get good marks for the sheer beauty of their big, athletic stride, but only absolute accuracy and complete obedience would secure Shaggy and Bramble a decent ranking. 'Never throw away a single mark,' said Felicity in training, over and over again.

Felicity, and their dressage trainer Miranda, watched from the other side of the white picket fence, arms folded, Miranda occasionally stepping forward to give advice.

Bramble watched Toby Fitzroy go in then – all too soon – a smatter of clapping at the end signalled her turn. She could hear his score over the loudspeaker: 63.5. Position twelfth.

He raised his hand to her in greeting as they passed each other and Bramble was disconcerted, her mind tugged away from the test in front of her.

'Focus,' hissed Felicity from the sidelines. 'Don't give away a single mark.'

Bramble dragged her tired, aching brain back to the test and, as she cantered in, everything cleared. All she was aware of was the steady rhythm of Shaggy beneath her, the contact of the mare's mouth on the reins and her own body straight and still as they cantered down the centre line and halted, four square, to salute the judges.

She took a deep breath and began a succession of rhythmical half-circles, feeling Shaggy respond to each twitch of the reins and every touch of her heels. The shoulder-in – beautiful. Bramble smiled. Then half-pass. Perhaps not as good. Bramble forced herself not to be distracted by the inevitability of lost marks. The crowd seemed to be silently concentrating with her, and all she could hear was the steady creak-creak of the saddle and the regular thud of Shaggy's hooves on the grass.

The slow bits were the hardest – getting a horse at the peak of its fitness and ready to run for its life to slow down and stretch out its neck in a relaxed, easy walk was often impossible – but Shaggy was at her sweetest and most reasonable. Then a collected trot, then another halt, not quite square, perhaps, and the rein back, always a little clumsy – more marks lost but don't think about that now – then into canter and more circles and serpentines. One last flying change and they were heading back down the centre line for the last time, in a rocking-horse canter, for a four-square halt, Bramble bowing her head to the judges.

Bramble knew she'd done well from the powerful burst of clapping that erupted over her head and, as she rode out, grinning and patting Shaggy vigorously, she looked up to where the electronic scoreboard registered a score of 42.5 and her position as third.

'Third!' squealed Helena, hugging Bramble as, safely back in the practice arena, she slid off.

Felicity, too, patted Shaggy enthusiastically and fed her mints. 'Don't forget, Helena, that two-thirds of the field are still to do their tests.'

'And most of the best riders still to come,' sighed Savannah, 'but fantastic start. Fantastic, well done Mum.'

Even with her mind still on the test, Bramble couldn't help noticing that Savannah and Tom were holding hands.

As the shadows lengthened over the afternoon the sun baked the ground. There were queues for ice cream and people fanned themselves with their programmes. Every time Bramble checked the scoreboard her heart crashed in her chest as she saw her position slip. By four o'clock, and in ninth place, she decided to concentrate on the party that night and forget about anybody else's scores. It only made her smile slightly to note that Toby Fitzroy had gone down to thirty-fifth, plummeting down the rankings even faster than she was. Teddy deserved better.

Savannah couldn't believe she was actually going to the cocktail party, the most coveted invitation of the year. The thick cream card invited riders and owners – and a guest each – to drinks with the Duke and Duchess of Beaufort in the main house. Eddie and Felicity had attended the grooms' party at Badminton village hall instead ('The only place to get the real gossip,' said Felicity, with a smile) but Nat, Bramble and Savannah – with Helena booked in months ago as her guest – queued up to be announced. Helena threw off her pashmina: 'It's so hot for May, really stifling. You'd have thought it might be cooler in the evening.'

Bramble fretted about Shaggy's legs on the hard ground. 'They're watering the course,' she said anxiously. 'But three more riders have pulled out.'

'Don't worry,' said Nat, hugging her. 'It'll be all right on the night, as they say.'

Savannah found that spending less time with her family, going to a different school and no longer being caught up in the desperate race for eventing success had given her a more relaxed perspective on both her irritating mother and her bumbling boyfriend. She had almost even forgiven him for being about to marry her.

'He's all right, really,' she'd said to Eddie the night before. 'He just goes on a bit. And he's so embarrassing.'

'They're all embarrassing. And my mum will have him if yours gets bored of him. She goes on all the time about how attractive he is, and how lucky Bramble is.'

'She wouldn't.'

'No, she wouldn't,' confirmed Eddie. 'But she is a bit desperate. Nobody has asked her out for about three months and the last man wore pyjamas under his trousers. Anyway, I think Nat's frightened of you. He's shy.'

'What?'

'Well, if you don't like him it makes things difficult with Bramble, so he's trying to get you on his side.'

'Well I wish he'd stop trying so hard.'

Savannah resolved to be nicer to him, even though Nat's idea of making conversation to a teenager was to tell her interesting facts.

'Did you know that the amount of goods sold by the trade stalls at Badminton are equivalent to the entire shopping area of a city?' he said as they shuffled along in the welcome queue.

She tried to think of a polite reply, such as asking which city – as there seemed to her to be quite a difference between the 'amount of goods' sold in Canterbury and, say, Birmingham – but he didn't seem to know.

'Don't you think it's amazing,' added Nat, turning to her just before they were about to be announced by a butler, 'that the Duke and Duchess stand at the door and shake everyone's hand as they come in? That must be over five hundred handshakes.'

'Mrs Bramble Kelly and Mr Nat Croft,' announced the butler.

Savannah heard the Duchess say how sorry she'd been to hear that Edward had died, and then it was her turn.

'Miss Savannah Kelly and Mrs Helena Harris.'

Then they grabbed a glass and were through, into a throng of people who all were all greeting each other like old friends. Savannah was overwhelmed by the huge hall, with its black-and-white chequerboard floor and massive family portraits.

'What you may not know,' whispered Nat in her ear, 'is that

this is the room where the game of shuttlecock was invented, which is why it's called badminton.'

Savannah had only the vaguest idea of what shuttlecock was, and hoped she wasn't going to be trapped with him and his relentless information all evening, but the press of people swirled them onwards and, free from her family, she was able to drink it all in. The first person she saw was Jez.

'How are you?' he asked gently, as if he really wanted to know.

'Fine.' She was surprised to realise it was true. She *was* fine. And she was pleased to see Jez, but that was it. She no longer felt dizzy and desperate for him to take notice of her. She was more interested in Tom, drinking lager back in the caravan, waiting for her to get back and tell her all about the party. 'What's Fireflight like?'

'He's a fantastic horse.'

'I hope you win.'

'You should be hoping your mum will win.'

'Oh, she's not going to,' said Savannah. 'She was lying ninth when we last looked and there were still about ten more tests to come, and then everyone tomorrow.'

'She's still ninth, I checked. Not bad at the end of the first day. There's still everything to play for.'

'Well, one of you must come first and the other second.'

He smiled and touched her shoulder. 'I'll do my best.'

Bramble saw quite a few familiar faces, but even more new ones. When she'd last come to this party, nine years ago, when Dom had still been alive, they had known everyone. Now she almost felt like an outsider, in spite of her successful season so far.

'Darling,' said a voice, kissing Nat on both cheeks.

Bramble turned to find a smartly dressed woman with deep lines of dissatisfaction etched around her mouth.

'Bramble, this is Penny Luckham. Penny, do you know Bramble Kelly, who's competing here?'

Penny Luckham leaned in very close. 'Didn't Jezzar Morgan come to you after he left my place?'

Bramble nodded. She wondered if Penny might be slightly drunk.

'Biggest mistake of my life, getting involved with him,' said

Penny in a slurred voice. 'I hear there was some problem with your daughter.'

'No, there wasn't.'

Penny drew back and tried to focus on Bramble's face, as if she didn't believe her. 'Really? I must have been misinformed.'

'You were,' said Bramble, aware of Nat hovering. Fortunately he had the tact to remain silent.

'Why did Jezzar leave your yard then?' Penny delivered the question with the victorious tone of someone who'd rumbled her opponent.

Bramble swallowed. 'He got a better offer.' It was almost true.

'Well,' said Penny, with an air of triumph. 'That sounds pretty typical. He stole some money and a pair of cufflinks from me. Took them off the mantelpiece. I had to call the police.'

It confirmed Nat's story. Bramble shrank away in dislike. It was none of her business, and she didn't want intimate confidences from someone she'd only just met.

Nat grabbed her elbow. 'Sorry, we must go. Lovely to see you, Pen.' And he steered Bramble through the oak-panelled inner hall, past the backs of hundreds of people – riders, owners, officials and members of the Beaufort Hunt. The party occupied the whole of the ground floor, from the great hall, past the stunning curved oak staircase, through a number of ante-rooms, then in to a sitting room that was nearly the size of all Lorenden's reception rooms together – although, oddly enough, it felt just as homely – and, finally, the ballroom with its glittering chandeliers, parquet dance-floor and little gilt chairs around the edge. Snatches of conversation emerged from the roar: 'You'll never guess who was seen coming out of Toby Fitzroy's lorry this morning', 'I didn't put the brakes on hard enough', 'Frances told me they paid a hundred and ninety grand for that horse', and 'He's just obsessed with mares, I don't know what to do about it'.

'Penny can be a bit intense sometimes. I thought you needed rescuing.' Nat came to a halt in the sitting room.

'Yes, thanks, she was awful.' Bramble was so hot she could hardly breathe. An old friend of Dom's, a rider who'd moved to the States, kissed her on both cheeks and she was just beginning to talk to him, when Nat grabbed her again.

'Bram, we need to find Savannah and make sure she's all right.'

Bramble disentangled herself. 'You go on without me.'

'No, no, I . . .' he broke off.

'Hello Bramble. And Nat.' It was Jez with a thin, nervous-looking woman.

'Is this some kind of joke?' Nat demanded.

'Bramble, this is Jenny Croft, an old friend of mine.' Jez introduced them.

'My ex-wife,' said Nat harshly. 'Now if you've had your little laugh, we really must go.'

'Oh Jenny, hello. It's so nice to meet you.' Bramble didn't think the woman looked mad or hysterical. Just tired and worried. 'Have you brought Gemma with you? I'd love to meet her, and so would Savannah.'

'She's staying with a friend.' Jenny bit her nails and then dropped her hand.

'We're going,' said Nat, taking Bramble's hand and dragging her off. 'Goodbye.'

'Nat, that was rude,' hissed Bramble once they'd battled through the crowds and were out of earshot.

'I don't know what he's playing at.'

'He's probably not playing at anything. He knows Jenny and asked her to be his guest. You're not worried that they're . . .'

'Of course I'm not fucking worried that they're having an affair. I'm more concerned that he's brought her down here to put you off your stride.'

'That's absurd. Why would he? It's not as if I'm going to win or anything. There are at least a dozen other riders he needs to put off their strides before bothering with me.'

She stopped. Not as if I'm going to win or anything. Well, she wouldn't with an attitude like that. Never give away a single mark, she told herself again. Never.

'Nat. I think you're making too much of this. Lots of people think their divorced partners are hell on earth, when they're really just normal people.'

He laughed and pulled her to him. 'Good old think-the-best-of-everyone Bramble. Listen, darling, I want to talk to you. About tomorrow.'

Bramble struggled out of his arms and looked up at him.

'I'm sure you'll be brilliant. And I'm sure there won't be any accidents. But I have to ask you what provision you've made for Savannah if something did happen.'

Bramble was chilled. 'My share of everything goes straight to her.'

'That's what I was worried about. Savannah's still young and she's very vulnerable. I thought perhaps you should write up a quick, simple trust so that someone could look after her.'

'Felicity and Helena would look after her.'

'Helena can't look after her own children, and Felicity will be off. She was talking about it the other day.'

'She didn't . . .'

'Oh she didn't want to distract you before Badminton, but I overheard her talking to Helena. You know her: she never stays anywhere long. What I was going to suggest – just as a temporary measure, and I'm absolutely 100 per cent certain it won't be needed – is that you make me a trustee for Savannah until she's twenty-one.'

Bramble couldn't take it on board. 'Doesn't that mean lawyers and stuff?'

'I hope you don't mind, but I typed something up. I just want you to be able to compete with complete peace of mind. You can rescind it all after Sunday, if you like.'

As they left Badminton House to walk back to the lorry park, past the tented city where stallholders were celebrating the end of the first day's takings by opening bottles and picnics, there was a massive rumble of thunder.

Bramble jumped as a bolt of lightning flashed across the horizon and huge raindrops began to fall. Then she let out a shriek of joy: 'Rain! Just in time.' She stuck her tongue out to taste the raindrops and Nat looked at her as if she was mad.

'Just what we need. Yes, OK, you're probably right. I'll sign.' She told herself it was nice, the way Nat thought of everything. He was so protective.

Chapter 38

The following day Bramble walked the cross-country course again. The rain, falling ferociously during the night on top of all the watering that had been done when the ground was rock hard, had turned parts of the course into a quagmire. Frantic pumping-out operations were taking place. Groups of riders and their trainers congregated around increasingly large puddles, shaking their heads as it continued to pour down on their umbrellas and big bush hats. Some of the most successful eventers, those who'd entered two horses originally, had already withdrawn the one that coped least well with hard ground. This left them with top-of-the-ground horses that would have skimmed comparatively happily over rock, but who hated mud.

Shaggy, who had a good dose of Irish hunter in her blood, would probably relish the change of going, but it would jump differently and Bramble, like everyone else, had to rethink her strategy. She stood beside massive brush fences, logs, gates and rails that seemed as large as she was, and clambered up on to the Bank and dropped down into the Sunken Road to try to judge what Shaggy would see, how far away she would take off and where she might land. The Vicarage Vee, with its gigantic ditches, terrified her as much as ever, and the Lake, the most famous obstacle in eventing, presented a classic opportunity for a thorough dunking. There were always the most spectators round this, drawn by the prospect of riders falling off. 'At least we won't get any wetter than we are already,' she sighed, raindrops trickling down her nose.

'Mind you,' said Felicity. 'The ground's been well prepared, so all we need is for the sun to come out again and it'll be perfect going.'

The sun did not come out.

Bramble decided to watch Jez's dressage test. Knowing that she could only slip down the rankings, she couldn't bear to check the leaderboard, particularly as Betsy Parker, the American, going just before Jez, scored an amazing 35.1 on the electronic scoreboard, registering 'Position: 1st' beside it. 'I could have slipped out of the top twenty by now,' thought Bramble. Betsy, with that score, would be pretty much unbeatable if she went clear in the cross-country.

Fireflight was one of those long-striding horses that would gain good dressage marks, and Jez emerged with a score of 39.8. 'Another one ahead of me,' said Bramble quietly to her boots, deciding that this was death by slow torture and that she had better either walk the course again or go back to the lorry. She couldn't resist a quick peek at the leaderboard on her way past, and was surprised to see that Jez was not far above her, in eleventh place, and that she had only dropped to fourteenth. There was still the afternoon to go, though, including a British Olympic gold medallist on a superb horse called Sunburst, who always scored brilliantly in the dressage, not to mention the current European champion and another rider who had won Badminton three times.

'Oh dear, I never really understand any of this,' said a hesitant voice from under an umbrella. It was Jenny Croft.

'In the dressage, the lower the score the better,' answered Bramble. 'That's all you have to remember. Then after that you don't want to get any more penalties. So the lowest score overall wins.'

Jenny smiled and Bramble, on impulse, suggested a coffee.

'This is so kind of you,' said Jenny, stirring the froth on a cappuccino. They had to pull their chairs in tightly to avoid the drips coming off the awning above them. 'And so kind of Jez. I couldn't believe it when he invited me. I've always wanted to go to Badminton, but . . . you know how things are.' She flashed a quick, nervous smile.

'Have you come all the way from Newcastle?' Bramble was still trying to equate her with the harridan that Nat had told her about.

'No, we managed to get a part-housing association, part-private ownership house near a good school this side of Bristol. It was a bit scary, moving us both away from where we had so many friends, but it's worked out.'

She must have seen Bramble looking puzzled because she added, 'My half of the house wasn't really enough to buy another house with, but we've been really lucky with this housing association thing. And there are lots of other divorced parents there, so it's nice for Gemma.'

Bramble couldn't think of a reply.

'Of course, it was a bit of an upheaval because I'd lived near Newcastle all my life. In fact, I'd grown up in the house we sold.' She clearly found Bramble's blank look disconcerting, because she began to gabble. 'My mother left it to me when she died. But that's divorce, isn't it? It hurts everyone. It's not anyone's fault, it just happens.'

'Why did you divorce?' Bramble asked, almost in a whisper. 'If you don't mind my asking?'

'Nat lost his job. He was working in a firm of accountants and they were taken over. And he got very depressed because we went quite heavily into debt. I got part-time work in a supermarket stacking shelves because I could choose my own hours and work round Gemma's school, but he thought it was too menial. It was as if I was proclaiming to the world that he couldn't look after us. So I don't blame him for getting angry. I wasn't very good with him – I used to make him angry all the time.'

Bramble remembered what Nat had said about Jenny's lies. 'Was there anyone else involved?'

'I don't think so. Well, not on my part. He was out quite a lot once he decided to re-train to be a blacksmith, and I don't think he . . . I did find someone briefly, after he left, and we hoped to . . . but, well, it didn't work out.'

'How sad,' said Bramble, trying not to show how shocked she was. A provincial firm of accountants, not a hotshot city job. A half-share in the house instead of losing it all. Nat walking out, not Jenny being unfaithful. Gemma in Bristol, not Newcastle. Either

Jenny was a pathological liar, or Nat was. And if Nat did have half of the proceeds of the house in Newcastle, why had he needed to secure his mortgage against her share of Lorenden? 'Look, it's been lovely meeting you, but I must check on my horse.'

'Oh, of course.' Jenny jumped up. 'I'm sorry, I didn't think. I've been jabbering on about myself. By the way, good luck tomorrow. I think you're so brave.'

'Have you heard . . .' said Hannah, Toby's groom, when Bramble, having struggled through the mud, arrived at the stables. 'Sunburst has got serious colic. They're operating on him now.'

That was the Olympic gold medallist out of the frame, thought Bramble, but she felt a sharp pang of sympathy for him. One minute he'd been a favourite to win, the next he was pacing up and down praying that his beloved horse would make it through the next few hours. It could have happened to any of them.

Her first instinct was to check that Shaggy was fine. She strode into the stables, down a seemingly endless corridor with dark red looseboxes down one side and windows along the other. Each team's space was neatly marked out opposite its box with an orderly pile of straw, hay, feed and an upended wheelbarrow. Shaggy was looking out, enjoying the bustle and the presence of so many other horses. Bramble went into the loosebox and laid her head against the muscular brown and white neck, stroking her shining coat. 'You and me, Shaggy. That's all that matters,' she whispered. Everything else was white noise. Who should she believe? Jenny or Nat? Nat, of course. But Jenny hadn't seemed like a liar.

Felicity appeared and ran her hand down Shaggy's legs, looking for invisible swellings or heat that – fortunately – weren't there. 'Hiya. You OK?'

Bramble nodded. Shaggy stretched her head round to nibble her shoulder affectionately, then pricked her ears towards another person approaching her stable.

'Oh, hello. You did a nice little test.' It was Toby Fitzroy, striding down the corridor like a king among his subjects. He was wearing a T-shirt that clung to his bulky chest and arms, heavily sculpted by hours in the gym.

Shaggy flattened her ears and shifted away from him.

'Hello, little pony,' he said, patting her. Shaggy's head shot up and she backed away.

'Sorry,' said Bramble. 'I'd rather you didn't.'

He raised both hands in surrender. 'Sorry. Sorry. Just trying to be friendly.'

Felicity looked up and gasped, and Shaggy responded by lashing out with a back leg. She was acutely sensitive to atmosphere.

'Shh, shh.' Felicity could hear murmurs and a scuffle as Bramble calmed Shaggy down, but it was like a faint buzzing outside. All she could see, ahead of her, were Toby's bare, muscular arms. She met his eyes in a shock of recognition, then down to his arm again. His right arm.

'When did you get that done?' She pointed to the mark of the rearing horse, etched between his elbow and his wrist.

'It's Merlin,' he said. 'The first Merlin. But you know that, don't you? I had this done when your father took him. Partly to make my father angry. He said it was common.' He lowered his arms and crossed them.

Felicity caught his wrist and pulled his arm out, twisting it to show Bramble the horse inscribed in blue on the tanned flesh. 'The tattoo,' she said. 'You were there.'

He looked down at her, then wrenched his wrist away with a slow, deliberate movement. 'You were stoned. You'd no idea who was there.'

'There was always something I was trying to remember about that night,' said Felicity, her shame, anger and guilt rising like a familiar, malevolent odour. 'It was you. There.'

'You were out of it. As you so often were.' She could see the scorn on his face. How he dismissed her, like everyone else, as a silly girl who'd deserved everything she had coming to her.

She raised her hand and slapped his face, and the slap landed flat. A superficial blow. She couldn't reach the man who lay beneath the sneering expression.

'Merlin was mine,' said Toby, ignoring her action. 'Then your family stole him, and you let him die.'

'No,' Felicity choked on the words. 'No, no, I never thought they could really hurt him. It was a freak accident, everyone said so . . .' She stopped. She couldn't reach Toby, make him realise, but she could change herself. Her own attitude to the rage that festered inside her.

'Yes. You're right.' She dropped her voice, quiet and dignified, and looked him in the eye. 'My irresponsible actions indirectly led to the death of Merlin. I'm sorry.'

Toby looked disconcerted. 'Well, that's not to say . . . I mean . . .'

She continued to face him. I have nothing to be ashamed of any longer, she told herself. I have nothing to run away from. Helena and Bramble know what happened and they didn't judge me. If anyone else does, then that is their problem not mine. She raised her chin slightly and straightened her shoulders.

Toby shifted from one foot to the other and Shaggy edged away from him again. 'I did what I could,' he said, as if the silence had been an accusation. 'I got you through the back door and pretended to be lolling, drunk, against it, so they had to wrestle me out of the way to open it. I got you a few minutes.'

Felicity sifted through her memory. The tattooed arm around her. Finding herself on the other side of a closed door. Yes, that was how it was.

'I was too frightened to do any more,' blurted Toby into the continuing silence. Felicity could see what a huge effort it was for him to admit it. 'I did manage to find the house phone and call the police, when I realised it wasn't just a game, but it was too late by then.'

Felicity felt Bramble move towards her, as if to defend her, but she stood straight and still, facing Toby.

'I thought that whole drugs world was exciting and unconventional and real,' he continued, 'different from what my parents wanted for me.' He looked at her. 'And so did you. We were both fools.'

'It was you who told Pa, wasn't it? asked Bramble, suddenly realising how it all slotted into place. 'Last year. Why?'

Toby studied Felicity, his arms folded again. 'We both missed the usual ferry crossing back from Punchestown and finished up on the last boat from Ireland. The grooms were asleep and there was hardly anyone else in the lorry drivers' canteen. It would have been silly not to share a table. So we had to talk to each other. We argued. About everything: about the past, about that summer and about whether he'd been right to buy Merlin and therefore stop me competing, and when I realised, from what he said, that he never knew the truth about what happened to you I threw it in his face.'

Felicity could feel fresh anger beginning to corrode her new calm. She took a deep breath. 'Did he ask you why you didn't stop them?'

'Yes. I told him there were too many of them. And I knew nothing about defending myself then. Or anybody else.'

She looked at his muscular physique, the result of hours of training. It had not been vanity that had driven him, but fear. A sheltered schoolboy's sudden realisation that not everybody had drawing-room manners. 'And you never wanted to be that vulnerable again,' she concluded.

'I never have been.'

They all stared at each other in silence.

'It's time for this to stop now,' said Bramble. 'Just stop. We owe you nothing. You are who you decided to be, you don't need to keep chipping away at us to prove how successful you are.'

'I know,' he said eventually, turning to her. 'We're quits now, at last. Teddy for the first Merlin.'

He turned on his heel and began to walk away.

'But I'm sorry,' he stopped and turned towards Felicity, wooden with the effort of apologising. 'No matter what you did, what happened to you was wrong. I'm sorry I didn't do more.' He smiled, the old, charming Toby smile that you saw on the society pages of magazines. 'Not that I suppose it matters now.' And he was gone, his boots echoing on the stone floor.

Felicity felt a huge weight lift off her.

'Are you all right?' asked Bramble, moving towards her anxiously.

'Someone has said sorry at last,' Felicity said, blowing her nose. 'That's what was so terrible, no one ever, ever saying it was wrong, no one apologising. That was what really made me feel worthless.'

'Why now, do you think?' asked Bramble as Toby's footsteps faded into the distance and she heard him laughing with one of the other competitors. 'What's changed him? Made him able to apologise?'

Felicity looked down the long corridor as if the answer was written at the end of it. 'Lottie's death,' she said eventually. 'It's changed us all.'

Chapter 39

Bramble woke up at five on Saturday morning, pulling on her wellies and struggling out through the mud to walk the cross-country course one more time, with a terrible sense of foreboding. The rain had pounded down all night, while thoughts of Nat and Jenny revolved in her mind, then the terror of going cross-country, then back to Nat again, and once more, over the cross-country course. Then to Felicity, who had come back to the lorry without eating supper and flung herself on to the banquette, pulling her duvet over her head.

But mainly Bramble rode the cross-country course in her mind, over and over, forcing her brain to accept that she could ride it well. Every time she heard her anxious monkey-chatter voice point out that, for example, Huntsman's Close, deep in the shadows of the trees, would be extra-slippery underfoot, she forced her brain to see herself steadying Shaggy for the tight turn, giving her confidence to go from light to dark because Bramble was her eyes, urging her on and out again. You did it, she told herself; you did it and it worked.

She didn't forget about the jumps that had easier, slower alternatives, either. She remembered Jez saying that you might start out with the idea that you would go round in the fastest way possible, but faced with an unexpected difficulty at a fence, you quite often had to take the long way round after all. 'I got really caught out once,' he'd said. 'Because I hadn't paid any attention to the alternatives.'

Shaggy was nippy and there were a couple of places where she could take the long route and have a reasonable chance of making up the time with fast footwork. And then the puzzle of Nat came back, and the heartache. She was glad he'd had to work on Friday, promising to be back on Saturday in time to wish her good luck, apparently not noticing the new distrust in her eyes.

Everyone was out walking the course, in sweeping waterproof coats, zipped up jackets and wide-brimmed rain hats, carrying umbrellas, assessing the ground with tense faces. Every effort had been made to drain the soil, but thirty-six hours of near-continuous rain, on top of ground that had been prepared for drought, spelt the possibility of injury – or even death – for rider or horse, and it would get worse as the day progressed, churned up by galloping hooves. On the other hand, a smaller field – and it was already a much smaller field than usual – meant a greater chance of being placed. And being placed meant being able to live her dream.

Green with nerves, Bramble wondered if she should pull out, whether it was madness to risk life and limb for a prize that was so far out of her reach. There were groups of riders around each jump, discussing their options and their horses' ability to deal with heavy going. They still had time to withdraw. Felicity, her eyes clear of shadows, pushed a cup of tea into her hand.

'What do you think?' asked Bramble.

'It's your call,' replied Felicity, brisk and businesslike again. 'Shaggy's a good, muddy hunter, but it's difficult going and she can go a bit mad.'

Shaggy was a fighter across country and it had taken all Bramble's courage not to put her in a stronger bit to gain more control. A horse as opinionated as Shaggy liked to feel in charge. She accepted the concept of partnership, but not of domination.

An out-of-control horse would be lethal on this ground, hurling them dangerously at jumps and slithering in the mud. Bramble took a deep breath and banished all negative thoughts. 'I'm going to run her, Felicity.'

In the end, sixteen riders pulled out, two of them above Bramble on the leaderboard, moving her up to twelfth place again.

On the big screens they watched the first dozen riders go and saw two falls. One horse refused, ejecting its rider against some rails with a sickening jolt, and the other pecked on landing, slipped and rolled over, nearly crushing its rider's leg. Both riders got up and walked away, albeit a little shaky.

As she arrived at the stables she bumped into Jez.

'Oh, hi.' She fidgeted awkwardly.

He stopped. 'You're on about half-past twelve?'

She nodded. There was so much she wanted to ask him. Have you been happy? Do you ever think about us, or were we just a brief mistake in your climb to the top? And so much she wanted to tell him. About the horses and how they were going, and that they no longer blamed him for Savannah's collapse.

'No one's gone within the time so far.' There was a warning in his voice as his eyes sought hers.

'It's the rain,' she replied. The words were like droplets, disappearing into the ground between them. She thought of Penny Luckham and the missing cufflinks, and of Nat and Jenny. So many lies. But who was telling the truth?

'Be careful. Take the alternatives if you're not sure.'

She tried to smile but she was too sick with nerves. 'You too,' she said. 'You too.'

'But Bramble?'

'Yes?' She didn't want to leave the bubble they stood in.

'I was right, wasn't I? You and Shaggy? You're good together. The best.'

'Oh Jez,' she hugged him, suddenly laughing. 'You are impossible. You've always got to be right.'

He drew back for a moment, then laughed too and she felt the roughness of his cheek against hers as he kissed her. 'Good luck,' he said softly. 'Good luck.'

It had been the embrace of brothers in arms, not the brief, formal touch of fellow competitors or the yearning entanglement of lovers, but something rare and special and warm. She was smiling as she helped Felicity tack up Shaggy.

By midday, Shaggy was on tiptoes with excitement, standing on her back legs and dancing round the yard. Nat arrived just before she left the stables and Bramble managed – just – to avoid a conversation.

'Good luck darling, did you sleep well?'

She shook her head, tightening Shaggy's girth. 'Felicity, have you got another hairnet? This one's torn.' Felicity handed one over.

'Nervous?' asked Nat.

Pulling her hair back in the net, she then bent down to re-oil Shaggy's hooves – unnecessarily – whipping her face out of the way of a kick just in time. 'Very,' she muttered to the flagstones.

'Are you OK?'

'No, I'm not. I'm about to ride one of the most difficult courses in the world, in the pouring rain, with a wildly over-excited horse under me. Felicity, can you give me a leg up?' She checked everything again: stirrup leathers, girth, bridle, reins – nothing must break.

'What's wrong?' asked Nat.

Cross-country gloves. She pulled them on and Felicity hoisted her up. She had hardly landed in the saddle before Shaggy clattered out of the yard, desperate to get going, spooking at the security guards and adding little rebellious bucks. It felt like riding a rocket. You could never be sure if everything was going to go as planned or whether you were about to crash to earth in pieces. The rain began to soak through her breeches.

Almost without turning her head, she could see Nat outside the stableyard arch, standing with his hands outstretched.

By the time she got to the start box, she'd worked a little of the fizz out of Shaggy, but she was still trying to prance a flamenco. Bramble managed to calm it down to an edgy waltz. Shaggy was an intelligent horse, and the bigger the occasion the more she was fired up by it. There was a real chance that she'd be too excited to start properly at all, getting penalised before they even got going.

When the official began his countdown Shaggy skittered sideways and stood on her hind legs again, but as soon as they heard 'Three, two, one . . . GO and good luck,' the little mare shot out of the start box towards the first fence, as if to say that it had been mad to doubt her. She just wanted to get on with her job.

It would be a question of holding her back – with all this mud, she would slip if she approached the fences too fast. Bramble, her weight up out of the saddle, had to work constantly to keep the contact with Shaggy's mouth. As the rain drove straight into her face, all she could see was between Shaggy's ears – thick grey clouds, a bedraggled haze of spectators, then the fences coming.

The first few fences steadied them, as Bramble's control and concentration communicated itself to the mare: we're a partnership, and we do this together. Shaggy obediently slowed down over the bumpy ground of the Medieval Village, picking her way with accuracy and over the fences without hesitation, but the Beaufort Staircase – two big banked steps down – was slippery in the mud, and Bramble could feel her hesitate. Go, she said with her legs. Go!

And Shaggy went – down one, down two – then pecked a little on landing, jolting Bramble forwards. She regained her balance and aimed for the little log pile straight in front. One, two, three, over. Then off and away without delay, flying to the next fence, Bramble crouched low against Shaggy's neck, giving the mare her head.

She quickly checked the large stopwatch on her wrist. Her time was good so far, and she allowed herself to take the longer, easier route on the next two fences, whipping Shaggy round instantly and off again.

But just as she was about to come up to the Sunken Road, ragged cries of 'Stop!' penetrated her concentration and she could see hands waving her down. Where was the fence judge? Who was looking after her time? Bramble reined Shaggy in, her heart beating wildly. An official hurried up. There was an accident on the course. Huntsman's Close. A short delay nothing more.

Bramble circled, trying to keep her mind on the work ahead, trying not to think about what might be happening down in the woods and keeping Shaggy moving, keeping her interested, but trying not to tire her out. She strained her ears to hear, worked out where she would start Shaggy again and tried to ignore the pelting rain and buffeting wind. She was beginning to cool down and stiffen up, and she worried that Shaggy was too, urging her in to a few trotted circles.

Toby, once again, had been the rider to go out immediately ahead of her and there was another rider further on. The thought

'I wouldn't wish this on my worst enemy' flitted through her head. Toby was known for his falls but he was considered almost indestructible.

Twenty minutes went by and Bramble began to shiver. If she felt like this, how must Shaggy feel? Starting out again with stiffened muscles was a passport to injury. The clouds above were so heavy it was almost dark.

'Is it Toby?' Bramble asked the fence judge.

He nodded. 'But he's fine.'

'Teddy – I mean, Be Good Be Clever?' Bramble thought of the magnificent grey, suffering through his rider's clumsiness.

The fence judge nodded again. 'I'm sure he'll be fine, too.'

Bramble thought he might be lying. She focused on the course again.

'It was the tight turn at Huntsman's Close,' added the judge. 'The horse slipped and they went at the fence all wrong and missed a stride.'

'Badly?' Bramble's throat closed up.

'Not badly.' The judge looked evasive. 'But be careful.'

But Bramble was running out of time. If she took another detour there would definitely be time penalties.

There was a shimmer of activity ahead and the official came to tell her she could start again. Shaggy began to pick up, her hooves flashing along the muddy ground, neatly popping in and out of the Sunken Road, splashing through the Lake and over the massive, looming barrels and table as if on angel's wings. But as they headed towards Huntsman's Close, Bramble felt Shaggy's hesitation, her own fears communicating themselves to the horse. The spinney seemed like a dark, menacing wood. To take the long route and lose the time, or risk the horse? She had ridden these fences in her imagination, over and over again, telling herself she could do them, so she banned her fears, urging the mare over the first giant log pile then wheeling her round to face the brush fences, feeling, with a sudden lurch of terror, the ground give way beneath her and her weight swing out of the saddle as Shaggy lost her footing in the mud. Both scrabbling to regain their balance, they righted themselves, but she had a split-second to decide between the long route – a sweeping curve and two low hedges – or the tiny narrow corner of the direct route. Her native caution versus her desire to win?

With a shout of defiance, Bramble spurred Shaggy towards the corner and they lifted over, pecking slightly as they hit the ground but steadying and heading for the gate. Another quick choice ahead at the next fence, up, over and down safely and off again.

But Shaggy was tiring and the mud was beginning to slow her down. Bramble could feel her own thighs burning with half-standing in the saddle for nearly four miles. Just two more fences. She glanced at the giant stopwatch on her wrist. They would have to go as fast as possible to make the time, and she spurred the little mare on again. She was so brave and fast, and so willing, with her ears pricked forwards and her legs speeding over the soggy turf, but the last two fences seemed a hundred miles away. You've got to keep going, you must keep going. The rhythm drummed through her head as she ignored her screaming muscles and Shaggy's heavier and heavier gait. You've got to keep going, you must keep going. Down the hill, steady and over, jolting on landing, a gasp from a knot of spectators as she lurched out of the saddle, a re-adjustment that stretched out, her toe desperately trying to find a flying stirrup, and still Shaggy galloped on, cheered on the people lining the last stretch of ground.

The last fence, the Mitsubishi Garden – a barrow of flowers with a roof to it – was straightforward but she had never jumped anything that size with one stirrup before. Clamping her legs to Shaggy's side, she clung on as Shaggy rose and dropped down, shaking her hard on landing and then they curved round the arena, through the finish, past the cheering crowds, then clenching her fist in exultation and almost falling off as they slowed to a walk.

Felicity took Shaggy's reins and began to walk her round in circles to cool her down, as Eddie took her saddle off and began sponging her down. Bramble, on legs that felt like jelly, staggered off to face a microphone wielded by Sally Clark, who was commentating on Badminton for the BBC.

'That last bit was a bit hairy,' she gasped, 'but Shaggy never gives up.'

'You've just made it inside the time – that was exciting,' said Sally, 'and very good in this field. You're now in fourth place.'

Fourth. Fourth: that was incredible. But, yet again, there was over half the field to go. She held back her elation.

'I see you're wearing a Pony Club badge,' Sally added.

'It belonged to Lottie Marsh-Robertson, a dedicated and talented young rider, and the ride was in her memory,' said Bramble, taking huge gulps of air. 'She stands for all the young kids coming through at the moment, who need all our encouragement and support.'

As she turned away Felicity hugged her. 'Well done. Shaggy seems fine.'

Bramble knew you could never be sure. She unbuckled her hat and felt the horse's legs. 'I hope I didn't crash down too hard on her back with that last jump. When I only had one stirrup.' The adrenalin began to drain out of her and she suddenly felt exhausted.

Then Nat was there, his big burly frame folding her in his arms, half-carrying her out of sight and finding a chair where she could sit down, her head in her hands.

'Teddy?' she asked, lifting her head up when she'd got her breath back. 'Teddy and Toby. They fell. Is Teddy OK?'

Nat shook his head and squeezed her hand.

Bramble covered her face again. Dear Teddy. Such a good-hearted, brave, talented horse.

As they led Shaggy back to the stables they passed Toby, carrying an empty saddle on his arm and a bridle on his shoulder, his face set like glass.

Bramble swallowed tears. She fell into step beside him, leaving Felicity, Eddie and Nat to continue ahead with Shaggy.

'Can I help you? Carry anything?'

He shook his head. 'Teddy was my responsibility.'

'I'm sorry.' Bramble knew what it was like to lose a horse, to have the vet shake his head and order the green screens erected around the fallen animal so that the public wouldn't see a bullet in the head. To ease off a saddle and bridle, carrying them away as the horse ambulance winched the body inside.

She walked alongside Toby, in step with him so that he wouldn't be alone on his journey back to the stables as the crowds turned their heads and pointed at the saddle that no longer had a horse. Other riders' faces changed in sympathy. Or blame.

'It was my fault,' said Toby.

'We all make mistakes,' replied Bramble, wishing she had more to offer than empty clichés. Teddy had been her father's last chance at a comeback, albeit as a trainer rather than as a rider. Losing him was like saying goodbye to her father all over again.

When they reached the stables Toby peeled off towards his loosebox where his grooms were packing up the rest of Teddy's kit, tears pouring down their faces.

In the end, there were only three other clear rounds within the time, one of them Jez's, one from Betsy Parker, the American, who was still nailed to the top slot, and one from a rider whose dressage had been unremarkable. Bramble, to her amazement, had only slipped down to sixth place, while Jez had risen to fourth.

But the showjumping was always Shaggy's weak point – she occasionally refused even to enter the ring – and they were also worried as to whether her legs had paid the price of her hard ride across country. Bramble, Felicity and Eddie spent the evening working on her. The stables were humming with activity as riders and grooms used every trick and treatment they knew to ensure that their horses came up sound the following morning.

Felicity strapped an ice pack on one of Shaggy's back legs, using one of her travelling boots to keep it in place.

Jez put his head over the top of the loosebox door. 'Well done.'

Bramble jumped up. 'And you. Fantastic.'

'How's Shaggy?'

'She seems all right, but that was a helluva slip in Huntsman's Close, and we're worried that she might stiffen up overnight.'

'Shall I?'

Bramble nodded, and Jez ran his hands down Shaggy's legs and back up to her haunches. 'If she's tweaked anything it might be a muscle further up.' He began to work his hands in small, circular motions over her muscular frame, and Shaggy's bottom lip drooped and waggled, as if to say 'Mmm, yes, there, up a bit . . .' Jez smiled. 'I remember she always loved a bit of shiatsu.'

'Jez!' It was Helen, Penny Luckham's groom, who was looking after Penny's horse three boxes up. Bramble had avoided her, not wanting to hear more poison.

Jez straightened up. 'Right, I'd better get on. She'll be OK.' He strode out and hugged Helen and they talked, mainly about Helen's impending wedding. When Jez went back to Fireflight, Helen was smiling after him.

'We all miss him,' she said to Bramble.

'Oh. Right. Well, I mean, er, we do too.'

'You know how most riders think the grooms don't care? They think *they're* the only ones who really care about the horses but we devote all our working days, and some of our nights, and the horses matter just as much to us. Jez was never like that. He always knew we gave as much as the riders do.'

Bramble stared at her.

'It was a bad business, the way he left,' added Helen. 'Terrible, really.'

'What actually happened?'

Helen looked over her shoulder. 'Penny's threatened me with the sack if I talk about it, but what the hell, I'm getting married next week and going to join another yard . . . Penny and Jez had been having an affair, but he met someone else so she threw him out. Just put his bags in the stables and refused to pay him. I was at her house a few days later and he rang the doorbell so I let him in. There was an envelope of cash with his name on it on the mantelpiece that he'd been left the previous Saturday by someone he'd ridden for several times, so he'd come to collect it. I gave it to him and we both left. Next thing I heard, Penny'd called the police and accused him of breaking in and stealing stuff. I made a statement and they dropped the case, of course, but she promised to make life hell for him, and to tell everyone he was a thief.' Helen sighed. 'Of course, some people wouldn't have believed her because she's done that sort of thing before, but Jez has such pride and he wouldn't have said anything against her in public. And stuff sticks. As soon as the police are involved there are always those who'll automatically think it must be true.'

'What about the cufflinks?' asked Bramble. 'I heard about some cufflinks.'

'They never existed.'

The stables closed for the night so that the horses could get some rest. Bramble smeared a last application of cooling gel on to Shaggy's legs, and prayed.

Chapter 40

By Sunday morning the rain had stopped, but the sun didn't come out. The riders sniffed the air. 'Good,' said Betsy Parker. 'Nice and cloudy. No rain, no sun to blind us or boil us. Perfect.' She so nearly had the Badminton trophy in her grasp. She could drop two fences and still win. Riders like Betsy very rarely dropped two fences.

Five riders withdrew their horses before the trot-up because of injuries. Everyone else was tense. Would the ground jury see a lameness that they hadn't spotted? Bramble thought she might seize up with terror as she trotted Shaggy up in front of Badminton House again, but the mare was on her toes, her ears pricked forwards at the applause from the crowd, acknowledging that 'Number twenty-seven, Chequerboard Charlotte – passed.' Bramble nearly fainted with relief.

Of the eighty-six starters there were now only forty-one horses going on to the showjumping, twenty-one in the morning and twenty, televised and going in reverse order, in the afternoon. They all felt like survivors, still keyed up and at the peak of their fitness but the tension had a strung-out, worn quality and the air no longer crackled with nerves. Bramble, like everyone else, was fighting exhaustion one moment and desperate to get going the next.

The afternoon seemed a long, long way away, like another country. After walking the course Bramble spent the morning watching the first group tackle the showjumping, spotting the difficult jumps and assessing their successes and mistakes. There were a lot of poles down at the treble, a series of three red-and-white striped fences about halfway round the course, and a number of riders also seemed to be dropping the last fence, marring an otherwise clear round at the last minute.

At twelve-thirty she went back to the lorry for a short nap, in the hope of lifting what had become an almost perpetual headache. Nat had been invited in to one of the hospitality tents for lunch, but she couldn't face talking to people and said that she'd rather be alone.

Clambering up on to the mattress over the cab, she fell almost immediately into that shadowy half-world between sleep and wakefulness. She thought she heard Nat warning her and wanting her to sign papers, but it turned into Jez, and then her father. There was a shadow, like that cold, evil mist, at the back of the lorry that she knew she had to fight off. It kept curling up towards her and only by jumping each fence cleanly could she escape it. But she was so tired, so, so tired, she couldn't go on jumping the fences to get away. At some point she would stumble and then she would be lost. She felt Shaggy under her, catching a leg on the fence and sprawling over it and she hit the ground with a crash that made her heart leap out of her chest.

Shaking, she sat up and looked at her watch. Time to get changed.

As soon as she'd tied her stock a ray of light fell across the inside of the lorry. The door opened and Nat stood there, blocking the way out. 'Darling,' he said. 'I might think you were avoiding me.'

'I'm not avoiding anyone. I just needed to be alone for a bit. Come on, let's go.'

Taking a folding stool and setting it in front of the door, he sat down. 'Actually, let's talk.' He splayed the fingers of one hand out and looked at them as if checking his nails. Bramble was reminded of a cat flexing its claws.

'Not now.' She looked at her watch. ' I'm really sorry, I don't have time. You know I don't. The procession is in forty minutes.'

'You never have time. I don't ask for much, but I am asking for your attention now, this moment. For five minutes.'

Bramble's guilt at always being the taker in their relationship caught her at the throat. 'I'm sorry, I'm really, really sorry. We can talk later. This evening, I promise.'

'Ah, but I've heard those promises before. It's always later, isn't it? There's always a horse to be seen to, a meal to be cooked, a form to be filled in, other people, Savannah . . . where's the time for us, Bramble? Where is the time for us?'

'Yes, but this is different. This is the most critical point in my career.'

'And it's the most critical point in mine,' he replied softly. 'I'm sorry to tell you this, but the business is going down the pan. As they so inelegantly say.'

'What do you mean?' White hot terror coursed through Bramble's veins, but her eyes flicked to her watch again.

'I mean, my dear, that the banks will probably be calling in your very generous offer of security some time soon.' He was watching her. 'I'm afraid you stand to lose a sizeable chunk of your inheritance. I think being a farrier was, perhaps, a mistake. There don't seem to be enough people around who want their horses shod. By me, that is.'

'What?' Bramble's knees began to shake. 'Why are you telling me this now?'

'Because you've always told me we should have no secrets.' He watched her carefully. 'And you've been talking to Jenny, haven't you? Without telling me about it? Listening to her lies, eh?'

'I don't have time to discuss this. I will talk properly later, I will, but now I must go.' She picked up her hat with trembling hands, her pulse crashing against her temples. Thud-thud, thud-thud. 'Let me past.' Thud-thud. She needed to focus on the challenge ahead, not think about hundreds of thousands of pounds being taken by an anonymous bank. Don't think about it, she told herself. Just concentrate.

Surely it couldn't be true? She tried to remember exactly what she had signed.

He folded his arms and leant back against the door. She opened the other one, to the horse compartment.

'The jockey door's locked from the outside.' He smiled. 'There's no way out there.'

Bramble couldn't work out what he was up to. 'Don't joke. I need to get out. Now. This isn't funny.'

'No, it isn't. Far from it, I can assure you.'

'Anyway, Jenny told me that you had divided the house between you. That you got half. So you can pay your own debts.'

'I rather thought she might have said something of the kind. Well, I can assure you that I don't legally have any money from that marriage. Trusts are a rather interesting thing, you see. My little blacksmith's business is what they call a shell company. The only person legally liable for its debts is you.'

Bramble, desperate, tried to push him away from the door. 'Let me out! We'll talk about this later.' She made no impact on his bulk at all. 'You destroyed Jenny, I won't let you destroy me.'

'Very spirited of you, my dear.' He laughed. 'Now Jenny is one of life's victims. She was going around with "doormat" written across her forehead. Somebody who couldn't say no without feeling guilty. Like you when I first saw you. There you were, chasing around cooking mounds of food, looking after everybody except yourself, being treated like a servant by that so-called celebrity sister of yours . . . well, I thought "there's a woman with an inheritance, who's lost her father and about to lose her way, and I can help her."' He laughed again. 'Help her lose, that is.' He unfolded his arms and put a hand out to her, winding a piece of her hair around his finger. She could smell his breath on her face. 'That's what you are,' he whispered, 'a loser, like the rest of your family. Only the old man had what it takes and he's gone. He never liked me, you know.'

'Nat, what has got into you? I feel I don't know you!'

'You don't. People like you never do.'

'What do you mean, people like me?'

'People,' he said, 'who are so overprivileged that they have no idea how tough you need to be to survive. That's why you always think the best of everyone. You don't know what the real world's like.'

She raised a hand to slap him, but he caught it neatly and twisted it round behind her. 'I don't think so, dear. Domestic violence never solves anything, I'm sure you would agree.'

It hurt, wrenching her shoulder, and she tried to resist her instinct to struggle. She couldn't risk an injury before the showjumping. 'Let go! I don't know what you think you'll gain out of this. I'll tell everyone—'

'Tell them what? And will they believe you? I'm in here trying to calm you down before the most important competition of your life. The pressure has got to you. You're hysterical. Have a drink to calm yourself down.' He let go and, with a quick movement, pulled out a bottle of whisky from the little cupboard beside the hob, unscrewed it and half-filled a plastic glass.

'I don't want a drink.' Bramble, rubbing her shoulder, tried to get to the door handle, but the space was so confined that Nat could stretch across to the cupboard without taking his foot away from the door.

'Oh yes you do.' Nat grabbed her, forcing the glass to her lips with almost super-human strength. She closed her mouth tightly. 'You're nervous, you're terrified,' he whispered. 'You need a drink to steady your nerves.'

She clenched her teeth and closed her lips.

'So, how shall we get you to open your mouth and take your medicine? Oh yes, I know. Your sister Helena and her beloved Ollie. I've been encouraging him to drink, you know. He wants to give up and get back with Helena, but I come back home after seeing you at Lorenden and tell him about the men Helena's been seeing and I open a bottle . . . he's got no willpower, no willpower at all.'

'You wouldn't be so evil!' blurted Bramble, and he shoved the plastic glass into her mouth and tried to hold it there. The whisky spilled over her face and her white shirt and stock. She spat it out, choking, but felt a few drops of burning liquid slip down her throat.

He drew back, almost throwing her across the lorry, and she landed on the banquette that they used as a bed at night. 'Hmm.' He sounded almost dispassionate. 'It's the sort of thing you see on the movies and which doesn't work in real life. Never mind. Perhaps I should just shove the whole bottle down your throat.' He looked at it. 'It might break, of course and that could get messy. I don't like anything that might leave a scar. People are absurdly hooked on physical evidence. Helena's come on to me, by the way. Her own sister's fiancé.' He cocked his head, as if to hear a noise. 'Hang on.' He suddenly threw himself on to her and placed a hand over her mouth.

She could hear Eddie's voice, and the sound of knocking on the door. Nat's weight was immense, almost choking the breath out of her as she tried to scream through the palm of his hand. His fingers pinched her nose closed and she could no longer breathe.

He must have calculated carefully, because when her lungs were tearing with pain and her brain almost losing consciousness, he removed his hand to let her take a few precious gulps of air, before closing it over her mouth and nose again before she could scream. Her legs, kicking futilely – and noiselessly – against the padded banquette, began to weaken and she heard Eddie's voice say, as if from a long way away, 'Nobody there. Let's try the grooms' canteen.' Nat let her take another two gasping breaths and clamped his hand over again, releasing it slowly after Eddie had gone.

Bramble couldn't get enough air into her lungs. She sucked it in, coughing and choking. Nat was sitting back on the stool, looking at her with amusement.

'You could have killed me,' she wheezed, lying back and trying to gather her strength.

'Oh no. You misunderstand,' he said. 'You've got it all wrong. I'm trying to help you. That's what I'll tell anyone if you make a complaint. I'll explain that you attacked me. You were, after all, the first one to raise a hand in anger, were you not?'

'Please, Nat, please.' She sat up. 'I have to get out there. This is so important, so very, very important to me. If you ever cared about me at all, let me out so that I can do the showjumping.'

'Oh, I cared. I even thought we could make it together. Until you talked to Jenny. It was all your fault, talking to Jenny like that. I warned you not to. We could have got a little house, and you'd have given up this competitive nonsense. I could have persuaded you, over time, that you didn't have what it takes and you'd have been grateful for it. Glad that you'd made a decision at last.'

Bramble wondered if she could break a window and shout for help. But the lorry windows were too thick.

'Wouldn't you?' he shouted. 'You'd have been grateful to have someone tell you to give up your foolish dreams and concentrate on real life. More whisky?' He looked at his watch. 'The parade will be starting now, you can't hope to make it. This is it, Bramble, this is the end. Because now you've missed this chance the will to win will fade again, won't it? You'll forget what it was like. You'll stop believing in yourself again.'

There was always a splinter of truth in his words. Tiny, sharp slivers of pain, getting under your skin and festering, poisoning your whole system, almost impossible to find and dig out. No wonder Jenny had crumbled.

Nat handed her the bottle in a chillingly friendly way. 'I take it that our engagement is off, by the way?' His voice was pleasant. 'That won't save you from the other matter, the money, but hey – what's money? People are what's important, that's what I always say.' He passed the glass to her in such a normal way that she almost took it.

There was no point in staying sober now, after all. For a fraction of a second she caught a gleam of triumph in his eyes and she threw the whisky bottle on the floor. The fumes rose into the air.

'Why Nat, why all this? What did you really want from me?'

He looked surprised. 'Half of your share of Lorenden, of course. While you're going round behaving as if everything had been taken from you, you're actually an heiress, you know. And if I married you and we divorced later you'd have to pay me off. Like Jenny did. Come on Bramble, wake up. Women have been doing this to men for generations.' He loomed over her like a great angry bear. 'All I've ever asked for,' he said, 'is something of my own that can't be taken away. That's why I put the money from the split with Jenny into a separate company. One that the divorce courts don't need to know about.

'You don't know what it's like to be left with nothing. Literally. Susan and I were married for eight years and when she died she left Serena – her daughter by a previous marriage – everything. *Everything*. I was turned out of my own home when she reached eighteen.'

'Was it Susan's to leave?'

He waved the issue of ownership aside. 'Susan's first husband had had to pay her off so she'd got the house. You lose some, you win some. It's only fair. My parents never owned a house so I missed out on the great property boom. But I thought Susan's was my home. I'd spent money on that house, put work into it . . . I was left, aged thirty-five, with nothing. Nothing. So I married Jenny and she insisted on getting pregnant, probably to tie me down forever.'

'Nat, that's not why people have children.'

'You are so naive,' he said, looking at her with distaste. 'Almost stupid, really.'

We can talk about this later,' said Bramble desperately, feeling as if the world had turned upside down. 'I need to get to the stables now.'

'No. I want to talk about it now. I want you to tell me what you think about Helena,' he needled. 'Coming on to me, I mean?'

'Helena comes on to everyone. She's an actress.'

'It was a bit more than that,' he said, taunting, and Bramble felt another quiver of fear. Would Helena betray her like that? Surely not?

'I don't care,' she said bravely, adding, 'Helena's way out of your league. You were imagining things.'

He slapped his knees and roared with laughter. 'Little kitty Bramble has grown claws. Who would have thought it?'

'I always had them. At my father's funeral, you saw a harassed, over-worked woman who let life walk all over her. That woman was never really there.' She paused. It wasn't entirely true. That woman had been there – she knew that – but someone else had been there too. The other Bramble. It was that other Bramble, the courageous one, who would get her out of here. She reminded herself that he didn't like to leave physical evidence. All she had to do was face him down and he would let her go.

'What you should have seen,' she continued, 'was someone who was grieving and shocked, and busy, but surrounded by her family and friends. Someone with an enormous amount of love in her life.'

She had never quite thought of it like that, but just saying it gave her strength. 'That's what you had to destroy, wasn't it?'

He gazed at her steadily. 'If it hadn't been for Felicity,' he said softly. 'I would have done.'

'Felicity?' Bramble was surprised.

'She made you all see things differently.'

'Felicity will come back and find me,' said Bramble. 'She won't let you get away with this.'

'And the lorry will still be locked with nobody here. Everyone will think you've lost your nerve again. They won't be surprised. All this has been a great strain for you.'

'Nat, why are you doing this? You know how important this is to me.'

'I'm doing it because I can, my dear, because I can.'

They faced each other in silence.

'By the way, my beloved, did you know that the paper about Savannah's trust you signed before the cross-country . . .' he inspected his fingernails delicately. 'The one you didn't read, as I knew you wouldn't. You signed your entire share of Lorenden over to me in the event of your death. Oh and you needn't think of screaming, because everybody has gone to watch the showjumping.'

Chapter 41

As Felicity tacked up Shaggy, she wondered where Bramble was. It wasn't like her to be late.

'Eddie, could you check the lorry? And the grooms' dining room? Take Helena's car, there isn't time to walk.'

Eddie returned fifteen minutes later, breathless. 'No one's seen her. And the lorry's locked. I knocked and tried to look through the curtains, but there didn't seem to be anybody there.'

'Fuck,' said Felicity. The horses and riders for the parade, the top twenty who were to showjump that afternoon, were clattering out of the yard, trotting to the main arena in ones, twos and groups, polished and gleaming in their cream breeches and dark coats.

Jez stopped beside her, as relaxed on his big prancing chestnut as a man in his favourite armchair. 'Where's Bramble?'

'I don't know,' said Felicity. 'She's vanished.'

'Nerves?'

Felicity sighed. 'Maybe. I think she was always more frightened of winning and what it might do to her, and to Savannah, than she ever was of getting hurt.'

'No, she wouldn't let people down like this. Something's happened,' said Jez. 'We've got to find her.'

'But the parade, it's in ten minutes. Jez, you've worked for this all your life, you can't screw it up now, looking for someone who may have gone missing of her own accord. Fireflight's owners would never trust you again. Nor would anyone else.'

'Bugger the parade. Eddie, leg Felicity up.'

They trotted briskly out of the quadrangle, overtaking other riders across the park and then taking a short cut through the cross-country course and breaking into a canter, slowing to a trot or a walk, parting the thick crowds of spectators. People turned their heads at the sight of Jez and recognised Shaggy. Felicity knew something was wrong. Bramble hadn't been sleeping. The five days of Badminton had stretched all their nerves to their maximum and it was as if they had been here for ever. That it would never be over.

They rode in to all the hospitality marquees in turn, past frantically protesting security guards, and looked over the heads of the guests. No Bramble. No distinctive gypsy hair. There were thousands and thousands of people milling everywhere. In some places the crowds were hardly able to walk at normal speed. How could you find just one person?

After forty minutes they stopped in despair. Felicity looked at her watch. 'Jez, the jumping started fifteen minutes ago. You must go. You can't miss this opportunity, you just can't. This is the most important day of your life. I can go on looking for her.'

'Who checked the lorry?'

'Eddie. He said there was no one there.'

'Did he go inside?'

'He said it was locked. He looked in the windows.'

'Let's go.' And Jez spurred Fireflight on across the car park, scattering a group of people who were opening champagne, and triggering off a volley of barks from all the dogs tied to car doors. Felicity followed him.

As Eddie had said, the lorry seemed deserted. They knocked and rattled, and tried to peer through the window, but it was dark and silent.

'Keys,' said Jez. But the door to the living quarters wouldn't open.

'Lower the ramp,' he said, unbolting the back of the lorry, and clattering up inside. He tried to pull open the door to the living area, but it wouldn't budge.

And then they heard Bramble scream.

*

Nat denied having threatened her.

'You're imagining it, Bram,' he said in his sweetest, most reasonable tone, when he'd opened up the door to Jez and Felicity. 'You and I have been sitting here while I've been trying to calm you down about the showjumping. She's never been so close to the top before, her nerves are shot to pieces,' he added. 'Perhaps you can say something to convince her that she can still go out there and at least get round the course in one piece.'

'I can do better than that,' said Jez, drawing his fist back and punching Nat in the face. As Nat fell back with a cry of pain, holding his mouth, Jez grabbed Bramble's wrist. 'Let's get out of here. We've got a round of showjumping to do.'

'Where have you been?' asked the official in charge of counting riders through to the main arena. 'You're due to jump in a minute and you haven't warmed up.'

'Don't worry,' said Jez, 'we've been jumping parked cars, picnic baskets and dogs on leads. We're quite warm, thank you.'

'How could I have been so wrong about Nat?' asked Bramble, trying to control her shaking limbs. She could never ride Shaggy in this state.

'Head games,' he said. 'He tortured Jenny mentally, always wrong-footing her, making her think she was mad. That's why I brought her here. I thought you should meet her and judge for yourself.'

'He pinned me down and held his hand over my mouth. I couldn't call for help when Eddie came round.' Her mouth still felt bruised.

A muscle of fury twitched in Jez's cheek. 'I should have hit him much harder.' He looked at her again. 'You look terrible.'

Bramble thought she might faint. She couldn't answer. Felicity took Shaggy's bridle.

'Get off.' Jez dismounted in one fluid movement as Fireflight's groom took his horse. 'Come here.' He wrapped his arms around her. 'Breathe into your diaphragm,' he murmured, 'here, like this. In. Out.' He began to massage her back, as if she was Shaggy after a hard day's hunting, saying words that Bramble could barely understand, words of comfort and calm, casting a spell over her that stilled her shaking limbs and cleared her head. The world around them disappeared. It was just her and Jez and a growing sense of peace and strength.

'He pretended he was going to kill me,' she whispered.

'He'll never, ever hurt you again. Never. Physically or mentally.' Jez's hands moved smoothly over her shoulders, releasing the fear and tension.

'There.' He pulled back to look at her. 'It's time to forget him. Go in and jump.'

She looked into his grey-blue eyes. 'Nat said his business was going bust,' she spoke in a rush, 'and that I'd lose a big chunk of money because I secured it, using Lorenden . . .'

Jez stroked her cheek. 'No. We've got enough on him, between us, to get him done for fraud if he tries that. Believe me.'

Bramble did. He emanated confidence. 'Leg me up, then,' she said, managing a smile.

'Bramble,' Jez called to her as she gathered up her reins. 'I've been meaning to tell you, you never lost your nerve. Your father lost his. He couldn't bear anything to happen to you. Not after Dom. He told me that. He knew he was holding you back, and that you needed someone else who wouldn't always give you the safe advice. That's why he asked me to come. For you.'

'For me?' Bramble was suddenly indignant. 'He wanted *you* to teach *me*? I'm just as experienced as you are!'

'OK, then off you go on that mad mare and prove it.' He laughed and slapped Shaggy on the backside, and Shaggy, outraged, shot into the air and into the ring.

It wouldn't have been the way Bramble would have chosen to start her round, but neither she nor Shaggy could afford to dwell on past insults.

'Come on,' she whispered. 'Let's show Jezzar Morgan what a mad mare and a middle-aged mother can do.' And Shaggy flicked her ears back. 'I'm listening,' she replied.

The fences required the tailored precision of the dressage arena combined with the heart of the cross-country. To jump them cleanly required rhythm and energy, but also control. Shaggy had it all when she chose but, as a horse trained to gallop over fixed timber fences, she could easily forget the fragility of the carefully balanced poles. She was inclined to be lazy over what she considered lesser challenges.

They cleared the first two neatly, but Bramble heard a whisper of a rattle behind her on the third. It wasn't followed by the sign of a pole falling. The crowd gasped, but the gasp fell away into a sigh of relief.

She gathered Shaggy up and aimed more carefully, this time at the treble: one, a stride, two, another stride, then the third jump. The arena held its breath and the poles stayed in their cups. Bramble was already looking at the next jump, which had a brilliantly striped insert that could have distracted Shaggy, but she lifted over it, and then they were facing a jump on a slight downhill slope. It would be easy to go too fast and crash into it, so she gathered Shaggy up again, hoping that she was still listening.

A big double coming up. Don't lose it, she asked Shaggy. Don't lose it.

Shaggy jumped in a beautiful rounded curve, up, down and a stride, then up again and down. One to go. So many people that morning had dropped the last fence. Bramble took a deep breath. Rhythm, she breathed into the mare's neck, rhythm. It was like a song in her head, and Shaggy picked it up. One, two, three, up and over, and suddenly the arena was ringing with applause, crashing around her ears like thunder.

'What a brilliant round,' said the commentator, 'from this charming rider, who is making a comeback to four-star after a number of years away. Bramble Kelly and Chequerboard Charlotte finish on their dressage score of 42.5, one of the few combinations today to manage it.' The leaderboard showed her in second place.

Bramble cantered out as Jez cantered in. As he went past their eyes met. 'Good luck,' she mouthed, and then he was off, focusing with the intensity she knew so well. She couldn't bear to watch. She had done everything she could. The rest was up to fate.

She slipped off Shaggy and gave her a special hug. 'So much for the horse nobody wanted,' she whispered in her ear, giving her a mint. 'And the rider everyone forgot about.' Shaggy nibbled Bramble's neck and Felicity took her off to cool her down. Bramble sat with her eyes shut and her fingers in her ears.

At one point she heard a gasp from the crowd and an expiration of air, the oooh-h-h that usually followed a pole down. She shut her eyes tighter but couldn't help hearing the applause a few minutes later. Was it polite clapping or a standing ovation? It was impossible to tell. She opened her eyes and saw Klaus Jürgen canter in as Jez cantered out and back into the practice ring.

Jez rode up to her, his grooms chasing after him. They took Fireflight's bridle and began working on the big chestnut, circling the horse round and sponging him down.

'Well?' she asked.

'Clear.' He picked her up and whirled her round, and she couldn't help laughing.

'That means you've knocked me down to third place, you beast,' Bramble said, surprised that she didn't mind more.

'Sorry,' he said, and kissed her, briefly, on the lips.

Bramble felt extraordinarily happy. 'I didn't dare watch.'

'Watch with me now, come on.' He took her hand and led her over to where they could see. He put his arm round her shoulders and she clasped his waist, feeling the thin cotton of his shirt and the hard, muscular body beneath. 'You know,' he mused, 'in some ways, I think Nat may have done us both a favour. We didn't see everyone in our section dropping poles so we didn't have preconceptions as to what we could achieve.'

'Klaus needs to go clear inside the time to stay in third,' said Bramble, intently. 'He hasn't got any fences in hand.'

'Did you love Nat?' asked Jez suddenly, not looking at her but watching Klaus.

'I thought Nat loved me,' replied Bramble after a pause, almost missing the question. 'And I somehow mistook that for loving him. I made him something I wanted him to be.'

Klaus, with his controlled, precise riding and big-striding horse, whisked over the first few fences as if they were nothing and the crowd murmured its approval. He shortened his reins and focused on the triple. Up and over. Up and over. There was a rattle of a pole landing. Up and over for the third time and another pole went. The crowd groaned. Klaus completed the round and fell down into fourth place, just below Bramble.

'I thought Nat was a safe choice,' she added, as she exhaled with relief, and exhilaration and adrenalin gave her a shot of self-awareness. 'I thought I didn't deserve any better.'

Jez flashed her a sudden smile. 'You were wrong. On both counts.'

The next rider, Hamish Woods, a buzzy, outgoing Australian on his eighth Badminton, had one fence down and dropped below Jez, pushing Bramble down to fourth again, and Klaus Jürgen down to fifth.

'I was stupid, wasn't I?' said Bramble, trying to conceal the disappointment of dropping another place and out of the top three. 'Thinking he was in love with me?'

'No.' Jez's eyes were fixed on the arena. 'Why shouldn't he be in love with you? After all, I am,' he said, speaking quickly, out of the corner of his mouth.

With only Betsy to come – Betsy the clear-round machine – Bramble told herself that fourth place was incredible. Better than she'd ever hoped she could achieve. And second for Jez. She was so busy preparing herself for not being one of the top three that she almost missed what he'd said.

'I love you,' said Jez again. 'Which *proves* you deserve better.'

Bramble still couldn't quite understand what he meant. She supposed, in a way, they all loved each other, all of them who worked together and competed against each other and understood the pressures of a life that no one else could understand. Embarrassed, she decided to make a joke of it. 'There you are again, Jez, always right, don't you ever suffer from self-doubt?'

'Hardly ever,' he said, with another sideways grin, as Betsy cantered in and circled. Almost immediately there was a smattering of groans from the crowd.

'Shit,' said Jez. 'That circle means she's gone through the start twice. Like Bettina Hoy at the Athens Olympics. It's a novice mistake. How could she do it?'

Betsy recovered herself and jumped the first five fences cleanly, taking the triple in style, and also the double, but her concentration must have been knocked because she knocked a pole flying on the last jump. She left the ring to sympathetic, but muted, applause.

Jez stared at the ring, his face white.

'Does that mean you've won?' asked Bramble, unable to take in what Betsy's mistake had meant. 'She only had one pole down, but she did go through the start twice. Jez, what does it mean?'

He shook his head. 'We don't know what penalties she incurred. And she had two fences in hand. And we missed the parade. I don't know if that counts.'

There was a silence as the judges conferred. The arena was buzzing with speculation and, in the practice ring, tension tightened everyone's faces. Betsy's grooms rushed to take her horse. Bramble saw her slim silhouette briefly, her hand covering her mouth and her shoulders shaking with tears, before the other American riders surrounded her, protecting her from curious eyes and cameras.

Jez swung her round towards him, his hands gripping her shoulders.

'I said I love you. Will you marry me?' asked Jez through gritted teeth.

At first she didn't know what he was talking about. 'What?'

He was paler than she'd ever seen him. 'You and me,' he said. 'I was right about Shaggy. I'm right about us.'

'Jez!' He was infuriating. He was joking, he must be.

'Sorry,' he said. 'I should have waited. Gone down on one knee. Taken you to a restaurant.'

'I've never heard you say sorry before.' Bramble tried not to think about it. A life with Jez. Someone to whom she had so much to say and with whom she had so much to share. Someone she now knew she had missed so much, so very, very much, that the last eighteen months seemed grey and drab when she looked back on them.

'Felicity,' she said, remembering how she had felt when she'd heard about Donna's story. 'You had an affair with Felicity.'

'No, I didn't.' He looked blank.

Bramble wondered if she'd stepped into another relationship where the truth was seen through a series of shifting mirrors. 'Donna saw her coming out of your flat one morning.'

'Oh, that.' His face cleared. 'She had a nightmare, you know how she does, and we stayed talking till about four in the morning. Then she fell asleep on the sofa and I put a blanket round her and went to bed.' He looked into her eyes very intently. 'Do you believe me?'

At that moment the loudspeaker crackled into life. 'In line with the decision at the Athens Olympics, Betsy Parker has incurred a fourteen-point time penalty for going through the start twice, which puts her in fifth place. The winner of this year's Badminton is Jezzar Morgan on Fireflight.'

Bramble punched the air. 'You did it!' she screamed. 'You did it.' The cameras and reporters rushed towards them, but Jez held on to her hand tightly, as if she might fly away.

'Do you believe me?' he whispered.

In the background the rankings were being read out. Hamish Woods second. Bramble Kelly third, Klaus Jürgen fourth . . .

'Third?' Bramble tried not to cry. 'I don't deserve it, it was luck. There are lots of better riders than me here.'

'It's always luck,' said Jez. 'Nobody can win without it. It's your turn. But Bramble, I need to know. *Do you believe me?*'

'Don't be silly,' she said briskly, to conceal the emotion. 'I've always believed you. No matter what anyone said.'

'Then marry me,' he insisted. 'This isn't sudden. I'm not just high on winning, I've missed you more than anybody I've ever lost in my life. There hasn't been a day when I haven't talked to you in my head or wished you were there beside me.'

Bramble thought of the fields at Lorenden and the horses grazing, and how often she had tried to look at them through Jezzar's eyes, and how many times she'd heard his voice in her head. Behind them, she was dimly aware of the arena being prepared for the prize-giving and the hounds of the Beaufort Hunt lolloping and jostling past on the way to give their demonstration. The press of people around them grew heavier and thicker as press and officials descended on Bramble and Jez, only interested in Jez, for quotes, interviews and photographs. He kept her hand in his.

She searched his eyes to see if he was teasing. She couldn't bear to feel a fool for a second time. To be deceived by hope, making something what she wanted it to be rather than seeing it for what it was. Nat's mocking face was still in her head.

'I won't ask again,' said Jez. 'Marry me.'

Bramble forced herself to be brave. She knew that if he said he wouldn't ask again, he never would. 'Yes,' she said, peeling her heart bare, afraid and exhilarated. 'Of course I will.'

'Please,' someone said, trying to detach her, 'we need a photograph of the winner on his own.'

'No you don't,' said Jez. 'I've waited too long for this.'

No one was quite sure whether he was talking about the Badminton trophy or the woman by his side.

Epilogue
Seven Years Later

'We're early,' said Jez. 'We could drive past Lorenden; show the children where you were brought up.'

Bramble wasn't sure if she could face it, but there were ghosts to be acknowledged.

Jez turned the car into the familiar lane, still lined with hawthorn berries and drying teasel heads, bedecked in cobwebs. There were polytunnels for the now-interminable strawberry season and a turning after that, into Ben's old field, leading to six new houses.

'Quite nice,' said Bramble, looking at their Kent peg-tiled roofs and long, low outlines. 'It worked. We sold to the right man. Look, Caz, Tash, I used to keep my pony in that field.'

Caspian and Natasha, aged six and four respectively, looked at the field. 'What, with the houses?' asked Caz.

'No,' said Bramble heavily. 'The houses weren't there then.'

They arrived at the bottom of the drive and Jez turned the engine off. The white-painted five-bar gates had been replaced with big wrought iron ones with gilt-tipped spears along the top. The name Lorenden Manor had been worked into the design. There was an entryphone beside the gates.

'Lorenden Manor, eh?'

'When my great-great-grandfather bought it, it was called Lorenden Farm,' said Bramble. 'He dropped the Farm bit to make it sound grander. I suppose it will finish up as Lorenden Palace. And everybody always used to be able to walk up the drive.'

'And straight into the kitchen. Yes, I remember,' said Jez, putting his arm round her. 'I should have known better, marrying you. I should have known that I'd never be alone with my own wife, in my own kitchen.'

'You don't want to be alone with me in the kitchen. You like everyone coming in.'

Jez squeezed her shoulders. 'I like what you like.'

Bramble thought about how much had happened in the seven years since she'd left. They had sold Lorenden to a developer called Brian Borthwick only weeks after Jez had won Badminton. Brian Borthwick had done up the main house and sold it on – to someone Helena described as a retired banker on his third marriage to a trophy wife – and built his half-a-dozen historically accurate eco-houses as well. They had sold quickly, according to the neighbours, but until now Bramble hadn't wanted to see them.

She'd been concentrating on her career. As well as coming third at Badminton, Bramble had won best female rider and Shaggy had won an embryo transfer for being the top mare. Shaggy became a working mother with her first two foals born to surrogate mares, while she and Bramble were picked for the British team for the European Championships, where the team got gold and Shaggy and Bramble had earned an individual silver medal. After two more successful years, Bramble retired her to breed from her full-time. Shaggy now had five youngsters coming through, two of whom were very promising, and Jez and Bramble had Caz and Tash who – they reminded each other constantly – might, or might not become the riders of the future. 'We mustn't force them,' Bramble kept saying. 'We must remember Felicity and Savannah.' 'And Eddie,' added Jez. 'Don't forget Eddie. Helena so wanted him to be a successful businessman or a city big shot.'

Jez had become one of Britain's top three riders and, with Eddie as his assistant, ran a yard of around twenty horses, riding up to six in each event. He was one of the few people who could make a living from it – he had sponsorship, advertising contracts and lottery funding, he taught riders and trained horses and sold horses on, wrote columns for magazines and newspapers and was even beginning to do some television commentating. He worked a fifteen-hour day in the summer and only a little less in the winter. But he and Bramble did it all together and, in spite of the separations for competing, they never ran out of things to say to each other. Although they still argued.

Bramble looked through the ornate gates with their Lorenden Manor inscription. 'The rose is still there. Up the side of the house. And the roof looks good. I think they've restored it all quite carefully.' The house, newly painted and serene, was almost unchanged and she could see the racehorse weathervane on the top of the stables. The drive had been newly gravelled and there were four cars parked outside, each one a byword for luxury.

The gates, though, cut her off from her past. The house was no longer an integral part of the lane and the fields around it.

'We could ring the bell. Ask if we could go in.'

Bramble shook her head. 'It's not mine any more.' She turned away to hide her face from the children. Jez took them by the hand and walked off down the lane with them, pointing out wild flowers, leaving her to say goodbye to her ghosts.

She spoke the names softly to herself, acknowledging each one in turn. Pa. She saw him in his flat tweed cap and long mackintosh, his spare figure striding up the drive, turning his face towards her with his beaky nose and the eyes that missed nothing. He had written that will, she thought, so that they had to learn to pull together as a family again. She, Helena and Felicity had picked up the worn threads of sisterhood and reworked them into something fine and strong and wonderful that could never be torn again. Helena had bought the one remaining unconverted barn and had turned it into an award-winning restoration while sending Roly and Ruby to the local school. It was strange that it was Helena, of all of them, who had turned out to be one of the swallows in the end, the one who had had to return to where she belonged. Bramble, once she'd left, had had to force herself to come back.

With an effort, Bramble summoned up an image of the mother she had barely known, a waft of lily-of-the-valley and soft embraces. And Dom, with his stocky build and huge laugh. She saw his dancing eyes in Savannah's, every time she looked at her.

Then Lottie, the skinny schoolgirl, with her endless eager questions and her hair scraped back from her face in a ponytail, carrying her saddle into the house and turning back for one last time to smile goodbye. She visualised Alan, the small, clever man whose generosity and love of his wife had made so much happen, and who had slipped away quietly from his confused twilight world in a matter of months. Pauline, beautiful to the end, had married a retired Brigadier for the last years of her life and had died in her sleep, aged eighty-one, only that spring. The horses, Ben, Teddy and the first Merlin. She watched them all go up the drive – the chestnut, the almost white-grey and the black – and turn for one last time before disappearing into the trees. The mist had released them all. It was gone from her mind for ever.

The front door opened and three children came running out. Two of them ran round the house into the garden but a little girl came down the drive.

'Hello,' she said through the bars of the gate.

'Hello,' Bramble replied. 'I used to live here when I was your age.'

The girl studied her carefully. 'I live here now.'

'Yes,' said Bramble, smiling. 'I've got another house.'

'Is it as nice as this?'

'It's different.' Bramble thought of the golden stone farmhouse nestling in the Cotswold hills, and the new modern stable barn they'd built with the money from Lorenden. Felicity had bought a cottage and a yard nearby and ran a re-training programme there, called Second Chance, for horses – especially racehorses – with problems. They'd had a great piece of publicity when Jez, six weeks earlier, had won Burghley on the first racehorse the programme had ever acquired, competing in Second Chance's colours. It had taken nearly ten years to get Merlin from a swamp in Louisiana to the top of his game.

The little girl was still watching her. 'Do you like your new house?' she asked again.

'Yes, I love it.'

'So you don't want to come back here?' She sounded anxious.

'No,' smiled Bramble. 'I don't want to come back.'

'Good.' The little girl studied her. 'I've got a pony.'

'What's its name?'

'Money.' She smiled, revealing two missing milk teeth. 'And when I grow up, I'm going to be the famous-est rider in the world.'

'I'll come and watch you,' promised Bramble.

'Look, I can do handstands.' And she cartwheeled up the drive and ran back inside the house.

Bramble turned and walked away herself, wishing them all back again just one more time. She missed each of them so much. Jez, a child's hand in each of his, knew exactly what she was thinking. He always did. He always had. It drove her mad.

'I'm not crying,' she said crossly, getting into the car without showing her face.

He passed her a tissue and she blew her nose, then fussed about her make-up and looked at her watch as he started the car again.

'Do you think Ollie has really stopped drinking?' she asked.

Jez was never surprised when she changed the subject suddenly. He was usually following the same well-known twists and turns of memory and speculation that her own mind took. 'Mmm. Oddly enough, I think hearing the way Nat manipulated him did him a power of good. I think he realised he had to do something for himself. And he's always wanted to get back with Helena.'

'I was quite disappointed when they got divorced. In spite of everything, I somehow always thought they'd make it.'

'Oh well.' Jez parked the car in the field opposite the church. 'As they say, you can never really understand a marriage until you've shared the bed with them and sat under their breakfast table.'

Bramble shuddered. 'I wouldn't dare. Come on. Now Caz, where are your shoes?'

It was the little church where Pa had been buried, and where they had all been christened. Where she and Jez had been married, and where two of Helena's weddings – albeit one a blessing – had taken place.

Helena and Savannah were both there, dressed in pale pink silk, and Poppy, Savannah's three-year-old daughter, was running up and down the aisle in a pale pink smock with a circlet of rosebuds on her head. Savannah and Tom had married at twenty, in a registry office, amid cries of 'you're both too young'. Now Savannah was in her last few years of vet's training.

Felicity – almost not late for a change – drifted up the aisle in a swirly red and orange chiffon kaftan, white jeans and high silver shoes, followed half a pace later by a distinguished-looking man in his sixties.

'Who's that?' hissed Helena.

'I haven't a clue. Don't you know?' whispered Bramble.

'All I know is that Felicity asked if she could bring someone. But you should know, you live closest to her.'

Bramble shrugged. 'I don't know if anyone is ever really close to Felicity. She meets men. I don't know where she finds them.'

Helena sighed, handing Tash a posy of flowers.

'Are you OK?' Bramble could see her sister's eyes focused on the road, waiting and worrying.

'Of course. You know what I've always said,' declaimed Helena, with a smile of relief as another car drew up. 'Your first marriage is about youthful madness,' she glared at Tom and Savannah, 'your second is about finding a man to support you while you bring up your children,' she looked down the aisle at Eddie and his girlfriend, who were marshalling the now teenage Ruby and Roly, 'your third is just hormonal – you think it's your last chance.'

The car door opened. She kissed Ollie. 'Where've you been? I was worried.'

'I didn't want to tell you,' said Ollie, whipping something out from behind his back, 'not until I knew I was sure.' He thrust a large, ugly glass trophy into her arms.

'What this?'

'Award,' he said. 'For my latest film script. I've only just come from the airport.'

Helena looked at it carefully. 'Good, darling. Well done.' She set it down on a pew. 'We'll keep it in the downstairs lavatory. Everybody always needs to go at some point.' Her mouth hovered close to his, almost in a kiss.

'Are you trying to smell if I've been drinking?'

Bramble had been present at this scene so often. Helena suspicious; Ollie angry. The man had been sober for seven years, thought Bramble. Give him a break, Helena. Just trust him a bit. She crossed her fingers, bracing herself for the storm that would erupt if Helena said yes.

'Yes,' said Helena.

Ollie's face darkened. But he took both Helena's hands in his. 'I nearly did. I sat at a bar and ordered a drink to celebrate. Now everything's fine I thought I deserved it. Just one. Then I thought of you, waiting for me, and I knew I could never have just one. I walked away, Helena. I. Didn't. Drink. But I can only do that if I know you're going to be there, waiting for me. It's always going to be there, Helena, it won't go away.'

Helena smiled. 'Neither will I.' She put her arm through his. 'Now I was just telling Tash and Savannah about marriage. The most important is, by the time you get to your fourth husband, you need to make sure . . .' She looked up at Ollie with real love in her eyes. 'That you marry your third husband all over again,' she concluded with a dazzling smile, setting out slowly up the aisle with him, followed by Tash, Savannah and Poppy.

She turned one last time and winked at them. 'Because at least that way you'll know what you're in for.'

Acknowledgements

Thank you to all those who took the time to share their expertise and experiences with me for this book, starting with event horse owner (and now breeder!) Rosie Dickens – who introduced me to so many people and explained so much, as well as providing the best egg rolls ever – and the Boucher family, especially Fiona and Marguerite Boucher; event riders William Fox-Pitt (with Tom Gittins and the Fox-Pitt Eventing Club – www.foxpitteventing.com), Simon Lawrence, Jonty Evans, Polly Williamson, Jane Lanyon and Jackie Jones-Parry and former eventer Victoria Sinnatt; fence judges Sue and Martin Sinnatt; legendary trainers Dot Willis and Rose Hart; JRN selector Sheila Barker; Jane Tuckwell of Burghley Horse Trials; Jane Davies of the Mark Davies Injured Riders Fund; Caroline Orme, author of *Celebrity Jumping Exercises*; eventing groom and equine journalist Lulu Kyriacou; Hilary Talbot; Prince Jezzar Giray (who kindly lent Jez his name); Julian Seaman of the Badminton Press Office, who took me behind the scenes and answered lots of questions exceptionally patiently; vets Penny Birchall and Deborah Baker; the Moorcroft Racehorse Welfare Centre; Di Arbuthnot of Retraining of Racehorses; Cassandra Jardine; Cantor Index for their hospitality in hosting talks by Zara Phillips and Captain Mark Phillips; Dr Teresa Holland of Dodson & Horrell equine feed specialists; Kent Police Press Office; Faversham Fire Brigade for their demonstration of how animals are rescued; and Vicky and John Clinch with Syndale Liberty (Liberty's demonstrations of horse loading proved especially invaluable).